MW01129314

STANDING TALL

To Velma —
Best Wishes,
Bill

WILLIAM WARDLAW

authorHOUSE®

AuthorHouse™
1663 Liberty Drive
Bloomington, IN 47403
www.authorhouse.com
Phone: 1-800-839-8640

Published by AuthorHouse   02/29/2012

ISBN: 978-1-4685-5962-0 (sc)
ISBN: 978-1-4685-5961-3 (e)

Library of Congress Control Number: 2012903962

"I took the Isthmus . . ."

Theodore Roosevelt

Speech at the University of California

March 23, 1911

PREFACE

After writing O'Reiley's Island, I had a number of readers who said, in effect, "I'd like to read more about this guy Thomas O'Reiley. I find him interesting . . ."

After several false starts, Standing Tall began to take shape in my mind and on paper. A lot was happening in the world prior to the First World War and Thomas would have been in his late twenties to early thirties. Life was good. He was successful, wealthy and married to a beautiful woman, but his life lacked some very essential elements.

So here is Thomas in a new role. Many thanks to all those who have encourage me to continue to write, taken time to read what I've written and given me valuable insights and criticism. Thanks especially to my wife Susan and to Ron, Beth, Cas, Celeste, Frank and Jo for their patience and help.

PROLOGUE

<u>Events: 1898-1903</u>

The several years encompassing the transition from the 1800's to the 1900's were tumultuous for the United States of America as it tried out its new-found presence as a world power. During the five or so years of shift between centuries, the United States experienced a monumental growth in its military capability; the navy was in the transition from sail to steam, expanded its capital ships from six battleships to eleven and its submarine force from none to eight. And during those few years, it experienced huge advances in technology. At the same time, it found itself deeply involved in three wars.

On April 25, 1898, the United States declared war on Spain after the battleship USS Maine blew up in Havana Harbor, Cuba. Upon declaration of war with Spain, the Pacific Fleet was ordered to attack the Spanish held Philippine Islands and on May 1, 1898 the Battle of Manila began. The battleship USS Oregon, at that time stationed on America's west coast, was directed to head for Cuba. The 14,700 mile cruise through the Strait of Magellan took sixty-seven days and heightened American thinking about a canal that would join the Atlantic and Pacific Oceans, a task that the French had twice attempted and twice failed. The Spanish-American War ended on February 6, 1899 after taking 2,446 American and 20,000 Cuban and Philippine lives. Spain sold the Philippine Islands to America for $20 million. Cuba, Puerto Rico and the Pacific Island of Guam were ceded by Spain to the United States.

However, the Filipinos had chafed under the Spanish rule and saw the United States as yet another imperialist usurper and thus the Philippine Insurrection against the American occupation began on February 4, 1898. This little war cost the lives of 4,234 American soldiers and 20,000 Filipino fighters. Philippine civilian casualties were estimated to be 200,000 to 500,000. The Philippine Insurrection officially ended on July 4, 1902.

In August, 1900, an expeditionary force of some 19,000 army and navy troops from the United States, England, France, Japan, Russia, Germany, Australia and Italy were assembled and prepared to move toward Peking to protect non-Chinese from the ruthless attacks by the so-called Boxers. Under the official name of Society of Righteous and Harmonious Fists this radical pro-nationalist movement had tacit approval of its actions from the Chinese Empress herself. The bloody Boxer Rebellion campaign against 70,000 Chinese Imperial troops, including 10,000 Muslim Kansu Braves, ended on September 7, 1901 after costing the lives of some 2,500 soldiers of the Expeditionary Force, 20,000 Chinese Imperial Troops and 19,000 civilians.

During this same period of history, America became fascinated with the new gasoline powered automobile. The first American gasoline powered car was built by the Duryea brothers and was first run on public roads in September, 1893. By the end of 1896, Ford had sold his first car. By 1901, Oldsmobile was producing its car and that year sold six hundred of them for $650 each. However, the horse remained the prime mover of transportation for many years.

Grover Cleveland was the President of the United States from March 4, 1893 until March 3, 1897. He was succeeded by President William McKinley who was assassinated and died on September 14, 1901. Vice President Theodore Roosevelt was sworn in as the nation's twenty-sixth President that same day.

In 1898, the United States annexed the Hawaiian Islands. By December that same year, Pacific Telephone and Telegraph Company had eleven thousand subscribers in San Francisco. Long distance telephone service was available between major cities but the Western Union Telegraph remained the main-stay for long distance communication for many years.

In October 1899, the simmering revolt of the Liberal party in Colombia finally exploded against the ruling Conservative Party, starting the Thousand Day War which eventually engulfed all of Colombia, including the Columbian Province of Panama. As it continued, the bloody war became drained of purpose while factions on each side argued among themselves. A peace treaty was signed on October 24, 1902 but Panama's fervor for independence from Colombia had not been quenched.

In 1899, the Wright brothers, Wilbur and Orville were experimenting to perfect control issues with their gliders. In 1900 they went to Kitty Hawk in North Carolina to start their manned glider test flights. In July and August of the next year, they were making manned test flights, gliding for distances up to 400 feet. During September and October of 1902, they made several hundred unpowered glides using still evolving concepts of control. They attached a gasoline powered engine to their glider and on December 13, 1903 Wilbur took the airplane on its first powered flight that lasted three seconds.

In 1900, United States instituted the Gold Standard Act, setting the price of gold at $20.67 per troy ounce to back up the American paper currency.

On September 8, 1900, a hurricane hit Galveston Island with such ferociousness that somewhere between six and twelve thousand people perished.

Paved inter-community highways and roads were still many years away. Effective management of the vast Sierra Nevada Mountains watershed was only a dream. Environmental ecology was in its infancy.

In 1903, at the age of 33, Thomas O'Reiley found himself in the midst of this maelstrom of events and social concerns. Born in San Francisco, he was the only child of poor Irish immigrants and had been raised by his widowed mother and worked all through his growing years to help support the household. In 1889, at the age of nineteen, Thomas fled the city aboard the sailing ship *Orion* bound for Australia, in order to avoid arrest and being accused of murder. During a ferocious storm, the *Orion* was sunk with all hands—except Thomas. He scarcely managed to escape to a small island where he lived in isolation for almost five years. The experience had left him scarred, both physically and emotionally. Finally, in an all-or-nothing endeavor, he managed to return to the place he loved—San Francisco. But things had changed. By 1895 the city had grown into a bustling, crowded, noisy metropolis. Thomas was now a wealthy man due to the discovery he made on the island. He was able to clear his name and in the process, met the woman he had seen only once, Amanda McPherson. He and Amanda married and they had three children.

But unrealized by Thomas, his isolation on the island had also deprived him of the rich, everyday human experiences that help cultivate the character, interpersonal skills and values necessary to live in society.

From time to time, Thomas was haunted by the terrifying memories and ghosts of his past, yet he was curiously drawn to the seclusion he had once abhorred; the years of discovery and self sufficiency amid natural beauty and splendor still beckoned to him like the mythical siren song.

CHAPTER 1

<u>Wednesday, February 11, 1903, Richmond, Virginia</u>
The Littleton Tazewell was a tawdry hotel situated on East Cary Street near 5th Street, close to the James River and away from the central district of Richmond. For years now it had catered to the lower rungs of society, usually those looking for a room they could rent for an hour or two.

The first to enter room number 212 was tall—an inch over six feet—and his long legs stretched out on the floor in front of him. When he had come into the room he wore a smooth leather overcoat that came to below his knees; he left it on as he sat on the wooden chair, leaned back and balanced on the two back legs. Under the overcoat was a black leather vest and white shirt with a dark blue cravat knotted loosely at the neck. A revolver was tucked under his belt, out of sight beneath the leather overcoat. He had waited for his visitors for thirty minutes but outwardly appeared to be unperturbed and relaxed, despite the lateness of the hour.

The small hotel room was dimly lit; the yellowish glow emitted by the single gas-lit sconce on one wall failed to reach into the gloomy corners. The lingering odors of various tobaccos, lotions and body odors accumulated over a third of a century only added another layer to the musty and damp aroma. Wall paper, once lively in color but now faded brown and stained with tobacco-smoke, covered the walls. Some years ago these walls had boasted heavily framed portraits of celebrated Generals of the Confederate Army but the portraits had disappeared along with the hotel's once heady reputation.

When he first entered the room the man had instinctively pulled the heavy drapes over the windows, creating a sense of privacy and muting the steady drum of the rain beating against the windowpanes. A faded gray bedspread covered the narrow bed; the threadbare pattern had long-since been laundered away. An unlit coal-oil lamp with its tall glass chimney sat on the ancient crocheted doily centered on a small side-table next to the head of the bed.

The man's face was tanned and deeply lined, resembling somewhat the gnarled bark of a cottonwood tree. Narrow crevices emanated web-like from the corners of his eyes and both sides of his nose. His lips were thin and expressionless; his upper lip was almost hidden by a thick mustache of coarse black and silver hair. His eyes were buried in two dark pits concealed in even darker shadows. One could only suspect that his pupils were dark. In the feeble light, the man's black hair appeared to be neatly trimmed and still carried the residual fragrance of his recent trip to the barber shop. Strands of silver ran through his hair, which he combed straight back and silver brushed each temple and tinted the fashionable sideburns that ended about mid-ear.

Outside, an opaque mantle of rain-heavy clouds completely obscured the light of the full moon. The sleeping city was firmly in the cold grip of mid-winter; it had rained—an unrelenting and icy, almost frozen torrent for three days and nights. The approaching morning would bring yet another bitter cold and wet work day for most of the city's population.

The two late arrivals sat on the edge of the bed facing him. They had nonchalantly flung their top hats and heavy wet overcoats across the single bed when they entered the room. The younger of the two was a congressman already marked by many north-easterners as a hopeful to become the nation's next vice President. The young congressman had been talking for fifteen minutes, leaning forward earnestly, gesturing and using every skill he knew.

The other, obviously older, was a wealthy railroad executive from Chicago. He appeared to be of enormous girth but narrow shoulders and a large head with fleshy jowls that quivered when he spoke with a voice that reverberated with implied status and power. His bulbous face was framed with elegant, fluffy white sideburns; a full white mustache with the ends waxed and carefully curled upward graced his upper lip. In spite of his apparent outward calm, the heel of his right shoe tapped nervously against the floor in a steady staccato drumbeat. His eyes continued to sweep across the room, taking in the tall stranger and the drapery-covered windows as if expecting something or someone to burst through. He sat quietly, mostly listening but interjecting occasionally with clarifications and specific details when his young partner couched his information in ambiguous terms and words. *This is no time to be vague*, he mused as he studied the silent man sitting across from them. Though this was the first time they had met, he felt an unexpected affinity with the stranger. Perhaps it was the deadly steadiness of the man's eyes; perhaps it was the cold exactness of the few words he had spoken; perhaps the unaffected manner with which he acknowledged his own expertise to carry out the task being discussed. And yet they knew very little about the man, only his reputation. That he was an expert there was no doubt. He had left a long record of his ventures across the United States. Rumors even led some to speculate that he had been involved in similar activities in Central and South America. The newspapers had occasionally headlined some of his more newsworthy actions but no one knew for sure what he looked like, or what his name was, or where he lived.

The tall man listened carefully, leaned forward at times to consult the map spread across the congressman's knees. This assignment would be difficult—*more than difficult*, he decided. From his point of view, there were quite a few loose ends, unknowns, opportunities for well-made plans to go awry. He offered a few suggestions, asked a few questions. Dates and times were critical. The window of opportunity was extremely short. He garnered the stream of information quickly, expertly, silently arranging it into sequences that had already proven successful, identifying gaps and pitfalls in the basic plan that he would have to deal with later. He accepted the individual documents as they were discussed; train schedules, security details, personnel folders, maps, itineraries of the central character—already updated in red ink and subject to further last minute changes. The gentleman operated on a tight schedule—most days were scheduled down to the minute.

He listened intently, leaning forward in his chair with the palms of his hands pressed lightly together, fingers spread fan-like with his elbows resting on the arms of the chair. He was motionless; no nervous foot tapping or knee twitches or facial expressions.

Tonight's meeting had been carefully arranged and there had been days of travel involved for all three participants. There were tremendous dangers for all three of them should the details of this meeting ever be known. The preliminary communication among them prior to tonight's meeting had been through hard to trace intermediaries; the final details of tonight's meeting—the time, location and passwords—had been communicated through cryptic telegrams. Tonight's introductions had been very brief; no handshakes, no amiable exchanges or small talk. The two men knew the stranger only by his reputation and the name under which he operated: *El Culebra*, Spanish for *The Snake*, a soubriquet given to him by a fellow soldier in another lifetime.

The money he had earned over the years had been excellent. This assignment could well be his most important and perhaps his last. It was, perhaps, time for him to retire from this business.

"Do you have any further questions?" the congressman asked as he leaned back and stared across at the figure across from him.

"No," the man leaned forward in his chair, his eyes boring into the man who had done most of the talking, "no other questions."

Few additional words were exchanged as the heavy packets of cash were handed to the tall stranger; half a million dollars in American money. One by one he slipped the packets into the leather valise he had brought with him. These three men would not meet again. They slipped quietly out of the hotel room and into the steady downpour. The last one out, the man known as *The Snake*, turned the collar of his leather coat up against the rain and hurried along the empty streets to the boarding house where he had taken a room only a day ago. He let himself in through the back door which he had arranged to be unlocked and crept quietly into his room. By dawn he would be leaving Richmond aboard an early-morning train bound for the southwest.

*   *   *

Monday, May 4, 1903 Pacific Ocean, west of Morro Bay, California
The small sailing ship wallowed in the smooth swells, its sails reefed so that it made minimal headway in the occasional wafts of the mild offshore breeze. At the moment, it displayed no flag of nationality but it could and would hoist one should it be deemed necessary. It was an old but well maintained square rigger of two masts. Built in the mid eighteen-eighties, it's sharply raked fore and main masts and extra-long bowsprit gave the ship the illusion, if not the reality, of speed and maneuverability. Originally designed and constructed as an armed privateer sailing under the Brazilian flag, it had been sold and modified and resold several times as the worlds navies modernized in the age of steam power and iron ships. Its exact nationality and ownership were intentionally vague, defined in a byzantine assemblage of complicated records. Its name changed quite

regularly; at the moment the name *Bonito* was written in dark lettering across its stern and if obliged, it's master could convincingly prove it to be a Peruvian vessel on a legitimate business voyage to Vancouver, British Columbia. Tonight she carried lighted running lights as she maintained bare headway in the dense fog that limited visibility to less than a half mile and her master had ordered extra lookouts fore and aft as a matter of due caution. It was the first night of the new moon and it would still be a few hours before the ship let her sails loose to make the dash under the cover of the fog and near total darkness toward the coast and into the difficult harbor at Morro Bay. There would be little time wasted near the monster, dome-like rock that squatted in the center of the bay; the passenger would be rowed ashore and the ship would depart as quickly as it had arrived, the thick fog providing additional concealment from curious eyes.

The man leaned silently against the starboard railing, a thin unlit cheroot stuck between his lips. He was the sole reason for the ship being here. Slightly built, he wore heavy denim pants and a thick, sturdy shirt under his sheepskin jacket, its collar turned up against the cold, damp air. A thick, nearly white mustache covered his upper lip; otherwise there were very few remarkable physical characteristics surrounding him. A western-style hat with a narrow brim covered his head; the hair that was exposed below the hat was graying and his face was lightly furrowed with age, or perhaps responsibility, or both. He was alone and silent at the moment but when he did speak, his voice was soft and composed; his English was slightly Spanish accented but very articulate.

His mission had been long in the planning and the man he was to eventually meet could put the plan into motion that would politically, militarily and economically change this hemisphere and affect the worldwide balance of power forever. Much blood had already been spilt and more was likely to saturate the soil of his country. Time was of the essence but it seemed to crawl far too slowly.

He carried with him a few maps and a generous supply of American currency. Should it prove to be necessary, a small collection of documents on his person would identify him as Juan Fernando Gomez, a rancher from a small border town in southwest-Texas. He had memorized a list of names and places that would help facilitate his overland travels in California.

The heavy mist had gathered with unusual speed, completely cutting off any chance of his seeing the mid-California coastal mountain range.

He had not been to California before; most of his prior travels to the United States had been to the big cities on the east coast. This trip had taken months of negotiation involving a few highly placed United States government officials. Similar voyages to the east coast over a period of six months had resulted in fashioning the basic strategy; this would be the last and most important trip. He would not spend many days in California; but if successful, his mission was certain to bring about profound changes in the world.

*   *   *

<u>Friday evening, May 1, 1903 San Francisco, California</u>
Thomas O'Reiley had never fully realized a fondness for the taste of wine, even the expensive Bordeaux imported from France that presently rested in his long-stemmed wineglass. The biting, acerbic liquid caused the inside of his mouth to pucker and left it dry and sour. Nor had he ever developed the subtle sensory nuances that to those around him apparently revealed the *rich, plum-like* fragrance coupled with *a delicate hint of cinnamon* that *softly brushes the back of the pallet* they seemed to be enjoying. His eyes swept around the room and settled on his wife Amanda. She was as beautiful and graceful as she was the day he married her, almost six years ago. She appeared to be engaged in animated conversation with three women but seemed to sense his gaze and turned her head briefly, returned his smile and raised her glass slightly in a graceful and private salute.

The high-ceilinged room was comfortably filled with Amanda's eighteen guests, though Thomas thought the room was perhaps slightly too warm. All the guests were wealthy; several were neighbors who occupied large Victorian-style homes on Nob Hill. They represented a cross-section of the prominent politicians, financiers, lawyers, businessmen and doctors of the city of San Francisco. Thomas watched as they circulated with practiced ease among themselves, nibbling at the abundant hors d'oeuvres delicately arranged on silver platters on the sideboard. The rumble of the men's conversations filled the room; solemn assertions among them—the talk of this hour would most likely be politics—caused nearby heads to nod in serious consideration. In amiable counterpoise, the women's refined gaiety seemed to waft through the empty spaces in conversation like an occasional aromatic zephyr or the delicate tinkle of fine crystal.

Thomas O'Reiley carefully tensed and released the aching muscles in his right leg, hoping the exercise would ease the dull pain radiating from the poorly-knitted bones—*how many years ago had it been*—and ironically the same leg recently injured. *I wouldn't be here if it hadn't been for Gray Hawk . . . In fact, this whole crazy idea wouldn't involve me at all if it hadn't been for Gray Hawk.* In a few days this would all change for him and he hoped fervently that he was up to the task that had been handed to him.

He glanced at the tambour clock on the fireplace mantle; the clock had been a wedding gift from someone, probably an aunt or uncle in Amanda's family. It was still a few minutes before eight o'clock. Then the hourly chime would announce that it was time for the men to retire to the parlor to conclude the evening with cigars and snifters of brandy. The conversation would converge on immediate concerns, usually political or financial in nature. The women would retreat to the dining room for tea and their talk would focus on those issues that were fundamental to ladies of their social status; women's organizations and guilds, charity associations, the arts and the city's museums. Thomas knew that Amanda was adept at steering and encouraging conversation and would assure the evening was a fruitful one for the ladies.

Thomas spotted Amanda's father, Handon McPherson, across the room and nodded briefly to him. Thomas and McPherson were business partners, controlling a variety of financially successful enterprises that dealt mainly with commercial construction. He watched as McPherson adroitly excused himself from the trio of men he was with and made his way across the room to Thomas's side.

"Ah . . . Thomas! Haven't had the opportunity to converse with you yet this evening." McPherson raised his wine glass in a short salute, glanced casually at his son-in-law. "You're looking fine, Thomas. Hope you're feeling well." He glanced at Thomas's leg. "And your leg is mending?"

"Healing well, sir."

"Good." He looked quickly around the room. "Looks like you've assembled a fine group."

"Amanda created the guest list, sir. Not one of my skills." He looked at his father-in-law. "You know that I would rather avoid this sort of thing." McPherson was three inches shorter than Thomas and slightly built. A widower of many years, his silver hair and beard were precisely trimmed, giving his face a handsomeness that betrayed his age and caused women to admire and whisper among themselves. His eyes though were tough and steady, sometimes cold and even devoid of emotion; they clearly reflected his devotion to the minutia of business. In many ways, Thomas admired his father-in-law but in even more ways he knew that he would never be like him. Handon McPherson had served as a construction engineer in the Union Army during the Civil War and brought that knowledge and experience with him to California shortly after the war. He settled in San Francisco and made his fortune during the city's years of rapid growth. Many of the city's landmark hotels and financial district buildings carried the McPherson signature and in a city beset with far too many disastrous fires, there was constant rebuilding that ran in parallel to the city's growth.

"As you know Thomas, these opportunities are necessary to keep our name before those who make decisions in this city. Once Congress approves President Roosevelt's Canal project, we'll see coast-to-coast shipping virtually explode and M. O. & C. must be part of it. Mark my words; there will be extraordinary financial expansion and construction as San Francisco becomes a major west coast seaport . . . and we will be a vital catalyst in that growth!"

Thomas listened half-heartedly. He had heard the same enthusiastic overtures many times. He wanted badly to discuss with his father-in-law the awful obligation he had just taken on but he had agreed to secrecy, even with Amanda. He shook his head and picked up again on McPherson's monologue. There was little doubt that his father-in-law was correct but for the sake of conversation, Thomas said, "we've already got the transcontinental railroad. Congress hasn't even decided upon a route for the canal and it will take years to build, if it ever is."

"The railroads won't be able to handle everything," McPherson continued. "Just look at what the state is already exporting to the east coast! Lumber, oil, fresh fruit and vegetables, cotton and rice! Soon it will be manufactured goods, imports from the Far East! And the west coast will need the iron and machinery and supplies the mid-west industrial states provide. Thomas, the canal between the Atlantic and Pacific will be built! We cannot simply *wait* for its completion. We must be ready! Our city must be ready!"

To Thomas's relief, the chime on the mantle clock began to slowly toll out eight bells. "I'm afraid that's my signal, sir. I must now play the role of congenial host."

McPherson nodded and watched as O'Reiley turned and addressed the group. "Gentlemen! If you would, please join me in the parlor for a fine Cuban cigar and a glass of Leland Stanford's most excellent brandy."

Across the room, Amanda smiled and took her cue from Thomas. "And ladies, let us retire to the dining room, away from the horrendous reek of the men's cigars!" Her announcement was met with polite laughter from the women and guffaws from the men.

The men seated themselves among the deep leather chairs and davenports in the spacious parlor; a variety of Cuban cigars were made available and Thomas distributed short-stemmed brandy snifters. The next several minutes were taken up with the exacting ritual of admiring and selecting cigars, then cutting and lighting them. Thomas poured the twelve-year old brandy from the cut glass decanter into waiting snifters. The men carefully puffed and checked the smoldering end of their cigars and murmurs and nods of indulgence filled the room—along with clouds of smoke. Thomas waited as the men settled comfortably into the deep chairs, found their respective ash trays and swirled the brandy in the elegant snifters, occasionally holding their glass to the gas-lit chandelier to admire and comment on the tawny liquor.

As host, it was Thomas's responsibility to get conversation started. The restless movement among the guests finally died down.

He leaned forward in his seat. "Mister McPherson and I were just discussing President Roosevelt's plans for the intra-ocean canal. It seems to be taking its time working its way through our Congress." He knew this would draw quick conversation, for the controversial topic was grist for the San Francisco Chronicle every day.

"Well, there seems to be general agreement that such a canal is necessary but there appears to be a sizable number who disagree that Nicaragua is the best place," one grey-bearded gentleman seated on the davenport offered.

A low rumble of murmurs greeted this announcement.

The silence returned, the discussion continued. "As you might suspect, Teddy Roosevelt will most likely get his way. After all, it's in the best interests of national defense that we provide a rapid means to get our navy from one ocean to another without resorting to going around the horn." The speaker was a well known businessman, young and dapper in appearance. "But from what I read, our President is much more interested in going through the Isthmus of the Columbian province of Panama, rather contrary to what the Walker Commission has already recommended."

"You're quite correct, Josephus. And a canal across the Panama Isthmus will cost the United States a hundred and ninety million dollars more than the Nicaraguan plan," the grey-bearded gentleman chimed in. Thomas recognized him as one of the Union Pacific railroad executives.

"There are simply too many impediments in attempting to go through the Panama Isthmus," a be-spectacled gentleman offered. "The French Canal Company tried it and twice they met with total financial disaster. And how many lives were lost to malaria and construction accidents? We'd be foolish to try. Besides, the Columbians, at the bitter end of a terrible civil war, are a sly bunch. They don't really want the United States digging a trench across one of their provinces; at least not without substantial financial benefits to themselves. I fear we could be at odds with the Columbians for years should we allow this to happen."

In one corner, an older gentleman straightened himself in the deep chair and leaned forward. "Well and in addition, there are quite a few that have . . . shall we say . . . a vested interest in a canal route through Nicaragua." Thomas noted that the man speaking was the owner of a large sugar processing company. He was a large man who walked with a cane and at the moment he used his cane as a pointer.

"What do you mean by *vested interest*, Cyrus?" The query came from an attorney, Ransom English. In his early forties English was a partner of a small but growing firm known for its position on seeking additional water for San Francisco.

"What I am saying is that some of us . . ." the man hesitated, glanced quickly around the room and a few raised their chins in silent acknowledgement, "have made substantial monetary investments in large tracts of land in Nicaragua. Since the exact route of the canal through Nicaragua has not yet been determined, tens of thousands of acres have been purchased for . . ." he looked carefully around the room, "shall we say *speculation*, especially near Lakes Managua and Nicaragua. Such a canal will need railroad right-of-ways, facilities for military protection, eventually homes and offices, supporting infrastructure for administrative personnel. Small cities will sprout up like mushrooms overnight." The speaker paused then added, "I think it would be a shocking mistake for Roosevelt to insist on going through Panama, especially in light of the findings of the Warren Commission."

"The Panama route would also force the United States to negotiate with the Columbian government," another chimed in. "Doing business with any of the South American countries extends our financial, diplomatic and legal efforts ever further away from our nation's borders. I, for one, am not so sure we ought to be entering into a long-term financial covenant with a South America country, in particular one that is only now emerging from a bloody three year civil war." He gave a quick nod to the gentleman with glasses. "Central American Nicaragua is a whole lot closer; much more convenient to step in to prevent trouble," he glanced around the room, "if you know what I mean. We've already had plenty of military experience in Nicaragua."

"The French Canal Company has a large amount of the canal infrastructure already in place in Panama," Thomas said. "The railroad, the ports, a great deal of the necessary blasting and digging equipment . . ."

"Old and rusting . . ." someone grunted.

"I understand," another added, "that a Panama route would require a complex engineering plan of raising ships through a series of locks . . ."

"So does a route through Nicaragua . . ." another voice.

"Depending upon the route . . ." the sugar company executive offered.

The gentleman in the corner chair stirred once again. "Well, I will say this. Roosevelt had better be damned careful and not over-extend his Presidential clout. It doesn't take much to get people all riled up. We live in a violent world; look what happened to President McKinley."

"The man who assassinated William McKinley was mentally unbalanced." The man who spoke up was a doctor. "He should have been locked up in an insane asylum instead of being strapped into a chair and cooked to death with electricity. Good God! The rest of the world must think we are barbarians!"

The last brought a muffled chortle from a few. "Hear, hear, good Doctor!" The voice of John Salvitti, a bank president, intervened and he raised his glass in mock salute. "Spoken like a true disciple of the Hippocratic Oath!" The gesture made brought more chuckles.

"What I'm saying is," the man in the corner went on after a quick glance at the doctor, "Roosevelt could end up with a bullet in his back if he's not careful. There are more than a few in Congress from his own party—and I dare say probably some right here in this room," he looked around the faces in the parlor, "who would not take lightly losing what they've invested in Nicaragua. The Walker Commission has studied the two routes; they recommend the Nicaragua route and the President should adhere to their recommendation."

"Well said!" a voice chimed in. "We've negotiated and signed canal treaties for fifty years! It's about time the United States of America made its stand and stopped being everyone else's punching bag! Buy the land rights through Nicaragua or simply take it, I say. Who's going to stop us?"

"I concur!" John Salvitti raised his glass again.

"We certainly don't need to get into yet another war over the issue, John."

"I'm not saying we should go to war with our good Nicaraguan neighbors. Put a couple of Teddy's big fat battleships off their coast and they would most likely sign anything you put in front of them."

Salvitti's comment drew more chuckles but the debate quickly grew fiery and centered on American financial interests in Nicaragua. Thomas listened carefully as the argument intensified; it seemed obvious that at least a few in the room had heavy financial investments already at stake. English pressed his argument supporting the Nicaraguan route and angrily expressed his zealous dislike of President Roosevelt, "The man's a damned stupid and arrogant fool!"

A few of the men avoided making eye contact with the brash attorney; the comment, among gentlemen, was sorely out of place and some quietly attributed it to the man's recent and tragic loss of his only child to diphtheria. The conversation drifted into uncomfortable silence; men puffed their cigars back into life, tapped off the ash and fidgeted in restless hesitation. The discussion had kindled an air of uneasiness among the guests.

"Well, of course," the silence was broken, "there is the situation in which our great city presently finds itself; namely, the lack of an adequate and dependable fresh water supply." The speaker had not entered the debate until this point. O'Reiley recognized him as Charles W. Madison, a member of the City Planning Board. "Just two weeks ago the Secretary of the Interior denied our filing for rights to the Tuolumne watershed. Our fair city shall soon be without water to support its growing population."

"Should we actually be stealing water from the Sierra Nevada Mountains that rightfully irrigates and supports the vast San Joaquin Valley's agricultural interests?" It was the doctor again. "The magnificent

Tuolumne watershed and the rivers and lakes that comprise it, is over a hundred and sixty miles east of our city . . ." His voice quivered slightly.

". . . and is inhabited almost entirely by a few uneducated Indians intent on perpetuating their minimal lifestyle," Madison interjected, glaring at the doctor.

"Perhaps that alone is substantial reason for acquisition by the city . . ." Anderson muttered to no one in particular.

"Well, we better do it before Roosevelt declares it to be yet another national park! In addition to the agriculture, think of the lumber and gold mining interests that would be affected!" The speaker, the sugar company executive, glanced at Thomas O'Reiley. "Thomas, you're in the lumber business. When do you think we will we run out of redwood trees?"

"We've not begun to put a dent in the vast California forests of redwood," Thomas stated, "in fact, we've surveyed perhaps only ten percent of them. There're hundreds of thousands of acres we've not even begun to cut. Timber demand is huge—commercial, homes, railroads. The cutting will go on forever, especially in the redwoods; they are impervious to disease and rot and the great redwood trees are found only in California. We've a natural resource here that will last forever and we will timber to meet the demand."

Madison leaned forward, his eyes fixed on Thomas. "What about the preservationists who are insisting that the federal government sets aside millions of acres of public land to forever be out of reach for financial purposes?"

"Well, I must say that I believe we should protect a portion of our national resources from over-zealous profiteers and corporate greed. Remember the damage the gold miners did up near Nevada City! Every year of hydraulic mining at the Malakoff Diggings added a foot of silt to our San Francisco Bay!" Thomas looked around at the assembled men. "A *foot* of silt! Our state capital of Sacramento was flooded and Marysville and Yuba City were once covered with twenty-five feet of mud . . ."

". . . and nineteen years ago, Judge Lorenzo Sawyer declared hydraulic mining illegal," English interrupted, his voice edged with sarcasm.

". . . after thirty years of damage by hydraulic mining had already been done! With careful timber cutting, our forests will restore themselves over time. Mountains don't grow back!" Thomas quickly shot back.

"But public opinion . . ." Madison once again started.

Thomas cut him off. "To hell with public opinion! Where else is lumber of that quality going to come from?"

There was a murmur of general agreement and the conversation once again fell silent before it shifted back to the canal issue. Handon McPherson took the opportunity to present an ad-hoc but detailed review of the series of treaties the United Stated had signed. Over the years, treaties had provided various means by which the United States could build and fortify, or not fortify, a canal across the Central American isthmus. Several nations had been involved in discussions and negotiations, including Great Britain, France, Colombia, Nicaragua and Costa Rica. Besides the issues in South and Central America, there were also concerns about emerging powers in Europe, namely Germany and Russia.

"Well, that sure as hell won't stop Teddy!" The banker Salvitti commented. "He appears to relish a good brawl!" The men laughed.

McPherson finished his historical assessment and a few took the opportunity to refill their snifters. The conversation moved on, more sluggishly now, listlessly drifting into local politics and the recent election of Eugene Schmitz, past President of the local Musician's Union, as mayor of San Francisco. Eventually the banter faded away awkwardly and some of the guests used the opportunity to glance surreptitiously at their pocket watches. The doctor stood and announced that it was time for him and his wife to head home, stating that he must catch the train in the morning in order to attend a meeting in San Jose. Thomas heard the mantle clock begin to chime ten o'clock in the background; one by one the rest of the men stood and stretched and began to make their personal leave-taking. Polite handshakes and comments circulated among the men.

Hats and top-coats for the men and shawls for the women were distributed as the group milled about in the wide foyer. The line of carriages inched forward as each departing couple bade good night and hurried to a waiting carriage's enclosed shelter. Thomas and Amanda stood at the front door and engaged each in final pleasantries; it was almost eleven when the last guests left. Behind them Xiang, their Chinese maid, was silently shuttling dishes, crystal and silverware to the kitchen to be washed, dried and put away before her day would be finished.

"Our home reeks terribly of cigar smoke, Thomas," Amanda said as she shut the front door. She wrinkled her nose. "It will take forever to get rid of the disgusting odor!"

Thomas smiled in spite of himself. "I agree that afterwards it is a repulsive smell. I believe we should have Xiang empty the ashtrays outside and open a few windows on the lower floor before she goes to bed. I think the fresh air overnight will help."

"Perhaps in a week . . ." Amanda muttered. She took Thomas's arm and they walked back into the dining room. Xiang had already cleared the room of tea cups and saucers and small plates, napkins and teapots. The table was shining and the room looked as if it had been unused. "Come, my dear Thomas, let's retire. I believe Xiang has everything under control." She winked at him, "besides, you will be going away shortly and I should like to offer *bon voyage* appropriately."

Thomas smiled and nodded, listened as Amanda gave Xiang her final instructions and followed his wife up the stairs to their bedroom on the second floor.

* * *

He wasn't sure just what had awakened him but he heard the mantle clock chime the hour of three. He turned onto his side and faced Amanda. The room was pitch black but he could sense her nearness as he listened to her regular breathing and became aware of the delicate essence of her presence. The fragrance was intimately familiar and arousing; a fragile and astonishing synthesis of exotic spices and flowers and sensual musk that he had learned to recognize whenever she was near. He felt he could pick it out from among others in a room crowded with women; it was her distinctively secret and unspoken message to him.

He rolled over once again, hesitated momentarily then quietly slipped out of bed. After pulling on his robe and stepping into leather slippers, he made his way downstairs and into his study; it was a large, comfortable room extending off the western side of the house. The room had magnificent floor-to-ceiling windows on three sides and from here, during daytime; he could look over the vast city to his left, watch the San Francisco Bay on his right and gaze toward the Pacific Ocean straight ahead. Tonight, however, was dark and moonless and the black sky was clear of clouds and coastal fog, though the thick cover would begin to ooze like an enormous white mantle over the mountains and through the narrow straits in a few hours as the air over central California, warmed by the early rays of sunrise, began to rise. He slid comfortably into a leather wingback chair next to

15

the western windows. The stars sparkled like millions of tiny diamonds strewn recklessly across the blackness of space but it took him only a few seconds to locate the revealing band of stars that comprised the mythical hunter Orion's belt. The remainder of the constellation Orion was low in the western sky.

He studied the constellation, as he did so very often, trying to envision the hunter's arms and legs, the drawn bow and the arrow that the ancient ones had seen in the grouping. Constellation Orion the Hunter was the namesake of the ship *Orion*, the ill-fated merchant-ship that had forever altered his life. *Orion* had been a brigantine-rigged ship carrying two masts that he managed to beg onto as a deckhand when he was nineteen years old, running for his life from the San Francisco police.

Thomas's mind slipped easily into the powerful memories of those months and years of long ago. Faces and names flashed through his mind; Pendleton the cruel captain, Madasu the African senior deckhand who had patiently shown him the ways of the sea, Robert Specter the shadowy first mate and the others; Pike and Knight, Paine, Alders, Simone who died from thirst, Chase and Perkins whom the captain forced to drink seawater until he too died. They were all dead now and resting on the bottom of the sea with the wreck of the *Orion*. Thomas alone had managed to get off the *Orion* alive and continue his struggle for survival. The ensuing years had been very difficult but he had matured, grown and adjusted to this new existence. The brutal experience had left deep and painful wounds on his body and mind that were slow to heal and these wounds left terrible scars, both visible and unseen. He had struggled those long years to stay alive and the episode had changed him forever. At last, after surviving a terrible journey alone at sea, he had been tossed like flotsam onto the rocky shores of Northern California, starving and broken.

Five long years away from everything he knew. He had finally returned to San Francisco and found the young woman with whom he had fallen in love all those years before. But he had also returned with more wealth than he could have imagined and it was this fortune that enabled him, the son of poor Irish immigrants, to marry his beloved Amanda and become business partners with her father.

Nearly eight years had elapsed since he had come back to San Francisco in 1895. Now he had a family, his wife Amanda and their three young children, James, Julia and Elizabeth. He had businesses to manage, a prominent standing in San Francisco society to uphold, important positions on various boards of directors. At times he had felt that responsibilities and circumstances, in fact the very people he loved, were closing in upon him, suffocating him, crowding him relentlessly, dictating and judging his every move and thought. San Francisco itself, the city which he had cherished and yearned for during his years away, had transformed into a bustling, noisy, vast and perplexing metropolis of nearly three hundred and fifty thousand people. Often times he had craved for time to be spent in personal solitude, for quiet, for peace, for the opportunity to be alone with his thoughts; to return, in some fashion, even if for a few days, to the solitary existence he had experienced on the island. Incredibly, his thoughts and recollections of those years tended to navigate around and avoid the episodes of appalling agony and dread, of awful desperation and terrifying visits from the ghosts of his drowned shipmates, as if his mind had stored these memories in a special, hidden location.

His father-in-law Handon McPherson had sensed that his son-in-law needed time away from his responsibilities and five years ago had invited Thomas to accompany him and several business and political acquaintances on a hunting trip in the Sierra Nevada Mountains. Reluctantly, Thomas had agreed to go and his life would once again be changed in ways he could not have imagined.

Now he had been called by the governor of California to assume an overwhelming responsibility that five years ago he would have immediately refused. The past five years had painfully wrought enormous transformations in Thomas's life.

CHAPTER 2

<u>Wednesday, August 16, 1898 San Joaquin Valley, California</u>
It was late in the afternoon when the seven men got off the train in the small central California town of Visalia. The summer air was fiery hot and dry; the scant shade was cast by a few dusty sycamore trees in front of the train depot. To Thomas, the little town appeared to be deserted or perhaps asleep; its main street was nearly empty of horses or carriages and not a single person was visible on the boardwalks in front of the dozen or so buildings that lined both sides. A sleepy, God-forsaken little town; not at all like the big, bustling city of San Francisco.

The men grumbled among themselves about the stillness of the air and the shimmering heat as they retrieved their suitcases and bed rolls and gun cases from the baggage car. Thomas had gotten to know a few of the men on the trip from San Francisco; Gene Alexander was in the plumbing business in San Francisco. He appeared to be about forty-five years old and was a little on the heavy side. Charles W. Madison, who the rest of the men referred to as CW, was on the San Francisco City Planning Board and had spent most of the trip in huddled conversation with Handon McPherson. Frank Barnwell was about thirty, tall and thin with a deep bass voice. Frank was a mechanical engineer working on the vast *Hech-Hechi* Water Project which would eventually bring a vast supply of drinking water into San Francisco. Thomas had found that the young engineer was relaxed and quite eager to explain the proposed workings of the monumental undertaking. The other two, Ralph Patterson and Harrison Fanning, had remained by their selves, playing cards and sipping whisky out of a bottle during the several hour train ride.

Thomas retrieved his gear; his father-in-law had presented him with a brand new Winchester Model '94 .30-30 deer rifle and leather scabbard several weeks earlier and had accompanied him several times to the sea shore to practice shooting. It had taken hundreds of practice rounds before Thomas began to feel at ease with the rifle but eventually he was able to consistently place shots within a small four inch target at fifty yards.

Handon McPherson had explained to Thomas that he had hunted in this area of the Sierra Nevada Mountain Range three or four times before. He had made all the travel arrangements for the hunting trip ahead of their arrival. Three open double-buggies waited to take them the fifteen miles to the cattle ranch that was owned by Hector Gordon and nestled in the transitional foothills at the base of the Sierra Nevada Mountains. Gordon would provide a guide for the hunting party as well as food and supplies and would rent them horses, saddles and tack for the four-day hunting trip. They would eat dinner and spend tonight at the Gordon ranch, then after an early morning breakfast, load their pack horses and saddle up for the ride up the Kaweah River, staying on the main river past the Northern Fork of the Kaweah, then continue generally eastward toward the four-hundred thousand acre Sequoia National Park, founded thirteen years earlier. Without any unusual delays, they should arrive at the secluded location just beyond the western limits of the park in time to set up their camp before dark. McPherson had used this remote camp site, situated some six or eight thousand feet above sea level, on previous hunting trips.

They stowed their rifles, bed rolls and canvas bags of spare clothing into the waiting carriages and within minutes were east of Visalia with the majestic Sierra Nevada Mountains spread across the landscape before their eyes. The air was clear, though it shimmered in the afternoon heat and Thomas could plainly make out the low, rolling, sun-baked foothills that gradually merged into the deep blue-green tree-shrouded mountains and valleys of the higher elevations. Far in the distance the jagged peaks and ridges of grey granite, the rugged backbone of the mountain range, caught the late afternoon sun's rays. Many of the further peaks shined brilliant white—still deeply layered with last winter's snow.

As if old and forgotten memories had been stirred, Thomas was struck with a nearly overwhelming sense of déjà vu as he stared at the mountains. He had been to and seen the Sierra Nevada Mountains before, particularly the mountains east of Sacramento where some of his lumbering interests were. He looked carefully, frowned. Coming from the unbroken flatness of the San Joaquin Valley as they approached the foothills, the steep rise of the deep-blue mountains beyond rose up like an island rising above the horizon at sea. He nodded to himself. That was it, of course. The memories of the small, deserted island as he had sailed away from it all those years ago suddenly surfaced and he found himself once again yearning for the solitude and peace the island had offered. No, he reminded himself, it hadn't been *offered* . . . it was instead an uncompromising, unforgiving *demand*; either fight daily for survival or face certain death. He had struggled to survive, alone with his thoughts and fears, alone with memories of what might have been or premonitions of what still could be. He had been utterly isolated, spending every day simply staying alive in order to eventually die on the island or to risk everything for the barest of possibilities to live. Five years of isolation! God! How he had yearned and ached for human companionship! He smiled as he recalled the injured sea gull he had befriended and named Frisco; his non-speaking but steadfast companion had actually even saved his life! He chuckled to himself.

Frank Barnwell was seated next to Thomas and glanced at him at the sound of his soft laughter. "Must be quite amusing, Thomas." His deep voice carried over the sound of the carriage.

"Just some very old memories, Frank. A long time ago, now," Thomas replied quietly.

"From your laughter, they must be good memories."

Thomas nodded. "Some are." These days it was difficult for him to talk about his experiences on the island. Too many people asked far too many questions, prying into his psyche and were morbidly curious regarding his physical wounds and scars that occasionally made themselves known. They wanted to know everything, all the intimate details, why and how and over the years his answers had become shorter and more abrupt as he enclosed the entire episode within a hard shell of self-protection, away from their *it must have been terrible* sympathetic observations.

"That's good. It's nice to have some worthy memories."

Thomas didn't immediately reply. The man sitting beside him seemed to be less curious than most who had inquired into his past. Thomas suspected that Barnwell was in his late twenties; perhaps five or six years older than himself. "Where did you go to school, Frank?"

"Stanford. I graduated eight years ago with an engineering degree. How about you?"

Thomas grimaced. "I'm without a college education." *Without any formal education* he acknowledged to himself.

"Well, you've done very well, if I do say so. Very well indeed." Frank pointed ahead at the foothills. "We're getting near the Gordon ranch. Ever been here before?"

"No. This is my first hunting trip."

"You'll like the Gordon's. Very nice people." He looked across and seemed to sense Thomas's discomfort. "I was the first one in my family to go to college. My father had only a basic education, up through the sixth grade. I grew up on a small cattle ranch north of Sacramento." He shook his head and laughed wryly. "My father was incredibly smart, even with his limited education!"

Thomas stared at the mountains for several seconds before he responded. "My father died in an accident when I was only a year old so I don't remember him. He and my mother were Irish immigrants. I . . . I lost track of my mother several years ago. I think she remarried and is living on the east coast somewhere."

Frank nodded his head and said, "I'm sorry." He studied the approaching foothills. "So you married Handon McPherson's daughter."

Thomas nodded slowly and smiled. "I sure did."

The three carriages turned up a dusty sycamore-lined drive. "Here's the ranch. They have a nice spread, around a thousand acres, maybe more. They raise cattle mostly but they're planning to get into citrus fruit as well. Oranges. Agriculture here in the valley's going to be big business someday. Going to require lots of water."

"Sounds like you've been here before."

"Once." The carriages pulled up in front of the ranch house. "Ah and there's Hector and Margarita!" Frank jumped from the carriage and greeted the couple, shaking hands with the tall and lanky Hector and sharing a hearty embrace with the short, dark haired woman. The rest of the men disembarked as well and Thomas joined them in meeting their overnight hosts. Hector shook hands solemnly with each man, carefully repeating every name and looking carefully into the eyes of his temporary guests. He was a few inches taller than Thomas and wore denim pants and shirt, in spite of the late afternoon heat. A sweat-stained and battered wide-brimmed hat protected his head from the broiling rays of the late summer sun. He introduced Margarita and she went around to each man and embraced him, repeating the names she had already memorized. Margarita barely came up to Hector's mid-chest; she was slender and startlingly alluring with features that opened easily into a warm and genuine smile revealing even and attractive teeth.

Within minutes the men were shown to their overnight quarters, an old but comfortable clap-board bunkhouse with enough beds for ten or more. A separate shower house was available for the men to wash up after their long trip.

The sun was just beginning to set when they entered the large ranch house for dinner. It was obvious that the structure had been added onto several times and was now spacious and open. The main room had at one time been the original house, built of white-washed adobe with massive hand-hewn beams supporting the cedar shake roof. An immense fireplace nearly filled one end of the room; a large, detailed map of California was positioned on the wall over an ancient wooden desk at the other end. Comfortable leather chairs were arranged to accommodate perhaps ten or twelve visitors. The group was ushered into the dining room and was seated around a long table where they were joined by Hector, Margarita and their two children, Ramon and Angela.

Thomas could see that Ramon would soon be the likeness of his father. Though just nineteen years old, he already stood over six feet tall, was wide shouldered and tanned from long hours in the sun tending the family's cattle herd. He spoke capably with a young but respectable sureness and strength in his voice, joining his father and some of the men in animated conversation about the futures of cattle ranching and citrus farming.

Angela would soon take after her mother, inheriting Margarita's petite figure and captivating attractiveness. Her impending beauty was already near full bloom at the age of seventeen; she nonchalantly informed the guests that she would be eighteen in less than three months. Like her brother, the suntan on her face and arms revealed long hours spent outdoors. Her black, silk-like hair was drawn back into a single long braid that she brought forward over her left shoulder. Her long eyelashes flashed as she spoke and stole fleeting, sidelong glimpses at the younger men, Frank and Thomas. Once, when Thomas caught her eyes as she glanced in his direction, he noticed the blush rise quickly above the open neckline of her blouse.

Shortly after eating, the hunting party joined Hector in the spacious living room and they met the man who would act as the guide on this trip. Hector introduced him as a long time employee of the ranch by the name of Beckley Weston. Beckley, or "Beck" as he quickly announced was his preferred moniker, was tall and slim, tanned and weather-worn with silver hair that hung loosely to his shoulders. He quickly and succinctly went over the arrangements: he would lead the group into the remote high Sierra Mountains, act as game tracker for a group—not to exceed three hunters—each day and dress out any game the hunters killed. They would remain in the area until each group managed a kill or until the entire party decided to return to the ranch. He would be responsible for preparation of meals but the hunting party would be responsible for their own horses and campsite setup and cleanup. There were few questions from the hunting party and Beck excused himself and left the room.

*   *   *

Morning arrived already warm and surprisingly humid. The faint purple hues of dawn were just beginning to lighten the eastern sky over the distant mountain peaks. The aroma of breakfast and coffee greeted Thomas when he entered the ranch house. Margarita had already prepared a generous meal of steak and eggs, biscuits and honey and was waiting, ready to serve the hunting party as they trooped into the dining room. Angela helped her mother deliver the heavy laden plates and platters, scrupulously avoiding eye contact with Thomas. Easy banter and laughter filled the room as the men finished the meal with steaming mugs of coffee.

Finally Handon McPherson broke into the stream of conversation; "Well men, it's time to ride. We have a long way to go and the hours aren't getting any longer or the miles any shorter."

The eight men pushed their chairs back away from the table, copiously thanking Margarita and Angela. Both of the women beamed and nodded self-consciously and Angela finally glanced at Thomas and blushed again as their eyes locked briefly.

Hector and Beck already had eight horses saddled and six more equipped with sawbuck pack saddles and panniers full of gear and provisions. Each man identified his personal rifle and scabbard already attached to a saddle and mounted his horse. Thomas's horse was a solid, six year old sorrel gelding. Hector and Beck had carefully sized up each man and the stirrups had already been adjusted to fit.

Beck organized the seven hunters and six pack horses into a single file and they got underway with Beck taking the leading position; Handon rode second in line and was the only one in the hunting party not leading a pack horse. Thomas was assigned as the next to last rider and led one of the pack horses. When he looked over his shoulder for a last glance at the ranch house he saw Angela standing alone near the gate and she raised her arm in a quick farewell gesture. He returned the motion and watched as she turned and started toward the house. Thomas didn't see his father-in-law turn and look back at the same time to check the riders behind him, nor did he notice the transitory look of uneasiness on McPherson's face.

The sun was touching the tree tops and the heat of the oncoming day was already in evidence. It wasn't long before sweat trickled down Thomas's neck and the leather saddle chafed at his thighs. He wasn't alone in his discomfort as he watched the riders ahead wipe away perspiration and squirm in their saddles. Beck led the party directly east until they picked up the slow moving Kaweah River where they stopped long enough for the horses to drink. The water was cool but Beck assured them that in a few miles it would be colder. They set out once again along the boulder strewn river with their guide carefully picking his way among the skimpy brush and rocks and fallen trees that lined the banks. In an hour, the scraggy brush changed to late-summer chaparral as the river canyon rose in elevation; the air cooled and Thomas found himself breathing in the almost forgotten scents of the surrounding feral wilderness. Three hours later they were among the scattered black oaks near where the North Fork of the Kaweah joined the main river. The air here was definitely cooler and when they stopped to water the horses, jackets were pulled out, ready to be worn a little later in the day. They ate a quick meal of cold biscuits and sun-dried beef, washed down with cold water from the river.

Beck eyed the position of the sun, hitched up the pistol belt around his hips. "Saddle up, men! We mustn't dally too long around here!" Everyone groaned as they climbed stiffly back onto their horses.

The trail slanted upward as they continued following the river, staying near the rocky northern bank. The deep canyon closed in on either side and the trees became more closely packed, the oak trees were slowly replaced by pine and fir trees at the higher elevation. The air became cool and crisp in the afternoon shade and the ground was covered with a thick, undisturbed carpet of needles and clumps of bracken, dogwood and manzanita, lupine and gooseberries and strong-smelling bear clover; only gray patches of bare rock and granite boulders broke through the dense forest carpet. Beck began to angle the hunting party away from the stream and the nearly invisible trail became much steeper as they followed a zigzag route up the precipitous side of the canyon. Soon they were above the tallest trees that filled the valley below and could look down at the Kaweah River, now just a narrow silver band several hundred feet below them.

Beck selected his way carefully, leading the train of riders and their pack animals among the rocky crags that formed the sharply sloping canyon wall, making sure that the foothold for the horses was sound while attempting to minimize the amount of upward lunging the horses and riders would have to do. Exposed on the southern edge of the steep mountain, the late afternoon sun beat directly down on them but the air itself was quite cool. The only sounds were the heavy breathing of the horses and the clatter of their hooves against the rocky path, the creak of saddle leather and the occasional cluck coming from the riders as they communicated with their horses. Their main focus was to stay in line with the horse and rider ahead and maneuver their horse around any obstacle such as loose rocks or an exposed tree root that might cause them to lose their footing or stumble. They crossed numerous rivulets that trickled clear spring water and what appeared to be inviting openings into the canyon wall but Beck led them on, continuing the slow climb, each switchback gaining a hundred feet or so in elevation.

Thomas lifted his eyes momentarily to absorb the majestic view. A mile ahead of them and further up the river canyon a massive pillar of granite like a medieval castle turret thrust its towering peak a thousand feet into the sky. More than two thousand feet below them the Kaweah River was now nothing more than a silver thread, nearly invisible as it wound among the granite boulders. The ridges of mountains repeated ahead, higher and higher. Lush green tree covered crests gave way to distant granite peaks eleven and twelve thousand feet high; lacerated by deep snow-filled crevices, the exposed spine of the four hundred mile long Sierra Nevada Mountain Range. Further to the south would be Mount Whitney, its peak over fourteen thousand five hundred feet above sea level; Thomas had located it on the map posted on the wall in Hector Gordon's ranch house the evening before. The cool mountain air was crystal clear, the cloudless sky deep cobalt. Tree-swathed mountains and shadowy canyons revealed the entire spectrum of green from near-yellow to dark blue, almost black. He looked around slowly and shook his head in awe; the sheer extent and splendor of the panorama were unlike anything he had ever experienced.

The climb continued for another hour. Then the terrain gradually changed and became less of a slope covered densely with trees and undergrowth. They stopped by a spring and gave the horses an opportunity to drink and rest for half an hour as the men climbed down to stretch and take in the vast scene spread before them

"How much further, Beck?" CW asked. "We going to make it before dark?"

Their guide checked the position of the late afternoon sun. "I reckon we will. Going to be a bit tight, though."

"Maybe a couple of hours?" CW persisted.

"About three, maybe a little more."

Some of the men groaned.

Gene Alexander turned to face Handon McPherson. "I swear, Handon. You sure know how to pick places to get away! Probably hasn't been a white man up here in fifty years!" he remarked.

"Hell, been a lot longer than that, Gene," Handon shot back and everyone chuckled.

"Don't know about you boys but my ass' 'bout rubbed raw," Ralph Patterson grunted. "I ain't used to riding horseback for ten hours straight."

"Didn't know you Johnny-reb artillery boys ever to ride a horse, Ralph!" Harrison Fanning commented dryly and everyone laughed.

The easy banter continued for a few minutes as the men paced about and stretched to ease their aching muscles. Thomas was beginning to feel more at ease with the collection of men about him. They were all either business acquaintances or political friends of his father-in-law and except for Frank Barnwell, were of McPherson's generation; conversations between the men revealed that Harrison Fanning had fought with the Union Army. Gene Alexander and Ralph Patterson had fought on the side of the Confederacy during the Civil War and occasionally voiced somewhat rancorous sentiments toward things associated with the North.

"Well, time to get back on your horses, boys," McPherson muttered, "lest you want to walk the rest of the way."

The hunting party rode easier now that the ground was not so steep. They had entered the deeper, high elevation forest. Beck identified the trees as they passed through, pointing out the orange-barked Ponderosa pines, the Sugar pines with their twenty-inch long seed-cones and tall and thin Lodgepole pines, so named because of their use by Native Americans in the construction of tepee lodges. Both red and white fir trees were interspersed with the pines and the forest canopy took on a dense, at times almost opaque thickness resulting in less undergrowth. In less than an hour another type of tree was seen and Beck pointed it out.

"That there's a Sequoia Redwood. We'll see some that are much larger."

The men stopped and stared. The tree was spectacular. Its trunk was likely ten or more feet in diameter and the lowest branches shielded the lofty crowns of the tallest pine trees.

Thomas gazed at the huge tree in awe. It was far taller than the largest buildings in San Francisco. "How long does it take for a tree to grow that big?" he asked.

Handon looked at this son-in-law. "That tree is probably over a thousand years old."

Thomas could only shake his head in amazement as they continued to ride through the enormous redwoods scattered among the forest but in less than an hour they stopped again to stare at another mammoth redwood tree. Its trunk at shoulder height appeared to be at least twenty-five feet in diameter; the bulbous base added another ten feet in diameter. A massive L-shaped branch about seventy feet up was close to six feet through and rose parallel to the main trunk another hundred feet or so.

"Four years ago I estimated its height to be right about two-hundred and seventy feet," Handon announced. "I'd guess it's near twenty-five hundred years old."

Beck continued to lead the group through the silent forest, from time to time entering canyons that shot off the general route, until finally they came to a small meadow surrounded by thick woods and a nearby vertical face of rock that effectively cut off the late afternoon sunshine.

"This's where we'll set up camp," the guide announced. "I reckon the cliff over yonder will protect us from the wind; the small creek over there will provide plenty of clear water and the woods a quick and easy supply of firewood." He glanced at the late afternoon sun. "We best git setting up, boys."

Though McPherson had camped near here in past years, there was virtually no sign of human presence in the area. Handon and the others had hunted together off and on for several years and they knew what needed to be done. Thomas helped wherever he could but found he hadn't but very basic ideas of setting up a hunting camp. He gathered rocks to stack into a fire pit and set about gathering firewood, breaking fallen branches into smaller pieces and hauling them into the protected meadow.

Darkness fell with surprising suddenness and with it the temperature dropped. The men pulled on heavier coats and hats and soon had a blaze going in the fire pit. Margarita had supplied them with a large chunk of beef which had been safely tucked away from the heat of the day. Beck skewered it and set it to roast over the coals at one side of the fire. Potatoes were tucked into the loose soil under the coals to bake.

They raised tarps overhead to shield them from possible rain and Thomas laid out his bedroll near one of them. While the others milled about the fire, he sat back and watched the stars as they popped out in the clear high altitude air. Orion would be rising in the eastern sky sometime after midnight this time of the year. It had been a long time since he had seen the full hemisphere of stars and the sight brought back memories once again; they absorbed his consciousness as he let his mind drift with his thoughts.

* * *

The sound of harmonica music awoke him and he stared into the pale glow of the circle of men around the fire. Gene Alexander was entertaining the men with songs he had played as a young man in the Confederate Army, Dixie's Land, Goober Peas, Southern Soldier Boy, and Stonewall Jackson's Way and several tunes that Thomas didn't recognize. He arose and joined the circle. The beef was roasted dark brown and dripping fat juice. He could smell the potatoes baking beneath the coals. Frank passed tin plates around. Beck sliced off thick slabs of meat and slid them onto the plates. Ralph dug out the steaming potatoes and speared them one at a time, dropping them onto waiting plates. Conversation stopped as the men ate. Thomas realized some of the older men were themselves lost in memories of years past, perhaps when they had desperately waged war and tried to kill each other.

Finally, the silence was broken. "Wonder if that old Indian is still around," Gene Alexander muttered between bites.

"Old Gray Hawk? Yeah, most likely." Handon answered.

"Who's Old Gray Hawk?" Frank looked up quickly.

Beck grunted and set his tin plate on a rock. "Just an old Indian whose been living in these parts for forty years or more." He turned and looked into the shadows beyond the dwindling light of the fire. "Probably out there right now, keeping an eye on us. That's why I always carry my trusty old Buntline when I'm up here." He patted the long barreled pistol at his side.

Frank turned and stared into the dark shadows surrounding them. "Well, I'll be! An Indian! Damnation! You ever see him?" he asked.

"Nope," Beck shook his head. "Never have."

"Well, how do you know he's out there then?"

"I don't but he'll let you know if he's there."

"Well, who is he?" Frank persisted, glancing around the circle of faces and settling on Handon. "Damn, Handon, you never let on about an Indian before."

Handon looked at Frank. "I guess the subject just never came up before, Frank." He stirred the fire with a stick, apparently in thought. "Well, the story goes that he was a young shaman. I guess you know that a shaman is supposed to have supernatural powers. Anyway, Gray Hawk was living with a tribe of Indians up near Columbia. It was a small tribe, maybe twenty or thirty, including children. Story goes that they were peaceful people, part of the Western Mono Indians that settled on the western side of the Sierra Nevada a couple of hundred years ago. In the winter, they'd come down to the foothills and then they'd summer over in the higher elevations to fish, hunt, gather nuts and berries. Apparently one summer they set up along a small river that a bunch of gold prospectors figured *they* wanted. They tried without any luck to convince the Indians to leave. Things got badly out of hand and the prospectors ended up slaughtering the whole bunch, men, women and children . . . raped the young women." He paused. "They dug a pit and threw the bodies in, along with the tepees and everything else the Indians left. Tried to burn it all up and conceal the massacre." He paused. "Gray Hawk wasn't there at the time; but when he got there two days later, he went completely crazy. Killed every one of those murdering prospectors—there were six of them. Cut off their manhood and slit their throats . . ." he paused and looked around the circle of faces, ". . . in that order. Left 'em stretched out in the sun for the authorities to find."

"Well, damnation . . ." Frank muttered.

"Anyway," Handon continued after another quick glance at Frank, "the army went after him, real hard at first but finally gave up chasing him after about ten years. Gray Hawk just knew the mountains and mountain ways better than the army did. Couple of bounty hunters have tried but they gave up, too. He's been seen off and on in these parts over the years.

29

Still has a price on his head but I don't think anyone's actively gone after him for years."

Frank asked, "So, you think he's still around?"

Handon shrugged his shoulders. "Far as they know."

"Well . . . Damnation . . ." Frank peered over his shoulder into the darkness.

* * *

Thomas awoke as the early morning sunlight streamed through the trees into his eyes. Three of the men were up and had re-kindled the fire, the rest were still rolled up in their bedrolls. Gene was digging through the pile of blankets that comprised his bedroll, mumbling to himself. Finally he stood up, a frustrated expression on his face.

"Hey! Anybody seen my harmonica?"

Frank and Harrison both shook their head.

"Had it right here last night," Gene muttered out loud as he bent over and sorted once again through the pile.

"Maybe ol' Gray Hawk made off with it," Frank teased.

"Now, that ain't even remotely funny, Frank," Gene growled.

Handon rolled over onto his back. "What's all the ruckus about, boys?"

"Gene can't find his harmonica," Harrison replied.

Thomas listened as the conversation bantered back and forth. He had slept well through the early part of the night and had awakened once in the hours before dawn. The night was hushed, not even the slightest breeze rustled the foliage high in the trees. The moon was new, the disk dark and absent of reflected sunlight. Constellation Orion was almost overhead and he had watched as the entire field of stars moved slowly westward. He had fleetingly sensed a shadow against the night sky as it moved rapidly across his field of vision but it was gone before he could rise up on his elbow. He had drifted off to sleep once again.

Beck poked the fire and carefully lifted the lid of the coffee pot. "Coffee's 'bout ready, boys."

* * *

The men divided into three hunting groups; Thomas joined his father-in-law. Their group would be led today by Beck. Frank Barnwell and Ralph Patterson comprised the second group, Gene Alexander and CW made up the third party. Harrison Fanning elected to stay at the campsite to protect it from curious bears.

They saddled up and rode off in three different directions. Thomas and his group headed further up in elevation, winding through deep canyons and dense forests. Twice Beck raised his hand, dismounted, studied the ground and muttered nearly inaudibly while gazing in the direction of the blurred deer tracks. In each instance he led them off on a route tangential to the group's heading, only to come up empty handed. From astride his horse, Thomas frowned slightly as Beck directed the hunters onto these futile excursions. By mid afternoon, they had traveled several miles without sighting any deer and decided to head back to camp. A half hour later a faint gunshot echoed among the mountains like distant thunder.

Handon grunted. "Well, someone got off a shot, at least."

The ride had unveiled a spectacular new world to Thomas. The vast stretches of seemingly endless mountain ridges, the scattered groves of huge Sequoia Redwood trees, the deep shadowy canyons with ice cold streams and the multitude of species of underbrush gave him something to look at and admire in every direction. Occasionally they paused on vistas that overlooked the lower foothills and the huge flatness of the San Joaquin Valley several thousand feet below and twenty miles west of their position.

Back at camp, Gene Alexander and CW were describing how they had spotted a large buck across a canyon and had worked their way closer on foot for over an hour. Finally CW had managed to get off a shot.

"I missed him! Nice big rack! Twenty-four, maybe twenty-six inches! Can't believe I missed him!" CW drawled. "Had him dead in my sights. Just a little downhill, maybe a hundred yards. Should have got him, easy."

"Looked to me like your shot was high," Gene commented. "Maybe we should'a sighted in, CW. Been a while since either of us fired our rifles."

"Maybe you're right," CW demurred.

The other hunting party rode in about an hour later. They hadn't sighted a deer all day.

That evening as Beck was fixing something to eat, Ralph let out a whoop from down near the creak. "Gene! I found your harmonica! Sitting right here on a rock next to the creek!" A few moments later he appeared carrying the harmonica and a feather. "Someone set it right on top this feather." He held it up for all to see.

Beck glanced at it then returned to his cooking. "That's a hawk's feather," he commented.

"Gray Hawk," Frank groaned. "Damnation! That ol' Indian was right here in our camp last night!"

*   *   *

Two more days passed with no luck for any of the three hunting parties. The weather turned cool and cloudy as an early autumn storm started gathering. On their third night, the wind picked up and streaks of lightning lit the sky, the thunder reverberating among the mountains. Cold rain drove the men under the tarps for protection and they remained there until mid-morning of the fourth day. At last the skies cleared; the noontime sun warmed the rain-soaked earth causing it to give off wisps of steam.

Beck glanced around and nodded. "Could be a good day if we get going. Deer'll be on the move after that rain."

Beck was right. Each of the three hunting parties got a kill before the day ended. CW had volunteered to remain at the camp, as sleeping on the ground and the cold rain had caused his knees and back to ache painfully. Ralph and Harrison, with the aid of Beck, had tracked a large buck and finally Harrison got a clean shot that dropped the animal immediately. Gene and Frank were even luckier; their opportunity came less than a half hour ride from camp when they spotted their quarry across a narrow ravine and Frank brought it down.

Thomas and his father-in-law had ridden back to the area they had hunted the first day. In the lead, Handon spotted deer tracks in the wet soil.

"Look there!" he whispered as he pointed. "Fresh tracks."

Thomas shook his head. "They're old tracks, Handon. Several hours, at least. Maybe more."

Handon stared at his son-in-law. "How would you know that? You've never even been deer hunting before!"

"See that spider web right there, across their path, Handon," he pointed. "Been there long enough to catch some debris from the trees. Deer would have knocked that web down had he gone through there after it was built." He turned to look at Handon. "I saw the same thing the other day when Beck was leading but didn't say anything because he's the expert."

"I'll be damned . . ." Handon muttered as he shook his head. "You got to be right, Thomas. Something you learned on the island?"

Thomas just nodded silently. Though the island had been devoid of four legged creatures, he had quickly adopted the habit of carefully studying his surroundings.

"Why don't you take the point, son?" McPherson moved his horse to one side. "Looks like you got some talents I didn't know about."

However, within half an hour Handon was the first to spot the large buck partly hidden and foraging within a thicket of young fir trees.

"Look there!" he whispered as he pointed. "That's a big one! Whew! Look at that rack! That'll make a nice trophy in your office!" He was already dismounting and pulling his handsomely customized Mauser G98 rifle from the scabbard. "You take the shot, son. I'd say it's about eighty yards. Nice clean shot for you."

Thomas nodded silently, dismounted and slid the Winchester from its scabbard. He slowly levered a round into the receiver, being careful to avoid making a noise and at the same time keeping an eye on the deer. The buck was suddenly conscious of their presence and turned his head to face them. Thomas shouldered his rifle, steadied on the stationary quarry and squeezed the trigger. The recoil made the rifle jump in his grip and the big buck staggered, fell to his front knees then struggled to stand erect. He turned and attempted to leap over a fallen log but his knees buckled again and he fell. The big deer struggled once more, desperately trying to regain his footing but the struggles were already weaker and his head fell to the ground.

"He's down. Excellent shot," Handon murmured.

Thomas shook his head slowly. He had already ejected the spent round from the receiver and was sliding the Winchester back into the scabbard. "Just not much excitement in it for me, Handon. Guess I'm not cut out to be a hunter like you. I've seen and experienced enough struggle for life, already." He pointed at the big deer, motionless now. "Not fair to him either. We ride up on him and shoot him from eighty yards away. He's alive one minute and dead the next. Just so I could have his head mounted and hung on my wall as a trophy."

"Nonsense!" Handon growled. "That's what hunting's all about, Thomas! Man against the wild animal in his natural habitat. The hunter pitting his superior skills against the instincts and cunning of the quarry."

Thomas looked at his father-in-law. "I guess I don't see it that way, Handon."

"Well, just how do you *see it* then?" Handon asked his voice edged with rare sarcasm.

"I see very little skill involved in sighting a non-belligerent animal by pure chance and executing it from a distance with a high powered rifle while it's standing still, looking with naive curiosity at its soon-to-be assassin. Where's the skill? I could have done the same thing with a stationary target made of wood and painted to look like a deer. We didn't follow the deer's tracks, nor did we locate him by observing and interpreting the signs of his passing through. We didn't investigate his habitat to determine where he has been and where he might go for food or shelter. We didn't skillfully work our way in close, attempting to blend in with his surroundings. So, where's the mystery? Where's the skill?" He looked at Handon. "What's the purpose?"

There were several seconds of strained silence. "That's all sheer nonsense, Thomas. We shall not talk about it anymore on this trip."

Thomas stood at a distance while Handon expertly field dressed the carcass and lashed it behind his saddle to be taken back to the camp. The silence between them stretched until they reached the camp and found Gene and Frank and their quarry already there.

By evening, the three hunting parties had each thoroughly prepared the carcasses and the portions—including trophy heads or antler racks—they would take with them. Lacking refrigeration of any sort, it was now imperative that they leave at first light for the Gordon's ranch. They packed up what they could. The unspoken opinion among the group seemed to be that all were anxious now to head for home. Thomas found that he was ready to leave and put the hunt and its memories behind him. He sat quietly among the group as they swapped stories around the campfire and celebrated by slowly roasting venison heart over the fire for their meal. Beck made a pan of corn bread to go with the venison and each took a few sips of whisky out of the bottle.

* * *

They arrived at Hector Gordon's ranch late the next day. Beck quickly said his farewells and with Ramon's help, began taking care of the livestock.

Angela stood to one side and Thomas was aware that her eyes followed his every movement, though she quickly diverted her gaze when he looked her way. Margarita took charge of the venison and Hector announced he would make sure the trophy heads were handed over to a local taxidermist to be properly prepared and mounted for future shipment to San Francisco.

It was dark when they finished the large meal Margarita had prepared. The men gathered in small groups to talk or play cards. Thomas took the opportunity to go outside and be alone for the first time in nearly a week. He walked across the wide drive until he came to the rail fence surrounding the corral, leaned against it and stared at the sky. The early first crescent moon cast very little light and the stars shimmered in the still heat of the early evening. Though he knew that he would never be a hunter like his father-in-law, the trip into the high mountains had already established a hold on his inner being. For the first time in years, he had found the possibility of genuine peace and solitude among the deep valleys and rugged peaks and the near holiness of the massive redwood trees and their quiet intensity. He knew that he would someday return . . .

"Mister O'Reiley?" The female voice behind him startled him and he spun around.

"Miss Angela," he stepped forward. "Good evening! Would you care to join me?"

"Please call me Angela and yes, I would certainly like to join you." She stepped closer and Thomas could feel the heat radiating from her nearness.

"I'll call you Angela if you agree to call me Thomas."

"I can only do that when my mother or father are not around. I'm sure you understand." She moved closer and nearly touching, stood beside him facing the fence. She put her foot on the lower rail and leaned on her elbows against the fence. "How did you like your hunting trip, Thomas?"

He turned and joined her at the fence, their arms nearly touching, aware of an unusual pleasure in their closeness. In spite of the near-darkness, he could see that she wore her long black hair loose and unfettered this evening. "I must admit that I doubt I shall ever truly enjoy killing an animal. Just not a part of who I am."

A moment's hesitation, then, "you took down a magnificent buck. My father said it was a good, clean shot. He doesn't make those kinds of comments very often."

He nodded slowly. "I didn't enjoy shooting him. I did it to only prove I could."

In the near darkness, she looked into his face. "Then . . . what did you enjoy?"

It took him several long moments to respond. "I suppose just being there in the mountains. I was spellbound by their . . . stark tranquility, their quiet beauty." He stumbled for words. "I think the incredible, boundless and amazing diversity of creation is astonishing, the deep, mysterious canyons and the silent power of the majestic snow-covered peaks . . ." He paused, shook his head slowly and chuckled. "I'm afraid I'm sounding rather poetic."

She remained silent for several seconds. "We get a lot of hunters through here and I don't usually hear them talk like that. They mainly want to brag about their hunting experiences. You know—the deer or bear they killed or the big buck that got away." She laughed lightly, her voice tinkling with amusement. "The ones that got away are always the biggest!"

They stood silently, nearly touching, for several moments. The faint sounds of crickets and cicadas and the odors of the late summer evening surrounding them. The air was motionless, warm. The sky blazed with hundreds of thousands of stars and the faint crescent of moon had already disappeared over the western horizon. From across the corral a horse whinnied softly, accompanied by the muffled sounds of its hooves as it pawed restlessly in the loose soil. In the tranquil stillness, Thomas was suddenly aware of the faintly perfumed fragrance of the young woman at his side. "I know that I like the mountains," he stated flatly as if setting an abrupt punctuation mark to his own thoughts.

"I certainly agree. The mountains are really beautiful." She turned once again to look at him. "I'm glad you like them. They're a part of my life." She paused and Thomas sensed that she was going to add something.

Finally she looked into his eyes and asked rather tentatively, "do you think you'll come back someday, Thomas?"

CHAPTER 3

<u>March 3, 1899 San Francisco</u>
Thomas read with some interest the article in the San Francisco Chronicle covering the proposed inter-ocean canal. Even the possibility of constructing a canal across the narrow stretch of land in Central America was moving at a snail-like pace, trapped in the web of political debate. Already the French Canal Company had gone bankrupt twice in its endeavors to construct such a canal and the current New French Canal Company had offered to sell their concession rights to the United States. Several major roadblocks stood in the way, financial, geographical, engineering and political.

Several commissions had studied prospective routes, leaning toward a canal through Nicaragua. The French Canal Company attempts to construct a canal through the Isthmus of Panama had cost thousands of lives and had shown little headway. Now their equipment lay, for the large part, rusting and disappearing under jungle vines. A proposed route through Nicaragua showed promise, taking advantage of the two large lakes—Lake Managua and Lake Nicaragua and a somewhat less mountainous path.

Congress met to discuss authorizing yet another investigation to determine the most practical route for a canal to be owned and operated by the United States.

<u>Monday, April 17, 1899 San Francisco, California</u>
Amanda's voice raised a notch, both in pitch and in volume, in spite of the children asleep in their rooms directly over their heads. "What do you mean; you're just going to *be away* for a few days?" She folded her arms across her bosom and tapped her foot impatiently. "You're going by yourself? You have a business to run, my darling husband! Have you told my father you will be taking a week away from the office? Why? I simply

don't understand, Thomas." Her frown turned into a look of desperate consternation.

"My dear Amanda, I don't suspect that you could understand." Thomas shook his head slowly. "I'm not sure myself that I fully understand. But I know that for my own sanity I need to distance myself from the increasingly difficult demands of our business and have some time to simply think . . ." he hesitated then added, "or to not think." He grimaced. "I need time to just . . . be. I feel that civilization is crowding in around me, virtually suffocating me. Every day I must deal with people that place tremendous demands on my time and vitality. I feel like a busy street juggler to whom someone has thrown several more items to juggle! I am surrounded by clamor; I am beset by demands; and I am haunted by the ugliness of corporate and political and even personal dishonesty. The only time I can pause to take a deep breath is when you and I go to bed at the end of the day. And then . . ." He shook his head.

She leaned herself onto his body and drew him close. "Thomas, my dearest Thomas," she whispered. "Our time together, our intimate time together is scarce but it is the best time of my day. I want you near me. I need your steadfast love and companionship. Your children need you . . ."

"You have my deepest love, sweet Amanda, as do our children. But," he hesitated, "I cannot fulfill any of your needs or desires if my own mind and body are so occupied with the external demands of this life that I don't have time to even *think* other thoughts." There were several moments of silence before he continued. "I will be going back to the lovely mountains that your father introduced me to last August. I shall be there for three days of repose and rejuvenation. I need you to understand that I *must* do this, Amanda. I will be away five or six days at the most and will return to your arms a new man."

She leaned back and gazed for several seconds deep into his eyes. "I believe you shall, my dear husband. But I shall miss you terribly."

*   *   *

A week later, Thomas stepped off the train into the mild early spring temperatures of the San Joaquin Valley. The little community of Visalia looked much as it did six months earlier but the spring rains had washed away the fine patina of dust that had accumulated on everything, giving the town a fresh look that would last only for a few weeks until the long dry summer began. The large sycamore trees in front of the railroad station had not yet leafed out but would very soon. A few horses with riders and a single carriage were moving slowly along the main street.

In spite of his father-in-law's obvious concerns and barely hidden wariness regarding Thomas's decision, Handon had reluctantly helped him make arrangements with the Gordon's for the necessary livestock and supplies for his private sojourn into the high country. A single carriage now awaited his use to get to the Gordon's ranch, he retrieved his baggage and placed it in the carriage. The train began to pull away from the station and Thomas felt a peculiar sense of separation, or division, of his life. There was a sense of freedom but at the same time a feeling of aloneness that surprised him and caused him briefly to consider that perhaps this was not a good idea after all.

By the time he reached the Gordon's ranch, he had pushed the earlier thoughts aside and was excited about renewing his acquaintance with the Gordon's. Although he was reluctant to admit it to himself he was looking forward to seeing Angela.

When he drove through the gate to the ranch, the Gordon's except for Ramon were waiting for him and greeted him enthusiastically. Hector pumped his hand and clapped him on the shoulder; Margarita stood on tiptoe to give him a hug and Angela followed suite, lingering only a fraction of a second longer than her mother. Over the evening meal, they questioned him about his reasons for wanting to be alone in the mountains and his answers were as vague as his own thoughts. He shared very briefly his exploits as a young man on the Orion, his years alone on the island and his recently discovered yearning to re-experience the solitude he had once dealt with in exile.

He joined Hector in the great room after dinner. A fire in the fireplace at one end was warding off the night chill and they pulled chairs up close to savor its warmth.

Hector shared with him his knowledge of the mountains at this time of the year. "I've been up there, Thomas. It could be very cold at night, freezing temperatures or worse. Build a good sturdy fire at night, bank it properly so that it'll remain alive all night, have firewood close at hand for the morning. Make sure to have water handy because creeks may still freeze up at night. Keep your food supplies out of reach of the bears; though it's still a little early for them, they'll be looking for food as they come out of hibernation. Have water and feed convenient for the stock. Days may be warm, especially in the sun, though there'll be drifts of snow in the shady areas and the canyons." He went on and Thomas carefully itemized these precautions in his mind. When he finally bid the rancher good night, Hector reminded him that the hours of daylight would be much less than he had experienced in August. "You won't have time to dawdle on your way up, Thomas."

Thomas made straightaway for the bunkhouse where he would spend the night but at the last moment changed his direction and walked through the darkness toward the fence enclosing the corral. He pulled the collar of his sheepskin coat up against the cold breeze and stuffed his hands deep into the pockets. When he reached the fence, he stood with his back to the ranch house, his emotions in conflict. Part of him waited eagerly and the other part harbored a feeling of guilt.

"Thomas?" the voice behind him called lightly.

He turned to find Angela several steps away, outlined against the diffused lantern light coming from the ranch house windows. The night was moonless and the overcast sky blocked out even the starlight.

"I was so hoping you'd come back, Thomas." she said as she stepped up closer to him. In spite of the chill, he could sense the aura of her nearness. "So, you're going again into the high country." The last was half statement and half question. He realized that her voice had changed somewhat in the six months since he had last spoken with her. It was, he thought, more . . . husky, more grownup. She leaned with her back against the fence, her thick sheepskin coat brushing lightly against his; neither of them made a move to put polite space between them. "I've gone up there every summer since I was a little tyke but I've never been up there at this time of the year."

"It'll certainly be different than the last time I was there." He leaned back, comfortable with her immature closeness.

There was a long pause before she responded. "I wish I was going with you, Thomas."

The last comment startled Thomas and he was awkwardly uncertain of how he should reply. In the few seconds of silence he allowed his mind to travel to places it had not visited for years. *That would be nice*, he thought abruptly and the notion surprised him.

Before he could respond, she spoke again. "I'm sorry, Thomas. I know that's not possible." She lowered her voice until it was barely a whisper. "It was only . . ." she tilted her head toward his, "a wish . . ." She stood on her tiptoe and quickly brushed his cheek with her lips. "Get some good sleep tonight." She walked quickly toward the ranch house, looking back just once to wave to him.

*   *   *

It was cold and the stars were still out when he awoke in the morning. He dressed quickly and headed to the ranch house where he knew Margarita would have breakfast prepared and coffee waiting. She greeted him with a warm hug and handed him a steaming mug of coffee. "Hector and Ramon are getting your horses and gear ready, Mister O'Reiley. Come! Sit and have breakfast. Hector says you should be off before sunrise! He is such a worrier! I think his head has a clock in it!" She laughed and set a plate of three fried eggs and a thick slice of pan-fried beef on the table in front of him.

Angela came into the room, slid into the chair across from him and smiled. "Good morning, Mister O'Reiley. You'll be getting an early start this morning."

"Yes. Your father suggests that I get started before sunrise."

She smiled and clucked her tongue. "My father is such a worrier!"

*   *   *

Two hours later Thomas was following the Kaweah River in the early light of dawn. He was astride the same horse he had ridden six months earlier and led the same pack horse. The countryside had areas of early morning frost that reflected the purple rays of sunrise. He stopped and allowed the horses to drink from the river but didn't linger. He figured he wouldn't stop and eat a midday meal, nor would he tarry around the giant redwoods. The time thus saved should get him to the camp site before darkness set in. He watched for memorized landmarks as he made his way among the boulders lining the river. By noon time he was high on the edge of the canyon wall looking down at the river far below. The clouds were beginning to burn off and the warm sunshine felt good, though the air still had a chill to it. Presently he crested the near-vertical canyon wall and before long passed the huge redwood tree, pausing only long enough to marvel at its immense size. *Two-thousand five hundred years old* he remembered his father-in-law telling them.

The way grew even less defined as he climbed higher in elevation. Some trees had fallen in winter storms, causing him to detour around them. One small stream now tumbled deep and wild with snow runoff and was impassable, forcing him to go further upstream to find a safe place to cross. The afternoon shadows were getting long and the air had turned much cooler. Landmarks were few and far between. There was no trail as such; in fact, few people had ever even been here.

With only a few minutes of sunlight left, he came upon the small meadow where the hunting party had established its campsite in August. Quickly now, he hobbled the horses and set about gathering a supply of firewood. Most of what he collected was damp from the winter storms but life on the island had taught him how to get a fire going even in these adverse conditions. The rough ring of stones he had arranged six months ago was still in place and soon the wood was crackling, sending up a shower of sparks as the blaze took hold, producing an expanding circle of light and warmth. He carefully arranged firewood, put water in a deep pot near the coals and sat near the fire savoring a few cold biscuits and venison jerky that Margarita had given him.

He allowed his mind to wander unguided through the labyrinth of thoughts and emotions; snippets of memories and events crowded and jostled for priority, clamoring for his attention. Some loomed large, like his thoughts of Amanda and the unanticipated attraction of Hector's daughter Angela, several years his junior. Some thoughts were irrelevant zephyrs that curled in like tiny wisps of smoke and his mind dispensed with them almost immediately. He closed his eyes and let his mind roam freely, unimpeded. It was late at night when he finally realized that the fire had nearly burned itself out. He rebuilt the blaze and stacked firewood close-by to keep it going through the night and then checked on the horses. The night wasn't as cold as he had expected and he threw down a tarp near the fire, rolled out his bedroll on top the tarp, removed his boots and climbed in fully dressed.

He awoke twice and added firewood to the blaze. Prior to the sunrise the temperature plunged and Thomas knew that it was approaching freezing. He was up and tending the fire when the sun crested over the distant high peaks. He fed and watered the horses and made himself a simple breakfast. He had no plans for the day—in fact, he had no plans for any of the three days he would be here. Probably he would hike to one or two of the higher vista points. There he could sit quietly in the sunshine watching and listening to nature. He had not brought the Winchester rifle with him, against the dour counsel of his father-in-law who argued that he should at least have protection against bears and mountain lions. To Thomas's contention that he had *lived in the wild for five years* without the aid of a rifle, Handon condescendingly reminded him that there had been no animals on the small island, *nothing larger than a damned sea gull.*

The morning warmed quickly and though there were patches of snow in the shaded areas, the air became almost spring-like. He busied himself collecting dead-fall Lodgepole pines, each about forty feet in length and stripped them of branches. When he had dragged a dozen of them into place, he set about making a rough six-sided corral for the horses using the pine trees as fencing around the perimeter. He utilized standing trees to attach the long poles, one at chest height and one at hip height. He laid it out so that one end of the corral straddled the creek which would supply the horses with a constant supply of water. The natural grasses and brush within the corral would provide some grazing food, at least for a few days at a time. Entrance into the corral was simply a matter of setting a single section of the fence on the ground. By late afternoon, he had the horses freed of their hobbles and loose to explore the new corral.

He had worked up a sweat in the afternoon heat. The hard work felt good and he become conscious of how little physical labor he had done in the past few years. He walked to the creek and rinsed himself off in the icy water realizing that the sun would soon be disappearing behind the mountains. He rekindled the fire and relaxed in its warmth. Sleep came easily that night.

Thomas awoke with the sun shining in his eyes; by noontime it had begun to warm the exposed slabs of granite and little wisps of steam came from the damp soil where the sunlight streamed through the trees. Thomas slipped a few biscuits into his pocket and set off to explore the area at the top of the sheer granite cliffs that bordered one side of the meadow. In less than a half hour he was sweating in the sunlight that reflected off the light grey granite as he followed a break in the granite that ran at a shallow angle up the cliff. Alternating winter freezing and summer heating had caused the rock to split and break over the ages creating a natural path about two feet wide and the climb was gradual. Vertical cracks intersected the natural path from time to time and were generally filled with small boulders and rocky debris. As he gained elevation, the view spread out below him in a panorama of green. The small creek near the camp site was visible as a thin silver thread that wove in and out among the trees. Further away, the forest closed in around the patch of meadow, carrying the carpet of trees beyond until they melded with the next ridge of trees a half mile away.

The pain struck his right leg with such suddenness and intensity that it caused him to gasp. His first thought was that his leg had snapped at the old injury and he looked down in surprise. The snake, which had been stretched out in the sunshine, still had its fangs buried in his calf, about three inches below his knee and even as he watched in horror the snake released its grip and struck again, lower this time. Thomas reeled in pain and fear shaking his leg violently in an attempt to get the snake to release. Finally the snake, which he quickly recognized as a rattlesnake, released its grip and dropped to the granite path then slithered back into a crevice. Almost immediately the area where the snake had bitten him began to burn as if someone had applied a red-hot poker to his leg.

"Oh, God!" The groan came out in sheer agony and terror through gritted teeth. Perched on the narrow rocky path two hundred feet above the green meadow, he quickly conceded he must either retreat or go forward. He had read several times in the San Francisco Chronicle of hikers in the dry hills south of the city that had been bitten by diamond-back rattlesnakes; many had died before they could reach help.

His only recourse would be to retreat and return quickly to camp . . . The horses, perhaps . . . Maybe he could somehow slow the advance of the venom . . . He slipped the bandanna from around his neck and made a quick tourniquet below his right knee. The pain was even more intense now, a torture of burning and throbbing as if a knife blade was thrust deep into his flesh. He turned and began the awkward descent, leaning against the vertical granite for support. He had traveled less than a hundred feet when the first flood of nausea swept over him like a wave of water, burying him in appalling pain. He doubled over and groaned out loud, shut his eyes against the agony, when he straightened, dizziness almost caused him to tumble off the narrow granite path. Perspiration exploded on his forehead and coursed stinging into his eyes. Before he reached the bottom of the cliff, he had doubled over twice again and ejected the contents of his stomach. Stumbling, dizzy, he tried to stay upright but the whole earth seemed to tilt on its side and he found himself lying on the ground, knees drawn up. Again he vomited; stomach muscles cramped; this time to bring up only bitter bile.

"Oh, God!" He moaned softly. "I'm not going to make it!" The pain was becoming excruciating, unbearable. "Amanda!" he whispered, "I'm so sorry! I love you, Mandy . . ."

Darkness swept in from all directions and folded about him like a soothing blanket . . .

*   *   *

The face directly above him was the perfect caricature of death. Wisps of smoke drifted from the nostrils and streamed from between the lips. One side of the face was stark white and the other side was black as coal; the junction of the two ran down the ridge of the nose. The sockets around the eyes were of the opposing colors. Long greasy hair hung loosely on each side, though some thin strands were gathered, braided tightly and decorated with small pieces of bone, wood and feathers. A weathered hand paused momentarily over Thomas's face and with a casual motion, swished the fumes away, only to be replaced with another long stream of acrid smoke from the lips of the creature Death. The lips barely moved but melodic sounds streamed from the appearance. Words that Thomas didn't recognize appeared to visually float above him in colors that he had never visualized before. When he let his eyes close, a montage of misshapen, distorted faces appeared to surround him and he was back once again on the ship Orion, tossing, pitching and rolling heavily in the angry sea. Some of the faces were howling like wild animals; their lips pulled back from their teeth; others simply stared at him with eyes that lacked any sign of life. The ship rolled hard to one side then continued to roll until Thomas felt himself sliding toward the abyss beside him. It continued to turn over and the screaming and howling reached a fever pitch; he was hanging from his bunk upside down, his fingers grasping for something to hold onto. The icy sea water came rushing in around him and darkness once more took him away.

A new sound awoke him; a low buzzing noise such as a bow being drawn across a cello string seemed to solidify the air, making it impossible to breathe; he struggled uselessly against his bonds. His limbs were clattering with uncontrolled shaking, like a wooden puppet on the end of its tethers. Drops of water were falling on him from somewhere; when he opened his eyes he saw Death once again hovering above him, this time with a leather pouch that dripped water. The face of Death pressed one end of the pouch to his parched lips. He sucked frantically to relieve the burning dryness of his lips; but his own lips refused to form the necessary seal, and the water merely dribbled uselessly onto his chin. The mouth of Death once again emitted a thin stream of smoke, this time directed at Thomas's mouth and nostrils. He gagged and coughed when the fumes entered his lungs and he vowed silently to never take a breath again, if necessary, to avoid the smoke. He tried to move his arms but now they seemed to be pinned to the floor, nailed perhaps with stout wooden pegs, as were his legs. Death hovered over him, crooning harmonious melodies that echoed and reverberated as if they were coming from deep within a cave. The voices began once again to howl and scream and the wind raged like a vile tornado of sound, smell and images of pain. A vicious shaking rattled and slammed and shook every fiber of his body until everything finally came apart; arms and legs and torso became separate parts of him, each filled with pain and consciousness as he floated thus disassembled watching with curious detachment from above as he slowly disappeared into the cloying embrace of the bottomless dark cave.

*   *   *

Angela saw the horseman approaching while he was still a mile away but when he got closer she knew that it was Beck. He had left three days ago to look for Thomas O'Reiley, at that time a week overdue. And now fourteen days had elapsed since Thomas had ridden into the high country. Beck was leading the horses that Angela recognized as the ones Thomas had used.

She stood waiting; her hand at her mouth to conceal the deep sob trapped in her throat. Beck rode up quietly and stopped in front of her, removed his hat. "I'm sorry, Miss Gordon," he said quietly. He shook his head. "Not a sign of Mister O'Reiley. He got there; I've no doubt about that. The rain two days ago pretty well wiped out any sign of him though." He hesitated, "you know, that young man was a lot more capable than we gave him credit for." He shook his head slowly. "I figure a bear got him." He shrugged his shoulders. "Maybe a mountain lion . . ." his voice faded off, perhaps so she couldn't actually hear his next words. "Didn't find any remains either."

Angela nodded slowly, her eyes vacant. "Thank you, Beck. I know that my father will want to hear everything. He'll have to send a telegram to Mister McPherson."

"I'll talk with him right away, Miss Gordon." He nodded, slipped his hat back on and rode on.

Angela shook her head in despair and tears flowed unimpeded down her cheeks. "Oh, Thomas," she whispered.

CHAPTER 4

<u>Thursday, May 11, 1899 The High Sierras</u>

Thomas slowly opened his eyes and found an unfamiliar image staring back at him. After studying the face for several long moments, he decided that the visage was that of an old man. His skin was the color of tree bark, smooth except for several prominent age-creases near his mouth and eyes. He had pale grey eyes and long grey hair that was gathered into a single braid behind his neck. It was a strong but gentle face, and nearly expressionless but for a slight frown that caused a single furrow at the center of his forehead; it had a look of curiosity or perhaps puzzlement. A fur cape of what was probably a bear skin was draped over his shoulders. The old man squatted next to Thomas and peered down at him, causing Thomas to suddenly realize that he was lying on the ground. He eyes slowly focused on his surroundings. He was inside some sort of rough hut, solidly constructed of small tree trunks and branches carefully stuffed and layered with moss and grass. The cracks and voids were filled with dried mud; it was warm and he smelled the smoke of a fire nearby. When he tried to move his head, a pain shot through him as if he had been stabbed and everything disappeared into the total blackness that swooped in around him.

The next time he awoke, the old man was not there. Cautiously, with only the barest movement of his head, he studied his surroundings. He was warm, lying on a thick pile of animal skins; pelts with the fur still on them, bear pelts and deer pelts and skins of smaller animals like rabbits and badgers. Two or three heavy bear skins covered him from his feet to his shoulders. He tried carefully to move his arms but found that he couldn't. He quickly gave up, for the minimal effort drained him and made him dizzy.

His muddled thoughts whirled in confused disarray. *Where am I? What happened to me? Where did the old man go? Who was he? I'm thirsty! Why can't I move?*

The old man entered, bent nearly double under the low overhead of the shelter. He had an armful of firewood and glanced immediately upon entering to find Thomas looking at him. He carefully put the wood near the opening and squatted next to Thomas. He still wore the cape of bear skin over his shoulders and roughly fashioned deerskin breeches that came to his mid-calf. His feet were bare. He nodded at Thomas. "You . . . sick," he said slowly, carefully sounding the words. His voice came from high in his chest, sounding almost as if it was being forced from a set of bellows.

Thomas nodded. "Yes . . ." is all he managed to squeeze out.

The old man nodded this time. With the first two fingers of his right hand curved, he struck at his left arm, mimicking a snake striking with its fangs. "Snake bite . . . leg . . ."

Thomas closed his eyes for a moment, then looked at the face above him. "Yes . . . I remember now." It had been a rattlesnake. "Where am I?"

"I live," the old man motioned around him with a sweep of his arm, "here." He pointed at Thomas, "I bring you here. You were very sick from snakebite. I watch the snake bite you."

"You were there?"

"I watch . . ." the old man pressed his spread finger tips against his skull, "from in here—not with my eyes. Then I go to find you. Then I see all," he motioned to his eyes, "with my eyes."

Thomas pondered these words for a long time. "Are you Gray Hawk?" he finally asked.

The old man smiled slightly, "I am called Gray Hawk."

Thomas nodded slowly. *Gray Hawk the shaman. What was it his father-in-law had said? The shaman had supernatural powers . . .* He pointed at himself, "I am called Thomas."

"Tah-moss."

"Yes." He closed his eyes with weariness.

"Now, I get you food."

Thomas simply nodded and went to sleep.

He woke up when Gray Hawk gently tilted his head forward and pressed a shallow wooden bowl of warm broth to his lips. He sipped and found the thick liquid to be rather gelatinous and rich but tasteless. He nodded. "Good," he muttered.

"Rabbit. Roots. Leaves . . ." Gray Hawk responded. "Good medicine for you."

Thomas finished drinking the bowl of thick soup and lay back. "Thank you, Gray Hawk."

The Indian nodded silently. "You need food. Sick many days."

"How many days?"

Gray Hawk frowned, finally opened his hand to show five fingers. He did this three times.

"Fifteen days?"

The shaman agreed. "Yes, fifteen. Snake bite very bad. You very close to die. I use very strong medicine."

Instant flashes of blurred memory of a face painted half black, half white and of acrid smoke; the face of Death that had hovered over him. That had been the shaman Gray Hawk. He nodded. "You have good medicine, Gray Hawk."

"You sleep, Tah-moss. We talk later."

*　　*　　*

Saturday, May 13, 1899, San Francisco

Handon McPherson and Hector Gordon had exchanged telegrams for several days as Handon requested more information and Hector did his best to respond to the distraught man's questions. Handon finally but reluctantly accepted the terrible facts; his son-in-law was dead, there was no body to bring home for burial; his beloved daughter was a young widow and his beautiful grandchildren would grow up without a father. Guilt sat oppressively heavy like burlap bags of grain on his shoulders; but he had done the best he could to console Amanda, so stricken with profound grief that she had been unable to even speak for several days. Just this morning, a memorial service had been held at Grace Church presided over by Bishop Nichols and attended by well over three hundred prominent San Franciscans. Now at her home on Nob Hill, Amanda circulated among the three dozen or so especially close friends that had been invited here following the service. Her house servant, Xiang, moved quietly among the crowd, serving trays of delicate hors d'oeuvres and cups of tea. Sister Mary Katherine, Thomas's special friend from the Saint Theresa by the Sea Hospital in Mendocino, was there and had provided crucial emotional support for Amanda and the three young children. Amanda had asked her to stay for a week or so until the family got its feet back on solid ground.

Later that evening, Handon sat with his daughter attempting to discuss her future. "Surely, Amanda, you will not want to remain in this large home. You and the children must find some place smaller and easier for you to manage."

Amanda stared at him. "I shall remain here, father! I am left financially well taken care of, as you know. This is the home that my dear Thomas had built as his wedding gift to me and I shall not leave it. I shall continue my obligations to charities and my civic duties. And I shall continue to raise Thomas's and my children in the only home that they know."

*   *   *

At about that same time Thomas sat with his back supported and legs stretched out in front. Gray Hawk was inspecting his right leg and the damage done by the poison venom injected by the rattlesnake. Thomas was surprised at the awful destruction to the flesh of his calf. His entire lower leg was red and swollen near twice its normal size. Near the actual injection site, the color turned to bluish-purple and the flesh appeared to be rotting, sloughing off in putrid clumps. Gray Hawk had made a poultice of ground leaves and berries and was carefully applying it to the wound. He studied the ferocious scars on his lower leg.

"Warrior?" he inquired, pointing to the puckered skin where broken leg bones had once sliced through.

"No."

"You have many scars. I think maybe you were soldier." The shaman studied him intently.

"Not a soldier." Thomas struggled as he thought of how to explain his time isolated and alone on an island. With a combination of hand signs he described his sailing on a ship that sank and how the island became his prison home.

"How long?" the Indian wanted to know.

He held up his five fingers. "Five . . . winters."

Gray Hawk nodded slowly. "Long time."

The conversation went on for a long time. They soon adopted a few mutual hand signs and Gray Hawk introduced a few words of his native language: *tape* for sun, *tamua* for moon and *paya* for water. Thomas grew weary and finally laid back and closed his eyes.

The shaman pressed the wooden bowl to Thomas's lips and he swallowed more of the thick warm liquid without even opening his eyes. When he next awoke, it was dark inside the hut and the old Indian was resting with his chin on his chest, his upper body braced against the side of the hut. The fire had fallen to a bed of ash-covered coals and the air within the hut was cool. Thomas turned his head to look through the opening and it was dark outside. His thoughts were clearer now and he had begun to remember the events leading to his being here, the ride up the mountains on the horse, the campsite, the new corral he had constructed, the near-vertical cliff of granite and the sudden excruciating pain of the snake's strike. The memory of the visit by Death came and went like an ocean fog driven by the wind. *No, wait. That hadn't been Death—it was Gray Hawk. Gray Hawk had saved his life. The painted face, the chanting melodies. Gray Hawk, the shaman. Gray Hawk, who as a young shaman had first mutilated and then scalped six men in a spasm of murderous vengeance. I've been here well over two weeks. The horses will be starving. Surely, I've been missed by now.* He fell back to sleep.

Over the next several days, his leg began to heal and the old shaman seemed pleased with his work. The flesh began to lose its deep purple color and the swelling receded, though dead flesh continued to slough off. At the end of his twenty-fifth day in the mountains, he attempted to stand with the help of Gray Hawk and discovered how weak he was and how painful it was to put even a slight amount of weight on his right leg.

The next day as he was relaxing in the sunlight outside the hut, the shaman disappeared for almost two hours. When he returned, he told Thomas that someone had been to the campsite; all of his equipment and the horses were no longer there. It had been a single rider leading another horse, fourteen, perhaps twenty or more days ago. The rider had tied one horse and left, and returned to the campsite three times, then had packed up everything and left again leading the three horses back the direction he had arrived.

Thomas nodded. Someone had come looking for him. Probably Beck, as he would know where he would probably set up camp. So, by now everyone would assume he was dead, the victim of a wild animal or a fall from a high cliff or his own lack of mountain experience. He grimaced at the thought. *Amanda, dear Amanda and our children. How would they cope?*

He knew that he would have to walk out of the mountains to the Gordon's ranch. It was a walk that would take two or three days, even if he was in good condition. He would have to survive without shelter, taking with him only minimal supplies and forced to live off the land. How long would it be before he could even put his full weight on his right leg? Tomorrow he would begin to exercise the injured leg.

Ten more days passed. The Indian began feeding him large meals of deer meat and roasted nuts and roots rich in starch. He walked a little more each day, leaning on a walking stick for support. Sometimes the ferocious pain made him so dizzy that he had to sit. The shaman watched him with interest, carefully checking the leg at the end of each day. One day, the old man led him to the nearby creek and a shallow pool where the water swirled slowly and was warmed by the sunlight. Thomas stripped off his clothes and waded in. The water caused the injury to throb but washed away the dried blood and accumulation of dried poultice that had gathered in the various crevices. He cupped his hands; brought the water to his face and scrubbed at the months-long accumulation of beard. While he was still in the pool, he rinsed his clothes and then put them in the warm sun to dry.

When he got out, the old Indian was sitting on a rock, watching him. "You leave soon?"

"Soon, Gray Hawk." Thomas felt the peculiar bond that had begun to grow between them and he felt the need to explain. "To be with my people, my family."

The Indian nodded. "Yes. Your family."

"Gray Hawk, you saved my life. I owe you much."

"Tah-moss," he used his hands to help communicate his thinking, "you and me. Good." He hesitated. "I watch," he again pressed his fingertips to his skull, "I see you again."

"Again?" Thomas could scarcely imagine coming back here again.

"Before winter, Tah-moss."

June 10, 1899, Washington, D.C.

On this day, President William McKinley appointed the first Isthmian Canal Commission, also known as the second Walker Commission, to carry out Congress' mandate to determine once and for all the best route to build a Pacific-Atlantic canal. Congress appropriated one million dollars toward the project, headed by Rear Admiral John Walker. The commission was charged with five separate issues: investigate the Nicaragua route, investigate the Panama route, investigate other possible routes, investigate the commercial and military values of a canal and determine what privileges and rights the United States ought to have with such a canal.

* * *

Gray Hawk's camp, The High Sierras

Two more weeks passed before Thomas felt that he was strong enough to attempt his trek out of the high country. His right leg was still raw and sore but there was little sign of infection or further putrefaction caused by the venom and the lower leg would now support his full weight. Walking was painful and could be accomplished only with a pronounced limp and occasional hop on his left leg, but he made himself a stout walking stick to help.

Using vines and the skills he had learned on the island, he wove a net sling in which he could carry some of the roots, nuts and edible parts of plants that Gray Hawk had taught him to eat, as well a small supply of smoked venison. The shaman gave him a leather pouch that held a day's worth of water, as well as a deer skin to protect him from either the sun or the cold. All of these went into the sling and finally Thomas strapped on the large knife and its leather sheath that had remained with him for years. When he did so, Thomas glimpsed the momentary shadow of envy in the eyes of his friend; but he had already decided not to part with the knife. The knife had once belonged to a dead man. Thomas had discovered the body; and when threatened by the actual killers, Thomas had been forced to flee from the police into a five year exile. The knife and the memories it evoked had been a part of Thomas's life ever since.

It was still early in the morning when Gray Hawk led Thomas away from the small hut where the two had remained. The deep forest surrounding them was warm and sunshine filtered down through the treetops to create varied patches of light on the forest floor. It took them two hours to cover the distance to the hunting campsite. It looked deserted and unused, almost as if the area had already been reclaimed by nature. The circle of stones used for a fire ring was covered with a layer of needles and debris from the trees.

They walked in the direction that Thomas remembered as heading for the edge of the canyon with the Kaweah winding its way in the bottom.

They passed the massive Sequoia Redwood tree. Gray Hawk told him that these huge trees were very sacred to his people, that they were charged with the care of all the forest around them and that some had lived since the earth was first formed. Some he said were even larger, hidden deep in forests many days walk away. Some had been badly scarred by fire, many had been struck by lightning and on occasion, a few had fallen like mighty warriors in battle to lay and someday become part of the forest soil.

They reached an overlook and stood studying the vast San Joaquin Valley far below and to the west of them. Many winters ago, Gray Hawk explained, the valley had been lush and green with huge herds of elk and deer roaming among its rivers and lakes; flocks of birds as numerous as stars in the sky had migrated in and out seasonally. All of this was before Gray Hawk was born but was known by his people, who had come to this side of the mountains many years ago. When Thomas asked "how many winters?" the old Indian could only reply, "many. Very many."

Gray Hawk accompanied him until the trail began the long switchback descent down the side of the canyon walls. The old man turned to Thomas and placed his hand on his shoulder. "Tah-moss, you are good man. This place for me marks the edge of the white man's land where I cannot go. Many of your people are not good and would choose to kill me. You are a good man. You come here again. I teach you many ways, many mysteries of my people. Make you stand tall among your people."

Thomas knew that the proposal was sincere and that an extraordinary honor had been offered to him. "Thank you, Gray Hawk. I honor your offer. I will come back. That is my word." He placed his hand over his heart as a sign of sincerity.

The shaman nodded. "I know."

*　　*　　*

The long hike down the canyon face was more difficult than Thomas had expected. Each step jarred his frame, especially his right leg. By the time he reached the huge boulders at the bottom, he was limping badly and the open wound on his leg was bleeding. He painfully hobbled to the edge of the river and bathed the leg in the cold water; afterward he studied the injury and shook his head. It had broken open from the stress on the muscles and blood flowed down his leg and into his boot. He would have to elevate his leg and rest from his hiking and hope that it would help the blood coagulate. He glanced at the position of the sun; it was getting late in the afternoon; it would be dark in less than three hours.

He awoke with a start. It was almost dark and the air had cooled considerably. His right leg was still propped on the boulder and he carefully let it down where he could check the injury again. It had stopped bleeding but the angry redness had returned and it was very painful when he touched the area.

"Not good, Thomas old boy," he muttered. He struggled to stand, but was hit by a wave of dizziness and nearly toppled over. "Need to make a fire . . ."

By the time he had collected a meager supply of dry firewood, it was dark and he was nauseous; the world around him seemed to tip crazily on its axis from time to time. He labored, his body now shaking with chills, to get a fire going at the base of a large boulder and then rolled himself in the deerskin Gray Hawk had given him. Moving as close to the small fire as he dared, he lay in the still warm sand and shut his eyes, his teeth chattering as spasms of excruciating pain shot up his leg.

It was completely dark when he awoke, rolled over and emptied the contents of his stomach onto the sand. He groaned in pain and absolute misery, reached over and weakly tossed another piece of wood onto the red coals of the fire. A shower of sparks shot upward and he followed them with his eyes. There were no stars overhead and he felt the first drops of rain splatter on his face. He moved awkwardly into a sitting position nearer the fire and pulled the deerskin closer about him and over his head. In just a few minutes the rain began to pour down, cold, soaking, near-vertical rain with drops as large as marbles. A lengthy flash of lightning lit the landscape momentarily, striking somewhere up river from his location and several seconds later the thunder rumbled and rattled through the canyon. He reached for the remaining pieces of firewood and tossed them onto the small blaze. He had experienced this kind of rain on the island and it could quickly extinguish a fire. He reached for the sling and took out a few pieces of smoked venison, put one in his mouth, closed his eyes and methodically began to chew the tough meat, forcing his stomach to not revolt. The lightning flashes lit his eyes through his closed eyelids and each resounding crash of thunder echoed up and down the river canyon. The deerskin kept most of the rain out but a steady trickle ran down the back of his neck like an icy finger. A solitary lightning strike nearby seemed to make the air around him shudder and the simultaneous thunder shook the ground. Thomas, shivering with cold, buried his head further into the deerskin, his knees drawn up to his chest; for the time being his overall misery surpassed the terrible pain in his leg.

He remained in this position as the rain poured from the heavens in what seemed to be an unending deluge. The deerskin became soaked through and now itself was simply a cold, soggy shroud that he managed to wrap himself with. The pitifully small fire had quickly drowned in the downpour and all that remained was a loose slick of rain-soaked ashes washing downhill to join the torrent of muddy water churning in the river. The coming of dawn was so gradual that he was almost unaware that the sky had turned from charcoal to a lesser shade of gray. The rain continued to fall unabated from the heavy cloud cover and he became aware of the angry, roaring turbulence of the nearby river, tumbling and roiling violently with the added rainwater that was flowing into the swollen torrent from hundreds of creeks upstream. He groaned in pain, reluctantly surrendering to the all-encompassing misery and cold, the surrounding violence and chaos, the noise and flashes of lightning, the body shudders and teeth chattering of fever and chills as he tried to roll into a ball of non-existence. Images and sounds beyond the present flashed like background lightning in his mind, replaying and mingling the horrors he had experienced on the ship and alone on the island. He was there on the island again, trying to stay out of the tropical storms that sped over the island, winds howling like a wild animal and rain blowing parallel with the ground with the force of pebbles being thrown at him. He ground his teeth, his lips pulled back and eyes shut hard and groaned in pain and fear, misery and isolation, close to the boundary of his human ability to cope.

CHAPTER 5

<u>June 17, 1899, The Kaweah River</u>

Sometime during the day the icy rain brought by the late spring storm turned into sleet. The lightning and thunder disappeared around dawn, although Thomas had no idea when dawn had actually occurred. Only barely conscious and soaked through and through, he huddled under the deerskin, teeth chattering, arms and legs shaking uncontrollably with the cold. As the temperature dropped near freezing, his body began to shut down. Already ravaged by infection and the toxic venom, the frigid temperature robbed energy from less vital organs and extremities. Soon his arms and legs were numb with the cold, fingers were stiff and refused to clamp any longer onto the deerskin; it slipped off his shoulder and it took monumental physical and mental effort to drag it back into place over his curled up body.

The bright sunshine struck him in his eyes and startled him into wakefulness. The rain had ceased and now the sky was azure and cloudless; the sun rested against the mountain tops but he didn't know if it was the morning or afternoon sun. He had difficulty remembering just where he was and the circumstances that got him here. He ran his tongue over his parched lips. His mouth was dry with a metallic taste and his ribs stabbed him painfully when he breathed. He felt the deep throb of pain from the snake bite and checked his leg; the flesh had turned dark purple, swollen nearly twice in size and the wound oozed a yellow excretion tinged with blood. He put his head back in frustration and shut his eyes. The hazy scene formed slowly in his mind, as if he was looking down while gliding bird-like high above. That was him at the river, stumbling toward the distant ranch house where he would find Angela and her father and mother, Hector and Margarita and their son, Ramon. He let the thoughts

58

roll slowly through his mind, repeating the names as if committing them to memory and wondering why exactly he was here and why he would be heading to the ranch house.

The Indian! Gray Hawk . . . He remembered the old man's face and having spent some time with him. How long had that been? Days? Weeks? And why?

The warm sun caused the deerskin to begin to steam and he slipped it off and laid it on a large boulder to dry. The sun, even though it was low in the sky, felt good on his body and he watched as the bright disk grew oblong and began to dip behind the mountain. He looked around him, just the swollen river on one side—the muddy water seething and rushing past him carrying broken trees and limbs, debris from the ferocious storm further up in the high country. To his left was the steep canyon wall with the narrow switchback path. He vaguely remembered making a fire but there was no sign of that now. It was suddenly darker and he tugged and pulled the half-dried deerskin back over his shoulders. In the shade now, he shuddered with fever and the chill cold that had reached deep into his viscera. The deerskin provided little in the way of warmth and he rolled himself tightly in the skin and stretched out sausage-like at the base of a boulder.

He slept fitfully through the night, waking several times shaking and coughing deep, chest-wracking convulsions that sapped what little strength he still had. When the sun finally came up in the morning he lay, only barely conscious, still rolled in the skin. By mid-morning, the sun had warmed the damp deerskin and he painfully crawled from the cocoon and tried to stand, leaning on the boulder for support and balance. He put the skin over his shoulders like a cape and took his first steps in the damp sand. His steps were awkward and infirm as he lost his balance several times, reeling in dizziness and falling against the rocks or landing in the sand. Spells of uncontrollable, wrenching coughs brought up reddish pink sputum and caused him to double over with pain; he wrapped his arms around his body in a half-conscious attempt to stem the impulse to cough up the liquid congestion that was slowly gathering in his lungs.

By mid day, he was gasping for breath in painful spasms and his nearly constant coughing was bringing up specks of blood. As he stumbled forward he began to notice that the trees had thinned out and that there was more sunlight reaching the ground. Faint, almost subliminal memories suggested that he was nearly out of the mountains and nearing the vast valley into which the river flowed. The ranch house had to be somewhere nearby . . .

*   *   *

Angela stood near the gate, her hand shading her eyes as she peered into the late afternoon shadows. Fair weather had finally returned after the freakish spring storm had inundated them with rain. Small creeks and large rivers had flooded well beyond their banks, wreaking havoc among nearby farmers and ranchers. However, her grandfather Luis Gordon had planned well and the Gordon ranch was carefully situated on higher ground, fifty feet or more above the flood stage of the nearby Kaweah River. Now with the rain over, Angela resumed her daily routine of searching out the approach to the ranch, the way by which Thomas must come if he was to return from the mountains. This was her evening ritual, for she believed that he would have to hike during the day and would arrive—if he arrived—late in the afternoon or early evening. Given the amount of time that had passed since his disappearance, it was a probability that her family felt was extremely unlikely and in fact her brother Ramon had taken her aside, put his arm gently around her and said, "it's not going to happen, Angela. He's not coming back." Her heart nearly broken, she had nevertheless maintained her vigil in spite of her family's open and frank skepticism.

The long tree-lined drive to the ranch's gate pointed south but it would be the easiest approach once a person reached it. The land east of the drive was rippled with low hills and small canyons; if anyone was following the river down, instead of attempting to cut across country, they would eventually come to the drive, a mile-long dirt road beaten smooth by sixty-three years of wagon, cart and horse traffic. To her right, the late afternoon sun was burning nearly horizontally through the haze of the wide San Joaquin Valley. It would be dark within the hour and she shook her head in anguish and fear. She glanced behind her to see her mother standing in the doorway of the ranch house watching her. Her father had reprimanded her last night at supper, admonishing her for continuing this useless vigil, saying, "you're only prolonging your own pain, Angela."

She turned back to look down the drive. The afternoon shadows were getting long and a cool breeze blew through the tall sycamore trees that were almost fully in leaf. She was about to turn back toward the ranch house when she glimpsed something at the end of the drive. It could have been an animal, for it was low to the ground; and she almost disregarded the vision before she shielded her eyes and studied it carefully. It was too large to be an animal, unless perhaps a deer of a small bear but then it stood on its hind legs and staggered forward before it fell once again to the dirt road.

She put her hand to her mouth to stifle a scream then muttered, "Oh my God! Thomas!" This time she let her voice pierce the air, "Thomas! Thomas!" as she stumbled the first few steps in that direction before she gathered her wits and yelled back at her mother, "It's Thomas, Mother! Help me!" Her feet flew over the hard packed earth as she sped toward the staggering and falling figure. When she had nearly reached the figure, it stood one more time, an arm raised in recognition; then it spun slowly and sank to the ground.

The form on the ground was hardly recognizable. His hair was unkempt, knotted and tangled with burrs and twigs and a thick beard covered his face. His lips were chapped and bleeding; numerous scratches and bruises covered his face and arms. But this right leg was what caught her attention; the lower pant leg was soaked with dried blood and exuded an odor which she, having lived her life on a ranch, knew all too well.

She bent down beside his head and lifted it gently to cradle in her arm. "Thomas, my dear Thomas. You're safe now. I'll take care of you," she whispered. "I won't let you die."

* * *

That evening Hector sent a telegram to McPherson that said:
> THOMAS ARRIVED AT RANCH TONIGHT
> STOP SEEN BY DOCTOR STOP VERY ILL WITH
> PNUMONIA LEG AND OTHER INJURIES STOP
> WILL NOTIFY YOU WHEN CONSCIOUS STOP
> CANNOT TRAVEL STOP MEANTIME UNDER
> OUR CARE STOP HECTOR

The telegram was delivered to Handon McPherson's office at nine o'clock the next morning. He immediately sent a reply to Hector:
> THANK GOD THOMAS ALIVE AND FOR YOUR
> CARE FOR HIM STOP WILL BE THERE WHEN HE

IS READY TO BRING TO SF STOP NOTIFY ME OF
ANY CHANGE STOP HANDON

His next duty was to visit Amanda and deliver the news which was greeted with shrieks of joy and near delirium, tears and laughter. Xiang launched into a lengthy Chinese song in her off-key style and the children started a frantic around-the-house chase that soon became free-for-all bedlam.

* * *

Five days went by before Thomas opened his eyes. During that time Angela maintained a nearly constant watch over him. She had insisted that he recover in her bedroom since it was closest to the kitchen where hot water was always available, where bandages could be hand washed then boiled to sterilize them and where special broths could be kept warm in case he awoke. At first her parents argued with her but in the end Angela was triumphant and her bed was prepared for Thomas. Margareta forbad her to be in the room the first night when she carefully bathed the sick man, frowning over the scars and almost becoming physically ill when she studied the damaged leg and the rotting flesh. She dressed him in one of Hector's night shirts, arranged the bed covers so that the corner near his injury could be raised for inspection and change of bandage. She raised his head gently and placed a pillow under it, pulled the covers up to his chin and finally allowed Angela to enter the room. Shortly after that, Doctor Chester Staunton from Visalia arrived shoeing everyone out while he inspected the patient.

Afterward he spoke to the family gathered in the great room. "I'm afraid the poor man has a very serious case of pneumonia, as well as a general overall poor state of health. He has a very high fever and fluid in both lungs. His right leg looks to have been rattlesnake bitten; the damage to the muscle tissue caused by the snake's venom is quite typical. He's very lucky to have survived that injury. He's obviously not eaten for several days and I doubt that he's had much water either. He needs to sleep as long as he will. Then he will need food, liquids at first then more solid food as he is able. He will want to sleep and just rest for several days at least. He should be urged to stand and walk as soon as he can or his leg muscles will deteriorate. His youthfulness is his best ally; he appears to have been physically fit except for some obvious injuries that appear to be several years old. Keep an eye on the leg injury; change the bandage at least twice daily. Infection has set in and he could still lose his leg to gangrene if we are not very careful. He should be in a hospital but the travel would probably kill him. So, what he needs is around the clock monitoring. Check the bandages. Replace twice a day. If he displays any sort of erratic behavior, I need to see him."

After the doctor left in his buggy for the ride back into town, Angela insisted on moving a chair into the bedroom where she could sit through the night. Margareta at first argued, then relented and helped move one of the leather chairs from the great room into the bedroom. Angela wrapped herself in a blanket and curled up in the chair. She rose up several times during the night to dab Thomas's face and forehead with a cool cloth and once peered under the blankets to study the injury on his leg. The bandages would need changing by morning.

She leaned over him, her lips close to his and whispered, "I'll take care of you, dear Thomas. My love for you will not let you die."

She slept in short spurts, always conscious of his restless movements, listening to his raspy breathing and the occasional mumblings about images that flowed through his mind. She assisted Margarita as she took the bandage off his leg, cleansed the wound and re-wrapped it with sterilized bandages.

One night as she sat listening to his mutterings and watching his body shake with fever, she lifted the sheet covering him and slid carefully in alongside him, her arm resting lightly on his chest and her lips close to his ear. She whispered to him, telling him about her life and dreams until she finally fell asleep herself.

She had maintained this regimen for five full days, leaving the room only to take care of her personal needs. She took her meals in the bedroom and tried several times each day to spoon a little warm broth between his lips but he only coughed and choked on it.

It was on the evening of the fifth day that his eyes fluttered open and he saw the face only inches from his.

"Angela?" he whispered hoarsely.

"Yes, Thomas, it's Angela. I'm right here."

By the next morning, Thomas was accepting sips of warm broth between long naps. His fever had broken and he slept peacefully for the first time in many days. Angela sat right beside the bed and held his hand when her mother or father was not in the room. By mid-afternoon he awoke once again.

"How did I get here, Angela?" he asked.

"You walked, Thomas. You don't remember?"

He shook his head slowly. "I don't remember very much, Angela." He frowned in thought. "I was with Gray Hawk."

"The Indian?" she gasped. "You were with that murdering old renegade?"

"He's not what people think, Angela."

"He murdered six men, Thomas. In cold blood. Mutilated them, too."

"He saved my life."

She scowled, "Gray Hawk saved your life?"

He proceeded to slowly tell her what he could remember of his time with the shaman. At the end of his account, he shut his eyes and drifted quickly off to sleep.

Tuesday, June 28, 1899 San Francisco, California

The San Francisco Chronicle carried the news item on its second page:

Thomas O'Reiley CheatsDeath Again

San Francisco businessman O'Reiley has returned to San Francisco after a solo early-spring hunting trip into the High Sierra Mountains became a near-disaster. O'Reiley suffered a grievous rattle-snake bite that nearly cost him his life. O'Reiley managed the ordeal with the eventual help of acquaintances in the area and yesterday returned to his home here to continue his recovery.

The article continued on, recounting his previous brush with death while spending five years alone on a South Pacific island.

The train trip back to San Francisco had been difficult and by the time he arrived at his home, he was exhausted. Amanda carefully took over his immediate care and forbad anyone from visiting him for nearly a week. She hovered over him as he slowly regained his strength, feeding him several small meals each day until he was able to feed himself. The open areas around the large calf muscles on the back of his leg healed slowly, though the doctor reminded him that muscle tissue that had putrefied and sloughed away because of the toxic venom would never grow back.

"This is not a thoroughly disabling injury," the doctor disclosed when Amanda was not in the room, "though it will most likely cause occasional pain and some impediment to walking."

"You mean a limp," Thomas suggested dryly.

The doctor shrugged. "Somewhat, perhaps. You're very lucky to be alive, Mister O'Reiley. Most men would have died with an injury of this magnitude. You may wish to consider the use of a cane."

Three weeks later Thomas was up and beginning his self-imposed daily exercise routine. At first his steps were painful and unsure, and on a few occasions the muscles on the back of his right leg cramped and shrieked in pain causing him to grimace and grit his teeth. But as the days went by and his walks became longer, the tissues continued to heal and the muscles adapted to his new stride. He concentrated on trying not to hitch his right leg up on each step but kept his step natural and free of any outward adaptation to his injury. He returned to work at his office, choosing to walk the two miles a day to and from work.

By the first week of September, he had made up his mind to return to visit the old Indian, Gray Hawk.

He had not mentioned the old shaman to anyone except Angela, deciding to keep his knowledge of the whereabouts of the outlaw Indian a secret. A little discrete research had revealed that there was still an active warrant for the Indian with a two hundred and fifty dollar reward—*Dead or Alive.*

* * *

Amanda refused to listen to his arguments. "No! I simply won't hear of it, Thomas! You can't even give me a good reason why you want to traipse off into the mountains again and risk your life! Don't you realize what your disappearance in the spring did to me? How could you even think about it?" She was on the verge of tears and shook her head to compose herself.

"Mandy, I don't expect that you will understand." He gathered her in his arms and drew her close. "I'm not sure I understand myself."

Handon McPherson was even more displeased. "You are on the threshold of making the biggest mistake of your life, Thomas," he warned angrily. "You're about to throw away everything," he repeated, "*everything,* you . . . and I . . . have worked for, not to mention your marriage to Amanda." His face was red and his hand was shaking as he waggled his finger in front of Thomas. "Damn it, man! Think about what you are doing!"

"I owe it to the man that saved my life." Thomas left a week later, promising to return in ten days.

When he arrived and got off the train in Visalia, Angela was there with the ranch buckboard to give him a ride out to the family ranch. He noticed that she had changed, even in the few months he had been in San Francisco. No longer a child in her teens, she was rapidly maturing into a young woman. Her slim, almost girlish figure had filled out and her face, he realized, was quite beautiful. From time to time he caught the faint scent of perfume and he smiled to himself.

He was greeted at the ranch by Hector and Margarita who inquired about his health and recovery. Ramon and Beck, they explained, were off rounding up strays from the cattle herd. After dinner that evening, almost as if by design, he met Angela at the corral fence. There was no moon that night and only the stars glittered through the haze that hung far above the great, flat valley. The temperature was still warm and the crickets and frogs began their evening chorus in the still air.

"I was hoping you would be out here, Thomas," she said quietly as she came up beside him.

His mind flashed back to the last time they had stood here. What was it she had said? *I wish I was going with you* . . . His thoughts whirled as he remembered his reaction: *that would be nice* . . . He caught the subtle fragrance of her perfume and felt the warmth radiating from her nearness.

His thoughts had delayed his response far too long and she stepped forward and started to leave. "I'm so sorry, Thomas," she whispered. "I didn't mean to interrupt your thoughts."

He gently took her arm and stopped her. "No, please don't leave." She stopped and swung around and suddenly she was in his arms and her face was buried in the crook of his neck. She turned her face up and their lips met, timidly at first, then pressed firmly as he gathered her with his arms around her waist and pulled her close. Her right arm encircled his neck and drew his face close to hers.

*   *   *

It was late afternoon the next day when he arrived at the campsite. After a quick check, he determined that there had been no visitors to the area over the summer. He set about getting the horses into the makeshift corral and was scarcely surprised when Gray Hawk stepped from the shade into the opening.

The shaman raised his right hand in greeting. "Tah-moss! You come back!"

Thomas raised his hand in reply. "I came to see you, Gray Hawk."

The old man nodded, "it is good."

Over the next four days, Gray Hawk spent every daylight hour with Thomas, showing him the variety of fungi, moss and plants, their leaves, bark and roots used in treating Thomas's snakebite. He showed Thomas how to dry and grind them into powders or mash them to garner the juices, how to combine them into a variety of medicinal compounds to treat anything from insect bites to open wounds, from a simple headache to an infected tooth or a case of diarrhea. Thomas took notes and collected samples as Gray Hawk led him through the forest, pointing out which vegetation was edible and those that were poisonous to humans. It appeared to Thomas that nearly everything that grew in the forest had a use. The old man agreed; "it is that way," he stated solemnly.

For Thomas though, the nights under the stars gave him plenty of time to think. Gray Hawk slept in the shelter but Thomas preferred to sleep in his bedroll in the open. It was there that his restless thoughts turned to Angela, his mind was crowded with conflicting doubts and desires, realities and dreams. He revisited those few intense moments with Angela time and again, relishing the sudden involuntary passions they had stirred within him and experiencing over again the ache and emptiness he was left with when she pulled away and withdrew to the ranch house. He was alone with his thoughts and a weighty sense of remorse that quickly dulled any desire to further explore their relationship.

The evening before Thomas left they sat close to the fire outside Gray Hawk's shelter. As the last pieces of firewood dropped into a bed of red coals with a shower of sparks, he presented Gray Hawk with a hunting knife and leather sheath similar to the one he carried. Even in the dim light of the fire, the shaman's eyes lit up with surprise and gratitude. "Ah! Like yours!" He carefully slid the blade from the sheath and stroked the edge with his thumb nodding as he looked at Thomas. "Very good!" he said quietly.

67

Thomas explained that the blade was made of German steel and that it would maintain a very keen edge if properly cared for. Germany, he explained, was a country that was known for making excellent steel many days travel and across a far-away ocean. The Indian nodded his understanding and grasped Thomas's shoulder in a show of appreciation.

When Thomas returned to the Gordon ranch, he found that Ramon had suffered an arm injury and was stuck at the ranch house temporarily unable to rope or handle a wayward and obstinate calf. Angela was out with Beck searching the foothills for a few last stray calves and would return to the ranch late that evening. By the time they returned Thomas had turned in. Angela was still asleep when he ate breakfast the next morning and bid his farewells to Hector and Margarita. Ramon gave him a lift in the buckboard back to the train depot in Visalia.

Chapter 6

<u>Friday, January 5, 1900, New Your City</u>

The four men sat in the hotel room crowded into uncomfortable chairs around the small table. The air was thick with tobacco smoke and the stench of cigar butts crushed out in ashtrays. They had been in the room for several hours now; their discussion usually muted, but at times their voices rose in anger or frustration. It would be unusual to find this particular group of men together in a room, much less to find them discussing a common concern. But these were men of great wealth, men who at one time or another could have easily put the others out of business. Now the stakes were huge and their only possibility of real success was to come together as a conglomerate, sharing the risk as well as the high potential for financial reward.

"There's still a possibility it could go the other way, John," one spoke up ending several long seconds of silence. He was a stout man with a mane of silver-gray hair whose brooding eyes stared at the maps laid out on the table. Extremely private, Ulysses Thaddeus McGarnet had made his fortune in the steel business and was now one of the richest men in the United States. Very few men ever referred to him in any manner other than as *Mister McGarnet*.

"Sir, there's always that possibility," John J. Ambrose responded softly. "We've got to make sure the odds are on our side, that there are no mistakes." He was older than the others and his corpulent face was framed by white sideburns. A rotund man who loved to eat, his forehead was beaded with a thin layer of perspiration. Strangely his lips were thin—almost lizard-like—with his upper lip nearly hidden by the white mustache. He was a railroad executive from Chicago. "We're all exposed out there pretty far . . ."

A third spoke up. His name was Sanford L. Parker but those that knew of him called Slim; those that knew him personally called him Mister Parker. The notable exception was McGarnet, who derisively referred to him as *cowboy*. Tall and thin, Parker addressed the others with a high pitched west Texas drawl. "Well, good God almighty, John, why don't you enlighten us with something we don't already goddamn understand! We're all floundering around in cow shit up to our goddamn crotch! I got everything I own and a few things I don't own, banking on this, just like you!"

The fourth man, Clarence O. DePallin, sat quietly and the others seemed to accept his silence as an introduction to share his thoughts. He was the youngest, perhaps in his early forties and a second term congressman from New Hampshire. He maintained control over the table by exercising his education, inherited social grace and self confidence. "Gentlemen! We've made some good purchases. We certainly need to solidify everything. Be ready, because it is going to happen! Congress is leaning our way and the public is generally behind them. We've got that attorney out in California working on the Esperanza property. That's the big one and he knows he's got our backing to make damn sure the deal closes, whatever it takes . . ." He glanced around the table quickly. Words had hidden meanings and the three others nodded in understanding. These were cautious men who seldom used explicit words that could come back to haunt them. "We've each put up a whole lot of money. This *is* going to happen, mark my words."

Tuesday, January 30, 1900, Frankfort, Kentucky

Republican gubernatorial candidate William Taylor narrowly defeated his two Democratic rivals, William Goebel and Wat Hardin for the governorship of the Commonwealth of Kentucky. Taylor's margin of victory over Goebel was so slight that the Board of Elections ruled that disputed ballots in some counties should be recounted. The result gave the election to Goebel. Republicans were extremely upset and Kentucky was close to resorting to civil war over the issue.

With results of the election still in dispute, William Goebel walked to the Old State Capitol this Tuesday morning accompanied by two bodyguards. A shot rang out from the State Building, followed by a second, third, fourth and fifth shot. Goebel was struck in his chest by one of the bullets. Moments after the shooting a man wearing a black leather overcoat was seen exiting the State Building carrying a long, leather case, the kind that would hold a hunting rifle. In the confusion immediately following the shooting, the man calmly disappeared into the gathering crowd of gawkers. Few could recall what he looked like, only describing him as tall with black hair, long sideburns and a mustache.

Seriously wounded, William Goebel was nevertheless sworn in as governor only to die of his wounds on Saturday, four days after he was shot.

*   *   *

Sunday, March 25. 1900, San Francisco

The city was quiet. Thomas sat in the light-filled office extending off the western side of his home. The sky was clear and blue. Sunlight sparkled off the waters of San Francisco Bay dotted with sailboats as the city's residents took advantage of the fair weather of early spring. The Presidio stuck out into the narrow passage leading to the Pacific Ocean, green and manicured, home of the United States Army in San Francisco. Further in, the island of Alcatraz stood alone in the current-whipped straits; the rocky outcropping was now the location of a military prison.

In January a bill had been introduced into Congress to authorize the United States to build a canal from the Atlantic to the Pacific through Nicaragua, in violation of a fifty-three year old treaty with Great Britain. After much debate the Congressional bill was defeated in March. The San Francisco Chronicle sat open on his lap to the page carrying an article regarding the recent signing of the Hay-Pauncefote Treaty in February. Yet another of a long string of agreements and treaties with the British, this one gave the United States the right to create and control a canal across Central America connecting the Pacific and Atlantic Oceans on the condition that all nations would be free to use this canal and that the United States would not erect fortifications to protect the canal. Once again American interests, often with differing agendas, were studying the feasibility of a canal after a four year hiatus while anti-imperialist Grover Cleveland was the President of the United States. Thomas had listened with bare interest as his father-in-law had argued the pros and cons of constructing an inter-ocean canal, an enterprise the French owned Panama Canal Company had twice attempted and twice failed.

Of more local interest was the small article that continued the debate regarding an alleged outbreak of Bubonic plague in the crowded section of San Francisco known as Chinatown. City and state officials stubbornly denied the existence of the disease in spite of medical and scientific evidence to the contrary, including a series of dead bodies showing up with confirmation of the disease. The city's residents were in an uproar. Only yesterday Thomas had suggested to Amanda that perhaps their Chinese house maid Xiang should remain at their house until the crisis ended.

Thomas let the newspaper lay open in his lap and stared out the window. The clarity of the air and view of the magnificent bay heightened his longing to escape the crowded city and all of its various troubles. His return from the high Sierras the previous September had entailed long and arduous days of restitution to Amanda and their children; however his collection of medicinal herbs and plants had given the family something to talk about and Amanda had enthusiastically taken on the task of determining the scientific name for each sample and pressing them for preservation and future reference. Thomas had carefully recorded each sample's medicinal value and use; this information was then transcribed and coupled with Amanda's skillfully drawn sketch of each sample.

The family disruption caused by his trip to the mountains slowly dissipated and life resumed its normal day-to-day business. Evening outings to the opera with Amanda, dinner parties, occasional get-togethers and formal dinners at their Victorian home on Nob Hill satisfied her yearning for social activity while his business enterprises kept him busy.

In spite of this, Thomas's mind was in silent and secret turmoil. The old Indian Gray Hawk had so much to teach him about life and survival in the mountains and it seemed to Thomas that the shaman was inordinately anxious to share this life-long accumulation of wisdom with him. He had begun to look forward to these twice-yearly mountain treks and his time with the shaman as a means of escaping, if only for a few days at a time, from the ever-increasing crush of city life and the multitude of expectations placed on being a prominent business leader. At the same time, he endured the cruel awareness that he had covetous thoughts—thoughts that he had no right to entertain—for the young Angela. When he thought of returning to the high Sierras, he also imagined her nearness and her voice and her embrace—and the soft touch of her lips. It was a startling yet exhilarating thought and one that he had more and more difficulty ignoring. The words of his father-in-law rang in his ears, *Damn it, man! Think what you are doing!*

Amanda stepped into the room quietly. "Thomas," her voice interrupted his thoughts, "father received a telegram from Uncle William's wife. Uncle William passed away quite suddenly late yesterday."

"Amanda, I'm so sorry to hear that." He stood and held his wife closely. "I know your father was very close to his brother even though they lived at opposite ends of the country." He had never met Handon's brother William, a prominent and well-to-do architect who lived in New York City.

"Father will need to go back east to help settle Uncle William's financial affairs as he is concerned that Aunt Luella is incapable of making those kinds of complex decisions. I'm concerned about him making such a trip alone at his age and I think that I should accompany him." She looked into his eyes. "Can you manage the children for a few weeks?"

Their son James was barely three years old and daughter Julia was eighteen months. "I think Xiang and I could manage quite well, Mandy." He hesitated. "Have you considered taking the children with you? Your Aunt Luella might enjoy seeing them. Xiang could accompany you and mind the children as well as provide some assistance with your father. It would also remove her away from the threat of the disease that appears rampant in her community, if even for a few weeks. I'll remain behind to keep an eye on your father's businesses in his absence."

"It's a dreadfully long train ride, Thomas," she replied thoughtfully, "but I'm sure Aunt Luella would enjoy seeing the children. I've not seen my cousins Kenneth and Margaret since we were just children ourselves." There was a sudden excitement in her voice. "We could visit some of the museums in New York City while father is occupied." She paused for several seconds, "let me think about it for a little while."

Before they had dinner that night, Amanda had decided that she would indeed take the children and Xiang, with her. Most of the evening was occupied by a whirlwind of packing clothes into trunks and getting the children ready. "It all seems so sudden. We'll be gone two weeks or more, my dear Thomas. I shall miss you terribly."

"And I shall miss you, Mandy."

The next morning, Thomas took his family and Xiang and their several trunks of clothes to the train depot where they were met by Handon McPherson. After a brief exchange, purchase of tickets and arranging accommodations on the train, Handon took Thomas aside and out of earshot of Amanda.

"I appreciate your willingness to remain behind, Thomas. Rest assured that there will be no need for you to involve yourself with my businesses; I've already left my senior assistant in charge. Hopefully, the experience will do him good." He put his arm around Thomas's shoulder and lowered his voice. "It might be a good time for you to take a week's respite and visit your mountains. I know that you look forward to those opportunities a great deal and your absence always concerns Amanda when she's left at home." He faced Thomas and looked into his eyes. "I do understand your need to escape the pressures of business and society now and then."

Thomas's father-in-law's suggestion surprised him and he studied the man's face but saw only sincere concern reflected in his eyes. "I shall certainly consider that, Handon. I appreciate your understanding and your suggestion."

* * *

He arrived in Visalia on the afternoon train two days later. Angela was there with the buckboard and greeted him with a discrete handshake and a smile as the other passengers and those meeting them quickly went about their business. The early spring air was cool and a stiff March breeze blew across the valley, causing people to turn their collars up and tuck their heads in. Bundled against the chill wind Angela and Thomas rode in restrained silence out to the ranch, exchanging only bare greetings and brief bits of news and comments on the weather.

It wasn't until after they had eaten dinner that they had an opportunity to talk. Margarita was in the kitchen cleaning up; Hector and Ramon had taken the buckboard to visit and help a neighbor. The sun had set and Thomas waited by the corral, his sheepskin coat buttoned all the way up and his hands thrust deep into the pockets. Angela walked toward him in the near darkness, silhouetted by the dim light coming from within the ranch house and joined him wordlessly. She also wore her sheepskin coat and pushed herself close to him, circling him with her arms. Her head was just below his chin and he nuzzled in her hair, breathing in the fragrance. They stood this way, silently, for a long time and finally he pulled his hands from his pockets and encircled her.

She pulled closer. "I missed saying good-by to you when you were here last," she said quietly.

"I know."

She whispered, "I'm glad you're here now."

Several seconds passed, "so am I." Somehow, the words didn't sound right in his ears and he felt the smallest of tremors pass through Angela's body.

She leaned back slightly and looked up at him. "This is very complicated for you, isn't it?"

He thought about her question for several moments, finally nodded, "yes, it is."

"I'm sorry Thomas. I think maybe I've made an awful mistake." She burrowed her head against his chest.

"I . . . I don't know," he replied hesitantly. "Perhaps we both have."

"I didn't mean to cause you any trouble."

"You haven't."

"I don't know why I . . . I don't know what I was thinking, Thomas." She pulled back again and Thomas saw tears on her cheeks. "I think I fell in love with you the moment I saw you. I just want to love you and for you to love me. I just want to be held in your arms . . ."

"I know, Angela." He held her tightly, not wanting to let her go. Finally, "I realize it just can't be that way, not . . ." he searched for words, "entirely."

She nodded silently, clutched him tightly and whispered, "I will always love you, Thomas."

"Angela . . ." he started.

"I didn't want this to happen. It feels just awful. I feel like something is dying inside of me." She pulled away and turned and half-ran toward the house.

Thomas watched as she disappeared inside the almost dark ranch house. *I understand, Angela,* he thought, *I too feel like some part of me just died.* At that moment he realized that he held core values and boundaries that molded and guided his life, some ingrained in him by his mother, others learned by observation of life around him; collectively, these were an unseen line in the sand and he had tentatively yet quite willingly stepped across that line with one foot. Now he had just as tentatively and somewhat unwillingly, pulled back.

Angela was not there at breakfast the next morning and the conversation between Ramon and Hector was about helping their neighbor during the night. Thomas ate in silence, feeling more like an outsider. But after breakfast Hector apologized, and the three men went to the barn and readied Thomas's horses and gear.

"Could be quite cold up there this time of the year, Mister O'Reiley," Ramon offered. "There's still a lot of snow at the lower elevations; but if the weather doesn't get any worse, it shouldn't be too bad."

"Thanks, Ramon." Thomas heaved himself up into the saddle and picked up the lead rope to the pack horse. "See you in five or six days."

* * *

The frozen snow covered much of the barely discernible trail and patches of ice made footing tricky for the horses. The switchback route up the side of the mountain was particularly difficult, as snow had drifted and frozen solid over the path. He was relieved when he at last rode over the crown of the bluff and onto more level land. Evidence of the recent hard winter was everywhere; fallen trees, their massive root systems torn from the ground or their trunks snapped off by high winds, lay at odd angles with their limbs poking into the sky still covered with green needles. Broken limbs and other debris littered the ground forcing him to detour several times. Swollen creeks, many still thickly covered with ice meant unsure footing for his horses, causing him to find alternate ways around these obstacles. By the time he reached the campground, it was late afternoon and a stiff, cold breeze was blowing. He knew that Gray Hawk's shelter was another ten miles further into the forest but had a sense that the old Indian was already aware of his presence.

The wait was very brief. The shaman stepped into the clearing, his right arm raised in greeting. He wore deer skin breeches and a thick fur cape covered the upper half of his body. He met Thomas with a grasp of his hand.

"Tah-moss! Good you are here!"

"You watch me," Thomas smiled and tapped his fingers on the side of his skull, "coming here?"

The old Indian nodded. "I watch you for two days, Tah-moss. You come with a heavy heart."

Thomas frowned at the Indian's intuition. *For two days?* He wondered *what does he really know?* "It is good to be here, Gray Hawk."

Gray Hawk simply nodded.

It took them another three hours to make their way to the Indian's shelter, taking the horses with them this time. Thomas threw a blanket over each and tied them loosely so they had access to the small creek and could rummage among the snow-covered undergrowth for something to eat. He took his few things into the shelter, food that he would share and his sleeping roll, the few cooking utensils, enameled plates and mugs he would leave with Gray Hawk. The shaman had a small fire going inside the shelter and it was warm although a thin pall of smoke hung as if suspended from the upper part of the hut.

They spent the evening talking and sharing the preparation of something to eat. Gray Hawk provided several thin roots to be baked in the coals; from the Gordon ranch, Thomas brought fist-sized chunks of beef that they roasted on skewers over the coals. He brought out the two enameled mugs and presented them to Gray Hawk, much to the shaman's delight. They filled them with snow to be melted over the coals and the shaman provided dried herbs that they brewed into a flavorful, hot tea. Their conversation, limited by the very small shared vocabulary and the blunt directness of hand signs and motions, cut quickly through nuances and innuendoes and double meanings. It was late before Thomas responded to Gray Hawk's early comment on his heavy heart and as they talked the Indian nodded his understanding of the concepts of moral values, truth, yearning and acceptance.

"I too, had a heavy heart, Tah-moss. Many winters ago. My family, my father, mother, sister . . . my wife . . . my boy child . . . all killed."

It was past midnight before the two went to sleep to the sound of the wind outside.

Over the next four days Gray Hawk spent long hours teaching Thomas about tracking animals, beginning with identifying the type of animal and moving on quickly to how to determine the direction and age of the track, how to determine the speed at which the animal was traveling, where it hesitated and where it made sudden changes in its attitude. Thomas was an astute student and quickly absorbed the gradations that seemingly minor differences in the shape and depth of the track made in its interpretation. He was surprised to learn how many animals, from small mice to larger rabbits and foxes and deer, left their footprints and marks in the snow and wet sands along the small creeks. The Indian taught Thomas how to walk without making sounds, how to blend in with the forest undergrowth and shadows, how to wait patiently without moving for long durations of time. He showed him how to determine if the animal he was stalking was male or female, how old it was and how much it weighed. He taught Thomas how to walk, crawl and slide along on his belly using every movement for a specific purpose. He taught him the elements of sight, smell and sound, wind and shadows. During the evenings he told Thomas how to cover his human odors by sitting a few minutes in the smoke of a fire or by rubbing his body with leaves or needles or branches of undergrowth. He showed Thomas how to apply streaks of black soot to his face and hands to break up their natural lines and shape and even how a few small branches and twigs of leaves tucked into his clothes could help him blend in with his surroundings. He demonstrated how to carefully place and shift the weight on his feet when stalking an animal in order to move silently through the woods and how to listen to the sounds around him, birds, insects, breezes—each sound or its absence having special meaning. By the fourth day, Thomas was able to track a rabbit and creep up on it until he was less than an arm's length away. Thomas could tell the old Indian was pleased with his progress.

The next morning Thomas said good-by again to the old man. "I will be back, Gray Hawk," he said, "in five or six moons."

"I watch for you, Tah-moss."

* * *

The weather had warmed somewhat over the days he was in the mountains and by the time he got to the Gordon ranch the late afternoon sun was shining. Angela met him as he rode into the area near the corral.

"Welcome back, Thomas!" She waved and walked over to where he sat on his horse. "How was your trip?"

"It was very good, thank you." Thomas studied the young woman for a moment. Something about her had changed in the last week. "You look well, Angela."

She smiled, "I feel good, Thomas. I think our . . . our *talk* the other night was what I needed, as painful as it was. And still is," she added wistfully.

He nodded. "I think that's true for me, also." He suddenly realized that he felt relieved of a sense of pressure and anxiousness that had been with him for several weeks and though her image had in fact visited him several times in the mountains, it lacked the hurt and longing that had accompanied such thoughts in the past. "I'm glad we talked."

*   *   *

Handon, Amanda, the children and their maid Xiang came back from the east coast on Monday, the ninth of April, five days after Thomas returned to San Francisco. Handon McPherson had settled his brother's financial affairs in New York and decided to close the architectural firm down in New York and move it to San Francisco. He offered its four senior architects the opportunity to relocate to the west coast city at the company's expense, an offer that three quickly accepted.

"It will be an excellent addition to our partnership, Thomas. To have an established and distinguished east coast architectural firm in our business portfolio will provide a myriad of benefits and new business opportunities."

Thomas nodded. His father-in-law was right; an experienced architectural firm under their wing would open up many new commercial options. Waiting for companies to bid on job opportunities takes a lot of time. "Who's going to run it, Handon?"

"I want Frank Barnwell to head it up."

"Barnwell?" Thomas could not help but express his surprise. "Frank Barnwell the engineer?"

Handon nodded. "He's got the education; Stanford graduate. He's got ten years of field experience. He's developed a lot of state and local contacts."

"When are you going to talk to him?"

"As soon as I can. I'd like to see the new company up and running by September."

CHAPTER 7

<u>Thursday June 21, 1900, San Francisco, California</u>
The San Francisco Chronicle reported that the incumbent President of the United States, William McKinley, was named the Republican Party's candidate for President in the upcoming November election. New York Governor Theodore Roosevelt was nominated for Vice President by a vote of 925 to 1 abstention. Theodore Roosevelt himself had cast the lone abstention.

Several pages behind these front page headlines was a single column article reporting that Quentin Montecristo, a lesser known but upcoming Louisiana republican politician from Lake Charles who had fought with Theodore Roosevelt's *Rough Riders* in Cuba during the Spanish American War, had been shot to death by an unknown assassin. Authorities reported that the fatal rifle shot was believed to have been fired by the assailant from a densely wooded area bordering the Montecristo family mansion near the Calsasieu River north of Lake Charles, in southwest Louisiana. Montecristo was killed as he arrived home and stepped out of his carriage following a private meeting in Lake Charles. The Montecristo name had been associated with the Lake Charles lumber industry for at least three generations and recently he had been negotiating with various wood and wood product industries in Japan.

What was not reported, however, was that the bullet that killed Montecristo was a heavy fifty-caliber round, especially designed to do massive bone and tissue damage when it hit. The bullet, which had been fired from a hundred and fifty yards away, hit him in the chest, crashed through his ribs and mushroomed into a squat projectile that utterly destroyed his heart before exiting through his back. Montecristo was dead before his body finished falling to the ground. Though not specific in detail, the paper alluded that he had been associated with sizeable and somewhat dubious financial investments in Nicaragua.

Thomas O'Reiley read the San Francisco Chronicle every morning as he enjoyed a cup of coffee and often times in the company of Amanda sitting in his sun-lit private office. He looked up often to gaze at the enormous bay that opened into the Pacific Ocean, well aware of the deadly beauty and fascination that the sea harbored. He often recalled the flimsiness of the small sailboat as he struggled to return to his homeland after years on the deserted island and would grimace when he thought of the frightening encounter with the huge shark and the crude, hand-fashioned barbed fish hook that had lodged itself in his left side. The puckered scar still revealed the self-inflicted parallel lines of rough stitching with which he had closed the wound. The scar on his side was just one of many, he thought—some which are not visible.

"What are you thinking about, Thomas?" Amanda smiled at him from her chair close by. "The sea?"

"You certainly know me, my dear," he replied. He let the newspaper fall to his lap. "I didn't know I was that transparent."

"I can read you like a book, my husband and when you get that look in your eye, I know something is going on." She sipped from her cup of coffee. "Would you like to talk about it?"

He laughed quietly. "Not much to talk about, Mandy. Just thinking about the long trip back to San Francisco from the island." He shook his head slowly. "The sea is so vast! So very huge and powerful; it can be both beautiful and deadly at the same time."

"It must have been simply awful but I'm so glad that you made it, Thomas."

"So am I. So am I."

She tilted her head and asked, "Do you miss it, Thomas?"

"The sea? No, I don't miss the dreadful hardships of my experiences on the sea, or the miserable existence aboard the *Orion*," he paused, "but there are certainly times that I long for the seclusion of that tiny, miserable island, Mandy. It was such a different manner of survival, of life itself; every day was unique; every day was a test for survival, every day offered new discovery about oneself. Some days were quite peaceful; others were a chaotic jumble of fear, pain, and confusion and utter, complete isolation. But some days I felt totally immersed in the intimate beauty, and peace and quietness of creation, an intense, almost religious hush broken only by the never ending murmur of the surf beating rhythmically against the shore; it was almost like the island's own heartbeat," he paused and laughed quietly, "and of course, the occasional squawk of the sea gulls, like . . ." he shrugged and his voice became whimsical, "my faithful companion, Frisco."

Amanda laughed softly with him. "Frisco must have been quite a true friend, Thomas. I can only imagine the intense complexity of your evening conversations." Her eyes twinkled with delight. "I should have been a fly on the wall of your hut."

"Ah! They were profound conversations, my dear." He said, mock seriously. "Very enlightening indeed."

Amanda looked at him steadily. "I think I understand why you have a need to retreat to your mountains from time to time, Thomas. I do really . . . try to understand. It's just that I worry so much when you are away. I worry that you will be become ill or seriously injured, or worse. I worry that you may not come home to me . . ." she struggled, "or that . . . something there might draw you away from me."

"That will never happen, Mandy. Never."

Monday, July 2, 1900, San Quentin Prison, California

The two men had served eleven years of their fifteen year sentence for murder; they had helped stab an itinerant gambler to death on the streets of San Francisco. With four years left, many would think that the worst part was over but for the two men, Clarence Chandler and Vernon Dyson, the worst was still ahead. Upon their release in four years, they would be transported under guard to Topeka, the state capital of Kansas, to stand trial there for the murders of a United States Marshall and his deputy. Their conviction for these cold-blooded killings was inevitable—they had left behind plenty of evidence and witnesses. The state of Kansas would quickly hang them.

Chandler and Dyson had no intention of allowing this to happen.

Eleven years is a long time in any man's lifetime and time in prison made it seem like an eternity. But San Quentin Prison was well stocked with criminals of all sorts, from petty burglars to deranged murderers. Exchanging *skills* among the inmates was widespread and one way to pass time. And so it was that Chandler, known as the Stick among the inmate population because of his tall slender build, learned the art of lock picking. Using a padlock stolen from one of the prison's workshops with nails bent and shaped into the various lock picking tools he had struggled under the tutorage of a dour old inmate for several weeks before he could even get the lock to snap open. Then many more months of practice followed until finally he could do it with his eyes closed or with his hands behind his back, or even with his wrists tied together with a strip of cloth—or all three handicaps at the same time.

Finally one day the old inmate had motioned to his student, tied Chandler's wrists together behind his back and stuffed a padlock into his waiting hand. It was a different padlock than the one Chandler had been practicing with for well over a year. For a moment Chandler was puzzled, then reached with his fingers into the hip pocket of his trousers for his set of *tools*, that had been perfected over time, each tool hardened by heating over a lighted candle until red-hot then plunged into cold water. He worked the torsion wrench in, twisted and held it with one hand. Then the half-diamond pick went in and he probed, feeling, sensing the tiniest of movements. He felt the pins move and click into place, one by one. Ten seconds later the lock snapped open. The old man clapped his hands silently and nodded. "Another year or two of practice, Stick and you'll be as good as me," he had grumbled.

*　　*　　*

Friday, July 20, 1900, Houston, Texas

The tall man peered out through the flimsy curtains onto the street below his hotel window. The meeting had been set up by means of carefully worded telegrams and was to begin within the hour. People in his occupation had very few reasons to meet with strangers. He turned once again to the small leather valise that lay open on the single bed in the room. Carefully secured within the open container were the four elements of his trade: an eighteen inch long Cataract Tool and Optical Company six-power rifle scope, the scopes mounting hardware, the twenty-seven inch long barrel of a German made Mauser rifle re-bored to accept a fifty-caliber bullet and machined to quickly and precisely join the fourth component, a Mauser bolt-action receiver also re-bored to accept a fifty-caliber round and its attached walnut stock. A small collection of hand-assembled fifty-caliber rounds resided in a side pocket of the case. The man had had the rifle modified for him by a firearms specialty company in New Orleans five months ago. The work had cost him almost five hundred dollars; part of that fee was to ensure that the work was completed in total secrecy.

It had taken the man only a few weeks to master this new killing tool. He had watched with professional satisfaction through the telescope as the bullet smashed into the chest of the pathetically pear-shaped politician Quentin Montecristo exactly where he had aimed from well over a hundred yards away. He had collected his fee without asking or answering questions as was his manner of doing business and left Louisiana by train two days later after spending one night pursuing his own unusual ritual of fulfillment.

He reached for the rifle components, expertly snapped the four units into position and inserted a round into the chamber, then shouldered the completed rifle. He had silently counted to less than five seconds. He disconnected the four pieces then did it again with his eyes shut. Still less than seven seconds. He frowned slightly. The problem was attaching the telescopic sight. The mounting brackets were small and fairly intricate. To ensure accuracy and speed, he would have to have them redesigned. The main difficulty was that the rear end of the scope was vertically adjustable to account for the distance to the target, which meant that the front of the sight must act like a precise hinge to accommodate the adjustment. Though slight, the fine-adjustment of the telescopic sight was essential for accuracy. Thoughtfully, he disassembled the rifle and carefully stored the pieces in the valise which he slipped under the bed.

The light tap on the door was not unexpected. The revolver tucked in the waistband of his trousers in the small of his back was already cocked. He slipped the door open a crack and peered at the two men standing there. Code names were exchanged and the two men entered the room.

The tall man listened carefully for twenty minutes. He asked only a few clarifying questions as he sat back, fingers pressed together. The task the two men were offering would require him to travel to Colombia in South America, specifically to Bogota, the capitol of Colombia. Colombia had been at war with itself for nine months, with the ruling Conservative Party being accused of fraudulent elections by certain radical groups and the Liberal Party. President Manuel Antonio Sanclemente was too ill to effectively manage the country. On May 28, eight weeks ago, the Liberals had suffered a bloody loss to the Conservative army led by General Prospero Pinzon at the Battle of Palonegro. There was a desperate move afoot in Bogota to replace the ailing Sanclemente with his serving vice-President Jose Manuel Marroquin.

"There is a man, a very powerful man in Bogota whose name is Juan Ramon Herrera. If the Liberal Party was to lose this man's financial and political support, the war would end quickly and there would be little contest for the presidency. If the Liberals were to win this war, the United States could give up all hope of any future negotiations with Colombia. That would not be in the best interests of the United States. Someone high up wants Herrera eliminated."

<u>Wednesday, August 22, 1900, San Francisco, California</u>

The August 15th assassination of wealthy Colombian industrialist Juan Ramon Herrera with political ties in Bogota, Colombia managed to make only minor headlines in the San Francisco Chronicle but his untimely death signaled the death-knell for the Liberal cause in Colombia, which had already failed to receive expected military reinforcements from Venezuela. While addressing a political rally in Bogota, Herrera was apparently shot from the upper floor of a government building some two-hundred yards away. The bullet struck Herrera high in his center chest; the force of the impact catapulted him back several feet. The assassin managed to slip into the panicked crowds and disappeared. Many Colombians placed the blame of his death on the ruling Conservative Party and a few felt the rebellious Panamanians had had a hand in the killing.

According to the Chronicle, Juan Ramon Herrera had made his fortune in the import-export business, dealing mostly with the export of coffee, hides and woolen textiles to the United States, almost exclusively to the California ports of Los Angeles and San Francisco since Colombia has no readily accessible commercial deep-water ports on its Caribbean shore.

Thomas read and reread the small article. There was something vaguely familiar with the article but he couldn't immediately put his finger on it. He let the newspaper flop onto his lap and stared at the blue San Francisco Bay. Bits and pieces of memory pulled together, like jigsaw puzzle pieces. It had been in the newspaper on a morning very much like this. The morning Amanda had joined him and they had talked. He had just put the paper down and glimpsed at the bay, just as he had now done. It was the killing in Louisiana; the Republican politician with the lumber industry background. He too had been shot with a rifle and the assailant had not been found. There had been no apparent motive for the assassination.

85

Thomas shook his head. *Politics, a dangerous business the world over.*

He had been very busy the last several months helping Frank Barnwell get the new architectural business established. Designed by its own architects, a new three storied building of contemporary design was constructed on Van Ness Avenue near Market Street to accommodate the offices and drafting rooms of the relocated company. The new building was designed to take full advantage of the most recent technical innovations: an electric elevator operated to haul materials, employees and clients between the basement and the three floors, overhead electric incandescent lighting provided greatly improved lighting in the spacious drafting rooms and offices, a powerful electric-powered ventilation system supplied a comfortable inside temperature, and the desk-top upright telephone connected them to many of the city's financial firms and other business associated with the construction industry.

The firm, now named *Sierra-Pacific Architects, Inc.*, opened its doors for business on September 10, 1900. Its street-side facade covered with polished white and black speckled granite from the Griffith Quarry in Penryn thirty miles north-east of Sacramento, won accolades from the city's business community.

Handon McPherson was there for the grand opening celebration, proudly ushering visitors from room to room. Everything was new, from the office furniture to the large tilting drafting tables and the best German-made drawing instruments and tools. McPherson had put emphasis on San Francisco's emerging preeminence as the major west coast seaport and business center. *California Champagne* from Korbel's Champagne Cellars in Guerneville was poured generously into waiting glasses; serving tables were laden with fresh seafood delicacies, local Italian and French cuisine, tidbits of California Monterey Jack Cheese, San Francisco Sourdough Bread and varieties of California table grapes. A sumptuous dessert table included petit fours, hand-made Ghirardelli Chocolate miniatures, orange sorbet and San Francisco's Pioneer Steam Coffee. Thomas introduced the guests to the company's President and general manager, Frank W. Barnwell, making sure business cards were exchanged. *Sierra-Pacific Architects* was off to an auspicious start and Frank Barnwell became the third member of McPherson, O'Reiley and Barnwell. Three essential elements of commercial construction in San Francisco were strategically anchored in M. O. & B: architecture and design, materials and supplies and construction.

A week later Handon off-handedly suggested that Thomas take a week off for a trip to the mountains, as that had seemed to have become Thomas's semi-annual routine. In fact, Thomas had already made arrangements and was on his way a week later.

He arrived in Visalia late Sunday afternoon, the 23rd of September. He was met at the train station by Angela, who greeted him with a warm but reserved hug. The ride to the ranch house in the warm afternoon air was pleasant and they exchanged accounts of their summer activities.

"Frank Barnwell?" She had asked, "didn't he come down here once before when you were here?"

"Yes. He came with us on my first trip here." He smiled, "surely you remember. You were so taken with him."

"All I remember is being taken by you, Thomas." She poked him in the ribs. "You were the most beautiful, handsome creature I had ever seen."

"Had seen?" he chided and chuckled.

"You still are, dear Thomas," she looked sideways at him. "You always will be."

"I missed saying good-by, last time."

"I thought it would be best that way. I didn't want to break down in tears in front of my parents." She glanced at him again, "but I missed it too."

They were silent for several minutes. Thomas's thoughts were a mixture of self-reproach and irresistible yearning. As he cast sideways glances her way, he realized that he still thought of the warmth and fragrance of her closeness and the touch of her lips. He recognized that it would take only an encouraging comment or evocative move by him, or from her, to re-ignite their brief but alluring moments of intimacy. He wondered if she was having similar thoughts but her eyes reflected only her concentration on keeping the buckboard centered on the narrow dirt road. He used the opportunity to study her profile. It seemed that she had continued to grow into adulthood during the last several months. Her features and her form had developed into mature shapes and proportions and the way she walked and spoke and held herself were reflections of her mother. Her skin bore the healthy, golden tan of an active outdoor life and her black, silky hair was always neatly arranged in a long braid or flowing loose. *I need to be very careful. It would be very easy to fall in love with such a young beauty.*

She seemed to read his thoughts. "What are you thinking, Tom?"

Her use of the shortened version of his name surprised him. It was something that few people ever did; only his mother, when he was just a boy, regularly called him Tom. Even Amanda rarely called him Tom, though he often called her Mandy.

"I like you calling me Tom," he admitted.

"Then just between you and me, you are Tom," she laughed.

He nodded. "I like that."

She steered the buckboard into the area in front of the ranch house, Thomas jumped down and was enthusiastically greeted by Margarita and Hector.

"We were beginning to wonder if you would not come back this fall, Mister O'Reiley," Margarita said as she gave him a hug.

"It's always good to be here, Margarita."

Hector shook his hand solemnly and Thomas looked around. "Where's Ramon?"

Hector shook his head. "Ramon is away for a few weeks attending some meetings in Sacramento regarding the future of citrus growing here in the valley. That industry will require a lot of water that we don't have right now. There are some that are looking at the possibility of building dams and canals to supply water for irrigation."

Thomas nodded his head. "I've spoken to Frank Barnwell about that." He went on to explain how Barnwell was now a partner, in effect, with him and Handon McPherson, in the commercial construction business in San Francisco. "So you are a little short handed. It's a good thing that you have Beck to give you a hand."

Hector shook his head sadly. "Well, I guess you didn't know; Beck left about a month ago, after all those years." He shrugged his shoulders. "He could get kind of cantankerous now and then but I hated to see him go, just the same."

"I'm sorry to hear that, Hector."

Hector nodded. "Well, I wish him luck. He said he was going to look for work up north somewhere."

Thomas settled into the bunkhouse and joined Hector, Margarita and Angela at the dinner table as the sun was setting. Conversation eddied around the citrus growing concerns and Frank Barnwell's new position with M. O. & B. The young man had made an impression on Hector and Margarita and only Angela remained silent.

It was late evening when Thomas finally bid the family good-night and headed for the bunkhouse. The moon was full and well above the eastern horizon. He sat in the ancient rocking chair on the bunkhouse porch listening to the night sounds around him; so much different than the city sounds of San Francisco. Here the gentle night sounds of cattle, the occasional restless foot-stomp of a horse in the corral, the rhythmic croaking of frogs around the water troughs and cyclic whirring chirp of cicadas in the sycamore trees seeped through the air almost like a gentle breeze. He could identify every individual odor, from the heavy animal smells to the light fragrance of the wild prairie grass that was drying in the late summer heat.

"Tom?"

He stood awkwardly as Angela stepped up onto the porch and stood next to him.

"I've really made things awfully complicated between us, haven't I?" she asked quietly after a few moments.

"I think things were already complicated, Angela, right from the beginning."

They stood side by side for several long moments. Finally she turned slightly and asked, "would you like to go for a walk?"

He smiled, "sure."

They stepped down from the porch and made their way across to the main gate leading to the long driveway. In the shadows, she linked her arm through his left arm and pulled close. In the late summer heat she was wearing a short sleeved blouse and her skin was warm against his. They walked slowly, silently and Thomas was aware of the haunting allure of her nearness.

"Angela, how are you folks handling things here without Beck? It seems like he was a big part of what you folks are about."

She hesitated for a few seconds as if gathering her thoughts. "Ramon has pretty much taken over Becks responsibilities here in terms of the stock." She glanced his way. "I suppose Beck was feeling kind of disillusioned," she paused, "and I guess in some ways . . . hurt. He told my father that he felt you had sort of . . . eased him out of the closeness of our family that he'd enjoyed for so many years. He implied that he had thought that someday perhaps he could marry the owner's daughter and help run the ranch. And then with Ramon probably taking over the ranch in a few years and already talking about getting into growing citrus and getting out of the cattle business, I think Beck just felt that he was not needed here any longer."

"I'm very sorry about that, Angela. I feel like I've helped create a very awkward situation for your family."

"It wasn't you." She smiled and changed the subject, "are you going to see Gray Hawk again?"

"That's what I plan to do."

"What's he like?"

"He's very lonely."

"How do you two manage to talk?"

"We use a lot of hand gestures. He's learning a little English and he's teaching me a few words of his language."

"I was raised being terribly afraid of him. You know—mountain legends and rumors about him being a deranged savage that stole little children and ate them and that sort of thing. You would be surprised if you heard some of the dreadful things he has been accused of."

"He's not like that at all, Angela."

"Well, I certainly hope not!" she laughed quietly.

The bright moonlight poked through the heavily leafed limbs of the sycamore trees. The warm air was still and cicada's metallic whirring rose and fell around them. They stopped and suddenly she was in his arms, her lips pressed to his; she held him tightly before she put her face to his chest and deep sobs shook her body. Thomas held her and let his face sink into her hair. Several minutes went by with neither saying a word. Finally her sobs subsided and she shook her head slowly and whispered, "I didn't think it would be this complicated, Tom. I don't know how I can be without you. I miss you . . . I want to be with you. I think of you all of the time."

Thomas continued to hold her; his own thoughts and emotions raging in conflict. Finally he said, "I know Angela, I know. I've some of the same feelings. I also know that for us to let this go any further would be devastating for you and for me."

"I just want to be with you," she sighed.

"I understand. It just can't happen, Angela."

Seconds went by before she whispered, "I know that it can't happen but that doesn't stop me from wanting it to happen." She laughed quietly to herself and added, "awfully childish of me, isn't it?"

"If it was childish we wouldn't be standing here talking about it."

She pulled away and wiped the tears from her eyes. The moonlight lit her face. "I'll always love you, Tom."

They walked back slowly toward the ranch house, holding hands and talking about his next-day trip to the high country.

CHAPTER 8

<u>High Sierra Back Country</u>

It was late afternoon when Thomas arrived at the hunting camp; a few minutes later Gray Hawk stepped quietly into the clearing.

"Gray Hawk! Good to see you!" Thomas greeted him.

"Tah-moss, my friend! Good you are here!" The Indian replied as he rested his hand on Thomas's shoulder. "Too long away."

"Yes. Too long," Thomas agreed.

The old shaman nodded then motioned with his head. "We go eat. Talk."

Two hours later they sat cross legged in the old Indian's shelter. He had prepared a freshly trapped rabbit and some small cakes made of ground acorns and nuts. They brought each other up to date on the happenings of the past summer. Gray Hawk talked about the ritual migrations and life cycles of some of the local animals, some of whom he had watched over the years as they had mated and raised their young into adults. Each animal had its own personality, its own peculiarities, he explained, not unlike human beings. One could only know this by spending many hours watching and tracking the animals to learn their ways. It was, he explained, a mysterious part of nature, of the connection between all nature and humans and between humans and the spirit world. Humans could not live in only a part of the world; they needed to understand and develop this connection with nature and the spirit world.

He smiled and pointed at himself, "I am still learning and I am an old man."

"Will you teach me?" Thomas asked.

The shaman hesitated, studied the white man that sat across from him. "I can help you begin to learn. What you learn is up to you."

Thomas nodded, "I want to learn."

The next morning, Gray Hawk presented Thomas with a pair of deer skin moccasins that he had made, as well as a hand-woven breech-clout and short deer-skin vest. "You must live like one of my people while we spend time together. I will teach you as if you were my own son."

Thomas knew that he had just been presented a great honor and he replied, "I will learn from you as if you were my own father." Something transpired that bridged the huge divide between the two men; one a father who had lost his son as an infant, the other a young man who as an infant had lost his father. Of different cultures, each had spent years of their lives in isolation. Both knew and understood cruelty and death, aloneness and self-dependence.

Thomas stripped and tied on the breech-clout, then slipped on the moccasins and leather vest. At first the minimal covering felt strange but he quickly began to understand its benefits as well. As the days quickly passed he learned that the moccasins gave him an intimate sense of the surface texture on which he was standing; the smallest pebble or slip of wood, the slightest resistance or give to his weight was immediately evident. The exposed skin on his arms and legs and chest provided him an abundance of information about the air around him, its modest temperature fluctuations, the amount of moisture it carried, even the tiniest variations in the direction from which small breezes came. With the increase of sensitivity of these senses, his other senses seemed to heighten as well. He began to hear sounds to which he had paid no attention: the sounds of birds, squirrels, insects and the gentlest breeze through treetops. His sense of smell increased and he took notice of odors that he had simply ignored in the past. The shaman taught him how to see among shadows and undergrowth, how to observe movement and how to sit for hours without moving. The old man showed him how to walk without making noise, how to blend in with the surroundings, even how to camouflage the angular shapes of his face with a few smears of dark soil or soot. He learned how he could take advantage of the direction of the wind to prevent his own scent from alerting an animal. Finally the old Indian began to teach him about the tracks that animals left on the ground as they moved about.

Tracks, both animal and human, the old man explained, were the track maker's connection with nature and the spirit. Everything about the animal: what kind of animal, how old the track was, the animals size and weight, its direction of travel, if and how it is injured, its pace, everything the animal did or even thought about doing would be revealed in the track it left on the earth. "Young boys of my people learn this before they are old enough to hunt. It becomes natural for them to read about an animal through its track." They spent all the daylight hours following and reading signs that animals had left on the ground. Thomas got down with his face inches from the track and studied as the old Indian was describing what he saw, the manner in which soil had been compressed, or had crumbled or slid, or had been shifted about. Sometimes when the animal walked across the rough forest floor covered with deep layers of decomposed leaves, the tracks grew almost impossible for Thomas to see; but the old man persisted, pointing out bent or displaced grasses, small depressions, tiny inconsistencies that had revealed the path of the animal. Sometimes the Indian would have to determine the direction of the animal and search further ahead to pick up the track again. He carefully made sure Thomas understood his process.

On the day before Thomas had planned to leave, the old shaman took Thomas out one more time. It was shortly after dawn and in a few minutes they picked up a deer track.

The shaman studied it for several moments, "how old is this track?" he asked.

Thomas looked at the series of tracks carefully. The sides of the track were crisp. A bent piece of grass was still struggling to become vertical again. "Fresh. Maybe fifteen, twenty minutes old."

"Buck or doe?"

Thomas walked along the track, pointed as he talked. The spacing between the rear tracks was narrower than the front tracks. "Buck. He stopped here, looked over his left shoulder." He moved on a few steps, pointed again. "Pissed here to mark his territory."

"How big?"

"Good sized. Two hundred twenty-five pounds."

The Indian nodded. "Find him."

Thomas followed the track, easily at first because they had picked it up in a sandy area near a small creek. He reached into the damp earth and spread smears of mud across his face and drew smears across his arms and legs to disguise their length. The deer had turned away from the creek into the forest and the track became more difficult to follow. Thomas worked the sunlight and shadows as the shaman had taught him and made out the faint impressions on the forest floor. The buck had stopped a few times, glanced over his left shoulder, perhaps conscious of the vague noises somewhere behind him. Thomas was suddenly aware that he was carelessly creating noise himself and slipped into the tracking crouch Gray Hawk had taught him, placing each foot with care to avoid stepping on a twig, feeling the surface carefully with his feet. The track veered off to the right; perhaps the buck was trying to distance himself from the occasional tiny wisps of sound that could be closing in on him. Thomas paused to check the air; there was a slight breeze but it was blowing right to left so it wouldn't be a problem right now. The big deer started climbing up a slope, not hurriedly but with slow determination. He wasn't yet spooked. A hundred yards up the slope the buck had once again paused and peered over his right shoulder, taken a few steps and turned again to the right, this time crossing a flat area of granite. Thomas had to get down with his face near the rock to make out the almost invisible marks left in the fine coating of pollen and dust layering the granite. The deer had gone straight across and eased into a copse of densely packed small trees and underbrush. Thomas motioned for the Indian to stop; they both dropped below the granite then cut around the outcropping, coming out below the compact patch of trees. They dropped to the ground and Thomas studied the thick growth ahead. *He's in there*, he thought.

The breeze was now coming more directly from behind them and they would have to be careful to not allow it to carry their human scent to the buck. He signaled to Gray Hawk and they backed down again to the granite. Thomas motioned that they would go around the granite in the reverse direction, go up the hill and come down on the undergrowth area from above instead of from below. The old Indian nodded.

It took several minutes to navigate back around the granite outcropping and move uphill a hundred yards. A fallen tree gave them visual protection as they made their way across the hill on the uphill side of the thicket in which the buck was hiding. From here, the rest of the way would require crawling on his stomach. Using deliberate and slow movements, he began the downhill crawl. Once among the dense thicket of small trees, he slithered under and around the branches noiselessly, each hand and knee placement carefully considered so as to be done in silence. He saw motion ahead and stopped instantly, frozen in position. It was the buck, pawing impatiently at the soil. Thomas moved carefully. From the small portion of leg that he could see, the buck was still facing outward toward the granite. Thomas signaled Gray Hawk and the Indian joined him.

It took twenty minutes to cover the distance that put them within fifteen feet of the buck. Thomas's estimate had been pretty close; the buck probably weighed two hundred and thirty pounds. Its antlers spanned nearly thirty inches. They watched for almost a half hour as the buck waited impatiently, chewing his cud. Finally the deer stepped out cautiously from concealment and continued his journey up the hill.

Gray Hawk clapped his hand on Thomas's back. "Very good, Tah-moss. You learn well."

Thomas hesitated for a moment, then, "I'm not a hunter, Gray Hawk."

"No Thomas, you are a hunter. You are not a killer. A hunter does not kill for pleasure. A killer seeks pleasure from killing."

Thomas nodded slowly as the shaman's words sunk in. "You are a good teacher, Gray Hawk."

* * *

Abilene, Texas

The man El Culebra was beginning to amass a small but solid fortune which he kept in deposits spread out through several banks in Texas so as not to bring any unwanted scrutiny into his life or occupation. By nature he was a quiet man who chose to be alone, or occasionally in the limited circle of men around a gambling table where he bet quietly and conservatively. He seldom drank more than one or two beers. On occasion he would solicit the services of a prostitute. When he was away from Abilene on business these encounters helped appease the smoldering, violent anger lurking beneath his fragile superficial composure. These ritualistic, often by chance, meetings left a succession of unsolved and gruesome murders that stretched from small town to small town across the Midwest and southern states.

As a young drifter, his father had joined the Confederate Army during the War Between the States but had become a deserter to join one of the outlaw brigades that terrorized Kansas during the last part of the war. Somewhere in a small farming town in the Oklahoma Panhandle, his father had dallied long enough to impregnate one of the local schoolmarms and he was the result of that unfortunate union. Unmarried and pregnant, his mother had lost her job as a teacher. After he was born, his mother turned to prostitution in order to support herself and her child. He remembered very little about his absentee father, mainly the times he would show up unexpectedly and beat his mother unconscious before pulling off his wide leather belt and starting on the young boy. When he was fifteen he had listened impassively when word came around that his father had been lynched by an angry mob in Texas for murdering a rancher and stealing his horses. Shortly afterward he ran away from home to start life on his own. His mother, then in her thirties, disappeared with another man soon after that.

The young man wasn't even certain of his own name; his father had always referred to him simply as *boy* and his mother called him *buddy*. Within a week of leaving home, he decided he would go by the name *Luke*, because it was short and easy to remember; he thought it sounded *masculine,* a name that would demand and receive attention. For a last name, if and when one was needed, he used one of several names like Forrest, Rivers, Hill and Woods. On his own at the age of fifteen, he had been forced to learn how to fight with his hands; and though he had lost a number of brawls, he eventually learned that there were no rules in a bar fight. He found that he could minimize his opponent's advantage by any means at hand. Once his adversary was slowed and confused from dirt thrown into his eyes, or broken finger bones, or an ear or nose or piece of cheek bitten off, he could ruthlessly and systematically continue his attack. Kicking, stomping, choking and bashing were lethal means of putting an opponent away, either dead or close to it. In fact, Luke came to enjoy the pain he could inflict on another human being.

Accused of murder in a hard-scrabble east-Texas town, he had ridden into southern Illinois to enlist in the US Army under the name of Luke Rivers and was taught how to handle a rifle. His superiors quickly discovered that he had better than average rifleman skills and he was soon being trained as a sniper. He saw action in 1898 when the United States landed on the island of Puerto Rico as a strategic move of the Spanish-American War. While serving in Puerto Rico, he discovered a perverse satisfaction in his ability to execute a man with a single rifle shot from a distance of a hundred or more yards; he came away with twenty-three notches on his rifle's stock.

Army life agreed with Luke and all went fairly well until he got in a fight with a drunken army lieutenant over the attentions of a young prostitute. The lieutenant got the worse end of the brawl, ending up with a violent scar that ran from his right ear across his right cheek and disfiguring his nose. The young sniper was stripped of his rank, spent six months in the stockade and was ordered to forfeit his monthly pay. He was given a dishonorable discharge from the army back into civilian life.

Luke spent the next several months drifting and stealing among the small towns strung along the Rio Grande border with Mexico. In the tiny adobe-built settlement of Ruidosa he got his first meaningful job. He was paid fifty US dollars to eliminate a pesky rancher named Adulio Hierra. Early one morning Luke followed the unlucky man to the banks of the Rio Grande and with a second hand Winchester 30-30, shot him off his horse. Luke quickly rode fifty miles across the barren landscape to Marfa; two days later he headed for San Angelo and then to Abilene.

In Abilene Luke eventually discovered there was a ready market for his unusual skill. Small time politicians, overly ambitious businessmen, quarrelling ranchers and farmers, unhappy wives and cheating husbands all found occasion to request his special talent. Over time, he established a loose network of listeners and informers. He rewarded those who brought him paying business; he cut, trimmed and nourished this network until its vine-like presence was in many of the saloons in the county. Luke was very secretive about his personal identity and the mysterious assassin eventually became known throughout the network only as *El Culebra*, or *The Snake*.

After the near-failure of his first truly important hired-assassin assignment, the Kentucky politician William Goebel, he replaced his off-the-shelf Winchester rifle with the carefully considered rifle of his choice. The killing tool was a highly modified, telescopic-sight equipped, German-made Mauser fifty-caliber rifle. He believed that high quality work demanded high quality tools. Originally manufactured to handle a 7.52mm round, Luke had the Mauser re-bored and re-rifled to fire a huge .50 caliber round. That provided the muzzle velocity, the bullet weight and size that he felt his new-found profession demanded. The gunsmith transformed the Mauser into a two-piece break down rifle that made it easy to transport. He had just recently paid another gun shop fifty dollars to redesign and construct a custom mount for the telescopic sight. The new mount provided a quick but very solid attaching system that enabled him to assemble the two parts of the rifle, the sight and insert a round in the chamber in less than five seconds on a regular basis in the dark or with his eyes shut.

His journey in July and August to Bogota, Columbia had been arduous but successful. After sailing from the border town of Brownsville, Texas to the Panamanian port city of Colon, he rode the trans-Panama railroad to Panama City. From there a small steamer took him to the western coast of Columbia. His journey continued overland by stage to Bogota. Once in Bogota, all he had to do was wait for the politician to announce his next move. Access to the nearby, sparsely occupied government building posed no problems and an unfinished empty room on the third floor provided a clear shot over some low trees to the plaza where the rally was taking place. On the fifteenth of August he had watched with perverted satisfaction through the rifle's telescope as the single blunt-nosed fifty-caliber bullet struck Herrera in the soft spot at the base of his neck, severed his spine and nearly decapitated him. Without haste, he broke the rifle and telescopic sight down into its three components, put them in the case, sauntered down the stairs and into the panicked crowd streaming through the narrow streets and away from the plaza. His return trip to Texas was uneventful other than a ten day wait in Colon as a soaking early-season hurricane swept through the Gulf of Mexico. It would hit Galveston, Texas at two in the morning on the eighth of September, killing more than six thousand of the islands residents.

Now back in Abilene, he had deposited the rewards of his trip to South America in a bank under the name of Luke Hill. For the past week, he had felt a restless urge and had trouble relaxing. This evening he decided he would prowl the alleyways and find a local girl who would serve to purge the bizarre restlessness from his mind. There were plenty of pretty girls in Abilene that liked to cater to the cowboys, especially young girls with long black hair . . .

*   *   *

The Gordon Ranch
Thomas had arrived at Hector Gordon's ranch late afternoon on the previous day after spending the week in the high mountains. After unpacking and seeing that the horses were taken care of, he had bathed quickly and joined the family in the big ranch house with plans to take the train to San Francisco the next day. As Hector and Thomas sat in the comfortable leather chairs in the great room, Hector filled Thomas in on the latest newspaper headlines, including what he had read about the hurricane that had struck Galveston Island in Texas.

"Six thousand dead!" Thomas exclaimed. "That's almost impossible to comprehend. And now, the local militia are shooting and killing looters!" He shook his head in disbelief.

After dinner, Thomas and Angela spent a few minutes next to the corral. The moon was in its last quarter, casting a subdued and pale luminosity over the countryside. Though the ground was still radiating warmth, the air temperature was cool for this time of the year. Hector had mentioned that he thought it would rain in the next day or so.

"How was your visit with Gray Hawk?" The question seemed strained and forced in her attempt to fill the vacuum that seemed to be between them.

"I had a good week with him," Thomas replied. "He's teaching me how to track."

"Sounds like fun." Her response was lightly tinged with cynicism.

He laughed. "It was, actually. I'm learning a lot from that old Indian."

Angela hesitated, then finally, "I'm sorry Thomas. I'm sure you are. I didn't mean . . ."

"It's all right. I know it doesn't sound very exciting to you but it is for me." He thought for a moment about revealing that he had even worn a breech-clout like the shaman but decided that she might believe he had gone completely insane. "I tracked a big buck yesterday and got within fifteen feet of it. He didn't even know I was there."

She looked at him and tilted her head. "Well, that really is impressive, Thomas." She sounded like she really meant it. There was a long lull in their conversation. Finally she asked, "will you be coming back in the spring?"

Thomas looked at her before he answered. Every time he saw her she had grown more mature and even more beautiful. Though she was not tall, she carried herself with an easy confidence that her mannerisms and bearing reflected. She's twenty-two years old now and would soon want to find a man who would fit into her life and she into his. *And that would not be me*, he thought. "I'll be back, Angela."

Their parting embrace was brief, the kiss a quick touch of lips to her cheek. Then she was gone.

CHAPTER 9

<u>Thursday, February 28, 1901 Beaumont, Texas</u>

Anthony Francis Lucas's oil well, Lucas # 1, south of Beaumont, Texas began gushing oil at 10:10 AM on the tenth day of January, 1901. With his wooden drilling derrick set atop *Spindletop Hill*, the drilling contractor had hit oil at a depth of twelve hundred feet; the resulting well produced over two and a half million gallons of crude oil a day. The discovery launched a flood of speculators, entrepreneurs and oil drilling equipment companies into Texas along with the usual crowd of hustlers, con artists, prostitutes and gamblers. New oil drilling companies were quickly formed, consolidated, bought and traded and with the ensuing rush of property lease claims and counter claims there was ample work for the man whose clandestine profession made him the ultimate resolver of disputes. The man went by various names, including Luke Hill, Luke Wells and Luke Lake. None of his clients ever saw him face to face, at least that they were aware of.

The local newspapers were full of deals that went bad, partners at odds with one another and bitter business feuds. Within three months after the *Spindletop* gusher, settling these disputes was keeping the assassin busy. Though the frequency of these killings elevated the anxiety level among those clamoring for their share of the action, it was not enough to bring things to a halt. And so the drilling—and the settlement of arguments by a well placed fifty-caliber bullet—continued along with the occasional disappearance of one of the prostitutes who had migrated into Beaumont and whose raped and violated body might eventually show up. Local newspapers sometimes covered these happenings but they were mostly interested in the latest oil gusher. The population of Beaumont swelled from a sleepy town of seventy-five hundred souls toward fifty thousand.

Hotel and boarding house rooms were becoming expensive and a city of tents was soon springing up on the edge of town. The steady influx of people was welcomed by the assassin as the growing population helped obscure his presence.

He had slept late this morning and awoke to the noise of the busy street below his hotel window. He squinted at the sunlight already streaming in through the window and wrinkled his nose at the ever present stench of raw crude oil that seemed to permeate everything in this part of the state. He'd been here nearly two and a half months now and had collected a handsome profit for his work which he had deposited in three banks under the three different names. Large amounts of money in this city rarely came under question but he knew that he would have to move on before too long. Perhaps two more weeks—three or four more jobs. Then he would have to goad his network into action again. Though he had been busy and the flow of money was good and fairly steady, it was nothing like what a big political job could bring in. Besides, he was beginning to miss the excitement of planning and bringing about the final sighting through the rifle's telescope and then the execution.

The job last night was typical of those of late. Joseph Reed, formally of Louisiana, had rolled into town eight weeks ago with his partner James Donovan. In short time, they had formed a company called R & D Drilling, borrowed enough money to buy some used drilling equipment and to construct a wooden derrick and then plugged into the earth to make a fortune. The plot of land they decided to drill on had no legal owner, at least as far as they could find with a quick and not very rigorous search and they laid stake to it. At nine hundred feet through the sand and rock, they struck oil, not a major gusher like Spindletop but enough oil to make sure they could borrow more money for their second and third drilling rigs. Donovan, though, wanted to sell out, take their significant profit and return to Louisiana. Reed didn't agree. As the weeks rolled by and the argument became loud and sometimes physical between the two, someone whispered a few words into Reed's ear. As an early spring thunderstorm trudged slowly across the land, Donovan reluctantly received one of Luke's fifty-caliber slugs in the center of his chest from a distance of two hundred yards. Donovan was dead by the time his body bounced on the street he had been walking on. It was still light when the assassin prowled among the back streets of Beaumont in search of a young prostitute to complete his evening's entertainment. The assassin nodded to himself; it had been a very satisfying night but it was time for him to move on.

*   *   *

Thomas O'Reiley sat in the early morning gloom and peered through the windows of his study. The city was fog bound by a thick blanket that stretched far past the Farallon Islands, some twenty-six miles beyond the Golden Gate. Alcatraz Island was cut off from view and he could barely make out the marina at the foot of the hill. The house was cool this morning and the rest of his family was still sleeping. Only Xiang was up and busy in the kitchen, singing in her off-key sing-song style.

He could hear the distant clang of the bell on the cable car as it made its way up Powell Street. Shortly, if the wind was calm, he would hear the squeal of steel wheels on the tracks as it made its left turn onto Jackson Street. He glanced at his pocket watch; the car was right on schedule. It was the first run of the morning.

The morning newspaper had not yet arrived and he sat with a map of California spread out on the desk in front of him. He knew that it was a certain sign of restlessness when he starting looking at maps. His finger traced the line of mountains bordering the eastern edge of the state—the great Sierra Nevada Range and stopped at the river he knew as the Kaweah River. *The Gordon ranch and Angela Gordon, would be right about here,* he mused. *Strange that I should still think about her as I do. Maybe it's not strange. The ranch hand and guide, Beck—wonder what became of him. Hector didn't seem to want to talk about having to let him go. And Gray Hawk.* Thomas let his finger follow the general route to the high mountains where the old Indian lived. *Early spring there. Still snow on the ground. Deep snow.* His mind flickered through the experiences he had shared with the old shaman.

"You'll be wanting to go soon, won't you?" Amanda's voice surprised him and he turned to find her standing in the doorway with two cups of coffee. "Coffee, Thomas?"

"Good morning, my dear." He arose and took the cup from her. "Join me? It's a little cool out here. I'll build us a fire."

"Not much of a view, either," she said as she took the offered chair. "This fog has just been awful for the past week. I do think the people are getting tired of not seeing the blue sky."

"I'll see what I can do about it, dear," he said seriously.

She laughed. "If anyone could change the weather, it would be you."

He chuckled as he busied himself for a few minutes arranging kindling wood and several small logs in the fireplace, then struck a match and watched as the blaze took hold.

Thomas sat once again, folded the map and slid it into a drawer in the desk. The wheels of the cable car squealed in the distance, combined with the clang of its bell.

"So, when will you be leaving, Thomas?"

He had been waiting for the question and he looked at her. "I've not really planned anything yet, Mandy. Business is taking so much of my time now with the architectural firm in full swing. Frank has done a superb job of getting things rolling along; so good, in fact, that your father and I can just manage to keep up with the new business. M. O. & B. had introduced new construction materials and processes into the business, which have meant locating and procuring these materials, some of which are not yet available on the west coast."

"Hmm. The fire feels wonderful. Thank you." Amanda commented.

We're sparring all around the issue, Thomas thought, *like two prizefighters. I will be going again and soon.* "I suppose I should make plans, Mandy. Certainly I do wish to visit the mountains sometime this spring."

"And your *Indian* friend?"

Thomas thought he detected a bit of cynicism in her voice. "Yes and my friend Gray Hawk also."

Amanda sat silently for a long time. "Perhaps I could meet him someday."

Thomas smiled. "I rather doubt it, my dear wife. I'm the only white man he's spoken to in forty years or more."

"Why is that, Thomas?"

He had never told his wife about Gray Hawk's history or that he had brutally killed the six men who had murdered his small tribe. It was not the kind of information that would endear Amanda to his relationship with the Indian. "He's an old man, Mandy, with a history that most white people would find quite appalling. He chooses to live in isolation. He is a shaman—what we might call a medicine man He lives very simply off the land."

"Then why has he befriended you, Thomas?"

Thomas remembered the old Indian pointing to his own head and saying *"I have watched you, Tah-moss."* Clearly, the shaman believed there was some mystical connection between them. "I truly do not know, Mandy."

* * *

The Washington, D.C.
William McKinley was inaugurated for a second term as President of the United States of America, coming into the presidency on a strong foreign policy platform. He rode in his carriage down Pennsylvania Avenue accompanied by his close friend Senator Mark Hanna of Ohio. Vice President Theodore Roosevelt rode alone in the following carriage.

* * *

The Gordon Ranch
"It's been a rough winter up there, Mister O'Reiley," Hector said between mouthfuls of dinner. "We got several feet of snow, even at the lower elevations. Hasn't been real warm yet, either. Probably a lot of snow still on the ground." He grumbled, "been pretty damn cold down here in the valley, too."

Margarita glared at her husband. "Hector!" she admonished, "watch your tongue!"

Angela looked across the table at Thomas and slipped him a subtle and nearly imperceptible wink. She had picked him up in the buckboard at the train depot and they had ridden through the cold afternoon weather to the ranch. Bundled against the cold, conversation between them had been restrained.

Ramon sat next to his sister and glanced from face to face as he pushed forkfuls of food into his mouth. "Been cold enough a couple of nights to freeze the water troughs solid. Makes me wonder how citrus trees would do in cold like that."

"I understand some of the farmers down south make smoke fires on cold nights," Hector said, "and the smoke keeps the frost from settling on the trees."

Ramon grunted, "sounds like someone's going to be up all night."

The family sat in the great room following dinner and a blaze in the fireplace took the edge off the chill air. Thomas found the conversation to center around their local conditions and problems: lack of irrigation water in the summer, what breeds of cattle seemed best fit for the irrepressible heat of the San Joaquin Valley, the future of the railroad in the valley and how it would affect the transportation of beef to the eventual marketplace.

Eventually Hector looked at the old family clock on the mantle. "Don't know about you folks but it's time for me to get into bed." He glanced at Margarita, "you coming, Margie?"

Before long Thomas and Angela were alone in the room, the fire still casting flickering shadows against the walls. They pulled the chairs up close to the fire and stretched their legs out to take advantage of the warmth. Angela reached across and took Thomas's hand in hers. She had just opened her mouth to say something when there was a loud pounding on the front door.

Angela jumped up and ran to the door, swung it open.

"Miss Angela! Sorry to intrude like this," a man's voice boomed. "It's Julia! We can't find her. She went out this afternoon and didn't come home. It got dark and she's still not back. I'm trying to round up some folks to help us look for her!"

"Come on in, Ted!" Angela said.

A big man lumbered in, wide-brimmed western hat on his head and a heavy coat that came to his knees. He nodded at Thomas before Angela had an opportunity to introduce them.

"Ted," she said, "this is Mister O'Reiley, Thomas O'Reiley. He's a regular guest here."

Ted thrust out his hand. "Mister O'Reiley. My pleasure, sir," as the two men shook hands.

"Julia. She's . . ." Thomas queried.

"Julia's my middle daughter. Thirteen years old. We need some serious help, Mister O'Reiley. She can't last long in this kind of cold."

"Ted owns the Stanton ranch just north of us."

Thomas nodded. "I'll go with you, Ted, if . . ." he looked at Angela, "I can borrow a horse for the night."

"You know you can, Tom. Why don't you go with Ted and I'll get the family up and started. We can all meet at the Stanton ranch."

Thomas found the rancher to be a man of few words as they headed for the Stanton ranch. The sky was clear and the stars glittered like diamonds.

The moon was about three-quarter full and cast a dim light over the landscape. The wind was icy, coming down from the high mountains to the east. Other than the steady drum of hooves, the night was quiet. Ted led Thomas at a slow gallop through the rounded hills and shallow canyons that made up the transition from valley to mountain. Presently Thomas saw the lights of the ranch house a half mile ahead.

When they pulled into the yard, a plump woman rushed out the door to meet them.

"Ted! Anything?" she hollered.

"I've got some help coming, Muriel. Gordon's are on their way. This here is Mister O'Reiley. He's staying over at the Gordon's place."

"Oh, thanks for offering to help, Mister O'Reiley!" She took Thomas's hand and squeezed it tightly. "Come in out of the cold. I have a pot of coffee on the stove."

The Stanton ranch house was a little larger that Hector's but equally comfortable. A large fire blazed in the fireplace and the main room was warm and cozy. Two other men were seated in the room and they got up as Thomas walked in.

Thomas introduced himself. "I'm Thomas O'Reiley."

"Peter Jenkins," offered the young, slender man as he stuck out his hand.

"I'm Jack Short," the other man, older, broad shouldered and muscular, shook hands as well. "I work for Mister Jenkins." He looked at Thomas, "You're not from around here, are you?"

Angela, Margarita, Hector, Ramon and Ted Stanton entered the room before Thomas had the opportunity to respond. Muriel poured strong black coffee into tin mugs for everyone as Ted Stanton explained the overall situation. He had a large map of the ranch on the wall. The ranch house was situated on the north-west corner of the roughly rectangular eighteen-hundred acre spread. It was bound on its eastern edge by the North Fork of the Kaweah, on its south-eastern edge by the Kaweah. A slanting east-west property line partly following a tributary of the North Fork identified the northern boundary. A north-south line designated the western edge. Ted explained that a local road marked that same line. The southern edge coincided with the northern limit of the Gordon ranch property. Ted indicated a rough line that divided the eastern and western halves. "Hills get pretty rough from here to the north fork. Cattle get lost in there all the time. They get back in some of those canyons and just aren't smart enough to get out."

"Which way do you think Julia would go?" Peter Jenkins asked.

Stanton shook his head. "Well, she wouldn't go north. That's Old Man Shingleton's spread. Julia's been afraid of him all her life. I think he's okay, just a little strange. Runs a few head, small operation. Widow-man for fifteen years or more. One of us should ride in and check with him." He put his finger on the map near the ranch house. "My bet is that she'd go toward the north fork. She's been fascinated by some old arrowheads she found up there last summer. She wouldn't go west; that'd just take her to the road. South? Perhaps but that'd take her down your way, Hector and you haven't seen her." He nodded. "I'd say east, toward the north fork."

"I'll swing by and talk to Shingleton, then ride along the northern boundary," Ramon offered.

"Jack and I will start here," Jenkins indicated the ranch house on the map, "and work our way down and toward the east. That's where that old barn was, isn't it, Ted."

"Yeah. Not much left there but that's a good idea. Sure need to check it out, Pete."

"Margarita will stay here with Muriel." Hector volunteered. "Ted, you and I take the northern third, along that rock ridge toward the north fork."

Thomas looked at Angela and she nodded quickly. "Angela and I will take the center third."

Ted pointed out landmarks so that the three teams would not overlap search areas. A small creek, rock outcropping, small stand of trees, the old barn all became sighting points for the three teams.

"We all have guns?" Everyone nodded. "Three shots means we found her. Two shots, repeated three times means we need help—pronto."

Thomas raised his hand tentatively. "A couple of questions, Ted. How much does your daughter weigh?"

"About sixty, sixty-five pounds."

"How tall?"

"Hmmm . . ." Ted glanced at his wife. "I suppose about four-feet ten."

"What color is her hair?"

"Black. Long. She's got it in a pony-tail."

"What's she wearing?"

"Blue denims. Red blouse, long sleeves. Sheepskin jacket," Muriel answered. "She had her hair tied up with a bandana, a red one."

"About how many hours has she been gone?"

"Six, maybe seven."

Everyone nodded. The information was good to have.

"Lanterns?" Thomas asked.

"In the barn. We'll top them off with coal-oil before we leave." Ted said. "More coffee, anyone?"

Everyone shook their heads. "Let's get going then."

The three groups headed to the barn, each took a lantern. After mounting their horses, they headed in three different directions and Ramon headed due north to locate and talk to Shingleton. Thomas and Angela headed away from the ranch house; Thomas swept the ground with his eyes. They had covered nearly a quarter of a mile before they came upon a sandy draw.

"Let's follow this north first, then south. If she came this way, she would have to cross over this sandy area. We might pick up her tracks."

He got down and walked slowly studying the sand. There were tracks; animal tracks of deer and probably coyote. They continued their search until they came to the large horizontal outcropping of rock that Ted had described. "This should be the northern end of our search area. I kind of hate to turn back but . . ."

"She could have just as easily passed across on the other side from where we started," Angela mused.

"No question about that. Let's go back."

It took them twenty minutes to get to their initial starting point and begin the sweep south. Fifteen minutes later, he found the girl's shoe prints in the damp sand.

"Here they are! She crossed right here. These are old tracks, several hours at least." He pointed as he spoke. "She climbed this shallow bank here and started off in that direction," he pointed. The land ahead was barely visible in the vague moonlight but he could see the undulating hills sprinkled with scattered scrub oaks. He tried to make out the footprints in the packed soil but it was difficult in the near darkness. Finally he got down close and shined the lantern light on the ground. "Here are her tracks. See these bent stems here . . ." he pointed, "and here . . . and here. She's headed in that direction, through that little low area."

They followed the tracks, occasionally losing them on the hard-packed dirt, then picking them up again several yards further. They led to a shallow area between two hills, became confused near a scrub oak tree. "Looks like she rested here for a while . . ." He studied the prints again with the lantern light. "Walked in this direction," he pointed, "toward that rock outcropping." For the next few hundred yards or so, the tracks were fairly easy to follow then the ground became strewn with small rocks and boulders. It took him a half hour to find the track again just before they led onto the huge slab of rock.

"Now it gets a little complicated," he said, almost to himself. The rock was rough granite, breaking out of the soil in a long horizontal run that was almost fifty feet wide sloping slightly following the gentle contour of the land, then downhill into the next shallow valley and part way up the side of the next hill. *Had she stayed on the outcropping? If not, where had she gotten off? If she had gotten off, had she turned left or right?* He studied the surface of the granite carefully with the lantern light. It wasn't bright enough to make out any dusting that may have been displaced by her footsteps.

"If you'll take the upper side, I'll take the lower side. We'll start here and walk the length, looking for where she may have stepped off the granite."

Angela nodded. "Let's get going, Tom."

They walked their horses along slowly as each studied the soil near the rock for any sign of the girl's footsteps. They were nearing the end of the outcropping before Thomas saw what he was looking for.

"Here they are, Angela! She stepped off here and . . . Oh, oh. This isn't good."

"What's the matter, Tom?"

"She slipped somewhere. See her footprint, turned on its side almost. Must have hurt herself. She's limping a little, here." He shined the light on the rock again and walked back in the direction they came from. "Look here, Angela. I'd say she slipped here, scraped her leg pretty good. I think that's blood on the rock."

She knelt beside him and nodded, "I think you're right."

"But she continues on in the same direction. Wonder why she didn't turn around for home?" He studied the footprints. The young girl was definitely limping and now seemed to be hurrying. A sudden cold feeling of dread swept over him. "We have to find her fast, Angela!"

"What's wrong?"

"She's really frightened. She's seen or heard something that's scared her."

Angela put her hand to her mouth. "Mountain lion . . ." she breathed. "We've had trouble up here with a big one killing some of our calves. His last kill was about a month ago, a few miles south of here near the north border of our spread."

"Let's go!"

They hurried along the barely visible track, stopping occasionally to study the footprints in the early spring grass. Twice they crossed shallow beds of sand—probably creek beds that ran only in the rainy season. It was on the second sandy bed that the track revealed an additional print. A large cat print, at least three inches across, had joined the little girl's foot prints. Thomas leaned close to the print. "These are fairly fresh tracks, Angela. Not even an hour old yet. It's a male lion, five or six years old. Probably weighs a hundred and eighty pounds, maybe more."

"You can tell all that from this track?"

"Yes and more." *Like, he hasn't eaten for several days,* he thought. "Let's go. We don't have a lot of time."

"Time for . . ." she queried, her voice trembling.

"She'll be an easy meal for that lion, Angela."

"My God, Thomas! We can't let that happen to her!"

"Where would she go? She must be headed someplace where she thought she could hide or be safe from the mountain lion."

"I don't know, Tom. I don't know a lot about the Stanton property."

"Let's go." He started again following the faint indentations in the new grass. Occasionally he had to stop and study the ground as the track became almost invisible. They crossed a sandy swale and the tracks were obvious—Julia's and the following mountain lion.

In a few minutes the track veered left. Thomas knelt by the tracks. "This is where she deliberately turned. She knows where she's going." The tracks led in the general direction of the opening to a narrow canyon. The tracks were strong, purposeful, in spite of the limp. "She's been here before. She knows where she wants to go."

He pulled his Winchester from the scabbard, levered a round into the receiver and put on the safety. He dropped the reigns and went ahead, leaving the horse behind. Angela put a rock on each set of reigns and followed him.

The canyon closed quickly on both sides. The bottom was a dry stream bed filled with small rocks and sand. The sides rose nearly vertical, cut through the earth when the stream ran high. The moon's faint light reflected on the bottom but the sides were in deep shadow. Large granite boulders lay strewn across the bottom forcing them to squeeze through narrow openings. The canyon appeared to end up ahead in a vertical stack of angular granite boulders.

"She's got to be up there," he whispered. "Maybe in a cave or slit in the rock where she can hide."

"I'll call to her." Angel whispered.

"Okay. Let's see what happens."

"Julia!" Angela's voice rang out. She paused, "Julia, it's Angie Gordon. Are you up there?"

"Angie!" The responding voice quavered.

The snarling screech from the mountain lion, the response to Angela's call and the ear-ringing crack of Thomas's Winchester all happened in the same fraction of time. The big lion had crouched on the rim on the canyon overlooking the rocky enclosure hiding the young girl. Upon hearing Angela's call, the lion had sprung toward the source. Out of the corner of his eyes, Thomas had seen the reflective glow of the big cat's eyes and had swung his Winchester into position. He caught the lion in mid flight with a shot that killed the big cat instantly. It bounced off the rocks not more than five feet from where they stood. A second shot would not be required as Thomas prodded the cat with his boot.

Julia scrambled down from her hiding place among the rocks and flew into Angela's arms. Before they made their way out of the narrow canyon, Thomas pointed his Winchester into the air and fired three carefully spaced shots.

* * *

It was well after midnight by the time they reached the Stanton ranch house. Angela insisted that Julia ride with her; the thirteen year old girl was sound asleep in Angela's arms as they rode in. Someone inside saw them through the curtained windows and the house seemed to explode with people pouring out to greet the trio.

One-thirty came and went before everyone had heard the story and asked all the questions. Muriel and Ted Stanton were practically beside themselves with the joy of having their child returned safely. Ramon and Hector were pleased to know that the predator that had been killing their calves had been destroyed. Angela could barely restrain herself from repeating her glowing report of the tracking and shooting that Thomas had done under such difficult circumstances. It was nearly three in the morning before the four of them finally returned to the Gordon ranch.

Angela took Thomas's hand after everyone else had gone inside and pulled him into the dark shadows around the corner of the house. She leaned into him, put her arms around his neck and kissed him passionately, long and hard on his lips.

"I am so proud of you, Tom," she whispered, "and I will always, always love you." Then she disappeared inside.

*   *   *

When Thomas awoke in the late morning, cold rain was pouring from the sky. *The air's cold, near freezing,* Thomas thought. *It's probably snowing in the mountains.* He got up, rinsed off quickly in the bucket of cold water provided for that purpose and dressed. After dashing across the space between the bunkhouse and the ranch house, he stamped the mud off his boots and entered the great room. Hector and Margarita were sitting in front of the fire and greeted him enthusiastically.

"You'll be staying with us a few days, Mister O'Reiley? Surely you won't be wanting to go to the high country." Margarita smiled invitingly.

Thomas smiled. "Thanks very much for the kind offer, Margarita. I believe I shall take you up on it." He had thought briefly about going up to visit with Gray Hawk but had decided that such a trip would be pretty close to impossible under the conditions. As much as he wanted to visit the old Indian, it simply wouldn't work out this spring.

The rain continued to pour down for the next two days. The various ranch chores were still accomplished but the rest of the time the family spent in the warmth of the great room. Card games, spelling bees, family stories and meals together filled the time and Thomas even spoke at length of his adventures in the Pacific Ocean. Margarita nodded her head quietly; now she knew the cause of the huge and ugly scars she had discovered while caring for Thomas. It wasn't until Wednesday, the eighteenth of April, that Angela took Thomas to the train station in Visalia.

CHAPTER 10

<u>Wednesday, May 12, 1901, San Francisco, California</u>
The San Francisco Chronicle announced that the President of the United States of America, William McKinley and his wife Ida would visit the city for a few days on the final leg of his California coast excursion.

A reporter for the local newspaper in Visalia, California, had heard about the recent incident at the Stanton ranch and decided to investigate. He wrote it up and it was published that week. Seeing that the main character in the drama was from San Francisco, he sent it by wire to the San Francisco Chronicle on the chance that they might be interested. It ran in today's Chronicle several pages back, fit in next to an advertisement for a funeral parlor:

Thomas O'Reiley Foils Death Again; It's The Third Time

Mister Thomas O'Reiley, local businessman and prominent figure about town, has once again had a close brush with death and survived. Readers may remember that O'Reiley suffered a near-fatal rattlesnake bite in May, 1899 while on a solo hunting trip in the high Sierra mountains. Recently, while visiting the same area near Visalia, O'Reiley was credited with tracking and finding a lost thirteen year old girl who was about to be attacked by a mountain lion. O'Reiley shot and killed the cougar. All of this occurred under the darkness

114

of night. O'Reiley's first brush with
death came several years earlier when he
was ship—wrecked on an isolated island
in the South Pacific.

Thomas read the small article with mild interest. His name appeared in the chronicle quite often, most generally associated with his business dealings although once in a while having to do with some social or civic function. He wondered briefly how the story had managed to get to the San Francisco newspaper, then folded the paper and laid it on the chair beside his desk.

President William McKinley was scheduled to visit San Francisco beginning today and O'Reiley had been given the select honor of escorting George Cooper Pardee, a rising Republican politician and past mayor of the city of Oakland, to the various political functions associated with McKinley's visit. Thomas had done his best to maintain a low profile when it came to politics but agreed to this assignment after the urging of his father-in-law. President and Mrs. McKinley were scheduled to attend the launching of the US Navy's newest battleship, the 17,500 ton *USS Ohio*, at the Union Iron Works in San Francisco on Saturday, the eighteenth of May.

The President and his entourage would arrive from Del Mar, near Monterey, on this last leg of his visit to California. The San Francisco welcoming delegation would meet him at one of the city's finest hotels, dine with him and then attend a reception. California Republican Governor Henry Gage would also attend. Governor Gage and his wife Francesca would sit and dine that evening with Handon McPherson, something Thomas was fairly certain had been carefully arranged by Handon. Thomas would be accompanied by his beautiful wife Amanda. Thomas smiled to himself; *her presence was sure to cause heads to turn. San Francisco society is wildly in love with Amanda.*

*   *   *

The reception got underway right on time with San Francisco's elite and wealthy rubbing elbows and keeping the small-talk carefully orchestrated. President McKinley and his wife Ida circulated casually through the crowd; the President shaking hands and listening carefully with his head cocked

67877

to one side. His wife Ida, considered generally to be in poor health, looked pale and appeared slightly withdrawn.

An aide brought the pair toward Thomas and Amanda. "Mister President. Mrs. McKinley, I would like you to meet Mister Thomas O'Reiley, one of our city's prominent businessmen."

"Mister President." Thomas shook the offered hand. "It is my pleasure, sir." Ida McKinley had stuck her hand out also and he took it in his, held it for only a few seconds as protocol demanded. "Mrs. McKinley. I'm very pleased to meet you." He in turn introduced Amanda. Within a minute Amanda was whispering something in Ida McKinley's ear and the two of them giggled like two schoolgirls.

The President spent a few minutes with O'Reiley asking about his business and his views on forestry management and protection of the giant redwood trees. Thomas was impressed both with the questions and the interest the President appeared to take in his responses. Quickly the aide moved the Presidential couple on and Thomas was left with Amanda. "What did you whisper to Mrs. McKinley?"

Amanda laughed. "She's such a dear! I told her these things bore you to death."

"I certainly hope you didn't!"

"I did. And she said Bill hates them too." Amanda giggled softly.

"Ah, Thomas." The voice came from George Pardee. Of medium height, Pardee sported a van dyke beard and handlebar mustache and eyeglasses that gave him a serious, studious appearance. He had received his medical training in Germany and by the early 1890's had become active in the Republican Party serving as Oakland's mayor from 1893 to 1895. During that time he began a long battle with Southern Pacific Railroad regarding ownership of the Port of Oakland. O'Reiley had met Pardee on several occasions.

"Mister Pardee. It's nice to see you, sir."

Pardee shook his head. "Let's dispense with the formalities, Thomas. Please call me George. Everyone else does."

"Very well, George," Thomas replied with a smile. He introduced Pardee to Amanda.

"Good. Now, Thomas, I'll get right down to business. I read an article in today's Chronicle that has your name attached to it. A very interesting story. I would be very pleased if you would tell me more about what happened."

Thomas went through the happenings of that evening, trying to downplay his own involvement but Pardee wouldn't let it pass that easily. He was an intelligent man and knew what questions to ask in order to pry more information from Thomas. How did he know it was a mountain lion? How did he know it was a male? How did he know how much the animal weighed? How did he know the young girl was limping from her leg injury? Was he by himself? How did he manage the killing shot under such stress, especially at night? By the end, Thomas had revealed everything he knew about the incident, including the fact that he was accompanied by Angela.

"That is utterly incredible, Thomas. Absolutely amazing. Where did you learn such practical and impressive skills?"

Thomas hesitated before he replied, "an old friend, George. An Indian."

"An Indian! Ah ha! Now I should have guessed! Quite remarkable!" Pardee continued nodding his head. "I've never met anyone with such incredible skills." He shook Thomas's hand once again and wandered off, still muttering to himself.

Amanda leaned close to him and whispered, "you didn't tell me that there was a young woman with you. Tell me about her," she looked at Thomas, "if you don't mind."

*   *   *

Steamship SS Buenaventura

The meeting in New York City had gone about as well as he had expected, although it had meant an additional trip via train to Washington, D.C. He was once again glad to be free of the stuffy New York hotel rooms where he had been forced to meet with a variety of highly placed government officials. Now aboard the small steamship bound for the Panamanian port of Puerto Panama he could breathe deeply and enjoy the tangy, spring air sitting in the warm sunshine.

Only a few minutes ago the *Buenaventura* had steamed into the Lower Bay through The Narrows that separated New Jersey from New York. Soon the heavy, long swells of the Atlantic Ocean would embrace the steamer and accompany them down the long eastern coast of the United States, until they eventually turned westward once again after clearing the southern tip of Florida and passing the westernmost tip of Cuba, then head south to his homeland. He had been away for over two months and was anxious to be reunited with his wife Maria and with his friends. Trained as a doctor, Manuel Amador Guerrero had spent years serving as the chief doctor on the Panama Railroad as well as dedicating twenty years to the Santo Tomas Hospital. Larger issues were at stake now and in spite of his age—he was presently sixty-six years old—he worked with a sense of dedication and vigor with which many younger men could not have kept up.

He stuck a long, unlit cheroot between his lips; sat back, took a deep breath and wondered where and how this undertaking would end, completely aware that it might cost him many years in prison or maybe his life. The civil war in his country had been going on for nineteen months. Conservative versus Liberal forces fought for control of the Columbian Province of Panama that continued to struggle without effective leadership. Economic conditions were deplorable and now both sides of the controversy had split into factions. The Liberal forces had twice suffered terrible defeats; the one at Palonegro a year ago was an especially bloody setback. Belisario Porras, exiled by the Conservative government in Bogata, had been recruited to lead the Liberal forces in Panama and was now working under General Victoriano Lorenzo. Both of these men were close acquaintances to the doctor.

This had been his third trip to New York City. The first two visits were expended just probing, asking questions and setting up future meetings. Some of the Americans he had met with had listened cautiously to his carefully assembled and multi-layered strategy. A few had bluntly rebuked his presentation and arguments and leaving during the early discussions, not understanding or knowing enough to do any real damage. But those who had listened had nodded their understanding and tacit approval. They would, they promised, carefully probe higher level officials for their thoughts. But in any respect, all agreed that final approval and implementation would require a much higher authority than any of them. Execution would demand a strategic advance through high political echelons, circumventing various agencies and working with staffs willing to move ahead with minimal authorizations. All of this must be done at the highest possible levels of secrecy. If the plan were to be somehow leaked to the public, *all hell would break loose,* was the way one senior official had bluntly stated the situation. Before he had left the last meeting, they had agreed on a series of coded messages that could be communicated by means of international telegraph.

* * *

San Francisco, California

"So, my dear husband, why don't you tell me about this young woman called *Angela*?" Amanda stood with her arms crossed, a position of irritation and defiance. Her eyes flashed but she kept her voice low, as the children were upstairs asleep and Xiang was probably still in the kitchen. She had waited until they returned home after the long reception to pose the question to her husband. Now she was waiting for an answer and Thomas knew that she would not budge until she knew everything.

"Angela is the daughter of Hector Gordon who owns the ranch near Visalia where I get the horses and gear for my mountain trips. Hector and Margarita, his wife, are good solid people. They also have a son, Ramon."

Amanda nodded. "And just how old is this *Angela*?"

"Probably her early twenties. Twenty-two maybe."

Amanda looked at him solemnly. "Is Angela pretty?"

"Well yes, she is quite pretty."

She nodded again, appearing to turn this new information over in her mind. "Well, do you like her?"

"*Like* her? Of course I *like* her. You wouldn't expect me to dislike her, would you?"

Several long seconds went by. "Thomas, are you having an affair with *Angela*?"

Thomas's heart lurched in his chest. "Of course not, Mandy."

Several seconds went by as Amanda stared into his eyes. Then the corners or her lips began to curl up and a broad smile broke out on her face. She began to chuckle and she shook her head slowly. "Oh, I certainly had you ill at ease, Thomas!" she managed to say through her laughter. "You looked so serious!" She collapsed in hysterical delight into his arms. "Oh, I love you, my dear Thomas!"

"Amanda! I should take you out behind the woodshed! First the wife of the President of the United States and then your own husband! You and your bizarre humor are going to get you into trouble, young lady." He joined in her laughter as she nuzzled into his neck, "but instead of the woodshed, I believe that I shall take you upstairs this very moment and teach you a lesson!"

She stepped back, rolled her eyes and pressed the back of her hand to her forehead in an exaggerated theatrical pose of female distress. "Terrors! Oh, dreadful punishment! Woe is me!" She winked at him, turned and sashayed slowly and enticingly up the stairs.

* * *

Abilene, Texas

The knock at the hotel room door was almost imperceptible; five carefully spaced taps. It was very late; Luke could tell that just by the low level of noise on the street below his window. He had left the window open to let in some of the cool evening air. He rose from the bed, fully clothed as was his recent habit, picked up his revolver from the side table and tucked it into his belt.

He tiptoed to the door and put his ear against the wood. He gently tapped just once and it was answered by two more taps. It was a code he had just recently initiated; the taps represented the day of the month—this was the twelfth day of May, the fifth month.

He cracked the door and peered out. He didn't recognize the man standing there but he seldom came face-to-face with this underground network of men who passed information along to him.

"I have a message," the man whispered into the crack.

Luke opened the door enough that the other man was able to squeeze into the dark room then shut the door behind him.

"The message," Luke prompted impatiently.

The man looked quickly around him, as if assuring that there was no one else in the room. "Bret Solomon in Sacramento."

"Bret Solomon in Sacramento," Luke repeated. "I'll pass it on." He let the man out, watched through the crack as he disappeared down the hallway, then shut and locked the door. The man would receive compensation for his time through yet another man whose job was to distribute money throughout his network every month and if necessary, repair or replace a broken link with a new recruit.

Sacramento. Luke nodded to himself; word of the competence of the man known as *El Culebra* was spreading far and wide. He'd be on the train before the next day was finished. *Bret Solomon*. Even that name could be coded. He would soon find out.

Later that day, he visited one of the banks in Abilene, withdrew some cash and packed a meager suitcase for the trip to Sacramento. The train would take him first to Los Angeles, then to Sacramento. The small valise containing his modified rifle would, of course, be in his personal possession throughout the trip.

*   *   *

Three days later Luke stepped off the train into the early summer heat of Sacramento. The town bustled with activity; the Port of Sacramento had barge access to the Pacific Ocean by means of the American River and then the Sacramento River which emptied into the upper San Francisco Bay.

It was warm and humid but the man left his long black leather coat on in spite of his mild discomfort. Sacramento was different than Abilene or Houston or any of the other large Texas towns he had stayed in. People here walked and talked with determination and without the easy languor of the Texas way of life. Men on the sidewalk stood face to face and spoke, using their hands as much as their mouths, it seemed. Women hurried with a sense of purpose on the sidewalks, often unaccompanied by men, their faces marked by concentration. Carriages and buckboard wagons vied noisily for space on the roads and men on horseback wove carefully among the tangle of traffic. It was intriguing and disconcerting at the same time for the man known as Luke who had spent his life in the south.

It took only a half hour to find a hotel and three hours later he was standing at the local newspaper office where he submitted a single-line personal to be run beginning the next day. It read: *"Bret S be at Golden Oak 9p EC."* It was the most convenient manner to make contact in a strange city. If this didn't work, there were still other means.

The Golden Oak was a large and apparently quite popular saloon on 8th Street near J Street, four or five blocks from the train station and three blocks from his hotel on G Street. Luke had visited it before going to the newspaper. The long bar stretched front to back down the left side; fifteen or twenty round tables with chairs filled most of the remaining space. A small raised stage at the back was apparently there for evening entertainment; an upright piano sat silent during his short visit. He bought a beer and lounged against the bar, watching the ebb and flow of patrons, waiting to see who knew who, who was the loner and who was popular, who was the serious drinker and who was there just for social purposes. He was sure some of that same crowd would be there tomorrow evening. He watched faces, especially the eyes, to determine who else was studying the crowd, who was keeping an eye open for someone they expected, or who glanced too frequently at the watch tucked into their vest pocket. He acknowledged that he too had been closely scrutinized by the regulars when he had entered the saloon. He would drop in several times again, just to become more familiar to those who surrounded him. No personal information exchanged—he never did that—just enough to become a vaguely familiar face in the crowd. He had learned, early on, that there was a lot of knowledge to be gained just by watching people.

He made three more trips to the Golden Oak that evening. On the last trip he was there at eight-thirty and stood at the bar toward the back where he could survey the crowd and the front doors. He had been correct; several of the faces were familiar from the day crowd but there had been an influx of new faces as well. Business men, workers, sight-seers, gamblers and pimps all mingled together. Some greeted one another with familiarity; many stood or sat alone. The conversation was loud and rambunctious and got even noisier in the evening with the piano playing. Business deals and hilarity merged with solemn discussions into a cacophony of racket that fully protected any particular conversation from eavesdropping.

The next day he repeated his visits. The bartenders began to acknowledge his presence and even responded with a quick nod and service when he simply motioned for another beer. Between visits he walked the streets of the city, mentally mapping out buildings, streets, alleys and shortcuts. He ate at three different restaurants, considered briefly buying some new clothes but decided not to. He had dispersed the big wad of bills from his banks in Abilene among the several pockets in his pants, shirt and coat and had been very careful not to display more than a few bills at a time. In his younger days he had often spotted a gentleman flashing large amounts of money that made for an easy robbery that left the gentleman sprawled in an alley with a large bump on his head, or worse. By the time he arrived at eight o'clock that evening, the usual crowd was already well into their evening of drinking.

He wandered once again toward the back of the bar. This time he had his revolver carefully stuck into the belt of his pants, covered by the loose-fitting leather coat. He nodded to the bartender, who simply drew him a beer and slid it down the bar to him as he had done for several of the regular customers.

Luke let his eyes carefully roam through the crowd, picking out the new faces. There were perhaps fifteen men whom he did not recognize. He quickly dismissed three; they were joined at a table and were already into their third or fourth beer, laughing noisily and loudly. A gray haired gentleman stood by himself in a far corner and seemed to be searching the crowd for a face. *A possibility.* Two others drained their glass of beer and wandered out the front doors, apparently gone for the evening. A bald headed man stood sipping slowly on his beer at the other end of the long bar and staring at the mirror behind the bar. *A possibility.* Three more had gathered at a table, apparently old friends. *Probably not any of them.* A well dressed gentleman with a heavy mustache had sidled up to the bar, glanced left and right then impatiently waved the bartender off. *A possibility.* A young man dressed in the manner of a ranch hand, stood leaning against the opposite wall, sipping occasionally at his beer as his eyes swept back and forth across the room. *A possibility.* Another man walked into the bar off the street and was greeted by the gray haired gentleman up front. *Strike him off the list.* A man with a neatly trimmed beard sat alone at a table facing the front door. *Waiting? A possibility?* Two others stood, bade farewell to those at a nearby table and left.

The possibilities were narrowing down. Luke glanced at his pocket watch. It was eight thirty. Still plenty of time. The bald man finished his beer, waved good-by to the bartender and wandered out the front door. Another walked in and greeted the mustached man at the bar; they stood side by side and ordered beers and dropped into intense conversation. Minutes went by as the piano player ran through a series of popular tunes. The young ranch hand drained his beer and motioned for a second. Luke watched as he was approached by a man he had earlier identified as a pimp. After a short interchange, the two walked out the door.

The list was getting short. The gentleman with the beard rose from his table and walked out the door. At about the same time, another man entered. Tall, gray haired, well dressed, he looked out of place in the establishment. A politician, Luke mused. The man looked slightly confused, glanced quickly around the room but his eyes settled on Luke. He went to the bar, squeezed in several feet from Luke, ordered a beer, slapped a large bill on the bar top and waved off the barman. His eyes caught Luke's in the large mirror behind the bar and they locked for several seconds. There was an empty table against the back wall and Luke wandered over to it and sat with his back to the wall.

The gray haired man continued to remain at the bar but his eyes followed Luke as he moved to the table. Finally he sidled over to the table, silently sought permission to join Luke and took a seat. His face was handsome, unlined with age, his hazel colored eyes clear. His hair was carefully trimmed.

"Solomon?" Luke asked quietly.

"Yes. Are you El Culebra?"

"I'm his agent."

"Agent?" Solomon glanced around the room quickly. "I thought I would meet him personally."

"El Culebra never meets his clients face to face. I'm sure you understand."

Solomon nodded nervously, glanced around the room again. "I don't like being here."

"Neither do I, but it's your meeting."

The gray haired man faced Luke and leaned just a little closer. "There's a job for El Culebra."

Luke simply nodded. Most negotiations started in this manner. Clients were usually uncomfortable talking about having someone killed.

The man continued. "What does he need to know?"

"Name. Location. Description. When."

Solomon nodded and took a deep breath. "Okay. Name's Richard Manhauser. He has a big spread east of here, near Fiddletown, up in the hills."

Luke waited.

"When can Culebra umm, handle it?"

"Three days after he receives the money."

Solomon glanced around and looked uncomfortable. "How much?"

"Five thousand."

Solomon sat back, hesitated. "That's too much."

"Okay." Luke pushed his chair back and started to get up.

"Wait . . ."

Luke sat back down again. "That's five thousand for his expenses."

Solomon shook his head. "Can't do it."

Luke tilted his head. "Oh, I think you can, Solomon. You just don't want to. Ten thousand for the whole job. Clean, done and finished."

"Five before and the remainder after."

"That's no good. All before, Solomon. That's the way El Culebra works. Take it or leave it."

Solomon sat back, pursed his lips, finally leaned forward. "How does the money get to Culebra?"

"I'm his agent. I get the money to him."

"I don't like this arrangement. How do I know you won't just take the money?"

Luke shrugged. "The work is guaranteed. Like I said, take it or leave it." He made the motion of pushing his chair back.

Solomon grinned wryly and held up his hand. "Okay, okay." He reached into his jacket pocket, pulled out an envelope. "I already figured that's what he would charge." He handed the envelope across the table. "You can count it if you want."

"I don't think that will be necessary." Luke tucked the envelope into his coat pocket. "One more question. What does Manhauser look like?"

"Big man, probably six three or four. Thirty five years old. Brown hair. Always wears a western style hat, white, broad brim. Lives at the ranch."

"Okay." Luke got up. "I'd be out of town for the next few days, if I were you. You and I won't be meeting again."

It took one full day to find and visit the Manhauser ranch. Located in the hills east of Sacramento, the large ranch house sat high atop a ridge; the location offered a clear view all around. On the second day he sat in the nearby woods and watched the day unfold. It wasn't long before Luke had identified Manhauser. The ranch hands all deferred to him with a nod of their heads and quick touch to the brim of their hats; presently his wife came out of the house arm in arm with him. Through his binoculars, the woman was also quite attractive, with long blond hair and a nice figure further enhanced by the clothes she wore. However, the distance from the protection of the trees to the ranch house was well over five hundred yards. He'd not tried a shot at that distance before. He'd have to wait until the man left the ranch.

The opportunity came mid-morning the next day when Manhauser walked out of the house, kissed his wife quickly and rode away on his horse. Luke followed at a discrete distance as the man broke off the main dirt road leading to the house and into the web of lightly forested canyons. It was an old path that wound among the hills and it revealed some recent use. Eventually Luke watched from the trees as the man arrived at a small, dilapidated cabin, an old line shack, tucked among the trees. There was another horse already tied there and when the man arrived the door to the cabin flew open. A young woman bounded out, greeted Manhauser with a long passionate kiss and embrace, tossing her long black hair as he allowed his hands to roam over her curves with obvious familiarity. Eventually the two went back into the cabin and shut the door. She was short, barely coming to the man's chest and well proportioned Luke noticed; he was particularly attracted to the long black hair that cascaded smoothly to the center of her back. Clearly, she was not Richard Manhauser's spouse.

"Well now," Luke muttered to himself, "this might be my lucky day."

* * *

San Francisco, California
The short statured gentleman knocked quietly at the door which was opened quickly by a young woman.

"Oh, Alex!" She threw herself into his arms, "I've waited all day for you! You've no idea how much I miss you when you're unable to be here with me."

He held her close and their lips met in a long kiss. "Dearest Sophia, I miss you as well! If only we could spend all our time together."

"We could, if you weren't already married to that vixen of a wife. She is a tyrant! She demands all of your time, especially on weekends. It's not fair," she pouted.

"Not fair, perhaps but a reality my dear." He had met the young woman eight months ago at a gathering of San Francisco attorneys. Sofia Jenkins was unmarried and had moved to San Francisco from Los Angeles. She worked as a secretary for a small legal firm and from the beginning Alex Dunsworth recognized that she was intellectually bright, easy to talk to and remarkably beautiful. Two months after their first meeting, Sophia became his casual mistress, lover and confidant. He felt untroubled, almost sheltered in the warm, sweet perfume of her embrace and was soon sharing intimate and confidential particulars of his life and ambitions as she listened admiringly with wide eyes; it was a trait his wife Nelle had never learned or even pretended to do. Once Sophia casually remarked that she had a brother in the Los Angeles area, though she never spoke of him again and Alexander was not at all interested in acquainting himself with her family relationships.

126

CHAPTER 11

The gruesome and apparently random double murder in the foothills east of Sacramento made the second page headlines in the San Francisco Chronicle. It was a lurid tale of infidelity involving the wealthy owner of a large cattle ranch, Richard Manhauser, age 36 years and the young and attractive wife of a prominent Sacramento business man. The newspaper avoided specific details but included enough insinuations that a reader could assemble the hidden particulars with little help. The two bodies were found by ranch hands when Manhauser failed to return to the ranch house that evening after riding out earlier in the day on an inspection tour of the property. Manhauser had been shot to death at close range; his nude body was sprawled on the rough wood floor of the small cabin, a single bullet hole in his forehead. The young woman had been found on the narrow bunk; the paper carefully and delicately worded the fact that she had been raped and violently mutilated before she died from a great number of stab wounds. She was Priscilla Solomon, the 34 year old wife of a wealthy but very private Sacramento businessman named Bret Solomon. Solomon was in San Francisco on the day of the murder to discuss the possibility of entering his name into the contest for Republican state senator. When he was notified of her death, observers said Solomon, who is 57 years old, went absolutely berserk, screaming and swearing and beating his head against the wall in a horrendous fit of rage and grief. He was finally subdued by an injection administered by a doctor.

Luke caught the train out of Sacramento and was back in Abilene two days later.

George Cooper Pardee read about the murder as he sat in his home in Oakland, California. Stunned, he could only shake his head in disbelief.

Bret Solomon was not only an acquaintance of Pardee's but an old and trusted friend whose relationship with Pardee went back many years. Solomon's first wife, a lovely lady named Bernice, had died of influenza after only four years of marriage to Solomon. The distraught Solomon had remained unmarried for many years. Pardee, as were others, had been taken by surprise by Solomon's eventual re-marriage just three years ago to a strikingly beautiful woman twenty-one years younger but Pardee had nevertheless wished the newly-weds well. Now it appeared that all had not been ideal in the May-September relationship.

Pardee recalled that Bret Solomon owned and operated a large cattle ranch in the Sierra Nevada foothills that bordered two sides of Richard Manhauser's choice and scenic property and Solomon had once admitted to Pardee that he had over the years approached Manhauser on numerous occasions with generous offers to buy the spread. According to Solomon, Manhauser had steadily refused the offers, even though the latest offer was well above what many would consider to be the property's market value. Pardee shook his head sadly, already planning to send his old friend a short sympathy note.

On that same day, Thomas O'Reiley had read the article with only mild interest. The gruesome murders had occurred far to the east of San Francisco and involved people that he did not know. Besides, his mind had already leaped forward to his upcoming trip to the high mountains and his visit with Gray Hawk. It had been a month since his last trip had been foiled because of the late snow that had buried the lower mountain elevations and of course, the hunt for the missing thirteen year old girl.

Amanda had already planned to take the children up to Cape Mendocino on the northern California coast for a week to visit Sister Mary Katherine, a Catholic nun who served at Saint Teresa by the Sea Hospital in Mendocino and who had become a close friend of the family. Sister Mary Katherine had offered the use of one of the small cabins at the hospital for Amanda and the children's use during their stay.

Unfortunately, the entire summer was to pass before Thomas finally had an opportunity to leave San Francisco for his retreat to the High Sierras. Another of San Francisco's disastrous fires raged unchecked across three blocks of older, wooden buildings and consumed one of Handon McPherson's major constructions. The huge blaze brought the seven-storied project to a complete halt, destroying six months of work in just a few late-night hours. Weeks went by before the huge pile of rubble and bent and twisted iron framework, pipes and electrical wiring could be painstakingly removed, put into waiting horse drawn drays and hauled away. Then the site had to be cleared and prepared for construction to begin anew.

All three of the business partners found themselves straining to get the vanguard project back on track; Frank Barnwell's organization poured over the building's blueprints and as a result of the fire, redesigned parts of the building incorporating the latest construction methods and materials to help prevent such disastrous infernos in the future. Thomas had to scramble to locate and procure building materials in the quantities and dimensions needed; Handon McPherson had his construction crews laboring extra hours to complete the work in a timely manner. In the end everyone was more than satisfied, and the extra effort received glowing accolades from the new building's owner and the city's fire department. But the summer had slipped by and it was late summer before everything was completed.

*   *   *

Buffalo, New York

President William McKinley and his wife Ida had arrived at the Pan-American Exposition on September 5, 1901 to attend a private reception and military review. On the morning of September 6, he visited Niagara Falls and then returned to the Exposition for a scheduled public reception that afternoon. At 3:30 that afternoon he proceeded to the Temple of Music building—the location of the reception. In spite of the security concerns of his secretary, George Cortelyou, McKinley insisted that he would stand in the reception line and shake hands with the public.

Cortelyou left the President's side briefly to shut a door. The great organ in the Temple of Music played *Traumerei*. Waiting in the line was a young man named Leon Czolgosz, the son of a Polish immigrant and an avowed anarchist who was determined to assassinate President McKinley. He carried a pistol in his right hand; the gun was hidden by bandages as if the hand had been injured. Czolgosz advanced in the waiting line and finally at 4:07p.m. stood face to face with McKinley. The President reached out to shake Czolgosz's extended and bandaged hand but before he could grasp it, the anarchist pulled the trigger twice.

One bullet deflected off McKinley's ribs and created only minor damage. The other bullet however, hit the President in the abdomen, pierced his stomach, hit his kidney, injured his pancreas and then finally lodged in the muscles of his back. In spite of the injuries, McKinley remained standing until an ambulance arrived eleven minutes later to transport him to a hospital. Surgeons could not locate the bullet and closed the wounds.

Over the next few days the President seemed to be recovering from these wounds. By September 12, he was taking in solid food; however, later that same day his health worsened and on Friday, September 13, his condition began to deteriorate very rapidly. A medical bulletin released that evening declared that his condition was most serious. President William McKinley died at 2:15 a.m. on September 14 of infection and gangrene.

The early morning Saturday edition of the San Francisco Chronicle notified the people of San Francisco Bay Area of the tragedy. Thomas O'Reiley had risen early as was his habit and was seated in the sun room reading the Chronicle. He leaned back in his chair and shook his head in incredulity as he scanned the extra-large headlines and read the details of the President's death. It had been only a few months ago that he had stood and talked to William McKinley; Amanda and Ida had enjoyed a few light moments of schoolgirl humor.

Amanda, wrapped in a loose robe, stepped through the doorway into the room, a cup of coffee in each hand. She was smiling as she asked, "Coffee, dear?"

Thomas turned, an aggrieved expression on his face, "Amanda, the President has died."

Amanda put the two cups down on a side-table; they rattled as she did so. "Oh, dear!" She pressed her knuckles to her lips and sat heavily, shaking her head. "Oh, dear! Poor Ida! What an awful, terrible thing to happen!" She looked at her husband, a sad, bewildered look on her face. "What's going to happen now, Thomas?"

"Roosevelt will be sworn in as President as soon as he arrives in Buffalo. It seems that he was at the family cabin in the Adirondack Mountains, hiking and climbing with some friends when the President passed."

Vice President Theodore Roosevelt arrived in Buffalo by train at 1:30 that afternoon and took the oath of office two hours later. He was just six weeks shy of his forty-third birthday when he became the 26th President of the United States of America.

* * *

The Gordon Ranch

It was two weeks after President McKinley's death before Thomas was able to travel by train to Visalia. The days following the tragic death were spent in national mourning and everyone followed the events unfolding on the east coast by reading the newspapers. It was a somber time.

Thomas spent the night at the Gordon Ranch. After dinner, he and Angela spent an hour talking at the corral fence. The evening was warm as the day's residual heat radiated from the dry ground. This was the dry time of the year during which the San Joaquin Valley rarely received rain. The sun began to set, becoming a huge orange ball that shimmered above the low valley haze, flattening in shape as if reluctant to drop over the horizon. For a few moments everything was bathed in red and orange; then the last sliver of sun slipped below the rim and only its soft glow remained in the western sky. It was a moment that Thomas had viewed many hundreds of times during his life on the Pacific island and during his near-disastrous journey back to the United States.

"What was it like, Tom?" Angela seemed to be reading his thoughts.

Thomas laughed quietly, "Am I that easy to see through?"

"Yes, you are. You were thousands of miles away just now."

"I thought I told you and your family about my . . . experiences."

"You told us what you did, Tom. I'm wondering what it was like for you. What were you thinking and feeling?"

Thomas hesitated. It had been so long ago, yet many of the memories were crystal clear, as if the events had happened only yesterday. "At moments, Angela, it was terrifying. At times it was beautiful beyond description. I was filled with awe and at times I was filled with disgust and fear. It was exciting and it was dreadfully tedious. I was lonesome; my only friend was a seagull." *Frisco,* he thought, *you were a true friend.* "At times I feared for my sanity and at times I thought I was about to die. I was in great pain several times, the kind of pain no human should have to experience and I knew I could either endure or die. I was hungry, cold, wet much of the time. There were times that I was completely out of my mind with illness, pain and fear." He paused. "That's what it was like, Angela."

She paused, finally asked, "What were your thoughts?"

"My thoughts? That I would never see another human being again. That I would die and nobody would know. That I was ready to do anything, even to forfeit my life, to be among human beings again. That life is most certainly more than struggling to stay alive from one day to the next."

"Do you believe in God?"

He waited a long time before answering. "I pretended to—maybe even thought I did—as a young boy, so that my mother would be happy. I don't remember if I called on God or not during those long years of struggle. I later met a Catholic nun who wanted to help me believe in God and in Jesus Christ. I'm not at all sure what I believe today."

Angela nodded in the growing dusk. "I pray for you every night, Thomas."

*   *   *

Thomas arrived at the old hunting-camp late the following day. The mountain air was fresh and warm in the afternoon sun. The familiar fragrances filled his nostrils and the afternoon hum and buzz of insects rode easily on the still air. He spent a few minutes repairing the corral, knowing that Gray Hawk would soon appear, almost as if by magic. The sun hadn't reached the tips of the mountains before he heard his name being called.

"Tah-moss!" The old Indian emerged from the thick forest. "I was afraid you would not come back. I watch for long time and finally saw you yesterday."

Thomas smiled. Yesterday he had been on the train and at the ranch house. "You have good *eyes*, Gray Hawk," he said as he pointed to his head.

Gray Hawk laughed and nodded. "I see many things, Tah-moss." He pointed at Thomas's things, "you come to my shelter?"

Within minutes they were walking through the warm late afternoon forest. Gray Hawk brought him up to date on what had happened over the months; Thomas was acquainted with the various large animals that the Indian discussed: which ones had moved, which ones had given birth, which ones were ill and which had died or simply disappeared; he talked about the large bear that he called *Crazy Bear* that roamed the woods, the buck with the distinctive left front hoof print, the doe that had last year given birth to three, the raccoon that lives near Gray Hawk's shelter, the small young brown bear that was curious but shy and others. Gray Hawk recognized most of the wild life that lived near him and they all had personal lives which the old Indian observed with care and respect.

"And, you, Tah-moss. What has happened?"

Thomas described his tracking of the lost child in the spring and his encounter with the large mountain lion, then the sudden snow storm that ruined his plans to visit the mountains.

The Indian nodded, "You did very well, Tah-moss."

"You taught me well, Gray Hawk."

The shaman studied Thomas for a long moment, looking deep into his eyes. "I feel some bad things have happened, Tah-moss," he said softly. "It is in your eyes."

Thomas frowned. "It has been a difficult time, Gray Hawk." He tried to explain the large construction project and the fire that brought it to a halt but was unsure the Indian could imagine a building over eighty feet high. "Also, our nation's President—our *chief*—was murdered not long ago. It has been a sad time for my people."

The Indian shook his head sadly. "You have a new chief now?"

"Yes. We have a new chief."

Gray Hawk was silent for several moments. Finally, "I would only say this to you, Tah-moss, because we are friends. Your people are a very violent people. My people would not kill their own chief."

Thomas nodded. "Many men are violent, Gray Hawk. Maybe it is in our blood."

*   *   *

Thomas spent the next three days under Gray Hawk's watchful tutelage. The old man declared Thomas to be responsible for hunting and preparing the meals, using the skills he had been taught. Dressed in the deerskin breeches and moccasins, Thomas spent the days tracking and catching small game using improvised traps and snares. They hunted roots and green shoots, leaves, berries and nuts, even the tender inner bark of some trees. Thomas prepared soups and stews, roasted rabbits and squirrels which they ate slowly, savoring the taste and smells. Gray Hawk carefully critiqued Thomas's efforts, suggesting ways to improve or change the flavor or consistency. He showed Thomas how eating certain insects and grubs could supply energy in an emergency. At first Thomas's stomach roiled slightly at the effort but he soon became accustomed to the crunch of insects and the squirming of grubs between his teeth.

"I will show you some other Indian ways, Thomas. Maybe you will never have to use them but they are good to know."

Now fairly adept at tracking, Thomas was aware of the many signs that an animal, or human being, left as they moved through their surroundings. Beside prints on the ground, there were broken branches, bent or broken stems, disrupted spider webs or patterns on the forest floor, tiny subtleties that most would never see or recognize. But as the one following the tracks, he was also leaving these same readable signs behind him; the Indian carefully showed him how and where to step, what not to touch or disturb, how to carefully cover or minimize his own tracks. Mountain lions, he explained, would sometimes loop back on their tracker and attack from behind. Animals that sometimes traveled in pairs, like bears, would occasionally separate so that one could follow at a distance as protection.

On their last evening, Gray Hawk complimented Thomas. "You have learned very well, Tah-moss. You are not as good as me but I have had many years of experience. And you have not learned all the Indian ways; that would take you a lifetime. You can track animals, trap them, cook them. You can stay alive under terrible conditions. You are very strong in your mind. When you return in the spring, you and I will put your skills to a test, as my people would do for one who is about to become a warrior. Then I will know how well I have taught you."

"I know you have taught me well, Gray Hawk."

"We shall see."

*   *   *

San Quentin State Prison, California

Chandler had planned their escape for two years and today would be the day. He and Dyson had worked for several weeks with a crew of fourteen other inmates to demolish and haul away the rusted and decayed remains of one of the last ships that had served as temporary prison quarters before the permanent prison was built. Now settled onto the bottom of the bay where it had been tied up for nearly forty years, the ship had been stripped until all that remained was a rotted skeleton of ribs and framework projecting above the water and the ancient stumps of pilings that had once supported the dock to which the old ship had been tied. Temporary planks attached to the stumps provided a walkway for the guards so that they could directly oversee the inmates as they worked on the wreck.

Four prison guards regularly escorted the work detail to and from the work site and hovered with shotguns loaded with buck shot while the inmates labored; each guard was responsible for four prisoners. The prisoners were shackled in pairs; six foot long chains tied them together, attached with a padlock to a chain belt worn by each man. Each day, the pairing assignments rotated but it hadn't taken long for Chandler to determine that the pattern of rotation was straightforward and thus predictable. Today he and Dyson would be paired together again.

Being Tuesday, he also knew that a barge would be coming across from San Francisco to shuttle inmates to and from the county and federal courtrooms in order to make appearances, stand trial and in some instances, be released. The number of inmates involved in this shuttle could number between six and fifteen, according to Chandler's observations.

As usual the prison work detail gathered in one of the narrow enclosures within the prison compound; the inmates were shackled—Chandler and Dyson together as Chandler had expected. They were led outside into the gray overcast and the guards took up their positions, two on each side and marched the work detail to the work site only a few hundred yards from the imposing walls of the fortress-like prison. Chandler could see the newer dock about thirty yards from where they would be working and where the barge would tie up briefly to exchange inmates. There was no sign yet of the barge but it could be out of sight beyond Tiburon Point and Angel Island. When they reached the water's edge the guards shouted their instructions; Chandler and Dyson were both tall men, over six feet and they were assigned to the deep end of the wreck where they had worked all these weeks. The water there was about thirteen feet deep at high tide and ten feet deep at low tide, murky with silt and pollution from the shipyards further up the bay.

Their job today was to attach steel cables to the rotting frames of the old ship and with the aid of horses on the shore, pry the timbers loose, drag and stack them at the water's edge. It was difficult work, as the only footing was the remaining framework of the old ship. They were mostly required to work in water up to their chest and occasionally go under water to attach the cables blindly to the rotting wood. Their guard, known as *Dog* among the inmates, stood on the temporary walkway fifteen feet away watching the slow proceedings with indifference; from time to time his eyes roamed the length of the wreck and peered out over the San Francisco Bay as he studied the spit of land—Point San Pablo—across the water.

They had been working almost an hour before Chandler saw the barge coming around Tiburon Point six miles away; he caught Dyson's eyes and nodded briefly. They both saw the group of inmates being shepherded from the prison to the dock, awaiting their transfer to temporary holding cells in the city. It took another forty-five minutes for the barge to arrive and tie up at the dock.

Chandler nodded to Dyson. He raised his right arm as if to stretch out a cramped muscle and across the way one of the inmates awaiting transfer to the city saw the signal. Moments later he shoved the man in front of him into one of the guards and in seconds an out-of-control scuffle was taking place among the shackled prisoners and guards. Chandler reached into his pocket, retrieved his lock picking tools and in less than half a minute both he and Dyson were free of the chain restraints around their waists and the connecting shackle. *Dog*, the guard that was supposed to be watching them, was nervously watching the furor thirty yards away and didn't see Chandler's hand come up to grab the guard's foot and to yank him into the water. Dyson wrapped the heavy chain around the guard's neck and pushed the panicked man deep under the water. The struggle was brief; the other guards were still staring and motioning at the commotion across the water. Chandler and Dyson took deep breaths and slipped under the water.

Chandler used long strokes of his arms and kicked his legs furiously to pull himself through the water. Blindly, opening his eyes for scant seconds at a time, he tried to stay near the bottom, hoping he was heading toward the rear of the prisoner barge. Within seconds his lungs were burning but he didn't dare to try to surface; the guards by now would surely be missing the fourth guard and would have their shotguns aimed at anything that popped to the surface.

He was going to have to surface! He fought the instinct to draw air in . . . A shadow passed to his right—the barge! Somewhere a sound like muffled thunder penetrated the water and repeated. The guards were shooting at something—or someone!

He passed beyond the rudder on the barge and finally had to raise his head. He sucked air in slowly to fill his starved lungs. With just his eyes and nose above water he looked back through the rudder mechanism. The bloody mess that had been Dyson's body floated fifty feet behind him and in their rage the guards continued to fire round after round of buckshot into the dead man. Chandler slipped silently to the far side of the barge, hiding below the overhanging curve of the old hull. *Stupid Dyson had managed to swim under the water for less than ten yards . . .*

The water was icy cold and Chandler was shivering. From here on he would be alone, not that Dyson was ever going to be much help. *Just as well he got shot . . .* Chandler peered carefully around the stern of the barge. Apparently someone had spotted the corpse of the guard and everyone, prisoners and prison guards, had crowded in to see. There was confusion, shouting, pointing at the spot near the old wreck. The guards didn't know what to do; who should go into the water to retrieve the body? Where was the guard's shotgun?

Chandler used the opportunity to slip around the barge and take up position between the barge and the dock. From there he could peer through the dock pilings and watch what was taking place less than a hundred feet away. He carefully worked his way toward the bow of the barge and reaching up slowly, slipped the mooring line off the cleat on the dock. Then moving aft again, he did the same with the second line. The barge floated free and Chandler gave it a gentle push away from the dock and into deeper water before he ducked under the water again and made his way around the stern of the boat. Ponderously, the barge floated away from the dock and into deep water and it was fifty feet from shore before a guard glanced in that direction and shouted an alarm. Once again indecision overwhelmed the guards, encouraged by the boisterous response of the inmates to their situation. In two minutes the barge had floated beyond immediate retrieval, well into the bay with Chandler clinging to the rudder mechanism. In another two minutes the barge was beyond shotgun range and Chandler pulled himself over the side and into the small cockpit. With a few turns of the hand crank, the diesel engine sputtered to life and Chandler steered the little boat away from the gray prison, the crowd of inmates and guards on the shore.

Inside the crowded cockpit he found a canvas jacket that evidently belonged to one of the guards and a filthy wool cap. He peeled off his wet clothes and spread them in the cool sunshine to dry, standing naked in the enclosure of the cockpit. He steered the barge along the rocky coastline, around Point Tiburon and around to the south side of Angel Island. Though there were several large homes on the mile and a half wide

137

island, for the most part it was deserted. He found a small cove with trees coming down to the shoreline and pulled the barge in as far as it would go, then secured it by tying the bow line to a tree. He pulled several branches off a tree and placed them over the stern of the barge in an attempt to camouflage the barge; the trees overhead would prevent anyone on the island from looking into the barge.

*   *   *

The moon was still in its first quarter and what little light it shed was obscured by the layer of fog that had settled upon San Francisco Bay. Within a few minutes of casting the barge loose of its mooring on Angel Island, Chandler had no idea where he was. He held the steering wheel steady, hoping that his course would land him somewhere on the city's fog hidden waterfront, just over three miles due south of Angel Island. If the tide was going out, the current could sweep the barge right through the straits and into the open sea. If the tide was coming in, he could be carried for miles down the length of San Francisco Bay. As it was, it was during the interval between tides, known as slack tide, when the tide was going neither in nor out. It was also a time that ship masters often chose to navigate the straits and not have to wrestle with the powerful rushing current of seawater at the ebb or flow of tides.

The barge brushed up against the rocky shoreline somewhere west of Fort Mason and Chandler quickly maneuvered the ungainly craft until it was pointed once again into the bay. Holding his dry clothes over his head, he lowered himself into the icy water then used the long boat hook to shove the engine throttle forward. The engine sputtered then caught and backwash from the propeller surged against him. He threw the boat hook into the barge as it moved forward into the bay and was soon out of sight.

Chandler was dry and dressed before the most fortuitous of accidents occurred. A large steamship heading to sea during this time of slack tide was carefully steering through the bay, sounding its fog horn to warn other ships of its presence; its navigation crew straining to see and maintain their position by means of familiar lights and channel markers. The barge, dark and low in the water and with no running lights, slogged forward through the rough water on a collision course with the steamship. A lookout on the bow of the steamship hollered a warning at the last moment but it was already too late. The heavy steel bow of the steamer crunched onto the barge and rolled over it effortlessly.

*   *   *

The Gordon Ranch

Thomas reached the Gordon ranch late afternoon the next day. The weather had taken a sudden turn; the air was damp and cool and the wind gusty as he rode in through the main gate. Big puffy clouds were scudding across the sky and piling up in a heavy dark mass against the high Sierra Nevada Mountains behind him. Angela greeted him as he was unloading his horses, giving him a friendly hug.

"Looks like you got back just in time, Tom."

He glanced again at the thick pile of clouds. "Isn't it early for a storm?"

She nodded as she followed his gaze. "Things can change real fast up there."

*   *   *

San Francisco

On Wednesday, October 2, the San Francisco Chronicle had carried the news of the attempted prison break at San Quentin Prison. One prison guard, Russell Doggett, had been killed by the escaping prisoners. One of the escaping prisoners, Vernon Dyson, had been shot and killed by guards. A second prisoner, Clarence Chandler, had managed to get away by stealing the prison barge but the barge had been struck and overrun late that night by a steamship, the three thousand ton *SS Xavier* en route to Vancouver, B. C. Prison officials announced that Chandler had apparently lost his life as a result of the collision. Only minor debris from the barge had been recovered; one item was a life ring with the words Department of Correction painted on it.

Thomas O'Reiley skimmed quickly through the pile of newspapers Amanda had saved for him. More interested in the business news within the city, he had paid scant attention to the prison break story.

CHAPTER 12

<u>Thursday, January 30, 1902, San Francisco, California</u>

The San Francisco Chronicle had reported on January 2nd that the steamship *SS Walla Walla* had collided with a French bark by the name of *Max of Havre* off Cape Mendocino, California. Forty-two passengers and crew of the five thousand ton, 336 foot long *SS Walla Walla* lost their lives when the steamship sank immediately following the accident. The twenty-one year old steamer had regularly plied the waters between Seattle and San Francisco carrying passengers and cargo. The *Max of Havre* made it into San Francisco for repairs, bringing with her the only three survivors from the *SS Walla Walla*. One of the passengers who died in the tragic accident was Nadellia Manhauser, the widowed wife of Richard Manhauser who had been murdered in May of the previous year. Once the courts determined there were no surviving family members, the Manhauser ranch was put up for auction and was purchased by Bret Solomon at a fraction of what he had previously offered Richard Manhauser.

In November, 1901, the congressionally appointed Isthmusian Commission on Interoceanic Canals voted eight to one to recommend building the Atlantic-Pacific canal across Nicaragua. The lone dissenting vote came from the only engineer on the I.C.I. Commission.

On January 4th, the U.S. House of Representatives approved a bill which authorized the construction of such a canal. But not everyone was pleased with these decisions; in particular a syndicate of Wall Street figures who had already bought out the defunct French Canal Company and were actively lobbying to purchase the equipment left in place in Panama by the New French Canal Company after their failed attempt. In addition, the original construction rights bought from the Columbian government would elapse in two years. The New Company was represented by Frenchmen Phillippe Bunau-Varilla and a New York attorney named William Nelson Cromwell. Cromwell and Bunau-Varilla started an intense lobbying effort to take the canal through the narrower Isthmus of Panama. Much of this intense maneuvering, largely political in nature, was unknown to the public. What tid-bits of information did emerge provided dynamic fodder for public debate.

Thomas O'Reiley sat quietly in the darkness of his sunroom, his mind wandering restlessly over these issues and other events covered by the newspaper. It was cold in San Francisco and the multitude of lights that usually glittered on and around the bay were hidden by the cold drizzle that had been steadily falling for the past three days. The chil, rain and early evening darkness had everyone slightly on edge and wishing to be able to enjoy the seasonable, though cool, outdoors.

The small wood fire in the fireplace had burned down to a few red coals that emitted very little heat. He glanced at his pocket watch; it was near eleven o'clock.

*   *   *

The Sierra Nevada Mountains

The four-day old storm had brought huge amounts of snow to the higher elevations; in some places the snow was already over twenty-five feet deep. Tonight it continued to come down—big, heavy, wet flakes that added to the already deep cover on the ground and bent boughs of trees until they either broke or sloughed off the gathering weight. It was silent; the snow muffled everything except the soft hush of the falling snow itself. Animals were out of sight, burrowed in deeply, curled up in rock crevices or caves or waiting in thick groves of trees that provided a little shelter from the falling snow. Nothing ventured out onto the deep snow pack. It was completely dark in the deep forest and even the days had been murky and gray below the heavy storm clouds. Temperatures hovered well below freezing and dropped still lower at night. Small streams, hidden by the deep layer of snow, had long since frozen solid. Tonight the icy wind started to pick up, first gently blowing the snow in swirls, then slicing sideways, packing the snow against the trunks of the trees and the rock outcroppings, carving monster drifts that moved and relocated, grew and disappeared as if they were alive. By the first hours of dawn the wind was screaming through the trees, howling in inanimate fury at anything that got in its way. Nearby a tall sugar-pine tree reluctantly gave up its root-grip on the red clay-like soil and fell with an earth-shaking, splintering crash whose sound was swept up in the shrieking gale.

When the storm would finally wear itself out, it would leave behind a broad path of destruction and more than forty feet of snow.

*   *   *

San Francisco, California

News of the week-long storm that had brought impassible snow to much of the Sierra Nevada range was written up on a second page article of the Chronicle. The infamous Donner Pass through which the Union-Pacific railroad traversed the mountain range was closed, and trains were backed up as railroad crews fought to clear deep drifts of snow from the tracks; some sections of track were buried by avalanches of snow over a hundred feet deep.

Thomas sat in his sun room, reading the Saturday paper and sipping his morning coffee. After reading about the terrible snow conditions in the Sierras, he could not help but to feel concern for the old Indian, Gray Hawk. What shelter had the old man sought to protect him from the cold? How had he managed food? He wondered how the snow would affect his own upcoming visit to the mountains later in the year.

The sun was shining on San Francisco, glittering off the whitecaps that rippled the waters of San Francisco Bay. Several of the more robust and wealthy San Franciscans were out on their sailing yachts, cutting in and out among the islands and challenging one another to impromptu contests. It was a spectacular day to take advantage of the sunshine and mild weather.

Of other interest was an article about the ongoing concern in San Francisco regarding the bubonic plague that was still frightening residents of the city. Though existence of the deadly disease was officially denied by both city and state health officials, occasional deaths were still being reported. Xiang had heard of cases among neighbors of her family that lived packed into crowded rooms in Chinatown.

*   *   *

Rancho De Pacifica, 10 Miles North of Santa Cruz, California

The tall, rather thin man pulled on his sheepskin jacket and slammed the wide brimmed hat on his head. Shoulder length silver hair hung loosely under the brim. The coastal ranch where he had found employment was nestled comfortably in one of the wide canyons that began at the sea and cleaved up into the coastal range of mountains that ended in San Francisco and stretched southward nearly the full length of the California coastline. The ranch was owned by a wealthy San Francisco attorney who showed up with his wife on the weekends to ride their horses among the hills and along the rugged coastline; the present owner, fifty year-old Alexander Dunsworth, ran thirty head of prize beef on the two hundred acres and enjoyed a cozy five-room house with three fireplaces. The well maintained outbuildings consisted of a carriage house, a barn and a small but comfortable bunkhouse for his hired help, at the moment consisting of the single ranch hand.

At one time the property had been part of a large parcel of land, or *ranchero* granted by the Mexican government to Señor Santiago Agusto Vincente in 1835. At the time of the granting, the property sprawled across thirteen thousand acres from the sea shore to the top of the Pacific Coastal Mountain range. The Treaty of Guadalupe Hidalgo ended the Mexican-American War on February 2, 1848 and resulted in Mexico ceding their lands in Upper California, New Mexico and Texas to the United States. When the United States took over the governing of California, holders of Spanish and Mexican land grants were required to present the titles of their land for confirmation. The legal costs for this process were enormous and many grantees were required to sell off all or portions of their property to pay for the legal fees. Santiago Agusto Vincente, the great-great grandfather of Esperanza Vincente, sold all but one thousand acres, which was also eventually sold and divided into smaller parcels.

Beck, as he was known by the Dunsworths, had learned all of this history from Dunsworth's wife Nelle. On this Saturday, as on most, the Dunsworths would be in residence. When the weekends arrived, the ranch hand simply made himself scarce, as little was expected of him when Alexander Dunsworth and his attractive wife were at the ranch. Since it was Saturday, he had gotten up a little later than usual, made himself a simple breakfast then went outside to chop and split firewood for both the bunkhouse and for the main house.

It felt good to swing the well honed double-bitted axe with force and watch the chips fly. The action seemed to release some of the frustration that often swirled through him. Finding work had not been easy and he regretted the lonesomeness that life had thrust upon him. He swung the axe with a smooth overhead motion hard at the end of the oak log. The log split with a loud crack and fell into two neat halves.

* * *

<u>Fort Worth, Texas</u>
Luke glanced out the window of his hotel room onto Main Street, the eastern edge of what the local's called Hell's Half Acre. Daytime traffic on the street was very sparse, mostly saloon keepers sweeping up the debris from the night before and the local law enforcement rousting the drunks still sleeping on the sidewalks and in the gutters. The wild cacophony of piano music had finally stopped about four in the morning and the raucous crowd of cattle men, gamblers and drifters had wandered off to get some sleep. Some would eventually wake up to discover that they had lost all their money at the gambling tables, some would awake in a strange bed with an unfamiliar woman beside them, some would wake up with a painful knot on the side of their heads and their pockets empty. Some would not wake up, ever.

Luke had spent the evening at Tall Charley's, one of the saloons on Russ Street near Seventh. Unlike most of those who had spent the night at the saloon, Luke awoke fresh and sober. He had nursed a single beer through the evening before he met with a man who called himself Andrew Goldman. The man was well dressed, well groomed, confident and articulate, though a little on the pudgy side. Luke thought he looked and sounded like a politician. At first, Luke was disinclined to take the job Goldman was discussing but it offered a very large sum of money in compensation.

"Nicaragua," the man had said, "Punta Gorda, Nicaragua."

Two days in a steamer out of Corpus Christi, Luke reckoned.

"The job takes place in Punta Gorda. No overland traveling involved, except to get to Houston."

Take the train to Corpus Christi, Luke quickly calculated.

"It's an easy in and out." Goldman insisted, "One, maybe two days in Punta Gorda."

"How would El Culebra recognize him?"

"Him?"

"The target." *Some people are really stupid*, Luke thought. "The object of this job."

The man nodded. "Oh, yeah. Well, it's a *her*, not a *him*. She has a big *hacienda* on the north side of Punta Gorda."

Luke raised his eyebrows. "A woman . . ."

"Yes, a woman." The man studied Luke closely. "Will Culebra have a problem with that?"

Luke shook his head, "not at all."

"One thing. He has to make it look like an accident."

"What do you mean, *an accident*?" Luke frowned.

"She is a prominent woman, very wealthy . . . an important woman in Nicaraguan politics and she has several very influential contacts in the United States government. There must not be an investigation that could connect her death in any way to the United States."

Luke nodded briefly then asked, "How many in the household?"

"Besides her, only a very small staff; a caretaker, maid, cook, perhaps one or two others."

"No husband?"

"He died four years ago. Malaria."

Luke paused, finally asked "what's her name?"

"Señora Isabella Laurencia Esperanza. Probably about forty-five years old."

"Isabella Esperanza . . ."

"Very old Spanish family. Owns a great deal of property. Used to have property in California, a big spread granted to them by the Mexican government, before the Mexican War."

"Isabella Esperanza . . ."

"Yes . . ."

*   *   *

Punta Gorda, Nicaragua

Luke arrived in Punta Gorda aboard the steamer *SS Charles Strong* out of Houston, Texas, along with sixty-four other passengers. He carried a small suitcase and the leather valise containing his Mauser rifle. It was mid-afternoon and the sun beat down ferociously. Most of the city's residents were just returning from their afternoon *siestas*. It was after three o'clock by the time he found and checked into a hotel. An hour later he was on horseback following the narrow dirt road that curved along the coastline north of the city. It didn't take him long to find the large *hacienda* belonging to Señora Isabella Laurencia Esperanza. He pulled off the road and studied the home with his binoculars. It was a long, low wood structure, very Spanish in architecture, with open windows behind wooden shutters, a red Spanish tile roof. All the wood was painted brilliant white. The front area of the *hacienda* was elegantly landscaped and manicured. The semi-circular carriage drive to the door was made of crushed sea shells. A few outbuildings consisted of a carriage house, a white painted corral and barn and a small building that was probably the servant's quarters.

He watched the building for about forty-five minutes, but saw no sign of activity other than a small curl of smoke from what was probably the kitchen chimney. By the time he got back to the hotel, he had constructed a rough plan in his mind. It would be different than his normal methods but it would work.

*   *   *

Corpus Christi, Texas

The arrival of the *SS Charles Strong* from Nicaragua solicited very little excitement at the busy waterfront. Luke disembarked with the other passengers and by the time he had boarded the train bound for Fort Worth; he had purchased a copy of the fledgling *Corpus Christi Chronicle* to read on the train.

He found the news article of his interest on the third page. Nicaraguan police were still investigating the tragic death of forty-seven year old Señora Isabella Laurencia Esperanza of Punta Gorda. The wealthy widow of Señor Edmundo Miguel Vincente had apparently died in a roaring fire that completely destroyed her coastal hacienda. Two of her housekeeping staff had also perished in the blaze. The inferno had reduced the house to a pile of gray ashes; only the red tiles of the roof remained identifiable.

Señora Esperanza had been a powerful vocal opponent of any plans to create an inter-ocean canal across Nicaragua, arguing that the country would benefit very little financially from the canal that would bring many years of international dispute, perhaps even more military intervention.

Señora Esperanza, the paper reported, was the surviving heiress of an old and wealthy political family that owned many hundreds of thousands of acres of Nicaragua ranch land. When she married Señor Vincente, their combined properties exceeded two and a half million acres, over thirty-nine thousand square miles, an astounding thirty percent of the total area of Nicaragua. This was of interest to some in the United States as most of the property lay squarely in the path of the planned canal but she had tenaciously resisted pressure to sell the property.

Luke nodded and smiled to himself. It was probably just as well the paper didn't describe the excruciating manner in which the strikingly pretty Nicaraguan lady had died; most people would have found the details to be horribly shocking. Luke however, had experienced profound, almost euphoric satisfaction in every long and intense minute of it.

The extreme heat, he was sure, had destroyed any evidence. Besides, he'd taken a few extra minutes to relieve the household of some exceptional pieces of jewelry and a small delicately carved wooden box of gold coins.

San Francisco, California

Thomas O'Reiley glanced quickly at his pocket watch. It was several minutes past six in the evening and Amanda would be waiting impatiently at home for him to arrive from his office. He had promised her a night at the theatre to see the British musical comedy Floradora, staged by a traveling New York chorus.

He muttered under his breath at the pile of invoices yet to be processed. *Damn this growing pile of paper! I was never cut out to be an accountant!*

His construction materials business had grown much faster than either he or McPherson had expected, especially since the architectural firm had been incorporated into the company now known as M. O. & B.. The rapidly-growing city needed new buildings to replace the fifty and sixty year old structures that had long served the city and were often destroyed by raging, out of control fires. Opera houses and theaters and restaurants were springing up all over town. Hotels and retail businesses, banks and government buildings, office buildings were all in desperate demand. Closer to the piers and the southern edges of the city, large warehouses were being purchased or leased as quickly as they could be constructed. In spite of his growing staff of estimators, buyers and planners and the small army of warehousemen and draymen, the amount of work was causing everyone extra long hours.

* * *

The man was well hidden, buried deep in the shadows of the thick shrubbery behind the home of Thomas and Amanda O'Reiley. He had been there since shortly after dusk after cutting through the empty lots behind the elegant Victorian house and slipping quietly into the densely planted privacy bushes running across the back of the property. He hadn't been in the city for several years and much had changed in his absence. It was busier, noisier, more crowded with people and buildings. Electricity and the telephone had arrived. Even a few horseless carriages were seen on the streets. The expanded piers along the waterfront hummed twenty-four hours a day with burgeoning import and export business. New streets had been added and old ones had been paved with cobblestones or asphalt, widened and well lit. Some had simply disappeared beneath the wheels of progress. Old acquaintances, the few that there had once been, had long since moved on or had become pathetic derelicts, filthy and habitually drunk. It had taken a few weeks of inquiring around in saloons to eventually learn the Nob Hill address of Thomas O'Reiley.

Through a convoluted, prison-warped way of thinking, he had over the years developed and nurtured a simmering hatred for the man whom he blamed for the eleven years he'd spent behind bars. The man he was waiting for had gotten away scot-free while he and Dyson had spent the best part of their lives in prison for murder. Now the once-poor Irishman imagined that he was well-to-do, safe and secure. Well, he would quickly learn otherwise. And his family would find out what it was like to experience the bitter side of life.

He heard the steady rhythm of the horse's hooves pulling the carriage even before it turned into the drive. The hansom pulled up and stopped in the light from the portico lamps on the side of the house. The gunman carefully pulled the pistol's hammer back with his thumb. From only thirty yards away, he concentrated on his two-hand grip that held the revolver unwavering. When the man stepped out of the carriage and turned toward the house, the shooter centered the sights on the man's topcoat covered chest.

The assailant held the sights steady, gently increased his finger pressure on the trigger; the pistol jumped in his hand and a bright spit of orange flame erupted from the barrel. His ears ringing from the report, he watched with curious satisfaction as the man convulsed from the impact of the .45

caliber bullet, clawing weakly at his left shoulder. He fell back against the side of the hansom, his face contorted in alarm, then dropped and rolled forward onto the steps, unmoving. The sound of the single pistol shot was still echoing among the other houses as the gunman quickly stood and made his way through the shadows to his carefully selected exit route.

CHAPTER 13

<u>San Francisco, California</u>

"He spent about an hour here." Thomas pointed to the imprints in the loose soil and glanced around quickly. "Probably doesn't smoke or dip tobacco. He's an impatient man, most likely not an experienced hunter, moved around trying to find a good place to hide. He knelt here—that's his left knee print. Took cover behind these branches. That gave him a clear shot, about thirty yards but that's long for a pistol. Probably right handed from his shooting stance." Thomas posed, hand held out as if grasping a revolver. "Stood up after he took the shot, turned and walked this way," Thomas pointed as he followed the prints in the loose loam among the shrubs. "He cut across the empty lot, followed this shallow curve on the hillside, crouching a little even though it was almost dark." He walked along the track, pointing out the salient features; "I'd estimate he weighs around two hundred pounds. By the length of his pace I'd say he's about six feet tall, slim build. Wears boots—notice the shape of the heel imprints—they're not riding boots. I'd say they're Justin's; look at the prints, nice sharp edges on the heels and soles—fairly new. Our shooter stopped here," he pointed, "and looked back, probably to make sure no one was following him." His eyes fell on the glint of metal among the weeds several feet away. "Notice that the length of his pace is shorter here; he slowed down, probably concentrating on reloading." Thomas stepped across, stooped and retrieved the brass casing, peered at it closely. "Colt forty-five long, handgun." He hesitated before he flipped the spent round to the police detective who was walking with him. "As you know, thirty yards is a little on the long side for an accurate revolver shot."

Thomas continued to follow the tracks on the damp soil. "The shooter turned again, looked both left and right and then continued toward the street. Look here," Thomas pointed to the marks in the soil, "he stopped again, turned back; probably thinking he ought to go back and look for the empty casing. He hesitated, decided not to, started back toward the street. He halted briefly again right here," he pointed at the prints in the soil, "probably to make sure no one was on the street, then stepped onto the street and stamped the dirt off his boots." He knelt on the cobblestone and peered carefully downhill. "I'd say he brushed the dirt from his left trouser leg right here," he pointed, "then his prints continue and disappear about thirty five feet down hill—probably got on his horse." He walked down hill and studied the empty road. "That's about all I can learn from what's here to see, Officer Kelly."

The police officer shook his head, "a hell of a lot more than I could have told you, Mister O'Reiley. Quite remarkable what you saw that I didn't. So, our man weighs about two hundred pounds, slim build, stands about six feet tall, right handed and shoots a forty-five caliber pistol. Doesn't dip or smoke tobacco, probably not the hunting type. Sounds like about half the men who straggle into the city for a weekend of drinking, gambling and girls."

"Except it wasn't a weekend, Officer Kelley. It was Wednesday night."

The policeman nodded. "How's Mister Barnwell feeling?"

"He's doing well for a man shot through the shoulder. The shot went through cleanly, didn't hit bone or major blood vessels. A few inches in any direction and it could have been real bad. As it was, he'll be out of commission for a week or two."

"Any idea why someone would want to try to kill him?"

"No idea at all."

"What was he doing at your house last night, Mister O'Reiley?"

"Mister Barnwell, my wife Amanda and I were planning to attend a show last night, *Floradora* playing at the new Pacific Theater. Mister Barnwell intended to meet us at our house so the three of us could attend together. I had worked late and was on the way home when the shooting occurred. I arrived only a few minutes after Mister Barnwell was taken into house by Doctor Cranston who lives just two houses away. Since the bullet had passed cleanly through, Doctor Cranston cleansed the wound and bound it here at my house." Thomas smiled grimly. "We didn't make it to the theater."

* * *

Thomas O'Reiley sat silently in his office, his mind recycling the thoughts that seemed to swirl unbidden through his mind. *Why had someone taken a shot at Frank Barnwell? Who would have known Barnwell would be arriving at his house that evening? If the shot was not meant for Frank Barnwell, then it could only have been meant for me . . .*

Doctor Cranston was with Frank at that moment in the extra bedroom upstairs and Amanda was waiting impatiently at the base of the stairs with a tray of light dinner to take up to him. Amanda had insisted upon personally caring for Barnwell for the few days he would remain in their home, a situation that Thomas found to be somewhat ironic. Frank had become a close friend of Amanda and Thomas and was a frequent visitor. In his mid thirties, Frank never seemingly lacked for female companionship and his business position had already begun to provide him the means to live very comfortably. He was known in the city's social circles as an available bachelor and with the political connections he had brought with him, became a popular figure in San Francisco government, especially as the city continued its search for a supply of water that could meet its ever growing needs.

Certainly that meant that Frank Barnwell could have developed a few enemies among those opposed to some of his ideas. *But, enough to cause someone to try to assassinate him?* Thomas shook his head in frustration. *No, that shot was meant for me, not Frank. But who and why?*

The doctor finally came down the steps, curtly nodded to Thomas on his way out.

"Tom?" It was Amanda calling. "Frank would like to see you."

Thomas climbed the curved stairs leading to the second floor and found the door to the extra bedroom ajar. He tapped on the door before he entered.

Frank was propped up on a pile of pillows, his left shoulder swathed in fresh white bandage that stretched across his chest and down to his elbow. A tray of food sat on his lap.

"Thomas!" Barnwell greeted him as he stepped into the room, "I feel like such a damned fool! You and Amanda waiting on me like this . . ."

Thomas shook his head. "If you're a fool, Frank, you're a damned lucky one! That shot could have killed you." He carefully closed the door behind him. "Besides, I think that bullet was meant for me, not you."

Barnwell frowned, "What do you mean?"

Thomas sat in the chair beside the bed and leaned forward as he spoke. "I've been thinking, Frank. Who would know that you would show up at my house that evening and at that time? I was late coming home from work and you got there about the time I would normally arrive." He paused. "I believe the shooter thought it was me he was shooting at. We're about the same height, dark overcoat, poor lighting. Easy mistake under the circumstances."

Frank grimaced, "Well, the same questions apply; who and why?"

"We have a few particulars to go by. Based on the prints left behind by the shooter, he's about six feet tall, weighs about two hundred pounds, is probably right handed, slim build, probably doesn't chew or smoke tobacco. It could be someone who is an experienced hunter but I rather doubt that. Shoots a forty-five caliber handgun. He shot from a distance of about thirty yards." Thomas quickly explained how he derived this information.

Frank frowned and was silent for a long time. "And you found a forty-five long casing?"

"Yeah. Of course, there's no proof it came from the shooter's pistol . . ."

Frank was silent for several seconds. "A Buntline Special uses a forty-five long."

It was Thomas's turn to frown. "Buntline Special?"

"A Buntline Special is what Beck carried when he led our hunting party into the mountains. It's a forty-five caliber handgun—actually, a Colt Peacemaker fitted with an extra long barrel. I believe Beck's pistol had a twelve inch barrel. Called it his *Buntline*."

Thomas nodded slowly. "I seem to recall that he did have a long barreled pistol strapped to his hip. His right hip. He was talking about the Indian, Gray Hawk, at the time."

"That's the one. I read about the Colt Buntline when I got back to Sacramento. Supposedly the longer barrel makes them a little more accurate. Some have sixteen inch barrels and are made to accommodate a removable stock. Don't see an awful lot of them around."

"But . . . Beck?"

"He fits a lot of the description, Thomas. Six feet tall, two hundred pounds. Slim build. Doesn't chew or smoke. Beck's a deer hunter," Frank shook his head, "and he shoots a forty-five caliber pistol with his right hand. Just something to think about."

Thomas was silent for several seconds. Finally, "according to Hector Gordon, Beck's supposed to be somewhere up north. Hector had to let him go a while back. He wasn't real specific why."

Frank glanced across at his friend. "Didn't have anything to do with you, did it?"

* * *

The San Francisco Chronicle had very little to say about the mysterious and unfortunate incident on Nob Hill, other than that the popular San Francisco businessman Frank Barnwell had been *slightly wounded* in an apparent random shooting and was recovering very well. The police department had intentionally decided to withhold the information that Thomas O'Reiley had ascertained from the trail of evidence left behind. However, there were no eye-witnesses of the shooters coming or going. In less than a week, the police realized that there was no further path to follow; the gunman had apparently disappeared. Though there were a number of unsolved shootings and killings in the San Francisco area, there was no evidence that could connect any of them to this instance

* * *

Gordon Ranch
Though Thomas was deeply concerned about the old Indian Gray Hawk and how he had managed the winter snows, the injury and subsequent recovery of Frank Barnwell had delayed Thomas's plans to visit the shaman until Frank was able to return to work. Finally, on the twelfth of May, Thomas had sent a telegram to Hector Gordon outlining his plans to make another trip into the mountains. The following day, Hector had replied by telegram:

DEEP SNOW STOP ACCESSIBLE WITH CARE
STOP SEE YOU ON MAY 26 STOP HECTOR

When he got off the train, Angela was waiting at the bottom of the steps and threw herself into his arms unabashedly. The sky over the San Joaquin valley was bright blue and the sunshine warmed the small town and helped dry the streets. The townspeople were out on the streets and sidewalks.

"Tom! I thought you were never going to come back!" She hugged him and he held her close, in spite of some of the curious stares from passersby.

"It's only been since October, Angela! But, it's good to be back, too."

"I know. It just seems like a long time! Hurry and get your stuff, Tom. I don't want to waste a minute of our time together."

She's grown even more beautiful in the last six months, Thomas thought. *Her hair is so beautiful. Her eyes . . .*

On the way to the ranch, Angela brought him up to date. "The winter was terrible, Tom. So much snow! We've never seen it like that. About three weeks ago it started melting and the rivers were all beyond their banks. The Kaweah is still running very fast. Lots of farmers in the valley were flooded out. Tulare Lake filled up and it's huge! We don't see that very often anymore. They're saying that most of the snow pack in the back country will stay on the ground all summer. We didn't get it as bad as they did up north some, where they got forty feet of snow! Forty feet! I can't even imagine that much snow. It's too bad we don't have some way to save all that water for when a dry spell sets in, or even distribute it to other parts of the state where they so desperately need water."

"It's going to happen someday. Frank Barnwell was working on those kinds of projects for the state before he came to work with us."

"Frank Barnwell! I remember him. He came down the first time you were here."

"He's the one. Frank's an engineer. Now he's heading up our architectural division. He had a tough time getting started. We got caught in one of the city's big fires and the new office building he designed burned to the ground; then we had to completely rebuild. Set us back almost six months. Then two months ago someone shot him. He's doing all right, but moving a little slow."

"Shot him?" Angela looked at him with a startled expression. "Who would do that?"

"We don't know, Angela." Thomas told her of the events on the evening of April the second.

"Tom, that's just awful! And you really think the ambush was meant for you?"

He nodded. "I think so. I don't know who or why but nobody would have expected Frank to be there at that time of the evening, whereas it was the normal time for me to arrive home from work." He thought about mentioning their suspicions about Beck but decided to wait.

Hector and Margarita greeted him with hugs and hearty handshakes. Even Ramon came out grinning and gave him several slaps on the back. "Mister O'Reiley! We are honored to have such a celebrity stay with us!" he said as he picked up Thomas's duffle bag.

Thomas looked quizzically at Hector.

"You made the newspaper headlines here in this part of the country, Mister O'Reiley. Seems that the big cat you tracked down and shot had been killing sheep and calves in this area for a couple of years. Some of the ranchers further north had even offered a reward."

Thomas shook his head. "I'm just glad we got him before . . ." his voice trailed off.

"We're thankful too, Mister O'Reiley," Angela chimed in as she cast a quick sideways glance at Thomas. "It would have been awful."

Hector broke into the somber conversation, "Well, come on, young fella! Let's get you settled in before it gets dark!"

*　*　*

It wasn't until after the family had finished eating and was sitting in the large great room that O'Reiley brought up the subject of the shooting of Frank Barnwell. Like Angela, the family was stunned by the information; he spent several minutes recounting the incident and his interpretation of the evidence the shooter left behind.

Hector was the one who offered Beck's name. "Well you know, Beck's pistol is a Colt Buntline; uses a Colt .45 Long. He's real proud of that pistol. He's right handed, tall, slim. Beck's a deer hunter. Doesn't chew or smoke tobacco." He paused. "He might have had cause to go looking for you, at least in his mind."

"What do you mean?" Thomas asked.

Hector waited several seconds before he answered. Finally, "Remember, Beck left the ranch a little over a year ago. I think it was a pretty hard decision for him to make. He'd been here at the ranch for fifteen years. I think he was beginning to think of himself as . . . well, like almost one of the family . . . with the young ones growing up and perhaps leaving in a few years, he could take on a larger role somehow. You come along and are . . ." he nodded briefly in the direction of Angela, "quickly accepted by the family, if you know what I mean . . ." Hector glanced around the table, "I mean that your presence here kind of made him feel shut out."

Thomas shook his head slowly, "I'm so very sorry Hector, if I have caused any trouble here at your ranch, I . . ."

"Mister O'Reiley," Hector interrupted, "you've done nothing wrong. You are always welcome here and we all look forward to your visits. No, the problem rests with Beck Weston. I have no ill opinions toward the man but his feelings were pretty well bruised. He'd cooled off a little by the time he rode out that afternoon; he said he was heading down to Texas but I found out later that he didn't."

O'Reiley frowned. "What do you mean?"

"I have a cousin, Diego Esteban, up north in Los Baños. He happened to see Beck in a livery stable there. Beck was having his horse's front shoe replaced. Beck had been watching the blacksmith while the work was being done; he'd normally be doing the work himself here at the ranch. Anyway, he told Diego he was heading up to the bay area to look for work."

"He was sure it was Beck?"

Hector nodded, "Yes, he was positive it was Beck. Diego has visited here many times and even went deer hunting with Beck a few times."

"And your cousin Diego, has he heard from or seen Beck since then?"

"I don't know. That's been several months ago. The last time Diego was here was in November. There was a family funeral in Terra Bella. Diego and his wife Nelida visited us."

The conversation slowly drifted on to the heavy snow of the past winter.

"It has been very bad, Mister O'Reiley, in the higher mountains." Ramon said. "Some places have reported more than twenty feet of snow. It's begun to melt at the lower elevations and the rivers are running very high. If you're planning on going up while you're here, you must be very careful."

"Angela mentioned that you've already had some flooding."

"We're very fortunate that our land is mostly above the river's flood stage. Some farms and ranches in the valley are under several feet of water."

The big grandfather clock in the great room began to chime the hour. Margarita glanced at the clock. "Well, my two handsome men Hector and

Ramon, it's almost ten o'clock. Mister O'Reiley will want to get an early start in the morning."

Hector and his wife bid O'Reiley good-night and Ramon exited shortly behind them, leaving just the two of them in the large room. The fire in the fireplace had receded into a bed of glowing embers; Thomas and Angela pulled their chairs up close to take advantage of the warmth.

"I am so glad you are here Tom, even for just these few hours." She reached across and took his hand in hers. "I do miss you."

CHAPTER 14

Luke strolled casually into the larger of the two banks in the small town of Snyder, some eighty miles north west of Abilene. He carried a small leather pouch that clinked when he dropped it on the counter in front of the teller.

The teller looked up at him quizzically. "May I be of some help?"

"Got me some Mexican coin I need to exchange."

The teller nodded. "Well, sir, I think I can handle that. Let's see what you've got."

The tall man untied the leather drawstring and poured the contents onto the counter. The teller took one of the coins in his fingers, adjusted his glasses so they rested on the end of his nose and examined the coin closely. "Hmm. These are Nicaraguan hundred-dollar gold coins. They're very rare. Never seen these in circulation." He squinted over his glasses at the tall stranger. "How'd you come across these, Mister?"

Luke leaned nonchalantly against the counter. "Won 'em in a poker game a while back, over in El Paso—never bothered to look at 'em that close. Hell, I thought they were just a couple of rich Mexicans from across the border." He shrugged. "Guess they were from Nicaragua."

The teller turned the coin over several times and shook his head. "Must have been pretty high stakes poker. Well, let's see what you got here." He slid the coins across the counter top, counting. He counted again and wrote a figure on a piece of paper. "Seventy three coins. I'll have to find out what they're worth. Right off hand," the teller rubbed his chin thoughtfully, "I'd say you have between seven-thousand and eight-thousand dollars here, face value, U.S. They could bring a lot more to a collector."

Luke frowned, "a collector?"

"Like I said, you don't see these coins in circulation. They've been mostly gobbled up by coin collectors."

Luke pursed his lips and nodded, "well, how soon can you find out what they're worth?"

The teller glanced at the clock on the wall. "I can have an answer for you in the morning."

The tall man nodded; he was tired of lugging the gold coins around. Besides, when he had once tried to use them, he was met with a shake of the head and "never seen anything like 'em before, mister. Don't know what they are. If I was you, I'd take 'em to a bank."

*　*　*

The Gordon Ranch

Thomas and Angela had sat in the two chairs in front of the fire until it burned down to just a pile of white ashes. Their conversation was sparse and Thomas savored her nearness and the occasional touch of her hand on his arm. It was after midnight when they parted with a brief embrace and the quick, brushing touch of her lips on his cheek that accompanied a whispered, "Good night, Tom."

The empty bunkhouse was cold and without wasting time, Thomas slid under the cover of the blankets. He tossed and turned for a long time, drifting in and out of restless sleep. Silvery light from the waxing crescent, still two days from being a first-quarter moon, streamed through the single window casting dark shadows in corners of the bunkhouse. Thomas was aware of the depth of silence around him, the stillness of the air that seemed to hang, curtain-like, poised in expectation. He wasn't sure exactly when the two eyes appeared just inches from his face. In fact, he wasn't even sure they were in fact eyes. Half asleep, he studied the large center pupils that appeared as fathomless caverns utterly devoid of light, like the sheer darkness of space between stars on a moonless night. Around the pits of darkness were wide surrounding iris's of gold that seemed to shimmer in the darkness. The eyes appeared to float with no apparent means of support and no surrounding facial features, human or otherwise. They didn't move or blink and they were completely lacking any expression or sentiment, yet they mysteriously communicated an undeniable sense of extreme urgency. They spoke to him in a tongue completely foreign; in fact the words were not even actual words but sounds that conveyed meaning that he heard from somewhere inside his head. Somehow he understood what the eyes were saying as they gazed at him as if to accumulate his absolute attention; the sounds and strange harmonies whirled and eddied and became colors that merged; separated and reformed into amorphous patterns and images that sang and chanted a repetitive mantra that expressed an unspoken critical urgency.

The eyes faded slowly into the darkness and finally disappeared entirely; he sat up quickly, as if suddenly awakened. The bunk house was silent; the moon had shifted position and little light entered the space around him. There was no breeze among the young spring sycamore leaves, no bunkhouse boards creaking or shingles rattling. It was the opaque quietness of the darkest part of night, long after the late evening mating clicks and buzzes of insects and the deep bellows of frogs had ended. Even the nighttime predators would have ceased activities by now. For the most part the natural world around him was motionless, quiet and asleep.

As he lay back on the bed, the significance of the images gradually became clear to him.

The eyes staring at him through the darkness had been those of a hawk.

*   *   *

Wednesday morning was warm—unseasonably warm according to Hector as he glanced uneasily at the pale blue sky.

"You must be careful, Thomas," he said quietly. "With this warm weather, the snow will melt very quickly."

O'Reiley smiled to himself at Hector's use of his given name. The rancher was usually very formal with his clients and preferred using last names.

"I'll be very careful, Hector, I promise you." Thomas had risen early and was ready before sunrise.

Hector Gordon nodded. "You have a troubled look on your face this morning. I still don't like the thought of you going up there alone, even after all these years."

Thomas grimaced. "Only been four years, Hector."

"Ah! Then that's even worse." They both laughed.

There was a pause as Thomas finished tightening and checking the cinches. "You know, Angela always wants to go up there with you," Hector said quietly, without looking at Thomas.

"I know."

Hector nodded and continued to gaze off at the mountains silhouetted against the purple eastern sky. "My little girl is growing up. Soon she will want a husband and children." He turned and looked at Thomas. "I hope she finds someone like you, Thomas. You're an honorable man."

O'Reiley didn't know quite how to respond and finally said, "Thank you, Hector. I know she'll find a good man and provide you with many grandchildren."

This made Hector laugh heartily, "Me! A grandfather! I'm not old enough!"

"You will be!"

Angela joined them and handed Thomas a bulging pouch. "Here's a little food for you, Mister O'Reiley. With the deep snow it could be very difficult to provide for yourself. This should last you three or four days."

"Thank you very much, Angela." he retrieved the pouch and fastened it behind his saddle. "You take very good care of me."

"It's all I can do when you ride off all alone like a crazy man into the mountains."

"Angela!" Hector lightly scolded his daughter, "You should not speak to our guest in that manner."

Thomas laughed. "Perhaps I really am a crazy man, Hector!"

Angela turned to Thomas. "I'm already saddled up, Mister O'Reiley. May I ride with you as far as the river?"

Thomas saw Hector's almost motionless nod behind Angela. "Of course, Angela. I would enjoy your company."

*　　*　　*

Rancho de Pacifica

The thin sliver of the emerging moon had set on the western horizon but the sight was not visible to Beck because the thick, early-morning coastal fog hid everything from his view. He sat motionless on the narrow porch of the bunkhouse, the tin mug of coffee that he had boiled on his small wood stove perched carefully on his right knee. He took a few moments to fish out and throw away the broken pieces of egg shell which was part of his coffee-making routine.

The landscape began to lighten with the approaching dawn. Lamps were not yet lighted in the main ranch house and only the barest wisp of smoke drifted from the fireplace that Beck knew was in the main bedroom; he had hauled firewood into the couple's comfortable bedroom many times for the attorney and his wife.

Nelle Dunsworth had decided to spend the week alone at the ranch as Alexander, her attorney husband, had business that would keep him away from the ranch for almost two weeks. Personally, she had questioned what kind of legal business would account for the need to spend nine days in Los Angeles. But she also anticipated some time away from her handsome, but often monotonous, husband who for several months had blamed his late night hours on a flurry of time-consuming work at the law office in the center of San Francisco. She occasionally wondered if Alexander was seeing another woman.

Beck knew all of this, including her intimating her husband's apparent disinterest in intimacy because just yesterday Beck and Nelle Dunsworth had spent well over an hour in lighthearted banter while he had carefully run the currycomb over the stabled horses. Though he had been extremely vigilant to avoid slipping into any presumed informality, he was acutely aware of her fleeting and sometimes clearly indiscreet glances as well as the natural, casual way she used his name. Nelle was several years younger than her husband and her carefully selected clothes simply emphasized her overall attractiveness.

He sipped at the cold coffee, glanced again at the still dark main ranch house. Sometime this morning he would propose that the two of them take a ride up into the deep, tree filled canyon that comprised the upper and seldom visited reaches of the ranch. He guessed that she would immediately suggest taking along a picnic lunch which would include a bottle of wine, because that's what she and Alexander did. With Alexander Dunsworth out of town, the conclusion of this day may bring some relief from the normal boredom of the weekend.

* * *

Near the Kaweah River

"I can see that you are worried about something, Tom. Does it concern you and me?"

O'Reiley smiled and turned toward Angela. "No. Of course not. I've been thinking about Gray Hawk and if he's managed to survive through this brutal winter. He lives in a tiny hut, Angela, in which I can't even stand upright. His only heat is a very small fire in the center of the shelter. He clothes himself in animal skins, sleeps covered with deer and bear skins. He eats food that he's saved over the summer, dried and smoked. He's gathered pine nuts and acorns. He eats roots and tubers, various kinds of dried leaves and tender bark from some trees and shrubs." He paused, then continued, "He's getting old, Angela. Between sixty and seventy years, I figure. Maybe even older than that."

"You really do care for that old Indian, don't you?"

"He saved my life, Angela." He almost mentioned the vision he had early this morning then decided not to. "With the terrible winter, he may need my help."

They rode in silence. The sun had risen above the highest peaks into a clear sky and the air was beginning to lose its nighttime chill. They could hear the deep churning rumble of the swollen Kaweah River nearby.

"I so want to go with you, Tom." The words were barely audible as she rode alongside him.

He looked at her for several seconds before he replied, "I know, Angela, I know. It's just not possible.

She hesitated as their eyes met, "If it *was* possible, would you take me with you?"

Thomas felt as if a knife had been twisted into his heart. His imagination wanted to chase the what if possibilities . . . it would be so easy, perhaps exhilarating . . . he grimaced, "Angela . . . please . . . I know this is not easy for you. It's difficult for me as well."

"Does that mean . . . *no?*" she persisted.

Several long moments went by. The breeze whispered through the trees. He shook his head. "It doesn't mean no," he answered slowly.

She smiled coyly, "Then it must mean *yes.*"

O'Reiley didn't respond. *To either deny or affirm her notion would simply be too heartrending,* he thought, *for both of us.*

* * *

Los Angeles, California, Legal office of Warner, Jenkins and Garcia-Rameriz, Esq.

Alexander Dunsworth arrived at the third floor office of the well known legal firm at nine o'clock. He was met by William Perceval Warner, the senior partner, and was introduced to Ramsfeld Jenkins and Antonio

Garcia-Rameriz, the two junior partners representing their client, Miguel Esperanza-Vincente, the surviving son of Señora Isabella Laurencia Esperanza and heir to the family's vast Nicaraguan properties. It was through this firm that Dunsworth had purchased a major portion of the one-time California Vincente Mexican Land Grant which became Rancho de Pacifica, though he had never met Edmundo Miguel Vincente or his heir Miguel Esperanza-Vincente.

"Señor Esperanza-Vincente should be arriving any moment," Jenkins commented as he shook Dunsworth's hand. Dunsworth merely nodded at the comment as he took his seat at the offered chair on one side of the long conference table. He opened his valise and carefully arranged the papers on the table. All they needed was the signature of Miguel Esperanza-Vincente; then he would hand the man a huge bank check to consummate the deal. It would give him a few extra days in the city away from the burdensome marital life that seemed lately to erode his freedom. The large ranch on the coast was Nelle's idea and it demanded more attention than he had patience or energy for. He would prefer to live in the city near his office where evenings could be spent in relaxed pleasure and weekends could be constructively occupied on case work, rather than suffering saddle sores from the endless horseback riding that seemed to entertain Nelle.

The door opened and a young gentleman entered and was introduced to Dunsworth.

"Ah, Señor Dunsworth!" The man's grip was strong and went with his athletic appearance. He was tall, good looking with a thin mustache and carefully trimmed sideburns. His mannerisms reflected the careful education and upbringing provided by his deceased parents.

"Señor Esperanza-Vincente," Dunsworth stumbled over the hyphenated name, "It is my pleasure as well. Please accept my sincere sympathies for the loss of your mother."

Antonio Garcia-Rameriz translated quickly for Esperanza-Vincente and the young man nodded solemnly, added "Gracias, Señor Dunsworth."

"Señor Esperanza-Vincente has asked that I translate for him, as he has difficulty with some English legal terms," Antonio Garcia-Rameriz said. Esperanza-Vincente nodded in apparent agreement.

"Gentlemen, shall we get down to business?" This time it was Ramsfeld Jenkins. He pointed at the chairs along the table and each took a seat.

Esperanza-Vincente leaned toward Antonio Garcia-Rameriz and spoke quietly near his ear.

"Señor Esperanza-Vincente has a few questions, if you do not mind," Garcia-Rameriz said.

Dunsworth nodded. "Of course."

"Señor Esperanza-Vincente would like to know if you are the same Señor Alexander Dunsworth that purchased a portion of the Santiago Agusto Vincente Land Grant near Santa Cruz?"

"Why, yes I am," Dunsworth replied, looking at Vincente. *How did he find out?*

Garcia-Rameriz spoke briefly to Vincente; the young man smiled then spoke for several moments to his translator.

"Señor Esperanza-Vincente would like to say that he is happy that the land of his great-grandfather is in such capable hands. He says he visited it once when he was a young boy, before it was sold."

"Please tell Señor Esperanza-Vincente that I would be honored if he would visit again."

Garcia-Rameriz spoke softly to the young man, who smiled and nodded to Dunsworth. He then turned to his translator and whispered for several long seconds into his ear. Eventually, Garcia-Rameriz turned back toward Dunsworth. "Shall we get down to business? My client has other pressing obligations today."

"Of course." Dunsworth was grateful to get on with the business at hand.

"Excellent. Señor Esperanza-Vincente would like to know what plans you have for the future of the property in Nicaragua."

Dunsworth nodded thoughtfully. "Certainly. Please tell him that the property is being purchased for long-term investment purposes."

Garcia-Rameriz spoke briefly to his client, who nodded in understanding. He in turn whispered into Garcia-Rameriz's ear.

Garcia-Rameriz cleared his throat before passing the young man's inquiry to Dunsworth. "Señor Esperanza-Vincente understands the premise of wealthy Americans investing in Nicaraguan land but he wants to know more . . . umm . . . specifically . . . how the property will be utilized." Dunsworth noted the transient glance from Garcia-Rameriz to his two law partners.

Dunsworth frowned slightly. This was supposed to have been already taken care of. Months of communication with Esperanza-Vincente had supposedly taken place through these Los Angeles attorneys and Vincente's agreement to sell the vast tract of over two and a half million acres had appeared to be a foregone conclusion, awaiting only the final legal actions to complete the sale.

"Please tell your client that the immense size of the property dictates that it be divided into smaller parcels for sale but we have not made any immediate plans."

Esperanza-Vincente frowned slightly as he listened to his lawyer whisper to him. This time his response was long and Garcia-Ramirez made fast notes as the man went on and on. Finally Esperanza-Vincente indicated he was finished and Garcia-Ramirez leaned back in his chair to study what he had written.

When he spoke, his face was unsmiling. "Señor Esperanza-Vincente is very much concerned, Mister Dunsworth. He says that the property has been in his mother and father's families for many generations. He says that the land is very historic, with great natural beauty and value. He says that it has provided for the two families as cattle country for several generations." He paused and cleared his throat, "He is also quite aware that it straddles an important route from the Caribbean Sea to Lake Nicaragua and that it might be the intention of the investors to realize a very large profit by selling that route to the American government so that shipping a canal can be built connecting the two seas." He raised his eyebrows and gazed intently at Dunsworth.

Dunsworth years in the court room had taught him how to remain composed. He smiled as he spoke, "I can assure your client that the investors we are referring to are prominent businessmen, trusted men of impeccable character and absolutely beyond reproach. As their attorney, I am not privy to their future intentions. It has not been a part of our negotiations." It was an absolute bold faced lie and Dunsworth knew it.

Once again Esperanza-Vincente appeared to listen intently and nodded as his attorney translated Dunsworth's response. A short and very quiet conversation transpired between the two and then Garcia-Rameriz reached into his valise and extracted a single sheet of paper, showed it briefly to his grim-faced client, creased it down the center and slid it across the table to Dunsworth.

Dunsworth reached apprehensively for the paper and unfolded it. There were five names carefully scribed on the paper in alphabetical order: Ambrose, DePallin, Dunsworth, McGarnet and Parker. Following each name was a dollar amount and a number that represented the percentage of the total entered at the bottom of the column. Dunsworth's name was followed by the major percentage—forty percent.

The room suddenly seemed to tip and Dunsworth fought to keep the astonishment from showing on his face. His right hand shook so badly that he casually slipped it under the table to hide it from the other attorneys. He knew all four of the listed clients; he had personally contacted and negotiated with each of the men named on the paper but he had been almost fanatical about not creating any sort of a traceable record of these dealings, instead committing the facts and names and figures to memory. Suddenly, like an electrical shock, the realization struck him. There was, in fact, one person beside Dunsworth who knew all the names on the list and the extent of their financial commitments. The awareness of who that person was and the fact that he had not already made the connection made him want to vomit. *Sophia. Sophia Jenkins. Ramsfeld Jenkins. Brother and sister!*

When he glanced across the table he saw the barely hidden smile on Jenkins' lips. There were long seconds of uncomfortable silence as Dunsworth looked again at the paper. Finally Garcia-Rameriz leaned forward over the table and glared at Dunsworth. "We know that you are in fact one of the so-called investors, Mister Dunsworth. You have not been negotiating on behalf of *clients*; you have been arranging a transaction as a major share holder of this investment group you have cobbled together. As the major shareholder, you would be in a position to put your partners to an extreme disadvantage when the property is resold, as I am sure you and your *clients* plan to do for a very large profit. I believe in the legal business that is called a conflict of interest." He paused as the young Nicaraguan leaned toward his attorney and whispered. Garcia-Rameriz nodded and then bent forward against the table and spoke very quietly and intently. "Our client has directed me to inform you that he has no intention of giving away this extremely valuable property to a group of *corruptos de América del Norte*." He smiled a toothy smile, "I'm sure you need no translation."

Dunsworth sat as if frozen in place.

There was another long silence before Garcia-Rameriz shrugged and smiled as if offering an apology. "However, he also respects a good business transaction. He has agreed to sell the property to your *investors* for exactly twice the amount indicated on the paper. It is, as you know Mister Dunsworth, still a very excellent price."

Alexander Dunsworth blinked his eyes in astonishment. "Sir, surely, you must have made a mistake. The price your client suggests is preposterous. It is . . ."

"Mister Dunsworth," Garcia-Rameriz interrupted, his voice no longer the well-practiced liquid-like courtroom modulation, "perhaps I do not make myself clear. You see, our client, Señor Esperanza-Vincente does not understand a single word of our conversation. He is as ignorant of the English language as a fence post." He turned slightly and smiled candidly at his client who nodded in apparent agreement and smiled back. "This is no longer an *offer to sell*; it is now *our condition of sale*. You see, *Señor corruptos de América del Norte,* we have sufficient information and evidence to request the Nicaraguan government to officially investigate the unfortunate death of Señora Isabella Laurencia Esperanza. We have been informed by various . . . sources . . . that there are particulars that link her brutal murder . . . I repeat, *Señor Dunsworth,* her *murder . . .* to a paid assassin from the United States, a clever man who goes by the *nom de plume El Culebra.* You and your partners may want to reconsider our offer before the investigation begins. It could be much more than simply embarrassing for all of you."

"This is a serious mistake! You are blackmailing me . . ."

Garcia-Rameriz shrugged. "If the shoe was on the other foot, perhaps we would see it that way as well . . ."

*　　*　　*

High Sierra Back Country

Because it was on the south side and caught the full day of sunshine, the switchback trail up the side of the mountain was nearly clear of snow. It wasn't until O'Reiley neared the top that the snow became a real factor. By the time he reached the enormous Sequoia the Indian called *Standing Tall,* the snow was a foot or more deep, with drifts and shady gullies with three or more feet of snow.

The air had turned much cooler and he flipped his coat collar up against the chill. It was late afternoon when he reached the old deer camp and found it covered by a thick layer of snow. He checked the perimeter of the camp and found no human tracks; Gray Hawk had not been here, at least during the past week or so. There were only a few hours of daylight left and he headed for the old Indian's shelter, still several miles distant. The snow became even deeper and it took him a long time to reach the shaman's shelter. O'Reiley entered the shelter and found the fire pit cold, even when he dug his fingers deep into the ash. He checked for signs of the Indian's activity. His fur wraps were missing, so he was probably out hunting. *He's usually back before dark,* O'Reiley thought. He checked once again outside and finally found prints left in the deep snow, heading away from the shelter area.

O'Reiley tied his horse and as an afterthought took his Winchester from the scabbard, levered a round into the receiver and started following the tracks. They led first toward the small creek, then crossed it and followed parallel to it upstream about a mile. The tracks were at least a day old; perhaps the old man had left as long ago as the previous morning. He stopped once and examined a good set of footprints. The pace appeared normal, considering the amount of snow. He didn't appear to be favoring either leg and seemed to be moving with typical determination and confidence, not pausing to look around. *He knows exactly where he's going.* Another quarter of a mile and the prints turned sharply to the right, followed a small ridge and then dropped down the side of a narrow canyon. The prints showed signs of the old man slipping from time to time and that was not normal. *I've got to find Gray Hawk! There's less than an hour of daylight left.*

He stopped short and listened. He had heard something . . . there it was again . . . not human . . . a snarling roar far in the distance but in the direction of the footprints. He increased his effort, plunging into the deep snow with legs that were beginning to burn under the physical effort. *Again! There's that roar! Closer this time . . .*

His breath was coming is short gasps now. *The roar once again, close now!* But this time it was followed by a different sound—a human, guttural roar of defiance. *Where? Where?* O'Reiley swept the area ahead and down the edge of the canyon with his eyes as he struggled forward in the deep snow. The footprints dropped quickly down the side, sliding, staggering, no longer sure footed.

It was then that O'Reiley saw the bear, now standing on its thick hind legs, waving the huge claw-equipped front feet and bellowing at the small human in front of him. The human roar came again and he finally spied the old Indian, his right thigh buried deep in the snow, the other leg slipping and struggling for a foothold. He held the knife that O'Reiley had given him in his right hand, poised and ready to thrust into the animal that was less than ten feet away.

The Indian growled once again, the sound echoing through the deep forest and he waved the knife in resolute though pitiful defiance. The massive bear bellowed in angry, rage-filled response, showing its huge teeth, then stood even higher on his hind legs before it lunged through the deep snow toward the old man. The Indian's lips were drawn back over his teeth and the warlike howl of fearless challenge roared from his lungs once again.

O'Reiley brought the Winchester up to his shoulder and snapped off a shot, immediately levered another round and fired again and then a third time. The first bullet struck the huge bear in the left shoulder, the second followed the same path and the third hit him in the thickness of his neck. Without a sound, the huge animal toppled forward onto the Indian as the three rifle shots echoed among the mountains.

CHAPTER 15

<u>Tuesday, May 27, 1902, Gray Hawk's shelter</u>
The long, slogging trek back to Gray Hawk's small shelter had been grueling; after finally putting the old Indian down and covering him with furs, Thomas had slumped weakly against the side of the shelter and nearly caved in to both the mental and physical exhaustion.

Thomas had pried the huge bulk of the dead bear off the Indian, rolling it to one side before he could even find the old man pressed into the snow beneath the carcass. Gray Hawk lay on his left side, his right leg buried to his hip in the snow. Thomas made sure the Indian was breathing, then went to work freeing his leg which was trapped between a large boulder and a fallen tree. Covered with several inches of snow, the tree refused to budge under his pulling and tugging. Almost six inches in diameter, the upper branches of the pine tree were buried solidly in the snow and the shaman's lower leg was wedged tightly between the rock and the trunk of the tree. Thomas used his knife and began carving away the bark and wood next to the Indian's leg, notching deeply on either side, then prying out the chunk of wood between. It had taken nearly a half an hour to free the man's leg and by that time darkness had begun to descend over the deep woods; the cold air sliced through his clothing. Thomas quickly felt the man's leg and decided that there were no broken bones or serious wounds to the muscles. The old man was breathing shallowly and was still unconscious; his pulse was weak.

Getting the unconscious Indian back to the shelter had taken every bit of energy and perseverance that Thomas could muster. He'd carried the old man diagonally across his back, the Indian's right arm looped over Thomas's left shoulder and his right leg carried in the crook of Thomas's right arm. With the added weight on his back, Thomas's feet sank even deeper into the snow and ice; each staggering step became an agony of balance and struggle in the deep snow. The sun went down behind the tall surrounding mountains and darkness fell. Three times he stumbled and fell under the burden, sprawling face down in the snow and weighted by the load on his back. The tiny crescent moon cast only a pale glow through the tree tops. Guided by memory and the vague trail of footsteps, he finally lurched into the cold shelter, exhausted beyond the ability to even think coherently.

It took almost half an hour before Thomas could muster the energy to get a fire started in the cold fire pit but the eventual warmth slowly penetrated the shelter and pushed the immediate weariness aside. He searched the hut and found some dried tubers, herbs and small strips of dried meat; then he started a thin stew cooking over the fire. He checked often on the old man but he was still unconscious, though his breathing had grown stronger. It took a long time for the icy water to boil and for the impromptu stew to begin to cook but eventually the inviting vapors swirled through the tiny shelter. Thomas helped himself to some of the thin broth, his first nourishment since leaving the Gordon ranch early that morning.

He heard the old man stir and leaned over him. "Gray Hawk. It's Thomas."

The shaman opened his eyes and blinked several times. "Tah-moss! I called for you," he said weakly.

"I heard you calling, my friend. I came as quickly as I could."

"I knew you would come, Tah-moss." The old man was fatigued and his voice quavered.

Thomas gently lifted the Indian's head and pressed an enameled mug with some of the broth to his lips. Gray Hawk sipped hungrily then nodded to let his head fall back. "The bear . . . what happened to the bear?" His eyes were closed as he asked.

"I shot and killed him, Gray Hawk. If I had been a few minutes later, you would have been the bear's dinner."

Gray Hawk nodded. "I know that old bear, Tah-moss. I have named him *Crazy Bear*. He has been around here for three winters. I have seen many of his kills." He paused. "He had bad poison in his heart. He killed because he got satisfaction from killing, not because he was hungry."

"Satisfaction?"

"I believe *Crazy Bear* had a terrible injury that he lived with. He did not understand the cause of his pain. We will see tomorrow, Tah-moss." The old man sighed wearily. "Tomorrow . . . I must sleep now."

Thomas watched as the Indian dozed off; after a few minutes of restless twitching, his breathing became regular and his face relaxed. Thomas put more small pieces of wood on the fire and checked that the deerskin flap was covering the entrance to the shelter. A small hole in the roof let the smoke out and the shelter slowly warmed. Thomas sat near the fire hugging his knees to his chest and listened to the old man's breathing. *How many years had the Indian lived here? If he was twenty years old when he had killed the six miners in 1850, he would be over seventy years old now. He would have been in hiding for over fifty years, avoiding contact with other humans, surviving entirely on his own. Living off the earth . . . Enduring terrible winters . . . Hunger . . .* Thomas shook his head and listened to the shaman's shallow snoring and occasional mumbled words in a language that he didn't understand; he wondered what sort of dreams and images confronted the Indian in his restless sleep. *Was he visited by the same kinds of nightmarish spirits and apparitions that had haunted and sometimes terrified him on the island?*

Thomas slowly lay on his side, put his head on the small packet of food that Angela had sent with him and fell asleep.

* * *

<u>Union Pacific Railroad, San Joaquin Valley, California</u>
Alexander Dunsworth barely heard the rhythmic clatter of the train's wheels as the overnight train from Los Angeles to San Jose rattled northward through the seemingly endless expanse of the vast San Joaquin Valley. Though he'd taken his dinner in the dining car and settled for the night in one of the sleeping compartments, sleep would not come and he spent the evening and now late night hours mulling over the events of the past day. He mentally berated himself for his own stupidity; how could he not have grasped the connection between Sophia Jenkins and her brother, Ramsfeld Jenkins, the attorney? He shook his head. How quickly he'd fallen for the tantalizing enchantment of Sophia's soft body, her indulgent attention to his rambling discourse, their shared glasses of wine and the long delightful evenings of intimacy. Sophia must have repeated everything he had naively shared during their private times together. He'd

been such a fool! He frowned. But even more worrisome was Ramsfeld's apparent knowledge about the assassin.

Dunsworth himself knew very little; he'd met a man, Bret Solomon, in Sacramento during a trip to a client there. Over drinks at an expensive restaurant, casual conversation had revealed common frustrations. A short time later he'd been contacted in his San Francisco office. The money had been agreed to and provided by the investment group; information was passed on, money exchanged. And then somehow it had happened far away in Nicaragua. Was it even possible that such a vague and fragmented trail could be traced back to him? Had he ever, even under the influence of her charm and excessive wine, alluded to the plan to kill the Nicaraguan woman? He thought not but he was uncertain. He'd have to make sure Sophia said no more.

Señor Esperanza Vincente, the well-dressed Nicaraguan playboy and sole heir to the family property, was going to be swindled by the corrupt legal firm in Los Angeles, not that it mattered a nit to Dunsworth. What mattered was that they had beaten him at his own scheme. He'd have to go back again to the small group of investors and solicit more money; their eventual profit would be less than what they expected.

He frowned—perhaps there was still another way. It would mean more risk on his part but more profit for him, as well. *Rancho de Pacifica.* He could use the ranch for collateral; the ranch was in his name, purchased as an investment before he'd married; Nelle would never even have to know. He could secure a short-term loan and the partners would not know either. His personal percentage of the proceeds would double when they sold the property in Nicaragua. Of course, he'd have to eventually deal with the legal records of the sale but that could be handled easily enough. As an attorney, he could *always* make the paper trail much more complicated, especially when dealing with a foreign country . . .

*   *   *

The High Sierras

Thomas awoke with a start. The old Indian had rolled onto his side and groaned. Light was beginning to creep through the openings around the deerskin flap covering the entrance to the shelter and the fire had died to just a few embers. Thomas stirred the coals and carefully placed more wood on them, blowing gently until a small flame licked at the newly placed sticks. Within minutes a small but warm blaze was going and the shelter quickly warmed. He put the remaining soup on to heat and checked the old man.

When he stepped outside the eastern sky was beginning to turn purple-gold with dawn and the crisp morning air hung motionless. Though snow still lay heavily on the ground, the air seemed to convey a sense of impending warmth. He walked to the small stream, squatted and washed his face in the icy water and drank from his cupped hands. The stream gurgled as it slid over the rocks and somewhere in the distance a blue jay squawked noisily; Thomas smiled to himself in the pleasure of his surroundings. The wisp of smoke from the small fire curled lazily around the shelter before drifting vertically and disappearing into the tall trees.

"You take pleasure in this morning, Tah-moss."

Thomas spun to find the shaman standing outside the shelter. "Yes, Gray Hawk. This is a good morning and I like it." He studied the old man for a few moments. "How do you feel this morning?"

The Indian nodded his head slowly. "Very tired. I feel like a very old man." Then he threw his head back and laughed, "Ha! I am a very old man."

Thomas brought out the food that Angela had packed for him and the two men shared the dried beef and biscuits. The shaman ate hungrily, relating how he had become trapped, spent the night and the following day in the freezing weather and being discovered by *Crazy Bear* just before Thomas arrived.

"I could not move my leg. The more I struggled, the worse it got. There was nothing for me to hold onto and my weight was on the wrong foot. I could not move. It was very cold. I had only my knife—the knife you gave me, Tah-moss. I thought I might have to cut my leg off. I called for you. That night as I tried to remain awake, I called for you, my friend. The next day I heard *Crazy Bear* looking for me. I knew he would kill me when he found me. But I am a warrior, Tah-moss. I would fight the bear to the death. I was ready. And you heard me and came and found me. You saved my life."

"And you saved mine, if you remember, Gray Hawk."

The old man nodded slowly. "Yes, I remember."

After they ate, the Indian said "we must return to *Crazy Bear*, Tah-moss. My knife is there. And I must say good-by to *Crazy Bear*." He watched Thomas's quizzical look. "You will understand, Tah-moss."

The trek back to where Gray Hawk was trapped took a long time. Both men were tired from the previous day but the sun began to warm the air and the warmth gradually instilled a fresh energy in them.

They found the bear's carcass where they had left it the night before. Thomas had never been this close to a bear and was surprised at the size of the animal. The clawed paws were several inches across and the claws themselves were almost three inches long. The Indian carefully inspected the carcass and finally called Thomas to look at what he had discovered. On the upper leg under the right front shoulder was a huge open sore; a rotted splinter still hung partially exposed with the rest buried deeply into the bears flesh. The fur had been chewed away around the wound but it had become infected and the flesh was putrefied around it.

"It is an old wound, Tah-moss. Perhaps two years. An accident. Perhaps he fell on a broken limb during a fight with another male bear." He shook his head. "It would be very painful. The terrible pain would make him act crazy." He stood alongside the huge animal and raised his arms high over his head and began to chant, his eyes closed and his arms motionless. His head moved and nodded occasionally as if listening, but the chanting went on for several minutes. Once he glanced quickly and motioned at Thomas as he stood silently listening. Finally the song ended and the final echoes died in the woods. The Indian turned to Thomas.

"I told him that my heart was aching that he had to die this way. I told him I was sad that he had such a terrible wound that made him crazy. I told him that someday he and I will walk together in the forest as friends without fear of each other. I told him that his spirit is free now, that he should leave peacefully, and that I will allow the earth to reclaim his flesh and bones as it should be. I told him I am sorry that I called him *Crazy Bear* and that even humans do bad things when we are badly hurt or injured. I told him that your name is Tah-moss and that you are a good man. I asked his spirit to not blame you as you were only saving my life. I told him that his next life will be without pain, hunger or fear, that it will be filled with warm sunlight, that he will always have much honey and fat berries to eat and cool streams to catch fish and to bathe." Gray Hawk looked solemnly at Thomas. "I told him that from now on we will call him *Ha Sook Inya—Bear that Walks with Pain.* That is what I told him."

Thomas nodded wordlessly, realizing how much of the Indian's language he now understood and how much they were able to communicate with

177

the hand signs they had used for three years and the English language words the shaman now knew and used.

* * *

<u>Rancho de Pacifica</u>
It was almost noontime and the thin wisp of wood smoke curled upward from the ranch house into the cool coastal air. Dunsworth glanced around quickly; it was an unusual time of day for Nelle to have a fire in the bedroom fireplace.

Everything seemed in order; it was quiet and Beck was nowhere in sight but that in itself was not unusual. He could be scouting for trees to cut for firewood or caring for the horses or riding to check on the cattle, or any of the numerous tasks that kept him busy through the week.

Early this morning Dunsworth had driven his own carriage over the narrow mountain road that connected San Jose and the small ocean-side community of Santa Cruz, planning to surprise Nelle with his early return from Los Angeles. He would take the rest of the day off then finish the week in San Francisco, making one last visit with Sophia. He had still not decided how he would confront her over the issue of revealing his confidential conversations to her brother. Besides, he was experiencing a sense of uncertainty now that his anger had had time to dissipate. The thought had already occurred to him that perhaps he should not act too hastily; after all, Sophia was a welcome and stimulating respite from his lackluster marriage to Nelle.

He looped the reins over the small handrail and stepped quietly onto the porch and through the unlocked front door. He was about ready to call out for Nelle when he heard the sounds coming from the bedroom. He stopped dead in his tracks and listened, his right hand still grasping the door knob. The sounds were unmistakable, the childlike giggling laughter of Nelle and the coarse mumble of the ranch hand Beck, then softly spoken words and faint whispers of pleasure amid the recognizable squeak of bedsprings.

The realization struck Dunsworth like a bolt of lightning; he felt the blood drain from his face and for a moment he had to hold tightly to the door knob or fall. *Nelle and Beck!* He shut his eyes for a moment as if trying to force his mind to remove the shocking certainty. *Nelle and Beck!* He opened his eyes and a pitiless composure seeped slowly through his body.

The custom-made solid walnut gun cabinet sat upright in the near corner. He always kept his two hunting rifles and a supply of ammunition stored in the cabinet alongside a loaded shotgun retained as a deterrent against intruders and predators. He had not needed to use the twelve gauge double barreled weapon for several months, ever since a pack of coyotes had been attracted to a young calf the that vet had advised that he hold for observation in the corral next to the barn. He reached to the top of the cabinet, slid the hidden panel covering the cavity holding the key to the cabinet and silently unlocked the heavy door. He knew the twelve gauge was already loaded with lethal double-aught buck shot; he lifted it gently from the rack, eased off the safety and cradled the gun in the crook of his left arm.

As he approached the bedroom door, the rhythmic high-pitched squeak of the bedsprings was joined by the couple's muted whispers and moans. Dunsworth nodded his head slowly as a ruthless smile creased his face. *This ought to be very interesting!*

He eased the door bedroom open with the toe of his shoe and caught sight of the two of them on the bed, sheets tangled and wrinkled, their naked bodies intertwined and glistening with perspiration. Their sounds filled the room and Dunsworth felt the cold flush of anger return. He pointed the shotgun at the pair.

"Beck, you son-of-a-bitch!" he shouted, "get away from my wife!"

The tall ranch hand reacted as if he had been stuck with a knife. Without even glancing in the direction of the voice, he scrambled off the bed, scraping up the sheet and draping it in front of himself in a feeble attempt to cover his nakedness as he backed into the corner. "Good God almighty!" he stammered, "What the hell are you doing here?"

Dunsworth motioned at Beck with the shotgun, "just shut your damned mouth and watch, Beck!" He walked over to the bed where Nelle still lay naked, her mouth wide open in shock, eyes locked on her husband with the shotgun now pointed directly at her.

Dunsworth slowly let the end of the shotgun barrel drop until it rested in the valley between Nelle's breasts. He was shaking his head sadly, slowly. "You dim-witted, pathetic whore," he said, just before he pulled the trigger.

The shotgun recoiled in his grip; the deafening blast filled the room and a spray of blood splattered across the walls and the sheet held by Beck.

Beck staggered, trying desperately to hide behind the sheet in the corner and distance himself from the grisly horror on the bed, his eyes wide and his face drained of blood. "Oh, my God! You killed her!" he groaned, "You killed Nelle!"

"That's *Missus Dunsworth* to you, Beck!" Dunsworth said quietly. The shotgun rose and pointed directly at Beck's head. "Except I didn't kill her. You killed her, you murdering bastard." He motioned with the shotgun. "Pick up your stuff. You have ten minutes to get your gear together and clear out. If you're not gone in ten minutes, I *will* find you and kill you. You better get out now, before I change my mind!"

Beck stood frozen in place for several seconds, his mouth working at forming words but no sound came out. Finally, he bent over, scooped up his clothing and boots and still grasping the blood-soaked sheet, hobbled to and through the bedroom door. Dunsworth heard the front door slam and he stood stock still, listening. In a few minutes he heard the hurried footsteps as Beck scrambled toward the corral and shortly after heard the horse galloping away, urged on by the strained commands of the cowboy hunched over in the saddle trying to make himself a small target.

Silence descended over the ranch, only to be broken once again several minutes later by a second shotgun blast that came from the Dunsworth's bedroom.

Two hours later Dunsworth secured his carriage, entered the wood-fronted sheriff's office squeezed into the line of buildings on the main street of Santa Cruz and slumped heavily into the chair across from Sheriff Joe McGee.

"Sheriff, my name's Alexander Dunsworth and I'm here to report a murder. Someone . . . somebody killed my wife, Nelle Dunsworth."

The sheriff sat up straight and pulled a sheet of paper in front of him, started jogging notes. "You say her name is Nelle Dunsworth?"

"That's right. She's . . . she was my wife. We have a spread a few miles north of here—Rancho de Pacifica."

"Yeah, I know where that is. Why don't you tell me what you know?" Sheriff McGee leaned forward.

"I've been out of town on business—Los Angeles. I'm an attorney. Got back last night on the train and spent the night in San Jose. I came home in my carriage this morning, about eleven o'clock. I . . . I found Nelle's body in our bed. She'd been shot . . . up real close . . . twice. Shotgun. First shot blew a hole in the center of her chest." Dunsworth swallowed and shook his head. "Second shot . . ." he shook his head again and looked down, "second shot took her head off." He rubbed his eyes and groaned. "God! It was horrible."

The sheriff looked at Dunsworth for several seconds. "I'm terribly sorry Mister Dunsworth. You just take your time. I know this is very difficult for you." He waited several seconds before he asked, "what else did you see?"

"Blood splattered all over the wall . . . the bed. My wife . . . Nelle . . . was on her back, naked. I figure he raped her then shot her."

The sheriff tilted his head, "Who raped and shot her?"

"My ranch hand. Beckley Weston. Goes by *Beck*. Been working for me for several months. He was just a drifter looking for a job," Dunsworth shrugged, "and I needed a hired hand." He paused and then added, "I suspect he's had a keen eye on my Nelle from the beginning."

The sheriff was writing rapidly. "Tell me why you think this guy Weston did it."

"I found my shotgun lying on the mattress of his bunk in the bunkhouse. I keep it loaded and locked in the gun cabinet in the main house. Both barrels had been fired. Beck was gone. He'd cleared out his gear and skedaddled. Clothes, bedroll, horse, saddle, everything. The murdering son-of-a-bitch high-tailed it!"

McGee nodded slowly. "Okay, Mister Dunsworth. Tell you what. I'm going to send one of my deputies out to take a look." He glanced at Dunsworth as he kept writing, then "You haven't touched or moved anything out there have you?"

"No sir," Dunsworth responded, shaking his head, "absolutely not! I walked in and came right back out after I saw my poor Nelle. Had to get some fresh air . . ."

The sheriff nodded and waited but Dunsworth was not going to add anything. "Good, then. My deputy Charles Watts will ride out there with the coroner and they'll take care of everything at that end. I'd like you to stay here with me while I write up a report, if that's all right with you."

Dunsworth acquiesced, his eyes downcast. "Sure." A few seconds went by, "I just can't believe this has happened to my poor Nelle."

Sheriff McGee leaned back in his chair, paused for just a moment, then turned and called through the partially open door to the room behind the wall, "C'mere, Charley! Got a job for you."

*　*　*

<u>Gray Hawk's shelter</u>

Gray Hawk and Thomas each sat cross-legged in the small shelter. The afternoon coolness had descended upon the forest; they built a small fire to roast the rabbit that Gray Hawk had killed on the way back from where the Indian had been attacked by the bear. Thomas watched in appreciation as the Indian quickly prepared the rabbit for the spit. There were no wasted movements, no awkward attempts. Every effort was clean and automatic. The knife flashed expertly and in minutes the job was done, the rabbit stuffed with herbs and roots, attached to the spit and set to roasting over the small blaze.

"You do that so effortlessly, Gray Hawk."

The old man smiled, "Easy after you've done it a thousand times, Tah-moss."

Thomas nodded. "You've been a good teacher, my friend."

"You are a good student." The Indian studied him closely. "You never told me why you wanted to learn the ways of my people."

Thomas didn't answer for several long moments. It was not something he had even thought through for himself. At first perhaps it had simply been curiosity, later, a desire to learn and master some of the Indian's skills. Now . . . he was not sure. Perhaps a desire buried somewhere deep within his psyche to lead a different life than the one that he had been dealt. He recognized his own need to get away occasionally from civilization and all of its various stresses, pulls and demands. The mountains . . . he had learned to love the outdoors and the wilderness with its many facets of weather and beauty. His thoughts drifted; the visions and memories of his experiences came and went . . .

He looked and the old man was nodding; Thomas realized that he had been talking and sharing his thoughts with the Indian for some time without even realizing it.

"I am talking too much, Gray Hawk."

The shaman smiled and shook his head, "No, Tah-moss. It is the first time I have been privileged to see within your thoughts and it is good that you tell me your story."

The two were silent for several minutes. The fragrance of the roasting rabbit began to permeate the small shelter and the warmth of the small fire felt good. Thomas took the opportunity to study the old man. He seemed to have aged in the few years they had known one another. The wrinkles in the Indian's face were deeper and there were more of them. His hands had a slight tremor to them and his eyes seemed not as bright. His hair had turned mostly gray and was thinner that it had been just those few years ago though he still wore it in a long, single braid that reached to the center of his back. His arms and legs were thinner and less muscled; the once solid and prominent chest muscles had begun to wrinkle and sag. Thomas wondered how the old man had managed to survive the brutal winter.

"I am an old man, Tah-moss," Gray Hawk said as if reading Thomas's thoughts. "Not many winters are left before I join *Ha Sook Inya* and the many friends that I lost during that terrible time many years ago. My body will return to the earth and my spirit will be free to soar," he smiled, "like a hawk. It is good that you and I have met and became friends, Tah-moss. I would have perhaps carried my hatred of your people to my death but no longer. In many ways, your people and my people are much the same." He poked at the fire with a stick. "It is sad that our people never learned how to live together in peace."

CHAPTER 16

<u>Thursday, May 29, 1902, Abilene, Texas</u>

Luke sat near the window of his second floor hotel room. The shade was drawn against the late afternoon sunshine that slanted in but he pulled it back enough to be able to peer at the street below. The daily scramble of people was drifting into the late day lull; shopping had been accomplished, business deals were settled; shops and offices were about ready to lock up for the day. In another hour the street would be taken over once again by the cowboys who would wander into town for a night of carousing and general hell-raising.

He slid the shade open a little further and looked up and down the dusty street. Perhaps it was time for him to move on, though he was partial to the lazy, dusty town where people tended to mind their own business. He had for a while considered moving his operations back to Louisiana but decided against that option. Then recently he had thought seriously about gathering up his earnings, scattered among several Texas banks to buy and run a saloon. But that scheme had also been short lived; he realized that he still anticipated the thrill of planning and setting up a kill with the heady rush of the moment when he pulled the trigger and watched the deadly impact of the fifty-caliber bullet. And, of course, he looked forward to the subsequent pinnacle of sadistic experience aided by an unsuspecting young woman who would pay the brutal and deadly consequence for her reckless choice.

What he really needed was a final challenging and high paying mission, something grand and important that would make the newspaper headlines—but the network had seemed, like a shallow desert arroyo in mid-summer, to have dried up. Perhaps it was time to personally extend a few cautious feelers outside of his network.

*   *   *

<u>Gray Hawk's Shelter</u>

The shaman sat cross-legged across from Thomas. He had told Thomas earlier of his plans to introduce him to the Indian ritual of the ceremonial smoke. Both men had bathed in the icy stream and then clothed themselves in their breech cloth and light leather vest. No evening meal was planned and the old Indian had started a fire outside the shelter in which he had placed several large stones to be heated until they were nearly red-hot. He had assembled around him the various implements of the ceremony: eagle and hawk feathers, a long ceremonial smoking pipe, small amounts of white and red and black powders, various herbs and leaves, gourds filled with water. He said little during this preparation while Thomas sat and watched with growing interest.

Finally the shaman secured one of the red-hot stones between two sticks and rushed it into the shelter and dropped it into the shallow fire pit on top of the glowing coals. He repeated this process two more times, then pulled the deer skin flap tightly over the opening to the shelter. The shaman sat quietly for several moments, then sprinkled water from one of the gourds on the stones. Steam rose in billows filling the shelter and coiling around them. He sprinkled some of the herbs on the hot stones causing the air to become heavy with an aromatic but pungent smoke. Thomas watched as the Indian dipped his fingers into the white powder and made stroke marks on his face. Gray Hawk motioned to the powder and to Thomas in an obvious invitation for Thomas to do likewise. Cautiously, Thomas dipped his finger into the powder and attempted to replicate the marks Gray Hawk had made. The shaman smiled and nodded, added some more herbs to the hot rocks, gathered up several feathers in his hand and used them to fan the smoke across to Thomas, then to himself.

The shelter was growing quite warm and Thomas had begun to perspire, the sweat running down his chest in rivulets. The shaman adorned himself with more powder marks, this time black on his forehead and both shoulders; Thomas did likewise. The marks became more fanciful; circles, spirals, arcs and jagged lightning bolts covered his chest. He changed to the red powder and covered both his ears, forehead and below his eyes in a mask-like pattern. Thomas did the same, feeling more at ease with each step of the process.

185

More water was sprinkled on the stones; and steam filled the shelter and his lungs; sweat ran in small streams down his neck and back and chest. The old man picked up the long smoking pipe, placed some herbs and leaves in it, lit it with a coal from the fire and puffed it into life. He sucked the smoke into his lungs and held it there, then passed the pipe to Thomas. Thomas inhaled the heavy non-tobacco smoke, nearly choking on the acrid yet sweet taste.

The old Indian began to chant. Thomas leaned back, sucked in another lungful of smoke and held the pipe out to Gray Hawk. The Indian took it and held it while chanting. *"Oo-oo-ha-ma-ma-cha-ha-ma-cha . . ."* The repeated ritual of splashing water on the rocks, adding herbs and leaves and passing the pipe went on for a long time. Thomas began to lose track of the passage of time; the small shelter grew warmer and the damp smoke thicker; he began to sense the walls around them expanding outward and the curved roof growing further away until they were sitting in a suspended cloud of steam and fragrant, sweet smoke. The old shaman began to chant once again and the chanting went on for what seemed like hours—or was it minutes—or days?

". . . na-hani-ha-ma-cha-mi-niwa . . ." A second voice, a deeper one, entered into the chant. Thomas felt his own chest vibrate with the intensity of the added voice and then he realized that it was his own voice that was accompanying the Indian, chanting, singing words and melodies that he did not recognize but that made perfect sense to him. He closed his eyes and chanted, singing in precise tempo and pitch; it felt natural and timeless from so deep within that it was as if his very soul was singing out loud. He heard the shaman sprinkle more water and felt the steam burst forth; the warm cloud surrounded him and curled and twisted into shapes and colors he never knew existed yet they seemed to have voices of their own. The sounds and images filled the tiny shelter that had lost its encompassing walls; he realized he was standing and dancing, shuffling and stamping his feet against the packed earth, bent nearly double and moving his arms and trunk in tempo with the rhythm of the chant. Animals of the forest joined him; Ha-Sook-Inya the *Bear that Walks with Pain* was there, as was the mountain lion he had shot and the deer he had shot and killed; flying among them was the gull, Frisco. There was a sense of peace among all the images and sounds that Thomas felt with acute warmth, throughout his entire soul. He didn't know how long he danced or if he even rested but when he awoke the fire was cold, the stones were barely warm and rays

of sunlight were streaming though the tiny spaces around the deer hide covering the door. He looked and saw Gray Hawk snoring across the tiny shelter, his face relaxed. The white and red and black ceremonial designs were blurred and smudged. The long smoking pipe was carefully hung in its place of honor along with the feathers and gourds.

* * *

San Francisco, California

Because Alexander Dunsworth was a well known attorney and member of a prestigious law firm in the city, the brutal slaying of his wife Nelle Nugent Dunsworth at the couple's weekend ranch just north of Santa Cruz made front page headlines in the San Francisco Chronicle. According the Sheriff Joe McGee, the suspected killer was Alexander Dunsworth's ranch hand named Beckley Weston, though he released no details of the murder. The sheriff stated that they had no clues as to the whereabouts of Weston but advised those living in the coastal range of mountains south of San Francisco to be aware that Beckley Weston, described simply as slender and about six feet tall, in his early forties with shoulder length gray hair, was considered a murder suspect, assumed to be armed and that they should exercise extreme caution if he was seen.

Handon McPherson read the article and sat back in his chair. *Beckley Weston . . .* wasn't that the name of Hector Gordon's ranch hand?

In less than an hour a telegram was on its way to his friend Hector:

HECTOR STOP BE ADVISED MAN NAMED BECKLEY WESTON WANTED SUSPICION OF MURDER STOP NOT SURE SAME MAN YOUR RANCH HAND STOP SAME GENERAL DESCRIPTION STOP BE CAREFUL STOP HANDON MCPHERSON

The telegram was delivered to the Gordon ranch two hours after it was sent from San Francisco to the Visalia Western Union Telegraph office. Hector Gordon cursed under his breath when he read the short warning from McPherson. *Weston!* It made sense since his cousin Diego had run into Weston in Los Baños and Los Baños was not more than a few days ride from Santa Cruz. *Damn Weston! First he raises hell here at the ranch then he tries to kill O'Reiley and now this!* Well, he would make sure that he carried a weapon until Weston was caught, and he'd warn the neighbors Ted and Muriel Stanton, as well.

*   *   *

<u>San Felipe, Panama Province of Columbia</u>

Even though the sixty-nine year old man was a doctor, his wife, Maria Ossa Escobar, was worried sick about his health. She hovered about him protectively, listened to every cough and sneeze as if it was a warning sign of imminent failing health. He traveled far too much, she often told him and too far away from home and her ability to lovingly care for him. The last trip had lasted months; he had come home utterly exhausted and had spent a week in bed recuperating as she nursed him back into health with hot tea, his favorite soups and homemade breads. Much of their married life had been like that; her husband had worked as a doctor on the Panama Railroad and spent twenty years at the Santo Tomás Hospital in Panama City located on the southern coast overlooking Golfo de Panama which was not far from their home in San Felipe.

But the doctor, Amador as his wife called him, repeatedly summoned his dwindling reserve of energy to accomplish the task he had set for himself. He walked daily to the small *Telegrafie la Oficina* to inquire as to whether a telegram had yet arrived for him. It had been six weeks since he had left New York City for the return to his native country. As each day went by without a telegram or message of any sort, he began to feel that perhaps the Americans were going to abandon him and ultimately, his country as well. He had risked much but many had risked much more and even given their lives for the cause. He could not let them down. Not as long as he had enough energy to get out of bed . . .

Today's visit to the *Telegrafie la Oficina* in San Felipe had been another disappointment; he walked slowly back towards his home, breathing in the warm tropical air and trying to appreciate the warm sunshine on his aching shoulders. He dug a cheroot out of his shirt pocket and stuck it in his mouth; it remained unlit, as Maria had insisted that he not breathe in tobacco smoke. He instead simply savored the tobacco flavor as he thought about the bloody civil war between the Columbian Conservatives and the Liberals. The future of the Isthmus of Panama remained uncertain as the war continued, though there were signs of overtures for peace from the Liberals. Panama itself was divided politically but reeling under the tough and punishing government of Columbia. Most favored complete independence from the South American country bordering on the south.

He thought through his plans for probably the thousandth time; if all went well, he would still have at least one more lengthy sea voyage to make.

*　　*　　*

Gray Hawk's shelter
Thomas came out of the small shelter into the early morning brightness. The air seemed especially fresh and clear as he inhaled; he was aware of the many odors and fragrances that rode on the gentle breeze. He could smell the smoky remains of the fire in the hut, though it had long since grown cold. He could even smell the deer skin that provided the waterproof covering for the shelter. He could smell the soil beneath his feet, feeling the individual grains of sand and sensing the delicate living aromas of the nearby trees, bushes and herbs. His eyes caught sight of a chipmunk as it scurried under the leaves littering the forest floor, and he could hear the sound as the creature hurried toward safety. Somewhere in the distance a blue jay let loose with a raucous cry of alarm and he was aware of the faint, almost inaudible sound of an animal sneaking through the underbrush. The green moss on the trunk of a nearby tree appeared intense and patterned with countless shades of green, each unique and each individually discernable. It was as if his eyesight had suddenly grown sharp, allowing him to see details that he never knew existed; and his sense of smell and hearing had sharpened a thousand-fold. Everything around him was its normal distance and at the same time sharply up-close and in acute focus, attuned and synchronized to all his senses.

He heard the old Indian stir inside the hut and shortly the shaman joined him in the sunlight. He studied Thomas for several long minutes before he spoke.

"Tah-moss. You are a new man today. I saw the change take place last night during the smoke ceremony. Your mind has been opened to many new ways; it has been awakened to some of the ways of my people, to some of the skills and mystical powers that I learned as a young man and that are now a part of me. I know that you will take council from them carefully and wisely use them. Your natural senses are now able to be honed to a new sharpness; be wisely aware of these new abilities. You must understand

189

and test these new strengths and teach yourself how to use them. You, like me, have some natural limitations. Our minds and bodies have tolerated the test of time. Old wounds remain old wounds. They are healed but the scars remain behind." He paused, as if to gather his thoughts. "Tah-moss, you must listen to your inner voice, for it speaks with wisdom not available when we choose to not listen. You must listen intently for sounds that are missing but should be present, for odors that are not there that should be. You must discover how and when to see what is not there and to sense all that is around you, even what you do not see, hear, feel or smell. Never doubt the truth and wisdom of your inner voice, Tah-moss. This inner confidence is deeply rooted in experience, belief and ancient mystery; listen to it carefully, especially before you speak or act. I tell you these things, Tah-moss, because you have become friend with me."

Thomas nodded. "Thank you, Gray Hawk for your wisdom and for your friendship. I listen with care and will always remember and honor your great wisdom and advice."

*   *   *

Chular, California

Beckley Weston had ridden hard to put miles between himself and Rancho de Pacifica and particularly between himself and Alexander Dunsworth. Whatever thoughts or convictions he had once held regarding the attorney, Beck now considered him dangerous and a clever madman. He also assumed that Dunsworth would tell the world that the man called Beckley Weston had murdered his wife, and that within a day or two he would be wanted and hunted by the law. If he was caught, the chances were good that they would hang him, regardless of what he had to say. His best chance was to simply disappear. And that's what he was doing.

He'd pushed his horse harshly to reach the tiny dirt-street town of Chular located in the eight-mile wide Salinas Valley and a few miles south of the town of Salinas where he had stopped quickly for something to eat. Chular offered not much more than a tiny Post Office and a few dusty board-and-batten fronted stores but he would spend the night here to give his horse a badly needed rest. Tomorrow he would continue south through the depressing string of little rural communities of Gonzales, Soledad, King City and San Lucas. He planned to spend his second night in San Lucas before he cut through the range of shallow mountains that separated Salinas Valley from the vast San Joaquin Valley. Once he reached the small railroad coaling station, *Coaling station A*, on the west side of the huge valley, he could take the coal-hauling train across the valley to Hanford, fifty miles east and slightly north of *Coaling station A*. From Hanford south to Visalia was a short ride. The weather was beginning to get warm and he was glad that it was not July or August that he was making this trip when, as the local people would declare, you could fry an egg on a rock exposed to the mid-afternoon sun.

It was late in the day and the air began to cool as Beck searched for a secluded place to spend the night. He found a gnarled, half-dead willow tree near a shallow gravel creek-bed, dried up except for a shrunken trickle of fetid water that would be gone in a few more weeks. In the few sun-warmed and slime-rimmed pools where the water moved sluggishly, small tadpoles swam, exercising their soon-to-be legs. He made his simple camp for the night, being careful to slide the Winchester under one side of his bedroll. He built a tiny fire in a natural hollow in the gravel and kept it going with dry sticks and rotted limbs broken off from the willow tree. When shortly after dusk the fire was reduced to a thin layer of ash-covered coals, he extinguished what remained using the side of his boot to cover it with dirt and gravel. He sat quietly in the gathering dark listening to the night sounds until he finally slipped off his boots and unconsciously checked the worn soles by pressing his fingers in the thin leather; if he was going to take refuge in the mountains, he'd have to buy new boots before winter set in. He stretched out on his bedroll and fell asleep around midnight.

*   *   *

Standing Tall, High Sierras

Thomas turned in his saddle looking back at the old Indian dwarfed by the enormous bulbous foundation of the huge redwood tree and waved; the shaman returned his gesture, turned and disappeared shadow-like into the forest. It was mid morning and Thomas was headed to the Gordon ranch on his way back to San Francisco. Gray Hawk had accompanied him as far as *Standing Tall*, the colossal Sequoia Redwood tree near the top of the switchback path that led to the Kaweah River far below. As they had approached the huge tree, the shaman explained to Thomas, "This tree is very old; it was old even before my people came here many winters ago.

My people believe that it has been here since the mountains were created, when even the rocks were first formed. It has stood through many storms and fires, through years of drought and winters of heavy snow. It is strong and does not bend or break to the demands of its surroundings. Though there are many other trees like it, my people have never found one as large and majestic as this tree. It is not sacred to us but we believe it has been given to us as a living symbol of strength, safety and of hope. It requires nothing from us. It is tall and strong, silent, powerful and proud. It is *standing tall.*" He had walked slowly around its massive circumference, his hand resting occasionally on the huge buttress-like root knees that came up to his chest. Thomas had met him after he completed his walk around the tree and the two had joined hands in the Indian manner, not palm-to-palm but each grasping the others wrist; then they had parted wordlessly.

The weather turned warm and the afternoon sun beat down on the narrow switch back trail. Thomas let the horse find its own footing and pace and simply sat, relaxed in the saddle. He concentrated on those things which Gray Hawk had taught him, the surrounding odors and fragrances, mere wisps of smell that he would have not noticed before, the pungent bear clover, the sharp fragrance of the wild onion, the resinous tarweed, the sweet gooseberries in bloom, the damp, loamy smell of the earth beneath the hooves of his horse and the coarse, sweaty tang of the horse and the leather saddle. The sky was clear and cobalt blue as he watched a hawk soaring so high overhead it was a mere speck; it circled and caught the warm updrafts off the steep mountainside and used them to gain even more altitude. The silvery thread to the river rushed between the boulders of the river bed; even from this distance, Thomas could hear the hushed growl of the water fed by the rapidly melting snow.

* * *

It was late afternoon when he arrived at the Gordon ranch and Angela rushed out to greet him as he dismounted.

"Tom!" she murmured as she threw her arms around him and hugged him closely, "thanks goodness you're back!"

"I'm back, Angela," he replied, "I'm back." He was aware of the warmth and fragrance of her skin, the closeness of their embrace and the huskiness of her voice. *It would be so incredibly easy to fall in love with her*, he thought.

Hector and Margarita came out of the house and joined them. Hector shook hands and Margarita gave him a short but warm welcome hug. Thomas was quick to notice that Hector had a holstered pistol strapped to his waist.

"What's going on with the pistol, Hector?" he asked, motioning to the revolver.

Hector glanced down at the Colt single action revolver, "Oh, of course. You've not heard . . ."

"Heard? Heard what?" Thomas looked quickly at Angela.

"About Beck," she said quietly. "We're a little concerned that he may try to come back down this way. He's wanted for murder up north."

"Murder! Beck? Who . . ." Thomas shook his head in confusion.

"We don't know who he killed, or even if it was him," Hector spoke up. "I got a telegram from your . . . from Mister McPherson yesterday. No details other than what you just heard. We're just being careful. I've warned the neighbors as well."

Thomas frowned. "Why would Beck want to come back here?"

Hector shrugged. "He knows this part of the country as well as any man. He's got experience in the mountains and foothills. The mountains are big and not many people live up there. There's plenty of game, plenty of water, plenty of places to hide. He could hole up in those mountains for years."

*   *   *

"I feel somehow responsible for what's happening here," Thomas said quietly as he leaned against the corral next to Angela. The sun had set but the temperature continued to be controlled by the heat that the ground had soaked up during the day.

"I don't understand. Why should you feel responsible?"

"I think it's something your father said about Beck and you and me . . . If I hadn't been here . . . if I hadn't . . ."

"Started to . . . fall in love with me?" She inquired quietly, looking up at him.

"Well, yes . . . something like that . . ." he felt a sudden loss for words.

"Tom," she dropped her hand into his, "The difficulty with Beckley Weston started a long time before you ever got here; he just didn't want to admit it. He wanted to be part of the family and though we treated him very well, he failed to realize that he really is . . . was . . . our hired hand. He's not my brother, or my cousin. It sounds mean and perhaps cruel but he's not even really a friend; he works for us on the ranch and has for years. He gets paid to be here . . . well . . . *got* paid to be here," she winced and corrected herself.

He shook his head slowly. "I'm still worried, Angela. What if Beck shows up here at the ranch, running from the law? If he's already killed someone, what does he have to lose? He's a dangerous man wanted for murder. Perhaps he's committed other crimes that we don't even know about." He held her hand tightly and looked into her eyes. "I don't ever want anything bad to happen to you or your family, Angela. All of you mean a great deal to me."

"Well, my father's started carrying his pistol . . ."

"I wouldn't recommend that your father get in a shooting contest with Beck." He put his arms around her and drew her close. "Angela, you don't have any idea how much you and your family mean to me. You are the closest to family I've ever had."

She smiled and looked up at him. "So, Tom, does that mean I'm kind of like a . . . sister to you?" she asked mischievously, her eyes twinkling.

He laughed quietly and held her even tighter. "Angela, you are much more than a sister to me."

CHAPTER 17

<u>Friday, May 30, 1902, Abilene Texas</u>
It was dark on the streets of Abilene and an unseasonably cold rain poured out of the sky, keeping even the usual crowd of restless cowboys lined up at the bars or sitting at the gambling tables while the locals stayed home and out of the drizzling downpour. Streets quickly turned to mud; deep puddles formed miniature lakes and streams that ran down the wagon ruts.

Luke sat on the edge of his bed and listened to the rain hammering on the roof and the slanted lean-to cover over the board sidewalk. Noise from the crowded bar downstairs had not yet risen to its usual Friday night pitch but the tinny melody pulsating from the out-of-tune upright piano slipped up through the floorboards into his room. Occasionally the high-pitched squeal of laughter announced the presence of one of the local prostitutes among the crowd of rowdy cowboys. At times Luke had thought that he should be more like the whoring, drinking, gambling men in the bar below.

For now he put those thoughts away. He had a job coming up soon in Dallas.

*   *   *

<u>San Francisco</u>
The funeral service for Nelle Dunsworth took place in the imposing Grace Church on Nob Hill; the interment procession wound its way slowly to well south of San Francisco for the burial since the city was in the process of relocating all of its cemeteries to a new location beyond the city limits. Alexander Dunsworth rode alone in the black-draped carriage following

the hearse, leading the line of nearly a hundred carriages carrying the influential attorneys, doctors and politicians of San Francisco and the grieving relatives of his deceased wife.

To the few friends who had spoken with him Dunsworth seemed miserably brooding and withdrawn, but they attributed the malaise to his wife's brutal death and showered him with compassion and well-meaning comforting words. In truth, he'd spent a large portion of the days since her murder in conference with Sheriff McGee in Santa Cruz. Dunsworth had the impression that McGee was spending an inordinate amount of time examining the murder, scrupulously poring over and probing every shred of information and evidence; Dunsworth was beginning to wonder if he had made a critical mistake somewhere. However, Sheriff Joe McGee had actually followed through on Dunsworth's account of the murder and issued a warrant for the arrest of Beckley Weston; so perhaps his concerns were for nothing.

It was stiflingly hot in the carriage and as the procession unhurriedly maneuvered through the streets of South San Francisco, his thoughts once again turned to Sophia. Although he was fairly certain she would have read about Nelle's murder, he had not yet attempted to contact her. Though his initial rage for her duplicity had somewhat faded, he knew he would have to make sure that such a lapse of confidentiality would never happen again if their relationship was to continue, which in fact had slowly become Dunsworth's optimistic wish. He would have to be very careful and insist that their friendship remain out of the public's eyes for at least a year. Eventually he would arrange for her to be seen as his *companion* at the theater or other social affairs. In the meantime, he felt certain he would be able to enjoy her sensuous charisma on long, languid weekends at the secluded ranch. In fact, he thought quickly, he might even invite her to the ranch next weekend if he could arrange to have it cleaned up by then. He leaned back, closed his eyes and allowed the imagery of their private escapades to occupy his mind. He smiled. *Yes, it would be very nice to be in her arms again, to breathe in her fragrance.* It would help take his mind off of Sheriff McGee.

*   *   *

The Gordon's Ranch
Thomas had arisen before the sun and was packed and ready to be taken to the train depot in Visalia. He shared early coffee and breakfast with

the family, lingered over a second cup of coffee as the table talk ebbed and flowed. No one questioned his activities in the high country. He felt fairly certain that Angela had somehow let the family know that he was spending his time in the mountains with the old Indian and that the subject was off-limits for family discussion.

The evening before Thomas and Angela had spent a few minutes, as had become their custom, lingering at the corral fence. The night had been warm and the air scented with the soft fragrances of mid-spring. Angela had come wordlessly to his side and nestled familiarly, resting her head against his shoulder. He had put his arm loosely around her waist and held her; they stood without speaking for several long minutes. The only sounds were those of the approaching summer, frogs croaking, the fleeting calls of a few nocturnal birds. Even the horses had seemed subdued with only an occasional thump of a hoof or soft whinny. It was restful, peaceful—the kind of life Thomas had yearned for.

Thomas reflected on their short time together during the late hours and the few words that they had exchanged, especially her comment regarding his falling in love with her. In fact, he wondered if he had indeed fallen in love. In spite of the reality that he was married and had a family, he was in some perplexing way, smitten with this young woman several years his junior. She was beautiful, warm and friendly, and obviously in love with him. Somewhat reluctantly, he had struggled to prevent their relationship from becoming more complicated but it had been difficult for him at times; he imagined it was equally difficult for Angela as well. So where would this lead? One path would lead to almost certain disaster for his family. Deep inside, he knew that was not the path that he should chose to follow but the realization wrenched at his heart.

"You're certainly quiet this morning." Angela's remark brought him out of his reverie.

"I'm sorry. I didn't mean to be rude."

The sun felt pleasant on their shoulders as Angela struggled to maneuver the buckboard into Visalia. The narrow wagon path, just beginning to recover from the winter rains, was rutted and pocked with holes and small rivulets. They drove in silence for several minutes, occasionally bumping shoulders as the buckboard bounced and swayed over the rough road.

"Is that the only way I'm going to get you to sit close to me?" she looked at him and chided.

Thomas laughed. "Guess I'm not very good company today, am I? I apologize." He slid close to her and put his arm around her waist. "I was thinking about us."

"What about us?"

He hesitated. "Our feelings for each other . . . why I feel about you the way I do."

Angela was silent for a few minutes. "How *do* you feel about me?"

"When I'm near you I . . ." he hesitated.

"I think I know how you feel about me when we're together. What about when we're apart, Tom? What about when you are in the high country, or in San Francisco?"

"I don't know. I think of you, Angela but . . . I guess I don't . . . *long* . . . for you." He turned to her, "I don't imagine that's what you wanted to hear."

There was a long period of silence as Angela steered the buckboard through a particularly bad stretc of road. "No, it's not what a girl likes to hear. But at least it's the truth and that's important to me."

* * *

Between San Lucas and Coaling Station A, California

Beck reigned in his horse and let him drink from the small creek that ran shallow in the narrow gorge between the sparsely treed hills. The noontime sun was beating down and he was sweating, even though all he was doing was riding on the horse. He figured he had gone almost halfway through the maze of canyons and narrow passes that would eventually lead him to the small town that had sprung up around the coaling station. The seldom-used trail was rutted; parallel lines of wagon wheel impressions connected the two small communities and the farms and ranches scattered among the mountains between them. These were low mountains, more rounded like hills really, with few as high as three thousand feet. They were dry in the summer and sparsely covered with scrubby oak trees, dusty tamarack and cottonwood trees that stayed close to the nearly dry creek beds. Mountain lion, coyote and rattlesnake country, covered with already-dry ankle-deep grasses, fox-tails and bull-head thorns and in early spring, wild flowers. There were a few sheep ranches, some cattle ranches, mostly just hills. Some early explorers had tried mining and a little further north they had discovered cinnabar, the ore that contains quicksilver. They had named the place New Idria, after its namesake, Idrija, in Slovenia. Quicksilver was vital in the gold mining industry and the mine had flourished, becoming America's second largest quicksilver mine. But around here, the hills were nearly devoid of humans, desolate, dry and hot, hostile.

Beck checked the angle of the sun. If he rode hard, he could reach the coaling station before dark, hopefully get a meal and a room for the night. He'd gone two days now without eating. His horse needed some substance also and was beginning to favor his right hind leg. A day's rest would do them both good. He knew that he was beginning to look like a man running from the law, unshaven, dirty and hungry. That alone would stir suspicion among town people who would see him as a stranger in their midst. He'd need a good story to cover his actions, a day or so of rest. A few good meals and some clean clothes would help. He might let his beard grow, just in case they managed to put out a wanted poster with a sketch of his likeness on it. He nodded to himself, *yes, that would be a good idea.* He had some money; perhaps he should buy a new hat as well to replace the worn and sweat-stained wide-brimmed Stetson he had worn for nearly twenty years. *Damned hard to break in a new hat . . .*

Dunsworth! Damn that man! Damn him and his craziness! Because of him, his whole life would change. Forever he would be hunted as a murderer, even though it wasn't true. But who would believe a drifter, a ranch hand over the sworn word of an attorney? He was as good as dead should he ever be caught. That simply could not happen. He would make his way back to the part of the country he best knew, find a small secluded place away from civilization and live there—if one would call existing *living*. But he knew the area; fish and game were plentiful. Shelter was not a problem—he could count seven or eight old abandoned cabins in the back woods that could be made weather-tight with a little hard work. Water was plentiful. He could go into town once or twice a year for essentials, if he changed his appearance. He'd need ammunition, some clothes, a few food-things, a half-dozen simple medicines.

Damn Dunsworth and damn O'Reiley as well. He's the one that started the ruckus at the Gordon Ranch in the first place.

"Let's giddy-up old man," he said quietly to his horse, "I reckon we got a ways to go." He started once again following the winding trail through the hills to the coaling station.

*   *   *

<u>Dallas, Texas</u>

The local Abilene newspaper carried a small article about an up and coming Republican named Tom Steel. He was a successful attorney in the growing city of Dallas. Married, he had two children and lived partly on inherited family money and partly from the proceeds of the legal firm he had founded seven years ago. Three years previous, Steel had been approached by the local Republican Party with the proposal that Tom run for the United States House of Representatives. He had agreed and after a slow but thus far successful campaign was busy giving speeches throughout the state of Texas. On this day, Monday, the second day of June, he was in Dallas preparing to give a campaign speech at one of the bandstands in a local recreation park. The crowd was expected to be somewhere between two and three thousand people. At two in the afternoon people had already begun to gather; a local band struck up patriotic songs and volunteers handed out small American flags. The people gathered under a bright sky, standing whenever possible in the shade of the huge oak trees that made the recreation park a desirable place to gather on a hot afternoon.

Steel was locally extremely popular with the people of Dallas, a city's son. He was tall, good looking, well educated, had a beautiful wife, Melody, and lived in one of the large homes in the old moneyed section of the city. He had held popular views on several issues involving local politics. His father had fought for the Confederacy during the war and returned home missing his left arm leaving the army at the rank of Lieutenant-General. He had made the family fortune in cotton and then cattle, leaving everything to his only son and heir, Thomas Bates Steel.

The bandstand was near the northeast corner of the park. It was a simple wooden structure about twenty feet long and fifteen feet deep with steps at either end. The band sat in three tightly spaced rows across the back of the stage with red, white and blue bunting draping the front and sides.

Less than a hundred yards to the north east of the bandstand and outside of the park was an old abandoned farmhouse, all the first floor windows now boarded up as it sat awaiting demolition. It was in this old wooden frame structure that Luke had positioned himself a day earlier. From one of the second floor windows, Luke had a clear view of the bandstand, yet the crowd of listeners would not be able to see the window because the canopy of shade trees would block their view.

Luke had had to pry the window sash up several inches and had arranged a stack of bricks as a seat. Under the cover of darkness, he had carefully practiced his escape route to the old dilapidated barn where his horse waited. He'd spent the night sleeping on the bare floor and ate beef jerky for breakfast and lunch, watching as the crowd slowly gathered in the park. He pulled his watch from his pocket and peered at it. It was a quarter past two. Fliers posted about the city announced that Steel would begin speaking at two-thirty.

Luke listened as the band struck up John Philip Sousa's *Stars and Stripes Forever* and he tapped his foot in time, recalling his days in the army when he had marched in step to such patriotic music. The crowd was stirred, waving flags and whooping when the band finished with a great and rousing flourish.

Now he watched carefully as the first speaker came to the platform; he would introduce Thomas teel. Luke picked up his rifle, carefully checked to make sure a round was in the chamber and the safety was off. He'd calculated the distance and drop; now he checked for any breeze that might deflect his bullet an inch or two. It was dead calm under the hot mid-day sun. People in the park were fanning themselves to stay cool, even in the shade. He shouldered the rifle, poked the barrel into the open space at the bottom of the window and sighted through the telescope; the man presently speaking filled most of the telescope lens. Luke calculated that his shot would hit Steel in the upper left back, rip through his heart and exit through his lower right ribcage. Steel would be dead before his body crashed onto the wooden stage.

The speaker finished and the crowd gave him a polite but not overly enthusiastic ovation; they were saving the cheering for Steel. Thomas Steel stepped up onto the stage. He wore a white wide-brimmed Stetson, sides turned up in the popular Texas style and was greeted by wild flag waving as the band struck up Sousa's *The Washington Post*. Luke hesitated only seconds before squeezing the trigger. The sound of the rifle shot was lost in the raucous shouting and band music. Tom Steel lurched forward as if he'd tripped and fell to the wood-planked stage. Luke carefully pulled the rifle back into the shadows and rapidly disassembled it into the three pieces, slipped them into the small case and hurried down the rickety stairs and out the rear door of the house. The crowd was still shouting, as yet not fully aware of the tragedy happening before their eyes. He heard the band music slowly begin to fall out of rhythm and the roar of the crowd dwindled which became instead a low anguished moan of disbelief, interspersed with a few horrified shrieks from women. He let himself into the barn, untied his horse and was three blocks away before the first few men arrived at the house looking for the assassin.

Luke slipped in unseen through a side door of the large downtown hotel and let himself into his third floor room. He lay back on the bed, perspiring and still breathing hard from the excitement. Several minutes went by as he replayed the events. He'd spend the night here, perhaps postponing the few hours of depravity with some young and attractive prostitute that usually capped off his killings. It seemed to be the only thing that released the residual rage that coiled within him like a tightly wound spring.

But then . . . perhaps he would wander onto the streets this evening and see what came to pass. It had been a long time and he needed the company of a young lady to calm his thoughts . . .

* * *

San Francisco

Thomas O'Reiley had arrived in San Francisco late Tuesday, taken a hired hackney to his home from the train depot. By the time he arrived home, the children were in bed asleep and he was greeted at the door by Amanda.

"Here's my husband the explorer come home!" she whispered in his ear as she hugged him tightly then pressed her lips to his neck. "It's so good to have you home, darling."

"It's good to be home, my dear wife!" His lips found hers and they held each other in a close embrace.

When they separated she pulled back slightly so she could see into his eyes, smiled and asked, "So, how was your Indian friend?"

"Well, Gray Hawk survived the winter," he began, then told her of his rescue of the old man and the killing of the bear. She listened with her fingers pressed to her lips as he recounted his trip to the high country, all except the mystical experience of the ritual with the Indian.

"My goodness! He's lucky that you arrived when you did. If you had been five minutes later, he would have been killed and eaten!" She shivered slightly at the thought. "That's two people whose lives you have saved in the high mountains, Thomas. It is starting to become a habit with you." She leaned back again and looked deeply into his eyes. "Do take care, my darling. I don't want to lose you."

It was on the way up the stairs to their bedroom that she said, "Oh, Thomas, I forgot to mention Alexander Dunsworth—I'm sure you remember him, the attorney?"

"Why, yes. What about Dunsworth?"

"Someone murdered his wife, Nelle Dunsworth, last week."

"Murdered? My God, Amanda, that's terrible!"

"I saved the Chronicle for you. It's just ghastly! Poor Alex Dunsworth came back from Los Angeles to find his wife slain in the most grotesque manner. I get sick simply thinking about it."

"I shall be very interested in reading all the gruesome details, my dear," he chided, "but tonight I have other, more, shall we say, intimate thoughts in mind!"

"Well, I was certainly hoping you would!" she giggled as she sashayed provocatively up the stairs ahead of him.

* * *

Thomas sat in his study and read the newspaper account of the murder. The sheriff in Santa Cruz had already issued a warrant for the arrest of Beckley Weston on suspicion of murder. Though the newspaper did not go into details of the murder scene, it was obvious from the imbedded insinuations and the manner in which the article was written that the killing had been carried out in a most brutal fashion.

Thomas put the newspaper on his desk and leaned back in his chair. *Beckley Weston? True, Beckley, or someone closely matching his description had almost killed Frank Barnwell with a pistol shot but somehow this didn't sound like Beckley. Beckley would wait for the opportunity and take a rifle shot from a distance like a hunter. And the newspaper had mentioned in the Dunsworth murder that the weapon used was a shotgun. Why would Beck choose a shotgun over his own familiar handgun? And lastly, what reason would he have to kill Nelle Dunsworth in the first place? Was it possible that with Dunsworth out of town, Beck had made an improper advance, been rebuffed and killed her out of anger?*

At least the problem was not his, though he was concerned that Beck might attempt to return to the area around the Gordon Ranch. Perhaps the man had headed for Canada or Mexico and freedom from the United States law. He remembered that not many years ago he himself had fled the United States to escape prosecution for murder.

* * *

San Francisco Police Headquarters

Shortly before dinner on Wednesday Thomas received a formal request from the Police Department to attend a brief meeting the following day to go over the attempt on Frank Barnwell's life. At ten o'clock he was sitting in the conference room at the San Francisco Police headquarters. Sitting at the table with him were Frank Barnwell, Officer Michael Kelly, who Thomas remembered as the police officer investigating Frank's shooting, Santa Cruz Sheriff Joe McGee and his deputy Charles Watts and two men from the San Francisco Police Department.

Police Lieutenant Urstan Scott led the meeting. "We have some new evidence to add to our investigations of the attempt on Mister Barnwell's life. Officer Kelly, if you would please review the evidence you and Mister O'Reiley discovered at the site of the attempt on Mister Barnwell's life?"

"Yes sir." Kelly referred to his notes. "According to what we found, the shooter would be about six feet tall, weigh about two hundred pounds, was wearing boots—probably Justins," he glanced quickly at Thomas, "fairly new. Not a tobacco user, right handed, used a forty-five caliber pistol that takes a forty-five long round." He held up the casing that he and Thomas had recovered.

Scott nodded. "Mister O'Reiley, would you say that fits the general description of Beckley Weston?"

"Yes sir. I know that Beckley carried a Buntline Special forty-five caliber revolver and he fits that general physical description."

"Mister O'Reiley, do you know a man named Clarence Chandler?"

"Chandler? Of course!" O'Reiley frowned, "Chandler and Vernon Dyson killed a man and blamed me for the murder. That was back in November of '89. Chandler's not out of prison, is he?"

Lieutenant Scott looked at O'Reiley. "Chandler and Dyson attempted to escape from a San Quinton Prison work party last October the first. Dyson was shot dead during the attempt but Chandler managed to take control of a motor launch and evaded the police. The launch was run over by a ship in the straits west of Alcatraz Island and we assumed that Chandler was killed in the collision. Chandler's body was never recovered."

Thomas leaned forward in his chair. "You're thinking he could be alive?"

"It's a possibility. Do you think he could have sufficient residual anger to attempt to murder you?"

O'Reiley nodded thoughtfully. "That's certainly a possibility. As I remember, Chandler would fit the general description of the shooter, though it's been many years."

Lieutenant Scot nodded. "We're keeping that possibility very much in our thinking, Mister O'Reiley. If I were you, I'd take extra precautions."

"Thank you Lieutenant. I'll certainly keep that in mind."

Police Lieutenant Scott then turned to the sheriff. "Sheriff McGee, if you would bring us up to date on your investigation into the death of Nelle Dunsworth."

"Yes sir. My deputy, Charles Watts was sent to investigate the murder scene while I interviewed Mister Dunsworth. I'll let him describe what he found."

Charles Watts nodded then leaned forward with his elbows on the table. "When I arrived at the ranch, the front door to the main house was shut but not locked. The door to the bedroom was shut. I found Nelle Dunsworth's body on the bed in the bedroom. She was naked and laying on her back on a bed sheet. There was a massive wound in her chest—obviously a shotgun wound at close range—probably touching as there were burn marks around the wound. The wall and the floor near the head and side of the bed were splattered with blood, except for one area in the near corner." He looked up and around the table before he continued. "Another shotgun blast . . ." he swallowed and shook his head quickly, "in the area of her neck had completely severed her head from her body. The shotgun blast had ripped through the pillow under her head and feathers were scattered all over the blood splatters. There were footprints in the blood splattered on the floor leading from the corner near the head of the bed toward the door to the living room. Whoever made the footprints was barefooted. They were large footprints; I would say a man's print. The footprints had feathers from the pillow settled on them." He paused as if to catch his breath. "When I looked over the rest of the house, I found the gun cabinet in the corner of the living room, the door unlocked and open. Inside the cabinet were two deer rifles, several boxes of ammunition—including shotgun shells—a small wooden box that contained what I would call *keepsakes*, a pair of field glasses, something that appeared to be folded legal papers bound with ribbon and a stack of twenty dollar bills totaling two thousand dollars. When

I had finished in the house and the coroner was still busy, I entered the cabin where the ranch hand Beckley Weston stayed. I found a bed sheet with blood splatters on it rolled up and apparently tossed into a corner. The cabin was empty of Weston's bedroll and personal gear and I found a twelve gauge double barreled shotgun—later identified as belonging to Mister Dunsworth—lying on top of the bare mattress. When I checked, both barrels had been fired and contained empty shotgun shells. Weston's horse and tack were gone from the barn."

Sheriff McGee nodded. "Thank you, deputy. Now I'll tell you what Mister Dunsworth told me when I interviewed him." He opened his notebook. "He arrived at the ranch about noontime; when he entered the unlocked house he found the bedroom door shut and his wife, Nelle Dunsworth, dead on the bed just as Deputy Watts has described. Mister Dunsworth stated that he did not touch anything, backed quickly out of the bedroom and then checked Weston's cabin where he found it just as Deputy Watts has described. He immediately left the ranch and came to my office in Santa Cruz. When I asked Mister Dunsworth about the shotgun, he described the gun cabinet and contents pretty much as Deputy Watts has already. He stated that the key to the cabinet was always hidden and that even his wife didn't know where it was—seems she detested guns of any kind."

Police Lieutenant Scott nodded. "Do you have an autopsy report?"

"Yes sir." He pulled a single sheet of paper. "According to the coroner, the cause of death was a single shotgun blast to the center of her chest that completely destroyed her heart. Death was instantaneous; copious blood from the massive wound flowed through an exit wound on her back and soaked into the mattress. A second wound, also an apparent shotgun wound, had entered her right neck at approximately a forty-five degree angle and had completely severed all connecting tissues and bone, effectively decapitating the body. After close examination, the coroner estimated this second wound occurred approximately *fifteen minutes* after the victim was dead." McGee looked up and around the table at the somewhat surprised expressions.

"So what brings you here, Sheriff?" Scott asked.

"When I issued the wanted bulletin for Weston, I was contacted by Officer Kelley here. He was surprised by the similarities of the two physical descriptions; his of the man who attempted to kill Mister Barnwell and mine of the man who has been charged with the murder of Nelle Dunsworth,"

Sheriff McGee stated, then looked at his notes. "However, there are a few details at Nelle Dunsworth's murder scene that do not add up properly. One is the blood spattered sheet found in Weston's cabin. How did it get there? Another is the bloody footprints leaving the Dunsworth's bedroom. Whose footprints are they? Whoever made them were there when Nelle Dunsworth was shot and the blood sprayed over the floor and wall and then left the room before the second shot was fired. Remember, they were *man-sized, bare footprints leaving* the bedroom and they had pillow feathers—*caused by the second shot*—settled on them. And lastly, there are questions regarding the shotgun. If the gun cabinet is always locked and the key hidden, how would Beckley Weston know how to get into it? And why would he *need* to get into it? He apparently carries a pistol, the forty-five Buntline Special we've heard about, and, as a ranch hand, probably has a rifle. Then, why didn't he take the stack of money that was right there in plain sight? And, why would Weston, fleeing the scene of his crime, pack all his gear, roll up his bedroll and *then* carefully place the shotgun—the murder weapon—*on the mattress*? Why not just throw it into a corner before he rushed to take his belongings? Why even take it to the cabin in the first place? Lastly, some questions regarding the statements of Mister Dunsworth. I asked him several times if he had touched *anything* and his response each time was *no*. If that is true, how did he know, without opening the shotgun, that both barrels had been fired?"

Police Lieutenant Scott frowned. "What are you suggesting, Sheriff McGee?"

The Sheriff waited for several long seconds before replying. "It's very possible that Beckley Weston may be the one who shot Mister Barnwell but I'm not convinced that he murdered Nelle Dunsworth." He paused and glanced once again around the table. "Let me tell you what I think actually happened."

*   *   *

Coaling Station A

It was blazing hot in the mid morning sun. The coaling station was mainly in name only as there was little in the way of structure other than the sturdy coaling tower with its hopper, bins, coal elevator and a single wooden water tower to mark its place. Most of the two dozen or so places of business were clapboard lean-tos in which the daytime temperature soared well above a hundred degrees. Recently oil had been discovered under the bleak landscape of the surrounding hills in what was now called the Temblor Pool and the few streets of the town were busy with horse-drawn wagons loaded with machinery, drill pipe and timbers with which to construct drilling derricks. A few of the larger buildings were of a little more permanent construction, signs of hope that the town would eventually take root in the hard soil baking under the broiling sun. A bank, a hardware store, a market and a few scattered businesses lined the hard-packed dirt main street shoulder to shoulder with saloons and a few wooden boarding houses.

Beck wiped the perspiration off his forehead and set his new hat back on his head. It would take a while to get used to the newness of the Stetson with the slope-front design but its design and brown color was markedly different from his twenty-something year old hat. A barbershop shave that removed the bushy mustache that he had worn since his early twenties and a haircut that shortened the shoulder-length silver-colored hair had also helped alter his appearance. Now when Beck looked in a mirror, a stranger looked back at him.

It took only a few minutes to secure a ride for himself and his horse on the daily train from the coaling station to Hanford. Though primarily a coal-hauling train, it did have one passenger car and a freight car in addition to the four coal cars and caboose. Pulled by a steam locomotive, the train shuttled daily between Hanford and the coaling station, hauling coal to fuel the Union Pacific Railroad locomotives that ran up and down the long, flat San Joaquin Valley.

The train departed the coaling station at two o'clock sharp and pulled into the Hanford Union Pacific depot an hour and twenty-three minutes later—right on time.

Beck stepped down from the passenger car into the motionless afternoon air, unloaded his horse and rode off toward Visalia, thirty miles to the east.

CHAPTER 18

<u>Thursday, June 5, 1902, San Francisco, California</u>
Alexander Dunsworth sat in his office at the legal firm located three
floors above Market Street. His return to work had been greeted somberly
by partners and staff tendering sincere condolences and offering to do
anything to help relieve his personal agony. He had replied as graciously as
he could, his bumbling words of appreciation interpreted as another sign
of his suffering loss.

With the heavy oak door to his personal office closed and secured,
Dunsworth sat and stared out the window at the buildings across the wide
street. The recent meeting with the attorneys in Los Angeles remained
heavy on his mind, particularly the unveiled threat to expose the murder
of *Señora Isabella Laurencia Esperanza*. It would be very difficult, indeed
almost impossible, to connect her death to him but linkage of the
murderer to him was a separate issue. He had taken great care to set up the
meeting with one of the assassin's network of informers, a man allegedly
from Sacramento and known to him only as Bret. Bret had referred to
the assassin-for-hire as a man known only as *El Culebra*. Money was
exchanged—a very large amount of money—and within a month the
deed was done; *Señora Esperanza* had been cremated in the conflagration
that destroyed her elegant Nicaraguan hacienda.

Somehow the Los Angeles legal firm had apparently picked up the
trail and was using this information as leverage to inflate the price of
the land transaction and there was nothing to indicate that they would
cease this extortion after the property sale was complete. The three
attorneys—Warner, Jenkins and Garcia-Rameriz—had become a major
stumbling-block to his plans. If they were out of the way, the threat would

cease and he could negotiate directly with Miguel Esperanza-Vincente. It was an idea that had quietly planted itself in his brain a few days ago.

He leaned back and closed his eyes in thought. With overnight train service now available between San Francisco and Los Angeles, he could be in Los Angeles and back in two days. It would be a grueling trip on the train but with some planning and a little luck no one would even be aware of his absence. He could take a few more days off from the office on the pretext of cleaning up matters at the ranch. After all, there were Nelle's personal belongings yet to sort through and properly dispose of and a few legal details were still pending. Certainly his partners would sympathetically understand. His vague scheme began to take on the shape of a plan of action in his mind. He walked through the various steps, locations, actions required. Timing would be critical, as would stealth and a certain degree of boldness.

He slid the center drawer open and reached in, his fingers searching then grasping his Remington pocket pistol, a palm-sized .41 caliber Derringer over-and-under. Almost every attorney he knew had a pistol close at hand in case a client began to turn violent. Known for its inherent inaccuracy at anything over a few yards, the Derringer was reputed to be deadly up close.

He slipped the loaded Derringer and four extra bullets into his jacket right pocket and stood. Though very small, the pistol weighed more than he expected and had a tendency to skew the lines of the jacket somewhat. He put his right hand in the pocket and cuddled the pistol, then adjusted the jacket until it felt comfortable. Satisfied, he nodded to himself. Yes, that would certainly do.

By mid afternoon he had excused himself from his office and taken the train to San Jose, where he bought a ticket for a sleeping compartment on the overnight train to Los Angeles that would leave late that evening. He then spent a few hours purchasing clothing at an unpretentious men's outfitter, Lloyd's Haberdashery, two blocks off the main street. Along with the necessary underclothes and accessories, he selected a pair of gray slacks and a blue plaid jacket, two white shirts with red pin-stripes and hard white tubular collars, a red four-in-hand tie and a dove-gray low flat-top derby. When he posed in front of the full-length mirror and viewed himself clothed in the new garments, he felt he looked quite dapper, especially compared to the dreary three-piece black suit he normally wore. After slipping on his seldom used reading spectacles, the image in the mirror was quite unrecognizable. He purchased a small, inexpensive suitcase in which he placed his other clothing, along with the Derringer pistol and four extra rounds of ammunition.

His anticipated visit with Sophia would have to wait for a few more days. He was glad he had not reprimanded her for talking with her brother Ramsfeld in Los Angeles. The less she knew the better.

*   *   *

When he arrived in Los Angeles, Dunsworth bought his return ticket for that night then visited the Western Union Telegraph office. The telegram was addressed and delivered to William Percival Warner, Senior Partner of the legal firm:

WARNER STOP JENKINS STOP GARCIA-RAMERIZ STOP MUST MEET TONIGHT YOUR OFFICE STOP CRITICAL ALL BE THERE STOP VITAL NEW DEVELOPMENT STOP 9 O'CLOCK STOP ALEX D

The telegram was received by Warner at four that afternoon and his reaction was predictable. He called his two partners into his office and shut the door.

"Who in the hell does that little piece of crap think he is?" he muttered as he read it to his partners. "Nine o'clock? What the hell?"

"Maybe he's just passing through town, Bill. Maybe the only time he can meet with us."

"That's just plain bull shit!" Warner uttered, obviously unconvinced.

"Wonder what the vital new development is?" Jenkins thought out loud.

"Sure as hell better be worth our time," Warner snarled.

*   *   *

Alexander Dunsworth was at the front door of the seven storied office building at eight forty-five. The door was locked, as he knew it would be as it was well after normal business hours. There were no lights on in any of the rooms visible from the street. The small suitcase was stashed around the corner of the building in a narrow alley behind garbage cans and out of sight. Traffic on the street was very light, mostly hansoms shuttling customers home from the evening out. Occasionally, a horseless carriage clattered by,

211

spewing fumes. Two streets over, the trolley rattled and clanged as it ran up and down the street. Dunsworth, dressed in his recently purchased attire, remained in the deeper shadows. It was a few minutes before nine o'clock when he spotted the three attorneys coming his way.

Warner spotted him, strode forward, habitually offering his hand but snarling, "Dunsworth, what the hell are you up to?" He stared at Dunsworth, "you're all dressed up like you're going to a goddamned New Orleans Mardi Gras."

"I have something that you will want to see," Dunsworth replied, struggling to hold back an angry retort.

"Well, that's horse shit! Let's see it."

Dunsworth shook his head. "We need to do this in your office."

Warner shook his head in obvious frustration and impatience, reached into his vest pocket and withdrew a key to the door. Seconds later the four men were inside the building and Warner relocked the door behind them. The legal firm was located on the third floor and they took the lift up. No one spoke and the atmosphere was tense. Only Dunsworth seemed at ease but his senses were alert, listening for any sounds that might indicate other people in the building. Since the lift by-passed the second floor and there were four floors beyond that, he finally had to ask.

"Building looks to be empty," he stated.

"Yeah, it is. Only a few of us *dedicated lawyers* are here this time of the night," Jennings said sarcastically. "Everyone else is home where they should be."

"Well, look, I'm sorry for the hour but this won't take long."

The lift stopped at the third floor and they walked into the faintly lighted hallway; Warner used a second key to open the office door. They stepped into the conference room; Jenkins and Garcia-Rameriz took seats at the far side of the conference table.

Dunsworth started to sit, then stood with a startled look on his face. "Damn me! I left my valise down at the street."

"What? Your valise is on the street?"

"I put it down behind some trash cans while I relieved myself in the alley. Forgot to pick it up. I'll just go down . . ."

Warner shook his head in disgust. "I'll go with you . . . got to unlock the front door."

"Look, I'm very sorry," Dunsworth said earnestly. "I had supper a while ago and a couple of beers and I had to take a piss."

"Happens to us all," Warner said tiredly. "Let's go."

Warner and Dunsworth retraced their steps to the front door; Warner unlocked it and Dunsworth squeezed out apologetically, dashed around the corner, picked up the light suitcase, then reached into the notch in the granite where he had hidden the Derringer and slipped it into his coat pocket.

When he stepped to the door again Warner frowned and shook his head, "thought you said you had a valise."

"I'm traveling light. It's inside the suitcase. One less thing to keep an eye on."

Warner grimaced, locked the door behind them and they got into the lift once again, Warner operating the controls. Dunsworth stepped toward the back of the lift, his hand gripping the Derringer in his coat pocket.

When they had passed the second floor, he brought the small pistol out quickly, cocked the hammer, pressed the barrel against the nape of Warner's neck and pulled the trigger. Blood and pieces of bone splattered against the control panel in front of Warner and the attorney slid to the floor without a sound, blood trickling from his ear, his dead eyes still open.

The lift stopped at the third floor and Dunsworth replaced the spent round before he opened the gate and stepped into the hallway, the cocked gun behind his back. He could hear the two men talking in the conference room and he stepped in quietly.

Jenkins started to stand up. "What was that noise? Sounded like a pistol shot!"

Dunsworth pointed the Derringer at Jenkins' chest. "It was," and pulled the trigger. Jenkins reeled backward, tipping over the chair. Garcia-Rameriz started to stand. Dunsworth swiveled quickly, pointing the gun at him. "Sit down, *corruptos de América del Norte*", he said quietly. "I'm sure you don't need a translator."

Garcia-Rameriz slid slowly back into his chair, his eyes locked on the Derringer pointing at him. Dunsworth pulled the trigger and the gun spit flame. The bullet struck Garcia-Rameriz squarely in the forehead. Calmly, Dunsworth replaced the two spent bullets, stepped over to Jenkins' body and fired again into Jenkins' head, then repeated the process with Garcia-Rameriz.

He removed both keys from Warner's body then dragged it into the conference room. It took almost twenty minutes to dump the contents of the office file cabinets and desk drawers on top of the three bodies. He stacked the wooden chairs, table and cabinets onto the pyre then struck a match to it, watching for a few moments to make sure that the mound was completely ignited.

He picked up his suitcase, locked the door to the legal firm's office, took the lift to the main lobby and let himself out onto the deserted street, locking the main door behind him. He dropped the keys into a storm drain and set out at a brisk pace to the street two blocks away that led to the train depot. Before he turned the corner he took one last look at the office building behind him. Flames were already erupting from three windows on the third floor and the flickering orange and red glow behind other windows indicated the blaze had already spread well beyond the conference room and was eating at the floors above it.

The overnight train for San Francisco, with a stop at San Jose, would leave in less than an hour.

*   *   *

There were only a handful of passengers on the Friday overnight train to San Francisco and no one had recognized Dunsworth; in fact he hadn't even spoken to anyone other than the conductor on the trip to Los Angeles or on the trip back. When he got off the train in San Francisco, he walked to the train depot's men's restroom and quickly changed into his usual business attire. He disposed of the new trousers and coat by dropping them into a garbage receptacle but decided to keep the hat, as well as the shirts and tie. Finally, he'd gone to his office late Friday evening and slipped the Derringer back into the desk drawer.

*   *   *

Abilene, Texas

The assassination of Thomas Steel had stunned and sickened the good people of Dallas. The sheriff immediately organized a search party but unfortunately, no one was even sure who or what they were looking for. It didn't take very many hours before the hiding place of the killer was found in the dilapidated old house but there were no clues other than signs that the killer had spent the night there in preparation for the shot that killed Steel. The killing made headlines throughout Texas and Luke read about it in the Abilene Reporter-News. The brutal murder of an unidentified sixteen year old prostitute the night of Steel's murder didn't even make the newspaper but then Luke didn't think it would.

He smiled at the newspaper's subtle insinuation that Steel's assassination had been politically motivated. That was exactly the reaction he had hoped for. Now he needed to begin to stoke that premise into a firestorm and he figured the best place to do that would be in Louisiana.

Shreveport, Louisiana was about fifteen miles east of the Texas-Louisiana border. The train would take him the hundred and seventy-five miles from Dallas to Shreveport in a little over four and a half hours. Dallas was approximately three hundred miles east of Abilene, about seven hours by train. Twelve hours overall, give or take. From Shreveport he could head up to Little Rock, then over to Memphis and then probably north. Luke figured to head east in the morning, after taking some money out of one of the local banks.

The noise from the Friday night horde of thirsty cowboys in the bar below his room was nearly deafening. Boisterous laughter was regularly interrupted by the sound of broken glass and crashing chairs and the high-pitched giggle of the barmaids. The piano player strained to keep the music above the noise level. The hotel room windows were open to the hot evening air and more noise rose up from the street below like a cloud of steam. Shouts and whistles of cowboys, the rattle of carriages and wagons, dogs barking at the chaos all fused together in an absurd cacophony of drunken celebration and manly bravado.

*   *   *

San Francisco, California

It was late evening in the city; Thomas and Amanda had finished an evening of dining and then the theater to see the hit musical comedy *The Toreador* by Tanner and Nicholls. It quickly had the audience laughing and tapping their feet, and near the end of the first act Amanda stood and shouted Bravo! after the chorus had finished *"If you want to know your passion in a floral kind of fashion"*. Her enthusiasm had been contagious and the entire audience quickly joined her. She had sat flushed and smiling as she squeezed Thomas's arm.

Thomas glanced sidewise at his wife. *She is the prettiest woman here. She's beautiful, intelligent, gifted, involved in the community, the mother of our three children. How could I even think of loving someone else? Why would I?*

She sensed his glance and turned to him, smiled and silently mouthed "I love you, too."

It was late when the hansom delivered them to their house. Their maid Xiang greeted them at the door, smiling and relieving them of their coats and his hat. She informed Amanda that children were fast asleep in bed, then turned to Thomas and handed him an envelope. He quickly recognized it as a Western Union Telegram and slipped out the folded sheet of thin yellow paper.

> MISTER O'REILEY STOP BECK SEEN IN VISALIA YESTERDAY STOP ALL CONCERNED HE IS NEAR STOP COULD USE YOUR HELP IF POSSIBLE STOP HECTOR GORDON

"What is it, dear?" Amanda asked quietly.

"Trouble, I'm afraid. Beck has been seen in Visalia. The Gordons fear he may retaliate by harming them in some way. Hector has asked for my help."

"Your *help*? What . . . why would he ask for your help? You're not a lawman . . . How could you possibly help?" she implored.

"I'm not sure, Amanda but they have asked. They have more than befriended me; they've been almost like parents I never had. I think I should go and see what I can do to help them." He looked at Amanda and took her in his arms. "I certainly hope that you can understand, dear."

She looked deeply into his eyes with such obvious love that her words surprised him. "I know you must go, my dear Thomas, though I don't fully understand. I know it is just who you are and you simply will not abandon a friend in need."

He could only nod in response.

She smiled and her eyes crinkled. "Well, my dear, since you will be leaving quite early, I think we should immediately retreat to the privacy of our bedroom and say our good-byes in a . . . mmm . . ." she smiled coyly and tilted her head to one side, "pleasingly *fitting* manner!" She winked at him as she added, "And the last one into bed turns down the light!"

*   *   *

Elsewhere in the city, Alexander Dunsworth continued to try to comfort the distraught and weeping Sophia Jenkins. She had received a telegram early that afternoon from her brother Peter Jenkins informing her of the untimely death of her brother Ramsfeld. The brother indicated that police were treating his death and the death of his two law partners as potential homicides, pending further investigation.

Somehow, Alexander had not been prepared for her outpouring of sorrow; and when he arrived looking forward to an exhilarating evening of intimacy following their several days of separation, he had instead been confronted with her inconsolable grief. Try as he may, there was nothing he could say or do that would comfort Sophia; and instead his efforts by and large resulted in yet another cresting wave of blubbering and uncontrolled wailing. Now, in order to not appear as the worst kind of indifferent cad, he would be obligated to spend the weekend with this bawling, snuffling woman in her bathrobe who at the moment did not appear at all attractive with smeared makeup, her hair in careless disarray, puffy eyes and a runny nose, red from near constant contact with her handkerchief.

The San Francisco Chronicle had carried a small article regarding the gruesome deaths on page seven revealing that the Los Angeles police were investigating the case as a multiple homicide and the fire as probable arson. Sophia had not read the article. Dunsworth was confident that his role in the killings had been well obscured. After all, he rationalized, many despairing people were dissatisfied with their attorney's council and some even took drastic actions. He was certain that all the partnership's legal documents concerning Miguel Esperanza Vincente and the property in Nicaragua had been destroyed in the fire along with all the rest of the firm's records.

*   *   *

The White House, Washington, DC

Theodore Roosevelt, the 26th President of the United States, was seated at a small table in the garden alongside the White House, his reading glasses perched on the end of his nose. Except for his shaggy mustache, he was clean shaven, having risen early in the morning as was his habit and breakfasted on eggs and ham and a cup of black coffee. The morning was still brisk, the air not yet warmed by the late spring sun, but he was comfortable in a collar-less long-sleeved white dress shirt. Spread on the table before him was a draft of the speech he would give in four days before the one-hundredth graduating class at the Unites States Military Academy at West Point. Pencil in hand, he was reading and pausing from time to time to look off into the distance to reminisce and then sketch in a few more revisions. It was important to connect the special presentation he would make later that same day with these cadets and the gallant role many of the graduates of the past had filled in the wars that fill the history of the United States: the Civil War, the Spanish American War, the battles in the Philippians and their recent role in the Boxer Rebellion in China.

He looked up as he heard footsteps behind him.

"Mister President, I hope I am not intruding."

"Ah, James," he motioned to his senior staff assistant to take the second chair. "No intrusion indeed! Please, have a seat. I'm putting some finishing touches on the speech I will be giving Tuesday at West Point."

"Thank you, Mister President. I will accept your kind offer of a seat. I do believe it will be a warm day today." He walked around to the other side of the table, slid into the offered chair and leaned back. "Oh, yes, the Centennial Commencement. Going to say a few words about the canal?" He paused then added, "Well, perhaps not, that would probably be of greater interest to our navy."

They both chuckled.

"No, James. I've decided to leave politics out of this speech—you know how the military dislikes politicians—all of our bumbling and fumbling around, debates and endless discussions, resolutions, treaties, bills, posturing and vote finagling. Action! That's what the military wants! Action! Right now! Not tomorrow! And I can't say that they're wrong. Ha! At least not all of the time. No, this confounded congress is so wishy-washy about the canal that we'll be lucky to have one built in fifty years! And the politicians wringing their hands about the money won't be here fifty years from now when the cost to build the same canal will have risen fifty times! Or more!" He pounded the table with the flat of his hand and papers flew off. "Sorry, James."

"That's quite all right, Mister President." The aide rose up quickly and captured the pages and handed them back to Roosevelt. "You were in the military, Mister President."

Roosevelt nodded as he repositioned the papers on the desk. "I was, James, because my nation called in its time of need." He paused, leaned forward with both elbows on the table. "James, listen to me. As you know, this Congress we now have is being coerced by a number of financial interests to build the canal through Nicaragua! *Nicaragua!* In January the House approved a bill to do just that! The route through Panama would be shorter and require fewer locks. Of course, we must deal with that bunch of scoundrels in Columbia. If only we could negotiate directly with a legitimate national *Panamanian* government."

"Pardon my forwardness Mister President but we must be careful that we are not seen as the neighborhood bully."

"But you are quite right, James. We must be the *friendly neighborhood policeman* on his beat armed with his night-stick, doling out constructive counsel and sharing his philosophy but ready—and able—to step in to prevent bloodshed between two powerful neighborhood gangs." He looked knowingly at his aide. Roosevelt took off his glasses and rubbed at his eyes. "Another major Panamanian advantage is that there are no active volcanoes in Panama. Now, granted, Nicaragua has not had a volcanic eruption for thirty-six years, or so they declare but should the U.S. build such an important inter-ocean waterway through a country that has had even a *single* volcanic eruption? I say *no*, yet our namby-pamby Congress is strongly considering just such a mistaken route. Money has incredible clout, James! And mark my words, there are speculators just waiting to make their fortunes; some may even be members of our own Congress! If I knew for sure, I'd have their hides tanned and nailed on the wall next to the door of their offices, by God!" He raised his hand as if to slam the table again but stopped short. "At least Senator Spooner had the raw courage to introduce an amendment to the bill! Ha! Let's see what the boys in Congress have to say about that!"

"I believe they've already begun the debate, Mister President."

"Good! You will keep me up to date, James?"

"Certainly, Mister President."

"Good! And James, one more thing. I'm thinking about a trip out west early next year. A little showing the flag so to speak. Los Angeles probably and San Francisco. James, I want to schedule a little private time for a side trip or two; I'm most interested in California's efforts to conserve their forests and water." He paused and leaned forward, looked closely at his aide. "James, I want these side excursions to be very discreet; no publicity—that's priority! No game hunting, no photographer, no crowds of celebrities or local politicians. I will need a very small security detail—only a few carefully selected individuals." He raised his hand against the startled look on the aide's face. "We'll talk about the essential details later, James." He paused, his eyes lit up as they took in the lawn and trees surrounding the White House. "Ah, ha! John Muir, the Sierra Nevada Mountain man—now by God, there's a man of my own heart! Hiked the length of the Sierra Nevada's backbone, they say. Bully for him! I'd like to meet John Muir! Maybe you could set that up for me, James." He carefully stacked the papers and put them on the table. "I need to make just one more addition to this talk. I'll be awarding the Congressional Medal of Honor to one of the cadets, umm . . ." he glanced at his notes, "Cadet Fourth Class Calvin P. Titus, for gallantry at Peking, China. Brave lad, that Titus! The *company bugler*, mind you! Scaled a thirty-foot wall, unarmed and under enemy fire, reconnoitered the area behind the wall, checked enemy tents and then gave the all clear signal to his fellow soldiers. We need more men like him!"

*   *   *

The Gordon Ranch

Thomas arrived in Visalia aboard the afternoon train and disembarked into the hot, mid-day sunshine of the San Joaquin Valley. The early-spring green velvet had already turned brown and spinning dust-devils swirled up dirt and debris in narrow, twisting columns. Thomas's telegram had arrived and Angela was waiting at the train depot for his arrival. She greeted him at the bottom of the step with a hug and kiss on his cheek. "I'm so glad you are here, Tom! We've been almost petrified with fear since learning that Beck is around."

"What about your sheriff? What's he doing to help out?"

"Sheriff Newton and his deputies have been tied up with a big shooting over in Springville. That's about twenty-five miles southeast of here. Family dispute over some property, we hear. It's got everyone in Springville riled up and the sheriff's just trying to keep people from shooting each another. All we have here right now is one of his part-time deputies, Silas Weaver. Silas's older than the hills and can hardly get on a horse any more. But for right now, he's the only lawman around."

O'Reiley shook his head. "I'm not sure what I can do, Angela but I'm here to help in any way I can."

"The murder Beck's charged with finally made the local newspaper, Tom. It sounded awful. He's got everyone nervous." She peered up at him. "I know you remember Ted Stanton and his wife Muriel; they're afraid Beck's going to swing by their place and do something terrible to Julia. Peter Jenkins and his family, Jack Short and his wife . . . people are terribly anxious. Everyone's carrying a gun, even me." She patted the pistol strapped to her hip.

"What would you do with it, Angela?" he inquired softly.

"I'm not sure, Tom," she sighed, "I just hope I would do the right thing."

By the time they arrived at the ranch house, the late afternoon sun was beginning its slide to the western horizon and had already taken on an orange glow from the dust particles lifted high into the atmosphere. The hot breeze had abated, leaving the air lazy, stirred now and then with lethargic currents and eddies that brought up little swirls of dust from the road.

"We badly need some rain, Tom. Haven't had any for three weeks and it's too early to begin the dry summer. Some of the ranchers are going to be really hurting." She shook her head. "The farmers who planted groves of citrus are already in trouble."

O'Reiley was somewhat taken aback by her mature outlook and concern. She had certainly grown and developed over the years—no longer the teenage girl with an adolescent yearning for a man several years older. *And me,* he wondered, *have I matured as well? Have I left behind my out of place longings for this young woman?*

His thoughts were cut short when Hector, Margarita and Ramon poured through the door of the ranch house to greet him.

* * *

Later when Hector and he were seated in the coolness of the ranch house, they were joined by the rest of the family.

"Why don't you tell me what you know about Beck at this point, Hector," Thomas suggested.

"Well, not much. Some folks in town thought they saw him; let's see, that would have been Thursday, the same day we sent you the telegram. Now, he'd done some to change his looks a little but what gave him away was his horse. Some folks in town recognized his horse; checked his saddle and found his mark—BAW—Beckley Weston, carved into the leather. I asked him once what the A stood for and he told me that was for Anderson, his mother's maiden name. They weren't sure and came out here to check with me since he'd been my ranch hand for such a long time. I told them yes, that's how Beck had marked his saddle. They described the horse and I knew it was Beck's. Seems Beck's shaved off his mustache and cut his hair but the rest of the description fits him. It's got to be him."

"Why would he come back this way?"

"Beck knows the country around here better than most folks, I figure. Lived here a lot of years, been up in the hills many times, knows a lot of places to hide."

"Where do you think he might go?"

Hector leaned back. "Well, been thinking about that, Thomas. He wouldn't go into the high country, least not yet. He'd find maybe a temporary place where he could set up quick and get ready for the winter. He'd be looking for something basic, shelter, water. Food for the long haul would be one of his big priorities right off. Have to be near some place to buy—or steal—some basic food stuff . . . flour, beans, coffee, salt, matches, that sort of thing. A man can live pretty simple if he knows how but Beck's not up on Indian ways; I don't think he could just live off the land. He could hunt for meat—and he'd be good at it—but he'd still need some basic supplies, maybe things like a frying pan and a pot . . . something to eat with and make coffee. He left here traveling pretty light. He'd want to get that all together before winter set in. Besides, he may need ammunition, winter clothes, some oats for his horse . . ."

Margareta and Angela rose up and said their good-nights.

The three men sat in silence for several minutes. Finally Hector said, "Well, I think if we're going to go looking for Beck, we need to go into town and notify Silas Weaver. I don't think he can deputize us or anything but at least we'd have told the law of our intension, just in case something bad happens," Hector glanced at the two men, "not that I think it will but just in case."

Thomas nodded, "I hope we can find Beck before things get out of whack and someone really gets hurt. Can you think of any place in particular where he might head?"

Hector shook his head. "Not right off-hand. Lots of places up there where a fellow could stay out of sight."

They spent the next hour going over possible places to investigate and finally decided to try to pick up Beck's tracks in the foothills. It would be slow going but if he had crossed out of the valley into the hills, Thomas was confident he could locate his tracks. Though the ground was dry, there hadn't been any wind to speak of, so horse tracks should last three or four days.

The three men went their separate ways when it got late. The lights in the ranch house were off, but the area was flooded by the light of the moon just one day past its fullness. The sky was cloudless but the stars were dimmed by the brightness of the moonlight and the persistent dusty haze of summer.

Thomas walked to the corral to find Angela there. The air was warm and Angela had on the low-necked blouse she had worn during the day. They stood near the rail fence surrounding the corral listening to the night sounds around them.

They stood side by side, each with a foot on the lower rail of the fence, leaning with their arms touching and resting on the top rail. They hadn't spoken since the meeting with the rest of the family had ended. Thomas sensed the natural fragrance of her skin and hair and the warmth that radiated from her; this awakened and stirred the restless feelings and desires that he had earnestly tried to dismiss; he thought *but do I really want to set these feelings aside?*

As if Angela was reading his thoughts, she turned to him, stood on tiptoe, slid her warm arms around his neck and pressed her lips against his. In the pale moonlight he could see her eyes slowly close. In a few moments the initial firmness of her lips softened and they parted slightly. He responded with his hand behind her head, fingers entwined in her hair, pulling her even tighter, closer to him. They remained in this fervent embrace with their lips together for a long time, neither of them willing, or wanting, to be the first to pull away, to initiate the separation. He felt her pulse increase and her warm lips became even more insistent . . . searching. When they finally drew apart she nestled her lips into the crook of his neck and he heard a soft sigh and her whispered words, "I do so very much love you, my dear Tom. And I fear for your life. No matter what, I don't want anything to happen to you." And he felt the wetness of her tears on his neck.

*   *   *

Thomas had slept very little, tossing and turning restlessly in the warmth of the night, his head a chaotic jumble of thoughts and images. When he shut his eyes, his mind overflowed with kaleidoscopic images of Angela and he experienced again those few moments of intimate contact; the soft, yielding warmth of her lips as they sought his, the liquid-like melding of her body against his, the wetness of her unembarrassed tears of fear and anxiety for him, his deep conflicting yearnings and self-anger . . . and her emerging young beauty and passion. He experienced again the wrenching hurt of physically letting go of her love, of emotionally feeling empty, of his arms and finger tips stretching, reluctant to surrender the last lingering instant of contact . . . as if it was to be forever . . . or never to be.

When he opened his eyes into the soft moonlight streaming through the door and windows of the bunkhouse, his thoughts shifted to what lay ahead today. Just he, Hector and Ramon were going into the mountains to look for Beck, based on Ramon's information. They had formed a basic strategy during the evening and though they believed it could be successful, there were still many risks; all three had emphatically said no to Angela's request to go with them. Thomas had brought them up to date on Sheriff McGee's thoughts; he could sense the obvious change in their demeanor and agreement that they didn't want someone along, specifically the somewhat frail part-time deputy Silas Weaver who might make a hasty decision that could lead to a tragic blunder.

The three men ate breakfast silently, each lost in their own thoughts. Margarita and Angela served them hearty dishes of fried eggs, thick slabs of pan-fried steak, biscuits with honey and cups of steaming coffee. By the end of breakfast the men had relaxed some and good naturedly accepted the ladies teasing about being the pokey posse but Thomas could see the uncertainty in Angela's eyes. As they walked out of the kitchen, she pulled him aside and gave him a tight, clinging hug kissing him on his cheek in front of her mother and father. "Please take care, Thomas," she said aloud, her voice quavering. Margarita smiled knowingly and tipped her head, shut her eyes momentarily and nodded in agreement. Angela pressed a bag of food into her father's hands. "That's to help keep the *perfectly pokey posse pluckily pressing in pursuit*," she announced, trying hard to keep a straight face and everyone laughed.

"Perfect!" Hector responded dryly and everyone laughed again. Tensions eased a little. Margarita and Angela each gave the three men hugs before they got on their horses. They would be traveling very light; each had a rifle in a leather scabbard attached to the saddle, a small bedroll, a poncho in case it rained, a small canteen of water. There would be no cook-fires, no change of clothes. The horses would have to forage for themselves. Each man carried a hunting knife; for Thomas it was the large knife that had been with him for so many years.

The three men rode into Visalia and stopped at the sheriff's office. They were met in the office by the bandy-legged deputy that Hector introduced as Silas. Silently, Thomas shared Angela's assessment that the old man might have difficulty getting on a horse. Thomas guessed the deputy to be in his seventies, thin and dried out like an old willow tree. But as the old man led them to a large map of the county posted on the wall his voice still spoke with authority and knowledge which impressed Thomas.

"Reckon you folks will start about here, near the south edge of Hector's ranch. That's almost due east of town and would be the closest place for Beck to enter into the foothills. Couple of folks spotted him in town a day or so ago but he's already cut and run. I'd guess he'd head straight for the mountains, rest up for a spell. He's going to need supplies and Hector, my guess is that he'd come to your place first. I've known Beck for a lot of years, just like you folks and I don't think he's a mean critter but fetch him up into a corner and no telling what he might do." He traced the Kaweah River with his finger. "I reckon he'd stay on the north side of the river. A little less human traffic there but he might could wander south of the river near Tharp's Peak . . . maybe Blossom Peak. I figure he'll stay this side of Red Hill, River Hill; gets too rough east of there. I reckon he'll stay inside of a rough circle, say from River Hill, over to Shephard Peak, west to Comb Peaks, down to Kaweah, maybe as far west as Davis Mountain or even a little north to Oak Knob. Outside of that area, country is pretty rough, though I ain't saying he wouldn't go there. He's a good horseman, least as I recollect." He stomped back to the big desk and opened the top drawer. He tossed a tin Deputy Sheriff badge to Hector. "Makes you legal, Hector. Least you're a county resident. I ain't going to swear you in or nothing like that." He looked at the three men, "Just don't do nothing crazy. I'd hate to have to explain to Sheriff Newton if things went bad. He'd be madder than a wet hen."

*　　*　　*

Near the Kaweah River
Beck let his horse stand in the slow-moving water at the edge of the Kaweah River. He figured he was several miles south and east of the

Gordon Ranch. It was already warm, though it was only mid-morning and he looked forward to getting to the cooler higher elevation by early afternoon. Beck had already assumed that he had been spotted in Visalia and that there would more than likely be a sheriff's posse coming after him. He had spent the evening before carefully mapping out in his mind the route he would take. He hoped the circuitous course would throw off anyone who attempted to track and follow him.

He'd picked up a few necessary supplies in town but the shop owner had begun to look at him suspiciously, so he cut his buying short, tightly packed and tied his purchases behind his saddle and spent the night camped on the Kaweah where it flowed sluggishly into the valley. Though he felt pressed to move on sooner than he had expected, it was good to be headed once again toward the familiar mountains. He'd spent a lot of years, even before Hector had hired him, riding these mountains searching for lost calves, tracking down predator coyotes and mountain lions, and occasionally deer hunting. He knew the landmark peaks, rivers and the small streams that flowed through deep and shady valleys about as well as anyone.

He clucked to get his horse moving again, guided him into the belly-deep water and turned him downstream. He had a long way to go.

*   *   *

"I figure he'll avoid trying to cut across our ranch," Hector said quietly as the three men rode out of town and toward the foothills, "He wouldn't want to stumble into me or Ramon. I reckon he'll head south of the river so as to by-pass Ted Stanton's and Peter Jenkins' spreads as well. Any further north and he'd have to travel too far across the open valley before he got to the safety of the mountains. He knows this country pretty well. There're a couple of nice little canyons that give good access to the high country, if you know which ones to take."

"Let's take a straight route towards the hills," Thomas suggested. "That should bring us in across the Kaweah south of your ranch and we can look for his trail along the river."

"That sounds good, Thomas."

It took them half an hour to reach the river and another half hour to locate Beck's campsite and the horse's prints. "New left front shoe," Thomas stated as he looked at the prints. "He's carrying some extra weight behind the saddle. And he's favoring his right rear leg some right now. My guess is the horse has been ridden pretty hard and needs a few days rest. That could change Beck's plans some if that leg begins to get worse. Here's where they went into the water. Beck paused here, and I think he spent a few minutes deciding which way to go." Thomas pointed downstream, "My guess is he'll go downstream a bit to try to throw any followers off. Let's cross here and head downstream for a ways, see if we can pick up his tracks."

Hector and Ramon both nodded wordlessly and plunged their horses into the river. It took the three of them another twenty minutes to pick up Beck's trail again nearly a quarter of a mile downstream. Beck had chosen a large slab of rock to exit the river and it had taken keen eyes to pick up the trail. But then the trail broke sharply toward the mountains and Thomas studied the tracks.

"He's got the horse into a trot, trying to put on some miles."

Hector stared at the range of foothills to their east. "I'd say he's headed for the canyon below Tharp's Peak. If he stays to the north of Tharp's Peak, he'll have fairly easy access to the river. If he tries to go south of the peak and around it, it'll take him way too far south. No advantage to him."

"Well, his tracks are pretty easy to follow here in the flatland. We're not in any hurry. Let's just stay on his trail, see where he leads us." Thomas clucked and his horse responded, moving ahead at a steady but easy pace. The hoof prints showed that Beck had stopped and turned around for a look over his left shoulder. "Checking to see if anyone's behind him."

"Can you tell how old these prints are?" Hector asked.

Thomas got off his horse and stooped to study the hoof prints carefully. One had landed directly on a small anthill and the ants had already removed the dirt that had fallen into their entrance and piled it up. "Couple of hours." He studied some other prints before he climbed back onto his horse. "Beck's getting a little nervous. He's turning around in his saddle every now and then to look behind him. Probably anxious to get into the hills for a little better cover. He feels pretty exposed right now."

"You think he's seen us?" Ramon asked quietly.

"I don't think so. If he had he'd have picked up his pace some. No sign of that. Just a steady trot. But that'll tire Beck as well as his horse. So he knows he better get into the hills and find some good cover, some water and a place to let his horse rest."

"Small year-round creek north of Tharp's Peak. Local people call it Stovepipe Creek. Eventually flows into the Kaweah. That's where he'll head."

Thomas nodded this time. "Sounds like a good plan."

CHAPTER 19

<u>Stovepipe Creek, tributary of Kaweah River</u>
Beck let the horse slow from the trot and rode him to the edge of the shallow creek. "There you go, old man," he said as the horse dipped his head and drank from the stream. He'd ridden the horse hard and the pace had been rough on the rider as well as the horse. He climbed down and let the reins drop to the ground. It was cooler here among the snarl of scrub oaks and short manzanita trees. The ground was covered with stubby ferns, tangled vines and bear clover. A few wildflowers—Indian Paintbrush and Lupine—poked their blooms up into the dappled sunlight. He'd selected a place to stop that was on a little rise from which he could look back over the route he had taken. The vast width of the San Joaquin Valley disappeared into the mid-day haze but he could see the three riders moving toward him across the flat valley floor several miles in the distance; he knew they had picked up his trail, though the horses appeared to be moving at a normal walk.

"Well, damn!" He muttered. There wouldn't be much time to linger by the stream. He'd let his horse rest for fifteen minutes or so, then he'd have to press on up the valley before cutting over the ridge to the Kaweah river. He lifted the horse's feet and checked each hoof. When he lifted the right rear he grunted when he saw that a sharp stone had cut into the softer frog. "That's why you're favoring that foot, isn't it?" He patted the horse's neck, "we'll give it a rest soon, old man but we need to keep moving right now." The horse nodded his head as if he understood Beck's words.

Beck scooped a few handfuls of water into his own mouth, wiping it with his shirt sleeve. "Sorry but we have to get a move on." He climbed into the saddle and clucked the horse into movement. He took one more look over his shoulder at the three riders, still several miles away. "Giddy-up, old man," he urged the horse.

* * *

<u>San Francisco</u>
Dunsworth had spent most of a miserable Saturday trying to console Sophia; he had finally accompanied her to the railroad station and saw her onto the train headed for Los Angeles and her brother's funeral. Afterward he returned to his office at the law firm and closeted himself in the room where he could think undisturbed. On a blank sheet of paper he listed the things that he had to take care of.

First, he was beginning to be very uncomfortable with the direction of Sheriff McGee's line of follow-up questions. The shotgun, the stack of money in the gun cabinet, the bloody sheet in Beck's cabin . . . the sheriff went over and over his discovery of Nelle's body—what happened before and what he did afterwards. As an attorney, he was used to this fine combing-over of details but mostly in dealing with financial issues—his area of legal expertise. He was beginning to see how a case could be built . . . The best thing that could happen is that someone would see Beckley Weston and shoot him dead on the spot before he got a chance to start talking . . .

Secondly, he would have to quickly finalize the Nicaraguan property purchase deal. That would mean a fact-to-face meeting with Michael Esperanza-Vincente, the sole heir and now owner of the huge tract of land. Without the legal firm in Los Angeles to advise him, the young man would hopefully sign an agreement that would benefit the group of investors. But Dunsworth didn't speak Spanish and Esperanza-Vincente spoke no English. That would mean a third party, the interpreter, would need to be present to understand the details of the transaction. And that assumed that Esperanza-Vincente would even agree to a meeting. Still, there were other methods available to him as a lawyer. Legally or not, he would acquire the valuable property. He had already received one telegram from the east coast investors asking what the last meeting with Esperanza-Vincente had brought about.

Thirdly, he had to somehow derail any investigation into his limited contact with the hired assassin who had killed Señora Isabella Laurencia Esperanza. It seemed incredible that the Nicaraguan government was insisting on an investigation in the United States. From all accounts he had managed to read, authorities in Nicaragua believed the tragedy to be the result of a tragic fire that had burned her hacienda to the ground. Nothing recognizable was left, not even the burnt remains of the beautiful lady. Nothing but ashes . . . Arson had not been mentioned.

Fourthly, he must decide what to do about Sophia. She had become almost incoherent over the death of her brother and now that she was in Los Angeles, he wondered if she would even return to San Francisco. He looked out the window at the building across the street. Sophia . . . She was unquestionably beautiful, marvelously bright, enjoyable to be with and incredible in bed, especially after they had shared a few glasses of wine. But love . . . he shook his head. A mistress perhaps but love . . . or marriage . . . was out of the question. He could not imagine her within his social setting, hobnobbing with San Francisco's rich and privileged. She would humiliate him and those around her with her frequently ribald sense of humor, a husky-voiced, earthy repartee that needed little clarification as to its gist. No . . . she would simply remain his secret, part-time mistress, well compensated to take care of his needs and to keep her relationship with him private and loyal.

Lastly, there were some lingering legal details he must take care of: the funeral expenses for Nelle, written replies to those who had so willingly offered their services in his time of dark despair, the need to select a suitable granite marker for her grave site, property deeds and wills to be straightened out and re-filed, the ranch house to be refurbished and made ready for possible sale. He leaned back in his chair, reminding himself that he must carefully pace his re-entry into the social world; the recently-widowed role would be fine for a few months but he would soon want to be out and among society, able to sit and share an evening drink in public.

*   *   *

Stovepipe Creek
Thomas studied the prints near the edge of the shallow creek and pointed out the essential marks.

"These prints are fairly fresh, two or three hours at the most. He stopped for a few minutes here to let his horse have a drink. He got off and checked all four hooves; he's probably aware by now that the right rear is giving his horse trouble. That could change his plans a little." Thomas looked closely at Beck's footprints. "Beck's boots are about worn out . . . sole's cracked on the left boot, heels are both worn down pretty bad." He thought about the boot prints left at the scene of the shooter who had tried to kill Frank Barnwell; those had been of fairly new boots—*probably Justins.* Judging by the shape of the sole, especially the toe of the boot, these prints were not made by an expensive Justin boot.

He looked at the sun; it was getting to be late afternoon. Their ability to follow Beck's trail was going to end when the sun set. The three men had decided to purposely travel light, bringing only enough food to have a few cold meals and a thin bedroll to ward off the night chill. Each carried a rifle in a leather scabbard attached to the saddle.

"I figure Beck's going to have to stop when it gets dark," Thomas said. "His horse is going to need some attention to that hoof. Could have a small rock in it, or could be just darned sore from some minor damage. In any case, his horse won't be able to go on more than a day or two."

"That may cut into his plans some," Ramon remarked. "He may have to head more directly to where he planned to stay, rather than try to throw off his followers."

"And it could slow him down, if the hoof gets worse," Hector added.

"Let's say he's three hours ahead of us," Thomas mused. "Could he get across the Kaweah before it gets dark?"

"Only if he went up and over the ridge."

Thomas looked at Ramon, "How hard's that going to be with a horse that's going lame?"

"Beck knows this country pretty well. I've been hunting with him a few times and he's got a map of this area in his head. I think he'll cut up the ridge at an angle so his horse won't have to work so hard. Probably go down the other side the same way. If he picks the right place, he'll end up right at the river."

*   *   *

Beck winced as his horse once again favored the rear hoof. The climb up the side of the ridge had been hard for the horse with his right rear hoof on the downhill side and taking most of the weight. Beck had cut back a few times to relieve the horse but such maneuvers only lengthened the distance he had to cover. The deeper forest had closed in around him, so it was impossible to determine how far ahead of his followers he was. Now with his horse getting lame, it was going to be even more difficult to pull further ahead. He pictured the terrain in his mind. Once he reached the peak of the ridge the Kaweah River would be to his left at the bottom of the ridge. If he stayed along the peak of the ridge he would ride eastward and parallel to the river until the ridge ended with another canyon that cut perpendicular to it; at the canyon's bottom would be Frenchman's Creek that flowed into the Kaweah. On the far side of Frenchman's was an immense, flat exposure of granite with the Kaweah on its left flank and its right buried deep into another ridge. The arrangement would provide three options: to the left and across the Kaweah, to the right and up Frenchman's Creek, or ahead and onto the granite. In any case, there would be no trail to follow.

*   *   *

"He's heading up the ridge," Thomas said as he studied the trail of bent and broken twigs and indentations in the pine needle covered forest floor. The three stopped and peered through the tangle of trees and chest-high brush. The ground rose up quickly up each side from the canyon bottom. "I think we can assume he knows he's being followed. He'll be looking for places where he can cover up his tracks. We've only got about two more hours of sunlight."

"The river's right on the other side of this ridge. Once he makes it over the ridge, he'll be right at the river. He *could* go across right there." It was Ramon. "But the river's deep and swift there. I think he'll look for someplace where he can cross easier."

"I think Ramon is right," Hector added. "You know, Beck once told me he never learned how to swim and he hates the river."

"So, which way? Up the river, or down the river?" Thomas asked.

"Well there's sure nothing downriver; just a steep river bank along the bottom of the ridge. In fact, the river curves somewhat along there and it's eaten away into the side of the ridge. In some places the drop into the river is forty or fifty feet."

"So if we continue up the canyon here, we'd come out at Frenchman's Creek?"

Hector nodded, "Yes but about half a mile, maybe more, from the Kaweah." He hesitated then added, "If he's going to try going up Frenchman's, we could cut him off."

233

"We could. What about crossings beyond where Frenchman's Creek merges with the river?"

"Hmm," Hector paused, "if I remember right, there's a long stretch of rock—smooth granite—there. It's almost flat and about a hundred yards long, maybe five or six yards across. Runs parallel to the river until it finally dips into the water itself." He paused again before he added, "That would be a convenient place for him to slip across the river. Besides, the river's shallow and wide there."

"Well, if we continue to follow his tracks, we'll know he's ahead of us. If we lose his tracks, we'll not be sure where he is and it could take a while to pick up his trail again," Thomas mused out loud. "I think we best just stay behind him."

* * *

The shadows were getting deeper and longer by the time Beck reached the crest of the ridge. Through the trees he could see the sunlight sparkle off the Kaweah River several hundred feet below him and the late sun shining on the mountain on the other side of the river. He sat quietly in the saddle, listening carefully for any sounds behind him. So far, there was nothing to suggest that the men following him were any closer than two or three hours back. The gentle rushing sound of the river came from his left and the late afternoon air was motionless and warm. The only odors were the smell of his horse and the leather saddle.

He turned in the saddle and stared along the crest of the ridge in the direction he had come. Somewhere back there the three riders were trying to guess what he would do next. He had only a few hours of sunlight left. The tiny sliver of two-day old moon would last only a few hours; then there would be utter darkness. He had to put some distance between himself and the men behind him. It would be getting dark by the time they reached the top of the ridge where he was. That could work in his advantage . . .

* * *

Thomas leaned over his horse's left shoulder to stare at the pine needle covered mountain side. "Getting harder and harder to make out his trail," he muttered to no one in particular. He had painstakingly followed the faint trail of hoof prints in the deep loam covering the ground, reading every minute clue he could discover. He'd seen where Beck had stopped on occasion, probably to listen over his shoulder and once to relieve himself. Beck's horse was beginning to get tired and it showed as more often favoring the lame right rear leg. "Another half hour and he's going to have to quit for the night. I figure we're about an hour and a half to two hours behind him."

"Reckon we've got about another forty-five minutes 'till we reach the top," Hector muttered. All three men were getting tired of being in the saddle and were feeling the early pangs of hunger beginning to gnaw at their insides. They'd sleep on the ground tonight, no campfire, no warm food, no coffee in the morning. The only solace was that the man they were following would be experiencing the same hardships.

They reached the top of the ridge in a little less than an hour. From there they could hear the rush of the Kaweah River below them. It was too dark for Thomas to get a good look at the tracks made by the horse ahead of them. Reluctantly, they decided to call it a night and make camp.

* * *

Darkness swept in quickly and Beck was forced to concede that he could go no further. He had turned and ridden back down the crest of the ridge toward the west—downriver—and had cut back and forth through the trees and brush, deliberately confusing the trail in the event the men following him would see that he had reversed directions. He would wait for the first rays of sunlight and continue downriver for another mile or so until he found the singular place just beyond the rockslide where the river spread out wide and shallow. That's where he would throw his followers off the trail.

* * *

Baker's Ridge, above the Kaweah River
Thomas slept restlessly, listening to the night sounds and the constant *shush* of the river far below them. The stars reeled overhead; the summer constellations bright through the tree tops. *Orion*, being a winter constellation would not be visible tonight. It was well after midnight when the forest sounds finally went away with the only disturbance being the distant rush of the river and an occasional breeze through the trees.

Thomas went over in this mind what he knew about Beck. He was almost certain that Beck had not been the one who had shot at Frank Barnwell by mistake. But that left Thomas pondering the question: *who would try to kill me and why? How does Clarence Chandler fit into this, if he does?* As a business man he certainly had disagreements with those he dealt with. Some of the disagreements had become quite vocal but none had ever reached the point of violence. There were those who favored saving the redwood trees and those who considered them a renewable resource there for humanity to use to its advantage. Never mind that it took a hundred years, or more, to produce a redwood tree that could be cut and turned into lumber. Though Thomas encouraged his own lumbering company to carefully cut and thin to promote new growth, he knew that the forest was left in sad disarray after his company had finished cutting. He finally drifted off to sleep with these thoughts on his mind.

He awoke as the eastern sky was just beginning to turn deep purple. The air was still and cold and his two companions were still sleeping, rolled tightly in their blankets. Thomas sat up and listened carefully, concentrating on the sounds he expected to hear; the soft voice of the rider putting the saddle on his horse, the leather snap of the straps being cinched up, the soft whinny of the horse, perhaps a tap of metal against metal as the rider eased himself into the saddle. But the air was still.

Thomas reached over and tapped Hector on the shoulder, made a motion to remain silent. Hector nodded and did the same to Ramon. Ramon parceled out chunks of jerky which they began to chew on as a vague substitute for breakfast. In the meantime Thomas circled the camp, trying to relocate the tracks of their query. He found where Beck had stopped but then Thomas frowned when he saw that he had turned back down the crest of the ridge in the direction of the river flow. The trail was extremely difficult to see in the deep forest ground cover of pine needles; he had to use the barest of clues to follow the trail. He listened carefully; the early morning sounds had yet to begin. The continuous burbling sound of the river below them filled the empty air. Thomas sat next to the two men.

"Beck's trying to throw us off his trail." Thomas kept his voice just above a whisper. "He's doubled back along the ridge crest. The way I figure it, he'll have to go on downstream until he finds a place shallow enough to cross. Or, he could drop back into the canyon we all came up and go on back to Frenchman's Creek, cut across there. Or, he could double back again and cross upriver while we're looking for him downriver. I think he's depending on us spending time tracking his every turn. What we really need is to know where he's headed."

"There's a bad rockslide area back that way. He'd be smart to get off the mountain before the slide," Hector said quietly.

"You know," Ramon spoke up, "what keeps coming to my mind is there's an old cabin—old wooden shack—perched on the side of a mountain ten or twelve miles up behind Old Man Shingleton's place. Hard to find and it's probably in bad shape but it's next to a small creek. I bet there hasn't been anyone living there for fifty years, maybe more. Beck said it's all overgrown, covered with vines and moss, real hard to see, even when you're right up next to it."

Thomas nodded, "Well, that sounds like the kind of place he might look for."

"Ramon, you're talking about the old Gilley place, aren't you?" Hector asked.

"Yeah, that's the place. I couldn't remember the name."

"It's a real old place," Hector went on. "A drifter called Sam Gilley put it up about fifty years ago; did a little trapping, hunting, that sort of thing. Some say he was wanted by the federals for something he done. He never registered a claim or anything. Then about thirty years ago he just disappeared. Never found him. Some of the local folks figure old Gray Hawk got him." Hector shrugged his shoulders and shot a quick glance at Thomas. "Reckon we don't know for sure. Mountain lion could have got him. Hell, any number of things could cause a man to disappear in these mountains."

"Well, do you think the place is still usable?"

Ramon frowned, "Sure could be. Water's right there. Pretty rough country though, lots of ravines, deep canyons, creeks, rock slides. And it's awfully brushy, lots of snags and trees down, thick cover of creepers, stink weed, rabbit-brush, vines, kit-kit-dizze, chinquapin, plenty of poison oak. It's plain tough to get through and it gets down-right nasty in the winter. I'd guess there hasn't been a burn up there for a hundred years."

"So, what makes you think Beck would know how to get there?"

"We were up near it once about three years ago when I was deer hunting with him." Ramon looked at Thomas, "he said he'd stayed there a few times when he went hunting."

*   *   *

Beck awoke and got up before the sun had started to lighten the eastern horizon. He slipped the saddle onto his horse, drew the cinches up tight, fastened his bedroll behind the saddle and slid his rifle into the scabbard. His stomach growled noisily and he grimaced at the hunger pang as he held out a handful of oats for his horse to nibble at. He ran his hand down the right rear leg, feeling for swelling but found to his relief that the leg was still okay. Ten minutes later he was in the saddle and steering the horse through the maze of trees that crowded the side of the ridge. It took him nearly an hour to reach the wide rockslide that dropped obliquely several hundred feet into the river below. The rockslide itself had happened many years in the past; the years of rain and snow had washed the dirt and sand into the river, leaving only chunks of fractured granite that varied from the size of small eggs to that of large barrels. It was a treacherous stretch, nearly a hundred yards across, where a single misstep by his horse could cause both of them a dangerous plunge into the river below. Over the years there had been several unanticipated landslides.

Beck got off his horse to study the slide area. Even in the faint glow of pre-dawn, there were no obvious paths across. Any course chosen would require the horse and rider to select a route with extreme caution and maneuver with extra care around the sizeable boulders that rested precariously on the rocky slide. If one of the boulders was to become dislodged, it could initiate another rockslide that would be certain to carry horse and rider with it. Beck walked uphill, studying the boulders and estimating their destructive force. Finally he found what he was looking for, a large, roughly cubic boulder that sat perched on one corner at an ungainly angle ready to tumble down the side of the mountain. Its path was sure to cause other boulders to join the out-of-control tumble toward the river, carrying with them rocks of all sizes and shapes—a rockslide.

He walked back to his horse and carefully led him onto the slide area, selecting every step after carefully considering its position on the face of the slide. It took him forty-five minutes to wend his way across the slide to the firm soil on the far side. Even there, Beck chose his path carefully, using deep pine needle ground cover to absorb the horse's hoof prints. He untied the lariat from the saddle and ventured carefully on foot onto the slide toward the boulder he had selected. When he got to it he warily made his way around it, studying the clutch of smaller rocks that held the boulder in place. One in particular appeared to be a main support, holding three other elongated rocks angled against the base of the boulder. With extreme caution, he slid the rope around the rock and knotted a loop. Taking the loose end, he retraced his steps back to his horse and tied the end of the rope to the saddle's pommel.

"Easy now, old man," he whispered as he eased himself into the saddle. He clucked softly and the horse stepped forward slowly until the rope became taut. He clucked again, gave a gentle nudge with his knees and the horse leaned into the pull. For a long moment it seemed that the rope would part but then it pulled the supporting rock from its position under the boulder. For a few long moments more it appeared that nothing would happen, then the huge boulder began to tip downhill with a grinding noise, pushing other rocks out of its path. Finally it broke free and began to slide and tumble noisily, taking others with it. Within seconds the entire inclined face of the rockslide seemed to be in fluid motion.

*   *   *

The three men heard the muffled rumble of the rockslide from where they stood. The earth appeared to tremble beneath their feet.

"What the hell is that?" Thomas whispered.

"Rockslide!" Ramon hissed. "I'll bet Beck tried to get across the slide area, started a slide. If that's the case, it'll kill him and his horse for sure!"

"How far is it from here?"

"Three, maybe four miles. Beck would have to get on the other side of it to get across the river."

"He'd have known that, wouldn't he?"

"Sure. He knows the rockslide; it's called Perdition Slide. If he wasn't in a hurry, he'd have gone up and around it."

Thomas frowned. *Something is not right.* "How long would it take him to go around it?"

"Couple of hours. It starts right up close to the top of the ridge. That whole area is unstable."

"Saddle up!" Thomas muttered. "Let's go! He may need help."

"If he was on the slide when it let go," Hector said quietly, "he's beyond help."

It took them an hour to locate the place where Beck had spent the night, identified only by an area of bent grass where Beck had laid out his bedroll.

239

The horse's footprints showed where he had stood throughout the night; he still appeared to be favoring his right rear foot. The trail that led from there was clear and direct. Obviously, Beck knew now where he was heading and was not concerned about trying to hide his tracks. The hoof marks curved slightly downhill about midway down the side of the ridge, then ran parallel to the river four or five hundred feet below. It took them another hour to cover the distance to the slide area. The early morning air still carried a slight sulfurous odor that rose up from the freshly pulverized rock.

"My God!" Hector muttered as he stared across the slope of shattered rock. "If he was on that when it let go . . ."

Thomas got off his horse and studied the prints. "Beck got off his horse here, walked downhill some then turned around and went uphill," he followed the prints, "until right here. Then he led the horse onto the rock." He studied the face of the rockslide. "He's either in the river, probably dead, or on the other side of the slide."

*   *   *

Washington, D.C.

It was late morning in Washington D.C. and President Theodore Roosevelt had sequestered himself in his study, going over letters and international news as printed in the major newspapers. His aide, James, knocked at the door.

Roosevelt had sent for him, so he simply bellowed, "Come in, James!"

"Mister President. You wanted to see me sir?" the aide asked when he stood in front of the President's desk.

Roosevelt took off his reading glasses and rubbed at his eyes. "James, remember our conversation when I was working on the West Point graduation speech?"

"Yes, sir."

"I mentioned I wanted to start pulling together a short trip to California."

"Yes, sir, I remember us talking about that."

"Good. I need a few things to assist me with my planning, James. I don't believe you'll have any trouble getting them for me." He looked up at his aide. "Please remember I want all of this to be very quiet, a very limited *need to know* basis."

"Yes, sir. Of course."

"Good. Now, I'm seriously looking at sometime in early May," he pulled open a desk drawer and retrieved a calendar for the coming year, "over a couple of weekends so as to give working folks an opportunity to see and hear me." He studied the calendar. "Let's plan to arrive in Los Angeles early on Thursday, the seventh of May." He paused, staring at the calendar. "Umm—going to be tight, squeezing this in but it's important. I've got to be back in Washington by the eighteenth. So, let's set it up to be in San Francisco on the fourteenth." He shook his head. "Gad, that's only five days!" He studied the calendar, running his finger across the days and weeks. "Well, right now, it's the best I can do." Without explanation to his aide, he put X's on the squares representing Saturday the ninth and Sunday the tenth. "You'll have to arrange train transportation, James and I'll give you some more information on that later; but it'll be a fast, non-stop run to California." He put his pen down. "Now, regarding the security detail. I mentioned that we would provide our own security, contrary to how past excursions have been handled." He slid a piece of paper across to his aide. "Here are the names of six soldiers from the Washington Detachment I want to accompany us. I know these men well from past expeditions with them. They're good marksmen, expert horsemen as well, and I know they are trustworthy. These men and only these men will comprise my personal security detail." He held up his hand to stop his aide's obvious objection. "You must notify them in sufficient time to allow them to arrange their personal time accordingly. James, this must all remain off the record. Names, dates, itinerary, everything is considered secret, do you understand?"

"I certainly do, Mister President."

"Good. Now, I will release certain, um . . . non-critical details of my plans as the time draws near but until then, this remains between us." He stared at his aide as if to ensure that the man completely understood. "No others, James."

"Yes, sir."

"Fine, that's settled. Now James, I want you to take care of one more thing. I need a map and I don't want one of those confounded tourist maps, James; they can't even correctly name the rivers! You may have to go do some arm twisting over at the Department of the Interior—you'll probably want to see someone at the Office of U.S. Geological Survey. Now, what I want . . . what I *must* have . . . is a topographical map—up to date from their latest survey data—of California's Kaweah River from the San Joaquin Valley to the Kaweah River headwaters and extending out . . . umm . . . let's say twenty miles on either side of the river. I'll grant you executive permission to throw my name around if you have to," the President laughed. "Now, it'll probably take more than one map to cover an area of that size. Get whatever you must. Anyway, you know how I enjoy poring over maps. One can learn a lot. You like looking at maps, James?"

The aide smiled. "Not particularly, sir, if I must say. An attractive lady's more to my liking."

CHAPTER 20

<u>Perdition Slide</u>

"I guess we best go on down and see if we can find him . . . or his remains." Hector muttered as he glanced quickly at the gray sky.

Thomas grimaced. "Hold on just a minute! I'm not sure . . ." He retrieved his binoculars from the saddle bag and studied the far side of the rock slide. "He just may have . . . ah! What's this?" He leaned forward, carefully focused the glasses, holding them rock steady. "Hoof marks! Dug in hard like he was pulling something. I think Beck has tried to flummox us again!" He put the glasses back and pointed, "He got to the other side safely, then somehow triggered the slide—I shouldn't think that part was very difficult."

"If he's on the other side of this slide, then he's only a half hour or so from where he can cross the river," Ramon murmured. "If we have to go up and around the slide, it'll put us even further behind him."

"My guess is that he'll take the shortest route he can because of his horse. He may want to be able to cut back and lead us on a rabbit chase but his horse is hurting. If there's a place where he can cross the river safely, he'll head right there. What we need to do is close the distance between us."

Hector nodded in agreement. "He'll be headed for a shallow area to cross 'cuz he doesn't know how to swim." He swiveled and looked at Thomas and Ramon. "I think the three of us know how to swim . . ."

It took them another half hour to find a place where they could approach the river and urge their horses into the swiftly moving, deep water. With only a little hesitation, the horses stepped into the water; the current pushed them downstream as the horses swam slowly to the opposite rocky shore. Their crossing had put them about a half a mile upriver from the slide.

"Let's head downstream a ways but keep your eyes open for any tracks coming from the river; he could have walked his horse upstream some after he crossed," Thomas urged as he turned downstream. "Might also want to keep an eye further downstream, in case he's still near the river."

Hector and Ramon both nodded their understanding and the three followed the gravelly river bank, carefully looking for any sign of Beck's crossing. They came to the slide area and Hector commented on the enormous amount of rock that had slid into the river, causing it to re-route itself around the blockage. The slide was over two hundred yards wide at the river and the recent rockslide had dumped enough rock and debris into the river to cut its width in half, forcing the river to create a new channel around the blockage.

"Keep your eyes open," Thomas reminded the two riders. "Going to be hard to see hoof prints in this gravel." Thomas had an uneasy feeling: *Beck knows exactly what he's doing . . .*

They rode slowly along the edge of the river, staring at the accumulation of small rocks and sand that comprised the shallow bank. They passed the area of the slide and Thomas noted that the bank on the opposite side was also shallow and would be an opportune place for Beck to bring his horse into the river. But the bank where the three rode was clear of any tracks. Thomas got off his horse to get a little closer to the gravel that lined the river for miles in each direction. *Beck could have led his horse quite a ways downstream before he came out of the river . . .*

Thomas checked the angle of the sun; it would be mid-day shortly and it had been at least two and a half hours since they last saw Becks tracks. After another half hour he drew up short and turned to Hector. "I think Beck's pulled another fast one. We're going to have to go back to where he crossed the slide and pick up his trail there."

Hector nodded reluctantly. "I think you're right, Thomas. "If he went back over the ridge, he's got a five or six hour head start on us." He glanced at the sky. "Clouds forming up. Probably going to be in for some rain this afternoon."

"I'm thinking about his horse with the lame foot. Could be Beck already reckons that he can't ride him any deeper into the mountains. Might be he's going looking for another mount."

Thomas nodded in hesitant agreement. "That means he could be heading for your place."

"Could be . . . but we don't know for sure . . ."

*   *   *

Punta Gorda, Nicaragua

Miguel Esperanza-Vincente sat across the table from the private investigator he had hired to look into the death of his mother and two members of her household staff in Punta Gorda. He had just returned from Managua, the nation's capital, where he had been since his recent trip to Los Angeles, negotiating with several North American shipping firms handling the family's growing coffee export business.

It was early afternoon in Punta Gorda and he had spent the better part of the morning at the burnt ruins of the family hacienda, supervising the removal of the remains of the fire, namely the curved, red roof tiles. He had already decided to rebuild the hacienda, using much of his father's original design and architecture. As each wheelbarrow load was carried away, he had the workers sift it through metal screen, searching for anything that could give them a clue as to what had caused the fire. So far, no new evidence had been revealed.

They had gathered a few facts, however. Thus far, while sifting through the ashes, none of his mother's expensive silver and gold jewelry had been recovered, not even melted into shapeless puddles of metal. Also missing was his mother's collection of seventy three rare Nicaraguan one hundred dollar gold coins. Minted in a small number in Great Britain for Nicaragua in 1898, the coins had remained uncirculated as the country lingered undecided as to the use of gold or silver for its large denomination coins. When it finally decided on silver, it made the uncirculated provisional gold coins a sought after collector's item. The whereabouts of the lost coins would have remained a mystery had it not been for the sharp eyes of an honest bank teller in Snyder, Texas who had taken them in on a currency exchange transaction and then sent them by courier to the Nicaraguan treasury. Government officials there had kept track of the location of the rare gold coins—exactly two hundred in total—and had eventually contacted Miguel Esperanza-Vincente to inform him of their recovery. They could be returned to Miguel Esperanza-Vincente once the transference of a large recording fee was completed.

Gomez Santiago, the private investigator, had made a trip on his client's behalf to Snyder, Texas and had spoken to the bank teller. The man was able to provide him with a reasonable physical description of the man who had brought the coins in for exchange. About six feet two inches tall, the man had said. Black hair with streaks of silver, silver sideburns and a thick black mustache with silver hairs running through it. Very dark eyes and a face deeply creased with wrinkles from the corners of his eyes, the sides of his nose and the ends of his lips—features unusual for a man that otherwise didn't appear very old—perhaps in his mid forties. The man did his banking business under the name of Luke Sage but had recently closed out his account. The teller would not reveal how much cash Luke Sage had withdrawn but reluctantly leaned forward and whispered, "*enough to buy up most of Abilene*".

Santiago had stayed in Abilene, hanging around the saloons that lined the main street, keeping an eye open for the man fitting the description the teller had given him. On the third day he saw the man, wearing a black leather overcoat in spite of the heat of the day, as he walked into the Western Union Telegraph Office. When he emerged ten minutes later Santiago tagged along behind him, half a block back and watched him enter the door leading to the hotel located over the noisy Aces High Saloon.

It had taken the private investigator two more days to learn which of the eight rooms upstairs belonged to Luke Sage and the next morning watched as Sage strolled casually away from the hotel and entered the barber shop. The two barber's chairs were both occupied and Sage nodded to the front barber and sat to wait in one of the straight-back wooden chairs.

Locked doors were not a major deterrent for Santiago and within minutes he was inside Luke Sage's hotel room. Quickly but with practiced precision, he went through the three drawers in the bureau, ruffling through the meager assortment of clothing. No papers, books, receipts, train schedules, loose change, ticket stubs. Nothing. He pulled open the door to the tall wardrobe and slid his hands over the empty shelves. Again there was nothing. He checked under the bed where he found the small valise. When he opened it he discovered the custom built .50 caliber break-down rifle and its telescopic sight. While not in itself anything damning, the find did provide some insight into the nature of the man called Luke Sage. He carefully replaced everything and let himself out of the room.

All of this information had been passed on to Miguel Esperanza-Vincente during their meeting.

"You've done very well, my friend," Esperanza-Vincente said in flawless English. "Now, if you're ready, I'll ask you to make another trip to the United States for me. This time to California."

Santiago nodded. "I'll leave tomorrow. I can be in California in less than a week."

"Excellent! I want you to go to San Francisco and learn what you can about an attorney named Alexander Dunsworth."

* * *

Kaweah River

"I think our best chance is to cross over by the slide and try to pick up his trail there, at least maybe figure out which way he's headed." Thomas said quietly. He looked skyward at the gathering clouds. "If it rains, there'll be little chance of following him."

"It's going to rain, for sure," Hector said. "I've watched these clouds for thirty years—we've got a thunderstorm coming soon, maybe in the next hour."

It took nearly an hour to cross the river and make their way back to the slide area. By then the air was thick with a heavy mist that soon turned to a drizzly rain. Thomas located the horse tracks and was able to follow them up to the top of the ridge but by then the rain had become a torrent, making it nearly impossible to see the horse tracks in the dense ground cover.

"Well, at least we know he's headed back down rather than going higher in the mountains."

"I'll bet he's going to try to find another horse," Ramon said quietly. "I sure would if I was him."

Thomas nodded in agreement. "Your spread's the closest and he knows your livestock. He could slip in there under the cover of the rain, swap horses and be gone in just a few minutes. If the rain keeps up, it'll cover his tracks pretty well. And it'll be dark right quick. I think we're going to have to wait a spell before we go out after him again." He looked at Ramon, "If you were Beck, what would you do next?"

Ramon wiped the rain off his face with his shirt sleeve, then, "I reckon Beck knows he's being followed; probably doesn't know for sure who's on his trail. He'll be thinking he threw us off back there, maybe make us believe he's headed for the high country. I'd still head for the Gilley cabin soon as I got a fresh horse. This rain came just in time for him."

A brilliant flash of lightning followed almost immediately by a loud crash of thunder punctuated his comments. "I believe we've got a good summer storm upon us," Hector muttered.

* * *

<u>San Felipe, Panama Province of Columbia</u>
The mid morning sun was reflecting off the warm waters of the Golfo de Panama. The sixty-nine year old doctor had just exited the *Telegrafie la Oficina* in San Felipe, bearing a small yellow envelope. He could scarcely conceal his anticipation as he walked briskly along the waterfront walkway overlooking the gulf waters. It took him twenty minutes to get to his house and he let the door slam shut behind him in his excitement. His wife, Maria, looked up briefly from her reading, recognized his animated expression.

"Finally?" she asked quietly.

"Si! Finally!" He stepped into his study, pulled the door shut behind him, sat at the big wooden desk and stared at the envelope for several long seconds before finally slitting it open. *So much depended on what the contents of the telegram said . . .*

He slid the single sheet out, unfolded it and spread it on the desk in front of him. He retrieved his reading glasses and perched them on his nose, tipping his head back so that he could peer through the lenses.

The contents of the telegram appeared to make no sense; it was a jumble of names and dates, congratulatory phrases praising him in detail on a highly technical medical paper he had presumably submitted for publication. He smiled grimly as he pulled his King James Version of the Holy Bible in English from its place on the shelf behind him and went to work decoding the contents of the message. The code was not difficult—that was why they had chosen this particular method to communicate—but it meant turning many pages, many references, even a few twisting mathematical exercises. But eventually the message was spelled out. He sat back and frowned, reading his scrawled handwriting.

"Madre de Dios!" he whispered to himself. "They have set a date! But, so far away!" He studied the figures again, double checking. "The ninth of May, next year! *Christo!* Not until next year! Eleven more months of waiting!" He pounded the desk softly with a clenched fist and reread the last portion. *More information will be forthcoming. Maintain absolute confidentiality. Travel arrangements will be provided. Do not attempt to contact us.*

He leaned back and closed his eyes. *Do the Americans not understand? So much to do!* The terrible, bloody civil war continues between the Liberals and the Conservatives, the ruling party in Columbia. A wrong

248

word, a political assertion that arouses someone's attention or a single correspondence can lead to someone quietly disappearing in the night or being dragged to prison for interrogation before being hauled away to stand for a few last terrifying moments before a firing squad. The war must end. Panama must be free of the distant yoke of control from Columbia!

*   *   *

The Gordon Ranch

It was raining hard by the time the three approached the ranch. A quick check of the barn revealed that all the livestock was there and that so far, Beck had not paid a visit. After putting their horses away, they entered the house and were greeted by Margarita and Angela.

"Did you find him?" Margarita asked.

Hector shook his head. "He got away from us and we think he may be headed back here to pick up a fresh horse."

"Here!" Margarita exclaimed. "Why would he do that?"

"Beck's horse is getting lame. He's been ridden pretty hard the past week or so."

"Do you think he'll make trouble if he comes by?" Angela asked quietly.

Thomas shook his head. "I don't think so, Angela. He just wants to get somewhere to hide from the law, or bounty hunters." He looked at Ramon and Hector. "I think it would be a good idea for us to keep an eye on the barn tonight. I wouldn't want him slipping in and changing horses while we're sleeping."

Hector nodded. "I think you're right, Thomas. Ramon and I will take the first watch, if you'll take the rest of the night." He looked at Margarita, "Got anything to feed three hungry men?"

*   *   *

The evening had been more than pleasant; Margareta and Angela had sat relaxed around the dining table, provided Thomas with an ample serving of homemade peach pie for desert and the conversation had been easy and casual. Finally Thomas excused himself after glancing at the big clock in the living room.

"I better get out to the barn and relieve Ramon and Hector," he'd said as he slid his chair back from the table. He stopped at the bunkhouse and retrieved his Winchester, made sure there was a round in the chamber and the safety was on, then headed for the barn. It was pitch-black under the cloud-filled sky as he slipped silently into the darkness of the barn, half expecting to surprise Beck sliding his saddle onto a fresh horse. He whistled softly to alert Ramon and Hector. The slow patter of the rain on the barn's roof obscured whatever sounds nature normally produced this time of the evening. The air inside was damp but not uncomfortably cool and pungent with the now familiar odors of the barn. The only sounds besides the rain were those of the restive movements and regular breathing of the livestock. After running his hands over each horse, he climbed the ladder to the hayloft and found the two men had taken a place where they could overlook the opaque rectangle that was the door to the barn. After a brief conversation, Ramon and Hector left and Thomas made himself comfortable, scrunching down among the dry hay with his rifle at his side. They hadn't exactly worked out what they would do if Beck made an appearance but they all agreed they didn't want it to get out of hand or turn into a deadly shooting match.

Within minutes his eyes adjusted to the darkness and he could see the interior of the barn as indistinct patterns of black and gray shadows. A flash of lightning somewhere far up the river canyon momentarily lit the barn through the cracks between the boards, followed several seconds later by the low rumble of the thunder. He felt for his rifle and pushed himself further into the loose hay. An unexpected tidal flood of exhaustion swept through him; his chin dropped slowly to his chest and his eyes struggled to remain open against the nearly intolerable weight of his eyelids.

The rain had stopped and the muted sound, a minuscule click, woke him with a start. There was complete silence now. Had he actually heard something? He strained to waken enough to concentrate and tried to replay the sound in his mind thinking it was most likely the latch on the barn door. He held his breath, straining to hear the slightest noise from the space below him, thought he heard a tentative footstep, then another. He slid his rifle out and cradled it in his arm. The footsteps stopped and he could hear the shallow breathing of the person below him. The ladder to the loft creaked as the person silently climbed, each step hesitant.

An indistinct shadow rose above the top of the ladder.

"Stop right there!" Thomas said quietly. "Don't even move!"

"Oh Tom!" It was Angela's startled whisper. "It's me, Tom! I've brought you some coffee! You about scared the life out of me!"

"My God, Angela! You gave me a start! I could've killed you!" Thomas whispered back. "You shouldn't be out here!"

"You don't want me here. Tom?"

"Angela, I think you know better than that. It's just . . . you shouldn't be here in the middle of the night . . ."

"Well, I won't stay very long. I have a mug of coffee for you. I thought you might be getting sleepy."

"I think I was dozing off a little, Angela," Thomas admitted quietly.

Angela came to where Thomas had settled in the hay and sat close to him, carefully handed him a mug of hot coffee. "It's very hot . . . be careful."

He took the hot mug from her and carefully balanced it near his side. The aroma of coffee seemed to fill the space around them.

"What time is it?"

"A few minutes after three o'clock," Angela responded in a whisper. "I couldn't sleep thinking about you out here."

"I don't think Beck is going to be coming here tonight."

"I believe you're right." She hesitated, "The rain's stopped, finally."

"There was some lightning up in the high country a while ago."

They sat silently for several minutes, their shoulders barely touching. Finally he put his arm around her shoulders and drew her close. She turned her head and her lips searched momentarily until they found his. She put her arm around his neck and slowly pulled their lips together, her tongue delicately probing as she let out a nearly inaudible sigh. His world seemed to tilt and spin as he struggled to find a position among the loose hay more comfortable for them both. They eased back into the hay and she lay on her back, her arm still around Thomas's neck, pulling him even closer into the tender warmth of her embrace.

*   *   *

Angela gently touched Thomas on his shoulder and he awoke immediately. She put her lips close to his ear and whispered, "Thomas, my love, I must go back to the house. My mother will be getting up shortly and I don't want her to find that I'm not in my room."

251

"I've fallen asleep," Thomas said quietly. "A fine guard I would make!"

"It's been very quiet, Tom. You were terribly weary. I kept watch for you." She brushed her lips against his cheek and murmured, "but the next time I won't let you fall asleep . . ."

She arose and swept the hay off her clothes. The deep purple of early dawn slipped through the spaces in board siding of the barn casting an eerie glow on the hay. Thomas watched as she shook her long hair and brushed the last remnants of straw from her shoulders. He found the mug containing coffee, now icy cold and he downed it quickly before handing the mug to her. "Thank's for the coffee, Angela and for keeping watch for me." He glanced around the barn, growing lighter by the minute. "I liked you being here with me." He hesitated before he added, "I'll wait some before I come to the house."

*   *   *

Abilene, Texas

Luke stared out of the hotel window into the early morning thunderstorm that had shaken and rattled Abilene for the past hour. Appearing first as a lightning punctuated ridge on the south-western horizon, the bolts of lightning and distant rumbling of thunder reminded him of his army days when artillery barrages lit up the evening sky and bombarded nearby ears, leaving them ringing for hours. Now the rain poured vertically in ridges that swept through town like semi-transparent curtains of water. The dirt street below had been reduced to a muddy quagmire and most people would stay indoors until the storm abated.

He finally sat back on his bed and stretched out, hands clasped behind his head. He had to admit to himself that he was tired, having spent three days on the train traveling from Springfield, Illinois. That had been the site of his most recent activity; a politician by the name of Gaspar Allovette was competing as a Republican candidate for a seat in the Illinois State House. Luke had found the name in the newspaper and soon discovered that Allovette was beleaguered by the reputation as a malicious distributer of political mud and rumors. The general population was not overly interested in his kind sitting in the state house as their representative. Luke decided he could do a favor for the people of Illinois as well as for his own reputation and set up his undertaking across the street from the old State

Capitol building where the candidate was scheduled to deliver one of his notoriously slanderous speeches. From a position on the vacant third floor of a new office building, he'd taken aim on the center of the politician's chest from a distance of two hundred and fifty yards. Gaspar Allovette had barely started his speech when the fifty caliber bullet smashed through his ribs and left lung; he died in less than five minutes in front of the stunned crowd who had gathered on the lawn to listen to and perhaps heckle, his discourse. Luke had spent the night in Springfield and taken the train out of town the next morning.

The string of killings with apparent political undertones had migrated up from Louisiana to Birmingham, Alabama then to Chattanooga, Tennessee and finally to Springfield. By then Luke was ready to take a few weeks off from his travels. The bait had been dangled out there; now it was time to see who nibbled at it.

*   *   *

San Francisco
The sun hadn't even begun to lighten the eastern sky but the man named Clarence Chandler had been awake for hours, unable to sleep with the train of thoughts that rolled through his head. Chandler had used the lock-picking skills learned at San Quentin Prison to his best advantage, performing small burglaries spread across the city over several months to establish his wardrobe and personal necessities and to provide him with a constant flow of cash to live on. He had used the daytime hours to wander the city, peer into store windows and visually inventory what was immediately available and to casually check the door locks upon which the owners depended to protect their merchandise. His burglary operations took place late at night when the businesses were closed and the store lights were extinguished; in the deep shadows on the street, he could pick the lock and be inside the shop in seconds.

He intentionally limited his thievery to a few items each time; a detail that often suggested to the store owners that missing merchandise had actually been taken by shoplifters during store hours. A shirt from this store, a pair of pants from that one . . . boots, underwear, shaving gear, belts, a warm coat, a hat . . . a few dollars from the cash drawer. He always left the shops orderly with merchandise neatly stacked and displayed and

253

the doors properly secured. Many merchants never even realized their store had been broken into and merchandise stolen.

The single major item he stole was a handsome Colt .45 Buntline pistol with a sixteen inch barrel. He didn't know much about handguns but he liked the unique, threatening look of the long barrel. He picked up a case of .45 Longs while he was there and took several practice shots in one of the wooded sections of San Francisco.

Chandler had eventually rented a hotel room and, with respectable clothing, a typical haircut and a precisely trimmed goatee, he was not recognizable as the same man who had recently broken out of prison. With no living relatives in San Francisco and his boyhood pal deceased, Chandler was now free to roam unrestricted about the city. For a while he frequented the saloons and brothels in the Tenderloin District but found little long-term satisfaction in evenings spent in a drunken miasma or with rented female company. However he did discover the back-alley gaming rooms operated by secret Chinese gangster associations or *tongs*. These smoke filled gambling dens drew clients from all sectors of citizenry from San Francisco and beyond; all were eager to lay bets against the roll of dice or the turn of a playing card or even tempt a few exotic Oriental games of chance. Wealthy bankers, merchants, plumbers and stevedores from the docks sat shoulder to shoulder and shared the fantasy of beating the odds under the observant eyes of the notorious *tong*. Within a few months Chandler had been warned that he owed a considerable gambling debt to one of the infamous *Tong* associations. With interest rates accelerating and accumulating daily on his gambling debt, Chandler was soon *persona-non-grata* in some of the city's Chinese run gambling rooms.

It was through these circumstances that just a week ago, while drinking alone at a saloon table, he had met Bret Solomon. Solomon was a wealthy businessman from Sacramento and long-time personal friend of George Cooper Pardee, ex-mayor of the city of Oakland. Pardee was presently being urged by the Republican Party to run for the Governorship of California in the upcoming general election.

It didn't take Solomon long to decipher Chandler's manner of speech, his body language and his general demeanor. A little careful probing revealed enough about Chandler's background to confirm his suspicions. Encouraged with a few drinks, Chandler was quite willing to unload his pent up restless anger and frustration. Solomon had a job that he needed taken care of and he sensed that the ex-convict Chandler was the right man for the task. Thirteen months had passed since he had paid the hired killer known as El Culebra to get rid of the neighboring rancher Manhauser but the assassin had murdered Solomon's young wife Priscilla as well when he caught Manhauser and Priscilla alone in their *love nest* situated on a remote section of Manhauser's ranch. Manhauser had died quickly enough with a bullet in his brain but Solomon's wife had been viciously tortured and raped before she was slashed and stabbed to death.

The night before, as the two men sat in the shadowy corner of a noisy back-street saloon called *Charley's*, Solomon had offered Clarence Chandler a deal.

CHAPTER 21

<u>The Gordon Ranch</u>

Margarita rose quickly from her seat at the breakfast table to answer the insistent knock at the front door. The rest sat in suspended positions of eating and turned to follow her as she went to the door and swung it open.

"Morning, Margarita!" The man's voice boomed through the open door. "Hope I'm not finding you at a bad time."

"Of course not, Ted! Come on in and have a cup of coffee with us,"

Hector rose from his seat and extended his hand to his neighbor. "Ted! What brings you this way?"

Hat in hand, Ted Stanton looked around the table quickly, acknowledging Ramon and Angela with a brief nod of his head, then set his eyes on Thomas. "Ah, Mister O'Reiley! I certainly didn't expect to find you here."

Thomas stood to accept the man's offered handshake. "It's good to see you again, Mister Stanton." He smiled then asked, "How's your daughter, Julie?"

"She's just fine! You're still her hero, young man!" Stanton laughed easily. "If she was fifteen years older she'd be after you!"

Margarita pressed a mug of coffee into Stanton's hand, "Please have a seat, Ted." She studied his face then asked, "Something wrong over your way?"

Stanton sipped noisily from the cup and nodded his appreciation. "You just might say that, Margarita." He glanced at Hector. "Had a visitor last night, Hector. I believe Beck Weston stopped by sometime during the storm. He took one of my horses."

256

Hector shook his head sadly. "Damn, Ted. I'm sorry. I'll pay for it of course . . ."

Stanton stopped him with a raised hand. "That's not what I'm here for, Hector. I know Beck pretty well and he wouldn't take a horse unless he was in pretty terrible need. And he did leave his horse with me—kind of a trade I guess. His horse looks pretty beat; he ain't quite buzzard bait but if Beck had ridden him much further he would be. Got a bad rear foot. I'll take care of his horse until he comes to get it."

"You know he's wanted by the law, Ted."

"I know that. Like I said, I know Beck pretty well and damned if . . ." he glanced quickly at Margarita, "sorry, ma'am . . . I mean, I can't figure him doing the things they say he done."

Hector nodded in agreement. "I don't suppose you have any idea where he was headed?"

Stanton shook his head. "He came and went during the storm. Just a lot of mud out there now." He glanced around the table. "Took along some oats, too. About twenty pounds. That'll last him about a week, maybe two if he stretches it out."

"Going to be pretty hard to pick up his trail now . . ." Ramon murmured.

"You going after him?" Stanton asked, surprise in this voice.

"Followed him up the canyon to Baker's Ridge two days ago. Almost to Frenchman's Creek. He doubled back on us and we lost him in the rain at Perdition Slide. We reckoned he was headed back this way but I never figured he make for your place."

Stanton frowned doubtfully. "What're you planning to do when you catch up with him?"

Hector looked around the table. "Bring him in, Ted. We're going to bring him in."

Two hours later they were saddled up again and Angela brought out another sack of food which Hector secured behind the cantle on his saddle. Angela came to where Thomas stood and leaned close to him. "Be safe, Tom," she whispered. "Please be safe."

Ted Stanton joined them and they rode east for about a half an hour, then turned north, cutting across the eastern edge of the Stanton ranch and not too far from where Thomas had killed the mountain lion—so long ago now. Stanton wished them success and split away toward his ranch house a few miles west.

The land was made of softly rolling hills, sparse with low scrub oak trees and some scruffy manzanita. An hour later they crossed over into what Hector figured was Old Man Shingleton's spread but a few miles east of the old man's cabin.

The land grew brushy with hills and narrow ravines. Plentiful scrub oaks and chaparral crowded in on them. Thomas halted and said, "Need to keep our eyes open now. Beck could have come across anywhere around here if he's headed for the cabin Ramon talked about. He'll probably figure that someone will be looking for him, so he'll try real hard to not leave a clear trail. If you don't mind, I'd like to lead from here."

Both Hector and Ramon nodded in agreement. They moved forward slowly as Thomas instructed them in some of the things they could look for.

"What we'll be looking for is a broken branch, bracken stepped on or knocked down, a piece of rotted wood stepped on and smashed, a small rock overturned or flipped, even a small depression in the forest floor where there shouldn't be one. It could be as obvious as a horseshoe print in the mud of one of these ravines but I doubt it. Beck's a hunter; he'll know what those trying to find him will be looking for."

It was almost mid-day before they found their initial sign that Beck, or at least someone, had traveled through on horseback.

"Ah, here we go!" Thomas muttered as he dismounted. "Look here!" He pointed to broad rings of plate-like fungus that had anchored itself to an old, half rotted log. "He rode by here and knocked off a piece of this fungus. Either his foot in the stirrup or maybe the horses leg." He studied the ground carefully. Chunks of rotted wood had fallen off the tree onto the loam and big black wood ants were busy hauling bites of wood from their maze of tunnels inside the log carefully dumping them in piles. He walked along the log, finally knelt down. "Here we go . . . He should have been more careful!" He pointed to where the horse had stepped onto one of the piles of wood grains so energetically deposited by the ants. A clear print of a horseshoe was pressed into the yellow-orange wood bits. He got back on his horse. "Beck . . . or someone, is less than twelve hours ahead of us."

They rode slowly, the brush covered slope getting steeper as the thick mantle of oaks began to change to thick pine trees and their saplings. The imprints left by the horse ahead of them were difficult to follow and the rider had more than once changed his direction radically to take advantage of terrain that would cover his trail. Rocky ridges, a small boulder strewn creek, steep canyons, deep swaths of ancient layers of pine needles, he had used each to his advantage. Ramon shook his head when asked if any of the surroundings looked familiar; Thomas agreed that one location looked pretty much the same as the next—dense shade with visibility limited to less than thirty or forty feet in any direction, thick undergrowth of saplings and ferns, bear clover and tangled berry vines.

It was mid afternoon when Thomas called them to a halt. The horses were beginning to tire from the constant steep grade they were climbing and even Thomas was getting tired of clinging to the uphill sloping saddle.

"This is pretty tough going," he groaned as all three dismounted next to a small cascade of water coming from a layer of rocks. The horses drank thirstily and the three washed their faces in the cold water. Thomas studied their surroundings. Downhill, there were small gaps in the dense cover through which they could catch occasional glimpses of the vast San Joaquin Valley far to the west of them. On either side and up the mountain, their view was sharply limited by surrounding forest. Vine covered fallen trees and branches created a relentless barrier, difficult to go through or over and apparently extending in every direction. But of course, the man they were following had had the same difficulty, forcing him to detour and backtrack around the maze of fallen trees. The three sat on a log, surveying their surroundings.

"I'm thinking we're getting close to that old cabin," Ramon offered. "It all looks the same but there's something familiar . . ."

The three fell silent for a moment. Thomas listened intently and signaled for the other two to listen as well. It was very quiet; no sounds of birds except the distant squawk of a Stellar Jay. He frowned as he remembered what Gray Hawk had taught him; the brilliant blue Stellar Jays with their distinctive swept-back crest tended to be nature's self-proclaimed protector, squawking a raucous alarm cry—a nasal *wah*—to warn other forest creatures of the presence of a predatory bird or animal—or a human being. The harsh warning call seemed to be coming from ahead and to their left, still far away and on the edge of their hearing range, a half mile maybe, perhaps even further in the motionless afternoon air.

* * *

The afternoon tranquility of the forest surrounded them like a warm cloak. Air hung motionless; narrow streaks of sunlight gleamed through the trees in golden beams reflecting off the suspended pollen and fine forest dust. After riding for another thirty minutes in the general direction of the sounds of the Stellar Jay, they had dismounted and secured their horses near a small stream. Thomas suggested it might be the stream that Ramon had mentioned as being near the cabin and all three dropped their voices to a faint whisper. They each pulled their rifle from the scabbard, made sure there was a round in the chamber and that the safety was on. Thomas checked the angle of the sun; it was now late afternoon—they had less than three hours of sunlight left. He reached into his saddle bag and retrieved the single folded sheet of paper that he had brought with him and tucked it into his shirt pocket. Rifle in hand, he led the way uphill through the snarl of vines and fallen trees, keeping the small stream about twenty feet to his right.

It took another forty minutes before Thomas got his first hint of human presence. He held his hand up and all three of them stopped. Thomas sniffed carefully, turning his head slightly; there it was—the faint hint of a cold embers, the almost imperceptible reek of ashes recently stirred or disturbed, perhaps even doused with water. The odor was almost lost in the warm air, blended with the myriad of other fragrances and odors of the forest; but when his mind concentrated on the odor, he could disengage it from the rest—almost like listening to a single conversation amid the babble of many voices. He knew they were close to the cabin. The air was absolutely still and there was no sound other than the sporadic buzz of insects and the faint trickle of water as it gurgled over the rocks in the small creek. Even the noisy Stellar Jay had conceded his strident alarm call, perhaps curiously waiting among the tree tops to see how the furtive movements on the ground below were going to play out.

The steep slope they had been climbing had begun to level off but the thick cover remained visually impenetrable. Small saplings grew side by side, interspersed with bracken and tangled vines that formed a thick, stubborn barricade.

"I think we're close," Thomas whispered. "Wait here for me. Don't move from where we are. I'm going to try to get in closer."

Hector and Ramon nodded anxiously, lowered themselves to the ground clutching their rifles, their eyes searching, trying to see through the thick entanglement surrounding them.

Thomas removed his hat and got on all fours, crawling between the saplings. He was quickly forced to go forward on his belly using his elbows to lever himself forward. He snatched a few branches of fern, jamming the stems in his hair, allowing the fronds to come down over his face and did the same with the long sleeves of his shirt to cover his hands. He dug into the loose soil and smeared the damp dirt on his face. He inched forward slowly, his eyes and ears alert to his surroundings, tuned to the slightest sound or movement. As dense as the undergrowth was, he realized he could be off his approach by any number of feet—or yards—or more. He squeezed under a half rotted log and felt several of the huge black wood ants drop onto the back of his neck. His right arm extended into a tangle of berry vines covered with thousands of tiny thorns that jabbed into his skin through the thin cotton of his shirt sleeves. To his left was an enormous pile of wood chips dropped by the wood ants, the mound crawling with hundreds of ants. He chose to go forward through the snarl of berry vines, the thorns snagging at his shirt and skin.

He almost didn't catch the brief glimpse of the cabin's old boards. He stopped and steadied himself. Thorns were painfully working their way into his skin through his shirt and pants and the disturbed ants were beginning to crawl on and explore the skin under his shirt. Suddenly through a narrow break in the thick screen of vegetation, just a small opening among the dense ground cover, he could see just a portion of the board siding of the cabin ahead of him; slightly to his right, about fifty feet away and closer to the small stream.

He made his way slowly to his left, dragging his rifle and easing under another ant-infested log, then inched his way parallel to the log, slightly uphill and closer to the old cabin. Wriggling over and under broken and rotted stubs of branches from the old pine tree, he continued until he figured he would be about even with the front of the cabin and thirty or forty feet to the left. From his position the area between the fallen tree and the cabin appeared to be densely filled with pine saplings and brush, though the ground had been cleared around the cabin. Carefully, slowly, he raised his head and peered through the natural screen toward the cabin.

His view was much better from here. He could see more of the cabin, at least the front and one side. The side nearest him was a plain board-and-batten wall, the rough-cut wood curled, split and turned gray with age. The front was similar with a single door and a small window with broken panes to the right of the door. The roof was a simple lean-to roof, slanted toward the stream, overgrown with moss and a thick layer of debris from the trees. A few ferns had rooted and grown in the natural layer of loam that had become part of the roof over the years. A section of rusty stove-pipe angled up from the back right hand corner and a large flat slab of rock perched on a few smaller boulders provided the single step from the ground into the cabin. Vines grew thick up the sides of the cabin, nearly enveloping the entire structure.

It was quiet. Even the raucous Stellar Jay was silent, as if studying the evolving situation on the ground.

From Thomas's vantage point he could see a flat area behind the cabin. A small building on one side, the door hanging crookedly on one hinge, was evidently the outhouse. A few crude, handmade pieces of furniture formed a rough chair and small table behind the cabin. But what caught his eye was the railing to which he knew a horse was hitched; though the horse was behind the cabin and out of sight, he could smell the animal's sweat and fresh dung.

Just then a man stepped from the dark shadows inside the cabin into the late afternoon light shining into the doorway. He cradled a rifle in the crook of his left arm. Thomas frowned; the man in the doorway had his hair trimmed to the popular length, wore a brown, slope-front Stetson. If it was Beck, his mustache was gone as well. The man frowned and stared both ways, as if looking for the source of a noise, then walked to the rear of the house and disappeared for a moment from Thomas's sight. When he reappeared he was carrying a small load of split firewood. Thomas studied the face closely through the branches of the trees. He nodded to himself. It was Beck Weston, of that he was certain.

*   *   *

The early morning light filtered down through the branches of pine trees overhead. It was still cool, especially as the three men had slept wrapped in ponchos and without the comfort of a warm fire as the night had grown damp and cool. A cold dinner of beef jerky and some of Margarita's biscuits had barely filled them and the same was offered for a quick breakfast this morning.

Thomas had returned to where Hector and Ramon were waiting the evening before, arriving just as darkness was beginning to firmly set in.

The moon had been full two nights ago and was still bright at night. He had slipped noiselessly among the two men and quietly explained what he had found only a few hundred yards further up the mountain. Ramon confirmed that, from Thomas's description, the cabin appeared to be the one Beck had shown him. They had eaten their cold dinner then rolled into their ponchos for the night.

After their cold breakfast Thomas went over his plan once again. They would split; Ramon would go uphill following the small creek; Hector would go forward and try to end up to the left of the cabin where Thomas had been. Thomas would go up the middle, placing himself directly in front of the cabin. Their approach must be made carefully and slowly, Thomas reminded them, without noise and without disturbing the low hanging limbs or the low brush that covered the ground. They checked their rifles one more time and Thomas showed Ramon and Hector how to camouflage their appearance with pieces of twigs and mud. He warned them to be vigilant crawling among the branches and limbs on the ground, watch out for the nettles and berry vines with their wicked thorns, try to avoid disturbing the wood ants, don't make sudden moves. There would be no means of communication or signaling between them. Take your time—speed was not a concern; he would wait until the sun was directly overhead before he made his move. Hector and Ramon nodded their understanding; they would be in position by then. All three of them would be armed with their rifles.

They each crawled off in different directions; Thomas followed the same general path he had used the afternoon before, avoiding the nests of wood ant as much as possible. The air was still and silent, the warm and humid atmosphere suggesting that the afternoon would be hot, perhaps even with the possibility of an afternoon thunder storm. There was no sound coming from the direction of the cabin but he got a faint whiff of the unmistakable odor of wood smoke and perhaps of ham or fat-back being fried. *Beck was up and probably preparing something to eat.*

It took him another hour before he caught his first glimpse of the cabin through the undergrowth. A pale hint of white smoke curled lazily from the rusted stove pipe. As he watched, Beck came out through the door and headed for the outhouse, casting a cautionary glance around as he went but obviously unaware that he was being watched.

He emerged from the outhouse and picked up an axe that was leaning against the side of the cabin, then disappeared behind the cabin. In a few minutes the sound of him chopping and splitting wood, interspersed with a few soft spoken words to his horse, drifted out. Thomas waited, glanced up at the sun. Another hour, probably.

He watched as Beck made several trips hauling firewood and stacking it next to the cabin door. He carried a metal pail to the creek, filled it and set it on a rock near the cabin and proceeded to wash his face and hands, used his shirt to dry himself off, then plunged the shirt into the water, scrubbing and wringing it before he draped it over a sapling in the sun to dry. Beck glanced around several times as if to assure himself that he was alone, then checked the position of the sun. It was almost directly overhead; he went back into the cabin as if he had decided to do something based on the sun's position. Thomas didn't want Beck to ride off for the afternoon and decided that now was the time. He hoped that Hector and Ramon were ready.

"Beck! Beckley Weston!" he called out loudly. Somewhere nearby the Stellar Jay squawked in alarm. There was silence from the cabin. He called again. "Beck! We know you're in there! We've got you surrounded, Beck! We need to talk!"

There was silence for a long time. Thomas could barely make out the shadowy figure moving around in the cabin. Finally the voice from inside the cabin called, "No need for talk. I ain't going to give up so you can just take me back up there and string me up."

"That's not what I have in mind, Beck."

"That's what you do to murderers, ain't it?"

"Are you a murderer, Beck?"

"Hell no! But I reckon that ain't going to make no difference!"

Thomas hesitated. *I hope Hector and Ramon are ready . . .* "Beck! I'm going to stand up so you can see me! I'm going to raise my rifle up over my head. I don't want you to shoot me, Beck but if you do, it'll be the last thing you ever do. That rotted wood cabin won't stop the storm of bullets that will take you down. You understand what I'm saying, Beck?"

The response took several seconds, then, "Reckon I do."

A quick vision of Amanda and the children passed through Thomas's mind. Amanda is saying *you're not a lawman! How could you possibly help?* "Good. I'm going to stand up now. I'm close to you, so don't be surprised." Thomas grabbed his rifle barrel with his left hand and raised it stock first above his head. He heard the sharp, surprised intake of breath from Beck, watched through the veil of branches as Beck raised his rifle and pointed it toward him. "Easy, Beck! There's rifles pointing at you!"

Thomas slowly raised himself through the saplings and scrubby brush until his upper body was fully exposed.

"O'Reiley!" Beck exclaimed. "What the hell . . ."

"I told you, we need to talk, Beck." He watched the man only forty feet away, saw the suspicion reflected in his eyes, the nervous left and right glances, the anxious flick of his tongue across his lips. Beck held the rifle steady, pointed at Thomas's chest, his trigger finger restless, caressing the side of the trigger guard.

"Ain't got nothing to talk to you about, O'Reiley!"

"Well, I think you do. Let me just ask one question, Beck. Did you murder Nelle Dunsworth?"

"Hell no! I would never have done nothing like that!" The tenor of his voice was different, positive, sure.

"Just to set things straight, Beck, I believe you. Now, you want to talk?"

Beck stared apprehensively into the surrounding brush. "You by yourself, O'Reiley?"

"No, I got help." Thomas watched as the rifle seemed to waver in Beck's hands, the muzzle dropping slowly until it was finally pointing at the floor of the cabin.

"Yeah. I reckon maybe I want to talk. I never was cut out to be a fugitive."

"I never was, either," Thomas said. "Listen, Beck, I'm going to set my rifle down, real careful. I'd appreciate it if you'd do the same. That all right with you?"

"Yeah, I reckon so. Don't have much choice, do I?"

"You always have a choice, Beck. Just have to think about the results of that choice." Thomas stepped forward, still holding his rifle over his head, until he was clear of the tangle of undergrowth, then leaned slowly over and put his rifle on the ground, all the time maintaining eye contact with Beck. "I'm unarmed, Beck. I don't even have my knife with me."

"I see that." Beck hesitated a few seconds, changed the grip on his rifle, leaned it against the door post and stepped into the sunlight. He seemed to relax some, slowly surrendering his hostility, then said abruptly, "I didn't kill her, O'Reiley. I didn't kill Nelle Dunsworth."

Thomas nodded. "Why don't you tell me what happened, Beck?"

Beck closed his eyes and shook his head slowly. "Nelle . . . Missus Dunsworth and I got along pretty good. We talked . . . she talked some about her marriage to Dunsworth. It was on shaky ground; she figured he was keeping a mistress up in the city. Dunsworth had to make a trip to Los Angeles, was supposed to be gone for several days. Nelle and I spent most of the day before together—riding the ranch, had a picnic lunch, drank a bottle of wine. One thing led to another . . ." He shrugged and looked at Thomas as if hoping for understanding. "When we got back to the ranch, she made us a dinner and we spent the evening at the house, talking, played some cards, drank some wine. Ended up in bed . . . my God she was so alone . . . and needy." He looked into Thomas's eyes. "I didn't know . . . I wasn't trying to take advantage of her, O'Reiley. I just never been around someone that . . . lonely. Dunsworth must have treated her like horse crap." He paused, shut his eyes momentarily again before he went on. "Anyway, morning came and we just stayed in bed, being . . . close. Suddenly Dunsworth busts in from nowhere, a double barrel shotgun pointed at us. I jumped like a scared rabbit . . . hell, I'm naked as a jay bird and in bed with his wife! I grabbed a sheet off the floor and held it in front of me . . . ha!" He snorted a rough snicker and shook his head, "like that was going to stop a load of buckshot! Dunsworth just walks over to his wife, puts the barrel of the shotgun against her chest and pulls the trigger . . . blood goes all over the place! I said something . . . I don't remember what . . . and he points the shotgun at me, yells that I raped and murdered his wife! Tells me to get out, now! I skedaddle, half way expecting him to shoot me in the back as I leave. I get to my shack, throw on my clothes, pack my things, roll up my bed roll and get the hell away from there. I reckon he's going to blame the murder on me and I just plain got the hell out fast as I could." He paused and looked at Thomas. "That's pretty much the way it happened."

"You didn't mention where your clothes were . . ."

"Well, in the bedroom. Pretty much in a pile at the foot of the bed."

"You grabbed them on your way out?"

"Yeah and my boots. Like I said, I was plumb naked . . ."

Thomas interrupted. "The shotgun. Was it Dunsworth's?"

Beck tilted his head to one side, "I reckon it was."

"Where'd he keep it?"

"In the gun cabinet, I reckon. I'm not sure."

"Ever see inside the gun cabinet?"

"No, I figure I seen the cabinet once or twice but it was always closed. I never spent much time in the main house; Dunsworth made sure that I *knew my place*, that I was only the *hired hand.*" His voice reflected the contempt he was feeling. "According to Nelle . . . ah . . . Missus Dunsworth, he kept the gun cabinet locked. She didn't even know where he kept the key."

Thomas frowned. "How'd that subject come up?"

"What do you mean?" Beck appeared puzzled by the question.

"How did you end up talking about the key to the gun cabinet?"

"Oh . . . Missus Dunsworth said she knew he kept quite a bit of money and legal papers locked up in the cabinet. She said if she ever had to get away from him, she'd have to break into the cabinet to get her some cash." Beck frowned and looked slightly perplexed.

Thomas nodded, looked straight into Beck's eyes. "Dunsworth shot her once, or twice?"

"Just once but that's all it took; blew a big hole right through her . . . blood went everywhere . . ." He shut his eyes momentarily and shook his head, as if trying to make the memory go away. "I reckon he still had a round in the other barrel. It was a side-by-side . . . scared the hell out of me; I reckon he was going to do the same to me."

Thomas nodded slowly. "I want to show you something, Beck. I want you to look it over. Take your time." He reached into his shirt pocket and pulled out the folded sheet of paper, stepped forward slowly and handed it across to Beck.

The man took it gingerly, unfolded and peered at it. His frown deepened as he read. He glanced up a few times, his eyes meeting with Thomas's. "That's . . . well, hell, that's exactly what happened. How did . . ." he ended, the question not finished.

"See the initials at the bottom?"

"Yeah. *J. M.?*"

"That stands for *Joe McGee,* the Santa Cruz County Sheriff. He wrote that up and initialed it."

Beck looked up, a puzzled expression on his face. "Why would he do that?"

"Because that's what the sheriff thinks happened. He thinks Alexander Dunsworth murdered his own wife and tried to set you up to take the blame."

*   *   *

Beck stood surrounded by Thomas, Hector and Ramon. All had put their rifles away and after the initial discomfort had settled into a casual conversation based on many years of mutual trust and relationship.

"Hector," Beck was saying, "I sure did some stupid things in my life but I reckon this was by far the worst! I really messed up and now I'm in hot water clear up to my neck!"

Thomas looked at Beck for several long moments. "Beck, there's still one thing we need to clear up."

"What's that?"

Thomas hesitated again, then asked, "Where's your Buntline Special? I noticed you're not wearing it."

Beck frowned. "My Buntline?"

"Yeah."

Beck grimaced and shook his head. "I had to pawn it off to get some money. When I left the ranch down here and rode north, I got as far as Los Baños and my horse threw a shoe—left front. I didn't have a cent in my pocket; the blacksmith in Los Baños set me up with this guy who loaned me some money in exchange for the pistol." He motioned to the cabin, "got the receipt in there, signed, dated and everything; he gave me a year to buy it back." He glanced at Hector, "I saw your cousin Diego in Los Baños. We had a couple of beers together and I know I mentioned it to him."

It was Hector's turn to shake his head. "Beck, from what you've told us you haven't hurt anyone or committed any crime. Let's get this mess up north cleaned up, then if you're interested, I still have a job for you at the ranch. It's going to be a few years before we can even begin to turn the business into a citrus ranch. Meanwhile, we'll need the revenue off the cattle to buy equipment, seedlings, drill water wells. Ramon here will soon to be going off to school for a couple of years. You know the ranch as well as any of us. We'll be needing a ranch foreman in a couple of years. If Ramon is right about the possibilities, we'll need several hands pretty much permanent to keep things going." Hector looked at his former ranch hand. "If you want it, the job's yours, Beck."

Beck put his hand out. "Hector, you know I want the job and I don't know how to thank you!" Hector and Beck shook hands, followed by Ramon who smiled and said, "Welcome back, Beck!"

They arrived at the Gordon Ranch late that afternoon; after Hector explained to Margarita and Angela what had happened up in the mountains, the family dropped back quickly into familiar camaraderie. Talk was light, purposefully avoiding Beck's experiences at Rancho de Pacifica.

CHAPTER 22

<u>San Francisco, California</u>

It was early evening in San Francisco and Alexander Dunsworth sat quietly in his office staring out the window. The sun was resting on the Pacific horizon but a thick layer of fog several miles off the coast blocked the view from those in the city. It would soon begin to turn dark and the lamp lighters would be out to light the remaining coal-gas powered streetlights that had not yet been replaced with modern electric incandescent lighting. The busy day-time street traffic was for the most part gone and the sidewalks were sparsely occupied with only a few late closing businessmen hurrying to get home. Some of the evening theater patrons would be taking to the sidewalks in an hour or so to occupy precious seats at the Victoria at Seventh and 42nd Street to see Sarah Bernhardt's *Hamlet*. He had briefly considered taking Sophia to see the famed artist but quickly realized that the production, done in French, would quickly bore her and then he would not be able to control her playful antics which were sure to embarrass him and those seated near him.

His most recent attempts to communicate with Miguel Esperanza-Vincente via the telegraph service had gone unreturned. Though he was concerned, he did not have reason to become panicked, yet. He had no personal experience with travel conditions in Nicaragua, nor did he have any real desire to visit the hot, humid country. Vincente would eventually get to his office—at least if it truly was located where his previous communication indicated. He belatedly realized that he should have taken a more active role in the basic communication with the wealthy Nicaraguan, perhaps even made a personal trip to the young man's country but that was all water beneath the bridge at this point. He would have to deal with the wealthy heir quickly, before other vultures swooped in, or before the young businessman decided to hold onto the valuable property for his own selfish reasons.

News of the negotiations out of Washington DC was particularly sparse. Congress continued to wrangle over possible routes for the proposed canal and the President alone seemed to support the idea of constructing the canal through the Isthmus of Panama, continuing with the earlier efforts of the French company. However, that would also mean negotiating with the South American country of Columbia, a risky and perhaps untrustworthy business. Thus far, the majority of voices in the congress that would publically address the issue favored the Nicaraguan route. Vincente's thirty-nine thousand square miles was right in the center of the proposed route, straddling the major river that would become part of the waterway between the Pacific and Atlantic Oceans for ships from around the world. There were millions—no—tens of millions of dollars of profit to be made for those who held the rights to property in the path of the canal. The investors from the east coast were getting anxious to close the deal with the young Nicaraguan.

Dunsworth wiped the damp accumulation of perspiration from his forehead. *Damn that bunch of crooked attorneys in Los Angeles!* They had brought him nothing but misery, including the murder of Nelle and the adverse attention it had brought on by the sheriff in Santa Cruz. At least he had successfully steered the murder investigation toward the ranch hand, Beck and with any luck, someone will shoot the bastard and bring a quick closure to the whole sordid mess.

He frowned for a moment. Perhaps there was another possible alternative. He could perhaps contact the assassin he had used to eliminate Señora Isabella Laurencia Esperanza and contract him to eliminate Beck. Would it be worth the cost? The hassle? The last time, the man had responded quickly to his inquiry, though through an intermediary. It would be something to at least consider.

He stared once again at the flimsy telegram in his hand. He could tell by the style that the message had been composed by DePallin, the only one of the four investors with any real brains. McGarnet the steel magnate was like an out-of-control locomotive. Ambrose the railroad executive was afraid of everything, including his own shadow. Parker was a big-mouthed Texas rancher who had more money than brains. If it was not for the money that Dunsworth would eventually realize from the deal, he would have dropped the foursome long ago. The telegram read:

MUST HEAR FROM YOU ASAP STOP STATUS OF NEGOTIATIONS UNCLEAR STOP RUMORS OF INCREASE IN PRICE STOP WHATS HAPPENING STOP REPLY

He'd have to hold the four impatient men off for a while, at least until he got in touch with Vincente.

*   *   *

Los Angeles, California

Gomez Santiago checked into the expensive hotel in the center of the large city. It was late evening and the steamship SS Gabriel from San Miguel had docked late at the Port of Los Angeles, having been delayed several hours by stormy seas off the western coast of Baja California.

Born in the United States to an American mother and Puerto Rican father, Santiago was an experienced private detective, having spent several years in the employment of the Mexican government as an *investigador especial* during a period of government uneasiness with its Northern neighbor. He was fluent in several languages including English and had lived for four years in Los Angeles while he attended college. It was there he met and became close friends with the wealthy Nicaraguan Miguel Esperanza-Vincente.

Santiago was of medium build and height, average weight and had no distinguishing scars or features. He kept his light brown hair and mustache carefully trimmed in the popular style and his clothing was nice but not remarkable in style. He was quite affable, spoke softly and seldom drank alcohol. Few people could accurately describe him, even after spending time with him. He had an encyclopedic ability to store and recall facts and information. He was perfect for the work that he did.

He began his investigation the next morning with a visit to the Los Angeles Police Department where he presented himself as an insurance adjuster for a client that had used the legal group of Warner, Jenkins and Garcia-Rameriz to litigate a large insurance settlement. Of course, the client had been informed that the legal firm had been completely destroyed by fire and all three attorneys had perished. All the records of his insurance company's case had presumably been destroyed in the blaze. What could the police tell him that might help his company put this issue to rest once and for all?

Though very limited on detail, the police detective he spoke with was able to tell him that the inferno most certainly had been a case of arson, although there was no evidence that kerosene or some other flammable fluid had been used, that the remains of all three men were located in the room where the blaze originated, that office furniture had been placed on top of the corpses to ensure they were totally incinerated, that enough fragments of one skull were recovered to determine that he had been shot in the head, that all office files had been dumped onto the pile before it was set ablaze and that there were no duplicate records kept off site. All that remained were ashes and very few charred fragments of paper, none of which could be used to determine who they represented or what information they had at one time contained. No, the other occupants of the building were not aware of unusual visitors that day. No, the men did not normally work late in the evening. Yes, the building is always locked during the evening, nights and on weekends; only the primary businesses have keys to the main door. No, there are no exterior doors that remain unlocked at night. All keys were recovered from the ashes except a missing key to the front door, which in spite of vigorous searching, had never been recovered. When the fire department entered the building, the elevator was located on the ground floor, as it normally would be. There was blood on the elevator controls which indicated that at least one of the attorneys had probably been slain in the elevator.

There were no witnesses near the building that saw anything unusual that evening. The three men had dined together earlier in the evening at a nearby restaurant and their waiter remembered them talking about a visitor they were expecting that night. Their talk apparently referred to the man in very offensive terms—according to the waiter—and indeed they used some *very vulgar* swear words which he was quite loath to repeat. The waiter got the impression from his casual overhearing while serving his table party that the visitor would be from San Francisco. The visitor's actual name wasn't used during the conversation—at least it wasn't overheard by the waiter.

How would one best travel from San Francisco to Los Angeles? He was told there is one train a day that arrives from the northern city in the early evening, then leaves for the same city shortly after midnight. It would arrive in San Francisco mid-afternoon. Had the police considered this? For the first time Santiago received a bureaucratic shrug of shoulders. No . . . too many people ride the train, too many places to get on and to get off. The combinations and possibilities were too overwhelming. There was no real evidence that the murderer had come from San Francisco; he . . . or she . . . could have come from San Diego, Albuquerque, Fresno, San Jose . . .

But what about the reference to San Francisco overheard by the waiter?

The waiter, a middle-aged immigrant from Germany wasn't absolutely sure . . . waiters aren't supposed to listen in on customers conversations . . . and he didn't want to lose his job . . . Upon rethinking about the encounter, the waiter began to waver and finally said he had maybe made a mistake . . .

Are there any surviving relatives of the three men?

The detective referred to the folder of notes. Garcia-Rameriz was not married and had moved to Los Angeles from Houston, Texas three years ago. No record of surviving relatives. Warner was married but his widow had packed up shortly after the funeral and relocated to the east coast to be closer to her family. Jenkins had at one time been married but his wife had died of pneumonia five years ago. He had a sister—the officer flipped through the file quickly—she had been nearly hysterical with uncontrollable grief at the funeral. Her name was Sophia Jenkins and she lived in San Francisco. The Los Angeles Police had no record of her whereabouts in San Francisco. Jenkins also had a brother, Peter Jenkins, who ran a ranch in the San Joaquin Valley.

Finished with his questions of the police, Santiago, fluent in German, made an attempt to contact the waiter but the restaurant owner said the man was no longer working there; he had failed to show up for work the day after the Police had interviewed him.

* * *

Santa Cruz, California

Sheriff Joe McGee glanced once more at the telegram in his hand. It had arrived late in the afternoon and had sat on his desk unopened for three hours while he was out investigating a break-in. The yellow paper shook slightly as his hand held it gingerly. He was caught in a dilemma and no matter what he did, his job as sheriff in Santa Cruz County could end abruptly. The telegram was from Thomas O'Reiley and had been transmitted from the Western Union Telegraph office in Visalia.

J MCGEE STOP PRIVATE STOP HAVE PERSON OF
INTEREST STOP YOUR SUSPICIONS CORRECT
STOP WAITING YOUR INSTRUCTIONS STOP
OREILEY

McGee carefully folded the telegram, slipped it inside the office safe
and spun the combination. He hadn't really thought this far along in the
process, nor had he thought O'Reiley had much probability of capturing
Weston. His thoughts about Dunsworth were only that: unproven
suspicions and puzzle pieces that seemed to fit roughly together, though
his file regarding Dunsworth was getting quite thick whereas Weston's
file consisted of very few sheets of notes; two different suspects with two
very different stories. What he certainly didn't need was Weston locked
up in his small jail awaiting trial with an irate population restless to put
the case to rest and a well-spoken attorney anxious to have the man tried
and most likely, due to the heinous nature of the crime, hanged for the
murder. Right now, if Weston was tried, McGee felt certain a jury would
convict him.

He sat heavily at this desk, pulled out a sheet of paper, pencil poised
and finally began creating his simple response.

*   *   *

Visalia, California
Thomas and Angela had ridden on horseback into town to see if there was
an answer to the telegram of the previous day. At the same time he would
send a message to Amanda to let her know that he would be on the train
home by Monday morning. The morning air was warm and smelled of
fresh grass that had already carpeted the open fields. Within a few weeks,
it too would turn golden, dried by the merciless heat of the San Joaquin
Valley.

Angela had been quiet as she rode close to his left side, knees nearly
touching, a smile that seemed to Thomas to light her face with radiant
sunshine. Finally he had to ask.

"What makes you so happy this morning, Angela?"

Her smile broadened, "You do."

Thomas frowned slightly. "Me?"

"You make me happy, Tom. I was so happy last night to sleep with my head on your chest, to hear your heart, to hear your breath, to feel your warm closeness."

Thomas thought of how quickly he had fallen asleep and remembered only laying back in the hay with his arms around Angela. She had kissed him and he had responded; that much he could remember, or at least thought he could remember. What would have happened if he had not quickly fallen into an exhausted sleep? Would he have actually made love with the young woman at his side? He could easily admit those thoughts were there and he knew that deep inside he harbored a obsessive desire to hold her, to allow himself to simply and fully succumb to her warm, moist, yet still inexperienced lips, to lose himself absolutely, completely within her youthful beauty, her lithe, arousing figure . . .

"I'm afraid of our relationship, Angela." He raised a hand to stop her protest. "The last thing in the world I ever would want is to hurt you in any way, or to ruin my friendship with your mother and father—or with Ramon. I respect your family deeply. I respect you as well, Angela. I don't know that I could resist responding to my own yearnings if the opportunity presented itself." He looked deeply into her eyes. "We've talked about these complications before, Angela. You know that I love you and yet I'm not even sure what I mean when I say that. I don't know if I am being fair to you, or honest with you, or if I'm taking advantage of your youthfulness, your inexperience in the matter of love. And I mean the deep, lasting, binding love between two people. I know that you love me and I don't know what that means to you. I know that I . . . I long to hear those words from your lips. I feel warm all throughout when I hear you tell me that you love me. But I don't know what those words mean to you. To you! Do you understand, Angela?"

Her smile remained but some of the light had disappeared from her countenance. "I think I understand what you're saying, my dear Tom. And I know that this . . . this relationship as you call it is very difficult for you and I wish it was otherwise. I spend too many nights not sleeping because I lay awake thinking about you and me. It's difficult for me as well, Tom. I try to keep our closeness, our . . . friendship hidden from my parents and my brother. It's like trying to cook without letting the cooking smells escape. I spend a lot of time . . . and emotions . . . keeping our life secret . . . and even though I suspect my mother probably knows something is changing, happening within me as I grow and change into a young woman, I know I cannot honestly speak of it with her." Her voice quivered slightly and Thomas saw the first signs of a tear forming. "Nothing will ever stop me from loving you, Tom. Nothing you say or do. Even if you do not love me like I love you."

Thomas reached across and took her hand in his, then drew their horses to a stop. He held her hand tightly and looked deeply into her eyes. "Angela, I never want to hurt you and I know that this has been . . . is . . . very painful. I have admitted my own confusion, my own inability to think things through logically, my own pain and discomfort with trying to . . . to be the husband and father I want to be . . . that I *have* to be. Dishonesty has no place in a friendship, or in the love that exists between two people." Angela smiled sadly and squeezed his hand in hers. "Dearest Tom, you have such beautiful, honest love to give. I shall always, always love you."

*   *   *

The elderly telegraph operator in the small Western Union office near the train depot located the message in the appropriate alphabetized cubby hole, handed it without comment to Thomas and sat back in the chair as the telegraph sounder rattled insistently. The operator glanced quickly at Thomas and Angela, then picked up his pencil and began to copy down the incoming message.

Thomas opened the envelope and took out the message from Sheriff McGee.

> OREILEY STOP URGENT PERSON OF INTEREST
> STAY THERE STOP MUST MAINTAIN SECURITY
> STOP WILL EXPLAIN WHEN YOU ARRIVE STOP
> SEND YOUR TRAVEL PLANS STOP

Thomas watched the telegraph operator, amazed at the gentleman's ability to mentally convert the string of irregular telegraph sounder clicks into letters and words and write them effortlessly on the pad of paper. He waited for a break in the incoming stream of messages. Finally the man stood and came to the counter.

"I have two messages to send, please," Thomas said.

The operator slid the blank message pad to Thomas and handed him a pencil. "Write 'em down, son. Helps me some if you print big. I'll send 'em out as soon as I can. Lot of traffic on that wire today." The telegraph sounder started to rattle. "Not for me . . ." the operator said after listening for a few seconds. "That one's for Bakersfield. BF . . . That's their call sign."

"You ever remember what you've sent or received?" Thomas asked.

"Hell no!" The old man barked a raspy laugh. "Most of the time I don't even think about what I'm doing! Most the time I set my mind on other things just to make time go by. Guess I been at this too long . . . started doing this during the War Between the States . . ." A crooked smile stretched across his face; he leaned forward across the counter, "I was just a young whipper-snapper then . . . . with Stonewall Jackson's army . . . 'till a rebel cannonball snatched my leg off. Get around now on my hickory-wood leg courtesy of the U. S. of A." He tilted his head, listened for a few seconds to the clacking telegraph sounder. "Well, I gotta go. VS . . . That's my call sign."

Thomas quickly finished the two short messages, motioned to the telegraph operator and put two dollar bills on the messages. The old man nodded and went back to his recording of words on a piece of paper.

They walked from the telegraph office to the railing where the horses were tied. The streets were nearly deserted; the midday sun shone from the cloudless sky and heated the air until it was comfortable. When they were on horseback, Angela rode closely alongside Thomas.

"Are we going to continue our conversation, or are we through?" she asked quietly without looking his way.

"*Are we through* makes it sound awfully final."

"Is it?"

"I hope not, Angela. God, I don't know what to hope for . . ."

They rode to the ranch in silence; it was a desperate, awkward, hurtful silence that neither attempted to break or close the eroding gap between them. When they entered the barn to unsaddle the horses, the curt silence extended until she had stored her tack and finally murmured "I'll see you at dinner," and left without glancing his way.

O'Reiley went to the bunkhouse to wash the dust from his hands and face then took the telegram into the house to show Hector and Ramon. Beck joined the three and they all sat in the leather chairs in the main room and talked about what the telegram was suggesting.

"Sound to me like the sheriff doesn't want Beck up north and he's saying to keep his presence real quiet down here as well. I think he's up to something." Ramon muttered.

"Like what?" Beck asked quietly.

"Sheriff McGee is certain you didn't kill Nelle Dunsworth." O'Reiley commented slowly. "I think he's hoping to buy a little more time to get his ducks in order and build a case against Dunsworth."

"The sheriff up there's taking a pretty big risk," Hector grunted. "He could lose his job over this."

"That's why we've got to keep Beck under tight cover here. We can't let any word of him being here get out."

"Well, so far, we're the only ones who know anything." Ramon said, almost under his breath.

"And we'll just keep it that way," Hector added, "whatever we have to do." He turned to Beck. "You'll have to keep out of sight, Beck. You never know who may just ride up for a little pow-wow, just to find out if we run across any trace of you in the mountains."

Beck nodded. "I'll set up camp in the back corner of the barn loft."

"Good idea." Hector mused. "You figure to eat with us here in the house. If anybody shows up while you're in the house, you go directly to Ramon's room 'till they leave. Understand?"

"Sure do. And I appreciate what you all are doing for me. One more thing. My horse is over at Ted Stanton's place. What are we going to do about that?"

Hector nodded quickly. "Thanks for reminding me. One of Stanton's horses is over here, too. We'll have to take care of both horses. If Stanton knew his horse was here, he'd know that Beck's around somewhere nearby. I'll go over and pick up Beck's horse; since Beck used to work here, Ted would likely think that was quite normal."

Ramon spoke up. "You know, Old Man Shingleton used to have a couple of acres of pasture land up behind his cabin. About a mile up the side of the mountain. He probably hasn't had any stock up there in years. Had a rough fence around it made out of cut saplings. Has water running through it, plenty of grass. What do you say I talk to Shingleton and see if he minds if we put a few horses up there temporarily. Could even offer him a few dollars. I reckon he won't ask any questions either."

"Good idea, son," Hector said. "Shingleton won't talk to a soul and if anyone was to come around and start making inquiries, he'll just pull out that old ten gauge of his and tell 'em they best move along while they still can."

*   *   *

<u>San Francisco, California</u>

The Union Pacific passenger train pulled into the depot and unloaded its human cargo into the brisk afternoon air. Gomez Santiago was among the last to step onto the platform, carrying a small suitcase. He looked around slowly, taking in the sea of faces and the flow of people towards a crowd of waiting carriages; some were met by relatives or friends or business acquaintances. Some, like Santiago, wandered alone off the platform among the rapidly thinning crowd. Within minutes the gaiety and conversation had subsided and the collection of hired carriages rolled off toward the city proper. Santiago caught the eye of a driver, nodded and the carriage rolled up in front of him.

"Where to, sir?" the driver asked as Santiago climbed into the seat.

"The Palace Hotel, if you would be so kind."

"Yes sir and that would be our very finest." The driver urged the horse away from the curb. "Your first time in San Francisco, sir?"

"Yes."

"On business sir, if I may inquire?"

"Yes, business."

"Should you require transportation in the city, I would be pleased to be at your service. Here's my card.' He handed Santiago a card with his name on it. "Most reputable carriage drivers know me. Should you need my services, just hail one of them and they will reach me shortly."

Santiago looked at the card quickly, nodded and put the card in his shirt pocket.

The driver maintained a running and quite knowledgeable monologue pointing out buildings and landmarks, interspersed with a humorous and well-practiced commentary on local particulars as they moved toward the tall buildings of the city's heart. The huge bay opened to their right, occupied by a plethora of ships of all kinds and sizes, and as they neared the city a virtual forest of masts of abandoned sailing ships, now rotting in the muddy tideland, seemed to fill the waterfront for miles. It took them only several more minutes to arrive at the huge Palace Hotel, a magnificent structure of nine floors offering over eight hundred guest rooms. The driver steered the carriage into the immense Grand Court and helped his passenger disembark. Santiago thanked the driver, committed his name to memory, tipped him extra well and then made his way quickly to the main desk. His reservation, sent by telegraph while he was in Los Angeles, was on file and minutes later he was in his room on the fourth floor overlooking New Montgomery Street.

The long railroad trip up the state from Los Angeles had been fairly comfortable, especially as Santiago had the advantage of a sleeping compartment. Though tired, he was not exhausted from his travel. He had dined on the train at lunch time, finding the food to be far better than the standard train fare that his travel experiences had expected.

After spending an hour scanning the San Francisco newspaper headlines covering the last few weeks, Santiago made his way to the hotel's large formal dining room where he dined on Monterey Bay Abalone *Meuniere* with garlic and fennel braised baby red potatoes, accompanied by a refreshingly cool glass of a California white wine proclaimed as an excellent choice by the elderly and somewhat rigid-faced waiter. Later as the evening chill began to sweep in from the Pacific, he went out to the sidewalk and walked among the evening theater-goers. It took him less than half an hour to locate the address that Vincente had given him, the address of Stevens, Porter and Dunsworth, Attorneys' at Law. The building was a plain brick structure, not magnificent by any means, crowded in as it was by larger buildings on either side. However, the firm's name was at the top of the list of occupants, elegantly inscribed in gold leaf on the large glass door that opened to the sidewalk. He noted that the several other occupants included a wholesale distributor, a shipping company, a property developer, an insurance company and a surveying company. He walked across the street and peered at the windows of the five story structure. There were no lights on in any offices, at least as he could tell from his position.

Back in his hotel room, he constructed a brief telegram to be sent to Vincente, walked to the main desk on the ground floor and paid in advance to have the telegram hand carried for him to the Western Union Telegraph office.

*　　*　　*

Punta Gorda, Nicaragua

Vincentes looked up from the sheaf of papers he was studying at the man who had politely knocked on the door to his office. He beckoned for the Western Union Telegraph messenger to enter.

The messenger extended his hand clutching the yellow telegram toward Vincentes, who took the telegram and pressed a coin into the messenger's palm.

"Gracias, Señor Vincentes," the man murmured as he backed out the door.

Vincentes sat deep in the leather chair behind the desk, opened the envelope with a practiced slash of a small pen knife, unfolded the enclosed telegram and studied it carefully.

VINCENTES STOP LOOKING FOR JENKINS SISTER IN SAN FRANCISCO STOP POSSIBLE SOURCE OF INVESTOR INFORMATION STOP SF ATTORNEY D WIFE SLAIN DAY AFTER YOUR MEETING IN LA STOP SUSPECT BEING HUNTED STOP SANTIAGO

CHAPTER 23

<u>San Francisco</u>

Gomez Santiago stood near the wooden kiosk from which the old man was busy selling freshly cut flowers to the early pedestrians, chatting and greeting each customer with practiced happy banter. Years ago the vendor had carefully selected this corner to place his stall across the street from the office building that contained the offices of Stevens, Porter and Dunsworth—Attorneys at Law. The clock on top of the Chronicle Building read 8:17 when Santiago saw the man he identified as Dunsworth approached the main door and entered. The detective waited twenty minutes then headed for the main door and went into the building. A directory on the wall of the foyer informed him that the legal offices of Stevens, Porter and Dunsworth were on the fourth floor.

An elevator gate rattled open and the uniformed operator peered into the foyer. "Going up, sir?" he asked.

"Yes, fourth floor please," Santiago replied as he stepped into the elevator car. The operator pulled the gate closed and operated the lever that caused the elevator to rise.

Santiago got off on the fourth floor and walked on the polished buff granite floor to the solid wood door that identified the offices of Stevens, Porter and Dunsworth. He opened the door into the small waiting area and was met by a receptionist seated at a desk to the right as he entered.

"May I help you, sir?" she inquired, glancing quickly at his informal clothing.

"Yes, you may. I would like to see Mister Dunsworth; I have no appointment. I am an attorney representing a client that had some recent dealings with Mister Dunsworth."

The secretary was already jotting a note. "And your name, sir?"

"Moran. James Tyler Moran. Attorney at Law." He reached into his breast pocket and withdrew the single business card, handed it to the secretary. He had found the card the evening before on the floor near the main desk at the hotel, apparently dropped by one of the hotel guests.

The secretary glanced at the card. "And the nature of your client's . . . dealings, Mister Moran?"

"It involves a real estate transaction."

She finished scribbling her note, rose and pointed to an empty chair. "Please wait here, Mister Moran. I'll let Mister Dunsworth know that you are here."

She entered the dark-stained six-panel door that bore a brass plaque identifying the occupant as Alexander Dunsworth, Esq. and pulled the door shut behind her. Several moments later it reopened and she motioned to Santiago; "Mister Dunsworth will see you now, Mister Moran."

Dunsworth stood behind his desk and extended his hand across the desk to Santiago. "Mister Moran. I'm Alexander Dunsworth. Please come in and have a seat. My secretary tells me you're an attorney?" It was half question and half statement, obviously the result of Santiago's casual non-businesslike attire. The business card was on the desk in front of Dunsworth.

"Thank you, Mister Dunsworth. I'm James Moran, James Tyler Moran from El Paso, Texas." He nodded, "You have a very nice office." He looked out through the large windows at the busy street below. "I'm an attorney in El Paso." He glanced casually around the office, taking in the bookshelves full of legal books. "I'm afraid my office is not quite this grand. Quite a bit smaller and without the view." He settled into the chair and leaned forward slightly. "I believe, Mister Dunsworth, that we have a mutual acquaintance." He watched as Dunsworth processed this information.

"From El Paso?" Dunsworth shook his head slowly, "I'm afraid I don't know anyone from El Paso."

Santiago shook his head, "I'm sorry, Mister Dunsworth. I've confused you. *I'm* from El Paso. Our mutual acquaintance lives in Nicaragua."

Dunsworth blinked rapidly and blanched but recovered quickly. "Nicaragua, you say."

"Yes, I'm sure you know him. Nice gentleman by the name of Miguel Esperanza-Vincente."

Dunsworth frowned as if trying to remember the name. "Esperanza-Vincente . . . ah, yes . . . he was attempting to sell some property in Nicaragua, if I recall."

Santiago smiled broadly. "Yes, that's the one. I thought you would remember him."

Dunsworth leaned back in his chair and studied the man across from him. "And you say you are an attorney from El Paso, Mister Moran? If I may ask, what brings you all the way to San Francisco?"

Santiago looked at Dunsworth, the smile still on his face. Presently he wagged his finger at the attorney and said, "Ah, Mister Dunsworth! That's what I like about you Californians! You get right to the point! That's very good! Texans would rather kick it around for a while, feinting and bluffing, trying to read the other person's mind, striving to get the upper hand." He nodded as if to himself, chuckled quietly. "You and I are going to get along very well."

Dunsworth, eyes somewhat narrowed, leaned forward while resting his elbows on the desk. "I'm not certain that I follow you, Mister Moran."

"Actually, I think you do, Mister Dunsworth. We both know that you were attempting to purchase a huge piece of property in Nicaragua from Señor Vincente and that in your last negotiation with him, he unexpectedly *doubled* the asking price. Sadly, very shortly afterward, the legal firm in Los Angeles that was representing Señor Vincente suffered a tragic fire that killed all three members of the firm and destroyed all records of the proposed transaction."

Dunsworth nodded. "Yes, I recall reading about it in the Chronicle. Tragic, indeed."

"Yes, very tragic." Santiago paused for several moments, glanced over his shoulder as if to ensure that the office door was shut tightly; when he spoke again, he leaned forward, his voice was very cautious. "Señor Vincente is experiencing, shall we say, *severe financial difficulty* at the moment and he's quite anxious to sell the property. He has asked me to reopen negotiations with you to reach a fast and equitable agreement." Santiago leaned forward until the two men were nearly face to face. "Mister Dunsworth," his voice was now barely above a whisper, "if we handle this very delicate situation correctly, we can both walk away afterward as wealthy men. Extremely wealthy men, I would say."

Dunsworth did his best to maintain a look of candor. "How much . . . um . . . are we talking about?"

Santiago let his eyes sweep over the ceiling, as if deciphering a mathematical problem in his head. "At least ten times that of Vincentes' last demand. With a little . . . mm, ingenious manipulation . . . we could have that property for ten cents on the dollar, perhaps less." He tapped the desk top with his finger, driving home the point.

Dunsworth sat quietly but his mind was working fast. Two and a half million acres, purchased at ten percent of the asking price. Its resale would amount to a good sized fortune, especially if he could close a deal without using the east coast investor's money. "And what happens to my . . . um . . . clients who want to buy the property?"

"They will have legally purchased a very large tract of useless Nicaraguan swamp and jungle, property deeds and all. Unless they are fluent in Nicaraguan legal language regarding property transactions and are familiar with complex and archaic Nicaraguan laws regarding land grants, it will be impossible for them to know anything is amiss until they attempt to sell the property." Santiago smiled quickly, "of course, some of the documents could subtly indicate their own malfeasance in the transaction, in which case they may choose not to pursue the matter legally."

"And your client, *Señor* Vincente. What happens to him?" Dunsworth murmured quietly, his eyes narrowed in thought.

Santiago shrugged. "We simply make certain that Señor Vincente will never know."

*   *   *

Dunsworth left his office early that afternoon on the pretext of visiting a client. If one of his business partners had looked out the window, they might have observed him purchase a bouquet of fresh flowers from the vendor across the street before he got into the hired hansom and gave the driver directions to the house he had rented for Sophia Jenkins.

Santiago trailed a few blocks behind in the hansom driven by Paul. This time the driver remained quiet; he had been told that the nature of this task was a very personal legal matter and that unless he wanted to be hauled into a courtroom as a witness, he should simply forget everything he saw or heard. For his cooperation, he was promised a more than generous gratuity.

Dunsworth's hansom pulled up in front of a small but tidy bungalow overlooking the Presidio and Santiago watched as the lawyer got out, paid the driver and approached the house, bouquet in hand. The door opened and he caught a glimpse of the attractive woman as she greeted her lover.

* * *

That same afternoon the train from Los Angeles arrived in San Jose and Thomas O'Reiley got off, retrieved his personal luggage and was greeted by the Santa Cruz Sheriff who had already made dinner arrangements for the two of them at the Montgomery Hotel in downtown San Jose. The sheriff promised Thomas that he would personally make sure he got home to his wife before the evening was over.

After they were seated at a corner table, the sheriff got down to business. "Tell me what happened down there, Mister O'Reiley."

Thomas spent half an hour recalling the hunt for Beck Weston and the final approach to the mountain cabin where the man had stayed for only one night.

"Took quite a bit of courage to stand up in plain sight like that, O'Reiley," the sheriff commented. "We could have been wrong, you know."

"Could have been but we weren't. I always had a hard time thinking that Beck would do something like that. He may be a plain old cowboy but he's not the kind to murder anyone, especially in that manner."

The sheriff nodded. "Having never met the man, I couldn't say one way or the other but I believe we have enough evidence to convince a grand jury to indict Alexander Dunsworth of the murder of his wife, Nelle Dunsworth. Once they do that, I'll arrest the bastard and let a jury decide what to do with him. If I had my way, they'd hang him."

Thomas nodded, his mind going back all those years when he feared his own death at the end of a hangman's rope. He even recalled with a slight shiver, his nightmare of the walk to the gallows, the feel of the rough rope that comprised the noose against his neck, the sudden drop . . .

"What will you need from me, Sheriff?"

"At this point, Mister O'Reiley, I think the entire case will be built on the evidence we found at the scene of the murder and on Mister Weston's testimony. My deputy will cover the murder scene in detail. We have the coroner's autopsy report. When we get to the jury trial, we may have to call on you as a character witness for Mister Weston. I believe the jury will find Dunsworth guilty."

Thomas nodded once again. "How long do you want Beck Weston to stay down south?"

"As far as I'm concerned, he can stay there until just before the jury trial gets underway. That could be two or three months."

"That's not real fair to the folks he's staying with."

The sheriff nodded. "I realize that. Just as soon as the grand jury issues an indictment he can come out into the open. But I wouldn't want some trigger happy cowboy taking things into his own hand by mistake."

O'Reiley nodded again. "What else you got for me, sheriff?"

"What do you mean?"

"Well, I hope there was something besides a nice dinner for us to meet."

The sheriff chuckled. "Well, you're right, O'Reiley. There is something else that I needed to talk to you about." He leaned forward and lowered his voice. "I have lots of contacts out here that keep me appraised as to what's going on. Part of the job, you know, is to prevent crime before it happens. Lots of folks hear things, pass it on to me. Names, dates, things like that. Every now and then something useful comes to light and we can move in and prevent something from happening." He glanced around the nearly empty dining room then moved closer to O'Reiley. "What do you know about a man named Chandler, Clarence Chandler?"

Thomas sat back in his chair and stared at the sheriff. "Clarence Chandler and two others killed a man in San Francisco in November, 1889. I happened to come upon the crime. One of the three men was Amos McPherson, the brother of the woman I eventually married. Amos died in a knife fight that night. Chandler and the other man, Vernon Dyson, were eventually sent to prison for murder."

The sheriff nodded. "Chandler and Dyson tried to escape from San Quentin Prison last October. Dyson died during the attempt—shot by the prison guards. We believe Chandler made good his escape."

"He's still on the loose?"

"Still on the loose. And I hear bits and pieces every now and then. Seems he's got himself into some big money troubles with the San Francisco Chinese gambling crowd. Word's going around that he's working for someone to get his gambling debts paid off." The sheriff looked up. "Ever hear of a man called El Culebra?"

O'Reiley shook his head. "Can't say that I have, sheriff. How does he fit in?"

"Culebra's a paid assassin. There's some talk going around that Chandler is trying to find this man Culebra. He's been active all over the eastern states and rumored to have made a few hits out west as well, maybe even some international jobs. We don't have much on Culebra but what we do have is that he's a vicious cold-blooded killer. He uses a fifty-caliber rifle to do his work. He likes to celebrate his latest killings by raping and then killing young women, usually within a day or two. I won't go into any gruesome details but savage butchery is his . . . *specialty*. Slow and calculated to produce maximum pain. There've been a few that I've heard about by means of various police reports that are circulated . . . makes the Dunsworth murder look like child's play."

"And Chandler's supposed to be looking for this guy?"

"That's what I hear, O'Reiley."

"What the hell for?"

Sheriff McGee shrugged. "Maybe he's planning on getting even with you for all the years he spent in prison while you were on the outside."

Thomas half rose out of his chair. "Are you serious?"

"I'm deadly serious, Thomas. I'm beginning to think maybe he's the one who tried to kill you a couple of months back. Could be wrong, though. Just wanted to warn you to watch out for your family and keep a close look over your shoulder."

*　　*　　*

Sheriff McGee was good to his word and Thomas arrived at his home on Nob Hill at a few minutes before midnight. He was greeted at the door by Amanda, who flew into his arms and held on with her lips solidly planted on his. She was ready for bed, dressed in a flowing nightgown that she had provocatively unbuttoned at the throat and down the front just far enough to reveal the soft curve of her breasts.

"I didn't think you were *ever* coming home, dearest," she whispered softly. "I want to hear everything about your trip but not tonight . . ."

*　　*　　*

San Francisco

Santiago waited until mid-morning before he made contact with the woman that had met with Dunsworth the night before.

His knock at the door of the modest bungalow was answered quickly by the same attractive woman.

"Yes?" she asked as she opened the door.

"Miss Sophia Jenkins?" Santiago asked quietly.

"Yes, I'm Sophia Jenkins."

"My name is Charles DeFoe." Santiago presented a business card which she took and quickly studied. "I'm an agent with a large insurance company that is investigating the recent arson in which your brother Ramsfeld Jenkins unfortunately died. I have a few questions I would like to discuss with you."

Sophia grimaced at the mention of her brother's death. "Certainly, Mister DeFoe. Please, come in." She backed into the house and opened the door fully. "I'm sorry, Ramsfeld's death was such a terrible shock. The whole thing was terrible. I still can't believe it happened."

Santiago walked into the tastefully decorated living room. A large window provided a panoramic view of the bay. Comfortable chairs were arranged to provide intimate seating. Sophia motioned to one of the chairs and she sat in another. "Now, Mister DeFoe, how can I help you?"

"Miss Jenkins, we're simply trying to set all of our records straight. I'm sure you understand with a loss of this magnitude, we need to be very careful. If you don't mind, I'll just gather the information that we need to know; it won't take long."

"Certainly."

"Now, Ramsfeld Jenkins was your brother."

"Yes, he was my *older* brother."

Santiago caught her emphasis on older brother. "Do you have other siblings, Miss Jenkins?"

"Yes, I have a younger brother, Peter Jenkins, as well."

"And where does Peter Jenkins live?"

"My brother Peter is a rancher. He owns a cattle ranch in the Sierra Nevada foothills near Visalia. I believe he's fairly successful."

"What can you tell me about the relationship between Ramsfeld and Peter?"

Sophia closed her eyes as if thinking. "Ramsfeld was the eldest son; four years older than Peter. Always managed to get what he wanted. Peter has had to work hard for what he has. Ramsfeld had a cruel streak that came out once in a while. Nothing serious but he could say things that really stung, just like a slap. You know what I mean?" When she glanced at Santiago, he saw the momentary flash of genuine hurt pass across her face.

Santiago nodded understandingly. "How often did you and your brothers get together?"

"Ramsfeld and I were more alike than Peter. Peter is quiet, reserved. A real hard working man but he shuns attention. You would probably call him a loner. I last saw Peter about three, maybe four years ago. Ramsfeld and I visited in Los Angeles several months ago. It was the last time I saw him."

"Miss Jenkins, do you know of anyone who would have had reason to harm your brother?"

She laughed quietly. "Probably lots of people would have liked to hurt him. Like I said, he had a real mean streak. As you know, he was an attorney and lots of people hate attorneys. But I don't know anyone who would do something like that."

"Were you at all aware of what your brother was working on at the time of the fire?"

Sophia shook her head. "We wrote back and forth about once a month, maybe a little more often than that. In his last few letters he mentioned something about a large real estate deal he was working on—something in Central America somewhere—he wasn't very explicit."

Santiago sensed she was holding something back. "Miss Jenkins, do you know a San Francisco attorney by the name of Alexander Dunsworth?"

The blood left Sophia's face and she sat quietly for several seconds before she recovered. "Alexander Dunsworth?" She shook her head as if trying to recall the name. "Dunsworth, you say? I'm afraid not, Mister DeFoe. Does this man have anything to do with my brother's death?"

"We don't really know. His name came up recently . . . I'm not sure of the particulars. My company audits its customers now and then has to do with liability insurance rates. Apparently Mister Dunsworth's name came up in one of these audits." He paused and opened the leather case of documents he had brought along with him, fumbled through the papers and finally lifted out a sheet covered with typewritten text. "Ah, here we are. Looks like Mister Dunsworth was working with your brother's firm regarding the purchase of property . . . ah, let me see . . . Señor Miguel Esperanza-Vincente . . . appears Mister Dunsworth represents some clients on the east coast. Hmm . . . Esperanza-Vincente lives in Nicaragua." He looked up, "that could be the Central America property you mentioned."

"Esperanza-Vincente?" She shook her head. "I certainly don't know, Mister DeFoe. Like I said, I'm afraid I don't know this Dunsworth person."

"I understand." He slipped the paper back into the case. Then, almost as if talking to himself, he murmured, "I wonder if this is the same Dunsworth who murdered his wife."

"Alexander's wife was brutally murdered while he was in Los Angeles . . ." Sophia volunteered defensively. "That was a week before the fire killed . . ." she hesitated, realizing her error of revealing her knowledge of Dunsworth's hereabouts. "At least, that's what I've heard," she added lamely.

* * *

Washington D.C.

It was mid-afternoon that same day in the nation's capital and the air was heavy with the remains of a late spring shower that would soon leave the area sweltering in muggy heat.

The traffic near the White House had diminished as the tourists ducked out of the rain, taking refuge in nearby restaurants and museums. The President of the United States sat in his office looking out the windows at the broad lawn that separated the President's residence from the public. His desk was cluttered with papers and several maps, the ones his aide James had collected for him, along with a ruler and a pad of paper on which he had written notes. The proposed trip to California was forming up quickly, even though it was still many months away. He would soon have to dispatch a team to set up the transportation and make arrangements for horses and a guide for the trip up the Kaweah River. Armed with his large magnifying glass and a ruler, Roosevelt had relentlessly perused the topographical maps, letting his knowledge of wilderness areas and U.S. Army experience with maps fill in the missing details. He finally selected the place where he and his security detail would spend two nights. According to his calculations, the proposed campsite would be a strenuous several hours ride from a starting point on the Kaweah River. It was part of a short, stubby valley running north to south, a small secluded meadow bordered on its eastern edge by a small creek at the base of a large sloped mountain and bound on the western side by the nearly vertical rock face of an imposing cliff. It was far enough removed from civilization to satisfy the accompanying security personnel's curiosity and he would be able to eventually respond to questions regarding the two days away from the public eye, should that be necessary.

And the location was remote enough from prying eyes to secretly handle the highly sensitive issue that was the driving force of this trip.

James informed the President that he had already spoken to the six men who would comprise the security detail, reminded them of the secretive nature of this trip to the west coast and that this information was highly classified. They were to not tell anyone, even their own family, about the trip. The itinerary, the dates, the locations, the means of transportation, the makeup of the traveling party were all highly classified.

The personal aide had spent many long hours with the President pouring over the maps, planning each day down to the minute, taking notes as Roosevelt dictated endless questions: where would they acquire horses for the trip into the back country? Who would be their guide? What sort of arrangements can be made to feed the traveling party while they were in the mountains? What sort of weather should they expect at that time of the year? How long would it take to get there? Roosevelt had finally selected the site, placing his large finger on the map, announcing, "Here, this is where we will stay. Let me know when the arrangements have been completed, James."

The President's aide studied the location on the topographical map carefully, seemingly puzzled by the maze of curved and swirling lines representing the surveyed shapes and altitudes of the mountainous location. "I'll get started on it immediately, Mister President."

The President finally pushed back from the desk, looked up at his aide and asked, "how are you on horseback, James?"

The aide answered wryly, "not very experienced I must confess, Mister President. However, I do believe that following this little expedition, I shall be a much better horseman."

"Bully for you, James!" Roosevelt had roared, laughing. "Never too late to teach an old dog!"

*   *   *

San Francisco
It was late evening in San Francisco. A thick fog had rolled over the city in the early hours of afternoon and now everything was slick with the cold

dampness. Streetlights struggled to shine through the heavy mist and from the bay, foghorns bleated mournfully.

When Clarence Chandler had begun to scratch around beneath San Francisco's smooth tier of dignified and well-to-do population, he found a whole other world of perverse values and behaviors. Of course, he had been aware of this since his early days as an unruly youth on the streets but now as an adult, especially an adult with a criminal history and the experience of being in prison, and possessing an entirely new language, new avenues appeared to open for him. The conniving underworld in which he now found himself tendered all forms of violence; robbery, assault, rape, murder, singly or in any combination or variety could be arranged with a quick nod or a slight tilt of the head if one knew the signals and the right people.

He had probed carefully among the longshoremen, the pimps, the bartenders, the crowds that gathered with curiosity around any human tragedy for information about the man known as El Culebra but little useful information had come to light. This much was known: the assassin was *probably* from one of the southwestern states, *probably* Texas and he operated within a tight network of informants that he *probably* paid. He also learned that the man used a large caliber rifle, again *probably* a fifty caliber rifle, to do his killing and that he was very good at what he did. Rumors scattered among the probable facts tied him to a number of political assassinations and others suggested that he had a predilection for attractive young women used for some sort of grisly ritual. Other rumors were easy to discard: that he had killed over eight hundred men and that he cut off the heads of more than half of his victims, that he was an agent of a South American country and that he was operating on behalf of an emerging anarchist political party in the United States.

He combed through these facts and rumors carefully, trying to put together enough information to eventually make contact with the assassin. Finally one night three weeks ago, he had been approached by a man who claimed to have access to El Culebra. When pushed for the reason Chandler wanted to make contact with the assassin, Chandler had suggested that he had a high-profile job in mind and needed someone of first rate skills. The man moved off into the gloom and Chandler had heard nothing since.

Chandler had decided that it was more than mere coincidence that the name Alexander Dunsworth had come up several times during casual conversations. He found that the man was an attorney in the city, that his wife had recently been murdered and that he owned a small cattle ranch on the coast just north of Santa Cruz as well as a home in San Francisco.

*   *   *

Santiago waited patiently in the tall shrubbery that separated Dunsworth's house from the neighboring house. He had been here since late afternoon and so far there had been no sign of the attorney. He checked his pocket watch; it was after seven o'clock and the air was getting cool along with the heavy fog that penetrated his clothing. He checked once more up and down the empty street; most people were already in their homes and lights glowed through windows. The attorney's house was still dark.

After one last quick glance up and down the street, he approached the front door, picked the simple lock and let himself in. He pulled the heavy drapes shut before he turned on the table lamp in one corner. The room was furnished with high quality furniture and accessories, comfortable and stylish with the characteristics of a bachelor's choice, a model sailing ship on the mantle, an assortment of antique brass nautical implements, a heavy cut-glass decanter containing whiskey and four matching stubby glasses. Dark coffee-colored leather covered the twin Victorian style button back armchairs and matching sofa. A built-in corner bookshelf held a comfortable collection of a dozen or so leather-bound books containing classic writings of Arthur Conan Doyle, Mark Twain, Alexandre Dumas and others, as well as a few exactly positioned pieces of brightly decorated Mexican pottery and a copy of the expensive *Times Atlas of the World.*

Santiago moved quickly through the rest of the house. The bedroom had been cleared of all things feminine; the closet was devoid of women's clothing, the dresser drawers contained only men's wear. One drawer held nothing but a set of gold wedding bands; a large men's band and a small woman's band, both snuggled into a small pillbox. The wardrobe held three formal black suits of different cuts and a selection of white shirts—some with narrow colored stripes—collars, cravats and two raincoats. Four pairs of highly polished black shoes sat on the floor of the wardrobe. A single, dove gray low flat-top derby sat on the shelf over the hanger rod. Santiago pulled it down and checked it. The sweat band on the inside was unsoiled; in fact the hat felt clean and smelled new with perhaps only the barest trace of smoke. Santiago checked the suits again. Nothing hanging there would match the informality of the hat. He frowned, replaced the derby on the shelf and shut the wardrobe doors. A heavy, tan and gray corduroy bedspread covered the bed. There was nothing stored under the bed. He gave the room one more glance before he entered the next room.

The room next to the bedroom was obviously his office. It contained a heavy roll-top desk—surprisingly unlocked—and a matching chair, a pair of glass fronted bookshelves, two filing cabinets, one upholstered side chair and a reading lamp. Santiago ruffled through the files quickly, not knowing specifically what he was looking for. He found buried within the papers a large group of receipts that covered various personal items including a receipt from Lloyd's Haberdashery in San Jose for two shirts (red stripes), a four-in-hand tie (red), a pair of slacks (gray), a coat (blue plaid) and a flat-top derby (gray), along with a fee for the tailor. It was dated June 5th, the day before the Los Angeles murders. Another receipt dated the same day, the fifth of June, was from Grissom Leather Goods in San Jose for what was obviously a low-priced leather suitcase. Buried among the receipts were two Southern Pacific train ticket stubs; one was for the early afternoon train from San Jose to Los Angeles dated the same day as the Haberdashery. The second was for a Los Angeles to San Jose train, the early morning train for passage on June 6th, the day of the murders. Santiago smiled; if nothing else, Dunsworth was certainly a meticulous record keeper. Santiago carefully folded the receipts and put them and the train ticket stubs into his pocket.

The remaining documents were mostly current and past client files. A few files contained deeds and legal papers regarding the property on the coast. From what he could determine Dunsworth had already started the process of re-mortgaging the coast property and having the name of his deceased wife removed from the deeds to the cattle ranch as well as his home in the city.

He did come across a file labeled simply *Sophia*. It contained papers and receipts regarding a house he apparently rented and assumedly rented for Sophia. There were also several recent receipts for expensive women's jewelry purchased at a well-known San Francisco jewelry store.

A quick check of the bathroom turned up only a few bottles of various lotions and basic medicines along with men's shaving and bathing paraphernalia. The kitchen appeared to be unused; cabinets contained carefully arranged dishware and glassware but there was no sign of even the most basic food supplies. The ice box was empty and was not even provided with ice. Dunsworth apparently ate in restaurants rather than at home.

There was no cash or gold to be found. A thorough search through the house failed to turn up a hidden safe or strong box or even a secret hiding place. After one last glance around, he let himself out of the house, carefully relocking the front door.

CHAPTER 24

<u>Monday, June 23, 1902, San Francisco</u>

Sophia sensed that Dunsworth had endured a strenuous day. When he arrived shortly after six that evening she had poured each of them a glass of red wine and they sat close to one another on the small sofa to relax. After reaching across and loosening his tie, she had casually remarked that she had had a visit from an agent from the insurance company. It was the company, she explained, that had provided liability insurance for her brother's Los Angeles company. Most of his questions were regarding the fire that had consumed the firm and all of its legal records, she added.

"What was his name again?" he had asked with feigned interest. He sipped noisily from the wine glass, leaned back and closed his eyes.

"DeFoe. Charles DeFoe." She sat back and crossed her arms over her bosom. "He was quite a nice gentleman, Alex. I'm sure it is just a matter of procedure."

"I'm sure it was. And what all did you tell him?" He sipped again from the glass of wine and watched her through barely opened eyes. The wine was good and in spite of his weariness he had designs on their evening together.

"Well . . . I answered his questions as best I could. He wanted to know what sort of relationship I had with Ramsfeld. He asked about Peter." She frowned and added, 'He did mention your name, once."

"What? My name?" He half raised himself from the chair then sat back down. "In what manner would I be of interest to him?"

"I don't know, Alex. And please don't get angry with me." She thought for a moment. "He mentioned that your name was associated with some sort of property sale in Nicaragua. A mister . . . oh my . . ." She shook her head in perplexity. "It was a Spanish-sounding last name . . . hyphenated.

Something . . . Vincente I believe." She looked at Dunsworth tentatively then added, "He said that you were representing some clients on the east coast regarding the property. He was also aware the . . . of Nelle's murder."

Dunsworth felt the blood drain from his head. He realized that of course, Sophia knew all about the east coast clients—she had given the information to her brother. And Vincente! Esperanza-Vincente! Was it just a coincidence that the man's name should come up twice in as many days? Events were moving too quickly. "What did he have to say about the east coast clients?" He tried to keep his voice even.

"Only that they were your clients."

Dunsworth shook his head slowly. He would have to move fast on the property deal that he and the Texas attorney, James Tyler Moran, had discussed. After meeting at Dunsworth's office for over an hour, they had moved to a secluded table in one of the many restaurants near his office. To his credit, Moran had obviously given this property transaction much thought. He had personal contacts in the government in Nicaragua. He knew what terms would satisfy Esperanza-Vincente, whom he described as "so rich he doesn't even know what all he owns." He knew precisely what legal documents would be needed to consummate the sale and how they could be manipulated by taking advantage of Nicaraguan law to reflect both the actual transaction and to camouflage the fact that the sale had gone for less than ten percent of the purchase price. Moran had clearly been fluent in Spanish and in the flow of Nicaraguan legal paperwork. He said he had the paperwork, all the legal forms with him. It would only require a few hours of Dunsworth's time and of his, to complete the forms. He assured Dunsworth that he could get the papers to Nicaragua in less than two weeks to attain to Esperanza-Vintente's signature . . .

"How will you accomplish that?" Dunsworth had asked.

"Miguel Esperanza-Vincente is extremely wealthy and a very active businessman. He has a staff that prepares contracts, bills of sale, agreements of all kinds for his signature." Moran smiled. "He foolishly signs piles of documents every day without even reading them. It will be just another paper awaiting his signature."

"I hope I haven't said anything wrong, Alex," Sophia interrupted his thoughts.

"No. Not at all, Sophia." Dunsworth answered and continued with his thoughts. Once the papers had been signed, Moran would have them legally filed in Nicaragua and the rest would be simply a matter of waiting for the United States to decide the actual route for the new canal through Nicaragua although there was little doubt that the canal would utilize the Rio San Juan, dredged, widened and straightened from the east coast to Lake Nicaragua. They would then trench across the ten mile wide isthmus that separates the large lake from the Pacific Ocean. The massive Esperanza-Vincente land grant straddled the Rio San Juan for nearly forty miles.

He and Moran would own the great bulk of property through which the canal would be constructed. Military posts to guard the canal would be built. Towns for the construction crews would spring up along the path of the canal. A railroad would have to be built over which to haul massive earth-moving machinery, supplies, construction workers, as well as the millions of tons of rock and dirt that must be relocated. Huge amounts of timber would be needed for railroad construction, housing for tens of thousands of workers, forms for concrete, storage facilities, repair shops, medical facilities, administrative buildings. Beef would be needed to feed the huge army of construction workers. Sand and rock would be needed for the hundreds of thousands of cubic yards of concrete used to construct the massive thousand foot long locks.

They could not afford to hesitate. He decided then and there to contact Moran tomorrow and set the wheels in motion. Without further comment, he got up, refilled their wineglasses and they tapped them together in mutual tranquility.

*   *   *

Washington D.C.
Clarence DePallin, the young congressman from New Hampshire, sat quietly in his hotel room alert for footsteps that he expected to hear coming down the hallway. It was nearing midnight. The trip to the nation's capital had come suddenly; notification by coded telegram had arrived just eighteen hours ago. It was easy for the congressman to move about the nation as he chaired two important congressional committees, the Natural Resources Committee and the Appropriations Committee, which provided him with ample reasons to travel.

He poured himself another tumbler of Tennessee whiskey, added just a dribble of water and sat back down. The telegram had not specified the reason for this trip to Washington but he knew it had to do with the situation in Central America. The subject of canal treaties was front page news on most American newspapers. Congress was still arguing whether the canal should be constructed through Columbia's Panama Isthmus or through Nicaragua. Incredibly, nearly around-the-clock lobbying efforts promising deals and trades, opportunities and under-the-table agreements rampaged unchecked through the Congress but the eventual selection was still a matter of intense debate, tipping one way then the other. Failed efforts by the French Canal Companies were presented as excellent reasons to not even attempt to build a canal. Those attempts had cost hundreds of millions of dollars, ruined scores of reputations, cost untold thousands of lives and had nearly sent France spinning out of control into fiscal insolvency. The Columbian government, aware that the opportunity was slowly slipping away, was anxious to realize the potential revenue from an inter-ocean canal and was talking now with other countries, including Germany and England.

DePallin was actively lobbying his congressional cohorts on behalf of a canal through Nicaragua, buying lunches and dinners for the opportunity to present and press home his points, following up by sending bottles of expensive wine with a short reminder note attached. It was not that he really cared, for technical reasons, one way or the other. But he stood to make a huge fortune if the canal should proceed through Nicaragua. This amount of money would allow him to do anything he wanted, because politics required access to money. DePallin was the consummate politician with his eyes focused on the highest seat in the government and the immense power that came with it.

He heard the cautious footsteps coming down the hallway. They stopped outside his room and shortly there was a light tap at the door.

DePallin got up, walked to the door and put his ear to the wood paneling. In a voice just above a whisper, he asked "What do you have?"

"An important dispatch from San Juan," the voice on the other side of the door replied quietly.

It had been a predetermined exchange of code words. He unlatched the door, opened it a few inches being careful to not reveal his face, reached his hand through the opening as the messenger slipped a large envelope into his waiting hand. Without a word he slowly shut and latched the door, then listened as the footsteps receded into the distance.

He opened the sealed envelope and slid the contents onto the bedcover. There was a folded map, a topographical map of wiggly lines. He read the designation of the map in the lower right hand corner and frowned slightly. Kaweah River, California. He unfolded the map and stared at the array of lines, the single dark line that was labeled Kaweah River that snaked into the high country; here and there map sections were still blank and awaiting eventual survey. In the approximate center of the map was a single penciled X.

He opened the folded sheet of paper that accompanied the map. It had dates on it and information regarding Teddy Roosevelt's planned secret trip to California and the Sierra Nevada Mountains. It listed his stops along the railroad route, the hotels where he would be briefly staying, the departure and arrival times of his special train, who, if anyone, would be allowed to spend a few precious minutes with the President, the names of his security personnel and how and where they were to be assigned and armed. It was all here, just as he had been promised. It even listed the small cattle ranch near Visalia where the Presidential party would be renting livestock for the three day trip into the high country and the name of the guide. Everything they needed to know . . . Things were coming together . . . It *was* actually going to happen . . .

*   *   *

The Gordon Ranch

Hector and his family sat around the dinner table. The late evening meal had been eaten and the table cleared when Hector asked for the family to remain. They all knew that this was when Hector would bring important issues before the family. Money concerns, immediate and long range plans, their neighbor's distresses, shortage of water, cattle illnesses, the questions of citrus farming—all had happened around this dining room table. They waited patiently.

Hector toyed with his coffee, stirring slowly while he got his thoughts in order. Finally, "you know that I had a visitor last week."

They all nodded. The man in the suit had arrived unexpectedly, and he and Hector had disappeared for half a day. Since then Hector had appeared unsettled and the feeling had influenced all of them. They had all been on edge for the last few days as each imagined what the visitor wanted. Had Hector decided to sell the ranch? Had he decided to forgo the idea of citrus farming? Did it concern Beck?

"He was from the United States Government. A man very high in government. What I will tell you now must not . . . *must not* . . . be repeated or discussed outside of this family. Do you understand?" He glanced around the table at his family.

Again they all nodded, though with unabashed curiosity in their eyes.

"We will be having another visitor next year, a very important visitor. He will be accompanied by several men and we will rent horses to them for three days for a trip into the mountains. Beck, if all goes well, will be their guide. Beck is the only one who will go with them. We will, as usual, provide food rations for three days, pack animals, tack. Their destination is not to be discussed, even in their presence. Am I making myself clear?"

Ramon nodded and mumbled "yes". Margarita and Angela nodded in understanding. So, what is different this time? The family had been doing this for years. All had frowns on their faces.

"The man coming here is the President of the United States—President Theodore Roosevelt."

Margarita whispered something to herself in Spanish, pressed her left hand against her lips and made the sign of the cross with her right hand. Angela blinked, shook her head, "Why?" she whispered.

"Why?" Hector echoed, "I guess because he wants to. The President does not have to have a reason." He hesitated. "I want all of us to work together to make this visit the best experience we can. That means our riding stock must be in excellent shape. Clean, curried, excellent health and well shod. Tack must be checked and double checked, repaired or replaced if necessary. I understand they will arrive in Visalia on the President's private train before sunrise, come here in rented buggies and leave almost immediately for the mountains. They will spend only two nights in the mountains, arrive here late in the afternoon and leave Visalia on his private train in the early evening. The President will have his own security people with him; these men will be armed and are experienced riflemen."

Hector's last comment draped a blanket of solemnity over the group as they realized that the need for armed men to accompany the President was meant to prevent any harm from coming to one of the most powerful men in the world.

"How many will there be in the group, all together?" Ramon wanted to know.

"No more than ten. Let's figure twenty horses. Sounds like a lot for two nights but . . . it's the President." Hector looked around at his family. "Now, I've also been told there will be another person arriving alone at roughly the same time. If he's not here in time to join the President's group before they leave for the mountains, Ramon will need to take him to where the President is. That's two, maybe three more horses."

Ramon whistled to himself and muttered, "That's cutting us very close." Those around the table knew he was speaking in reference to the family's working herd of thirty horses and he saw his father nod in agreement. "Who's the additional man?" he added.

"I don't have a name or any information about him, only a password that he'll use to identify himself." He looked solemnly around at the faces of the family he loved. "Remember, for those few days, we are responsible for the President of the United States. Not one word of this is to be disclosed to anyone, no matter who it is." He looked around the table again, letting his eyes rest on Angela for a few extra moments. "No matter who."

* * *

San Francisco

Clarence Chandler sat in a dark corner of a back alley saloon in the Tenderloin district called *Charley's*. It was filled with its usual clientele made of those addicted to the hazy life of spending most of the day and night in saloons, such as this one, their brains solidly under the influence of far too much alcohol. The overwhelming stench of stale and spilt beer combined with the acidic and nauseating odor of unclean bodies gave the air a thick, noxious feel and odor. Even deeper in the shadows, Bret Solomon sat with his back to the wall, pushed away as far as he could from the crowd.

"My God, Chandler! Couldn't you find a nastier place to meet? *Charley's* for the love of Christ!"

"These are my kind of people, Bret. You don't like them?"

"They might try taking a bath at least once a year. That would help a lot."

"I'll let 'em know."

Solomon sat quietly looking at Chandler. He felt entirely out of his element in the run-down saloon but no one was looking at him. It was a strange feeling to be so completely ignored. "So, what have you got?"

"Not much. A few loose ends . . . unattached strings . . . some names . . . Thought I'd run a few past you. See if anything rings a bell."

Solomon leaned close to Chandler over the table. "If anyone recognizes me in here . . ."

"Nobody in here even knows who you are, Bret. Your kind don't hang out in places like this, remember?"

Solomon raised his hands in a sign of surrender. "Okay. Okay . . . What do you have?"

"Bits and pieces. He's from Texas. Likes young women, especially those with long black hair."

"I know. My wife had long hair . . . beautiful . . . shiny black. God, it was wonderful . . ."

"Yeah. Well he enjoys tormenting them . . . sexually . . . before he kills them. He kills them slowly, like he's enjoying that, too."

"That's the way he killed my Priscilla . . ." He shook his head. "That son of a bitch sliced her into so many little pieces . . ." His voice quivered slightly.

Chandler interrupted him. "He's done jobs all over. The states, eastern, midwest . . . here in California, maybe in South America, maybe in Central America."

Solomon nodded. "That's all stuff I've heard before."

Chandler looked sharply at Solomon then continued. "Usually uses a fifty caliber rifle. Probably was army trained. Some talk that he did a job in Nicaragua. Killed a politically important woman there. There was a big fire. In and out. That's what I heard. In and out."

"What does that mean?"

"Went in, did the job and left right away. Didn't spend any time there. In and out. May have taken a few souvenirs."

"What kind of souvenirs?"

"Gold coins, jewelry."

"When was that?"

"Early June."

Solomon nodded. "I can follow up on that. If he's from Texas, he probably left from Corpus Christi. Could be some names on the passenger manifests."

"Do you know someone by the name of Dunsworth? Alexander Dunsworth?"

Solomon frowned. "Dunsworth . . . Sounds familiar . . . Yeah, I remember. His wife got murdered a while back. That was in June as well. Why? Did he do that job?"

"No, at least it doesn't look like it. The name came up a few times. Nothing in particular, just . . . you know . . . I had the feeling every time his name came up that I should already know something associated with him. Like he's at the top of the pile, the big gun, you know what I mean?" Chandler paused. "I think he's an attorney. I'm fairly sure he has a mistress. Got her name and address. I'm going to check her out."

Solomon nodded. He also had heard Dunsworth's name when he had first tried to track down the man called El Culebra. "Check Dunsworth out but be careful. He could make a lot of trouble for you."

* * *

San Francisco

Thomas O'Reiley had awakened very early and slipped out of bed without disturbing Amanda. The house was still and cool. Their children were sound asleep in their bedrooms and Xaing was still asleep in her private room near the kitchen. The house held the recognizable odors of his family fully imbedded in the walls and furniture. It was an odor that offered him familiar comfort and a sense of peace. He spent a few minutes trying to separate out individual odors and felt he could determine the faint musk of Amanda, the delicate child-odors of the girls, the strong boy-smell of his son. All were intermingled with meals past, wood smoke from any of the homes fireplaces, odors from the kitchen, smells brought in by visitors.

He made his way carefully through the dark house to his office and sat in the big chair by the window. It was still dark outside and the stars hid behind a thick layer of clouds. He left the room dark and his thoughts turned to the discussion Sheriff McGee and he had the previous afternoon. Chandler! He hadn't thought about the man for years, considering him safely held behind bars at San Quentin Prison. Now he had escaped and was roaming the San Francisco streets. Was Chandler the one who had tried to kill him? That would at least provide some possible explanation for the shooting. And having unsuccessfully tried once, would he attempt again? Were Amanda and their children in any danger? What did Chandler know about him? What did Chandler know about Amanda? About the children?

O'Reiley considered the options that would provide some level of security for his family. The most obvious and probably the best, was to relocate his family until the situation was resolved. Amanda's deceased Uncle William's widow still lived very comfortably on the east coast. She had written a few times and suggested that Amanda and the children come back again for a visit. It had been two years since Amanda was last there.

* * *

The day opened with heavy gray overcast and a light drizzle falling. Amanda found her husband in his office and she brought in cups of coffee for them, took a seat near the small fireplace that heated the glassed-in room. They left the room lighted by the diffused sunlight that struggled to make it through the clouds. They sat quietly for several minutes, both lost in their own thoughts.

Finally O'Reiley knew he would have to bring up the subject of his families security. "Mandy, I spoke with Sheriff McGee from Santa Cruz yesterday. He's the one working on the Dunsworth murder on the coast."

"I remember." She said. "Why would he want to talk with you?"

"Sheriff McGee has a number of informants that pass information on to him. He has reason to believe that the man who shot Frank was Clarence Chandler."

She put her hand to her mouth as if to stifle an automatic protest. After a moment she nodded her head. "Does Sheriff McGee think he was trying to kill you?"

"That's a pretty good guess. And McGee thinks he might try again."

Amanda shook her head slowly and her eyes filled with tears. "It isn't fair, Tom. It just isn't fair. He can take away our freedom, our sense of security, our peace and replace it all with fear and anxiety. Our children..." she shook her head sadly. "Does Sheriff McGee have any idea where..." she looked at O'Reiley with a helpless, almost defeated look.

"No. Chandler has gone deep underground, like a mole. He's apparently deeply in debt to the Chinese gambling mob. If he can't manage to pay them... well, his life is at stake."

"So . . . what's he doing? Where could he get money . . . it must be a lot of money? Holdup someone? Burglary? Rob a bank?"

Thomas didn't answer her question. The more Amanda knew, the more in danger she would be. He just shook his head. "Mandy, I think you and the children should go back to the east coast and spend a few months with Uncle William's wife. You would be safe, and she would love to have you there. The children would thoroughly enjoy the change of scenery. Take Xaing with you again to help manage the children."

"Oh, Tom! I couldn't leave you like that with your own life in jeopardy."

"Mandy, right now we have to think mainly about our children. As long as they remain in San Francisco, they are susceptible to whatever Chandler wants to do. He could kidnap any of them, hold them for ransom—or worse. If he has it in mind to get even with me he could do it in any number of ways."

Amanda looked at him; her eyes filled with deeply felt love for her husband. She shook her head slowly as a tear streamed down her cheek, "Oh, Tom . . . I love you so . . ." She slipped out of her chair and knelt at his knees, put her arms around his waist. "You'd be careful during our absence? You wouldn't take chances? You'd eat properly?" She smiled at this last request.

"Mandy, I will take excellent care of myself."

"How long would we have to be away?"

"Chandler can't remain hidden forever. He's a wanted man, a murderer, Mandy. The sheriff's looking for him, as are the police. Sooner or later, he'll make a mistake and he'll go back to prison."

"I would much rather that it is sooner than later." She looked at him, eyes reflecting her love. "I will miss you terribly, Tom."

PART 3

CHAPTER 25

<u>Tuesday, July 1, 1902, New York City, NY</u>

The four men sat in straight back chairs around a table in the luxury hotel suite that they had rented for this one night. Before the night was through, the suite would be unused except for their meeting; as usual they would depart individually and go their separate ways. Clarence DePallin, the congressman, had quickly taken control of the meeting and two of the other three appeared, in general, to acquiesce to his leadership. Even the often cantankerous Ulysses McGarnet listened without injecting his personal criticisms or suggestions as he leaned back staring at the ceiling and took in the information. DePallin, he ruefully admitted to himself, had done a thorough job. The railroad executive, John Ambrose, also unconsciously nodded in agreement, even though the stratagem DePallin was laying out to them sounded somewhat complicated in its planning and execution. The only one openly expressing his variance with DePallin was the tall, skinny Texan rancher, Stanford Parker. His voice, nasal and whiney, sounded to the others around the table like he was being strangled; McGarnet cringed as Parker leaned into yet another whimpering, circuitous disagreement.

"Good God almighty, Cowboy," McGarnet finally slapped the table in exasperation. "Give it the hell up! He's got a goddamn plan! What the hell have you offered besides a whole belly-full of your whiney, picayune complaints?"

"Ya'll just listen up!" Parker pushed his chair back and stood angrily. "I got as many dogs in this fight as you do! I'm saying we're making this about as complicated as building a cook-fire in the middle of a Texas gulley washer!"

"Gentlemen! Let's calm down! Sit down, Mister Parker," DePallin ordered quietly. He somehow had the ability to get their attention without raising his voice. "It's not *difficult*." The Texan grimaced and slipped back into his chair; the fracas around the table quieted. "Look at the advantages. The target's going to be miles from the nearest medical doctor. It'd take at least a full day to move him, even if they thought it would do any good. The shooter can get away in any direction he chooses. It'll be late afternoon so he'll have at least half a day head start and that's supposing they will even attempt to follow him, which I seriously doubt they would given who they are dealing with. Also it'll be too late to start to move to the nearest doctor, which means they'd have to wait until the next morning, assuming he's still alive."

"All I'm saying is, we can pull off the same thing by stopping the goddamned train somewhere in New Mexico and take care of it way out in the desert," Parker whined, his eyes downcast.

"Except that the shooter would have to take out a six man security detail. I shouldn't have to remind you that our man's weapon is a precision high powered rifle, not a handgun. He's a sniper, not a Texas cowboy with a six shooter."

"Well, it sure ain't what I'd do, if I was heading up this show," Parker grunted, gulped the remains of his glass of whiskey and slammed the glass in a show of disgust onto the table top.

"Well, you aren't heading up this show and the rest of us agree with DePallin's plan." It was John Ambrose that spoke up and his pronouncement appeared to put the note of finality on the discussion.

"We're agreed then?" DePallin asked.

The three other men nodded their acceptance, though the Texan avoided eye contact with DePallin as he barely dipped his head in mute approval.

DePallin spoke up. "I'll get a telegram off to Dunsworth. He'll make the contact from that end."

"You know," it was McGarnet speaking, "I've been thinking. This is going to cost us a ton of cash up front. I'm thinking that a couple of us should meet this guy before we turn the money over to him. You know, put a little pressure on him."

"What kind of pressure do you have in mind, Mac?" DePallin asked quietly. The use of the shortened version of McGarnet's name caught the others off guard. Nobody ever referred to the steel executive in that overly familiar manner. Absolutely nobody—ever.

McGarnet stared for a few seconds at DePallin. "Well, now, let's just stop right here for a moment and get things straight! The name's *Mister McGarnet.* A few select and intimate friends who have known me personally for a very long time are allowed to call me *McGarnet.*" He continued to glower at the congressman. "You hardly know me at all, sonny."

DePallin nodded slightly, just once, apparently indifferent to the rebuke, took a small sip of whiskey from the tumbler in his hand. "What kind of *pressure* did you have in mind?"

McGarnet, his face still flushed, leaned back slightly. "He needs to know who's paying the tab and that we have the power to do anything we care to. He follows *our plan,* "he glanced quickly at DePallin, "to the letter. No damned slipups or mistakes. No last minute changes. No improvising on his part. He gets the one shot—that's all. It has to be a good, clean kill. We've already talked over the possibilities and alternatives. There won't be any second chances. It's our money! He goes by our rules, or else."

DePallin raised the tumbler and peered through the amber liquid, turning it to catch the light of the lamp on the corner table. "Or else what?" he asked casually.

McGarnet rotated his head slowly and looked hard at DePallin. "It's your goddamned plan, Mister Congressman. You figure it out. I just don't want to have my neck stretched at the end of a rope if he messes things up!"

*   *   *

San Francisco

Dunsworth had spent the last two days sequestered with the Texas attorney John Tyler Moran. Meeting in Moran's hotel room, they had assembled the package of complex legal forms required by Nicaraguan law to transfer ownership of real estate. Composed in Spanish legal language, they were for the most part incomprehensible to Dunsworth and he accepted Moran's explanation and interpretation as the stack of forms slowly began to grow. Moran showed him the survey sketch and where the papers precisely denoted the government survey information for the Esperanza-Vincente property. Dunsworth whistled quietly as he viewed the actual property layout, much of it straddling the river that would someday become a major part of the trans-isthmus canal through Nicaragua. Other identical papers showed the immense tract of useless mosquito infested jungle and swamp-land far to the north that described the property that would be mistakenly purchased by the *eastern clients*. Dunsworth and Moran had both signed the papers as legal representatives for their clients and Moran sent them by private courier to Managua, Nicaragua for Esperaza-Vincente's signature before they were legally filed. The last thing Dunsworth must do is come up with the money to close the sale. That would be accomplished by splitting the client's investment money; the major portion would be Dunsworth's half for the Esperanza-Vincente property with the remainder used to purchase the useless swamp-land on behalf of his clients.

Dunsworth knew that as soon as the sale was completed and they realized his duplicity in the swap of property, the east coast clients would be after him with a vengeance. The problem, of course, was that the President of the United States was privately, if not publically, fixated on building the canal through the Isthmus of Panama. If that was the decision reached eventually by the United States Congress, the Nicaragua properties would be practically worthless as investments. But, if the Congress decided to build the canal through Nicaragua, the Esperanza-Vincente property could skyrocket in value.

The telegram from DePallin arrived at Dunsworth's office the next day and he stared at it with little enthusiasm. The telegram read:

HAVE INFO WE NEED STOP TIME YOU MAKE
CONTACT STOP HE MUST MEET WITH US STOP
DETAILS TO FOLLOW STOP CD

"Damn!" he muttered. This wasn't something he enjoyed at all. He'd done it once before when he'd set up the Nicaraguan job on behalf of the same east coast investors. That time he had made the acquaintance of a gentleman from Sacramento who over a few drinks told him of a man who would take care of problems for a fee. His new contact, a businessman from Sacramento had once used the hired killer himself. Dunsworth had eventually made contact with the assassin through a middleman named Sharp—Gabe Sharp—a railroad man who traveled extensively and would make sure the request reached its intended recipient. Dunsworth eventually traveled to Fort Worth, Texas under the name Andrew Goldman to meet the assassin. After a short discussion, the assassin had agreed to the job, taking the money in advance for his service. The job in Nicaragua had been completed with no complications and had been a good test of the man's skills and resourcefulness. Dunsworth set out to once again find the man called Gabe Sharp.

It took nearly three weeks of late evening searching among many of San Francisco's seedy bars and saloons to locate the go-between. Sharp assured the attorney that he would make the contact within one week, two weeks at the most. A contact place, date and time were arranged.

*   *   *

Abilene Texas

The request reached the assassin late one evening. The man who brought it to Luke's hotel room had arrived that afternoon on the train.

"I'm told that the man needing your help has used you once before."

"Do you have a name for me?"

"Andrew Goldman."

Luke grimaced. "I remember him. A persnickety lawyer. Little on the chubby side. Pink cheeks."

The visitor nodded. "There's something else."

"What?"

"There's another guy up there asking a lot of questions about you."

Luke frowned. "A lawman?"

"No. Broke out of prison is what I hear. Word's going around he murdered a couple of drifters several years back."

"He have a name?"

"Yeah. It's Chandler. He's a loner but he's got a chum he drinks with every now and then." The visitor made a face as if straining to remember. "Solomon. Yeah, Bret Solomon from Sacramento."

"Okay. You did good. I'll take care of it."

After the visitor left, Luke sat on the edge of his bed and thought. Solomon. The one who had hired him to take out a neighbor up in the foothills. He remembered the details of that job and smiled, shook his head at the memory. It had been good. Damned good. He wondered for a few minutes just how the Sacramento businessman fit into this. *Could Solomon have hired the drifter Chandler to extract revenge for the killing of Solomon's wife?*

*   *   *

San Francisco

The large house on Nob Hill seemed empty and was too quiet for Thomas O'Reiley since Amanda and the children had left for the east coast. He even missed the sing-song chattering of Xiang as she worked in the kitchen.

Thomas and Frank Barnwell had dinner together a few times but even that seemed contrived and irrelevant. He was well aware of the constant shadow of Chandler over everything but realized there was little he could do except keep a sharp eye out for anything different or unusual.

Business was slow and after two weeks he decided he would take a week and travel to the Gordon ranch and make a quick trip to the mountains to visit Gray Hawk. And, he had to admit, to spend a few minutes with Angela.

*   *   *

Visalia, California

Three days later he stepped off the train in Visalia into the early summer San Joaquin Valley heat. It was not quite like the dry, furnace-like temperature of August but it was still a drastic change from the cool sea air of San Francisco.

Angela met him at the depot with the buggy and greeted him with a tight embrace and a quick brush of her lips across his. Her eyes shone and glistened with joy at seeing him but Thomas felt the stares of a few of the local men absorbing this show of affection and he suddenly realized that he felt some underlying nagging discomfort. He quickly put it aside as they got into the buggy and headed for the Gordon Ranch.

"I am so glad you're here Tom!" Angela said as soon as they were underway. "It seems like such a long time!"

"It's not really been that long! How's Beck doing?"

"He's doing well. My father is concerned that someone may ride out to the ranch and recognize Beck, so he keeps him out with the herd during the day." She laughed. "There's really not too much to do with a herd the size of ours except sing to them to keep them happy!" She laughed again. "We had a nice turnout of calves this spring and we don't have to worry as much about the mountain lions hauling the young ones off."

"I'm glad that Beck's okay."

"Do you have any idea when his trial might start up north?"

O'Reiley shook his head. "Haven't heard a thing about that."

"Well, Beck's been talking about going to Texas to visit his brother after the trial. I guess his brother's health isn't too good."

"You think he'll come back?"

"Well, we—that's my family—have talked about it. We think he may stay there if his brother is getting frail. If his brother was to die . . . I don't know what Beck would do."

"What are Ramon's plans?"

"Oh, he'll be going off to school for a few years, I suspect. He's really interested in the citrus farming thing."

"That's going to leave your folks pretty shorthanded, isn't it?"

Angela glanced at him. "We've talked about that too. Things are pretty stable here at the ranch. Doesn't mean there isn't a lot to do but we've sort of gotten into a way of doing things. I'm a lot more helpful than I was three or four years ago. I guess my father figures I can take over Ramon's part."

Thomas nodded. "What do you think?"

This time Angela looked steadily at Thomas. "Tom, I . . . I know that you and I don't have a future together, as much as I'd love to." She hesitated for a few seconds. "Wishing . . ." she turned her head away for a few brief seconds, "wishing can't make it happen." She made a sad attempt to smile but Thomas saw her eyes were ready to spill over with tears. "I'm a rancher, Tom. Born into a rancher family and brought up as a rancher. Maybe someday I'll meet someone who wants a rancher wife." She looked straight ahead for several seconds then turned again. "But I still mean what I've said all these years. I will always love you, Tom. Always."

O'Reiley could only nod. Words wouldn't come.

Angela steered the buggy into the lane leading to the ranch house. He noticed how large the trees had gotten over the years. Everything was beginning to take on a mature appearance. The family had planted oleander bushes between the trees and they had grown until they were several feet tall, filling both sides of the lane with their bushy greenness and white blossoms. When they arrived at the ranch house, he noted that it too had begun to look different; planters in front held flowers, exposed wood beams had been whitewashed, flat pieces of flagstone formed a walkway. The bunkhouse had had been whitewashed as well and a large area in front of the porch had been laid out with flagstone and several bent-wood chairs sat invitingly in a circle. The shower house appeared to have been rebuilt and enlarged and a flagstone path united the two buildings.

"It looks really nice, Angela. When did all this happen?"

"My father's been working at it over the years. Some of the changes and improvements are so subtle you just don't notice them. But recently he's put a lot of effort here at the house and the bunkhouse. There's not an awful lot for him to do with Beck, Ramon and me all here."

"Well, it certainly looks nice!"

She smiled. "Just be sure you tell my father!"

They were greeted by Hector and Margarita in front of the adobe ranch house with the usual handshakes from Hector and hugs from Margarita. They told him Ramon was out with Beck rounding up, castrating and branding this year's calves and would be back by dinner time.

Thomas spent a few minutes washing up after the train trip and joined Angela and her mother and father in the coolness of the adobe house. They talked and laughed easily and were still sitting in the comfortable leather chairs when Ramon came in the front door and enthusiastically greeted the visitor. Thomas noticed how mature and grown Ramon had become; his hands were callused and his handshake strong and earnest. He clapped Thomas on the shoulder as a friend might do, a sign of intimacy that had slowly developed over the years. The young man had grown tall and had filled out, arms muscular, his face tan and seasoned reflecting a combination of his father's determination and his mother's vibrant beauty. His voice was full and he spoke with certainty and authority, his words coming from deep within his chest. Ramon, like his sister, had developed and grown into a mature adult. In some respects Thomas knew that they looked to him as an integral part of their tightly knit family. And for the first time he recognized that Hector and Margarita had been close to him, almost as parents, over these years—not in the sense of discipline or guidance but as loving, supportive parents. For a brief moment he imagined himself referring to Hector and Margarita as mom and dad and the thought brought a lump to his throat. The only family he had ever known was his Amanda and the three children and it was still in the early developing years, leaning heavily upon Amanda's education and direction. Their children, he knew, would be expected to attend a college and become professional, contributing adults in society. This thought caused him to reflect upon his own experience as a child and young man. Fatherless and then motherless, he had essentially no education. He was wealthy beyond most people's imagination and yet he had come by this prosperity not through any particular skill or effort but more as a matter of luck during his five years as a sole survivor on the island . . .

"Mister O'Reiley?"

Thomas shook his head and realized the rest of the family was looking at him. "I apologize," he said quickly. "I was day-dreaming."

"We saw you sort of drift away," Margarita said quietly. "Are you feeling okay?"

"Certainly and again I apologize for my unsociable behavior. I guess the trip down on the train tired me out. Hector, I meant to tell you how nice your ranch looks. Looks to me like you've spent a lot of time on it recently. Anything special coming up?"

Hector looked at his plate as he responded. "No, nothing special."

Angela jumped in. "Father, tell Thomas about the visitors you had a few weeks ago."

Hector grimaced and shot a quick glance at his daughter. "No big deal. A couple of government men from Washington, D.C."

"The government checking out your beef?" Thomas lightheartedly inquired.

"No. Nothing like that. They said they were interested in maybe someday building a road up to the park. Wanted to hear what I thought about it." As he spoke, Hector kept his eyes averted from Thomas's.

After dinner, he and Angela walked to the corral together. She no longer felt that she had to sneak their time together away from her parents. They stood and watched wordlessly as the sun settled into the low haze of the immense valley to the west. In the last minutes of daylight the blinding brightness of sun slowly turned into a brilliant orange disk that at first perched on the edge of the world. Gradually and subtly it changed shape, casting off rays of red, purple and orange as the last sliver of the orange disk slipped below the horizon. Angela held Thomas's hand tightly and they remained quiet, watching the far western skyline change in hues of gold that became red and then deep purple. Finally darkness replaced the faint glow as the coals of a fire might fade and eventually extinguish at night, to be replaced by the full moon rising over the high mountains

After several minutes Thomas said, "It sounded like your father was pretty reluctant to talk about the men from the government."

"He's been real secretive about it. I thought maybe he'd open up a little and tell you. That's all he's told Ramon and me but I think my mother knows something too. I can tell because it's hard for her to keep a secret."

"Well, it's probably nothing."

"I don't know. They spent an awful lot of time checking out the stock, the tack, saddles, everything. Even looked at the horse's shoes. They seemed to be particularly interested in the horses."

Thomas shook his head. "I'm sure it's nothing to worry about."

"I hope you're right." She turned to Thomas. "You were lost in thought in there, Tom."

He nodded, "Yes, I was."

"Do you want to talk about it?"

"It was nothing that involves you and me directly, Angela." He took both of her hands in his. "You're family . . . all of you . . . I don't know how to tell you without introducing even more complications in our friendship . . ."

"Tell me, anyway, Tom. You so seldom appear lost in thought that I'm curious what was happening."

He chuckled softly. "You know that I had no family as I was growing up. I was suddenly aware this evening of how much you, your brother, and mother and father are like family to me. I never even knew my father. I best remember my mother as a boy in my teen years. And they were difficult years as my mother strained to keep us fed and a roof over our heads. Now I have no family . . . except yours."

She looked at him for several long moments. "I believe I know what you're thinking. If my family is your family, it would make you and me brother and sister." She smiled. "That certainly would complicate our relationship!"

"Will you let me hold you, even if you are my *sister*?" he teased.

"If you didn't hold me, I would be awfully upset."

He put his arms around her and she snuggled close to him, her lips resting on the crook of his neck. "You smell so good," she whispered, "I miss that when you're gone."

He kissed the top of her head, breathing in the aroma of her hair.

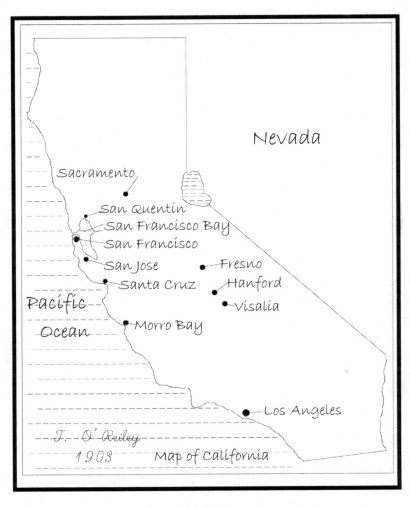

Map #1

Thomas O'Reiley's map of California showing cities and towns.

Not drawn to scale.

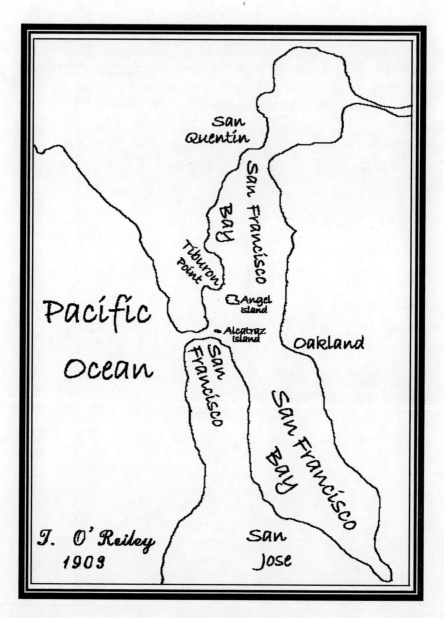

Map #2.

Thomas O'Reiley's map of the San Francisco Bay area.

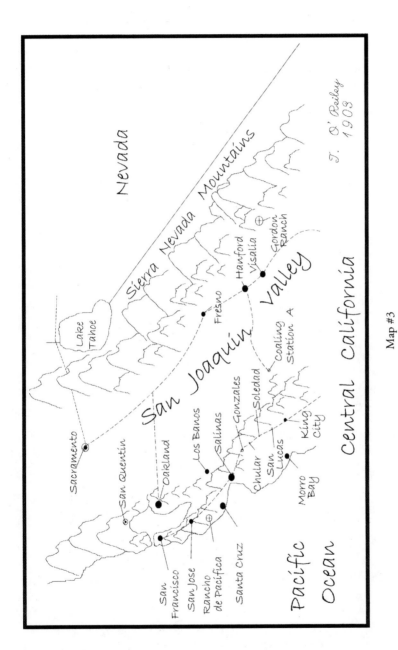

Map #3

Map of California's San Joaquin Valley showing towns and railroads.

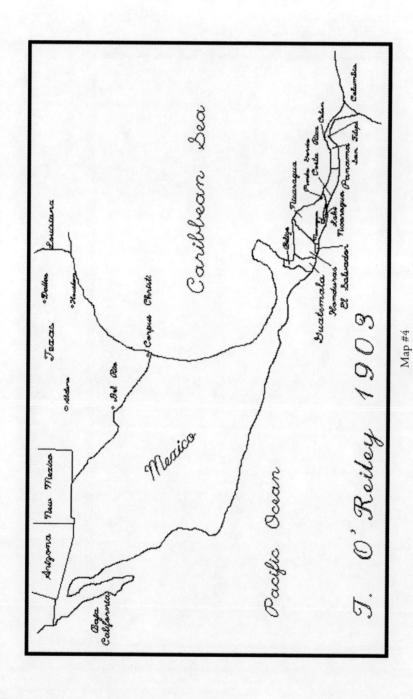

Thomas O'Reiley's hand drawn map of Central America countries.

Map #4

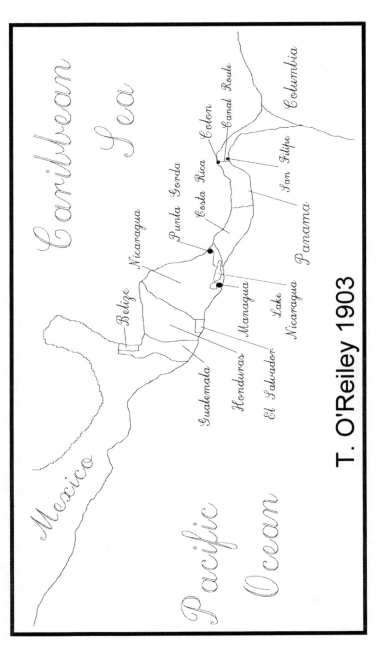

T. O'Reiley 1903

Map 5

Thomas O'Reiley's map of the lower Central American countries.

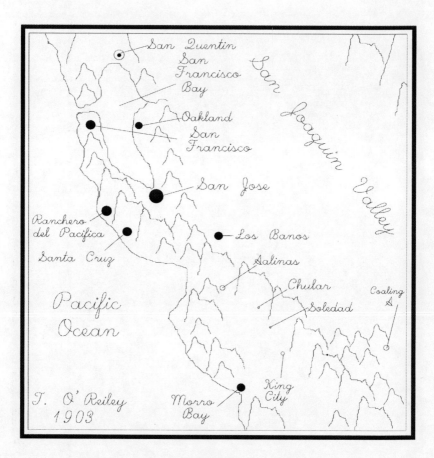

Map #6

Thomas O'Reiley's map of California's Coastal Range of Mountains.

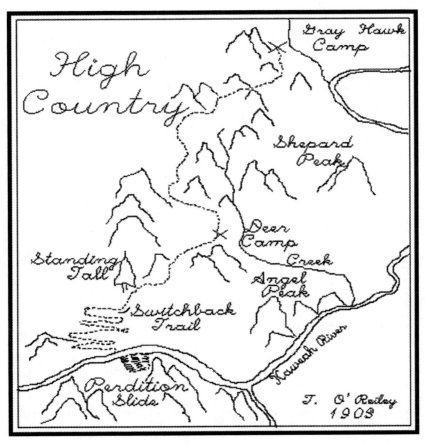

Map #7

Thomas O'Reiley's sketch of the high country. Not drawn to scale.

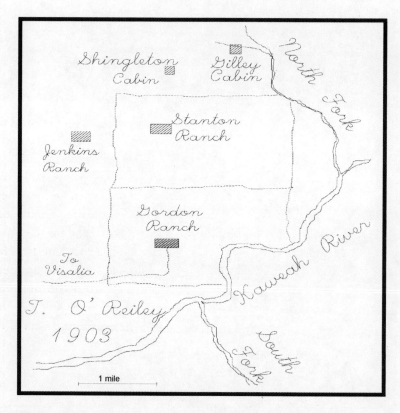

Map #8

Thomas O'Reiley's map of the area around the Gordon Ranch. Approximate scale showm.

CHAPTER 26

<u>Sunday, July 6, 1902 Kaweah River</u>
By mid-day the following day he was on the switchback trail leading up the shear face of the canyon enclosing the river. He and Angela had spent the best part of an hour out by the corral last night, making small talk. Each of them had avoided the subject of their awkward relationship but before they parted company, Angela had gently pulled his face to hers and their lips met in a long kiss that made his head swim. He felt her tongue gently slide across his lips and then probe, searching for the tip of his tongue; she let out a little kitten-like sigh when they met and her arm around his neck tightened. He pulled her close so that their bodies were tightly pressed together and he could feel her heart beating in the intimacy of their embrace. They held the kiss for what seemed to be long minutes and then Angela broke away, brushed his cheek with her lips again before she turned and headed for the ranch house.

*   *   *

Now it was mid-morning and the early summer sun beat on his back, the heat soaking through his shirt and warming his skin. The horse was leisurely plodding along, taking the sharp turns easily and naturally, the pack horse behind following almost step for step. Thomas let the aromas fill him, the trees, the musky smell of the horses, the damp soil. The air was especially clear and when the trail turned toward the east, the range of high mountains south of the Kaweah River glistened in sharp contrast to the sky. Deep canyons among the tallest peaks appeared to be filled with snow; during the warm days of summer some of it would melt and become the water that filled the several large rivers in the watershed. It would be the water his friend Frank Barnwell hoped to manage one day to help provide irrigation for the vast San Joaquin Valley, water needed for the Gordon family to realize their dream of commercially growing citrus trees.

Two hours later he rode by the huge tree that Gray Hawk called *Standing Tall;* he paused for a few moments to take in its astounding size and majestic presence. *How could, why would anyone,* he wondered, *ever cut a tree like that into lumber?* He marveled at the fact that the largest tree on earth, a member of the conifer family, would have such a diminutive cone barely the size of an apricot, whereas the pine tree put forth a cone as long as a man's arm elbow to fingertip.

Another hour found him at the old deer camp and he was not surprised when Gray Hawk stepped out of the shadows and greeted him with a raised right arm.

"My friend Tah-mas! I saw you coming! I knew I would meet you here."

Thomas laughed and they greeted one another as old friends; Thomas saw that the Indian was beginning to show his age. His face had more creases and his arms and legs seemed thinner and less muscular. But the shaman's eyes were still bright and his skin still taut.

That evening they sat together as they shared a meal of roasted rabbit and rich tasting bulbs the old man had dug from the soil which he buried in the coals of the fire to cook.

"So, you knew I was coming to see you?"

"I saw you."

Thomas smiled. "When ? When did you see me coming?"

"Two days ago. I see much smoke and noise; the white man's steel horse. I see you sitting, watching." He made motions with his hands to indicate scenery passing before his eyes.

Thomas nodded. "I took the train from where I live to the town near the Gordon Ranch." He had explained several times his relationship with the Gordon family. "Spent one night there."

The old Indian nodded and looked Thomas squarely in the eye. "Good."

Thomas sensed that the shaman was aware of the difficulty he and Angela were having with their relationship but knew that the old man would not broach the subject. Perhaps he would share some with him later as he greatly respected the shaman's wisdom which seemed to always strike obliquely at the heart of the matter.

Later, in the early evening, they sat in silence watching the sky grow dark and the fire burn down to a few embers. Sitting in the near darkness, the old man finally broke their silence. "How is your chief?" He asked quietly.

"My chief?" Thomas repeated.

"The white people's chief."

Thomas nodded head. "Our chief's name is President."

Now Gray Hawk nodded. "I would like to meet him."

"You would like to meet our President?"

"Yes. I would like to meet your *Prez-i-den*. Have parley with him."

"What would you say to him, Gray Hawk?"

The Indian sat quietly. Minutes passed but Thomas waited patiently. He knew that Gray Hawk was thinking and composing his response. "I would tell," he started, "I would warn *Prez-i-den* of the danger to his life."

Thomas frowned. "Danger?"

"Yes. Your chief in danger."

Thomas sat quietly for a long time. The old shaman had several times demonstrated his unique ability to sense future happenings, even as he had done today knowing of Thomas's arrival. But Gray Hawk had never shared his images of events taking place far away and most likely had little, if any, idea of where the nation's capital, the President's residence was located.

"Tell me of what you have seen, Gray Hawk," Thomas asked quietly.

The Indian nodded slowly. "I will tell you. Three days ago, I was near where we left Bear that Walks In Pain. I go often to visit his spirit because I think my spirit will soon be joining his. We talk about many things. I find a sign." He paused for so long that Thomas started to feel that the shaman was finished with his explanation but then he spoke again. "I find a powerful sign on the forest floor. It was a very large feather, a white feather of the great eagle's tail, a sign to my people of the chief. The feather is unspoiled. It is different than most eagle feathers I have seen. The end of the feather is gold in color the length of my finger. I see this feather on the forest floor. It is a sign. As I look at it, the sound of thunder," the shaman used his hands to indicate the explosive suddenness, "loud, sudden and near, rips the air apart and I know it is the sound of the white man's rifle. I hear the sound and see the feather and I know that the white man's chief is to be killed. The white man has killed their chief before. We have talked. That is my vision. I have thought much about what I have seen."

Thomas sat quietly for a long time, thinking about the old man's revelation and its implications. There was no doubt in Thomas's mind the shaman was sincere in his thoughts, because he had heard such stories and visions from him in the past. The shaman had an uncanny ability to see very clearly some distant event but many times Thomas was able to tie in other factors such as weather or seasonal changes, or of cyclic events that occurred with some regularity. But he had to admit that the vision just recounted caused a ripple of goose bumps to sweep over his arms.

President Roosevelt's popularity ebbed and flowed with the seemingly endless discussion of the eventual canal. Many accused him of abusing his position as President to unduly influence and bully the Congress. Some accused him of outright imperialism. Many believed the whole idea of an inter-ocean canal was foolhardy, for after all, previous attempts had failed and nearly bankrupted France. If Roosevelt was to order the canal to be built, there would be many angry people. And the old Indian sitting next to him knew nothing about the far reaching events that swirled around the nation's chief.

"The President is many days travel from here, across many rivers and mountains, Gray Hawk. He lives in a place we call Washington. Many of our important people live in Washington. Many men there form a council to advise the President on important matters."

The Indian nodded. "I understand council. The Indian people have council as well. These things I tell you will not happen far away in this place you call Wa-sin-ton. It will happen very near to where we sit."

Later that evening Gray Hawk pulled the feather from a leather pouch and handed it to Thomas. "You take this, Tah-mas. Perhaps if you show it to your chief . . . *Prez-i-den* . . . he will hear you."

The feather was as the Indian had described. It was a feather from the group that form the eagle's tail feathers; it was long, reaching from Thomas's elbow to mid-hand. It was unblemished and the smooth vane was intact with no breaks. The feather was as white as snow except for the last three or four inches and that part was, as Gray Hawk had said, brilliant gold in color. Thomas carefully accepted it from Gray Hawk's hands, recognizing that the old Indian considered the feather as having special powers.

* * *

San Francisco

The train arrived from Los Angeles in mid-afternoon. The tall rugged looking man from Texas got off carrying in his right hand the small leather case that held the three components of the high-powered sniper rifle. His left hand gripped a small matching leather suitcase with clothing to last three or four days. The full-length leather coat felt good on this cool day in the city. Half an hour after his arrival he was checked into one of the smaller but still pleasant hotels in the heart of the city. Within an hour he had located the attorney he was to meet and sent a message to his office by messenger telling Dunsworth where and when to meet him. He had selected a restaurant with a bar near the hotel; the bar was dark, even in the daytime and offered secluded seating that minimized the possibility of conversation being overheard. He stretched out on the bed and flexed his arm and leg muscles to rid them of the stiffness brought on by spending so long on the train. He still had five hours before he met with Dunsworth.

Dunsworth heard the messenger enter the firm's office and listened to the brief conversation between him and his secretary. In a minute she brought in a sealed envelope. He asked the secretary to please close the door to his office before he ripped the envelope open, read the short note inside. He glanced at the clock on the end of his desk and nodded to himself. The message stated that El Culebra would meet him at ten o'clock at the French Restaurant, an upscale place off the main streets offering good food, strong drinks and near-total seclusion for clandestine meetings between lovers, businessmen and disreputable politicians. The table would be arranged under the name Rivers.

Dunsworth slid the desk drawer open, pulled the Derringer and a box of shells from the safe place at the rear of the drawer. He quickly checked the tiny pistol, opened the box of ammunition and inserted a shell in each of its over-and-under barrels. *Better safe than sorry*, he thought. He slipped the Derringer into his coat pocket and decided he would spend the next several hours with Sophia.

It was nine-thirty when Dunsworth climbed into the pre-arranged hansom and headed for the French Restaurant. He had enjoyed the company of Sophia and planned to return after this meeting. He sensed that she had finally shaken off the despair over her brother's death and was becoming once again the sensual, sexually exciting women he yearned for. The evening had turned cold and a heavy fog seeped through the city's streets causing auras around the streetlamps and painting everything with a gray hue. Even the lights at the French Restaurant seemed to have difficulty penetrating the dense mist.

It was even darker inside the restaurant while he waited just inside the door until the maître d' approached him. "Mister River's, table please," Dunsworth spoke softly. The maitre d' simply nodded and Dunsworth followed him through the darkness to a booth in the back corner fully hidden in the cave-like darkness. Dunsworth slid into the vacant seat without introductions. They didn't shake hands or acknowledge each other in any way. After a few minutes Dunsworth's eyes adjusted to the darkness; and he saw the man across from him and recognized him as the same man with whom he had negotiated the Nicaraguan job.

Several long seconds went by. Neither spoke. They could both hear the muted conversations around them but the words were not intelligible. Finally the tall man spoke. "You're Dunsworth."

"I am." Dunsworth answered quietly. "You and I have done business once before. I have another . . . business venture . . . to offer El Culebra. It entails some travel and probably a great deal of personal risk."

"His work always entails personal risk. Just tell me what you want done."

A man walked near the table, evidently searching for a familiar face, paused and slowly walked on. Dunsworth leaned far across the table so that his face was only inches from the other man. "I want El Culebra to kill a very prominent politician," he whispered.

"He can do that."

"The job must be done to our exact specifications."

"Our?"

"A small . . . committee . . . shall we say."

"What kind of specifications?"

"Where, when and how."

The assassin leaned back in the deep seat, apparently in thought. Dunsworth sat back and waited. Finally the man leaned forward again, "Keep talking," he said.

"In California, in May."

"So far, he can handle that."

"In the high Sierras."

"As long as he knows where it is, he can handle it." He hesitated, "The beneficiary of this action is a he this time?"

"It is." Dunsworth leaned forward again. "However, I need his agreement before I can divulge the exact details."

"Agreement? That's a little preliminary, isn't it? He doesn't even know any specifics to agree to."

"I understand your concerns but unless I have his word that he will accept the assignment, I can't give you any further information."

The tall man frowned, slid sideways in the seat, leaned forward and said, "I'll have to talk with El Culebra." He paused, "Meet me here, same table tomorrow night, same time." He disappeared into the darkness.

Dunsworth waited several minutes alone in the dark before he got up and followed the man out.

Culebra spent the late evening in his hotel room. He felt uneasy regarding the possible assignment Dunsworth had hinted at but he had the feeling that a job to kill a very prominent politician could demand a very high price.

That same night, Clarence Chandler sat in a dark corner of Charley's in the Tenderloin, nursing a single beer and watching the swarm of drunks crowding against the bar. He had just received word from a man whom he had not previously met that the assassin who called himself El Culebra was in town and would meet with him the next evening.

At seven thirty the next evening, Culebra waited in the shadows of the warehouses lining one side of the pier where he would meet Chandler. He wasn't used to the cold, penetrating dampness of San Francisco and had turned his coat collar up against the cold wind off the bay. It was another gloomy night, similar to the previous night. A thick gray blanket of fog had settled over the bay and replaced the clear afternoon air with an opaque miasma that muted sound as well as the pale light shed by the streetlights at the end of the pier. He waited impatiently for Chandler.

It was quiet, with only the distant foghorn in the bay breaking the silence with its mournful bellow. Minutes passed and Culebra began to wonder if Chandler had come to the pier even earlier than he had and was perhaps waiting in the shadows for him to make a move . . . make a mistake. Culebra had left his rifle at the hotel; it wasn't meant to be used in this kind of situation. He was almost ready to step out of the shadows when he saw the vague silhouette of a man walking toward him, back-lit by the streetlight. The man appeared to be looking into the shadows near the row of warehouses and occasionally peering over his shoulder toward the street. Culebra let the man walk past him about ten yards before he stepped out of the shadows and quickly closed the space between them. His shoes crunched slightly on the rough timbers that comprised the main deck of the pier.

Chandler spun around quickly to his left, his knife ready in his right hand, blade up and ready to plunge into Culebra's body. But he was not fast enough; Culebra used his left hand to grab Chandler's right forearm, twisted it outward, pulled the man closer and in a single motion drove his own knife deep into the man's belly. Chandler gasped and his head drooped as if he was inspecting the wound. Chandler's knife clattered onto the boards. Culebra grunted as he pulled his knife blade upward, viciously sawing through skin, muscle and intestines as Chandler let out a low groan. He began slumping; and Culebra placed his left hand on the man's chest and gave the dying man a shove backwards. Chandler collapsed backward onto the rough boards, his momentum pulling the knife clear. Culebra leaned over, slashed one time across the man's throat before he wiped the blade on Chandler's jacket. He gave Chandler's knife a brief glance before kicking it into the water. He didn't bother to check the man's pockets; the dead man would have nothing that Culebra needed or wanted. He put the toe of his boot under Chandler's ribs and rolled him toward the edge of the pier. Twice more he repeated the rolling; then Chandler's body slithered awkwardly feet first over the side and splashed into the murky water of the bay.

Culebra slipped back into the shadows and listened. There were no unusual sounds. The fog horn bleated again; the forlorn sound echoed among the islands in the bay and the mass of warehouses that served the city's shipping industry. He stepped out of the shadows and walked quickly to the streetlight at the end of the pier. He would meet with Dunsworth next. He felt the familiar urging and knew that before the night was through, he would find a woman, most likely a prostitute, to complete and satisfy the ritual of Chandler's death. He would be on his way back to Los Angeles on the morning train, then on to Abilene. But he had to deal with the attorney first.

He was waiting in the same seat when Dunsworth arrived at ten o'clock. The lawyer slid in across from him. This time Dunsworth had a tumbler of whiskey in his hand and he offered to get the same for El Culebra but the assassin shook his head. A few patrons wove their way among the tables, greeting others or looking for a vacant place to sit. They sat in total silence for several minutes, taking in the muted conversations around them, the clink of glasses and the occasional slightly out-of-control giggle of a woman. It reminded Dunsworth of Sophia's giggle after she had finished three or four glasses of wine.

"I think El Culebra will agree with your terms, so far."

Dunsworth nodded and sipped from his glass of whiskey. "Good. Then I will tell you some more about the job." He leaned forward again until his face was only inches from the assassin. "He will be provided with anything he needs to do the job. His travel expenses will be fully paid. We suggest that he hires a horse rather than try to travel with his own; we have information for him regarding that. He should plan to be two or three days ahead of the beneficiary and plan his escape route well ahead of time. The shot must take place in the late afternoon to prevent anyone from effectively following him. He must not leave any evidence behind; no spent cartridges, no scrap of clothing, no tobacco, nothing. Then we suggest that he leave the United States, at least for a few years."

Culebra grunted at this last suggestion. "I'm not sure El Culebra can do that. He still has to work for a living as they say."

"There will be little need for him to be concerned about money once this job is completed. He will be very adequately compensated."

"How adequately?" Culebra leaned forward, closing the distance between them.

Dunsworth gave him the figure the committee had agreed to.

Culebra nodded and leaned even closer. "Who do they want eliminated?"

"The President of the United States."

*   *   *

Culebra spent a few hours in his hotel room, before exiting back onto the street well after midnight. He walked in the shadows of the streetlights and the lighted advertisements of the bars and saloons. He spilt off the main street and followed a dark, narrow street, listening to the occasional murmur of conversation or drunken giggles that spilled from the darker shadows.

The voice called to him from a darkened doorway. She sounded young, perhaps hoping for one last customer before quitting for the night. He approached her and was pleased to find that she was indeed quite young, perhaps fifteen years old. The top of her head came up to his chest and even in the near darkness he could see that her hair was long, falling to the middle of her back and dark, perhaps even black. In minutes they were in the small bedroom on the second floor of the building.

She removed her clothing in the light of a single candle on a chest of drawers and waited on the bed while he undressed. When he was through with her, he killed the young girl as slowly as he could, pressing her light frame onto the bed, pinning her thin arms and legs under his weight. His hand covered her mouth and nose cutting off her air, preventing her from making a noise. He relaxed slowly as her feet slowed their feeble thrashing and her struggles to breathe began to lessen; he experienced arousal again as he felt her heart beating frantically, drumming and thudding before it became erratic, slowed and then finally stopped completely as she relaxed noiselessly on the bed. He pulled his knife from the scabbard strapped to his lower leg, pressed its razor edge to her flesh and began to make the meticulous, deliberate incisions. He was in no hurry now though he would have savored the experience more if the circumstances would have allowed her to scream, shriek and howl like a deranged animal throughout the terrifying fear and agonizing pain. Each cut held some carefully considered fiendish and perverted symbolism for him; at least at first and then the lust, wanton satisfaction and the smell of warm blood all began to fuse together, bringing on the inevitable spasms of ecstasy that goaded him into the final manic frenzy of stabs, slashes and visceral incisions that left little to recognize as having at one time been a human being. When he finally leaned back, breathing hard; his shaking hands and forearms were covered with her blood. He wiped the blood off on the threadbare covers, averting his eyes from the dark mass of mutilated flesh in the center of the bed, blew out the candle, dressed in the dark and quickly crept down the rickety stairs to let himself out by way of the unlocked door into the silent alley.

* * *

Gomez Santiago stepped aboard the early morning train for Los Angeles that would put him in that city around noontime. From Los Angeles, he would take a steamer to Puerto Sandino on the Nicaraguan Pacific Coast, some thirty miles from Managua, where he would meet with Miguel Vincente-Esperanza.

CHAPTER 27

<u>High Sierras</u>
The small party of men rode horses down the narrow path. Six of the men wore uniforms and western style hats and were armed both with holstered side arms and Winchester Model 94 lever action rifles in scabbards. Their horses, identical red chestnut sorrels, were well groomed and their saddles and tack was immaculately maintained. They rode two ahead and four behind the seventh man. He rode a Sabino white, sitting high in the saddle and was dressed in an all-white suit of clothing. He wore eye glasses and had a bushy mustache and a broad face. On his head sat an Indian war bonnet made of eagle feathers that ran down his back and trailed behind his left leg nearly to the stirrup. The feathers were brilliant white except for their tips, which were gold in color. This rider was unarmed and both his bearing and riding reflected an obvious aura of dignity, command and power; his distinctive eyes looked straight ahead. The seven men rode silently in this strict formation; the only sound was the soft padding sound of the horses and the squeak of the leather saddles. Trees lined both sides of the path, crowded closely together and separated occasionally by dense undergrowth and an occasional boulder.

Thomas saw the shadowy form of a man flitting among the thick growth bordering the path. The figure moved quietly and swiftly among the trees, maintaining a position several yards ahead of the party. Thomas tried to signal his concern but the party rode ahead, oblivious of the danger that appeared to be stalking them. The shadow figure suddenly stepped from behind a boulder into the path, lifted his arm and pointed a pistol at the man in white. Thomas's cautionary shout caught in his throat, stuck, rendering it impossible for him to call out his warning. The riders all started in surprise and the six simultaneously reached for their side arms but the stranger was already in position and his finger tightened on the trigger. The long-barreled six-shooter spat out a tongue of flame and jumped in his hand; the man in white lurched in his saddle. The sound of the pistol shot echoed and echoed among the mountains and Thomas sat up straight on the bear skin that he had been sleeping on. His body was covered with a sheen of perspiration in spite of the early morning coolness.

Gray Hawk's bed was empty. Thomas lay back wearily; the night had been long and restless, the terrible dream relentlessly occurring over and over with only minor variations; sometimes the assailant would jump from the bushes to the center of the path, or he would hide behind a boulder, or the man would be one of the soldiers, or the man would suddenly appear as if by magic in the center of the path. In his dream Thomas was positioned as a nearby observer, somehow elevated above the scene as it unfolded, helplessly unable to come quickly enough to the President's aid, always too late, his intended warning shout constricted in his throat before the solitary pistol shot shattered the calm and the man dressed in white lurched in the saddle . . .

Thomas closed his eyes for a few moments. He knew that the dream had most likely been influenced by Gray Hawk's unnerving and prophetic vision of America's Commander in Chief being shot. The vague and featureless man who did the shooting surely represented the unknown factors; who was this assassin, when and where would he strike? Was it only a fearful vision with little substance, or could the shaman actually see into the future?

He arose, put on the breech cloth and slipped the leather moccasins that Gray Hawk had made for him onto his feet. The air was still cool with the morning sun just beginning to reflect off the taller tree tops on the nearby mountain peaks. Gray Hawk was nowhere in sight. Thomas figured that the old man had left to find something for the two of them to eat. He wandered down to the small creek, washed his face in the icy water and returned to the campsite.

He thought about this visit with Gray Hawk. The old Indian's age was much more apparent now than it had been in previous visits. His arms and legs were thinner, the skin a little looser and tended to sag. The bones of his upper body were showing through thinner layers of muscle; even his hair, almost completely turned silver, was beginning to thin. His still rugged face was filled with new creases and dark pouches claimed the spaces below his eyes. His voice no longer had the timber and volume, the vitality that it once had. His hands, no longer the strong firm hands, shook slightly. Only his eyes remained unchanged; they were still powerful, the eyes of a shaman, able to penetrate right into the center of Thomas's head to see beyond the visible. Thomas sensed that the old man would not have many seasons left and would someday, perhaps soon, be walking with Bear that Walks with Pain. He was saddened by the thought that the shaman would most likely die alone, perhaps while out hunting, maybe during his sleep with no one there with him to help ease his transition into the other world, or to grieve for him when he died and to properly care for his earthly remains, to sing the ancient chants to ease his spirit in the journey to the next world. Thomas looked around, so little left at the end of life, a few animal furs, a hunting bow and several arrows, some articles of clothing made of carefully tanned deer hides, a half a dozen objects that represented special times or moments to the old man—a piece of crystal clear quartz, a broken sea shell, some colorful feathers, the sacred smoking pipe, a small leather pouch that contained various healing powders and herbs, tiny animal bones and small stones to be used during his solitary rituals and ceremonies. The knife that Thomas had given him had never left the shaman's possession.

Thomas heard the old man approaching; he was chanting, his voice wavering in the morning air. "Ah-wee-ah-ha-ma-ra-see-na . . ." His eyes caught sight of Thomas. "Ah, Tah-mas! I see you finally wake up! I am awake all night with your snoring!"

Thomas laughed, "Old friend, your snore is like thunder that shakes the ground!"

The shaman laughed this time and dropped his leather bag on the ground near the cook fire pit. "I have gathered something for us to eat."

It took Gray Hawk only a few minutes to prepare a rough gruel of roasted nuts and a few slender tubers, quickly ground against a flat stone and boiled with water. Thomas ate it, tentatively at first, then with relish when he found the taste to be quite pleasant. The old Indian talked and talked, telling Thomas about the last winter and spring, the migration of animals, which ones had given birth, of the various birds he had seen and what that meant in the way of future weather. One subject ran on to the next. He talked about the trees, which ones had budded out on time and which had not. He talked about the rain and snow and ice, the melt and the runoff and what it would mean for forest life. He talked about the cloud patterns, the direction and intensity of the wind, the color of the sky in the morning, mid-day and evening. It seemed to Thomas that the old man had a reason that corresponded with every act of nature and every act of nature, every creature, every living thing, indeed, everything, was interconnected as if by an infinitely large spider web. There was no such thing as a solitary, disconnected action, either by man or by nature.

This reasoning would allow him to predict what the weather would be like tomorrow, next week, next month and next year, which animals would be abundant, which nuts and berries would grow in profusion, which trees would produce seeds or nuts. Thomas suddenly realized the shaman was sharing a lifetime of experience and knowledge because he knew he was going to die.

"Gray Hawk, my friend," Thomas interrupted, "what have you seen that causes you to share your life in this way with me?"

"Ah, Tah-mas, you can see me," he pointed to the side of his head, "you know me."

"Yes, I see you. This is not like you."

The old Indian looked down. "I have seen signs, omens. My life here is almost finished. I have so much I want to tell you."

"I understand, Gray Hawk. You have walked this ground for many winters, seen many things; you understand many things. You know that someday you will walk beside Bear that Walks with Pain."

"Someday, perhaps very soon, I will walk beside *Ha Sook Inya*, Bear that Walks with Pain. But my time will come too quickly; my time to go to the next life will come but not as an old man. I have seen signs."

Thomas studied the face across from him. Gray Hawk kept his eyes averted. "What signs, Gray Hawk?"

"I have seen the signs. I know these secret omens. They are very old signs of my people. They are always right." He finally looked up and into Thomas's eyes. "They tell me that I die soon. Not as an old man."

Thomas frowned. That was the second time Gray Hawk had used the phrase *not as an old man*. "What do you mean *not as an old man*?"

The Indian looked at him, his eyes searching Thomas's face. "It means I will go to my next life before it is my time. It means someone will take my life from me. The signs tell me that I will die at the hands of another man."

Thomas shook his head in frustration. "Who would want to kill you, Gray Hawk? You've not hurt anyone! You have lived in peace for many winters. Very few people even know that you live here."

"Only you, Tah-mas, know where I live."

The old shaman's comment sliced like a sword into the very depth of Thomas's soul. Had his presence, his presumed friendship put the old man's life in jeopardy? Had he erred in assuming that the shaman had wanted a friendship with him? Did the old Indian think that he would somehow bring an end to his life?

It took more questions for the shaman to reveal when he had seen these warning signs. The old man had stumbled onto them while hunting. "At first I could not believe what my eyes were seeing. I sat nearby and just looked at the omen for a long time. I knew what it was telling me. When I was with my people I read this sign for old men many times." He looked at Thomas and his eyes revealed a sadness Thomas had not seen before. "I saw the sign of my death one day before I saw the other sign, the omen telling me of the vicious murder of your chief."

*   *   *

San Francisco

Dunsworth lifted his glass of wine and perfunctorily clinked glasses with Sophia. He had spent the entire day in his office; the Texas attorney had finally left with the completed papers for the transaction. The money was deposited in the bank to be transferred to the appropriate bank in Nicaragua. In a few days he would be half owner of some of the most valuable real estate in the Central American country and the four east coast investors would own several thousand acres of useless jungle swamp land. All now awaited the Congress and President Roosevelt's decision. Construction of the canal would demand thousands of acres for timber, administration and housing buildings, railroads, rock and gravel for concrete. All would be available—for a price.

Sophia sipped delicately at her wine but her face showed disappointment and some irritation at Dunsworth's palpable lack of attention. After missing three evenings of his company, she had anticipated a little more of his attentiveness this evening but his thoughts were obviously somewhere else. He had absent mindedly uncorked the bottle of French wine and unceremoniously poured the two glasses; he had not mentioned the play that he had promised to take her to the next evening.

"Alex. Are you still here, darling?" she finally asked.

"Huh? Oh, I'm sorry my dear." He winced at Sophia's words as if he was startled from a deep sleep. "I have so many things on my mind! Please forgive me!"

She shook her head sadly. "You mustn't let such things disturb you, Alex. You know you have a tendency to do that."

"Yes, yes I know," he replied impatiently. He longed to reveal all that had transpired over the past few days but couldn't trust her to keep the information to herself. All he had done was speak to an acquaintance of the assassin; the man was simply part of the assassin's vast network but he could be hauled into federal court and charged with conspiracy to commit murder. If the President was indeed assassinated as a result of that conversation, he and the other four would be hung by the neck. Then there was the swap of properties on the legal documents. Eventually the east coast investors would discover his duplicity; they might even send the assassin after him. And besides that, he was growing weary of Sophia's persistent comments that tended to single out his obvious numerous human frailties; these became matters for never-ending debate followed by implied remedial action. He decided that it was Sophia's suppressed mothering instinct since she had never had a child.

He also was experiencing some rising second thoughts about the Texas attorney. He realized, much too late, that he had simply taken the man's word for a number of things; was the man even in reality an attorney? Were the papers they had both signed and initialed countless times really what they were supposed to be? After all, he spoke no Spanish and had relied entirely on the Texan's translation. He could, in a court of law, if necessary, swear that the signatures on the documents were clever forgeries; but that would not account for the cancelled checks and deposits of hundreds of thousands of dollars that belonged to someone else. And suppose his relationship with the Los Angeles law firm eventually came to light. Though he assumed that the murders and subsequent fire had left no trace of evidence that would implicate him, there could always be some incriminating trace lurking somewhere: a letter, a note sitting unread on one of the partner's brief case at home or in a jacket pocket hanging in a closet. Even Sophia, if she really tried, could assemble a scenario that would tie him into the murders. Then there was Nelle's death and the escape of the wanted man, Beckley Weston and the seemingly endless investigation by the sheriff in Santa Cruz. If only he had someone to confide in . . .

"You must get some sleep, Alex dear. You know that you are not getting a proper amount of rest. Perhaps we should limit our time together to, say, four nights a week. That would give you at least three full nights of sleep, though I would dearly miss our time together. Perhaps it would make our limited time together more precious. What do you think?"

There was no response; Dunsworth's mind was already engaged in the monster spider web of problems beginning to enmesh him.

Sophia set her wineglass down hard. "Alex, are you even listening to me?"

*   *   *

<u>On the train, East of Los Angeles</u>

The assassin sat alone in a seat on the east-bound train out of Los Angeles thinking about the last few days. The anonymous man that he had killed on the San Francisco dock meant nothing to him. The fact that the man had carried a knife and was ready to use it was proof enough that he had been up to no good and verified his original belief that the man was out to kill him; perhaps he had been hired by someone, he didn't really care about those details. But his mind shifted to the young girl he had ravaged—that was worth dwelling upon, often. Though not fully satisfying all his cravings, the experience in itself was different and suggested a new perspective on the ritual. He recognized the fear of being discovered by other occupants of the building and he had despised the self-enforced silence; he liked—no, he *enjoyed* listening to the hysterical screams and whimpers of terror and agony as his victims began to realize what was happening to them and fought, perspiring, squirming, bucking and twisting, to get away from the razor sharp knife as it did hideous things to their bodies, slowly . . . always slowly. But the necessary silence had introduced a new dimension of furtiveness, of secrecy that had not been present before, mysteriously elevating the intensity of his euphoria and ultimate carnal satisfaction. It was something he would remember in the future.

His meeting with the attorney preyed heavily on his mind and he had churned it over and over, looking at it from all angles, analyzing the possibilities of success and potentials of failure. He had never attempted such an action; most of his kills had been simple and easy to set up for execution and escape. This job would demand skills he was less sure of. He

345

was not a man familiar with mountain skills, nor was he an accomplished horseback rider. Living out-of-doors was something that he had never enjoyed; he preferred some of the basic animal comforts of a bed and a roof over his head, somebody else to cook his meals, though from time to time the needs of the work had caused him to suffer primitive conditions for a day or two. This job would require several days, perhaps even more, exercising these more basic skills. It would demand his ability to provide himself with food and water, seek or make shelter wherever he could find it. He had no doubts about the actual shooting; that would be the easiest part of the entire enterprise. He thought, too, about the man he was going to kill. After all, he was just another man; he had already ended the lives of more men than he could remember. And there would most certainly be someone already slated to fill in the void; the United States would survive without its President, not that it mattered to him. The nation would still insist on starting wars, spreading its influence to parts of the world that didn't care one way or the other. There would be more armies in the future and more trained snipers who would eventually find their way to do what he was doing.

The money offered was tempting, as were thoughts of moving to South America or Europe. It was certainly only a matter of time before some unexpected slip up would cause his identity to be revealed and then a nation-wide manhunt would begin to close in on him. His range of freedom would become smaller and smaller, until at last he was found trapped in a house, ridden down in the desert or hiding in a thicket of trees. Then it would be over. If he was taken alive, they would hang him. He had imagined the hanging many times; the harsh hemp rope around his neck, the heavy hangman's knot partly resting upon his left shoulder, a black hood slipped over his head closing out all light and the sudden fall, his last human sensation, straight down into nothingness. Unless someone made a mess of the hanging, it would be over before he was even aware of it—painless, no lingering thoughts or feelings. Like *falling* asleep—he smiled at the wry humor of the words.

He had felt a lingering distrust of the San Francisco attorney. During their discussions, he had said that the committee would want to meet with him personally. At that point he would be given the exact details of the job, including maps, train tickets, directions, everything he would need. But afterward, he would be a hunted man. If everything worked as it should, his identity would still be a mystery but there was always a small chance that something would go wrong.

*　　*　　*

<u>High Sierras</u>

It was time for Thomas to leave Gray Hawk and return to San Francisco. He had spent the hours listening to the shaman's enormous knowledge of mountain ways, his beliefs as a shaman, the ways in which he interpreted nature's signs. He kept telling the old man that he could not possibly remember everything he was being told. The old man simply smiled and replied that he would remember what he needed to remember when it was needed. No one, the shaman told him, ever forgot what they needed to know to survive.

When the parting became reality, Thomas looked at the old man, feeling that this might be the last time he ever saw him.

The Indian smiled. "I know your thoughts, Tah-mas. I will see you again. You will return and we will see each other. That I promise you." He raised his right hand in salute to Thomas. "My friend."

"My friend," Thomas replied, his right hand raised as well. It was a ritual that they had begun early in their friendship. It simply realized that a great friendship existed between them. There was no promise of return, or sorrow of leaving. Nature itself would dictate the future. But Thomas was fully aware of the vision Gray Hawk had experienced regarding his own death and felt an additional burden of responsibility toward the old man.

Five hours later as the sun was beginning to fall behind the western trees, he rode into the Gordon's ranch. That evening the weather was perfect as he and Angela stood by the corral fence watching the last vestiges of sunlight shift into the darker hues of red and purple as night fell around them.

"How was Gray Hawk?" she asked after they had stood silently for a long time.

"He's getting old, Angela. I'm afraid that he won't live very much longer. This winter, perhaps the next winter as well. By then he'll be too weak to hunt for himself . . ."

"I'm sorry, Tom. I know he has become a good friend for you."

"I'll be back next spring. Hopefully, I can help him, someway . . ." He felt her hand on his arm, a light squeeze.

"There may be nothing you can do for him."

"I know that, too. But I should try."

347

She just nodded her head and they lapsed again into silence. The evening sounds of nature began to stir around them. "I don't think," he started, "that I'll ever tire of these sounds. They'll always remind me of these times together. You and I. The sounds, the fragrances of winter, spring, summer and fall in the air, the beautiful sunsets, the moonlight, the closeness of the stars overhead. I will always have them with me."

Her hand on his arm tightened and she turned toward him. "My dear Tom. I've made your life so complicated and I'm sorry. But I'm not sorry that I love you as I do and my only hope is that you believe and understand my love. I wish it could be different but I can accept that for what it is. I want to believe that you love me in some way—your own way and perhaps it's different from the way I love you."

"I do love you, Angela. I know that and it confounds me. For me to wish that things could be different is to wish that I did not have a beautiful wife and three gorgeous children. And if that were true, then I would never have met you. We know one another and we do have a wonderful love for each other but it has to remain simply that way; it cannot go further; it cannot be different for us. I've anguished over this Angela and I've wondered if a man can . . . could love two women at the same time."

She pulled herself into his arms and put her arms around him holding him tightly. She was silent but Thomas could feel the restrained sobs that racked her small body. They remained that way for a long time, silent, holding one another tightly.

Finally she pulled away and Thomas knew she was looking at him, even in the darkness that surrounded them.

"My dear Tom, I do love you and I always will." She pulled his head down and their lips met, fused together as neither wanted to pull back. Her lips pressed and he felt her tongue sweep across his and he pulled her even more tightly to him. The kiss lasted for a long time and finally she loosened her arms and their lips parted, reluctantly.

"Angela, I love you in ways I don't even understand. Please just accept my love for what it is."

* * *

San Francisco

Bret Solomon saw the small article on an inside page in the Chronicle. A man's body was found floating in the bay, brutally slashed to death.

A member of the police force had seen the body and identified it as an escaped prisoner by the name of Clarence Chandler. Chandler had escaped from San Quentin and had been assumed dead after the barge he used during his escape had been run over and sunk by a merchant ship. Photo identification from the San Quentin prison files verified his identification.

Solomon read the article and realized that the assassin El Culebra had probably been in the city. Somehow word had reached El Culebra that Chandler was looking for him, perhaps Chandler had even let it slip that he was planning to kill the assassin. But surely El Culebra would not travel to San Francisco merely to eliminate a pathetic braggart who talked too much. That meant that El Culebra had been in the city for another reason. Solomon frowned. What would bring El Culebra to San Francisco? Someone in San Francisco wanted El Culebra to eliminate . . . who? An enemy? A rival? A political opponent? Something was going on . . . He decided to keep an eye on the local newspapers for the next several weeks to see what transpired.

Well, Solomon decided, so much for Chandler and his outstanding debt to the Chinese gambling gang. Life would certainly go on without him. The only thing that disappointed Solomon was that Chandler failed to get rid of the assassin. Solomon shook his head sadly, remembering the horror of hearing that his wife had been brutally raped, tortured and stabbed to death after the assassin had shot her lover, Richard Manhauser, to death in their secret love-nest in a remote section of Manhauser's ranch.

CHAPTER 28

<u>Wednesday, July 16, 1902, Managua, Nicaragua</u>
Gomez Santiago had spent well over an hour behind closed doors of the import-export office of Miguel Esperanza Vincente reviewing what he had learned and accomplished in San Francisco. Vincente bent over the official property transfer documents Santiago and Dunsworth had completed, studying them carefully.

"So, Dunsworth believes he has purchased the Vincente property, all two and a half million acres of it with you as co-investor."

"That's correct, Miguel. I established a price I knew he could not turn down, yet would require a major portion of his financial holdings. He is very much, how do you say it, *out on a limb*? He has mortgaged the rancho for the additional funds he needed. He will soon be informed that through a minor error, my name does not appear in the documents and he is in fact the sole owner of the property."

"That should make him extremely happy to think that he has squeezed you aside as a partner and it's entirely legal! You did very well, Gomez. Very well." He peered at the documents again. "And he will be the owner of property that is described in this document?"

"That's right. I have contacts in the government records department who located the property he has purchased. It's been for sale for over ten years. The owner was willing to almost give it away. It is mosquito and snake infested swamp land, part of a very old land grant that he inherited. Even if Dunsworth was able financially to drain the property, all he would have is two and a half million acres of almost bottomless mud, rotting vegetation and snakes. Even the natives are afraid to go there."

"And what about the investors from the east coast?"

"They will end up with their two and a half million acres and a complex, nearly irresolvable paper trail that implicates Dunsworth's full involvement as a scheming attorney who cheated his clients out of several millions of dollars by means of a fraudulent land deal in Nicaragua. They will be in the courts for many, many years. If the American lawyers ever manage to untangle it, Dunsworth will certainly go to prison—if he's still alive."

Vincente nodded his approval. "Very good! Let's make the necessary changes to the documents and get them filed. That way you can send the paper that indicates the documents have been properly filed."

"Let me show you how simple that will be. It took me several days to arrange the documents so this could be done." Santiago carefully paged through the two sets of documents, located the selection of pages he was looking for and quickly rearranged them, tapped the two piles to square them up. "There. It is done. Two legal and complete documents, properly signed and witnessed, soon to be legally filed with appropriate filing fees and purchase money deposited in the banks. Dunsworth will receive this set that describes him as the legal owner of two and a half million acres of Nicaraguan property, carefully identified in the document. The investors will receive the second document which is completely legal, giving them full ownership of two and a half million acres of real estate—legally described by precise longitude and latitude descriptions—located beneath several hundred feet of sea water fifty miles off the west coast of Nicaragua." He laughed, "It will be a long term investment."

Vincente paused for a moment before he continued. "And what did you find out about the assassin?"

Santiago leaned back in his chair. "I believe he is the same man I saw in Abilene. Sophia Jenkins was not much help but I followed Dunsworth several evenings and on two separate occasions he met the man in a very secluded lounge. I tried to listen in on their conversations but was not able to get close enough. But I'm certain the man he met with is the man called El Culebra."

Vincente frowned. "Dunsworth and Culebra? That is very interesting. What could they be doing?" He tapped the desk with a pencil.

"Well, interestingly, there was a murder on the docks while I was there, which of course is fairly common in a city as large as San Francisco. The man killed was named Clarence Chandler, an escaped convict and there were a few interesting similarities. The man was brutally knifed, gutted would be more accurate and his throat slit; he hadn't been shot from a distance as most of the others. But later that same night, there was a young Mexican girl, fifteen years old, who was raped, tortured, viciously mutilated and killed. Among the information we have gathered on the assassin, covering a dozen or so murders, that is one of his perversions. However, the questions then become, did Culebra kill Chandler? If the murderer was Culebra, why would Dunsworth hire him to assassinate a moneyless vagrant, an escaped convict? If Dunsworth didn't hire him, who did? And if no one hired Culebra to kill Chandler, why did he? And lastly, what was El Culebra doing in San Francisco?"

"You're sure you saw El Culebra?"

"Yes. I'm certain."

"Could Dunsworth have hired Culebra to kill the lawyers in Los Angeles?"

"It's possible but I think Dunsworth did it himself. First, it wasn't Culebra's style, though granted, it's very similar to the death of your mother. It wouldn't have been very difficult for Dunsworth to travel to Los Angeles, kill the three attorneys, set the fire and return to San Francisco—all in less than twenty four hours. I had an interesting talk with the conductor on the train. He remembers a man making the round trip from San Francisco to Los Angeles and back in one night. He said it was unusual, although not unheard of. He remembered that man specifically because of his clothes; he was all dressed up—his words were *like a New Orleans pimp*—and he wore a light gray flat-top derby." He pulled the receipts from Dunsworth's house from his pocked and spread them in front of Esperanza. "I found a hat of that description in Dunsworth's home in San Francisco. It had barely been worn and it didn't match any of the clothing in his wardrobe. It looks like he got rid of the trousers and jacket, kept the rest. Train tickets to and from Los Angeles fit perfectly. And incidentally, did you know that Dunsworth's wife was murdered less than two weeks before the Los Angeles murders? He's up to something; maybe getting ready to leave the States in a hurry. I just have to dig a little deeper."

Vincente stared out the window. "So, we know that Culebra stays in a hotel in Abilene, Texas. We're *fairly certain* that Culebra traveled to Punta Gorda to murder my mother, stole her gold coins and jewelry and eventually cashed in the gold coins. Dunsworth *probably* met with Culebra in San Francisco but we don't know why. Culebra *probably* killed a vagrant and dumped his body in the bay but we don't know why. Dunsworth *probably* killed the three law partners in Los Angeles because he was being squeezed out of making a property sale in which he stood to make a lot of money. Dunsworth's own wife was murdered and we don't know why. And now Dunsworth has a mistress who was the sister of one of the Los Angeles lawyers. Dunsworth and El Culebra."

*   *   *

San Francisco, California

Thomas entered the quiet home on Nob Hill and set his suitcase on the floor of the foyer. The house felt strangely empty and abandoned with the absence of Amanda and his children. They were still in New York and would be there at least another week. He walked slowly through the home, each room, breathing in the familiar odors and fragrances of his family, even the smells in the kitchen that kindled thoughts of Xiang with her sing-song voice and her cooking skills.

He had decided that the next day he would meet with Handon and Frank to bring himself up to date on what was happening with the business. But this evening he would settle into his favorite chair in the sun room and catch up with some of the daily newspapers that had collected on the front stoop. He found something to eat after rummaging through the kitchen, set himself a plate and took it to the sun room. The sun was almost set, leaving the sky tinted with a brilliant spectacle of orange, pink and purple swirls. He took his time eating the snack, watching the wonder of the changing western horizon as dusk and then darkness fell upon the city. He lit the oil lamp that still resided on his desk; he had been reluctant to convert this room to electric lighting, though most of the rest of the home was now lighted with electric sconces or table lamps. He supposed the next modern marvel would be a telephone in the house; Amanda had already mentioned how handy it would be for the family. *Then,* he mused; *I suppose we shall have to purchase an automobile.*

He organized the newspapers by date and took his time perusing through the pile of papers, experiencing the luxury of feeling rested and relaxed. The paper dated June 28 revealed that the United States Congress had authorized itself to purchase the concession to build the Panama Canal from the French canal company for forty million dollars, even though a final decision had not yet been made of the route of the canal, or even if the canal would be built through Panama or Nicaragua.

*   *   *

Alexander Dunsworth had not missed the small newspaper article either and reading it sent chills up his back. He had just invested everything he owned into the acquisition of the prime Vincente property in Nicaragua. He was either going to come out of the deal a multi-millionaire, or nearly penniless. In addition to investing all his available liquid assets, he had mortgaged the ranch on the coast; the San Francisco home, purchased barely two years ago, was already highly mortgaged. Everything hinged upon Congress giving the go-ahead to construct the canal through Nicaragua. The Texas attorney had eloquently spoken of that probability with such unflinching assurance, even bluntly alluding that he had powerful political contacts deep within the United States government. Dunsworth had felt himself being swept up in the enthusiasm. The recent approval to buy the French concession to build the canal through Panama was sure to anger Columbia, convincing them that the United States was circumventing negotiations with them. And Columbia was a tough negotiator, or so he had heard . . .

Then there were the east coast investors who would eventually learn that they had purchased useless property. They would come after him with vengeance in their hearts. He would have to leave the country, perhaps for Brazil before they were able to catch up with him; perhaps they may even decide to pay the assassin El Culebra to put a bullet in his back.

He reached for the cut glass decanter, poured himself a second tumbler of whiskey and glanced around his home. Of course, all of these treasures would be left behind; the colorful Mexican pottery, his collection of books, the handsome ship model and his attractive assortment of nautical paraphernalia that women always cooed over. He wasn't even interested in the sea or ships; the few times he had gone sailing on the vast San Francisco Bay he had been violently sea sick, embarrassed in front of friends and miserable.

There was, of course, Sophia to consider. He enjoyed her intimacy, at least most of the time. But he knew that in spite of whatever feelings she had for him, she was simply a lonely and forlorn companion whom he blatantly exploited when he was lonesome or needed sexual satisfaction. She was not and never would be, an essential part of his life; and he had brutally murdered her brother. The thought of her vengeance if she ever discovered the truth was truly fearful.

And there was still Nelle's murder to be dealt with. That damned sheriff in Santa Cruz keeps digging and looking! Why would he not just take what evidence he had and capture, arrest and hang that good-for-nothing Weston? Why was he continuing to investigate? What did he expect to find? Dunsworth sipped at his whiskey as he went over and over the events of that morning, mentally walking through each minute step by step, seeing the events in some sort of slow-motion. Even the deadly blast from the shotgun seemed to erupt slowly, spewing flames and a load of double-aught shotgun pellets into the soft valley of flesh between Nelle's creamy white breasts. Blood, flesh and bone erupted upward and out, spraying the bed linens; the walls and the sheet that Beck Weston had held in front of himself in a pathetic attempt to protect himself from the expected second deadly blast of the shotgun. Then there was that snake Beck, crab-walking across the blood speckled floor toward the door, naked and barefoot, grabbing his clothes as he scurried out of the house. *What a wretched, contemptible sight that had been!* Maybe he should have unloaded the other barrel right then into the back of the son-of-a-bitch and blown a hole clear through him. But through his eyes as an attorney, that option became very complicated, very quickly. *No, it had been handled correctly.*

He sat up straight with a sudden, almost convulsive movement. *The footprints!* Why had he not thought of Beck's footprints before? He shut his eyes and forced his mind to replay that part one more time: Beck holding the sheet in front of himself; the blood splattering the sheet, the walls and the floor; Beck slinking, cowering in front of the shotgun, toward the door, his footprints visible on the splattered, bloody floor and then his bloody feet leaving even more prints across the pine floor to the door! He shook his head. Did McGee see that same thing? Was he wondering how the prints came to be? *Son-of-a-bitch!* How had he overlooked the prints? How could he explain their presence? His eyes got wide. *And the goddamn bloody sheet! If Beck had actually shot Nelle, how did the sheet get covered with blood splatter and why would Beck take it to his cabin?* He squeezed his eyes shut. Now he couldn't even remember what he had told the sheriff! He'd have to sit down with McGee to remind himself what he had already said. Dunsworth tipped the glass and drained the remaining whiskey into his mouth, reached for the decanter and sloshed the tumbler full again. "Shit!" he muttered. "Goddamn it!"

*   *   *

Dunsworth took the next day off, rode the train to San Jose and rented a carriage to take him through the narrow coastal mountain pass to Santa Cruz. It was mid afternoon by the time he arrived in Santa Cruz when he jumped hurriedly from the carriage and slammed through the door to Sheriff McGee's office. McGee was seated behind his desk.

"Whoa there!" he said. "Don't bust up my office coming in!" He looked and saw that the visitor was Alexander Dunsworth. "Well, Mister Dunsworth! I was just thinking about you. Come on in and have a seat." He motioned with a pencil to the straight backed chair across from him. "Coffee?"

"No, thanks anyway, Sheriff."

McGee put the pencil down, put his elbows on the desk and leaned forward. "Well, what brings you to Santa Cruz in such an all fire hurry?"

Dunsworth sat down in the chair, carefully crossed his legs and leaned forward. "I've been thinking, Sheriff. You know, about the murder. The thought came to my mind last night . . . you know, just sitting thinking about poor Nelle and all . . . and I wondered why Beck took that bloody sheet into the bunkhouse? And how did it get all covered with blood in the first place?" He looked up at the ceiling as if thinking. "I mean . . . if he shot poor Nelle . . . which he did . . . how did the sheet get bloody? I think . . . someone had to hold the sheet up for it to get splattered with poor Nelle's blood, God bless her soul. I mean, you could see the outline of the sheet on the wall. Someone had to hold it up and they couldn't do that and handle the shotgun at the same time, could they? What I'm thinking is that Beck must have had help. There must have been two men in that room, Sheriff."

McGee leaned back quietly, nodding his head as Dunsworth spoke. When the attorney was through, he continued to nod as if in agreement for several seconds. He leaned even further forward collaboratively, lowered his voice. "You know, Mister Dunsworth, I been thinking along those very same lines. I'm glad to hear someone else could see the circumstances same as me. I've been wondering about that sheet for some time now and I do think you're right. There had to be two people in that room when your wife was shot to death. The question is—who else was there beside Beck? Who else would want to do such a dastardly thing to your poor wife? You know there are those bloody footprints to consider, too . . ."

Dunsworth nodded quickly, "Beck probably met someone . . . maybe right here in Santa Cruz. Most likely got all liquored up, got a little crazy, thought they could have some . . . fun with poor little Nelle, with Beck knowing all along that she was alone at the ranch."

McGee nodded carefully. "That's smart thinking, Dunsworth. I could check with the local saloons, see if anyone remembers Beck and another man drinking heavy. Might be a little hard now, with so much time passed . . ." He stared at Dunsworth. "You're pretty good at this kind of thinking, Dunsworth. Maybe you should run for District Attorney. We could sure use someone with your brains running that office. You got any more ideas? I can use anything you give me."

Dunsworth wrinkled his forehead as if in thought, slowly started to shake his head. "No, can't think of anything right at the moment, Sheriff. Sure would like to see this finished up, though. It presses heavy on my heart when I think that Nelle's murderer is still running around free and loose." He looked up at McGee. "Have you heard anything about the whereabouts of Beck?"

Sheriff McGee shook his head slowly. "No, sir. Haven't heard a word. It's like he walked off the edge of the earth. We'll certainly keep our eyes open but right now he's just plum disappeared. Could be in Arkansas or Tennessee by now."

"Good Lord, Sheriff, let's hope not! We got to put this thing to rest, let poor Nelle's tortured soul slumber in peace!"

McGee smiled knowingly. "I'm working on it. And I appreciate your ideas and I'll follow up on 'em. Maybe it'll help us put the murderer behind bars."

"Better yet, we should hang the son-of-a-bitch!" Dunsworth muttered.

Sheriff McGee nodded slowly in agreement. "Anyone do what he did should be hanged."

*   *   *

El Culebra alighted from the train in Abilene, stiff and a little sore from the long ride across the California desert, Arizona, New Mexico and the western quarter of Texas. He had given the conversation with Alexander Dunsworth a lot of thought during the long hours on the train. There was certainly a lot to consider. But one element continued to ride to the top of his thinking: the money. It was, after all, what he had set out to accomplish. One last job from which he could begin to lead a life of leisure, surround himself with all the accouterments of luxury: a nice home, fancy clothes, nice belongings, women . . . The offer Dunsworth had made was close to assuring that. But if they wanted his skills that badly, perhaps he could extract a little more money from the committee the attorney had alluded to. Besides, he had reasoned with himself, the final job would force him to flee the country of his birth, of his language, of his culture. Not that he was opposed to the idea of taking up residence in Rio de Janeiro; from what he had heard, it was a place of strikingly beautiful women, warm sunshine and clear ocean water. Perhaps even Peru or Chile though he knew nothing of South America's Pacific coast countries. On the other hand, he had thought, they would know nothing about him as well.

In any case, it would take a lot of money. Money to get there . . . money to establish himself there. He wondered briefly what an American dollar was worth in Brazil. He would have to check with the banker in Abilene. He could perhaps be a millionaire several times over in Brazil. He decided he would contact the attorney in San Francisco and insist on more money. Dunsworth had left his office address with El Culebra with instructions to send any telegraphs there by courier.

It was late afternoon and the dry heat bore down on Abilene without compassion. When he found the Western Union Telegraph office, he composed the following message:

ALEXANDER D STOP I ACCEPT JOB STOP NEW CONDITION STOP DOUBLE FEE OR WILL REVEAL PLAN STOP MR RIVERS

He included the address in San Francisco where the telegram was to be delivered, watched as the telegraph operator sent the message. The operator nodded to El Culebra when it had been acknowledged as received by the San Francisco office.

Culebra was sure that Dunsworth would reply within a day or two.

* * *

Dunsworth had barely taken his seat in his office when his secretary came in with the distinct yellow telegram envelope in her hand. He frowned as he took it from her, motioned for her to shut the door as she left the room. He slit the end of the envelope and shook out the flimsy sheet of paper. He read the message quickly and half-stood, his face and neck red as a wave of anger coursed through him.

"You son-of-a-bitch!" he whispered. "You rotten son-of-a-bitch!" He crumpled the message and slammed it into the trash can next to his desk. "You goddamn bastard!" He stood and walked to the window shaking in anger and stared malevolently at the crowd of people on the sidewalk, enraged and itching to strike out at someone, anyone . . . . The four men back east will be furious. Hell, more than just furious! They would be after his blood! They should be the ones negotiating with the goddamn assassin, not him! Let them figure out how to placate the double-crossing son-of-a-bitch! Double the money or else! Who the hell does he think he is? Would he really expose the plan? He sat again at his desk and began to compose a message to be sent to the east coast.

*   *   *

Clarence DePallin carefully opened the Western Union telegram envelope and read the brief message. After reading it twice, he folded the paper and stared at the opposite wall in his Washington D.C. office.

> MESSAGE FROM OUR EMPLOYEE STOP JOB ACCEPTED STOP CONDITION CHANGED STOP DOUBLE SALARY OR WILL DISCLOSE PLAN STOP ADVISE

Just how much had the west coast attorney Dunsworth told the assassin? How much of the actual plan did he know? Did he know names, locations, dates? What would be the potential fall-out if the assassin went public with what he knew?

DePallin leaned back in his chair and considered the situation. The Texas *cowboy*, Stanford Parker, would most likely come completely unhinged with the news and commence his useless stream of bellyache whining and I told you so objections. John Ambrose, the railroad executive, would hear mainly the threat of being exposed and propose drastic action against the assassin to cut off any possibility of that happening. Ulysses McGarnet, the steel company owner, would put everything into terms of dollars: how much will this cost? What would our potential net profit be if we paid him what he demanded? What sort of guarantee or assurance could they stipulate before they handed over this much money?

DePallin considered the options. The amount of money, though very large by most common standards, was not unattainable. Any one of the four of them could most likely pay the entire amount with only minor financial strain. DePallin was probably the only one who tended to weigh all facets of the plan, consider all the various factors: risk, probability of success, potential of long term monetary gain, personal reputation and the like. Of the four—actually five counting Dunsworth—he understood the two main aspects of the project the best: First, the purchase of the Vincente property in Nicaragua, which, according to Dunsworth was now an accomplished fact. Second, the effort to ensure the Congressional vote for the Nicaraguan canal route. The second was where the largest risk resided. Both routes had strong points and both had weak points. The commission created by Congress had strongly recommended the Nicaragua route. But President Roosevelt was strongly opposed to that route and leaned heavily toward the Panama route. If Roosevelt was eliminated as a strong Panama voice, Congress would most likely vote for the canal to be constructed across Nicaragua.

And now another matter had come to light. A dispatch from their man on the inside of the White House had revealed that Roosevelt was planning a secret meeting with the influential Panamanian revolutionary leader, Doctor Manuel Amador Guerrero, during the President's short stopover in the Sierra Nevada Mountains. It appeared to DePallin that this clandestine meeting may have in fact been the singular reason for Roosevelt's brief excursion into the Sierras. If their plan to assassinate Roosevelt was successful, culpability could be, by implication, placed squarely on the Panamanian people, virtually assuring a Congressional *yes* vote for the Nicaragua route in reprisal.

DePallin would have to convene the committee and listen to their whining and complaining but in the end they would agree to the assassin's demands out of fear if for no other reasons. DePallin would relay this information to Dunsworth and set the location, date and time for a face to face meeting with the assassin.

CHAPTER 29

<u>Friday, July 25, 1902, Del Rio Texas</u>

The wiry Texas cattleman, Stanford Parker, leaned back against the bar in the Del Rio saloon called simply the Longhorn. It was an all-around name that covered the saloon, the hotel and the restaurant that filled half a city block on Ogden Street across from the railway and close to where he would soon load another five thousand head of beef bound for the slaughter houses in Chicago and Kansas City. He owned a lot of Del Rio, including the Longhorn complex and two other, not so upscale hotels, the Texas Hotel and the Del Rio and three bars. He owned the cattle yards, pens and the loading docks next to the railroad, making a tidy sum off every head of cattle that passed through the chute onto the waiting cattle cars. He also owned over a hundred thousand acres of prime grazing land to the north of the small town, a hundred times the amount of land owned by his nearest competitor, James English. The Parker family had settled in the area back when it was known as San Filipe Del Rio. Marriages, acquisitions and land purchases had enlarged the Parker family empire over the years. Nowadays people meeting a Parker on the street would doff their hats in greeting, move over into the street mud or dirt in the event the boardwalk was crowded, which usually happened only on Friday nights when the cowboys came to town to spend their pay on women and liquor. Stanford Parker was politely referred to as Mister Parker, at least when in his company. But truth be known, not many people liked the tall, whiney-voiced land baron, including his wife, Jennette Parker, who had been married to him for twenty-two years. Five years his younger, she had grown to detest his constant quibbling about . . . well everything. Whether it was the food on the table or the amount of lean on the beef, he would find reason to argue, disagree and bicker over the tiniest issue.

Jennette had long since stopped paying any attention to his nasal whining and simply grunted to let him know she was listening. The union had produced no children, a fact for which she was ever grateful.

If Stanford was aware of this, he didn't show it. When in his company the citizens of Del Rio stood and listened in courteous attention to his wrangling, nodding in agreement or shaking their heads sadly at his dire declarations of doom, be it the weather, the price of beef or politics. Stanford didn't like Mexico, Mexicans, the Mexican border, people who dealt with Mexicans, Mexican art, Mexican pottery or even anyone who had visited Mexico. As a matter of fact, he didn't like anyone who even looked like a Mexican; Stanford didn't like anyone who was not enclosed in white skin and spoke *American like a Texan.* That was the way his daddy raised him. Mexicans were not welcome in the Longhorn and at the first inkling of trouble he would not too gently remove them from any of his other holdings.

He didn't hate them; he just didn't recognize them as regular human beings. They were okay to load with burdens like a mule, or to use to install miles of barbed wire fence in the mid-September heat but even then he would not have fairly paid them if it had not been for the silent threat of retaliation by others.

Today he was holding sway with several of the town's minor landowners and businessmen. It was late afternoon and they had gradually assembled in the saloon for an afternoon beer and the opportunity to spend a few minutes in the comparative coolness of the dark interior of the Longhorn. Stanford Parker had been there since a little after lunch time and had already downed several beers, his nasal voice going up an octave and becoming raspy to boot, along with an occasional slurred word. The locals winked carefully to one another as Parker moved into some of his favorite subjects. He had already dispensed with Mexico and the Mexicans and anything else south of the Rio Grande, which he claimed should really be named Big River, at least the American half.

"And I'll tell y'all something else!" he continued after taking a long noisy swallow of his beer. "You know who else ought to be goddamned shot?"

The men standing around looked at one another. "No, Mister Parker. Who might that be?"

"The goddamn President Roosevelt, that's who! Sons-a-bitch is going to ruin this country! We ought to just get rid of the goddamn sons-a-bitch!"

"Well, that's pretty drastic action, wouldn't you say, Mister Parker?" The man asking the question was J. B. Talbot, President of the small bank in Del Rio.

"Hell, no, J. B!" Parker stared at the banker as if he'd uttered a heresy. "If someone doesn't do it real quick-like, we could be in for a lot of hurt!"

"Well, I don't figure there're too many people that would try to do something that crazy." Talbot said as he glanced around the circle of faces.

"Ah, shit, J. B! Don't you bank on it!" He chuckled at his own play on words. "I happen to know some folks up north that're willing to put up the money to have it done, all neat like."

"Well, that's those damn scheming Yankee's for you!" one of the other men added and everyone chuckled.

Talbot frowned slightly, then asked, "What kind of money they talking about, Mister Parker?"

"American dollars, my friend. Good old American dollars and lots of 'em."

"You saying there's something in the grist mill right now?" Talbot asked.

Parker smiled a lop-sided smirk. "Hell, J. B., don't be surprised when it happens, 'cuz it's going to happen, mark my words. It's going to happen and with that sons-a-bitch out of the way, Congress'll build a canal where it damn well wants!" He swallowed the remaining beer. "Hell yeah!"

*   *   *

Later that evening J. B. Talbot sat at the desk in his modest house in Del Rio. Parker's words still replayed in his ears. He'd known the obnoxious Texas cattleman for well over thirty years, had done his banking for nearly as long. Over the years he's loaned Parker money to buy real estate in town, make it through some early difficult years and finally fifteen years ago financed a large part of Parker's Circle SP ranch. About five months ago, the cattleman had come to him with an unusual request; he wanted to mortgage nearly all his holdings—the ranch, the hotels and bars and the loading pens for a large amount of money. He needed it, he had said, to close a big money deal up north. The bank, he'd promised, would get it all back and more, in less than a year . . . Just needed to keep it quiet so word didn't get out. Reluctantly, Talbot had loaned him the money, written up the papers placing heavy liens on the property and Parker had walked away. Nothing further was said until today and the drunken talk he'd heard bothered him greatly. Parker was well known for his vocal ranting against most things political, or for that matter, with anything he basically disagreed with. He'd more than once vented his rage and frustration regarding the actions of President Roosevelt and the Inter-ocean canal. His words today suggested a plot, perhaps a death plot against the President and he seemed pretty sure of himself. *Had that been his big money deal up north?*

He drummed his fingers against the desk in frustration. Finally he pulled a sheet of writing paper in front of him and began jotting a letter to his brother, William Talbot. William, or Bill as he was informally known, was the District Attorney in Los Angeles. The two brothers used the U.S. Mail to keep their relationship whole and corresponded almost weekly with one another. The least he could do, Talbot thought, was to get the issue off his chest and share his concerns, imagined or not, with Bill. By the time he was finished and had the letter sealed and addressed, he was beginning to have second thoughts about his suspicions and he came close to tearing up the letter. Finally he decided to post it and let his brother have a good chuckle.

*   *   *

Washington D.C.
"Mister President, you wanted to see me sir?" The President's aide stood in the doorway to President Roosevelt's office.

"Ah, yes, James! Come in, come in." Roosevelt took his reading glasses off and laid them on his desk. "Shut the door behind you, please."

The tall aide carefully shut the door making sure the latch caught so that a breeze would not unexpectedly blow it open. He took the offered seat across from the President. "If you've not yet been outside, Mister President, you really should take a few minutes to do so. The weather is beautiful! One of those rare perfect Washington D.C. days, especially as we approach the heat of August."

"I shall do exactly that, James. Thank you! Mustn't miss the opportunity when it presents itself." He smiled a sort of impish smile. "One would think our forefathers could have found a more hospitable place to put the nation's capital."

"Perhaps the price was right, Mister President."

"Ha! Perhaps so. Perhaps so." It was his style of indicating that small talk had lasted long enough. "Tell me how plans are progressing for our trip to California."

"Quite well, Mister President. We've made arrangements with the railroads to put your private train-car in the line for the entire trip from Washington to Los Angeles, to San Francisco and back to Washington. We will arrive in Los Angeles mid-morning on Thursday, the seventh of May. You will stay two nights at the Hotel Wilshire and we will leave early the morning of the ninth. Our departure will get us into the small town of Visalia—that's in the great San Joaquin Valley—and from there we'll travel by carriage. We'll bring those along with us on the train and go to the ranch of," James referred to his notes, "Mister Hector Gordon. The men we sent out to check it out say that it will be quite comfortable, though a little rustic. The Gordon family all check out well. They will provided horses and supplies and a guide into the mountains. We will depart for the mountains on the next day, Sunday, the tenth, arriving at the camp site that afternoon. I understand it is a six or eight hour horseback ride." He waited for Roosevelt's comments.

"Ah, bully, James! I'm looking forward to it already. Now, the man who will meet us there . . ." The last was framed as a question.

"He's been notified of the date and location. He will meet us at the Gordon ranch the morning we leave for the mountains. If we miss him there, we'll go on and send the guide back to wait for him."

Roosevelt nodded his head in understanding. If there was any part of the plan he didn't like, it was this short window of opportunity to make this covert connection with this crucial contact. But he had been assured by those who had set up the clandestine meeting that it would work. History would certainly be changed if he did not.

"Very well, James. And we will leave . . ."

"We will leave the camp the morning of Wednesday, the thirteenth, overnight at the ranch and take the train to San Francisco on the fourteenth, arriving there early evening. We will spend two nights at the Palace Hotel . . . usual dinner, possibly a short speech, etc. Leave San

Francisco for Washington, non-stop, on Saturday the sixteenth and arrive here on the eighteenth. You will be back in your office on Monday, the eighteenth of May, Mister President."

"Good! Now, James, the railroad people fully understand what we want done with the Presidential train-car and the two cars for the security detail during our layover in Visalia."

"Yes, Mister President. That has been explained in great detail and they have assured me that your demands will be fully complied with and with the utmost secrecy."

"Excellent, James. And our security detail. Are they prepared?"

"Yes sir, with one exception. One of the gentlemen . . ." he again referred to his notes, "Sergeant Armstrong Tenor, had an accident and I have replaced him with another from the same group. The new man is Corporal John London. Very trustworthy man, I'm assured. Excellent horseman. Sharpshooter."

A small frown crossed Roosevelt's face. "John London? Never heard of him."

"Well sir, there are over two thousand soldiers in the Washington detachment. It would be quite unusual to know each of them by name."

Roosevelt nodded. "You're absolutely correct, James. And Sergeant Tenor? How badly was he hurt?"

"I'm afraid he fell into some bad luck, sir. I was notified that he was assaulted three nights ago while walking back to the base late one night. He was alone and took a knife between the ribs, left side. I'm told the wound was not of a lethal nature and he'll recover, be on his feet in a week or two but in no shape to undergo the rigors of a security detail assignment. The ruffians stole his wallet containing eighteen dollars and left him bleeding beside the road."

"A whole month's pay. The poor lad . . ." Roosevelt shook his head sadly before he asked, "What does Corporal London know about his upcoming assignment?"

"I assume very little, Mister President. The detail has been ordered not to discuss the assignment with anyone, even with each other, until they are on the train headed for Los Angeles."

"That's probably the best way to keep things under wrap."

CHAPTER 30

Gomez Santiago arrived in San Francisco on the afternoon train from Los
Angeles and quickly registered at the Palace Hotel. He placed his leather
satchel on the small desk and withdrew the sheaf of legal documents that
he would hand over to Alexander Dunsworth the next day. All the papers,
carefully hand duplicated from the originals, were properly stamped and
initialed certifying that the original papers had been recorded and filed
with the Nicaraguan government. Written in Spanish, the papers were a
complicated maze of declarations, clarifications, historical data including
the intricate elements of property transfer, longitude and latitude,
dimensions, landmarks and such. Most attorneys in Nicaragua, even
though trained to comprehend such convoluted documents, would merely
page through the stack without reading, making sure proper signatures
were included, purchase money transferred, fees had been collected and
that impressive wax seals were affixed. Most American attorneys would
not even take time to do that.

Santiago had sent Dunsworth a telegram from Los Angeles, suggesting
they meet on Thursday, the twenty-first of August to review the papers
before they were turned over to Dunsworth who would handle sending
the east coast investors their copy.

*   *   *

The next morning Santiago headed first for the San Francisco Police
Department. He introduced himself as an attorney from Dallas, Texas by
the name of G. W. Whiteman representing an uncle of Clarence Chandler.
Mister Chandler, Santiago patiently explained, was listed as an heir to

some money left by the death of the uncle, a Mister Thomas G. Edwards of Dallas, Texas who had passed away several months ago. The family had been trying to locate Mister Chandler who was last known to live in San Francisco. A distant family friend had read in the newspaper of Mister Chandler's death. As the family attorney, he was here to verify the death and date of death of Mister Chandler so the disposition of the will could be taken care of.

The policeman listened politely, then led him into the vast room of records where two clerks filed or located various records based on a constant stream of demands. The policeman introduced him to one of the beleaguered clerks who listened impatiently while Santiago went through his request again. In the meantime the policeman excused himself and left.

"Chandler, you said? Clarence Chandler? Name's familiar, seems like I've seen it recently. What was the date?"

"Sometime in early July, I believe."

"Hmm. Early July . . . Well, there are a lot of records waiting to be filed, could be among those, or could have been filed already. I'd guess it hasn't been filed yet; we're about three months behind on filing." He looked at Santiago, "You're an attorney?"

"Yes. I'm an attorney in Dallas, Texas."

"Well, I imagine you know what you're looking for, Mister Whiteman. Why don't you take a look," he pointed at the several stacks of legal papers on tables, "and see if you turn up anything. Just give me a nod if you do. If you don't, you may have to start searching through the file cabinets. They're in chronological order and cross referenced alphabetically. If you don't turn up what you're looking for, it probably means we don't have it."

Santiago thanked the clerk, took off his jacket and began searching through the piles. It took him three hours to find the thin file marked Clarence Chandler.

The file produced a poor quality prison photo of the man's face and a copy of his prison records. He was sentenced to prison for fifteen years for the fatal stabbing of an unknown vagrant on November 22, 1889 and was awaiting his eventual transfer to Kansas to stand trial for the fatal shooting of a US Marshal. He had been an average inmate at San Quinton Prison until he escaped on October 1, 1901. He was believed to have been killed in an accident in the San Francisco Bay but had apparently escaped that incident, living in San Francisco until he was stabbed to death on or about July 7, 1902. The hand-written autopsy report was included;

Victim Clarence Chandler had been first stabbed in the lower abdomen; the knife wound, approximately seven inches deep, entered slightly to the left and three inches below the navel before being pulled upward in a sawing motion approximately seven inches, cutting through the rectus abdominis muscle, puncturing the bladder, severing the small intestine in four places and severing the transverse colon. A second wound was a horizontal cut approximately 7 inches long and 1.5 inch deep across the victim's neck just above the larynx, resulting in complete severance of the carotid artery and jugular vein. The cause of death was loss of blood due to the neck wound, though the abdominal wound would ultimately have caused his death as well. The body had been in the water for about twelve hours.

Personal effects included clothing, boots (Justins), wallet with four dollars, key (unidentified), ankle-type hunting knife scabbard (knife missing), three small scraps of paper (two with barely discernable ink hand printed: ORILEYCALSTWPOWEL *and the other* SOLOMAN-CHARLEYS 11P.

The report included a rough sketch of the man's body with marks showing the locations of the wounds and a single tattoo, probably done in prison, on his left arm. The coroner had made a rough sketch of the tattoo: a skull with a knife thrust through it and the word death below it.

Santiago glanced about the large room; no one was looking his way as he carefully slid the autopsy report from the file, folded it quickly and dropped it into his pocket. There was little else in the report that may be of use.

He made eye contact with the clerk, gave him a quick salute and nod and indicated he would be leaving. The clerk nodded and went back to his filing.

Santiago took the report to the hotel room, unfolded it and put it on the small desk. On a piece of hotel stationary, he wrote the string of letters ORILEYCALSTWPOWEL and stared at them. After several attempts of organization he ended up with ORILEY CAL ST W POWEL as the most probable arrangement.

He went to the main desk and spoke to the man there.

"I'm looking for a gentleman named O'Reiley, a friend from long ago. I know he lives in San Francisco but I don't know where. Can you perhaps help me?"

The deskman smiled. "There are several O'Reileys in San Francisco, sir." He glanced at the business suit Santiago was wearing as if gauging his social status. "Perhaps you mean Thomas O'Reiley, partner in the firm of M.O.& B? Mister O'Reiley lives on California Street—a very nice neighborhood."

Santiago nodded. *CAL ST* "Ah, yes, I do believe that would be the one! Now, one other question. I've heard mention of a place named Charley's. What can you tell me about it?"

The deskman's face fell and he glanced both ways as if to ensure he was not being overheard, leaned slightly across the desk toward Santiago. "Sir, I do believe you have been badly led on. The only place of business by that name—if I may use the term *business*—is a scandalous saloon in the tenderloin district. It is a decrepit and filthy little hole-in-the-wall off of Turk Street near Jones." The deskman leaned closer and lowered his voice until it was barely a whisper. "Rather notorious reputation among the other businesses in the area if you know what I mean. I can suggest several much more suitable to someone of your station. Sir, I strongly recommend that you avoid Charley's."

Santiago nodded, adeptly slid five dollars across to the deskman who picked it up just as covertly with no change of expression and murmured, "Any time I can be of assistance, sir. My name is William."

"Thank you, William. Oh, perhaps there is one more thing. Could you direct me to the offices of M. O. & B? I'd like to surprise my friend Thomas O'Reiley."

*   *   *

The hotel deskman had directed Santiago to an address on Van Ness Avenue, a few blocks north of Market Street. It was a walk of several long city blocks from the Palace Hotel but the day had turned cool with a heavy bank of fog laying a few miles off the coast waiting to creep in upon the city a few hours later. Santiago took his time and it was early afternoon by the time he stood in front of the newly constructed offices of McPherson, O'Reiley and Barnwell.

Thomas O'Reiley was seated behind his desk when his secretary came in. "There is a Mister George Whiteman to see you, Mister O'Reiley."

O'Reiley stood up and stepped around his desk to greet the gentleman as he entered. "Mister Whiteman, I'm Thomas O'Reiley. Please come and have a seat. Would you like a cup of coffee?"

"No but thank you very much." Santiago replied as he shook O'Reiley's hand, moved toward and sat in the offered chair.

O'Reiley dropped into the facing chair and casually crossed his legs. He had never seen the man before, but had an immediate liking for him. "I'm afraid I don't know you, Mister Whiteman."

"I'm sorry to come in like this, unannounced. Let me introduce myself. I am an attorney from Dallas Texas. I am doing some research for a client of mine. Your name came up recently and I'm just following up. If you don't mind, I'd like to ask you a few questions."

O'Reiley nodded slowly. "Do I know your client?" It would not be unusual for a client of MO&B to hire an attorney to resolve some issue or another.

"Probably not, Mister O'Reiley. His name is Vincente Esperanza."

O'Reiley shook his head slowly. "I'm sorry but I'm not familiar at all with the name. Perhaps you could tell me what this is regarding."

"To be perfectly honest with you, Mister O'Reiley, I'm not sure myself what this is about. Let me please ask a few questions and perhaps we shall both be enlightened." He waited.

O'Reiley nodded. "Very well, Mister Whiteman. Ask away."

"Well, we already know that the name Esperanza means nothing to you."

"Never heard of it."

"What about the names Jenkins, Garcia-Rameriz or Walker?

O'Reiley frowned. "Seems I remember reading something about them recently . . . are they the three attorneys that were murdered recently in Los Angeles?"

"They are the ones, Mister O'Reiley. What do you know about that triple murder?"

"Only what I read in the newspaper, when was that . . . several weeks ago now."

Santiago nodded. "What about Sophia Jenkins?"

O'Reiley shook his head. "Never heard of her."

Santiago sat for several seconds before he asked, "Alexander Dunsworth?"

O'Reiley leaned back. "I know of Dunsworth only as a local attorney. I've never used his services or the services of the law firm he is with. I understand Dunsworth's wife was murdered recently."

"That's correct. She was killed on May the twenty-eighth."

O'Reiley sat silently, wondering if the man across from him was probing into his knowledge of Beckley Weston. But the attorney sat silently, studying O'Reiley as if not sure what to ask next. Finally he asked, "Does the name Clarence Chandler mean anything to you?"

"Chandler!" O'Reiley nodded his head slowly. "Yes, I knew . . . well I didn't actually *know* him . . . many years ago. *Met* him would probably be more accurate. I read in the newspaper that he was found murdered recently."

"Yes. He was the victim of a very brutal homicide." The attorney studied O'Reiley for several long moments. "Do you have any idea why Chandler would have your name and address in his pocket when he was killed?"

"My name and address?" O'Reiley asked incredulously. He shook his head. "I have no idea. I haven't seen the man in thirteen years." O'Reiley frowned, hesitated. "Wait . . . there was an apparent attempt on my life in April, the second I believe . . . the pistol shot wounded my partner Frank Barnwell instead. The details are all in the report filed by the police. Chandler was later determined to be a possible suspect. Is that what this is all about?"

The attorney appeared to ignore his question. "How did you happen to . . . meet Chandler?"

O'Reiley stared at the attorney, then shrugged and gave him a brief summary of the altercation that had occurred thirteen years ago and the resulting five years he had spent as a fugitive in isolation away from family and everything he knew. He talked about his eventual return to San Francisco and marriage to Amanda McPherson and the business partnership with Amanda's father. As far as he knew, he told the attorney, Chandler had been in prison since the murder and had died shortly after escaping from San Quinton.

The lawyer nodded, then asked, "What do you know about a man names Soloman?

O'Reiley shook his head, leaned back in thought. "I recall having read something a man named *Solomon*. His name popped up in the newspaper quite some time ago, as I remember, quite a grisly story. His wife was found brutally murdered along with her lover. I believe the gentleman lives in Sacramento or perhaps in the foothills east of Sacramento but I'm fairly certain he spells his name with an O—Solo*mon*."

Santiago sat silently, finally asked, "What about a man named El Culebra?"

O'Reiley shook his head. "Never heard of him." He looked at Santiago for several seconds. "Are you certain you're talking to the right person?

"I think I am, Mister O'Reiley. It's pretty complicated. Let me try to explain it to you."

*   *   *

San Francisco

Alexander Dunsworth had already decided he would take half a day off and travel to the ranch, bringing Sophia along as his guest. They would take the train to San Jose and he would drive the carriage over the pass to Santa Cruz and up the coast to Rancho de Pacifica. They would arrive early evening. He had paid to have the bedroom cleaned and repainted, the mattress had been replaced and closets emptied of Nelle's clothing. Tonight he would fix them a light dinner, open a bottle of wine and build a cozy fire in the fireplace . . .

He needed time away from the city and the office. The Texas attorney, James Tyler Moran, had come by his office the day before, left both sets of property documents with him after carefully steering him through the maze of signatures and assuring him that all was legal. At one point Moran seemed to hesitate slightly, as if he had seen an error but quickly moved on though his face had taken on a worried appearance. They went as well through the east coast investors documents; Moran suggested that Dunsworth send them by US Mail to the investment group as soon as he could. He had brought the documents into the office this morning, carefully wrapped them, addressed them to Clarence DePallin and had his secretary take them to the Post Office.

He had felt a brief sense of relief that the documents were on their way to the east coast but at the same time was concerned that somehow they would discover his duplicity, even before they attempted to sell the property.

He thought back on his talk with Sheriff McGee and felt that it had gone fairly well. At least the sheriff had accepted his theory of a second man being present at the time of the murder. He would have to continue to build, somehow, on this angle.

But right now he was just plain tired. Tired of the Los Angeles mess, Nelle's murder, the Texas lawyer, El Culebra, the east coast investors, tired of thinking about all the things that could happen and everything else that seemed to be closing in on him. A nice long weekend with Sophia would sooth his jangled nerves and everything else that needed soothing.

He checked his pocket watch. It was shortly past noon; the morning had dragged by sluggishly. His law partners had left for early lunch which usually lead to shots of whiskey and had already planned to go sailing on the bay this afternoon. The clerical staff and secretaries were yawning in boredom and broadly hinting that it would be a *nice day to go to the beach.* He'd have to find something for them to do this afternoon in his absence or they would spend the remaining hours in useless chit-chat about marriages and babies. He made a lengthy list of make-work projects that would keep them more than busy all afternoon, dropped it on the office manager's desk on his way out the door.

Two hours later he and Sophia were in a hansom headed for the train depot. She had packed a small suitcase for the weekend and he already had a separate wardrobe at the ranch. They would stop in Santa Cruz on their way through to pick up food items and wine to last the weekend. Sophia was almost giddy with happiness and it raised his spirits some to see her excited and looking forward to finally be visiting Rancho de Pacifica.

The sun was setting over the Pacific when he at last wheeled the carriage into the final approach to the ranch house. The air had cooled but it was still quite comfortable; at least it had been in the sun. A fire would feel good though. Sophia had lost some of her enthusiasm during the long trip and was sitting wrapped in a shawl with her eyes shut. The riding horses were somewhere in a large fenced grazing area and would have to be rounded up and brought to the barn for currying. But he could perform the task, allowing Sophia to see another facet of his manliness. He would have to split some firewood also. He smiled at the thought of her admiring his skill and form.

He brought the carriage to the steps of the front porch and helped Sophia descend to the rich, mulch-covered ground. The air was cool and smelled fresh and earthy, tinged with the smell of the close-by ocean. It was, he thought, going to be a perfect weekend.

*   *   *

San Francisco
Thomas sat in the glass-enclosed sun room, watching the rain pour down in sheets that drummed against the windows in a steady rhythm. The shower had crept ashore late Friday night, coming it seemed from nowhere, blown by a gentle wind that smelled like the sea. The precipitation was refreshing and gave everything a clean look, getting rid of the constant dust and soot from the city's manufacturing plants that beleaguered the city. Thomas had made it home from his office an hour before the drizzle started and now it had rained on the city for two and a half days.

Thomas had built a steady fire in the fireplace that needed only very occasional tending, so the sun room was warm and sun looked like it was ready to come from behind the clouds. He had sat in his leather chair next to the windows but his mind drifted as he attempted to read today's Chronicle, stubbornly returning to the meeting with the man who had called himself George Whiteman at least at first until he admitted his ruse and told Thomas his real name—Gomez Santiago. He was, he disclosed, a private detective working for his friend Vincente Esperanza who lives in Nicaragua. Santiago and Esperanza had gone to college together in the United States; Esperanza later inherited the vast family fortunes and Santiago had gone into detective work. Esperanza had called upon his friend's services after his mother had been murdered in Punta Gorda in March. Shortly after that a group of investors from the east coast made overtures to purchase the Esperanza property in Nicaragua. The discussions quickly took on the characteristics of a property scam and Vincente Esperanza decided to ensnare those planning to steal the valuable property under false pretenses. That's when Esperanza hired the Los Angeles attorneys Warner, Jenkins and Garcia-Rameriz, who agreed to represent him in face to face meetings with the American investors, represented by Alexander Dunsworth. Sophia, Jenkins' sister in San Francisco, kept the attorneys apprised of what Dunsworth was up to. Things became much more complicated with the unexpected murders of

Warner, Jenkins and Garcia-Rameriz in June. Esperanza sent Santiago to try to find out who had murdered the three attorneys and look into the possibility that Alexander Dunsworth was responsible for their deaths. During Santiago's investigation, Dunsworth was seen to be in discussion with a man known as El Culebra who is suspected of being a highly paid assassin. During his visit to San Francisco, it appears that El Culebra killed a man by the name of Clarence Chandler. Santiago checked with records of this murder and was led to the names of both O'Reiley and someone called Soloman. Santiago's follow-up on O'Reiley had led to their meeting and discussion. He had also determined that Sophia was Dunsworth's mistress and that there was no apparent connection between Dunsworth and Chandler. Santiago went over the evidence (clothing, hat, train tickets) that suggested that Dunsworth was the man who had murdered the Los Angeles attorneys after arguing over the price.

That left three unanswered questions Santiago had told him. First, what was the assassin doing in San Francisco and why was Dunsworth talking to him? Second, why did the assassin murder Chandler, a low-life prison escapee with no apparent connection to any of this? And third, who is Solomon and why would Chandler be planning to meet him at Charley's?

Thomas decided during their discussions that he would share the strong belief of both he and Sheriff McGee in Santa Cruz that Dunsworth had murdered his own wife and placed the blame on another man. Thomas left Beck's name out of the discussion.

Finally, Thomas had asked "Why would a group of investors want so badly to purchase the Esperanza property in Nicaragua?"

"They stand to make many millions of dollars if the United States decides to construct the canal through Nicaragua."

Thomas shook his head. "Seems like a bad bet to me. What happens if congress decides to build through Panama instead?"

"These men are determined to not let that happen."

"How could they do that? Roosevelt will probably get his way with Congress and we'll build through the Panama Isthmus . . ."

"They simply would not let that happen."

Thomas blinked. Dunsworth represents a powerful group of speculators who are buying millions of acres of land in Nicaragua. El Culebra, an assassin, is in San Francisco talking to Dunsworth. *Planning an assassination? An assassination to stop Roosevelt before he could influence the final decision? He* shook his head. *It couldn't be . . .*

Santiago saw the horrified look on Thomas's face. "Now you understand why this is so important."

"Who else knows about this?"

"No one . . ."

CHAPTER 31

<u>Saturday, August 30, 1902, Rancho de Pacifica</u>

It was midday and with the rain brought on by the unexpected storm, Dunsworth and Sophia were snuggled down within the ranch house. The weekend had thus far been everything that Dunsworth had anticipated. The evening before he had carefully fixed two steaks and made a salad for the two of them. They opened a bottle of wine to go with dinner and a second bottle as they relaxed in front of the cozy fire in the fireplace. Half-way through the second bottle, Sophia had sprawled leisurely onto his lap; what few reservations she had, had been washed away by the wine. In the radiance of the warm fire they had boisterous, uninhibited sex, finally pausing long enough to finish off the bottle of wine before picking up where they left off. With a third bottle of wine they at last retired to the bedroom to continue their escapade, finally dropping off to sleep sometime in the hours after midnight.

Now Sophia sat near a window, a book in her lap and enjoying the sound of the rain and the residual warm glow of the night before. She glanced at Alexander who was seated at his desk in the far corner.

"Alex, dear! Whatever are you so occupied with that you have your back to me?"

Dunsworth turned his attention unhurriedly from the documents in front of him and rotated slowly to face Sophia. He had been debating with himself whether to share the recent land purchase with Sophia.

"Sophia, I've made a financial investment that will make me a very wealthy man. Remember I mentioned that I was working with a Nicaraguan named Vincente Esperanza? Well, the attorney from Texas that I have mentioned to you, James Tyler Moran, offered to be my financial

378

partner and we have bought the land, two and a half million acres, for a very good price."

"Is that the property that the east coast investors hired you to purchase?"

"Well, yes. To be frank, we have cut them out of the deal and instead sold them another vast tract of land."

"Good gracious, Alex, won't they be terribly angry?"

Dunsworth sat quietly while he composed his thoughts. "Yes, they probably will be but that could be years from now. By then, I will no longer be able to be located."

Sophia sat still, her eyes boring into Dunsworth. "What do you mean, Alexander? Where are you planning to go? And are you planning to go alone?" The tone of her voice had taken on a sudden iron-like quality.

"Now, Sophia, now is not the time to get upset! We can talk about that later! Come here and take a look at this property deed! It's in legal Spanish."

Sophia rose up out of her chair and crossed the room to stand at his desk. Silently, she lifted the sheaf of papers and studied the series of seals and signatures. She frowned as she shuffled through the papers.

"Sophia, don't tell me you can read Spanish!"

"I studied Spanish when I was in college. It's a useful language if one lives in southern California." She paused, looked back and forth between two pages. "Alex, dear, this is a very handsome document but I don't think it's what you believe it to be."

*   *   *

Penacook, New Hampshire
Congressman Clarence DePallin gazed through the wide living room window overlooking the Merrimack River. Trees were just beginning to reveal the end-of-summer look; dry and dusty appearing and in a few places already turning yellow. The view from this window was one of his favorites; it revealed the size and splendor of the DePallin estate that had been in his family for five generations. The family money came from the cotton mill industry and the DePallin family at one time had owned several large mills. In the mid nineteenth century James Estavus DePallin had diversified and began quarrying marble. Both industries grew exponentially and assured the family wealth for several generations to come.

Clarence DePallin decided to go into politics while attending college. He had no great dreams of changing the world or even making life better in the United States. Instead he saw it as a simple road to fame. He grew to enjoy rubbing elbows with political big wigs, the late night meetings in smoke filled rooms, trading favor for favor that went along with politics. In 1896 he was elected as the Republican Congressman to the House of Representatives in Washington. D.C.

The tangible, heady experience of power was vital nourishment to his ego. It was second nature to him to make deals, to stroke and caress those that could improve his lot, build his power base and put in the good word with those still above him in the world of political power. He would, he knew without any hint of doubt, someday be the President of the United States of America. He would, he believed, be the most powerful man in the nation and his years as President would be looked at as the best, most decisive, most productive in the history of the United States.

To that end, he had sought to gain some vestige of control over the eventual inter-ocean canal. He wanted to be immediately involved in the route, design and use of the canal. He wanted to dictate the terms of agreements with Nicaragua. The under-populated Central American country might just become another state, just as Utah had joined on January 4, 1896.

If . . . if the canal route went through Nicaragua. If it did not, it would most likely pass through Panama. That could be a political disaster for the United States and for him in particular. He had hung his hat politically and financially on the route through Nicaragua. His voice had helped sway other members of congress, both in the House and the Senate, to his way of thinking. He'd backed up his conviction with a huge portion of the DePallin family money, found three other men who would match his investment and an attorney in San Francisco to spearhead the deal making. The initial plan was to buy a choice area of land but the landowner, a powerful Nicaraguan woman, had refused to sell. DePallin had told their attorney, Alexander Dunsworth, to make it happen. Within weeks, the woman had been killed in a tragic fire and her son was now in the dealer's position. Soon inquiries had led the California attorney to believe the son was willing to sell. A suspicious fire killed the three Los Angeles attorneys representing the wealthy son and negotiations appeared once again to be in jeopardy. Unexpectedly, the son himself through his attorney had reopened communication with the San Francisco attorney.

Now, things were back on track. A deal had been made, the land purchased for an extremely good price and the legal documents now rested on the desk at which he sat. The San Francisco attorney had even removed his name from the investment group, leaving it in the hands of the four original investors.

DePallin had studied the documents. Of course they were written in Spanish, very legal and proper Spanish, completely undecipherable to him. In fact, he knew of no one on the east coast who could even read ordinary day-to-day Spanish. The documents with long paragraphs of legal language were stamped with several impressive seals: some were plain wax seals, others were embossed wax seals with little blue ribbons that accompanied various signatures and initials.

It all looked very magnificent.

It was all worthless if Theodore Roosevelt was able to convince Congress to build the canal across the Isthmus of Panama.

But plans were already underway to make sure that did not happen.

*   *   *

Foothills east of Sacramento, California

Gomez Santiago spent two days locating the man named Bret Solomon, eventually finding him living in a large ranch house near a tiny settlement named Fiddletown east of Sacramento. Surrounded by the oak-tree sprinkled foothills, the house sat atop a hill overlooking the surrounding hills, dry now at the end of summer.

Santiago arrived at the house, noticing immediately that it was showing signs of badly needed repairs: the paint was dirty and chipping around the doors and windows; several panes of window glass were cracked or broken; the steps to the broad front porch were dangerously worn and rotting.

When he knocked at the door, he heard rustling from inside the house but it took several minutes until the door was opened slightly.

"Yes?" the man had said through the narrow crack.

"Mister Bret Solomon?"

"I'm Bret Solomon."

"Mister Solomon, my name is Jonathan Madison. I'm an attorney. I would like to speak to you regarding the unfortunate death of your wife, Priscilla."

"What do you want to know?"

381

"I wonder if I may come in, Mister Solomon. I will not take long."

The door opened wide. "Come on in." Solomon said over his shoulder as he walked across the large room, turned and sat heavily in an overstuffed chair. "Come in. I won't hurt you."

Santiago entered the room, took a seat across from Solomon. It took only a few seconds for him to see that the house was in sore need of housekeeping. Table surfaces were covered with piles of paper, empty coffee cups, mounds of dirty clothing and a fine patina of dust. He settled into the chair and studied the man across from him. The face was lined, unshaven. Hair was in disarray and shabby looking. The man's shirt was soiled with food and stained with perspiration.

Solomon had apparently sensed the visitor's survey. "Kind of a mess, isn't it?" He glanced around the room. "I hate it but I don't care anymore."

Santiago simply nodded. "Mister Solomon, I'm sorry to have to ask you these questions but I've been hired by a relative of Mister Richard Manhauser to look into a few things regarding his and Missus Solomon's deaths."

"Go right ahead, Mister . . . what did you say your name was?"

"Madison. Jonathan Madison."

"Go ahead, Mister Madison. I've been asked before."

"I'm sure you have, sir." Santiago made a pretext of pulling a sheet of paper from his satchel, studying it for a moment. "How well did you know Richard Manhauser?"

Solomon nodded slowly. "Manhauser once lived in this house. I owned an adjoining piece of property. I used to raise cattle but I no longer do. I had talked to Manhauser many times about purchasing his property so that I could increase the size of my ranch. He refused. Over the years, the gulf between became a matter of profound separation and eventually anger." He shook his head. "It's all so . . . ridiculous . . . now. But then, I would do nearly anything to realize my dream." He stopped, as if finished.

Santiago felt he knew where the monologue was heading but took a different tactic. "How do you know a man named Clarence Chandler?"

Solomon half chuckled and shook his head slowly. "Chandler? Poor, stupid Chandler. I met him in one of those Chinese gambling dens in San Francisco. I am, among other illnesses, a gambling aficionada. When I met Chandler, he was getting into very deep debt to the Chinese. They have a method of handling those who owe them and don't repay." He made a slicing motion with his finger across his throat. "They kill them as a warning to others. I offered Chandler an opportunity to work for me and in turn I would pay off his debts."

"You offered to employ him here on the ranch?"

Solomon laughed. "Heavens no! He couldn't earn enough money here in a lifetime to pay off what he owed."

Santiago frowned. "What, then?"

Solomon gazed out through one of the dusty windows and took so long to reply that Santiago thought perhaps he wasn't going to answer. Finally, Solomon faced him. "He killed my Priscilla."

"Chandler?"

"No, I'm sorry. Have you ever heard of a hired killer by the name of El Culebra?"

"El Culebra? Tell me what you know about him."

"I heard about him . . . overheard a conversation. For money . . . a large amount of money . . . El Culebra would kill someone for you."

"How did you get in touch with this *El Culebra*?"

"I put the word out. Like spreading seeds. Just a hint here, a hint there. Pretty soon a man got in touch with me. Things happened quickly then. I met with his agent, though I think the agent was actually Culebra. Made a deal, gave him the money. A few days later Manhauser was dead."

"You hired Culebra to kill Manhauser so you could buy the ranch."

Solomon nodded slowly. "Yeah. He killed Manhauser and then he killed my wife, Priscilla."

"I don't understand."

"Neither did I."

Santiago shook his head. "What happened?"

"My wife Priscilla and that son-of-a-bitch Manhauser were having an affair. Right under my nose! Culebra found them together in a line shack back in the hills. Shot Manhauser between the eyes but took his time killing and raping Priscilla. They wouldn't even let me see her body . . ." He paused for a long time, looked away as if struggling with his emotions. "If I hadn't hired El Culebra . . ." his voice tailed off and he shook his head.

"So you hired Chandler to kill Culebra?"

"Yeah. That was the idea. Of course, Chandler didn't have a chance against Culebra. Culebra slaughtered him."

"How did Culebra know Chandler was looking for him?"

"Who knows for sure? He's got eyes and ears all over the place. He just took care of Chandler while he was in San Francisco on other business."

"Other business?"

"Sure. You don't think Culebra would come all the way to San Francisco just to kill Chandler, do you?"

"Come from where?"

"Somewhere about three or four days travel from here."

"How did you get to know Chandler?"

"Ha! Met him at a gambling house, like I said. He knew the Chinese were going to kill him if he didn't pay up."

"Do you know someone by the name of Dunsworth?"

Solomon wrinkled his forehead. He shook his head. "Don't know the name."

"How about Thomas O'Reiley?"

Again Solomon shook his head. "Sorry I can't help you." He studied Santiago, "You going after Culebra?"

"Maybe."

"Well, if you catch up with the son-of-a-bitch, put a bullet in him for me, too."

"So, what do you do now, Mister Solomon?"

"Not much except sit here and drink, get a little older every day. Sold off my old ranch and the stock a while back, thinking this is where I wanted to be. I was wrong, of course. Get into town once in a great while. You know, without Priscilla, it's just not the same . . ."

CHAPTER 32

Friday, September 5, 1902, San Francisco
Charley's was exactly what Santiago expected it to be: an unpainted, dilapidated store-front saloon with uneven floors, a single long bar down one side, a dozen or more round tables taking up the remaining space. The air stank with the odor of old beer, whisky, cigars, sweat and a variety of other human odors. The bar top was sticky with an unwashed accumulation of spilled beer and workingman's grime. The single front window overlooking the sidewalk appeared to be painted over; actually it was several years' accumulation of smoke and various human vapors that had made the glass barely translucent. Those who happened by on the sidewalk could only see vague shadows through the glass.

It was after eleven o'clock when Santiago cautiously walked into the crowded room. Chairs around the small tables were all occupied and the bar was crowded with all forms of humanity from the obvious derelict to the somewhat less destitute workingman. Voices rose and fell as arguments bloomed, lived short life spans and died just as quickly. Some staggered to the back door that opened into a narrow alley to relieve themselves and returned even as they were fastening the fly on their trousers. An occasional burst of laughter punctuated the thick air but few seemed to even notice it. The occasional rattle of dice provided a drum-like tattoo infrequently ended by a whoop of temporary excitement.

Santiago squeezed up to the bar near the back door and eventually caught the eye of the busy bartender. The bar man wiped his grimy hands on his pant legs and ambled up to Santiago.

He leaned across the bar toward Santiago. "What'll be, mate?"

"Anchor Steam."

"You got it." He turned to the beer taps, placed a questionably clean glass under one and expertly filled it, casually skimming off the excess head with his finger before his slid it in front of Santiago.

"Twenty-five, mate."

Santiago shook his head. "Steep. Must be pretty good."

The barman started to reach for the glass but Santiago motioned surrender with his hands.

"Just making conversation," he said quietly. "I'm looking for a man."

"Lot'a people do, mate. He got a name?"

"Chandler. Clarence Chandler." Santiago saw several heads swivel toward him when he said the name.

"Chandler. Let's see now. I seem to recall someone by that name used to come round once in a while. Drab looking guy—word got round that he'd done time up at the big house but escaped. You reckon that might be the chap you're look'n for?"

"Sounds like it might be. You know where I can find him?"

"Potters Field. Bloke got gutted couple'a months ago then ended up floating in the Bay." The barman turned as he heard a call from down the bar. "Gotta tend the customers." He gave Santiago one last look before he turned and walked to the other end of the bar.

"I might could 'elp ya some." The man standing nearby, one who had looked his way at the mention of Chandler's name, sidled up closer to Santiago. "I use'ta know Chandler pretty good."

"Well, let's talk, then." Santiago signaled the barman to bring the man another beer. "How did you know Chandler?"

"Well, the man 'e comes in 'ere lots, mostly sits alone, you see? E'd drink four or five beers then I'd wander over and sit with 'im. E'd buy me a beer or two, same as you, while we talked. Once 'e started talkin, there wasn't no stoppin 'im. Talked about 'is time inside, 'ow 'e learned to pick locks, 'bout the friend 'e lost in the escape. I tell ya, I 'eard them stories many a time." The man swallowed long at his beer. "'Bout three weeks before 'e got killed, 'e starts asking around about somebody to do a big job for 'im. 'E drops the 'int quite a few times. Most everyone 'ere thinks 'e's daffy. Then one night this man walks in, a stranger like you, asks about Chandler and somebody points 'im out. They talked for a bit and the stranger left. Next night Chandler walks in 'ere early, 'as five or six beers and leaves. Next thing we know 'e got opened up like a pig at slaughter."

He shook his head sadly, took a deep pull at his beer. "Stranger left. Never seen 'im again."

"What did this stranger look like, you remember?"

The man squinted as if it helped his memory. "Yeah. Tall guy, little over six feet I'd reckon. Mean face. Lots of deep wrinkles, like cracks, from 'is eyes and 'is mouth. Black hair but 'ad lots of gray. Big mustache. Oh yeah—and 'e 'ad a long black leather coat that 'e left on, even though it was 'ot in 'ere, it being July and all."

*　　*　　*

San Francisco

Dunsworth and Sophia sat on the davenport in her house, the papers making up the complex deed to the Nicaraguan property spread between them. Sophia had on a pair of reading glasses; Dunsworth had never seen her wear them before. She was going through the deed line by line, pausing and studying various parts with great concentration, often flipping back a few pages.

"Alex, my dear, I think there is a mistake here."

"Damn it! Moran is supposed to be the expert! How could he have made a mistake?"

Sophia looked once again at the page she had been studying. "Well, Alex, it may not be that bad! It looks to me like you, Alexander Crandell Dunsworth, are the sole owner of the described property. There is a default paragraph here that gives Moran the option to recues himself to avoid conflict of interest and he selected that option—here's his signature right here and the witness initials, here."

"Why would he remove himself as a partner?" Dunsworth frowned. "It doesn't make any sense."

"Unless he simply made a mistake. These are very complicated papers, my dear and though they're written in Spanish, they're obviously based upon Nicaraguan law. There's a lot of old history of the property: it was originally a grant from the King of Spain; then it was surveyed and purchased; here are records of various purchases to add to the property, partial history of taxes paid and late payments, liens, many names . . . It would take an expert to plow through all of this and know for sure what they had read. But it appears to me that you are legally the sole owner." She looked at him. "It may not be too late to have the error corrected . . ."

"Hell with that! He's the expert! He'll have to come after me through the Nicaraguan courts!" He paused, frowned, "What about the money? He put up half . . ."

"Hmm. It looks like the purchase price did not change. That's a real bad mistake, Alex. Whoever owned the property will only receive the half you put up. No . . . wait . . ." She studied the pages, shifting back and forth. "This is so complicated! It could be that . . ." she frowned, "I think that part will come out okay. If nothing else, they may come after Moran for the other half, even though he would not be a partner."

"That could take months in the courts. By then I'll be . . ."

"Where, Alex *dear*?" She asked. "Just where will *we* be?"

Dunsworth knew this was going to be an issue in the near future. He had no plans to include Sophia in his future, nor did he even have a firm plan where his future may take him. Certainly he would have to leave San Francisco; as soon as the Congress made its decision, the east coast investors would be after his hide and now Moran would be looking for him as well. Actually, the Congress decision as to the route of the canal could come any time; but of course, it would take months before the surveys could be completed and the United States started purchasing property to suit its needs.

* * *

San Francisco

Santiago told Thomas he was going to visit Sophia one more time. He felt certain that she knew more than she was telling him and he thought he could get her to talk with a little persuasion.

The next day, after making sure Dunsworth was at his office, Santiago knocked at Sophia's door. When she opened it, she appeared startled and then said, "Oh! Mister DeFoe. I didn't expect to see you again." Hesitantly, she at first kept the door open only a small crack then opened it wide. "Please come in."

"I'm sorry to arrive unexpectedly like this, Miss Jenkins but there are a few things I'd like to discuss with you." He stepped into the living room and sat in one of the straight back chairs. Sophia sat in the large overstuffed chair across from him.

"How can I help you, Mister DeFoe?"

"Well, I have a few more questions regarding Mister Dunsworth." He saw a quick shadow of concern pass over her face but she smiled and nodded pleasantly.

"I hope that I can help you."

"I hope you can too. Now Miss Jenkins, you said Dunsworth was working on a land transfer in Nicaragua, is that correct?"

"Yes, I believe that's what I told you."

"Yes. He was working with the firm of Warner, Jenkins and Garcia-Rameriz during this time. Were you aware of that?"

"Yes, I was . . . they were representing the owner . . . Mister Esperanza-Vincente." Sophia sat up straight on the edge of the chair.

"That's correct, Miss Jenkins. Are you aware that he was there the night your brother and the others were murdered?"

"That can't be possible! He was in San Francisco . . . perhaps at the ranch . . ."

"I have proof that he was in Los Angeles, Miss Jenkins."

"Oh, dear God! You must be mistaken, Mister DeFoe."

"I wish I could be, Miss Jenkins but unfortunately, I'm not. There is very strong evidence that Alexander Dunsworth, either by himself or in alliance with someone else, shot and killed the three attorneys and set fire to the office. As soon as the Grand Jury meets, they will issue an indictment for his arrest."

"Oh . . ." the cry came out almost as a kitten-like mew. She covered her mouth with her left hand as if to block the words that waited to come out. "My God. Oh, my God . . . this can't be true, Mister DeFoe."

"I'm so very sorry, Miss Jenkins. And I need to let you know that the sheriff in Santa Cruz is investigating the possibility that Dunsworth murdered his own wife."

This last was too much. Sophia let out a long, anguished cry before she bent double and surrendered to the deep sobs that shook her. Between heavy sobs she wailed, "Oh, my God! Oh, my God! It can't be! It just simply cannot be! What has he done? What has he . . . why?" She looked up once, "He murdered my brother?"

"It appears certain that he did, Miss Jenkins."

Another long sorrowful wail greeted this last statement. "It's too much! Too much!" Her sorrow suddenly took a turn in its expression. Her eyes narrowed in rage and the words were forced out between clenched teeth. "That son-of-a-bitch! That goddamned murdering son-of-a-bitch!"

"Miss Jenkins, I'm sorry but for your own safety, I suggest that you find a safe place to stay while this takes its course through the legal system. Do you have any relatives . . . ?"

"None here in the city. Perhaps my brother, Peter . . ."

"Would he offer . . . ?"

"I believe he would. I could send him a wire him this afternoon though I wouldn't have a reply until sometime tomorrow . . ."

"In the meantime, Miss Jenkins, perhaps you could stay at a hotel? I would suggest the Franciscan Hotel. It's quiet, very clean."

It took Santiago two hours to help Sophia gather and pack her things. He hired a hansom to take her to the Franciscan Hotel after she assured him that she had adequate money with her.

*   *   *

Alexander Dunsworth got out of the hansom when it pulled up at the familiar house where Sophia lived. He held a small bouquet of flowers he'd purchased from the vendor across the street from his office. He rapped on the door and waited patiently but after several seconds frowned and knocked a little louder. When the door still did not open, he pulled his house key from his vest pocket and let himself in.

"Sophia?"

There was no answer to his call. He put the flowers on the table and circulated through the rooms. The house seemed unusually empty; her toiletry articles were not in the bathroom, her book not in its usual place alongside the davenport. He frowned and, suddenly apprehensive, checked the bureau drawers in the bedroom.

"What the hell?" he bellowed. A quick glance into the wardrobe confirmed his findings; she had taken all her belongings and was gone. Nothing of hers remained in the house. He felt the angry rush of blood to his head and he pounded the table top with his fist. They had argued quite loudly the other evening regarding their future together. By the end of the evening they were not speaking and he left her place to spend the night at his own house.

Sophia knew far too much. She knew about the property swindle involving the east coast investors. She knew about the apparent errors that would cut James Tyler Moran out of any dealings with the valuable piece of property in Nicaragua. She had intimated that she was suspicious that he may have had something to do with her brother's murder and with that thought in her mind, she might even be pondering Nelle's murder.

Like a train out of control, this whole thing was starting to come off the tracks.

Where the hell was Sophia?

CHAPTER 33

<u>September 24, 1092, San Francisco</u>

Thomas O'Reiley had wired Amanda that the threat was over and that she and the children could safely return to San Francisco. On this day he waited impatiently for the ferry bringing passengers from the train depot in Alameda across the bay and south of Oakland. The air was cool and damp; as late afternoon approached, the breeze off the bay was quite cool. At last the profile of the ferry appeared south of Buena Vista Island cutting through the bay toward the Ferry Building where Thomas waited.

Amanda waited until most of the crowd had disembarked before she attempted to bring the three children and Xaing to the pier alongside the ferry. The children all rushed to Thomas and threw their arms around him, chattering about all they had seen. Eventually, Amanda scooted them away far enough that she could get close enough to Thomas to hug him.

"I've missed you Thomas, so very much," she whispered in his ear. "It seems like years. I'm so glad to be home."

Thomas kissed her, put his hand behind her head to pull her closer. When they finally parted, he whispered, "I've missed you too, darling Mandy."

Thomas had arranged for two carriages to be waiting to bring the family, their luggage and Xaing who had stood smiling silently in the background.

By the time they reached their home on Nob Hill, the sun had set. Xaing quietly went to her kitchen and before long delicious odors came from the room. By the time Thomas and Amanda had put away the children's clothing, Xaing rang the tiny bell that indicated that dinner was ready. The table was set for the family and Xaing brought in steaming dishes of food.

"Xaing, I've missed your excellent cooking!" Thomas exclaimed. "I think that I should not let you go away again!"

The maid smiled self-consciously, blushing lightly with this complement. She bowed slightly and backed quickly into her kitchen. A few minutes later they all heard Xaing singing softly in her native language, off key and tunelessly but the familiarity brought smiles around the table and helped the family realize they were together again.

Later when the children were asleep and Xiang had retired to her room, Thomas and Amanda sat close together in the sun room, sharing a glass of wine. Amanda told Thomas of all the places she, the children and Xaing had visited, the sights they had seen, the plays they had attended. The most exciting event, Amanda told him, had been the trip to the Statue of Liberty where the children had been allowed to climb the stairs inside to the very head and look out the windows there.

Finally, after a long pause in their conversation, she asked, "What happened to Chandler while I was gone? Why was it suddenly safe for me to come home?"

Thomas hesitated for a few seconds, afraid to put a damper on their time together. Finally, "He was killed, Amanda. Someone stabbed him and threw his body into the bay. He'll never threaten us again."

"Do they know who did it?"

"No. Whoever did it left no clues."

Amanda considered this for a long time, finally simply nodded. "He's gone. That's good." She took his hand and raised it to her lips, kissing his fingers slowly. "I've missed you, Thomas. I thought about you every day. I prayed that you were safe."

"I've missed you also, Amanda. The house seems so empty without you—and of course the children but especially you. Your presence in our home seems to fill each room with light and life and a kind of warmth. And our bed seemed awfully empty and cold."

"Why, Mister O'Reiley, that almost sounds like an invitation to join you in bed; I certainly would not want my husband to feel lonely and cold . . ."

"Well, Missus O'Reiley, you are quite astute. Perhaps you would care to join me upstairs in an authentic celebration of your return."

"And just what do you have in mind?" She snuggled her lips into the crook of his neck, making little nibbling sounds.

"Skyrockets, spinning pinwheels and firecrackers!"

393

"Ooh . . . that sounds deliciously exciting!"

*   *   *

Abilene, Texas

Luke sat in the hotel room overlooking the dusty street that ran parallel to the railroad track. Since his return from San Francisco late in July, he had spent almost all of his time in this room, leaving only for necessities such as eating and haircuts. The weather was hot, typical for this time of the year in Texas and he felt cooler when not moving around in the heat.

The solitary time also gave him the opportunity to think about the upcoming job in California. After he had sent the telegram to the San Francisco attorney accepting the job and at the same time making his demands known, he had received only the briefest of telegraph replies:

AGREED STOP WILL SEND MORE INFO STOP

He knew that he would meet with the committee the attorney had mentioned and they would certainly not be happy with his threat. But they had agreed and that meant a lot of money, a great deal of money, would change hands. They had agreed to pay in advance. From that moment on he would be a wanted man.

He would shoot the President of the United States of America and kill him. For that he was to be paid an amount that exceeded what most people would earn in three lifetimes. He would have to figure out how that much cash could be handled. Even in the largest denominations of paper money, it would present a fairly large pile. And he already had other large amounts stashed in banks all over Texas. He would have to consolidate those accounts, carefully so as not to raise any suspicions. Certainly by the time May rolled around, he must have all these details taken care of. The money must be transportable, disguised in such a way as to not draw attention. It must be readily available, interchangeable at a given rate for goods or services. It must be recognizable and exchangeable in foreign countries—not like the damned Nicaraguan gold coins! It must retain its set value and not be up to the whim of a banker.

He had spent many hours mulling over these worries and as of now still did not have a solution. Several ideas but none that handled all his concerns; he had considered investments in stocks or bonds, purchasing art treasures, diamonds, gold. He knew he was far out of his element in dealing with this much money. He must have the answer in less than eight months.

He tried to picture the fine cross-hairs in the telescopic sight on his rifle centered on President Roosevelt. He'd seen pictures of the man: husky, broad shouldered, robust face, hair quaintly parted in the middle and combed each way, reading glasses like a school teacher tethered with a black string, ears that laid flat against the side of his head and a bushy, walrus-like mustache. Would the man be facing him when he pulled the trigger? Would he even know that he'd been hit by a fifty-caliber bullet? Would he die standing on his feet, or would he lay fallen on the ground, bleeding out slowly through his mouth and nose while those around him tried frantically to do the impossible.

The Sierra Nevada Mountains. He'd seen them but had never been among them. Only knew what he'd heard: taller than any other mountains in the United States, air so thin that breathing becomes difficult, a mountain range over four-hundred miles long, winter snow packs that reached twenty, thirty even forty feet in depth, trees bigger around than some houses in Abilene, Indians that still scalped unlucky white men that wandered too far into their territory, big blue lakes so deep they have no bottom, waterfalls with a quarter of a mile drop, great vertical slabs of rock stretching up a half mile . . .

He figured he would have to spend some time on horseback. He was by no means an excellent horseman; in fact, he knew he was just barely satisfactory. The right clothes, the correct boots would help. He would check at the local livery and talk to the young stable hand there, at least enough to learn the right language and what questions to ask. He had ridden horseback very little while in the army; the Cavalry did the riding; soldiers like him marched or rode in the back of wagons. His mind wandered back to the army days, the attack on Puerto Rico in 1898 when he had taken his first live target out during the Battle of Yauco. Following that were more, mainly Spanish and Puerto Rican officers, at Guamani River Bridge, Coamo, Silva Heights and Asomante. That's when his army chums started calling him *Hombre de Culebra*, the Snake Man; which quickly became simply *El Culebra*.

He'd have to toughen up some because he'd be spending long hours and probably long days in the saddle. He'd let himself get a little out of condition living in hotels and riding trains.

And the food issue . . . he'd never enjoyed, rightly never even learned cooking, even when it was easy. The few times he'd been forced to overnight without food and shelter, he'd survived on beef jerky, hard biscuits, and water from a canteen. Lucky it hadn't rained. He could do that—for a day or two. But then a man's stomach begins to mutiny; it does corrupt things that can completely disable the hardiest man. He didn't need to be gripped by stomach cramps and gas or worse still, *Montezuma's Revenge* as they had called it in Puerto Rico, that can catch a man by surprise any time day or night. Within a day or two a man can be put down, so ill that he can scarcely wiggle, much less think through and complete a complicated task.

Well, he had eight months to get ready. He'd set up a daily routine, just as he had while learning to be an army sniper. It took practice. It took time. It took patience. He had plenty of each.

* * *

San Francisco
Sophia peered out her fourth floor hotel room window at the Friday evening crowd that was beginning to fill the sidewalk. She had barely left the confines of the hotel since that evening a little over two weeks ago when Mister DeFoe had helped settle her into the room. The hotel boasted an excellent dining room that provided meals and a glass of wine or two in the evening and a small collection of books for long-term guests.

It was certainly not a bad place to have to stay but she would have preferred a little more personal freedom. She'd sent a Western Union telegram to her brother Peter, asking if she could come to spend a month or so with him. He replied the following day that he was in the midst of making major repairs to the ranch house; this would not be a good time—perhaps in a month or six weeks. His negative response wasn't a great surprise to her.

She'd had plenty of time over the past few weeks to think about Alexander Dunsworth and what DeFoe had told her. As much as she hated to admit it, she had suspected Dunsworth was up to no good as he told her about the property deal he was working on. Nor was she surprised that her brother would react to the information she had sent to him as he did; he had not inherited their father's sense of ethics and morality. But it was hard for her to believe that Alexander Dunsworth would resort to multiple murders to sooth his anger. He had shared very little with her about the death of his wife Nelle; she had assumed the topic was simply too painful for him. But now she wondered. He had taken on a sort of preoccupied, dispassionate personality after the murder, sometimes spending hours staring off at nothing, refusing to talk or even answer her questions. Now, of course, he had intentionally refused to correct an obvious error on the property deed, cutting his attorney friend out of the swindle.

She felt she knew what his thoughts about her were: she was his paid mistress, reasonably beautiful, rather mediocre of mind and thought, embarrassingly candid at times, rather skilled in bed, entertaining but not exactly the type of lady he would feel comfortable introducing to his business acquaintances.

She had at one time not too long ago believed that she was in love with the man and that he might be in love with her but that fantasy fell apart. His passion was limited to money, power and control. And he would do almost anything to achieve his selfish dreams. But . . . murder? Yes, she decided, he would even resort to murder.

So, what was she to do? Mister DeFoe had said he was leaving the city for several weeks, perhaps longer. She was comfortably accommodated in one of the city's better hotels and she had enough money to last several months. If money became an issue, she could always go back to work as a legal secretary. But Alexander Dunsworth was *out there* somewhere and he would be very angry by now. Angry enough to kill.

*　　*　　*

The late-summer storm had blown in from the Pacific with a force that surprised even the old-timers who had lived in the city most of their lives. The surf pounded the cliffs below the magnificent seven-story Victorian Cliff House that had recently burned and then had been rebuilt by Adolph Sutra. Curious sightseers lined the boulevard that curved along the cliff to watch the gigantic rollers come in from the Pacific and crash thunderously against the rocks. The wind howled and carried the spray flung upward by the surf nearly a city block taking with it men's bowlers, ladies hats and umbrellas.

The storm reached far inland as well. The heavy clouds laden with rain blew up against the Sierra Nevada Mountains and began to let loose the hundreds of millions of gallons of water they held suspended. Low areas around Sacramento, barely at sea level, quickly flooded. Further south the huge valley began to saturate and water filled the Sacramento and San Joaquin Rivers; the lesser rivers, the Kern, the Merced, Stanislaus, the Kaweah and the Kings quickly reached highest recorded levels and were soon overflowing their ill-defined banks as they penetrated into the valley flatland. Tulare Lake, at one time the largest freshwater lake west of the Great Lakes, had slowly been deprived of its natural water source but with the rains it spread once again across miles of farmland. Citizens of the larger cities, Sacramento, Stockton, Merced and Fresno hunkered down as the deluge of rainwater flooded streets and lapped at the doorstep of their houses.

In the Sierra Nevada Mountains, the rains caused landslides, small rivers and creeks became rushing torrents that carved into hillsides and undermined huge trees that then became victims of the wind, toppling them by the tens of thousands.

Further north, the Russian, the Eel and the Trinity Rivers filled and overflowed.

It was, according to the San Francisco Chronicle *The Storm of the Century*. Damage to property was estimated to be close to a million dollars.

The city of San Francisco managed to avoid most of the damage, though a few low places were completely inundated by muddy flood waters. Construction work slowed and finally halted as the porous soil turned to thick, clinging mud. Some homes built on the sides of San Francisco's hills simply slid downhill, coming to rest against their neighbors.

Thomas sat in the sun room watching the residual rain continue to fall but with much less force. The storm had lasted nearly five full days. People were forecasting sunshine, more out of desire than any real scientific observations. The huge surf had retreated and normal waves crashed against the coastline now devoid of curious sightseers. Thomas put the newspaper aside after reading the latest reports of damage in the central valley. Just then he heard the knocker on the front door; Xaing shuffled through to answer it. He heard her, then a man's voice and moments later she escorted Frank Barnwell into the sunroom.

"Frank! Good to see you. Please, have a seat. What brings you out on this rainy day?"

"Actually, I'm here because of the rain, Thomas." He looked out the windows. "Hopefully, it's beginning to reduce some."

"I believe it is." Thomas studied his long time friend. He has grown more mature over the years with just a brush of distinguished looking gray hair at his temples. He kept himself immaculately groomed and Thomas had to admit his clothing style and fit certainly was enviable. Of course, the man was still unmarried and he made a very good salary. He waited for Frank to open the conversation.

"Thomas, I have something that I need to discuss with you. It is quite personal; so I would ask that you not share this with anyone, at least not yet." He looked at Thomas until he saw the confirming nod. "The rain has created havoc throughout our state with the exception of the southern portion—Los Angeles down to the border. But elsewhere we've taken a beating. Millions of acres of farmland are under water. Miles upon miles of river water are creating entirely new courses through rich farm and ranch land. Cities are inundated, utilities flooded. Telephone and telegraph offices flooded. Electrical generating plants the same. We can only guess how many homes and business have been seriously damaged." He paused. "Of course, you have already read of this in the Chronicle." He gazed quietly out of the window before he resumed. "I have received a call from my old department with the State of California. They are spread terribly thin. They have three crews of two men each in Northern California assessing damage and preparing recommendations for not only how to initiate recovery efforts, but how to prevent this from happening again in the future."

"They've put the rest of their resources into the San Joaquin Valley but they came up one man short. They have asked me to lead the team assessing the Kings, the Kern, the Merced, Stanislaus and the Kaweah rivers. Of course, you realize this means that I would have to resign my present position with M. O. and B. I've given that a great deal of thought, Thomas. Though I have done well with the architecture firm, it is not my real area of expertise." He held up his hand to stop Thomas's interruption. "I'm a trained engineer. We don't need a trained engineer to lead Sierra-Pacific Architects. We need an expert manager. I have someone in mind who could take over the leadership of the company without losing a beat. He's one of my leading architects but has been the one I lean on when it comes to managing a particular situation. His name is Emerson Cartwright. He came out west when the company closed up in New York and has been an asset for these years."

Thomas was nodding his head. "I remember Emerson very well and was quite impressed when I met him for the first time. If I remember correctly, he pretty much led the effort after the building burned to find new ways to prevent similar casualties in the future. A good man. A good selection."

The two men spent nearly an hour discussing the situation. Thomas poured each of them a tumbler of whiskey and they sipped it slowly as their conversation ebbed and flowed. The pros and cons of Frank's leaving, the ability of a new man to pick up the responsibilities quickly, the effect on the overall business were all topics open to discussion. Finally there was a long period of silence.

"So, Thomas, you agree with my plans?"

"Reluctantly, yes. I know from personal experience that one must find what truly makes him happy and pursue it." He looked at Frank, "So, when are you considering this move?"

"As soon as possible, Thomas. What do you think about this coming Friday, October the third?"

"I believe we best run it past Hanson but I should think he would not have a problem, other than suffering the loss of a good friend and a member of the organization."

Frank Barnwell nodded slightly and Thomas could see that there was something else on his friend's mind. He waited and watched as Frank struggled with whatever it was that was tying him in knots. Finally Frank looked straight at Thomas.

"I have one other request, Thomas. This may not be as simple to solve."

"And that is . . . ?"

"I would like to borrow you away from your job with M. O. & B. for a month." Again he held his hand up against Thomas's objection. "Let me talk, Thomas. There is no one around that knows the lower Kaweah River any better than you. Not that you've been to its headwaters on Mount Kaweah at thirteen thousand eight hundred feet; I would dare say very few people ever have been there. But you know the lower stages of the river and that is where the efforts must ultimately be made to do something that will prevent this from happening again. You have a keen sense of what should be left untouched; we engineers sometimes trample without thought on people and what is sacred in our haste to make things better."

"I appreciate your thoughts, Frank but certainly there are others . . ."

"There very well may be, Thomas but I am asking for your help."

There was a long silence while Thomas considered all that he had heard. "Two of us away from our desks at the same time may throw Handon into a fit of apoplexy, Frank. But, let's talk to the old codger."

*   *   *

<u>San Francisco</u>

Handon McPherson had listened quietly as they two men he often thought of as his sons presented their case. As they expected, he peppered them with questions and arguments. Frank Barnwell's resignation from the company was already a fore drawn conclusion and he heartily approved of Frank's recommendation to move Emerson Cartwright into the position. It would require officially changing the name of the company to M. O. & C. but that could be handled quite easily. He would contact the Chronicle and they would run a small article about the change in name and why the change came about. He was not quite as enthusiastic about having a new man at the helm of the architectural firm at the same time his manager of the supplies division would be away. Thomas knew who he would slip in to temporally fill his position and finally Handon nodded. "So be it, gentlemen. Now, off with you two to save the world, by God!"

Amanda was even less happy than her father; but being that Frank was the instigator, she finally relinquished and dubbed the two men her intrepid explorers. The three celebrated Monday evening by going out to one of the upscale restaurants in town. Amanda was up to her usual frolicsome mood and had used the afternoon to visit a shop in the city where she purchased a handsome sterling silver hand compass with a crystal face for each of them with their names engraved on the back. With great solemnity she presented each his compass, along with a warm kiss on the cheek. "Just come back," she said quietly. "Please come back."

CHAPTER 34

Two days later they had arrived by train in Fresno where they met with the other two-man teams and discussed their basic strategy. Using geological survey maps they would chart out the locations of main water holding ponds, depths of rivers at their crests and any changes in the paths of the major rivers. They would make note of any other potentially useful information such as landslides caused by the rain, property lines and structures that had been affected by the flooding. Following the meeting, they continued by train to Visalia where they had agreed to start, since Thomas's familiarity with the area would help them learn what they were up against before they went into areas they were unfamiliar with.

Neither man was prepared for what they found. The little town of Visalia was now on the eastern shore of what had once been Tulare Lake. The usually dry lake now spread across the huge valley; an inland sea of over seven hundred square miles. The rivers that once fed the lake had been diverted for farming use. Its depth was not great and without constant input from the rivers it would soon recede until it was once more a mere puddle and then it would dry up completely during the first hot summer.

The Kaweah River was one of the sources that fed the ancient lake, along with the Kern River and southernmost tributaries of the Kings River and the Tule River, which come in south of the Kaweah. All these rivers had reached levels they had not experienced in at least fifty years. They would concentrate on the Kaweah River first.

It was too late to attempt to take a buggy out to the Gordon's ranch, so they slept that night in the only hotel in town that had any room left.

* * *

The next morning they rented a buggy and headed for the ranch. The road, which had never really been a road but was rather a set of wagon wheel and carriage tracks, was now deep and slippery mud, even though the rain had nearly stopped. By the time they reached the ranch, both were saturated with rainwater.

When they pulled up in front of the Gordon's ranch house, Hector was the first to come out. They had neglected to telegraph the family and let them know of their plans but Hector greeted them with his usual friendly handshakes and claps on their backs. Soon Margarita and Angela were there with hugs and embraces. Ramon, they explained, was away from the ranch once again attending a conference. The two men went directly to the bunkhouse, changed into dry clothes and returned to the main house. Margarita and Angela were already in the kitchen and hot coffee was set out as the men sat in front of the roaring fire in the fireplace. Frank carefully explained why they were there and what they planned to accomplish. Hector nodded and provided excellent first-hand knowledge of the storm-initiated flood. Once again, he explained, they had been fortunate that Hector's grandfather had built his home far enough above the flood level of the Kaweah River. Many people today, he went on, were building houses of convenience and spectacular views of the rivers. Several such homes were under water or had been entirely swept away. Peter Jenkins, he said, was one of those who had suffered loss; Peter had built his home on a small bluff overlooking Mill Creek that fed the Kings River. Usually a slow moving and picturesque creek, the rain had swollen the creek into a raging river that had washed under the bluff and most of Jenkins' house tumbled into the creek. "He just finished several months of work on it, too." he added. "He was planning on his sister coming down from San Francisco."

Hector showed them the high-water mark where the Kaweah River had overflowed its banks and washed across the southern end the Gordon's property. Thomas looked across to the other side and estimated that the river at that point had been two hundred yards across and at least thirty feet deep. He knew that Frank would be calculating the flow of the river at flood stage in terms of so many hundreds of thousands or millions of cubic feet of water per second. The figures would help him determine if and where and how the river could be contained or diverted to prevent this from happening again. A dam on the Kaweah right here would flood ranches up both sides of the river up into and well beyond the north and south forks of the river. All for the *possibility* of another once-in-a-lifetime storm such as the one they had just experienced.

Frank and Thomas joined Hector, Margarita and Angela as dinner was served at the family table. Talk was of the storm, damage done and the possibility of preventing such happenings in the future. Frank Barnwell was in his element as he talked eloquently of long range plans the state had to supply Sierra Nevada water to the huge and fertile San Joaquin valley. "It will someday," he said seriously, "produce enough food, vegetables, fruit and melons to feed all of the United States. On top of that there will be cotton and grains . . . it can and will all be grown here. Hector, you will be growing oranges, lemons and grapefruit that will be shipped fresh in refrigerated railroad cars to the east coast. California's exotic produce: figs, dates, artichokes, grapes . . . Grapes! California is already producing wines that are taking prizes in Paris." He stopped, nearly out of breath. "But we have to have water. Not only have it when and where we need it but control it so that a single flood does not undo tens of thousands of hours of work." He paused, "and mark my words; many people in California will not be happy. Some will say the water belongs to everyone. Some will say we're stealing their drinking water. Others will say we are ruining the environment." He glanced at Thomas. "None of this is going to happen overnight. Perhaps it will happen in my lifetime but I certainly want to help it happen."

After dinner, they went into the great room and sat in front of the fire to continue the discussion. Thomas could see that Hector and Margarita were following Frank's enthusiasm calmly; both were in their late forty's and it would not happen in their lifetime. Angela sat and listened carefully and Thomas imagined she was mentally accepting the possibilities and envisioning the Gordon ranch as a major player in the overall scheme. She doesn't realize, Thomas thought, that already wealthy speculators were buying up tens of thousands of acres of rich land up and down the valley. Frank Barnwell was not the only man with a vision.

Hector and Margarita wandered off to go to bed and Frank excused himself, headed for the bunkhouse. Thomas sensed that everyone had left so that he and Angela could be alone and the thought made him uncomfortable. She seemed to sense his uneasiness.

"Are you all right Tom?"

He laughed quietly. "I think so, Angela. It seems that everyone suspects that you and I are . . ." he paused, not knowing quite what words to use, "that we're more than just good friends."

Angela took his hand in hers. "I don't know what my parents think, Tom. I know that they trust you as if you were their own son. I believe they would be very angry if I ever caused trouble between you and your wife."

"What have you told them about you and me?"

She was silent for a long while. "I have told them everything, Tom. That I love you more than if you were my brother. I have told them that nothing imprudent has happened and that as a gentleman you respect and treat me as a lady. I've spoken to my mother quite frankly about you and she has warned me of the risk I am putting us in."

"Have you told her about our . . . closeness, our kisses?"

"No. Tom. That is far too personal and it is only between you and me. Our close times together are precious moments. You have no idea how terribly I want you to love me, Tom. And I know that you do love me but with only part of your heart; I work hard to understand and be contented with that portion of your love. Should it ever be different for you, I will be waiting."

*　　*　　*

The next morning Thomas and Frank were up and had a quick breakfast while it was still dark. The day was just beginning to dawn when Frank went ahead on horseback with Thomas following. Frank had his transit with him and as the day progressed they took a number of sightings up the north side of the river until they well past the south fork of the river. Crossing the river was still not a possibility as it still ran deep and very swift carrying broken trees and limbs with it. Unable to cross, they returned the same route and were at the ranch by late afternoon.

"Tomorrow I'd like to go downstream some. I've thought about it and this just may be a case where a large water holding area could be built."

"You mean a dam."

"A dam would hold many millions of gallons of water for use throughout the dry summer, Thomas. It's water that otherwise drains into tributaries of the San Joaquin River and finally ends up flowing into San Francisco Bay. The Kaweah flows all year and a large clear-water lake could

405

exist, with capacity to store excessive rain like we've just experienced. It would supply water for tens of thousands of acres of produce or fruit or cotton."

"And it would put some of these small ranches under fifty feet of water."

Frank nodded. "It may. But it would be small price for such a huge possibility."

"Unless you are the rancher whose property is going to be flooded by a man-made lake."

"Like the Gordon's."

"Yeah, like the Gordon's."

"They would be compensated, Thomas. The state would buy their ranch at a fair price."

"But their way of life, a life several generations have spent here on this ranch, would be forever gone. How do you compensate for that?"

Frank smiled. "That's why I brought you along, my friend."

*   *   *

The next day the two rode into the valley and under Frank's direction made numerous sightings along the Kaweah River below the Gordon ranch. Frank pointed out to Thomas where a dam could be placed that would back up the river and produce a lake of between fifteen hundred and two thousand acres.

"How does that translate into gallons of water?"

"Well, it would be difficult to calculate without many more measurements because of the terrain but on the surface an acre-foot of water contains three hundred and twenty-five thousand, eight hundred and fifty-one gallons of water. So, just taking the surface area, one foot deep, a two-thousand acre reservoir would contain over six hundred and fifty million gallons of water—in just the top foot. If the reservoir averaged fifty feet deep, it would hold well over four billion gallons of water."

Thomas shook his head in wonder. "I can see why you get excited about this Frank. I had no idea."

"It's so damned important to California, Thomas. A hundred years from now they will still be looking for more water. We can't wait until then to start figuring out how to better utilize that natural resource."

It was late afternoon when they rode into the Gordon ranch and were greeted by Hector.

"Good to see you back." he said as they dismounted, "You boys got it figured out?"

Frank smiled, "Well, the way I see it, Hector, the worst that could happen is that you would have several hundred acres of land bordering a beautiful lake—someday."

Hector laughed. "Well, maybe someday I can handle it but not today. Come on in and let's have dinner and let's talk. I'd like to hear what you found."

*　　*　　*

San Francisco

It had been five weeks since Dunsworth had last seen Sophia. Her disappearance surprised him since he had not known her to be one who acted rashly or under her own initiative. But now it was as if she had simply vanished and he didn't have a clue where she might have gone. She used to have a brother in Los Angeles—that is until he got himself murdered. Dunsworth wondered if she had any inkling into his own culpability in her brother's death. How could she? No one had even mentioned the triple murder to him, no one had asked where he had been that night, no one had even asked if he knew the murdered men.

No, he assured himself, he was safe on that one. Nelle's murder was a little more problematic but he felt reassured after talking to Sheriff McGee who seemed to readily agree that there must have been a second person present during the murder. And no one had even thought about looking into his finances which was good; for if they had, they would find that he was in financial debt way over his head, having had to re-mortgage the ranch property and put up all the cash on hand that he had in order to swing the property deal in Nicaragua. But the payoff would be even more than he expected with the error Sophia had found in the legal papers that effectively cut the Texas attorney right out of the deal.

And no one had tied him, even remotely, to the murder of the wealthy Nicaraguan woman, though he resented the east coast investors using him to be the go-between person with the assassin. So, where did the Los Angeles attorneys get their information? There's still a loose end out there somewhere and as long as it was loose, there could be trouble.

Now he had to wait for Congress to make up their mind; however it went Roosevelt, would be out of the way anyway.

The recent revelation from their spy in the White House that Roosevelt would be meeting with a high level Panamanian would help support evidence that the Panamanians were at least partly responsible for his death. No one, not even the Congress, would approve of the United States building a canal through a country that was implicated in the murder of the United States President.

How much did Sophia know? She didn't know about him murdering the three lawyers. She didn't know about him murdering Nelle. She didn't know about the Nicaraguan woman. So exactly what did she know? What or who was her source of information? Where was she? She had mentioned the visit from the attorney named DeFoe, Charles DeFoe, if he remembered correctly. *What was it she said about him?* He was with an insurance company investigating the arson . . . *What did he know? What had he told Sophia?* A sudden thought came from nowhere; wasn't it strange that both he and Sophia should be visited within days by attorneys that neither of them knew? Certainly he knew nothing about the lawyer from Texas named John Tyler Moran other than the man talked a good line and seemed to know exactly what was necessary to handle the land transaction. But then, according to Sophia, there was a huge error in the deed that apparently Moran had not picked up on. Or had he? How would it be to Moran's advantage to not be a partner in the ownership of thirty-nine thousand square miles of prime property straddling the route the canal would take through Nicaragua? At the price they . . . no . . . he had paid for the property, he would stand to get a return of ten dollars on the dollar. A one thousand percent return on investment at the minimum.

And he hadn't heard anything from the east coast group, even though they had received their property deed at least six weeks ago, so apparently they had not picked up on the deception. When it became time to sell the property, only then would they discover that the longitude and latitude points that spelled out specifically the boundaries of the property they now owned actually consisted of two and a half million acres of useless swamp land. But by then, he would be gone. Great Britain probably, at least somewhere that English was spoken.

But where in the hell is Sophia?

CHAPTER 35

<u>Thursday, October 16, 1902, San Francisco</u>
Sophia Jenkins was getting tired of spending her days in the fourth floor hotel room. She'd eaten her meals in her room, most of the time skipping breakfast. On a few occasions she went to the comfortable lounge late at night where she often caught the disapproving glances of other patrons; women weren't supposed to be in bars and lounges unescorted. But she yearned for a glass of wine and on occasion, a shot of good whiskey before she went to bed. *Damn Alexander!* She was certain he'd be looking for her. Perhaps he thought she'd run off with the lawyer Charles DeFoe; she didn't even know where he was from!

This evening she ventured downstairs at eleven thirty and entered the cozy and semi-dark lounge. The bartender recognized her and pointed to a secluded booth in the darkest corner. "Whiskey, please Phillip," she said quietly as she walked past him. He nodded and by the time she slid into the booth, he was there with the whiskey, straight up.

"Thank you Phillip," she said evenly. "Seems quiet tonight."

"It is for a Thursday, Miss Sophia. Must be the weather. Will anyone be joining you tonight?"

"I don't think so, though I can always hope." She chuckled the throaty, alluring laugh that she knew men liked.

"You going to be staying long . . . I mean at the hotel, Miss Sophia?"

"Depends on what you call a long time, Phillip. I think I've already been here a long time. Trouble with a man, you know?"

He grimaced and shook his head sadly. "Well, Miss Sophia, if you ever need my help, I'm right here."

"Thank you, Phillip. I'll remember that."

She watched as the barman walked back to his place behind the bar. He was older than her by fifteen years or more she estimated; growing bald with the horseshoe-shaped crown of silver hair neatly trimmed. He wore an attractive mustache, something she generally did not find all that good looking but his seemed to fit his face, neither too small or too large or bushy nor waxed into something unnatural and bizarre. He had a friendly face and a gentle demeanor, spoke with deep voice that was soft but carried well.

*   *   *

Alexander Dunsworth had spent the last five evenings wearily searching the lounges and bars in San Francisco, convinced that that's where he'd find Sophia. He knew of her weakness for a glass of wine or a shot of whiskey to calm her down before she retired for the night. If she was at a hotel, it was a good guess that she'd visit the hotel's lounge or bar late in the evening. So far he'd visited nine hotels, dropping in a little before midnight, just long enough to take a slow saunter among the booths where unattended ladies usually tended to sit or were often seated there by the barkeep. So far his search had turned up a few female prospects for future consideration but he hadn't found Sophia. Raw anger boiled in his veins when he thought how she'd packed her things and slipped away from the house without a single word, no good-by, no thanks, not even "see you later". He wasn't sure what he'd do if he located her but he had to find out just what she knew and didn't know. If she said the wrong thing to the wrong people, his whole life could come down around him like a house built of playing cards.

He'd begun wearing his overcoat during these searches, not because the weather was especially cold but because the deep side pockets provided plenty of space to hide the Remington .41 caliber Derringer pistol. He wasn't real sure why he felt better with it in his pocket but he liked the sense of power and control.

The search usually kept him out until after midnight and he was close to abandoning the entire endeavor. The Franciscan Hotel catered to the middle-upper-class cliental and tonight it was the second hotel on his list.

The lobby lighting had been dimmed in the late evening hours as new guests were generally not expected at this hour. He asked the desk clerk, an elderly gentleman with a pot belly, to show him where the lounge was to be found. The clerk graciously led him to the door to the darkened lounge with the words, "I hope you have a nice evening, sir". Dunsworth's quick glance around the lounge revealed several shadowy booths around the perimeter of the room and he ambled by them just as he if he was looking for a person he was expecting to meet.

Sophia had glanced up when his shadow blocked the filtered light from the lobby and she recognized the silhouette as that of Alexander Dunsworth. Desperately she attempted to shrink into the darkest corner of the booth. Phillip apparently saw her movement, caught her frightened expression and nodded his understanding. She watched as Dunsworth continued to stroll around the booths, peering quickly into each one. When he got to Sophia's booth, he stopped and turned toward her.

"Well, well! If it isn't little Miss Sophia. Where have you been little lady? I've been looking for you. We have things to talk about." His voice had a rough, almost snarling sound to it.

"Go away and leave me alone, Alex! You and I are through. I know what you've done and it makes me sick to my stomach! Just leave me alone! I want you out of my life!"

"Well, Sophia, that's not going to happen that easily! Like I said, we have things we need to talk about—in private!"

"Alex, please. Just leave me alone."

Phillip came out from behind the bar and walked toward Dunsworth. "I think the lady has made herself clear, sir," he said calmly. "Why don't you just leave her alone?"

Dunsworth spun toward Phillip and his right hand came from the coat pocket, Derringer in hand. He pulled back on the hammer, cocking the small handgun. "Why don't you just mind your own business?"

Sophia eased herself out of the booth and stood behind Dunsworth. "Alex," she pleaded, "please put that away! Is this the only way you can solve problems, by shooting someone? I don't want any trouble."

"You already have trouble, Sophia." He waved the Derringer at Phillip, "Get back behind the bar."

Phillip stood his ground, shaking his head. "You've got no right to point that thing at me, mister. Like the lady just said, we don't want any trouble."

The elderly deskman had sensed the turmoil in the lounge and made his way to the door, stepped in and walked toward Dunsworth. "Hey! Put the gun away, mister. No guns in here!"

Dunsworth swung toward the man, now several feet away, the Derringer pointed at his chest.

"Alex, for God's sake! Put the gun away!" She reached for his right arm, intending to push the gun away from the direction of the old man. The touch of her hand on his arm startled Dunsworth; his hand jerked in reflex. The detonation of the .41 caliber round sounded like a crash of thunder in the enclosed space. The old man stood for a few seconds, staring down at the sudden splotch of red on the white shirt he was wearing. Then his knees went out from under him and he collapsed in a heap on the floor.

Sophia shrieked in horror and stared at the man on the floor. "Alex! Oh my God, Alex, you shot him!"

"I didn't shoot him. You did Sophia. You grabbed my arm and pulled the trigger. You killed him!"

Phillip had knelt down beside the old man and after several seconds he looked up at Dunsworth. "He's gone. There's no pulse. You shot him through his heart. I'm going to have to get the police. I think you better sit down and put the gun on a table where everyone can see it. The police might get a little testy if they came in here and you were still holding the pistol."

Dunsworth nodded, placed the Derringer on the nearest table and sat in the chair. His mind was already working on how to shift the blame onto Sophia.

*   *   *

The Gordon Ranch

Thomas and Frank had spent a week and a half already finishing the measurements and sketches up and down the Kaweah River for the site that Frank was proposing as a future dam site. The days were long, from sunup to sunset and the weather was typical October weather; unpredictable. Some days it was cold and dreary; others were warm, almost summerlike. Thomas had little time to spend alone with Angela as he and Frank continued in the evening after dinner to make a permanent record of all the figures they had recorded during the day. Thomas was amazed at how much Frank knew about the dynamics of rivers, how fast or slow they flowed, how much water they carried, how water tended to react to obstacles in its path. He could even make some tentative predictions on how much electrical power could be derived from water stored behind a dam, something that was still in its infancy as the United States rushed to become electrified.

Often Angela was already in bed by the time the two men blew out the lamps and retired to the bunkhouse. But this evening, Frank had been the first to give up. "I think I'm going to hit the hay, Thomas. I'm guessing we're about through here and we need to be moving back north some to do the Kings River before we move on to the Merced and Stanislaus Rivers."

Angela was in one of the big chairs with a book where she had been all evening.

Thomas nodded. "I'll be there in a while, Frank."

After Frank had left, Thomas walked over to Angela. "Like to join me out by the corral, Angela?"

"I've been waiting for better than a week for you to ask me!" She smiled and quickly set the book aside. As they stepped off the porch she reached for his hand and held tightly as they walked across to the rail fence around the corral. They stopped and faced each other. The moon was two days short of being a full moon and its brightness spread across the land illuminating everything with a soft, cream colored light. She turned and suddenly she was in his arms, their lips together, her urgency reflected by the strength of her kiss.

"Oh, Tom, how I miss you holding me, kissing me," she said when they finally separated. "Don't let me go, Tom. Ever."

"Angela, we know that can't happen. I haven't made it any easier for either of us. I do want to hold you and I . . . I yearn for your lips on mine . . . I shouldn't be doing this and I know it. I have to be careful of my feelings for you and I guess I'm not being careful enough. It would be so easy, Angela . . ."

"It's what I want, Tom."

"I know and that makes it even more difficult. It's like I'm standing at the edge of a cliff; I can either move back toward safety, toward sanity, or I can just let myself fall forward effortlessly. It would be so easy to let go and fall . . ."

"I think I've already fallen, Tom. I want you to join me."

"Angela, regardless how badly I may want to, you and I both know that's not possible."

* * *

New York City

Clarence DePallin sat in the large leather chair where he could see who entered the exclusive men's club. Almost hidden among the buildings that were beginning to reach for the sky in the center of the city, its main entrance was carefully manned by a uniformed doorman who amiably declined admittance to those gentlemen who were non-members. DePallin liked it here; many of the city's influential men hob-knobbed in the comfortable lushness and exaggerated splendor. The atmosphere always smelled of carefully maintained leather, freshly waxed wood, quality whiskey and smoke from expensive Cuban cigars, the fragrances of wealth. Voices were never raised, but rather they were obscured by strategically placed potted palm trees and the background murmur of contented conversation. It was a place where extremely private conversations could and did take place.

DePallin saw Ulysses Thaddeus McGarnet as he came in, handed his top hat and overcoat to the doorman. The steel magnet let his eyes sweep across the room quickly nodding very slightly when he saw DePallin.

DePallin stood and shook the man's hand. "Mister McGarnet. I'm glad you could make it."

McGarnet dropped into the leather armchair next to DePallin. "Make it fast, DePallin."

"Soon as John and Sanford are here."

"You can bet they aren't busting their butts hurrying." McGarnet grumbled.

DePallin nodded as he acknowledged the railroad man's entrance at that very moment. "Here's John."

McGarnet looked at this gold pocket watch. "Well, that shit-kicking Texas cowboy has four goddamn minutes."

Ambrose walked over with his heavy, faltering footsteps that he claimed to have had since his early days on the railroad, before he came to power through dint of political aptitude and ruthless management that propelled him up the organization ladder. "Mister McGarnet. DePallin. Sanford here yet?"

"Should be here any minute," DePallin said.

414

"What's this all about, DePallin?"

"Wait 'till Sanford gets here."

Sanford Parker ambled in through the front door looking as far out of place as one could be: blue denim pants, a western-cut light tan shirt, cowboy boots and a fringed leather coat topped with a western style Stetson. Heads turned and a low buzz filled the usually polite level of conversation.

"Couldn't he make himself a little more conspicuous?" McGarnet asked sarcastically.

"Wants everyone to know he's from Texas . . ." John Ambrose muttered, "as if you couldn't tell anyway, soon as he opens his mouth."

Parker spotted the three, waved and sauntered across the room to join them. He glanced around the room as he settled into the waiting chair. "'Bout as fancy as a high-class Mexican whore-house." His high, scratchy voice penetrated the low murmur of conversation like a sheep's bleating. "Been here long? I need me a whiskey to wash this New York dust down." He glanced around the room, then looked at DePallin. "What do you have to do to get some dammed service in here?"

"We can take care of that later, Sanford."

"If you say so, boss." Parker sat back in the chair stroking the fine leather. "What's on your mind?" He placed his Stetson carefully on his knee.

"Okay, let's keep our voices down." DePallin urged the three others to move in a little closer. "I have some recent news from our man in the house." He looked around to make sure the others were following his cryptic reference. Heads nodded. "Big Ted is expecting company while he's camping in California." He looked at the others and received head nods again. "An important man in Panama politics, political leader of the revolutionaries."

He saw three different expressions in response to his announcement. Sanford Parker appeared impassive; DePallin thought the Texan really didn't understand the ramifications. Ulysses McGarnet nodded slowly, his expression connoting immediate understanding. John Ambrose frowned, his mind running through the possible implications.

"So? We got another crazy Central American revolutionary who wants to pow-wow with Big Ted. So what?" Parker bleated.

McGarnet stared at the Texan with obvious disgust. "How did you ever get so damn rich, *cowboy*, with the brain of a grasshopper?"

"Come now, *Mister* McGarnet, no need to get nasty!" Sanford Parker started getting out of his chair;, his raised voice caused heads to turn their way again.

"Sit down, Parker and shut your trap!" DePallin said softly and the Texan complied. "What it means, in case you are unable to grasp the significance, is that the whole assassination will look like the Panamanians had a hand in it. The Panamanian revolutionary wants to talk with Big Ted. Talks do not satisfy the Panamanian's demands. A Panamanian assassin shoots Big Ted. Big Ted's security people say that the Panamanian signaled the assassin. No one wants to do business with these back-shooters. Canal won't go through Panama; it will be built through Nicaragua. Guaranteed."

"How do you know for sure that the security people will do what you just said?" McGarnet asked.

DePallin smiled, "Because I just recently got one of my hand-picked men on the security detail. Corporal John London."

"How did you manage that?" asked John Ambrose.

"Pulled a few strings, called in a few political *promises*. I've known Corporal London since he was a child. He's ambitious. He's from Penacook, same as me. I've already talked to him. He'll do exactly what I tell him."

"Well goddamnit, DePallin!" It was McGarnet. "We all agreed on a plan! You know better than to make changes without discussing them with us."

"Yeah! This guy London could go blabbing off at the mouth, no telling what he might say!" Parker whined, sensing an opportunity to strike back at the obnoxious congressman.

"Wait a minute." It was John Ambrose. "I think we better listen to Clarence here. I think there's some merit in starting the rumor, like he said, that the Panamanians had planned the assassination in case their talks with Big Ted failed. We don't even have to know what the meeting is going to be about. We don't care. Panama takes the blame and they get cut out of the canal deal for good."

"Wait a minute, now! How come all of a sudden, *Clarence* is the only one that has any brains?" Parker complained. "How come he's the only one we listen to?"

"I can't believe this is coming from the one who wanted to do the job in the middle of the Arizona desert!" DePallin muttered to no one in particular but saw the quiet affirming nods from McGarnet and Ambrose.

"So, is that all? That's the reason we spent two days getting her?" It was Parker once again, his nasal voice carrying across the room and again heads turned with looks of obvious censure.

"Parker, shut your goddamn mouth, now!" DePallin ordered none too politely, his voice low and menacing.

"Who made you the boss?" Parker challenged.

DePallin shook his head in frustration. Parker's behavior was drawing unnecessary attention to the foursome and men seated in the room would tend to remember faces associated with the ungentlemanly behavior. "Parker, if you want to leave and head back to Texas, I'm sure we finish up without you."

"Well now, ain't you the stiff necked trail boss. No thanks, *Boss*. I reckon I know my place and I'll just let you *gentlemen* carry on lest I say something that might embarrass you." He sat back in the chair, crossed his arms and stared at the other three men.

"Okay, we have a problem that we need to talk about." DePallin lowered his own voice so that the others had to lean in to hear. "Dunsworth. Our attorney Alexander Dunsworth has become a big problem."

CHAPTER 36

The San Francisco Police Department was faced with a particularly difficult situation. Someone had shot a 68 year old gentleman by the name of Oliver Perkins with a Remington .41 caliber Derringer in the lounge of the Franciscan Hotel. From a distance of less than eight feet the single slug had gone through the man's heart and lodged in his spine, killing him nearly instantly. The weapon was found at the scene in plain sight resting on the top of one of the small round tables that dotted the floor of the lounge.

There were two suspects in the shooting and one witness. Each of the two suspects blamed the shooting on the other person. The witness backed up the story of the female suspect, Miss Sophia Jenkins. The other suspect, Alexander Dunsworth, was a successful San Francisco attorney.

Miss Jenkins claimed that Dunsworth had entered the lounge with the intention of frightening or perhaps shooting her, that he had pulled the gun and pointed it at the witness, Phillip Goode, when he tried to intervene. She said the hotel employee, Oliver Perkins, entered the room; Dunsworth swung his weapon toward Perkins and when she tried to brush his arm from that direction, he had pulled the trigger and killed Perkins.

Mister Dunsworth laughed at the lady's attempt to shove the blame off onto him. He stated he had entered the lounge simply to have a late night drink. When he attempted to make polite conversation with a single female sitting alone in a booth, the bartender, Phillip Goode, attempted to intervene. The woman, Sophia Jenkins, had pulled the Derringer, obviously a woman's weapon, from her handbag and pointed it in confusion first at Goode, then at Perkins when he entered the lounge. Dunsworth grabbed at the pistol but was unable to prevent Jenkins from pulling the trigger and fatally wounding Goode.

The police were caught in the middle: a respected attorney's statement sworn on the Holy Bible versus a bartender and a *lady of the night,* as they glibly put it, who both swore their statements were true, even placing their hand on the Holy Bible the police provided.

All of this was stimulating grist for the San Francisco Chronicle and ran on the front page for almost a week while the two sat in the San Francisco jail. According to the police, they were also investigating other *disassociated criminal incidents* that one or the other, or maybe both, had possibly been involved with, including the recent murder of Alexander Dunsworth's wife, Nelle Dunsworth and the recent murder of Ramsfeld Jenkins, Miss Sophia Jenkins' brother. Ramsfeld Jenkins had been killed at the same time as his two law partners and all three bodies had been incinerated in a purposely set fire.

*   *   *

Clarence DePallin had seen the headlines on the Chronicle when he walked by the newsstand near his Washington DC office. He'd purchased the paper and quickly took it to his office, locked the door and read it completely.

The police investigating Dunsworth! How far would they have to dig before they found something with the names of the eastern investors? What happens if Dunsworth starts to bargain in exchange for lenient treatment? Is that why he removed his name from the Nicaragua property deed? How could they make sure Dunsworth didn't talk about things that could unravel the plan?

He had felt the tightening sensation in his chest as he realized the possibilities. That's when he had called for the meeting. Now the other three men knew and they could share the concern with him.

"We've got to shut him up some way." John Ambrose stated quietly. "He's the direct link to us. If he goes down, he'll take us with him."

"That damn attorney! Got the brains of a Mexican piss ant!" Sanford Parker exclaimed in his nasally voice.

"Yeah, thanks. That helps a lot cowboy." McGarnet murmured sarcastically then turned his attention to the other two. "Do we know anyone out there who could take care of Dunsworth?"

"Be pretty tricky; him being in jail." Ambrose muttered.

"But it can be done." McGarnet stated. "Been done before."

"What if we got him out on bail?" DePallin wondered out loud.

"Then what?" Sanford ventured.

DePallin smiled. "Then we get rid of him."

There were several moments of silence as the men considered the idea.

"Might work. We'd lose our bail bond money . . ." Ambrose muttered.

"Small loss compared to everything else." DePallin said quietly.

They sat there; the only sounds were the low buzz of gentlemanly conversation in the room, the occasional clink of a glass.

"Means one of us would have to go out there, assumed name and all, to bail him out. Then . . ." McGarnet said.

"Then we get rid of him. Gun, knife, dynamite, rope, fall off a cliff . . . who cares how we do it. Take him out somewhere where people don't usually go, put a pistol to his head and pull the trigger. Bam! Troubles are all over." It was Sanford and the three others looked at him.

"Are you volunteering, Sanford?" DePallin asked.

There were several long moments of silence. Finally Sanford spoke. "I'll do it if no one else will. Be like shooting a coyote or putting down a lame horse."

"It will take some fancy maneuvering to bail him out." Ambrose offered quietly.

"I'll be his long lost cousin from Texas."

"What about the woman?" Ambrose asked.

"Now, I ain't killing the woman. I reckon I draw the line there." Sanford stated flatly, shaking his head for emphasis.

The four men sat quietly for a long time. This was headed where they had hoped it would not go: actions that directly involved them. It was so much easier to pay someone to do the difficult or illegal or dirty work. Asking someone to kill another person was another thing. They had paid Dunsworth to be the go-between for them. Their hands were still clean—well mostly clean—but they wouldn't stay that way when Dunsworth started talking to the police. The woman was an unknown factor and, according to the paper, possibly a prostitute. Her level of credibility with the police would be pretty low.

Finally DePallin spoke up, "Leave the woman alone. We've just got to take the risk that she doesn't know anything." He faced Sanford Parker. "You sure you want to do this, Parker? You're taking a lot of risk."

"I don't relish doing it, if that's your question. I'll do it so that nothing else happens that can come down around our necks."

DePallin looked around the faces. "Anyone have any comments?"

There was silence.

"Okay, Sanford. You just drew the low card. How soon can you get out there?"

*　　*　　*

Campsite on the Kings River

Thomas and Frank had ridden hard to get to their next project on the Kings River. Although the water level had fallen considerably since the storm, it was quite easy to see the high water marks on the river banks and where the water had flowed out onto the flatland of the valley. The canyon that held the main river was quite narrow at places.

"The Spaniards called the river *Rio de los Santos Reyes*—River of the Holy Kings." Frank explained. "It has several branches both upstream from where we are and downstream. Some provide water into the river and some take water from the river. It's quite a complicated watershed."

They spent days taking measurements and making sketches of possible locations for dams.

"This right across here would be my choice, if it were mine to make." Frank pointed across an expanse with the river several hundred feet below.

Thomas looked down. "Take a mighty high dam, Frank. Think we could build something that big?"

"Perhaps not today but in ten, fifteen, twenty years, yes. New technology, new tools, new materials, it's all coming, Thomas, and when it does, lots of things will change. Just like they will in your business as new building construction materials, and new tools are introduced. Your customer's needs will be different and if you don't bend to meet them, you'll go out of business."

Thomas sat back and thought for several minutes. "So, the idea of the Gordons moving from cattle to citrus farming . . . you think that's a good idea?"

"Absolutely! They're a small-time cattle ranch. In ten years their ranch will be just an expensive hobby. They couldn't keep up with the rancher with eastern financial backing who has ten thousand head of cattle on twenty-thousand acres of grazing land. They'll not even depend on grazing land, eventually; they'll buy feed and have it brought in. It'll be cheaper; they can control what their cattle eat and how much fat they put on; that will control the price they sell it for. The Gordons will have their acreage making money for them. They'll be among the first to get into the citrus business in this area. They'll be pioneers in the field. They're already thinking about what to do during a hard freeze, how they would water their orchard, what kind of diseases their trees may have and how to control them, how many people it takes to handle the growing season and how many during the picking season, where and how they market their crops. It'd be exciting to be part of it!"

"It's just hard for me to think ahead that far, Frank."

"Well, I think you do in your own business. You're just not aware that's what you're doing when you look over new construction methods and materials when a salesman calls on you to show you his company's latest technology. Your mind says *hey, that'd save us so many hours when we're doing this or that*, or *that would make a lot neater or easier or safer or better or cheaper or stronger or whatever* . . . that's the way you change to keep up. I've watched you, Thomas."

"Guess you're right. Just never thought of it in those terms."

"You're no different than the Gordon's. You don't have to have an engineering degree to think, Thomas."

Thomas nodded. *I think ahead but I'm not aware that I'm doing it. What about Angela and me? The future. Why and how . . .*

Frank interrupted his thoughts. "Looks like I hit a nerve, Thomas. I'm sorry if I said something . . ."

Thomas shook his head. "Just got me thinking about . . . about other matters. Personal stuff that I've not been thinking about in the right way."

There was a long period of silence then Frank asked quietly, "About Angela?"

Thomas looked over at his friend. "I'd hoped it wasn't that obvious."

"She's quite obvious, Thomas."

Thomas remained silent for a while, somewhat embarrassed by the revelation that his relationship with Angela was that noticeable. "It just started as a friendship and . . ." the words wouldn't come.

"Have you . . ."

Thomas could guess what his friend was asking. "No. I've been careful to not let it get that far. Sometimes it's been very difficult."

"I can imagine. She's grown to be very pretty."

"Yes, she has."

"Does Amanda know anything?"

"I don't think so. We've talked about Angela a few times. I think she has wondered from time to time . . ."

"Thomas, I know she has. She's talked to me about your trips to the ranch and to visit with your Indian friend. She has tried very hard to trust and believe in you."

Thomas shook his head. "I feel like such a fool. I know that Amanda loves me more than anything and here I am yearning for the company of a woman several years younger than me . . ."

"Angela is very pretty, Thomas. It would be quite easy for any man to feel as you do."

*   *   *

San Francisco

Alexander Dunsworth sat on the bed in the jail cell. He'd been there nine days so far. The grand jury had met and he was formally charged with the murder of Oliver Perkins. A trial date had yet to be set. He had not posted bond; almost everything he owned was now mortgaged to purchase the Nicaragua property. He had been allowed to hire an attorney and he'd gone outside of the law firm he worked for, selecting instead an attorney he had once worked with named Patrick Kirkpatrick. The two had talked and Dunsworth reiterated the same story he had told the police. When he asked Kirkpatrick what was happening with Sophia Jenkins, he replied that she was also being charged as an accessory to murder but separate from him.

Dunsworth went over his carefully crafted story, even demonstrated how he had unsuccessfully tried to rip the Derringer from Sophia's hand. The more he told the story, the more he began to believe it himself. He must have left the Derringer at Sophia's house at one time or another. After Sophia left, he began searching for new female companionship. He didn't recognize Sophia in the dark shadows of the lounge. Only when she rose up with the Derringer in her hand did he recognize who she was. It began to make sense in his head. The fabric of the story began to take cohesive shape and texture. He could feel it. He could relive it. He could experience again the emotions of surprise, fear, desperation and finally realization that a man had been killed before his very eyes.

He repeated the sequence to himself, adding detail of those things peripheral to the small space he had occupied. He saw the bartender advancing. He envisioned the placement of the round tables. He remembered exactly how the deskman, Oliver Perkins, had been dressed, the surprised look on his face when the bullet struck him. It was a good story. He would work on appropriate facial expressions to use during his practices. A jury would hear his narration of the details, would themselves experience his fear and desperation.

He practiced the story, carefully tuning it here and there, making minor changes in the inflection of his voice. He didn't want it to come across as rehearsed, practiced. It needed to sound somewhat nervous, reluctantly dragged from his memory as if telling someone about a nightmare dream. He practiced closing his eyes, even wiping an imaginary tear away. He ran his tongue nervously over his lips and bit his lower lip as if feeling the pain when the bullet struck the elderly gentleman. A good touch! A little more practice and he could sit in the box before his peers and mold them like clay. And Sophia? She would probably get ten years for manslaughter. When she got out, he would be somewhere far away, living like the Vanderbilts, the Morgans and the Carnegies.

* * *

In another wing of the jail, cells were provided for the relatively few women that ended up waiting for the legal system to either set them free or move them to prison. Among those woman, prostitutes, vagrants, shoplifters, some with charges of battery, sat Sophia Jenkins. She was like a gem among ordinary rocks. Her dress spoke of money, her hair of careful attention. Her voice, however, entertained the girls as Sophia chose to call them, with ribald humor and bawdy one-liners. In spite of her obvious culture, they liked this salty woman who sat among them accused of murder.

Sophia had hired an attorney also, a young man she had known a number of years who was at the legal firm where she had at one time worked. Martin August was in his late-twenties, tall, slim and quite attractive; Sophia's cell mates nearly swooned when he first showed up.

He listened carefully to her story, taking numerous notes, asking clarifying questions now and then. She provided the name of the single witness to the killing, Phillip Goode. He raised his eyebrows when she told him of her visit from the man called Charles DeFoe and his claims that Dunsworth had killed his own wife, as well as the three Los Angeles attorneys. She told him everything she could remember Dunsworth ever telling her, including the names of the east coast investors. He listened as she spelled out everything she knew about the man. When she was finally finished, he looked across the table at her and smiled.

"Miss Jenkins, I don't believe we have anything to worry about." He got up from his chair. "I need to talk to some people and do a little detective work. This is Saturday. I'll see you again not later than next Wednesday; that would be the twenty-ninth."

*   *   *

When the train arrived in San Francisco, Thomas O'Reiley stepped onto the platform only a few steps behind the tall, skinny man dressed in western style clothing complete with riding boots and a tall gray Stetson, a clothing style most city-folks would refrain from wearing and would simply call *cowboy clothes*. Thomas only noticed him because of this unusual clothing.

Frank Barnwell had stayed behind to complete the figures and sketches he would need to present his report to the state water commission. Thomas had thought a lot about the discussion the two men had regarding the delicate situation between Angela and him. His friend's last words to him as he boarded the train were: "Don't do anything you'll regret, Thomas."

I may have already done something I shall regret, Thomas thought as he hailed a carriage. It took about thirty minutes for the driver to reach Thomas's house. It looked so nice from the street, even if the few trees were beginning to lose their summer green and would soon be turning brown and dropping for the winter. Amanda had the lights on inside glistening through the windows, giving the home a warm, welcoming look. The sun would set in just a few minutes and the San Francisco air would turn cool and damp. *A fire in the office tonight and a glass of wine,* he thought, *with Amanda.*

*   *   *

425

Sanford Parker had taken a hired carriage to the Twin Peaks Hotel, checked in at the front desk and arranged to have a rented carriage delivered to the hotel for his use. He would be in San Francisco for about three days, he said. He was using the name Francis J. Watson, from Oklahoma City.

That evening Parker took the carriage into town and located the main jail. From there he toured the city looking over the waterfronts, the vast Army Presidio, the rugged Pacific coast with the Cliff House and lastly the Twin Peaks area filled with dense, overpowering woods. He took the carriage from the Twin Peaks back to the jail. The route was fairly straight forward. His plan for the next day was taking shape.

He found a saloon in the Tenderloin, parked the carriage a few blocks away and walked to the noisy saloon. Although the clientele was different than the saloons in Texas, the rest was familiar. The long mirrored bar down one side, round tables scattered across the rest of the space. This saloon had a small stage at one end and a piano player was trying to keep the music flowing with the mood of the crowd. A few women, clad in gaudy attire that emphasized the best parts of their well endowed figures, wove slowly among the men striking up conversations, telling jokes and selling drinks.

Parker sidled up to the bar and ordered a whiskey neat. When it arrived he turned to face the noisy collection of men seated at the tables. When one of the women looked his way, he lifted his head in a come here motion. She responded quickly and stood near his side, hand on hip.

"What can I do for you, mister?" she asked in a sultry voice.

Parker let his eyes roam over her figure. "What's your name?"

"Josephine. What's yours?"

"Francis." The name popped out without Parker giving it any thought.

She tittered quietly. "That's a girl's name, isn't it?"

"Not where I come from."

"And where would that be?"

Parker allowed himself a broad smile. "Oklahoma City."

"Yeah? Will you buy me a drink, *Francis*?"

Parker slipped his arm around her small waist and drew her closer. "Sure, *Josephine*, why not?"

*   *   *

When the sun came in through the hotel room windows the next morning, *Josephine* was gone from the rumpled bed as he knew she would be. That was okay. He checked where he had carefully concealed his money and the pistol; they hadn't been disturbed. He chuckled. He wasn't a greenhorn when it came to dealing with prostitutes. And besides, he hadn't been so intoxicated that he had not experienced pleasure from what *Josephine* was doing, at least until he'd drifted off to sleep a few hours before the sunlight beamed through the window.

He got up, took a bath and shaved, languishing away the morning hours. He'd eat a late breakfast at the hotel before his day began.

*   *   *

Thomas awoke as the sun streamed in through the bedroom windows. Amanda was beside him on her side with her face toward him. She was still asleep and Thomas allowed his eyes to feast on the simple beauty beside him. Her face was relaxed and her lips formed a satisfied smile. Her skin, unblemished, had no lines or creases and was a healthy cream color only slightly tanned. Her hair, a sort of golden-red was luxurious, full and shiny and falling across her shoulder and partially covering her neck. He could see the transition to the supple curvature of her breasts that were hidden by the delicate silk night gown that she had put on before they had finally decided to go to sleep.

She was beautiful and she loved him dearly, without reservation, honestly and fully. She could be completely herself when in his company and she was. There were no limits to her love for him; there was no part of herself she would not honestly and willingly share with him.

Intuitively Thomas knew all this without hesitation,. He had never had a reason to doubt. He asked himself, *what about my love for her? Am I as honest with my feelings, my wants and my needs, my love for her as she is with me? Have my feelings toward Angela affected my love for Amanda? Have I wounded the special and unique husband wife bond between us and would Amanda ever tell me if she sensed that I had?*

"I can hear you thinking my dear husband," she whispered softly, her eyes still closed. "I hope they are good thoughts."

Thomas smiled to himself. *She can read my mind. She knows me . . .* "They are very good thoughts, my beautiful wife," he whispered softly into her ear.

"Perhaps," she continued to whisper, "before our children awaken, we might continue what we started last night . . ."

"I believe that is an excellent idea."

*   *   *

The Gordon Ranch

It was late afternoon when Angela decided to saddle up her horse and take a ride out toward the northeast corner of the ranch. She liked it there; the summer golden grass-covered foothills were gently rolling and sparsely covered with small oak trees. The air was beginning to cool after the summer heat and much of the smoky, dusty haze that usually hung in the San Joaquin Valley had dissipated allowing the flat valley to spread out before her like a huge map. Far across the valley the horizon was broken by the bluish line of coastal mountains.

Angela needed a place to be by herself for a while to think about the inner commotion that was causing her nights to be spent in sleepless tossing and her days in restless and unfulfilling anxiety. It had all started while Thomas and Frank Barnwell had been at the ranch. *What's happening to me,* she wondered. *I thought I knew what I wanted and where I wanted to be. Why all of a sudden am I feeling this way?*

The questions and thoughts circulated like an endless stream of chatter in her mind. She felt torn and even a sense of betrayal when she allowed her thoughts to migrate beyond the familiar settings she had established long ago.

Why did Frank have to come here? Why didn't he start his project somewhere else? Why do I feel this way about him?

She didn't want to allow herself to think about him. She had forgotten, after so many years, how handsome and sophisticated he was; how knowledgeable and articulate he could be. She had forgotten his expressiveness, the dark blue eyes, his face with the almost-hidden smile that seemed ready to burst out at any moment, the hair carefully combed in the most recent stylish manner.

Why had my heart beat so hard when I first saw him after all these years? Why had I tried so hard to keep my feelings for Tom from changing? Had they?

She loved Thomas—she knew that beyond any doubt. But . . . suddenly something was different. Thomas had been exciting in a strange, very young woman sort of way, an adventure, perhaps, that a young lady needed to experience to prepare for *real life* or even *real love.*

Haven't I felt this way about Thomas? Haven't I felt that my love for him was forever?

She knew very little about Frank Barnwell, other than he had recently left a partnership with Thomas and his father-in-law to join the state of California's search for a way to better manage it supply of water. *Did he already have woman friends? Was he already in love, perhaps waiting for marriage? Would he even be interested in me?*

These painful thoughts and questions had made one thing perfectly clear. Thomas had been candid regarding his anguish and confusion about their relationship. It could never go anywhere further than where it was and perhaps that was already too far.

The thoughts brought tears and a sense of loneliness she hadn't experienced for years.

CHAPTER 37

<u>Friday, October 31, 1902, San Francisco</u>

Sanford Porter was dressed in the conventional cut business suit that he had brought with him from Texas. He hardly ever wore the suit, though his wife Jennette insisted that he have it *just in case*. Black pants, black shoes, high buttoned waist coat, white shirt with a stiff collar and a business-like four-in-hand. A black overcoat and a gray Homburg completed the attire. Porter looked at himself in the large oval mirror, gave the waist coat a little tug and nodded in satisfaction. In spite of his dislike of the suit, he felt he cut a fairly handsome figure that people would remember. And that was exactly what he wanted.

He searched within his suitcase and found the small packet of papers prepared by a friend. They appeared authentic on letterhead stationery, complete with county and state seals and signatures. It specified that he, *Francis J. Watson of Oklahoma City, Oklahoma was a citizen in good standing and had placed fifty-thousand dollars in trust at the Southern Bank of Oklahoma for the express purpose of paying the required amount of bail bond to release Alexander Dunsworth from the San Francisco Metropolitan Jail into his custody until the date of his trial.*

Of course, they were all forged papers and there was no money in trust and he wasn't Francis J. Watson.

He removed the pistol from its hiding place. It was a unique firearm in that it had started as a Colt revolver. Porter had the barrel shortened to a mere three and a half inches and the pistol grip's size and shape customized to fit Jennette hand shortly after they were married. She had wanted a weapon she could use in self defense in the wild parts of western Texas. The modified pistol was more accurate than a Derringer and certainly less bulky than a full sized Colt. She had never even fired the pistol and Porter eventually retrieved it for his own use when traveling. He had fired the pistol enough times to know its fearsome kick and middling accuracy. He slipped shells into each of the six cartridge chambers, spun the cylinder, liking the metal to metal sound it made. He had made sure there was a simple but secure hiding place for the pistol under the carriage seat.

It was early evening when he got into the carriage, slipped the pistol under the seat and snapped the reins to put the carriage into motion. There was a very light drizzle in the air, more like a heavy fog than a rain. He was glad he had brought along his overcoat. It took him about twenty minutes to reach the San Francisco Metropolitan Jail and turn the carriage over to the livery. He walked to the broad steps in front and was soon inside speaking to the Police Sergeant behind the desk.

"I've looked over your papers sir, and everything seems to be entirely in order." The sergeant shuffled through the papers one more time and handed them back to Porter. "The bond has been set at forty-thousand dollars, Mister Watson. If you wish to make a draw against the trust fund specified in the letter, we'll accept that," he pointed, "at the cashier's window. In the meantime, we'll get Dunsworth ready to be released and bring him here to be turned over to your custody."

Porter nodded and said, "That will be fine."

Fifteen minutes later a thinner and somewhat dazed Alexander Dunsworth was led into the waiting room. He looked quizzically at Porter.

"Alexander, you most likely don't remember me. I'm your second cousin on your daddy's side, Francis J. Watson from Oklahoma City." He put out his hand and Dunsworth shook it hesitantly. "I heard about your situation here in San Francisco and thought that you could probably use some help, even if it was only paying the bail bond so you could enjoy your freedom until the trial."

"Well, I . . ." Dunsworth stammered.

Porter cut him off with a nonchalant wave of his hand. "We'll talk about it later. Let's be off, Alex. Some good dinner and a drink will do wonders to freshen your outlook. I have a carriage waiting." He turned and waved at the Police Sergeant as he steered Dunsworth through the doors and into the evening, saying in a very quiet voice, "Just don't say anything until we're in the carriage."

Dunsworth simply nodded and followed the stranger.

In less than five minutes they were in the carriage and Porter had pulled it onto the main thoroughfare. Dunsworth had said nothing until then.

"Who in the hell are you?" he finally asked. "I don't have any cousins, first, second or whatever by the name of Watson."

"You do now." Porter smiled. "At least for a while." He looked at the attorney. "You don't know me, do you?"

"I haven't the slightest idea who you are."

Porter laughed. "Does the name Porter ring a bell? Sanford Porter?"

"Porter?" A few seconds went by before Dunsworth's chin dropped in astonishment. "Sanford Porter? From Texas?"

"That's the one."

"Why . . ."

"We met several days ago and decided that you shouldn't be sitting in jail. I volunteered to come out here and get you out."

"But . . . why? I don't . . ."

Porter held up his hand. "Enough questions. How about you and me stop and have a drink? I'm drier than a sun baked horned toad in August."

Porter had already spotted a saloon on his previous drive around town and within minutes they were tied up in front and sitting inside at a small table. The bartender poured two whiskeys and brought them to the table.

Porter raised his in salute. "Well, here's to the canal going through Nicaragua."

Dunsworth nodded, lifted his glass; they touched and both men drank the shot of whiskey in a single gulp.

"DePallin got the package of papers you sent him." Porter looked up, signaled the bartender for another round. "Said they looked very good." He smiled, "pretty fancy with all them seals and signatures and all!"

Dunsworth nodded. "That's legal Spanish. Damned hard to read and understand."

"Yeah, that's what DePallin said. He did manage to notice that you had removed your name as one of the partners. He was a wondering why you did that." He leaned back as the bartender delivered the second round of drinks. "In fact, we were all a wondering."

Dunsworth had not expected this to come up in a one-on-one meeting. He looked at the mirror behind the bar and put on his best serious lawyer face as the fabrication formed quickly in his mind. "Well, actually, it was pretty simple. When I researched the Nicaraguan laws I found out that in cases of this type—large land transactions—there is a legal limit on the number of partners. This is done to prevent large groups of investors from crowding out the small investor, sort of their version of *spreading the wealth*. Believe it or not, four investors is the maximum number. Beyond that, the property must actually be sub-divided between groups of investors of equal size, or if that is not possible, the land itself must be spread among the investors in equal parcels. It's all quite complicated. It would take a long time and enormous legal and court costs, to divide a section of property as large as that one into five individual parcels of land of equal value. I simply removed myself as one of the partners and assumed that after the sale the remaining four—you four—would each share a portion of the proceeds with me." He glanced at Porter, his face serious. "I hope I have not assumed too much." His quickly invented argument sounded awfully flimsy and it was but he smiled and finished, "It was that simple, or complex, depending how you look at it."

Porter looked at him for a long time. "Nicaraguan law?"

"Yeah," Dunsworth nodded, "based on an archaic Spanish legal system. It's very complicated."

Porter shook his head as if in amazement. "Well, here's to it." He raised his glass and swallowed the liquor. Dunsworth followed and signaled the bartender for a third round.

"God, this stuff tastes good after drinking that stinking jail water!"

Porter nodded. One more and Dunsworth wouldn't know what hit him. The bartender sat the glasses down and swept up the empties.

The two men sat for another fifteen minutes making small talk. The saloon began to fill with regular patrons and the noise level rose. Porter used the noise and growing crowd of people as a reason to exit.

"Getting too crowded for me, Alex. What do you say we find a place to have dinner and a few more drinks?"

"Sounds good! That jail slop is bad enough to make a dog puke." He tipped his glass back, draining the last vestige of whiskey before he slammed the shot glass down. "Let's go!"

They got into the carriage and Porter clucked the horse into action. Dunsworth leaned back, relaxed and smiling. "I was just thinking about poor old Sophia. She's still in jail. Loving the wonderful accommodations and food, I'm sure." He chuckled to himself.

433

Porter steered the carriage toward Twin Peaks. Dusk had fallen and darkness would follow in another fifteen or twenty minutes. It was a new moon tonight; darkness would be complete. The air had turned much cooler and people on the sidewalks had turned up their collars against the cold. He turned onto Market Street which eventually became Portola Drive heading south past Twin Peaks.

"Where we headed?" Dunsworth asked, his head rolling as he spoke.

"Place I know where the food is great, the women are beautiful and the liquor is cheap."

"Sounds like my kind of place," Dunsworth muttered.

They continued a short distance past Twin Peaks, then turned west and began to climb the winding dirt road into the woods. Darkness began to close in around them.

"Hope you know how to get back out of here," Dunsworth said nervously.

"You don't have to worry about that, Alex. Just enjoy the ride. We'll be there in just a few minutes."

"Never been back here before." He was swiveling his head about, straining to see where they were. "You sure this is the place?"

"Absolutely certain." Porter found a wide spot where he could turn the carriage around. "See? Here's where we get off, Alex. Just a short walk from here."

"I don't see anyone else." Dunsworth stared into the darkness. "You sure you have the right place?"

"There's several different ways to get here. Come on, let's go."

Alexander Dunsworth stepped down from the carriage and stood rather unsteadily. "Damn dark here, Porter." He took a step, nearly fell and swore loudly as his foot got tangled in a root.

"Right up that path, Alex. Believe me, you'll really like it here."

Dunsworth struggled to not fall in the darkness. Tree roots wound across the surface of the ground and rocks protruded among them; branches swept across their faces. The soil was slippery and the attorney was laboring hard. "How much further?" he gasped.

"I think we're almost there," Porter said as he pulled the pistol from his pocket, cocked it quietly behind his back. Dunsworth was only a few feet ahead of him as he pointed the pistol at the back of his head. He pulled the trigger and the gun erupted, spewing an orange flash that lit the surrounding trees for an instant. The heavy slug hit Dunsworth in the hollow at the base of his skull, tore through his spinal cord and exited as it created a huge bloody crater where his nose had once been. He fell forward without a sound as the echo of the shot continued to ricochet among the hills. Porter stood over the still body, nudged it once with the toe of his shoe. The attorney was dead.

He turned quickly and hurried back to the carriage, turned it around and within minutes was going north on Portola Drive. Thirty minutes later he was in his hotel room, having slipped in unnoticed through a rear entrance. He poured himself a shot of whiskey, gulped it and poured another. *Just like putting down a lame horse.*

He thought he'd take a bath then maybe go out for a few drinks and see if he could find Josephine again.

* * *

Thomas O'Reiley sat in the deep leather chair in the sun room and watched the sun come up and lighten the city. Wisps of fog blew up and down the streets and he heard the clang of the cable car as it crossed a major intersection not far away. He unfolded the Chronicle and spread it across his lap, took a sip of the scalding hot coffee from the cup in his desk. Amanda was still asleep in the bedroom and the children, though awake, were still in their rooms. Xaing was in the kitchen getting the menu set for the day and beginning preparation of breakfast. Saturday mornings had become special for the family and one of the luxuries was a special late morning breakfast.

Thomas studied the headlines on the front page of the paper; mostly national or international news. The paper was still covering the terrible eruption of the Santa Maria volcano in Guatemala on October 25th that had killed some six thousand people. Located in the southwestern Guatemalan mountains, the twelve thousand foot tall volcano had erupted earlier in the year with a loss of two thousand lives. Already, some were speculating that Nicaragua, separated from Guatemala by Honduras, might suffer similar earthquakes and thus raised the question: was Nicaragua a geologically safe country through which an inter-ocean canal should be constructed?

Thomas turned the page to more local news and was startled by the article headlined: **Local Attorney Found Slain**.

The short article spelled out in some detail the location of the murder and stated that there were no witnesses. Alexander Dunsworth had been

435

released from jail on a bond earlier that afternoon. It went on to cover the case against Dunsworth awaiting trial and that the bail bond had been covered by a man named Francis J. Watson of Oklahoma City. Police were looking for the man for questioning. He was described as about five feet eleven inches tall, weighing about one hundred seventy pounds, reddish-brown hair. When he was last seen in the company of Dunsworth, he was wearing a black business suit.

Thomas sat back and stared out the windows. Strange that Dunsworth's name should pop up again. He remembered the talk he had with Sheriff McGee regarding the murder of Dunsworth's wife, the murder that Dunsworth had blamed on Beck Weston. So someone had wanted him dead. But why? Surely not because of that murder. Beck, as far as he knew, was still in hiding at the Gordon's ranch. Maybe he needed to take a day off and visit with the sheriff again. And what about Santiago's assertion that Dunsworth had met with an assassin? What the hell was that about?

* * *

Sophia Jenkins also got the news of Dunsworth's death from the newspaper. The jailer had brought the paper to her cell after reading it; he had recognized the name and realized the connection with Jenkins. She read the article with shaking hands, forcing herself to remember this was the man who had lied under oath about the murder of Oliver Perkins and tried to shift the blame onto her. *So who would want him dead? Who would pay the bail bond and then kill him? And why?*

Charles DeFoe had said that Dunsworth had murdered the three attorney's, including her brother. *A possible connection there.* She sensed that Dunsworth had cheated the four east coast investors through fraudulent deeds. *Another possible connection.* There was also the case involving Dunsworth's wife, Nelle. When she counted the number of persons whose murders could be linked to Dunsworth she was startled. *Five, at least!*

Later in the day she had a visit from Martin August, her attorney. He was smiling when they sat together in the tiny visiting room.

"Miss Jenkins," he began, "I know you've heard about Alexander Dunsworth's murder. That, of course, closes the door on his case; you can't try a dead person for a crime." He paused, "In your case his death removes the prosecution's only witness; though I believe if the case had gone to trial, we could have torn holes in his testimony. So as the case

436

now stands the only other person remaining is our defense witness, Phillip Goode. There is no one to refute his testimony. I believe I can have this case dismissed in a week or less."

Sophia felt the tears of relief begin to well up and she pressed her hand against the young lawyer's hand. "How can I thank you, Martin? How can I ever thank you enough?"

*   *   *

Sanford Parker read the short article while reading the newspaper in bed. He had returned the evening before to the same saloon called *Marker Inn* in the Tenderloin where he quickly found *Josephine* again. It took little encouragement on his part to talk her into spending another night with him; after all, he willingly paid twice the usual amount of money and his amorous proclivities were not excessively weird or bizarre. She had left before the sun rose and he rolled over and went to sleep, waking only when the hotel's room service knocked at his door to deliver coffee and the newspaper.

By early afternoon he was at the train station, dressed once again in his western style clothes. With any luck, he would be back at the ranch in Texas in three days.

He'd stopped at the Western Union telegraph office and sent a simple message to DePallin:

LAME HORSE WAS PUT DOWN STOP PARKER

The hours went by slowly as the train made its way over to the broad San Joaquin Valley. The flat, featureless terrain rolled by mile after mile as Parker peered through the window. It seemed nearly as barren as the scrub land in western Texas. They crossed a few rivers and the train rolled steadily on, stopping for several minutes at some of the larger towns in the valley.

He was awakened as the porter announced that the next stop would be Visalia. Parker peered through the glass into the early evening gloom. The Sierra Nevada Mountains were barely visible much further to the east. *The mountains don't look so damn big to me. We got mountains taller than that in Texas.* As they stopped in Visalia, he remembered that their contact inside the government had told them that the President would stop in Visalia and get his horses and supplies from a rancher nearby. Parker noted the size of the town and the rustic appearance of its streets and buildings in the bleak late fall weather. *No better than some of the small towns in Texas.* He shook his head in incredulity. *Why in the hell would the President of the United States want to stop for several days in a place like this?*

He tipped his hat over his eyes, leaned back and went back to sleep.

*   *   *

Washington, D.C.

Clarence DePallin got the telegram when it was delivered to his office in Washington D.C. that Monday morning. The short message was straight and to the point: Alexander Dunsworth had been dealt with.

DePallin had to give the disgusting Texan credit; he did what he said he would do and another loose end was eliminated. He wondered briefly if there were any more loose ends waiting to ensnare them. The only possibility that came to mind was the assassin, El Culebra. He'd never met the man, in fact, as far as he knew, few people had met him. According to Dunsworth, one dealt only with the assassin's underlings. Well, they would be changing that soon enough because they were planning on a face-to-face meeting with El Culebra, probably in February.

DePallin rubbed his eyes wearily. Everything seemed to take far too long. Congress appeared to be dragging its feet, afraid to make a decision regarding the path of the canal. If he was the President, he thought, he'd put an end to this useless dilly-dallying, step in, make the decision for them and they could all go to hell.

Certainly, he thought, he *would* be President of the United States of America one day, one of the most powerful men in the world. The phrase sent a shiver up his spine, *one of the most powerful men.* He let his mind run with that thought for a while. How would *one of the most powerful men* exercise that power? How would it feel to have such power? How would other men react to that power? What would he do using that power while in office, to ensure that his name became part of history—to ensure there were portraits of him, statues of him, streets named after him, perhaps his name carved over the doors of important federal buildings, schools, universities. How would it feel to have a huge navy battleship named after him, or to have an engraved image of his countenance on one of the nation's large denomination bank notes?

It would feel good he decided, in fact, very good. And he would make it happen for the simple reason that power was for those few who were destined to know how to use it, control it and make it work for them. Power was for the elite, like him.

* * *

San Francisco

The Chronicle reported that George Pardee, the Republican candidate for Governor of California, had won in the general election by a very slim margin over the Democrat Franklin Lane, the Socialist Gideon Brower and the Prohibitionist Theodore Kanouse. Pardee won with a plurality of less than one percent.

Pardee had graduated from University of California at Berkley, had then attended the Cooper Medical College in San Francisco and had received his doctorate from the University of Leipzig in Germany.

Pardee had served one two-year term as Mayor of Oakland, California from 1893 to 1895.

CHAPTER 38

<u>Wednesday, November 19, 1902, San Filipe-Panama Province of Columbia</u>

Doctor Manuel Amador Guerrero and his wife of many years, Maria Ossa Escobar, had gone to bed shortly after the sun had set. Amador had blown out the solitary lantern in the bedroom and let the moonlight stream in through the single open window. The atmosphere was pleasant and slightly humid. Through their bedroom window they could hear the waves of the Gulf of Panama brushing against the shore. It was a peaceful sound that had lulled the couple to sleep for many years.

Doctor Amador Guerrero was having trouble getting to sleep tonight. In fact he had been experiencing sleepless nights for several weeks, much to Maria's concern. Amador was normally a patient man—at least to an extent. But this was stretching his patience beyond something that a man of his age should experience.

Where was the message from the United States? Had it been intercepted by the police and was he going to be dragged through their interrogation again? In spite of his encoded message to his contacts in the United States, he felt vulnerable. Had they even received it? How would they respond? And even more importantly, when would they respond?

He rolled over onto his side, hoping that the new position would let sleep come to him. He could hear the clock ticking in the other room, mocking his impatience. Another sound, nearly inaudible caught his attention. A footstep, perhaps? His eyes instantly opened and his hearing became heightened. Another. Yes, it was a footstep on the gravely-dirt that made up the walkway to his house. It was quiet now. He waited in anticipation. Police? *God protect me!*

A single quiet tap on the front door. *It's not the Police!* They wouldn't resort to a soft, single tap. He slipped out of bed quietly so as not to waken Maria and walked barefooted across the cool tile floor to the front door. He put his ear to the door. Nothing. No sound at all. Perhaps he had been imagining things; he was turning, ready to return to bed when the single tap repeated itself.

He returned to the door, quietly slipped the bolt and opened it a crack.

"Who is there?" he whispered.

"Señor Manuel Amador Guerrero?" The voice was that of a man's, a raspy whispering.

"Sí. I am Doctor Amador Guerrero."

"I am told to deliver this envelope to you." The corner of a large envelope came through the narrow space of the door. "Hurry, Señor. I must leave quickly."

Amador gripped the envelope and pulled it through. "Gracias," he whispered.

The man on the outside did not respond. Instead Amador heard the very soft footsteps retreating into the darkness. He shut the door and slid the bolt back into place.

Amador was torn. The man who had delivered the envelope had taken a great risk and Amador wanted badly to light a lantern to see what was inside the heavy envelope but he knew that would not be a good idea. Government spies were everywhere and a lighted lantern in a house at this time of night would ignite their curiosity requiring a visit, perhaps even including a demand to open the house to their investigation. No, he would have to wait until morning. Now he *knew* he would not sleep!

*   *   *

It was slightly after dawn when Amador crawled out of the bed leaving Maria to snooze comfortably in the extra space. He went into his office, drew the curtain across the single window, shut and locked the door. He hefted the large envelope in his hand; it was fairly heavy but not bulky. He lifted the envelope knife from his desk, found a loose corner on the envelope and slit it open. Another envelope was inside; it was sealed with red sealing wax, embossed with an impression of an eagle, two at each end. A single thin red ribbon ran through all four wax seals. To open the envelope now, he must break at least one of the seals. A minute later he dumped the contents of the second envelope onto his desk. The first thing he noticed was a plain sheet of white paper. On it was printed:

NOTICE! IF ANY OF THE SEALS ON THE INNER ENVELOPE HAVE BEEN BROKEN OR IF THERE IS <u>ANY</u> EVIDENCE THEY HAVE BEEN TAMPERED WITH, <u>YOUR SECURITY HAS BEEN COMPROMISED</u>. DESTROY THE ENTIRE CONTENTS OF THIS PACKAGE AND THE ENVELOPES IMMEDIATELY! YOUR LIFE MAY BE IN DANGER!

Amador looked carefully at the seals. Red sealing wax, each was complete with no apparent attempt to lift them or tamper with them. "I'm getting too old for such things," he muttered to himself.

He found American money, almost a thousand dollars, train tickets, overland stage tickets, a list of addresses and names, a paper that contained information to be used by him. It identified him as *Juan Fernando Gomez*, a farmer from a small town named Verhalan, some thirty miles south of Pecos, Texas on the Toyah River. His farm consisted of a little over three hundred acres on which he grew melons. The paper included names of people in Verhalan who knew him, the name of his bank and the name of his wife, Abella. It was all a fabrication.

He must commit all this information to memory and destroy the paper.

A second sheet of paper provided him with his travel details. He would be met at San Filipe by a square rigged ship of two masts named *Bonito* of Peruvian registration. The ship would be carrying papers showing it on a business trip to Vancouver, British Columbia. The ship would deliver him to his destination, Morro Bay, California and would pick him up at the same place three weeks later. His travel plans detailed the times and destinations of the overland stage coach he would use. There were names: Morro Bay, San Luis Obispo, Paso Robles, Hanford, Visalia, a rancher named Hector Gordon, alternate plans and railroad tickets in case something went terribly wrong. He read quickly through the papers, finally found what he was searching for; he would meet with the President of the United States of America on May 11 and 12. The location of the meeting was described only as a *remote wilderness area*. He would either meet the President at the ranch or be escorted on horseback to and from the remote wilderness area by one of Roosevelt's own security men.

There were several more pages of details, dates, times, places, topics of discussion with the President.

He leaned back, feeling a little dizzy and out of breath. It was going to happen. Even though it was still six months away; it was actually going to happen!

He slid the papers back into the envelope and slipped the envelope into the narrow hiding place behind the bookshelf, carefully operating the disguised latch that locked the shelf securely against the wall. Not even Maria knew of this concealed hiding place.

*　　*　　*

Washington, D.C.
Corporal John London sat on the edge of his bunk in the army barracks near the nation's capital. Around him were other members of the Capital Guard as they were called; most were getting into their dress uniforms for an evening in the city of drinking and carousing. Most did not plan on spending any time in their bunk this weekend. London decided he would wait until the crowd of soldiers cleared the barracks building before he showered and dressed. He had no place in particular to go and though he liked to drink, he had decided to be especially vigilant and not get drunk. Drunkenness most often led to trouble and London was trying very hard to stay out of trouble.

He was still surprised that he had been personally approached by Congressman DePallin and asked to fill in on a special detail involving the President of the United States. The Congressman had approached him as if he had been a long-time friend, though the two had grown up on opposite sides of the town. DePallin came from wealthy stock whereas London's family was nearly constantly in debt. Both his parents held menial jobs and when his mother passed away four years ago, he had joined the Army to relieve some of the financial burden on his father.

DePallin had sat with London for nearly two hours and told him about the special detail. First, the general information: protect the President on a trip to and from California, including a top-secret meeting in the Sierra Nevada Mountains. The young army corporal felt a sense of pride in being asked. The entire assignment, he had been carefully warned, was very highly secretive. London understood this. There was, however, a second part: the congressman quietly informed him of the special task that he and he alone would be responsible to carry out. Though he may not immediately understand the overall significance of this duty, it was at the very heart of the assignment. When he had been fully briefed on what he was to do and to say, London began to have second thoughts. This began to sound very political, deceitful and well . . . dishonorable. Not that London had much *honor* to begin with, as he was reminded by the congressman. There was that scandalous situation in his last year at school that could have brought the wrath and complete disgust of the town upon young John London and his father. DePallin had pulled strings to cover up the repulsive episode and was now extracting his pound of flesh. Failure to follow his directions, DePallin warned, would result in London's dishonorable discharge from the army and then trial and conviction in a civilian court followed by time in the penitentiary plus years of personal and family disgrace. The young woman involved, the only daughter of a highly respected state official, was still in the New Hampshire state asylum for the insane and would most likely be there the remainder of her life.

London had shuddered inside. The memory of his irresponsible teen-age crime had left him ashamed and shaken. He would, he assured the congressman, follow his orders completely.

London still broke out into a sweat when he thought about the warning. He had been careful over the years to avoid excessive alcohol for fear that he would say something that could bring everything down on his head. The problem was, like most soldiers, he enjoyed drinking and he enjoyed women.

*　*　*

Del Rio, Texas

Sanford Parker had spent most of the day standing at the bar of the Longhorn sipping whiskey and drinking cold beer. It was good to be back in Texas and to be among Texans who didn't have that *California accent* that made their speech sound funny. Hell, he'd enjoyed the stay in San Francisco, especially the long nights with the prostitute Josephine. He could have stayed a few more nights for more of that . . . but Jennette's wrath, bad enough as it was, would have been too awful had he stayed any longer than he did.

The small crowd of hangers-on laughed at his jokes and snickered at his description of California people, their fancy *cuisine* and their manner of dress. He awed them with stories about the cable cars and the huge Cliff House. Most of his listeners had never been out of the county in which they were born. But it hadn't taken long for the conversations to take on a political overtone.

"What's their take on the canal, Mister Parker?"

"They all want one, so long as it's not built through San Francisco."

His reply got the expected laugh.

"What about Teddy Roosevelt?" someone asked.

"What about him? They'll tell you how they feel about him soon enough."

"What d'ya mean, Mister Parker—soon enough?"

"Hell, he's going to be out there in May. Now, why our great President—explorer and adventurer that he is—would want to spend more than ten minutes in some of them little towns is beyond me."

"Little towns? Los Angeles ain't little, last I heard."

"Well, he's going to spend two days there. Two days. But he's spending *five days* near some paltry clod-buster town that I could spit across with the wind in my face. Visalia? Any ya'll ever hear of Visalia?"

Heads all shook in unison. "Don't reckon we have, Mister Parker."

J. B. Talbot stood several feet away. He'd been in conversation with a salesman from El Paso and overheard the last part of the interchange. "How do you come by all this information, Parker?"

Parker frowned. J. B. Talbot was the only man he knew in Del Rio that got away with not calling him *Mister Parker*. "Got my own sources, J. B. Straight from the horses' mouth, as they say. Ole Teddy's going up to the mountains to take a look at one of them California redwood trees. They say they got some up there over two hundred feet tall."

There was a rash of whistles and disbelieving shake of heads.

"Hell, reckon them Californian's will say anything!" Parker chuckled. "They even got a lake out there so deep they claim they can't find the bottom!"

"No bottom?"

"That's what they say. Lake Tahoe, it's called."

Another round of incredulous whistles. "Did you feel any earthquakes while you was there, Mister Parker?"

"Hell, yes! The ground out there shakes all the time. Makes your bed shake and squeak all night!" He winked at the group of men and received an appreciative laugh.

*   *   *

<u>San Francisco</u>
Sophia Jenkins waited patiently while her lawyer completed what had to be done to release her from jail. Martin August had managed to have her case completely dropped due to lack of evidence. He had suggested to her that she go back to the rental house where she had lived for two years and live there until all of Dunsworth's legal affairs were settled and that could take years. He had, as far as August could determine, no relatives on either his father's or mother's side. But the law would have to determine that for legal purposes. The second cousin that had paid his bail bond seemed to be a figment of someone's imagination as preliminary investigations revealed no one by the name of Francis J. Watson lived in Oklahoma City or within that county.

In the meantime Sophia realized she would have to go back to work. In a sense she thought it had been good while it lasted. He had been a steady companion, had never seriously mistreated her and he bought her nice things. The only problem was he was a crook and a ruthless murderer. And someone knew that and made sure Dunsworth got what he ultimately deserved. Sooner or later the legal system would have caught up with him; he would have been dragged through the courts, humiliated in front of his peers, convicted of at least four murders and most likely hung by the neck and buried in a pauper's grave. Now, legally, he was innocent until proven guilty. And he would never be proven guilty. As Martin had said, "*you can't try a dead person for a crime*".

"You're free to go, Sophia!" Martin August came around the corner smiling. He handed her a sheaf of papers. "If you would allow me, I would be pleased to give you a ride home."

*   *   *

Thomas O'Reiley sat quietly at the desk in his office at home. The sun had set about thirty minutes ago and he had lighted the gas sconce over his desk. He had been sitting there for nearly an hour, his mind going over and over all that had happened in the past few weeks.

Finally he pulled a pad of paper and began listing the names that he either knew or had heard of over this same period. He started with those he knew:

Beckley Weston
Hector Gordon
Frank Barnwell
Sheriff Joe McGee
Gomez Santiago
?George Whiteman
?James Tyler Moran
?Charles DeFoe
~~Clarence Chandler~~

He put a question mark in front of those he suspected were also Santiago, and crossed off Chandler's name. Then he listed those he had heard mentioned but did not personally know:

Sophia Jenkins
~~Alexander Dunsworth~~
~~Oliver Perkins~~
~~Ramsfeld Jenkins~~
~~Warner~~
~~Garcia-Rameriz~~
~~Nelle Dunsworth~~
Solomon (Soloman?)
El Culebra

He drew a line through those names who he knew were deceased. He counted seven as deceased. It was not an impressive list except when he counted seven as deceased and five of those as *probably* killed by Alexander Dunsworth according to the newspaper. Clarence Chandler was killed by *person or persons unknown*, according to the newspaper.

So, what was the significance of these names? How were they tied together, if they were? He decided that he would try to speak to Sheriff McGee and Sophia Jenkins in the next day or so, as his own name had been discovered on Chandler's body along with that of Soloman.

*   *   *

Thomas had little difficulty in obtaining the address where Sophia Jenkins was living; it was all a matter of public record since she had been jailed and released. It was eleven in the morning when he pulled his carriage in front of the neat bungalow overlooking the huge Presidio. Sophia answered the door after his second knock.

"Yes?" she simply asked.

"I'm very sorry to arrive unannounced, Miss Jenkins. My name is Thomas O'Reiley," He handed her a business card which she glanced at quickly. "I wonder if I may take just a few minutes of your time. I have some questions I would like to ask."

"Everyone has questions, Mister O'Reiley. Could you tell me what this is in regard to?"

"I wish I could be a little more explicit, Miss Jenkins but I guess that's why I'm here. I'm not completely sure myself what this is about."

"All right, as long as you're not from the newspapers, Mister O'Reiley, I guess it would be okay." She opened the door and motioned him in. "Please have a seat."

He sat in the overstuffed chair; she sat primly on the edge of the davenport. "Now, how can I help you?"

Thomas took a deep breath. "Miss Jenkins, I seem to be caught up in the middle of something that I know nothing about. My name was found on a dead man. I had a visit from a man who said he spoke with you. Do you recall Charles DeFoe?"

"Certainly. He dropped by here and asked some questions regarding my brother, Ramsfeld Jenkins. Ramsfeld was murdered in Los Angeles on June the sixth, along with his two law partners. Mister DeFoe said he had evidence that Alexander Dunsworth killed them."

"Did he say what sort of evidence he had?"

"He mentioned train ticket stubs, some articles of clothing . . ."

"You have another brother named Peter?"

"Yes. Peter lives on his ranch near Visalia. The storm ruined most of his house."

Thomas suddenly realized the resemblance between brother and sister. "I've met your brother Peter."

She stared at him for several seconds then smiled broadly. "Of course! Thomas O'Reiley! He mentioned you in one of his letters. Let's see . . . must have been a year and a half ago! You helped track down and kill a mountain lion. Saved a neighbor's daughter's life! It's a small world, Mister Thomas."

He smiled. "A long time ago now." He paused. "How did you get to know Dunsworth?"

Her face clouded for a moment. Then she shook her head as if clearing away bad memories. "I met him at some sort of legal get-together. I was working as a legal clerk. We met and one thing led to another. I became, please excuse the expression, his mistress."

"Did you know Dunsworth was married?"

"Oh, yes. He described his marriage as . . . well, dull."

"Did you ever meet his wife?"

"No. I never even saw her."

"Mister DeFoe mentioned that he thought Dunsworth was working on some sort of property deal in Nicaragua. Do you know anything about that?"

She looked at him for a long time, as if deciding what she should reveal, if anything. Finally, "I guess it doesn't make much difference now, does it? Yes, he was working with my brother's firm in Los Angeles on a very large piece of property that an investment group on the east coast wanted to buy." She hesitated again then shrugged her shoulders. "He was engaged in some sort of swindle on them." She shook her head, "Property deeds, papers were falsified, somehow. He was working with an attorney from Texas named James Tyler Moran. Mister Moran supposedly had all the inside information, political contacts, that sort of thing, in Nicaragua. He's the one that got all the signatures and seals on the papers, had them recorded. Would you like to see them?"

"Certainly, if it's not an inconvenience."

"They're right here." Sophia crossed the room and removed the sheaf of papers from a desk drawer, handed them to Thomas. "They're in Spanish."

"So I see. I wish I could read Spanish."

"I can read Spanish, Mister O'Reiley. Is there something in particular you are looking for?"

"No." He flipped through the pages, noting the many seals and signatures. "It's quite a document." He looked at Sophia. "Have you read it?"

"Parts of it. It's very complicated. I don't understand a lot of it, you know, with the Spanish legal terms and all. It has the history of the property through at least three generations."

Thomas shook his head and handed the papers back to Sophia. "Did Dunsworth ever mention a man by the name of Chandler? Clarence Chandler?"

"No. I'm sure he never mentioned that name to me."

"What about a man named Soloman, or Solomon?"

449

Sophia started to shake her head then frowned. "Wait a minute. He did mention that name to me once quite some time ago. A man named Solomon . . . his wife was murdered up in the mountains east of Sacramento. Oh! I remember now . . . it was in the newspaper . . . a double murder. The Solomon woman and her lover—I don't remember his name—were found shot to death. She had been tortured and mutilated. It was quite gruesome. Alexander said something about they had been killed by a paid assassin. I wonder how Alex knew his name . . ."

"What about a man named El Culebra?"

"El Culebra? He mentioned one time that he had to get in touch with someone—he was very secretive about it. He wouldn't tell me who it was. I know he was very late several nights, smelled like he had been in a saloon. I think Alex did mention the name El Culebra a few times. Culebra is a Spanish word meaning snake."

Thomas recalled Santiago's revelation that Dunsworth had met with the assassin at a lounge. "Do you know if Dunsworth was ever personally in touch with El Culebra?"

Sophia shook her head slowly. Her face suddenly tilted slightly and she looked sad. "You know, I always listened to Alex. He said his wife never listened to him. He always wanted to talk, you know . . . about what he was doing, what he wanted to do . . . he was lonely, I guess, like me." She struggled and finally wept silently. "I'm sorry. It is just all too much."

Thomas sat quietly for a few minutes, acknowledging Sophia's deep personal sorrow. Finally, "What did Dunsworth do for the investors on the east coast?"

"He worked as their legal attorney in arranging for the purchase of the property in Nicaragua. That's how it all started out." She shook her head sadly. "He hated them for the way they kept piling more things on him. They were using him. They made Alex their middle man, who had to take care of all the dirty work for them. It put him in jeopardy while it protected them and he hated that. I think that's why he didn't have any regrets about cheating them with the property deeds." She paused gathering her thoughts. "I know there was something about a woman in Nicaragua that he anguished over for weeks. I think they wanted her killed and they made it Alex's job to make sure it was done but I don't know for sure. That was sometime early this year; I think maybe March."

Thomas nodded. "You mentioned *property deeds* indicating there was more than just the one you showed me. Were there others as well?"

Sophia nodded and stared at the ceiling. "Yes, there was a second deed that he sent to the investors back east. It was very similar to the one he kept but the property descriptions were different. I have the feeling these properties have something to do with the inter-ocean canal and it being built in Nicaragua. Alex said that when that happened he would be very wealthy. That was his first insinuation that he had future plans for himself and that I was not going to be included. That and Mister DeFoe's opinion that Alex had killed the attorneys in Los Angeles and possibly his own wife caused me to rethink my relationship with Alex." Thomas could see a tear beginning to form in her eye. "I started to see him for what he actually was. I left and rented a room at the Franciscan Hotel. That's where he found me and you know the rest."

"One last question, Miss Jenkins. Can you provide me with the names of the investors Dunsworth was working for?"

*   *   *

Santa Cruz, California
Sheriff Joe McGee sat back in his desk chair and stared at the pile of papers on his desk. There were several full pages of handwritten notes, ten pages of an autopsy report, several hand sketches, witness statements, newspaper clippings and a medium-sized cardboard box that contained a variety of evidence: a bloody sheet, two empty shotgun shells, a key . . .

It had all been gathered for naught. McGee's prime suspect, Alexander Dunsworth was dead, a victim himself of foul play. A bullet had entered his head from behind and blasted much of his brain through a large hole in the front. McGee had gathered this, personally convinced that Dunsworth had murdered his own wife. The other suspect, Beckley Weston, was legally still at large and the grand jury had decided he should be brought to trial. Things could go badly for Weston should he ever come to face a jury. Whereas the evidence against Dunsworth was all circumstantial, the evidence against Weston was mainly Dunsworth's deposition, sworn to and sealed in front of a judge. Even though Dunsworth was now dead, his sworn statement would be read in court carrying the credence of a respected attorney, a victim himself of foul play. In fact, a jury might even find reason to consider that Weston himself may have murdered Dunsworth.

So far there was no physical evidence in the Dunsworth murder. The bullet that had killed Dunsworth had been lost after exiting Dunsworth's head, buried somewhere among the rocks and tangled roots and a lifetime of leaves and debris from the closely packed trees. They did have the vague description of the stranger from Oklahoma City whom several witnesses stated they saw with Dunsworth shortly before he was killed. Of course, telegrams that shuttled between the San Francisco police and the Oklahoma City police quickly revealed that no such person as Francis J. Watson lived in or anywhere near Oklahoma City. The documents Watson had submitted to the San Francisco police all proved to be clever counterfeits. Watson had simply disappeared.

Joe McGee knew where Weston was and that thought was enough to keep him awake at night. Convinced of his innocence, McGee had overstepped his authority by turning a blind eye when Thomas O'Reiley captured him in the mountains above Visalia. Weston was still there, somewhere, waiting for his trial.

This lapse in judgment would probably cost him his job as sheriff, McGee mused. He'd been the Santa Cruz County sheriff for going on thirteen years. It wasn't a very high paying job but he liked the work and had managed to maintain some semblance of civility in the small ocean town and the rugged mountains that divided the ocean from the large San Francisco Bay area.

Not sure of the eventual destination of the accumulated evidence, McGee packed it back into the cardboard box and slid it under his desk.

* * *

San Francisco

The eagle soared so high that it was a mere speck from where Thomas stood alone and high of a rocky cliff. From here he could see for many miles around; his view unbroken and in sharp detail as he felt the cool breeze blowing against his skin. From high above him he heard the high pitched, raspy *kree . . . kree* of the eagle. When he looked up again the eagle had come closer and Thomas could see the golden eyes of the beautiful bird centered on him. The tail feathers were clearly visible and were as white as snow, except for the last few inches that comprised the tip of the feathers; that part was gold in color and they shimmered in the bright sunlight.

The eagle put its strong wings into motion effortlessly and rose confidently in the air, soaring and turning in tight circles, higher and higher. The *kree . . . kree* sounded far away now but Thomas could hear the wind as it whistled through the eagles feathers as it formed itself into a plummeting sword, dropping faster and faster with its curved beak thrust forward and its talons open, braced for the impact. At the last possible instant the eagle swerved, cut sharply to its left screaming its warrior cry and rose from the dive, twisting, spiraling higher and higher. Thomas saw the single feather separate gracefully from the beautiful bird, a single magnificent tail feather that appeared to have powers of its own as it sailed, soared and darted until it settled softly at Thomas's feet.

When Thomas tried to locate the eagle once again against the cobalt sky, it was not to be seen. Somewhere, perhaps from the very edge of the earth came the cry once again, *"kree . . . kree"*.

Thomas, dressed in the breeches and vest and moccasins that Gray Hawk had made him, sat beside the feather which began to speak to him in the language of the eagle . . . or was it music? Or perhaps both and Thomas simply felt, not attempting to understand what it was saying, sensing the feeling-sound-words sink into his flesh with hot and cold sounds and smells and color sensations.

Thomas sat cross-legged next to the feather, his head back and his eyes closed, feeling the intense energy like the powerful light beam from a steam locomotive streaming into his inner self. He heard chanting words . . . *ah ya, tah ya, so say, ah ya, tah wa, nah wa, tah no, tak ni . . .* The chant continued but Thomas chose to let the words, sounds, colors, odors and vibrations penetrate into his viscera to become part of him. He sensed Gray Hawk was nearby but the old Indian was silent, observing, watching Thomas carefully. Thomas began to join in the chant, knowing the words and melody and colors without thinking; then he stood and put his arm-wings out, lifted effortlessly into the sky and soared in huge sweeping turns alongside the great eagle high over the earth to the very edge and into the vast darkness beyond that was forever. The eagle spoke to him without sound and Thomas listened. The message was clear and frightening and spoke of future events and happenings; the eagle advised Thomas that he must go forward, regardless of the pain, regardless of the loss and that some events were of greater importance than life itself.

Thomas continued to sit with the feather in front of him as the words and chanting melodies and colors all joined inside him and he could feel them all coalesce within him like a magnificent form of energy and knowledge that he had never before experienced. The feather spoke one last time and Thomas listened carefully and then he knew and he spoke to the eagle: "you speak the truth."

When Thomas awoke, Amanda was at his side; her smile, face and perfume so familiar they were part of him. Part of him . . .

*   *   *

Thomas remembered his dream as he sat in the sun room and watched the sun light the higher places in the city as it began its sweep across the sky. He could still feel the presence of Gray Hawk and feel the cool wind over his body as he had sailed with the eagle.

Amanda came into the room with two cups of coffee on a small tray. Setting one in front of Thomas, she sat in the other leather chair carefully balancing the cup in her lap. "So, my dear husband, when will you be leaving?"

He frowned. "Leaving?"

"You will be leaving soon, I know. I could hear it in your mutterings last night. You were very restless and you muttered words that I didn't understand, some sort of mumbling gibberish. But I heard you speak plainly of Gray Hawk twice. I can only assume you've had some sort of . . . supernatural . . . contact with your shaman." She looked at him waiting for his response. "Am I correct?"

Thomas smiled. "Amanda, you are truly amazing. Yes. That's all I can say about something I don't fully understand. I was with Gray Hawk last night. He was here. It was an urgent meeting . . . an urgent message he was attempting to deliver to me."

"It all sounds mysterious and spooky, my dear Thomas. I certainly hope you have not slipped over the edge. I'm not sure that I can reach you there in time to grab your hand."

"I'm entirely sane, Amanda dear. I've learned a great deal from being with Gray Hawk over the years. He's taught me how to listen to the most inner part of myself, the place that most people never, ever visit. I . . . dreamed I was at that place last night. I hesitate to call it a dream, for it was real to me. I could hear, feel, smell, touch the sensations; they were all very real."

"Like a nightmare or a bad dream . . ."

"No, it's not at all like a bad dream, Mandy. It was like experiencing a sudden enormous truth. Like suddenly understanding a basic concept within something very complex. Like solving an enormously complicated riddle of words, shapes and colors on my own. Like finding something precious I had lost a long time ago. Like hearing a voice that I haven't heard in years and immediately knowing who it belongs to. Like all of these things happening at the same time . . ."

Amanda nodded. "I think I have begun to understand the profundity of your experiences with Gray Hawk, Thomas. I don't understand the experiences but I do understand that they are very precious and significant to you."

* * *

The Gordon Ranch
Thomas arrived at the Visalia railroad depot mid-morning and found Angela waiting for him with the buckboard. He had sent a telegram early in the morning before getting on the train, hoping that the Gordons would get it before he arrived. They had, and Angela drove into town to pick him up.

The weather was cold and overcast, quite typical of valley weather this time of the year. The dense fog, called a *Tule fog* in the valley, had not yet made its annual appearance but the air felt damp causing Thomas to pull the collar of his coat up over his ears.

Angela had greeted him warmly, yet he felt that her usual zeal was missing. He decided quietly that it had been unfair to her and her family to drop in on them with only a few hours notice. He would only spend a night there before he went into the high country to find Gray Hawk. She brought him up to date on what was happening at the ranch. Ramon was once again off to school near Sacramento. He was becoming very excited of the prospect of raising citrus crops and the visit from Frank Barnwell had seemed to provide his interest with a boost of possibility.

Old Man Shingleton had passed away two months ago. Jack Short, who worked for Peter Jenkins, had found him dead when he had dropped by the Shingleton spread one afternoon. The old man had been dead for some time. The Shingleton property was put on the auction block and sold off for back taxes. Angela's father had bought it, mainly as a place for Beck Weston to stay out of sight until his case came to trial. They had not heard of the death of Alexander Dunsworth and what complications this could introduce.

Beck had settled into the old Shingleton place shortly after the property became Hector Gordon's. The old cabin was cleaned out and repaired; Beck moved in quietly. Hector felt fairly certain that the Stantons, Peter Jenkins and Jack Short were aware that Beck was living there but the subject remained off-limits and the questions were not asked.

The weather had been very dry after the terrible storms of October. The water had receded leaving some places completely devastated with top soil washed away revealing a layer of rocky gravel. The Gordon family had fared very well with only the lower end of their property scrubbed by the Kaweah River. The river itself had returned to its normal flow although the current still brought debris from the higher elevations.

Their talk focused primarily on events and local news. The ride to the ranch house was fast and when Angela pulled up near the barn, she turned to him.

"Tom, I've neglected to tell you that my folks are up north attending a funeral. We have the place to ourselves tonight. I hope that is all right with you."

Thomas sat almost stunned. "Angela, I wish you had told me. I would have gotten a room in Visalia. I wouldn't want your folks to hear that . . ."

"It's going to be okay, Tom. I want you to stay here tonight. I'm a good cook and I'll make us dinner and breakfast. Please, Tom."

Thomas sat quietly. It was too late to try to get back into Visalia before dark. The thoughts of being here alone with Angela quickly surfaced. "I'll spend the night in the bunkhouse as usual, Angela."

She smiled with excitement. "Great! You get cleaned up and I'll go put something together for dinner."

By the time he had cleaned the travel dust off and gone across to the main house, Angela had a fire blazing in the fireplace and there were delicious odors coming from the kitchen. She smiled greeting him with a spatula in hand.

"Have a seat Tom. I'll have dinner on the table in just a few minutes."

When he sat at the family dinner table, she brought in a steaming plate of beef strips in gravy and mashed potatoes with a serving bowl of fresh green peas.

"It looks and smells wonderful, Angela."

She smiled, "My mother is a good teacher, Thomas." She took the seat opposite him and passed the dishes toward him. "Hope it tastes good."

"I'm sure it will."

They spent the mealtime in light banter, relaxing and laughing at the simple things of their day-to-day lives. It was lighthearted and fun; when they finished Thomas offered to help clean up the kitchen. She accepted his offer and they worked elbow to elbow to scrub the pans and dishes; their easy chatter from the dinner table continued.

Later they sat in front of the crackling fire in separate deep leather chairs since there was no davenport in the Gordon ranch house. She reached across and took his hand in hers, interlacing their fingers. They sat quietly for a long time listening to the snap and pop of the logs in the fire. When he looked across at her, she had her eyes shut, a relaxed smile on her face.

She seemed to sense his looking at her. Without opening her eyes she said softly, "I love you, Tom."

"I know you do, Angela. I love you too."

She smiled and replied, "I hope it always stays like this."

Several seconds went by, "It will if we allow it."

She nodded. "I know."

They sat quietly again, letting the fire warm them as they basked in the heat and glow of the red-hot coals. Finally she got up and selected a few more split logs, tossed them onto the bed of coals. She turned and faced Thomas.

"May I join you in the chair, Tom? I feel so far away from you."

He looked at her and smiled. "Certainly. I think I can find room here for a beautiful young lady."

She sat lightly on his lap, her left arm around his shoulders as she leaned back, and put her head on his right shoulder. He could smell the fragrance of her long, silky black hair and looked at the long eyelashes that emphasized her eyes. *My God, she's so beautiful.* He put his right arm around her waist and pulled her close. She moved slightly and he felt her lips pressing against the crook of his neck. She placed her right hand on the side of his face and pulled him to her lips, moist and slightly parted. They searched for each other's lips, found them and they merged, pressing, parting slightly. Their tongues met and swirled slowly, intertwining, probing. She let out a small sound and pressed harder, more persistently against him, breathing quickly. His left hand reached across and found the buttons of her blouse which easily became undone. His hand cupped the smoothness of her breast and she gasped *"Oh Tom!"* and pressed harder against his lips. He felt the softness of her skin and pulled her closer, then brushed his hand over her breast feeling her swell under his touch, feeling her breath coming in short gasps, feeling her whole body responding, aching for his touch, aching . . .

She broke away quickly, her eyes searching for his, unaware perhaps that her breasts were uncovered. She shook her head, almost sadly. "Tom, my dear Tom. I can't do this, as much as I would passionately with all of me want this to continue. I can't. I'm so sorry. I haven't been fair with you; you have struggled so hard to be honest and true to me and to your own wife. Oh, Tom, I've wanted so badly to hold you and to have you hold me and feel our skin together and to make love with you . . . Please try to understand."

He nodded slowly. "I do understand Angela. You've shared your thoughts and feelings; they are like mirror images of mine. I want you, too Angela but I can't ever have you in that way. I will always love you in some way, but we can never ever love each other in that deepest, most profound, most personal way. We are two people who must try to remain as modest acquaintances to each other. You have your life and I must have mine."

She buried her face in his neck and simply nodded. Her blouse remained unbuttoned and he could still see the soft curve of her breast, the creamy color of her skin. He was tempted to reach out and stroke her breast to rekindle the passion that they had only moments ago but instead he closed his eyes and tugged her blouse to cover the captivating beauty of her vulnerability.

It is over, he thought. *It is over and done. There would never be a return to what was or even to what was possible and there could never be second thoughts or feelings of remorse or misgivings. What once was, is gone.*

They sat like that for a long time, long enough for the fire to die into a gray pile of ash. Neither spoke; neither moved. He held her tenderly but not ardently as lovers might. Their hands touched from time to time almost as if to assure one another they were still there. They occasionally whispered to each other as if sharing something profound but the words were not important; what was important was to maintain the significance of closeness with another human being. It was a moment that for each of them would last a lifetime.

*   *   *

Thomas awoke as the sun struggled to break through the early morning clouds. The bunkhouse was cold; he hurried to dress and then went across to the main house. Angela was in the kitchen and she smiled as he came in.

"Well, sleepyhead! I was wondering if you were going to stay in bed all day! Here's some coffee." She handed him a mug with coffee and cream, just as he liked it. "I've put some food together for you and Gray Hawk. It should last a few days."

"You're an angel, Angela! I'd take you with me to introduce you to Gray Hawk but he would probably roast you over a fire for dinner. I hear that's what he does with young ladies."

"You're quite wrong, Thomas O'Reiley. He stopped doing that years ago."

They ate together and neither spoke of the events of the evening before. It was as if a curtain had been lifted, a curtain that had veiled their relationship in secrecy, in deception, in the need to be careful of what was said and who it was said to. They both knew that there would be difficult times ahead that moments would raise memories and feelings but the freedom of what they had now was so much better.

"Thomas, before you go, I have something I need to tell you about last night."

"Angela, I don't need any explanations."

"But I need to tell you." She hesitated, took his hand in hers. "Frank Barnwell came back by here after the two of you left at the end of October. He had to spend another week making surveys. We . . . we spent a lot of time together. He's so much like you, Tom. He's a gentleman, polite, respectful. He and I talked . . . a lot. I think I may have fallen in love with him and now I understand how you must have felt. I could not . . . last night . . . do something that I might regret in my relationship with Frank . . . and I don't even know if there is a relationship. I only know that all of a sudden he was important to me . . . I hope you understand, Tom. I really do."

He smiled at her. "Angela, I understand completely. I knew last night that it was never going to be the same again for you and me. I didn't know why but I'm glad it is someone like Frank. He's a good man." He took her other hand in his. "He's a lucky man."

*   *   *

It was late morning when he finally started the switchback trail up the sheer face of the canyon wall. It was cold and the air was damp. At times he could feel the mist freeze to the outside of his coat. He kept moving, wanting to reach the old deer camp before the sun set. He finally felt the steepness of the trail lessen and then he was on the top of the mountain looking down through the watery haze at the river, far below. Now he was able to pick up the pace some; he was soon in the silent company of Standing Tall and shortly later reined in at the deer camp. He hadn't even dismounted when Gray Hawk appeared as if by magic from the gloom and greeted him with a raised right hand.

"Tah-moss! My friend. I called for you. You heard me! I knew you would come."

"Gray Hawk! I saw you and knew. It is good to see you."

"And you! Come, we must go before the sun hides behind the mountains."

Thomas reached out his hand to the Indian. "Come, ride with me Gray Hawk."

The old Indian smiled. "Many winters since I've ridden a horse, Tah-moss." But he grasped Thomas's hand and with surprising agility, bounded up behind Thomas. "Ah," he said, "feels good! I must get a horse!" He laughed hard and long, nearly choking on his hilarity. "Old Indian buy a horse! Ha!"

It was almost dark when they reached Gray Hawk's shelter. Thomas noticed that he had built a skin covered smoke house; Gray Hawk told him that he had deer meat inside drying and being smoked to preserve it through the winter. "Not so easy for this old Indian to hunt rabbits in cold winter time now."

They quickly unpacked the things Thomas had brought and took them into Gray Hawk's shelter. It was all familiar to Thomas now: the low roof made of bent over saplings, woven tightly and stuffed with moss layered with mud baked dry for many years and now covered with a gray layer of soot from the years of fires inside the hut that provided warmth and heat for cooking, the familiar bear skins, the sacred pipe in its place of honor, the small collection of enameled pans and mugs that Thomas had brought up years ago. Gray Hawk's carefully constructed bow and the quiver of arrows, his collections of small items of great and personal significance to him. The piles of tanned hides, the carrying baskets carefully made of inner bark from trees and against one side an ample supply of firewood carefully arranged in preparation for the cold nights ahead.

The odors of thousands of cooking and warming fires that the hut had endured, the smell of the hides and furs, aroma of meals prepared and eaten here, the faint tang of the sacred herbs and leaves that the shaman smoked in his pipe, even the faint musk-like smell of the old man embedded in the rough structure and the furs were all familiar and satisfying to Thomas. He suddenly realized the similarity of this old Indian's hut and the one he had built and lived in for so long on the island and the thought that their lives had been lived in some sort of parallel of loneliness, quest for survival, exploration of their natural surroundings and eking out those precious moments of pleasure and beauty.

Gray Hawk entered the shelter quietly and Thomas didn't realize his presence until he spoke.

"Yes, Tah-moss, we are very much alike and very different at the same time. I am old enough to be your father. You have become as a son to me. A father must try to leave the earth a better place for his son and the son should try to leave the earth a better place for his son. I have not had enough time to teach you everything a son should know but I have done what I can in the short time we have known each other."

Thomas nodded. "Gray Hawk, you have been my father and have taught me well. I will spend my life learning and passing on to my son what is important to know. Our lives are different; our people are different. But some truths are the same for all people."

Gray Hawk nodded solemnly then broke into a wide smile. "We will celebrate this visit. Come, let's eat. Old man is hungry! We have much to talk about. I want to hear about the vision you had that brought you here. I think we will smoke the sacred pipe tonight."

*   *   *

The glow of the small fire cast a faint orange aura in the shelter. The two men sat across from each other; the meal they shared had been well prepared by Thomas, using some of the beef he had brought with him from the ranch. He had roasted it until it was almost black on the outside but full and juicy when he sliced into it with his knife. They had roasted tubers that Gray hawk had found that day and finally some nuts carefully

461

warmed by the fire until they opened on their own. Gray Hawk had brewed a strong tea from dried leaves and blooms of flowers he had collected in the springtime. When Thomas sipped the tea from the enameled mug, it was strong and slightly bitter but the aroma was sweet. He felt it as it moved into his body, warm and relaxing.

Gray Hawk took the pipe down from its place selecting herbs and thin slices of bark and roots and packed them into the bowl, lit them with a stick fired by the central fire and puffed until the mixture was well caught. He handed the pipe to Thomas who took it carefully in both hands, nodding his thanks to the shaman before he sucked at the pipe and felt the searing smoke in his lungs. He was careful to not cough, though his eyes watered from the strong fumes. Two deep pulls on the pipe and he nodded and handed it back to Gray Hawk.

The Indian puffed on the pipe, once lifted it by both hands as if presenting it to an unseen spirit, then handed it once more to Thomas. They shared the pipe until there was nothing left to burn in the bowl and he put it down carefully.

When he spoke, his voice sounded deep and far away but was strong and virile. "I know what you saw in your dream, Thomas. I was there with you. I brought the great eagle to you."

"I knew you were there Gray Hawk."

"The great eagle has been my dream-companion for many years. I wanted to bring him to you so that you may learn from him as I did. After my time, when I am walking beside *Bear that Walks with Pain*, he will be your dream-companion. That was the message of the single feather he left you."

"I flew with the great eagle, Gray Hawk."

"Yes. I have flown with him many times. It is his way of telling us that we can do many things, that we are not tied to the earth, though we think we are." He smiled. "I saw you lift yourself into the air with strong wings and soar beside the great eagle. The great eagle was pleased that you would do that."

"It just felt natural," Thomas said.

"That is the way of much of life. It is natural. Even death is a part of life. There is sadness when a loved one dies but the sadness is not for the loved one; it is sadness for self, that we are not able yet to join them in that great journey."

"The great eagle spoke to me of moving forward even through great pain or great loss," Thomas said. "He spoke to me about some events being of greater importance even than our own lives." Thomas hesitated. "The great eagle had tail feathers with gold tips and powerful talons. He was very strong and powerful."

Gray Hawk nodded. "The great eagle was telling of your leader, your chief. He is strong, a warrior. That is important for you to remember."

Thomas frowned. "I don't understand what this means, Gray Hawk."

"When the time comes, you will understand. That is why he took you to the edge of the earth where darkness begins and everything becomes forever."

* * *

Fresno, California

Frank Barnwell looked at his handwritten report one more time. There was still a lot to do but at least he would be able to give a comprehensive report to his superiors when they met in two days in Sacramento. He paged through the sheets of sketches showing rivers and dams and new lakes with estimates of acre-feet of water each would store. Engineers could later calculate the amount of electrical power each could supply if equipped with dynamos to take advantage of the stored water. That was not his immediate concern. He felt compelled to look at preventing monster floods and loss of water like they had recently encountered.

He would be heading to the State Capital the next morning and would not have time to travel to Visalia again to visit Angela. He had discovered his longing to be with her as soon as he left the ranch the last time he was there. They had spent many hours together, riding, talking. It had suddenly seemed like he had known her all his life, that their being together was natural and perhaps meant to be. He had been careful to not overstep his welcome with her and had departed after only giving her a modest good-bye hug. She had spoken of her and Thomas's relationship but only in the way that suggested they were casual friends. Frank had, of course, spoken with Thomas and understood the intensity of their relationship; although he did not want to trample on that bond, he knew that he wanted to know Angela better. He was, he admitted to himself, seriously attracted to the young lady.

But what about Thomas he wondered. Thomas was among his best friends and though they had little in common, he had a great deal of respect for the man; Frank could only imagine the self-reproach he must be experiencing due to his problematic relationship with Angela. It was not his place or desire to come between Thomas and Angela but he knew that if things progressed much further, that would be the natural outcome. And that could end the years of friendship he and Thomas had shared, and just as well could destroy any future chances he had of becoming an important part of Angela's life.

Finally, he positioned a sheet of paper on the desk, dipped his pen into the ink and began writing a letter to her.

My Dearest Angela, it began . . .

* * *

In the mountains above Visalia, Thomas was getting ready to bid Gray Hawk goodbye. The weather had definitely turned colder and the clouds began to slip lower, heavy with possible snow. Thomas was reluctant to leave the old man, as his age was taking a toll on his physical abilities. He walked now with smaller steps, slower and a little uneven. His arms, once full and muscular, were thin and the skin hung loosely. Hands were wrinkled and no longer capable of grasping the knife with ease to prepare a rabbit for roasting; now it was work. He slept more, even in the middle of the day he would cover himself with a bear shin and snore loudly.

Thomas was not sure the old shaman would make it through the approaching winter. He helped gather a good supply of firewood, broke it into small pieces, stored it in the back corner of the hut and outside against one wall where it would be easy to retrieve. He and Gray Hawk checked the drying venison and rearranged some, kept the small smoky fire going. Gray Hawk probably could move the dried and smoked deer meat into the hut in a week or two. They made one last trip to the bog area where they dug cattail roots from the ground. These would be dried to provide a starch-like vegetable later in the winter. Thomas knew now what to look for while searching for food and came in several times with baskets of roots, nuts and tender pieces of bark that could all be eaten. Finally, he felt he had done all he could for the old man; it was time to depart.

"Gray Hawk, my friend. Please take good care of yourself this winter. I will return in the spring after the snows have stopped. I will look forward to seeing you again."

"Tah-moss, you have been a good friend to me. I will be here waiting for you."

They bid each other goodbye with the raised right hand and Thomas clucked his horse into motion, leaving the old man behind. After he had gone a short distance, Thomas had to brush the tears from his eyes.

CHAPTER 39

Thursday, December 4, 1902, San Francisco

Thomas read in the San Francisco Chronicle that the Santa Cruz County Grand Jury had issued a warrant for the arrest of Beckley Weston, present location unknown, to stand trial for the murder of Nelle Dunsworth on May 28, 1902. A trial date had not yet been established.

Thomas had met with Sheriff Joe McGee just four days ago to talk about the situation with Beck. Both men were concerned that someone could simply stumble onto the location of Beck and something really bad could happen, possibly resulting in the death of one or the other, or even both men. Though McGee was not enthusiastic about keeping Beck in his jail, it would at least alleviate that problem.

McGee had spent a few hours going over the case against Beck Weston as he saw it. The only real case the state had against him was the signed statement Dunsworth had made, implicating Beck as the murderer. McGee easily saw where Weston's defense could raise questions with that testimony but nevertheless their case would rest upon that statement and the physical evidence as found and recorded by deputy Charles Watts. Was it enough to convict Weston? Probably not on its own according to the sheriff, but the public had been further infuriated by the shooting death of Alexander Dunsworth and already rumors had started tying Weston to that murder as well. Some rumors even insisted that Beckley Weston had been seen in a San Francisco bar in company with and conversing with the stranger who had called himself Francis J. Watson from Oklahoma City. The only way to absolutely refute that was to admit that Beckley Weston had all that time been allowed to freely roam the mountains east of Visalia.

Thomas could see that Beck's situation was by no means a certain acquittal by a jury and Sheriff McGee was in full agreement. In spite of the uncertainties and the disruption to Weston's life, the best thing was to get him locked up in the Santa Cruz jail to await his trial.

Sheriff McGee had eventually decided to have his deputy Charley Watts take the train to Visalia to pick up Weston and accompany him back to the Bay Area in manacles.

Thomas had telegraphed Hector Gordon and gave him the essential details. Deputy Watts would pick up Beck on Wednesday, the tenth of December, in time to get Beck and himself on the northbound train. The pick-up would occur at the Valley Hotel in Visalia where Beckley would spend the night with Hector guarding him.

* * *

Santa Cruz

Thomas looked through the bars on the small jail cell that held Beck. Beck glanced up and saw Thomas; immediately jumped up and came to the bars, sticking his arm through to shake Thomas's hand.

"Mister O'Reiley! It's good to see a familiar face!"

"Good to see you too, Beck. Let me see if I can get Sheriff McGee to get you out of there for a while. I'm sure there's a meeting room somewhere in here."

Five minutes later the two men were sitting across from each other at a table in a visiting room. "Beck, I'm sorry the way this is turning out but given the circumstance, I had to agree with Sheriff McGee that this was the best place for you."

"Well, of course, I'd rather be somewhere else myself. The sheriff and I have talked and I understand where he's coming from."

"I'm going to get you an attorney, Beck. I know a couple that will do a good job for you."

"Mister O'Reiley, I'm not going to be able to pay you back very quickly . . ."

"Don't worry about that. I just want to make sure you have someone who is working in your best interest."

"I certainly appreciate that."

"Is there anything I can get for you? Sheriff McGee told me you can have books, most anything like that."

"I reckon some books just might help pass the time, Mister O'Reiley. That would be very nice."

"I'll make sure you get a stack to choose from."

Beck hesitated for a moment, then asked, "Mister O'Reiley, how are the Gordon's doing? I saw Hector but you know him, he was taking the job of guarding me very seriously." He chuckled. "How did they make out from the storms?"

Thomas brought him up to date and talked about the trip that Frank Barnwell and he had made to the storm area. They talked for some time about the effect that Frank's suggestions for dams would have on the ranchers and farmers.

"You reckon I'll have a job there when this is over?"

"I can't speak for Hector but I believe they want you to come back. Miss Angela mentioned that you have a brother in Texas you are concerned about."

"Yeah. He's been laid up for a long time. Doctors don't rightly know what is the problem and I reckon it's just getting worse."

"Sorry to hear that. You planning to head down that way?"

"Depends. I reckon if he's still alive when I get out of here I'll mosey down that way."

Thomas nodded. "Sheriff said they don't even have a trial date yet."

"Yeah. reckon I could be sitting in here a long time."

* * *

Managua, Nicaragua

Gomez Santiago and Esperanza-Vincente sat in the deep leather chairs in exporter's office. Santiago had spent the day telling Esperanza what had happened in San Francisco. Ramsfeld Jenkins' sister Sophia had been cleared of any wrong doing in the killing that ended with Dunsworth being jailed. Dunsworth was now dead, the case remaining unsolved and the police slightly baffled, unsure as to the motive. The assassin known as El Culebra had apparently visited San Francisco and spent some time meeting with Dunsworth but it appeared there was no tie in between El Culebra and Dunsworth's murder. However, it appeared that the assassin had killed a man named Clarence Chandler with connections to a Bret Solomon in Sacramento and Thomas O'Reiley in San Francisco.

The property swindle had worked as planned, although the property Dunsworth had purchased would end up in court as part of his estate; though Santiago was almost certain that the lawyer had mortgaged almost everything he owned to purchase the useless swamp land. Perhaps the ruse would be uncovered by the courts but there would be no one to contest the deed anyway. The second piece of property, some thirty-nine thousand square miles of sea floor that had been purchased by the east coast investors would take years to untangle. In the meantime their investments would be tied up, probably for the remainder of their lives. Their children or their children's children would have to deal with it.

Santiago told Esperanza-Vincente that he felt there was still unfinished business regarding the assassin El Culebra. Though there was some circumstantial evidence tying him to the murder of Vincent's mother and household staff, there was no solid proof that would hold up in court.

"I'll keep looking, Vincente. Something will turn up that will put the noose around his neck. Meanwhile," Santiago said, "I have a feeling there is something going on involving the assassin that we're unaware of."

*   *   *

San Francisco
Christmas week was upon the city and the O'Reiley household joined in by putting up a tall Christmas tree decorated with strands of popcorn and cranberries along with a few homemade decorations constructed by the children. Evenings were full with invitations from neighbors and friends and the O'Reileys themselves had a party planned for this evening. Mostly the guests would be comprised of Amanda's friends that shared her interests in the various charity and civic activities with which she found satisfaction.

Xaing had spent the day preparing hors d'oeuvres, cookies and cakes. Thomas had put together a punch which he sampled and *adjusted* occasionally throughout the day. When the guests arrived, the home was warm with a crackling fire in the fireplace and candles scattered among the various tables and fireplace mantles. The tree was the center of attraction and the party ended up with most people standing around the tree. Someone suggested a few Christmas Carols; Amanda sat at the grand piano and led them in a dozen or so carols. Someone else had brought a copy of Clement Clarke Moore's *T'was the Night Before Christmas* which was read aloud and the adults listened as they had when they were children. The evening ended with one last toast to a *Merry Christmas and a Happy New Year*, then final hugs and handshakes at the door as party-goers headed for their carriages.

When the house was quiet once more, Amanda turned and hugged Thomas. "Oh Thomas, wasn't that wonderful? Everyone had a good time and it was just so nice to have them here. Thank you my dear husband for putting up with the idiosyncrasies of your wife. I hope you had a good time. It looked like even Peter Strauss enjoyed himself once he got a few cups of your punch in him. And that was a wonderful punch dear." She rattled on in excitement until finally she stopped and giggled. "Perhaps I'll have just a little more punch myself." She ladled out two cups and handed one to Thomas. "Merry Christmas, darling."

"Merry Christmas, my beautiful wife."

"Let's go sit in the sunroom, Thomas. Without any lights."

They walked into the darkened room. The late city lights sparkled around them and a few homes in the neighborhood still had lights on inside. Thomas sat in the deep leather chair and he was somewhat surprised when Amanda sat on his lap, her left shoulder snuggled against his right shoulder. They generally saved such intimate moments for the bedroom.

"Are you comfortable, Thomas?" she asked.

"It's perfect." He put his arm around her and she melted into his encirclement, her face radiant in the faint glow through the windows. He reached and drew her face close to his and their lips met softly, scarcely touching at first. She let her lips brush against his cheek and his eyes; when their lips came together again, it was with rising passion and ardor that urged their embrace to become even less restrained, their lips to search and discover and join together, melt together comfortably. She closed her eyes and wrapped her arms around him, pulling him closer, tighter. He put his hand behind her head, gently drawing their lips together, merging them, fusing them. She let out a tiny cry and her tongue probed for his. After what seemed time unbounded, she pulled away just enough so she could whisper, "Let's go upstairs, my love. I need you desperately."

*　　*　　*

Abilene, Texas

Luke had spent the evening in his hotel room above the saloon. The usual mid-week crowd of cowboys had arrived late evening and the piano had banged out crowd pleasing melodies for hours on end. Luke had taken the opportunity to thoroughly clean his rifle, carefully disassembling it and cleaning each component with a piece of white cloth, then reassembling after each piece had been lightly oiled. He ran the bronze rod and brush through the barrel and followed it with a clean white swab until the gun barrel looked like shiny silver when he looked through it at the light. He wiped the stock, carefully inspecting it for any irregularities, then gave it a quick wipe-down with the oil rag. Satisfied with the rifle itself, he turned his attention to the scope and its mounting hardware. Giving everything a close visual inspection, he cleaned the exposed lenses carefully and packed everything away. There were eight rounds of fifty-caliber ammunition in the case that he carefully inspected each for dents or imperfections in the brass casing and the lead slug. Finding everything to his liking he wiped them down and put them back in the case.

Luke realized he was simply finding ways to occupy his time. The weather was bitter cold, windy, blowing snow and frozen rain horizontally, much to the misery of anyone outside. He had spent several weeks moving from town to town to withdraw the cash from his bank accounts. He now kept everything in a small wooden box under his bed. He had taken his cash in the form of paper money of several types and denominations spanning amounts from ten dollars to one thousand dollars. Some were Gold Certificates, some Silver Certificates, some were simply labeled *Treasury Note* and some *United States Note*. He had decided that the variety of notes would most likely assure him redemptive capability regardless of where he was. Counted, sorted and stacked, the certificates represented well over two hundred thousand dollars. With the money coming from his next and last job, he would indeed be a very wealthy man. He would have to find an ordinary-looking yet heavy-duty, lockable leather case capable of carrying the total amount. He would also carry a small portion of cash in the form of gold and silver coins. These were generally acceptable anywhere, quickly and without too many questions.

He had decided that he would make his escape from the port of Los Angeles by steamship to Buenaventura, Columbia. It was a small seaport but large enough for him to disappear into the multi-national population. He would have to learn the language and if that became a major roadblock, he could go by steamship to any of several United States territories in the Pacific where English was spoken. He was twenty-seven years old, though his facial appearance and skin texture made him appear as a man in his forties or fifties or older. The life he led had hastened to cultivate the gray hairs in his thick mustache and sideburns and those that were now almost an equal part of his long shoulder length hair. The deep lines and creases in his face were largely inherited from the man who had fathered him twenty-seven years ago.

He had thought a great deal about the job he had accepted and although he still did not have the detailed information, he had been told enough to encourage him into a self-preparation discipline that included hours of target practice among the mesas and mountains of New Mexico, spending days at a time on solitary bivouac learning to start and maintain small nearly smoke-free cooking fires and sleeping with the barest of bedrolls on the hard ground. Little by little he honed these skills, learning to disregard the discomforts and inconveniences of existing without the comforts he was used to. He'd spent days and nights in the rain and cold and equally miserable days in the hot direct sun of the desert. Sandstorms, snow, fog, rain, wind and darkness all became a part of his catalog of experiences, each lending some portion of knowledge to his ability to survive. He'd forced himself to eat creatures and plants he would have never eaten before. This regimen had also toughened him some; he lost several pounds that he had gained in the ease of hotel living. He practiced some with his pistol but only for the sake of overcoming bad habits and learning how to draw and shoot quickly. He had finally quit this exercise; he admitted to himself that he would never be a gunman.

In the mornings after he had awakened and before he ate, he even practiced a few of the exercises the army had taught him and he discovered that his body responded by re-building muscles that had disappeared under the thin layer of fat.

By the end of April, he figured, he would be ready in all aspects to assassinate the President of the United States of America. All he needed were the details that Dunsworth had promised he would receive. And the money.

*   *   *

Washington. D.C.
President Theodore Roosevelt had spent the evening in the relaxed company of a few friends. Activities in the nation's capital had come almost to a complete halt this week before Christmas. A light snow had

covered the city with a blanket of white, much to the delight of some and concern to others.

President Roosevelt and James had met earlier in the day to review the President's plans for the California trip that was coming up in a little over four months. Some minor adjustments were made in the itinerary; some short layovers were added, some were cancelled. Most of the changes reflected the political give and take of the ongoing Panama Canal dispute.

James had assured the President that all was ready for the trip. The various railroad segments upon whose tracks the Presidential railcar would travel had all been notified of any special requirements and all had replied that they would be prepared. The security detail had been training regularly and was practicing weapons training daily at the firing range. James told the President that John London, the single replacement to the detail, had fit in well in the security detail; he was well liked by the others and as it turned out, was an excellent marksman.

Roosevelt then gave James authority to announce the planned trip, including the major stopover places, to the press. The side trip into the Sierra Nevada Mountains was of course to remain a secret and would not be announced ahead of time, although the President himself would probably allude to it afterwards during the layover in San Francisco.

CHAPTER 40

Clarence DePallin sat in the swivel chair in his Washington office staring out the double windows at the wintry scene. The lightly falling snow had given everything a powdering of white including the now bare branches of the trees across the way. The few carriages on the street left parallel tracks that crossed and swerved in a multitude of patterns that eventually disappeared under a fresh layer of snow. Those outside were bundled against the cold, overcoats and top hats for the business men and government employees, heavy mackinaws and caps for the working class trudging to fulfill their multitude of tasks. Ten more days until Christmas and it looked like the population had already begun to celebrate the holiday with good cheer.

Ten days until Christmas. A week after that and the new-year would be upon them. The coming year would be a pivotal one for the United States, DePallin thought. The canal issue would be decided and following the assassination of Roosevelt, the country would be experiencing the presidency of the now serving as Vice-President, Charles W. Fairbanks.

DePallin was faced with an issue that he wasn't sure how to handle. The death of Alexander Dunsworth, though it had diminished the problem of possible leaks in their plans, had also severed the only known ties to the assassin, Culebra. Admittedly, he had failed to think that all the way through when the four of them decided to eliminate Dunsworth. Dunsworth had never told them how he arranged to meet with the assassin. Dunsworth seemed to believe the man lived or stayed primarily in Abilene, Texas. One of the four of them would have to go there and seek him out. The most logical person would of course be Sanford Parker, himself a Texan. Sanford had surprised them with his well thought-out plan to kill Dunsworth which was executed without a single slip-up.

But Parker was a loose cannon, possibly even more so after the Dunsworth affair. Parker, however, wouldn't be required to negotiate or even meet face-to-face with El Culebra; he simply had to determine the most expedient way to communicate with him. The telegraph, most likely—it's much faster than U.S. Mail. But to whom do we send it? How does he reply and who does he reply to? And can we trust Parker to carry out the assignment without bringing everything crashing down around their heads?

And lastly, would Parker even agree to the task? It would take him away from his ranch for several days. Perhaps a larger share of the profits, say increasing from twenty-five percent to maybe twenty-eight percent would be sufficient inducement. He'd pass it by the other two, Ambrose and McGarnet, before he ran it by Parker.

DePallin was pleased with his recruitment of John London. The boy had already pleased his superiors and was apparently well liked by his peers. The two had met a few times very quietly and DePallin had carefully described the soldier's tasks while he was attached to this special detail. Although London sometimes appeared to be reticent, he nodded his complete understanding of both the job at hand and the consequence of failure on his part to fulfill the mission.

* * *

Del Rio, Texas

Sanford Parker picked up the letter from Clarence DePallin on his daily trip by the Post Office where he always took a few minutes to ogle twenty-one year-old Betty Lou Hershey who worked behind the barred window. The small building was empty except for the two of them; after Sanford had retrieved the envelopes from his Post Office Box, he stopped at the window and stared shamelessly at the ample bosom barely hidden by the low-cut blouse. She continued to count postage stamps without looking up.

Finally she glanced up and asked, "What can I do for you, Mister Parker?"

"I reckon you could do all sorts of things, Miss Betty, if you had a mind to," he replied as he winked at her.

"Mister Parker," she paused long enough to stare him in the eye then went back to counting stamps, "if I did that for you, you'd have a big ol' heart failure and die."

"Be worth it . . . I'd sure be happy!"

"So would the rest of us," she muttered. "Don't hurry back." She then stacked the pile of postage stamps, shaking her head in disgust.

Sanford left chuckling to himself. He thought *she's a cute little heifer that I wouldn't mind checking out. Maybe I will someday.* He let his mind roam around among these thoughts and generate images as he walked checking through the envelopes. He stopped in his tracks when he came across the one that had come from DePallin. "Now what the hell?"

He glanced both ways suspiciously, as if expecting someone to catch him opening a secret communication. He walked in through the front doors of the Longhorn and into the small space he referred to as his office that he more often used when he wanted to be alone in the company of a woman. He locked the heavy door, sank into the chair behind the desk and slid the paper from the envelope.

He read through the single page quickly then read it again, carefully studying the exact wording. "Well, now, ain't that just a big crock of manure?" he muttered. "Reckon I got myself a promotion to trouble handler." *He'd give me a three percent raise? Three percent of say a million dollars? Thirty thousand dollars? So each of the other three toss in ten thousand each . . . that's nothing to them!*

But he sat and thought about the offer. *Not bad money though, for what, maybe a week's work?* He got up, went to the Western Union Telegraph Office.

"Afternoon, Isaiah. Need you to send a wire for me."

*   *   *

Washington D.C.
The telegram was delivered to Clarence DePallin's office and he opened it immediately.

> DE PALLIN STOP WILL LOOK FOR LOST HORSE
> PER YOUR REQUEST STOP WILL GET BACK TO
> YOU STOP SANFORD

DePallin smiled. Parker would do most anything for money. He was surprised that the Texan hadn't insisted on more percentage. Doesn't make much difference—there will be plenty to go around once the property is sold. But, it was going to take a lot of cash to pay the assassin and so far neither Ambrose or Parker had put up a single cent. McGarnet had already deposited his share, a quarter of a million dollars, in the Chicago bank account, as had DePallin. A lot of money for one bullet in just the right place. The two holdouts had the money; they were just sitting on it until the last minute.

The congressman leaned back in his chair and lit a cigar. His share of the land sale could be enormous, ten or twenty times what he had invested. Money was always useful in politics and he would put his share to good use. He would probably have to find a woman and get married. People wanted a *family man* in the White House as a sign of wholesomeness and stability. He had not had time for women in his climb through the political labyrinth, nor was he very interested but it would be a necessary step and the lure of money would be helpful there as well. Thus far in his life, women were paid for sundry and usually very temporary purposes and then quickly discarded. He had never experienced a personal relationship with a woman that he could consider as anything beyond a casual friendship.

His own mother had barely been a part in his life. His father and mother had slept in separate bedrooms on different floors of the family mansion. Meals had been eaten alone and separately in the huge dining room under the vigilant eyes of the household staff. The occasional times Clarence had seen the two together had usually ended in minor disagreements that escalated into angry arguments and eventually screaming, swearing and slamming doors. Both were gone now; his father eventually drank himself to death and his mother had thrown herself off the pier into the swirling Merrimack River behind the home one winter night. Now Clarence DePallin lived in the huge thirty-four room mansion by himself. His staff of fifteen resided in the servant's quarters, a separate two storied house some fifty yards from the main house; from there they went through the daily rituals of preparing meals, changing linens, doing laundry, sweeping and mopping, washing windows and caring for the vast property. DePallin could care less. The property was well endowed with DePallin money set aside in a trust fund.

*   *   *

Abilene, Texas

The northwest wind was howling down the streets of Abilene when Sanford Parker got off the train in the late afternoon. Though it was Friday, the town seemed to still be recovering from the New Year celebration. The streets were quiet except for the wind. Only a few stores had customers. Those that were out were bundled for the weather in sheepskin jackets, gloves and western style hats. Collars were turned up and backs braced against the wind that had traveled a thousand miles across the vast western prairie.

Parker checked into one of the three hotels in town, then went to the saloon that was situated next door. The crowd there was quiet as well, with men sitting in small groups at the tables and several lined up at the bar. The piano player went through a series of short melodies and then repeated them. No one seemed to mind.

Parker took a place at the bar and ordered a whiskey neat, tipped it back and swallowed, then pressed his glass forward for a refill.

He looked around the room slowly. Fifteen, perhaps eighteen men. Cowboys, mostly. Three could be merchants or lawyers wrapping up deals before the weekend.

He had thought a lot about how he would go about this task. No one even knew for sure that the assassin lived in Abilene. Dunsworth had seemed certain but no one knew the source of his information. He had talked once about the killer, describing him as tall and thin, shoulder length black hair with gray in it. He had a face marked by deep lines from the corner of his eyes and from his nose. He had a thick, heavy mustache and wore a long black leather coat.

Parker glanced again around the room. No one even came close to that description.

The bartender had poured his second drink; Parker took it and sat at a vacant table. It didn't take long before one of the businessmen wandered over.

"Mind if I sit?" he asked.

Parker shook his head slightly, "Glad to have the company."

"Nasty weather out there." The man stated as he slid into a chair. "The name's Fogleman. Dan Fogleman. Don't think I've seen you around here before."

Parker thrust his hand out. "Frank Jarvis. Glad to know you, Mister Fogleman. I'm from over San Antonio way."

Fogleman grasped his hand and shook it, "Glad to know you, Frank. Call me Dan! What brings you out this way?"

"Cattle. I'm a buyer for an outfit in San Antonio."

"Well, we've got plenty of cattle 'round these parts."

"I suspect you do. I'm looking for a couple of Black Angus breed'n bulls." Parker eased back in his chair; he could talk about cattle for hours.

Fogleman shook his head. "Now, that narrows the field quite a bit. Only have a few ranchers around here working with Angus. Might be able to steer you in the right direction though."

"Much appreciated, Dan." He looked at Fogleman, "Now, what is it you do here in Abilene?" He caught the bartender's eye and ordered another round.

"Own the gun shop down the street. Specialize in modifications, scopes, large bore hunting rifles. Folks around here take pride in their huntin' rifles."

"That so? What's the largest bore hunting rifle you worked on?" The bartended dropped the two whiskeys on the table and left.

"Oh, hell! Got some out there over fifty caliber but they're mostly for big game hunting. Lots of wealthy men down here go to Africa where they can bag themselves a lion or a rhino. Few of 'em even brought back elephant trophies."

"Whew! Rifle that size must really pack a wallop!" Parker shook his head for emphasis.

"Takes a big man to shoot one of them canons. Yes sir! Now, I worked on a real pretty fifty caliber not too long ago. Started out as a German Mauser but you would never know it now. Beautiful piece—bored it out to fifty caliber. Has Cataract telescopic sights," he leaned forward conspiratorially, "and those beauties are damned expensive. Had it built as a breakdown." He shook his head. "You'd pay a lot for a piece like that."

"Why would he want a breakdown?" Parker inquired.

"I don't know for sure. Must travel a lot with it. Hardly ever see the guy. Stays around here someplace. Name's Luke something. Don't rightly know I ever heard his last name."

Parker put on a puzzled look. "That wouldn't be the guy that always wears a black leather coat, would it? Tall, kind of thin, black hair . . ."

"Well, that just might be him. Like I said, I hardly ever see the man. Sounds like him, though. Keeps pretty much to himself."

"Well, I bet that's the guy! Luke, something."

"Yep, that's him."

479

"Hell, ain't it a small world!" Parker laughed, lifted his shot-glass in a mock toast.

*   *   *

Parker spent the night at the hotel but was up early the next morning to have breakfast at the hotel dining room. There were only six others having breakfast and the man Parker was hunting for wasn't one of them. He finished early and hurried down the street to another hotel and took a seat in their dining room, ordered a cup of coffee and breakfast. He'd been sitting there a little over thirty minutes when the man stepped in.

Parker knew right away it was the man he was looking for, even if he hadn't been wearing the long black leather coat. The man was cautious, carefully looking over the sparse population of breakfast eaters. His eyes met Parker's, hesitated for a fraction of a second then moved on. He took a seat at a table near the back of the dining room, near a door that Parker figured led outside. The other men eating paid no attention to the stranger.

Parker got up slowly and saw the stranger's eyes quickly shift and lock onto him. *The man is cautious.* Parker eased across the room, keeping his eyes on the man he knew was called Luke.

He reached the table, nodded quickly to the man, pulled a chair into position and sat across from him.

"Hope you don't mind if I join you for a few minutes," he said quietly.

"I mind," the man growled as he continued to stir his cup of black coffee.

"Just going to take a few minutes of your time, Luke."

The man tensed and his eyes narrowed. "I don't know you."

"You know me; you just don't know my name." Parker looked around quickly. "I'm with the east coast group. You did a job for us in Nicaragua and you have a job coming up in May for us."

Luke stared at Parker for a long time as if deciding whether or not to acknowledge the statement. Finally, "How'd you find me?"

"Pretty easy when you know where to look."

Luke sipped slowly from the mug of coffee. "So, now that you found me, what do you want?"

"You hear about Dunsworth?"

Luke shook his head. "The fat little attorney out in San Francisco?"

"That's the one. He got himself killed. My partners and I just needed to figure out how to get in touch with you since he's not around any longer. In case we have things we need to . . . talk over. Know what I mean?"

"Reckon I do." He stuffed a large bite of breakfast into his mouth.

Parker reached into his shirt pocket, drew out a folded sheet of paper and slid it across to the stranger. "Here's directions on how to reach us and how we can reach you. You're going to want to check at the Western Union Telegraph office every other day for a message for Eugene Sherman, just like it says. Any messages you send our way are to be addressed to Madison North at that address. It's all there on that paper. If we don't hear from you within three days after we send you a telegram, we will assume you are either dead or no longer want the job. Three days. Remember that. If you send us a message, we'll get back to you in less than twenty-four hours. Learn those names, commit them to memory then get rid of that paper."

Luke looked at Parker then nodded. "I got it. Anything else?"

Parker stared into the pitch black eyes of the assassin, shook his head. "Just make sure you remember it, Luke." He got up, placed the chair back where he got it and walked out without looking back.

When he got to the side walk, he drew a deep breath. That man is scary, he decided. *Talking to him was kind of like trying to talk down a rattlesnake.* Now he needed a drink, real bad.

*   *   *

When Clarence DePallin received the telegram from Porter early that same afternoon he smiled. That damned Texan had more gumption than he had given him credit for. The telegram from Porter was straight and to the point:

> DE PALLIN STOP OUR MAN UNDERSTANDS
> COMMUNICATION SETUP STOP EUGENE
> SHERMAN IN ABILENE STOP MADISON NORTH
> IN DC STOP SUGGEST CONFIRM SOON STOP

Parker spent the rest of the afternoon in the bar sipping whiskeys and watching the crowd of cowboys as they came and went. His train wouldn't leave until early the next morning. He didn't see Luke any more that day. At seven-thirty he had a light dinner in the hotel dining room then went to his room.

*   *   *

Sanford Parker was on the train headed south out of Abilene for Del Rio when Clarence DePallin printed the message for El Culebra on a lined paper at the Western Union Telegraph office in Washington D.C. The telegram was short:

> EUGENE SHERMAN STOP CONFIRM RECEIPT
> OF THIS MESSAGE STOP MADISON NORTH

DePallin stood around long enough to see the telegraph operator operate the sending key to transmit the message to Abilene, Texas.

It was after five o'clock that afternoon when the Western Union Telegram was delivered to his office:

> MADISON NORTH STOP MESSAGE RECEIVED
> STOP EUGENE SHERMAN

Abilene, Texas

Luke wasted little time moving from his hotel room in Abilene. The ease with which the man from the east coast group had found him all too easily convinced him that he must relocate or risk further problems. He knew of several hotels nearby and selected a small family run hotel on the western edge of the city. Two stories high, the second floor provided only four rooms and a common bath but the rooms were nice sized. Only two of the other rooms were occupied, one by a young school teacher, the other by an elderly couple that he rarely saw. The first floor offered a very small dining room with a back exit door and four dining tables. Large front windows provided a view of the Southern Pacific Railroad tracks across the street. There was no bar or saloon and the owners let it be known that they did not want alcohol in the rooms either.

Luke spent some time attempting to determine just how the man had tracked him down but eventually gave up. Although Luke was not well known in the town there were unfortunately, some that provided services for him such as haircuts, laundry and of course, the hotel itself. He'd been there better than three years, so it was probably time to move on anyway.

Since his personal belongings were quite sparse, it took him very little time to relocate to the new hotel. Run by an older couple, the new location was quiet and the food was more than adequate. Neither one of them inquired into what Luke did, nor how he spent his time.

The young school teacher had the room directly across the hall from his and he saw her quite regularly. He figured she was about twenty three years old. She was fairly good looking in an ordinary way, with a trim, almost thin figure, healthy complexion and long brown hair brushed straight. She dressed very properly; her blouse was plain white, full enough to reveal little of the figure beneath it and buttoned tightly at the neck and wrist. Her long pleated skirt, generally either blue or black, covered her narrow hips and went almost to the floor. Luke thought her legs were probably long but the length of the skirt hid that as well. When the two met in the hallway from time to time, her smile was quite prim and proper but certainly not off-putting. She vaguely reminded Luke of his mother, or at least what he thought he remembered as a child. The memories triggered strange and bothersome thoughts and images to his mind.

Luke had very little experience with women except for the randomly chosen prostitutes he had brutally murdered after each assassination. Somehow those carnal encounters seemed to fully satisfy the myriad of thoughts and urges that otherwise surged through him unchecked. In a few instances, such as the lady in Nicaragua and the woman at the cattle ranch near Sacramento, the prime victim and the sacrificial victim had been inseparably woven together into the complex fabric of the assignment.

But this young woman left him with confused, contradicting thoughts and feelings. He had heard men talk of *loving* a woman, and yet he had no idea of what comprised love. For the most part, women in his life had been prostitutes or noisy, drunken, pathetic creatures that existed on the ragged edge of society. His own mother had become one of them after his father was hanged.

Was this *love* that men talked about physical like being *warm* or *hungry* or was it mental like being *angry* or *lonely?* Was it something that you purposely let in like opening a door to the blistering hot wind, or was it something that slipped in quietly as a warm breeze through a window left open? No one had ever defined love for him. If he had ever loved, he had no memory of the sensation. Nor could he remember a time that he had felt himself as being loved. He was uncertain that he would have recognized it even if it did happen.

It took him several days to learn that her name was Ida—Ida Hubbard from Kansas City, Kansas. In that same amount of time he discovered he could wait patiently for her to come home from her day of teaching school and the two of them could sit at a single table to dine together in the hotel's tiny dining room where talk was subdued and sociable.

* * *

<u>San Francisco</u>
Thomas read the Chronicle's coverage of President Theodore Roosevelt's plans to visit the state of California in May and of his planned stopovers in Los Angeles and San Francisco. San Francisco immediately put plans into motion to welcome the President in a big way. A parade would carry him from the train station to an as yet undecided location where he would speak to the local citizens.

As usual Handon McPherson managed to get seats for Thomas, Amanda and himself near the President for a dinner and planned speech to the city's progressive leaders and businessmen. But this was all five months from now.

George Pardee had been inaugurated into the office of Governor of California a week earlier on the seventh of January, and had sworn to eradicate the bubonic plague that was still infesting San Francisco. The previous governor, Henry Gage, had steadfastly held that there was no plague. Thomas remembered with a smile the meeting with President McKinley and Pardee's reaction to Thomas's retelling of his tracking and killing the mountain lion. "Amazing! Absolutely amazing!" the Republican politician had muttered over and over.

The San Francisco weather was quite warm for this time of the year and many people had taken their sailboats out of temporary storage to enjoy the sunshine on the open water of the bay. From his study in their home on Nob Hill, Thomas could take in the vast expanse of the bay including Alcatraz Island and more distant, Angel Island. The sailboats with their white sails spread skimmed back and forth across the cobalt-blue water, some jockeying for position in ad hoc races, others just delighting in the wind, sun and spray.

Amanda came into the study and sat near Thomas, who had decided to take the day off from work. Thomas put the Chronicle aside and leaned back. He could tell from her face that Amanda wanted to talk about something.

"Yes?"

"I was just thinking, Thomas, we've not heard from Frank Barnwell in some time. I do hope that everything is satisfactory for him. It seems strange to be this separated from him."

"I'm sure he's simply very busy, Amanda. The work that he was doing when I was with him was quite complicated and all we were doing at that time was gathering information. He would have to still interpret that information and then formulate plans around the results. It seemed easy enough to talk about putting a dam here or there but I can only imagine the complexities of such an undertaking."

"Well, I'm sure you're right, dear. I just miss seeing him from time to time."

"I miss him as well. He is a very competent and strategic planner; he kept the entire company moving forward with his incorporation of evolving design and construction improvement." He paused. "The State of California has a very good asset in him."

"Do you think it would be appropriate to invite him to spend a weekend up here with us? We could go to the theater one evening, have dinner at that Italian place he liked, what was it . . . Joe's?"

"It certainly wouldn't hurt to offer an invitation, Amanda. I don't know whether or not his schedule would permit him to take the time away from work."

"I will go write him a letter immediately, Thomas." She stood up and swished out of the room.

Thomas sat and thought about the last few words Angela had shared: *"He and I talked lot. I think I may have fallen in love with him . . ."* It had not surprised him to hear the words. She was young and would be wanting marriage and a family. Frank was the right age and well educated. Money would not be a problem for him. It was a natural relationship. He closed his eyes momentarily and thought of her lips, her fragrance and the intensity of her being close to him. It had been . . .

He shook his head in frustration. He simply must not allow those kinds of thoughts to be part of his conscious thinking. *But why is it so damned difficult?*

*   *   *

Penacook, New Hampshire
Clarence DePallin sat in the straight back chair pulled next to a small table. The Merrimack River flowed by several hundred feet away across the snow covered area that would be covered with closely clipped grass

most of the year. He held a tumbler still half full of Tennessee Whiskey in his hand as he read the article in the newspaper.

United States Secretary of State John M. Hay and Doctor Tomas Herran of Columbia had signed a treaty that would allow the United States to lease a six-mile wide strip of land across Panama. In return for a one-time payment of $10 million and annual payments of $250,000, this lease would remain in perpetuity.

DePallin sipped slowly at the whiskey. This treaty would of course have to be sent to the United States Senate for their advice and consent, reviewed by the Foreign Relations Committee and then returned to the Senate for approval or rejection. If approved, it would be sent to the President for ratification. The process is slow and sometimes cumbersome but it did give opponents several opportunities to put a torpedo in it. DePallin would be quite busy in the oncoming months.

*   *   *

Washington D.C.

Corporal John London, with a towel wrapped around his hips, stepped out of the shower in the barracks that housed the special security detail. His fellow soldiers were in various stages of getting ready to bunk down for the night. Some were already asleep, their snores filling the large room with hand-saw intensity. Two were sitting on the edge of their bunks, writing letters or taking care of some insignificant soldiering detail. London peeled back his top sheet and spread himself out on the narrow bed. The soldier in the top bunk, Peter Haas, was in bed causing the bedsprings to sag under his weight in a parabolic arc that dropped to less than two feet above London's bunk.

London lay with his hands clasped behind his head and listened to the noise slowly diminish around him. At ten o'clock sharp the sergeant would look in through the door calling *lights out!* before operating the switch than turned electric power off the three incandescent lights that lit the barracks.

They had been drilling conscientiously for the past several weeks, a practice that started even before he had joined the outfit: rifle practice twice daily, both short and long range through the various shooting positions, marching and running for mile after mile carrying heavy packs and then practicing horsemanship in formation and in mock attacks and responses. They had started at six this morning and had not returned to the barracks until eight this evening. Hard work. Minimum rations. The only blessing was the weather. It was cold but not frigid and there was no rain to soak their clothing and flesh through to the bone.

London had been called twice to speak with Congressman DePallin, although never was the rest of the detail aware of these private meetings. DePallin always asked how he was doing and London always gave him the upbeat response, *"Going great! Nice bunch of guys."* Somewhere in the ten minutes they would spend together, DePallin would ask how he felt about the special assignment he had been given. Again London gave the Congressman what he wanted to hear, *"Not a problem, Mister DePallin. I will carry out my orders like a good soldier, sir."*

"Good," was always the Congressman's reply, "just remember the consequences of failure."

London had thought hard about the consequences of failure. He had also thought hard about the consequences of success, something the Congressman never talked about; in fact, the Congressman had never mentioned success.

"Lights out!" The Sergeant shouted and moments later the room was dark.

*   *   *

Abilene, Texas

Luke had waited patiently outside his room for the footsteps of Ida Hubbard to sound on the wooden steps leading to the second floor of the hotel. He had gotten to recognize them over the past month and they seemed to have a special sound about them that pleased him when he heard it. They had begun eating dinner together in the hotel's dining room and these times had become important to him. He'd watched the few others that ate there to see just how they handled their eating utensils and how and when they placed their napkin. He watched as men stood and helped their female partners get seated. He observed the eating habits of these people and attempted to emulate them. He realized that he had lived a life of the crudest of social graces. Now he felt compelled for some reason to learn respect and courteous behavior. These he felt were what Ida expected and he wanted to live up to her expectations.

He had shared virtually nothing about his life with her other than he lost his mother and father when he was a young lad, that he had been on his own for many years now. She never asked him where the money came from that he spent on their dinners nor what he did all day while she was teaching at the local school.

He began shaving more often, had his shirts laundered and pressed, combed his long hair neatly, always thinking, perhaps unconsciously, *she would like this.*

He learned that she was raised as a farm girl in rural Kansas, had gone to school and spent two more years learning how to be a teacher. Her mother and father still lived on the farm where her father raised wheat. She had no brothers or sisters but she had always wanted to travel, to *see the world,* she said.

Their dinners together took longer and longer as the two got to know one another and spent the time learning about each other. So it surprised neither of them when one evening following dinner, he invited her into his room so they could continue their conversation. She sat on the bed while he occupied to only chair in the room. Their conversation had been light and they had both laughed and enjoyed the moments. When she stood to leave, it seemed only natural that she would end up in his arms, awkwardly at first, then with a little more fervor as their arms encircled each other tightly and finally their lips met tenderly, softly, gradually began searching . . .

Finally she pulled away, somewhat flustered and breathless and walked across the room. She opened the door and glanced back quickly, smiled at him, then left and pulled the door shut. He heard the door to her room across the hall open and shut as he stood and stared at the door to his room. For the first time in his life, he felt what he thought might be the faint tingling of genuine care for another person . . . for a woman.

The next night after dinner, they retired once again to his room and when the door was shut she readily fell into his arms; they held each other and kissed with growing fervor.

It was long past midnight when she finally eased free of his embrace, crept from under the blankets and started to gather her clothes. When he began to mumble in protest, she whispered in his ear reminding him that she still had to teach come sunrise. But tomorrow would be Friday, she prompted him and there was no school on Saturday.

*   *   *

It was two in the afternoon when he remembered that he needed to check at the Western Union Office. There was a telegram for Eugene Sherman:

> EUGENE SHERMAN STOP MUST MEET 2-11 LITTLETON TAZEWELL HOTEL E CARY ST RICHMOND VA STOP 11PM STOP MADISON NORTH

Luke swore softly as he read the telegram. He would have to respond. The message he sent in reply read:

> MADISON NORTH STOP I WILL BE THERE STOP EUGENE SHERMAN

He checked the train schedule. The last train he could take and still arrive in time was the 4:15 pm train on Sunday. It would get him to Richmond, Virginia at 2:30 pm on Wednesday, February 11th.

Damn! It meant he would have to leave Ida for about a week. For the first time ever he felt pulled against his will. How could a person have that sort of power . . . control . . . over another? He felt the anger building inside of him. No! It wasn't Ida that was causing the conflict. It was him. He wanted . . . what? Her company. Her passion. Her tenderness. Her love. He wanted . . . her—Ida.

*   *   *

That evening they ate quietly at their usual corner table. The elderly couple that ran and worked at the hotel seemed to understand that the young couple wanted extra time and they went out of their way to provide them with privacy and let them sit long after the few others had left.

When they reached Luke's room they stood together closely for a long time, just standing, cheeks touching, arms around each other. In a while they each explored with their hands, roaming gently; then they took their time undressing and getting into the bed. Luke reached across to the table and turned the lantern low . . .

489

CHAPTER 41

<u>Saturday, February 6, 1903, San Francisco</u>
Frank Barnwell arrived at the O'Reiley home promptly at 6:30 pm and was greeted at the door by Amanda who put her arms around him in a close hug.

"Oh, Frank! It's so good to see you!" she murmured. "I'm not sure I like you being so far away that we can't visit from time to time."

"Sacramento isn't that far away, Amanda," he chided.

"Perhaps it just seems so," she responded as she led him onto the living room to greet Thomas. The two men shook hands and Thomas led him to the sunny room that was his office.

"I'm glad you were able to come, Frank," Thomas said as the two men seated themselves in the deep leather chairs. "I imagine you've been pretty busy."

"We're trying to get all this data pulled together. We've made a few presentations to interested agencies but I'm afraid that any real work in this area is still years away. We're getting some opposition from a few of the large farming groups and from some of the San Joaquin Valley cities that we're *stealing their water*. They can't see the long term effects of doing nothing."

Thomas nodded his head. "Well, they have the right man to do the job."

"Thank you for the compliment but sometimes I wonder if I'm just pounding my head against a wall."

"It'll pay off eventually, Frank."

The two men continued to talk about their mutual interests and the continuing progress in the construction business. San Francisco was busy adopting new construction codes as the city began to grow vertically with multi-floored buildings now using steel beam construction. Amanda came in and sat with them for a while, then left to supervise the dinner arrangements.

Thomas took the opportunity of her absence to raise the subject. "How are you and Angela doing?"

Frank smiled knowingly. "We've been seeing each other quite regularly. I hope this is not upsetting for you, Thomas,"

Thomas shook his head. "I hope things work out for you two. She is a wonderful young woman and she deserves a man in her life that can provide her with what she needs. I hope that you're that man, Frank."

"Thanks. To be very honest with you, we've talked about the possibility of marriage."

Although he had expected the announcement, it set Thomas back some before he was able to extend his hand and offer congratulations. "Wonderful news, my friend!"

"Well, nothing is going to happen for a while. I'm busy up to my neck in this project. It will last another six months or so."

"How's Angela dealing with the delay?"

"Of course, she's excited, Thomas. There are a whole lot of things going on in her family as well. Ramon has returned from school and is very excited about their plans to convert to citrus farming. Hector seems to have some big shin-dig going on in May, but he's very secretive about it. In fact, none of them will even talk about it. They smile and glance at one another whenever I touch on the subject but they become tongue-tied and nothing comes out!" Frank laughed. "Whatever's going on, they're keeping it to themselves."

Thomas couldn't resist asking, "And how's Angela?"

Frank looked at Thomas closely. "She's doing very well, Thomas. There are times that I believe she thinks of you, misses you. I recognize a kind of sadness, like talking about the death of a friend. It may take her a long time to get over the friendship you two shared. We'll work that out between us. We've got a whole lifetime ahead of us. I do intend to marry her, Thomas."

Thomas nodded. *I understand that sadness*, he thought. "I'm happy for both of you. Is this something that we can share with Amanda this evening?"

Frank smiled. "I certainly don't know why not. We've already told Hector and Margarita."

*   *   *

<u>Abilene, Texas</u>

Luke and Ida spent most of the day in his room, alternately talking and making love. He was amazed by the creamy smoothness of her skin and of her fragrance that seemed magically to emanate from her in a way that fit her personality, her beauty. It was as if the odor had been specifically designed for her. He had never paid attention to the odor of a woman. It was tantalizing, erotic and *special*. It was her. He knew he would always remember it.

They shared their life stories, although Luke had little he could tell her about. He had spent time in the army, served during the Spanish-American war. He had traveled for *business purposes* much of the United States and had been to Central and South America. He too had been raised on a ranch, or perhaps it was a farm, depending upon how you defined it. His father died when he was a young boy, his mother had run off not long afterward. He had been on his own all his adult life.

"What sort of business are you in Luke?" She asked.

"It's a very private business. I work for large corporations and wealthy men. I travel quite a bit. Usually these trips last a week or two."

"What do you do for them?"

"Well, you could say I'm in the personnel business."

"Personnel?" she asked, her head tipped to one side.

He nodded slowly. "I work with them take care of trouble makers, slackers, problem people." He hated the lie.

"I didn't even know that kind of business existed."

"It's relatively small. That's why I end up traveling a lot." He paused, "Which reminds me. I must leave tomorrow afternoon for Richmond, Virginia to meet with a client there. I should be back here a week from today."

He could see the look on her face. It was disappointment. His being away for a week was a disappointment for her. "I'll be back, Ida. I promise you that."

She smiled, her face tinted with the feelings that ran through her. "I'll miss you. I've never met someone who I would miss so much. Please, please don't leave me, Luke." The beginnings of tears formed in her eyes.

"I won't do that to you, Ida, I promise." He drew her close to him and they kissed and his hands moved over her body and she melted into his arms.

*   *   *

<u>Sunday, February 8, 1903</u>

Luke was on the train the next day, traveling with only a small leather satchel of change of clothes and the gun case. Ida had inquired as to what was in the case; he told her it contained the tools of his profession, alluding to books and such. He had not wanted to lie to her but the situation left no alternatives. As he watched the countryside whirl by, he thought of all he had done in his short lifetime. Looking back, some he regretted yet he recognized the awful monster-creature that lived within him and that controlled much of him. It required such terrible, violent actions to keep it satisfied, such inhuman and sadistic acts that often Luke had felt that someone other than himself had committed them. Yet the blood and gore was right there on his hands and arms, and the monster that lived in him was sated, at least for a time.

With Ida, it will be different, he vowed to himself. *Ida has helped me find a new side of myself. Ida cares for me. She cares for who I am. And I care for her. I've never felt that before. That terrible thing inside me has always demanded blood. Perhaps this will be different.*

The train roared across central Texas and into Dallas, where he boarded the train that would travel through many of the southern states and then gradually turn northward to Richmond, Virginia.

*   *   *

<u>San Francisco</u>

Thomas sat alone in the office staring out the windows at the few lights sprinkled on the bay. A sliver of the waning moon slipped down close to the western horizon. It was a little after three in the morning. Something had awakened him and after a few minutes of restless tossing, he had slid out of bed and into his bathrobe and slippers. The sky was clear and the winter constellations were slowly revolving toward the western horizon. He sat, just listening for a long time. His thoughts came in bits and pieces at first, jumbled and in no particular order. He thought of his life aboard the sailing ship Orion and before that his life as a teen-aged boy trying to earn money in a society that looked down on the poor Irish immigrants. The murder of Amos McPherson and his escape from the police to the Orion. The sinking of the Orion in the storm and the terror of being

493

alone in the sea. He remembered the small bump on the horizon and the hope that it was an island and the interminable swimming toward it in fading hope. He had made it and lived in isolation on the island. There had been no other human beings for years and then his determination to sail somehow back to civilization with the horrors of that journey. He had somehow succeeded and eventually, almost miraculously, found the young lady he had met only once but had dreamed about all those years. They married after a short courtship. *Amanda. Lovely, dear Amanda. Other than my own mother and dear Sister Mary Katherine, I'd never been alone with another woman until I met you. Perhaps there's an emptiness in my life that I've been trying to fill.*

*   *   *

Richmond, Virginia

Luke got off the train after it pulled into the depot in the Richmond. It was raining ice-cold rain, almost frozen with the wind trying to blow it sideways through every slit and opening in one's clothing. It was early afternoon and the sun remained behind a thick layer of clouds that hovered above, dumping their load of water on the city in massive sheets.

Luke waved down a hansom and directed the driver to the Littleton Tazewell Hotel on East Cary Street. The driver nodded. The hotel was well known for accommodating those who could not afford the city's more prominent and sumptuous hotels. Old and rundown, the hotel had a seedy reputation that matched its appearance.

The windblown hotel sign swung wildly over the sidewalk as Luke entered and went straight to the desk. "Yes, we have a room reserved for Mister Eugene Sherman." The hotel clerk looked into the icy eyes of the man standing across from him. "How long will you be staying, Mister Sherman?"

"One night."

"Certainly, sir. Would you care to pay in advance?"

Luke placed a fifty dollar bill on the counter and the clerk made change for him. "Room 302 sir, up the stairs and to your right." He handed Luke a single key.

Luke climbed the three sets of stairs and found room 302. He put his ear to the door and listened carefully. No sound coming from the inside. He reached under his long leather coat and gripped the revolver, then put the key in the lock and unlocked the door, pushed it open slightly. A quick look inside showed him that the room was empty. He walked in and across to the heavily draped windows that looked out over the street below. The rain slashed against the glass relentlessly and he let the drapes fall back into position.

The furnishings were comprised of a single bed, a chair, a corner desk, a corner wardrobe, an oil lamp on the desk and two gas sconces on one wall. Dark and aging wall paper covered the walls. It smelled as if someone had lived in the room; body odor was thick and mingled with the smell of cologne and cigars.

Luke walked outside into the hall, locked the door to the room and went back down stairs and out into the late afternoon rain. He had seen another hotel on the way to the Littleton Tazewell about two blocks away. He had no intention of spending the night at the Littleton Tazewell.

He walked the single block to the Chesapeake Hotel and found it to be about the same age and condition. They had a room he could rent for a single night. Luke pressed a second fifty dollar bill into the clerk's hand and the clerk returned the change. "Room 108, Mister Sherman. Right through that door," he pointed, "and to your left. Last door on the right."

Luke nodded in reply and found the room. It was in about the same neglected shape as the other but that mattered little to Luke. The rear door leading from the hallway to the outside was more interesting to him; he checked the lock and found that his room key, with a little persuasion and wiggling, could unlock the ancient lock. He tried it three more times to assure himself that it worked.

He went into his room and lay down on the bed. Bedsprings were broken and the mattress was thin and lumpy but he was asleep in minutes.

He wasn't sure what woke him up but of course he was never sure. It could have been someone in the next room locking or unlocking the door, or it could have been someone placing a hand gently on the door to Luke's room. He listened without making a sound then he heard the footsteps over head, in the room on the second floor.

He pulled the watch from his pocket. It was after seven o'clock. He had four more hours until the meeting was to begin. He walked out to the desk clerk, who pointed out several different places where he would find something to eat. Fifteen minutes later he was seated at a table in the rear of a small diner. The food was only adequate but there was plenty of it. He refused an alcoholic drink, electing to be stone sober when he met with his new clients. This was usually how it worked; he would meet with prospective clients posing as El Culebra's agent. But the two men he would meet tonight knew who he was; they would be able to identify him, even help an artist draw a facsimile that could be printed on a wanted poster. There were altogether far too many places where the job could completely unravel. But it would be his last job as Culebra. He would be wealthy beyond his wildest dreams. He would live in luxury in a foreign country, perhaps with Ida at his side, if everything worked out as it should.

At ten thirty he walked in the rain to the Littleton Tazewell and found his room. After carefully checking his surroundings, he unlocked the door and entered. The room was as he had left it; he lit the two sconces on the wall and the single lamp on the side table then pulled the chair into the corner away from the door. He sat, his leather coat adjusted so that his hand could find the revolver in a flash, if it came to that. He pushed back, leaning the chair on its two back legs, balanced. He waited, listening to every creak and snap in the old building and to the rain that thrashed against the window panes. His watch came to eleven o'clock, then past. The minutes ticked slowly by. Ten minutes past the meeting time. Twenty minutes past. At last he heard the footsteps as they climbed the stairs. Two men, talking in subdued voices. He heard one say, "There it is. Room 302." The doorknob rattled and then there was a light tap at the door.

Luke got up slowly from the chair and walked to the door. He unlocked the door and turned the knob letting the door swing inward. The two men stood outside.

"Can I help you gentlemen?" Luke asked quietly.

"Looking for a man called Sherman. Eugene Sherman."

Luke eyed the two men. "And you would be . . ."

"Madison North," replied the younger of the two. "May we come in?"

Luke opened the door and motioned them in. Both man removed their damp overcoats and flung them on the bed before taking seats themselves on the edge of the bed facing the single chair. Luke sat again in the wooden chair and leaned back. No one spoke for a long time. Finally Luke said, "It's your meeting, gentlemen."

"My name is . . ." started the young man.

"I don't want to know what your name is." Luke interrupted. "I don't want to know anything about you. The more I know about you, the more I put you at risk."

The young man nodded quietly. "Very well. Let's get down to business." He reached into his satchel and withdrew a large envelope. He spread the contents onto the bed cover, picked up a government map, opened it, turned it in Luke's direction and began. "Right here," he pointed with his finger, "is where the target will be camping. It's high elevation—about seventy-five hundred feet. We don't know what the terrain is like; all we have is this topographical map. But as you can tell, there are many deep valleys and rock cliffs. We want you to be in position as soon as they make camp. But you are to wait until another man joins the party."

The other man, older with white whiskers whispered something in the young man's ear. "Yes, the additional man may come up at the same time as the target. I'm not sure how to identify him other than he has white hair and a white mustache. He's an older gentleman."

"I was to take out only one man."

"You still are. The President is your only target. I trust you can identify President Roosevelt?"

"I've seen plenty of pictures of the man."

"The President is your target. The other gentleman must be there at the time you take the target down. Do you understand? This is critical."

Luke nodded. "I understand."

"If the other man never shows up, wait until the best possible moment and then take down the President. For the sake of thoroughness, it would be best if you wait until late afternoon to do it. That makes it too late in the day for them to take the target, if he is only wounded, out of the mountains for medical help."

"He won't be merely wounded. He will be very, very dead."

"Good. I like your positive thinking but there is always a chance of something happening."

Luke nodded. "I always make sure nothing just *happens*."

"Good." The man reached for a packet and handed it to Luke. "Here are train tickets. Abilene to Los Angeles, Los Angeles to Visalia, California. The President and his party will get off the train at Visalia and rent their horses at a ranch near there. From there they will go by horseback into the high country. You should plan to be set up when they arrive. You should plan your escape route ahead of time. The second set of tickets is from

Visalia to Los Angeles. We assume you will be making your own plans from that point on."

Luke nodded. "What sort of protection will the target be getting?"

"There is a six man security detail; U.S. Army. One of them is one of my men. He has a special assignment to carry out. There isn't any way of identifying him separately, nor would you need to." The man hesitated, "I must warn you, these men are well trained in all aspects of fighting; they're tough as railroad spikes and mean as rattlesnakes. They're all sharpshooters and one in particular is extremely accurate. They're well trained in hand-to-hand combat. They can live off the land for weeks on end."

"Thanks for the information."

The man nodded in reply and pulled another sheaf of papers from the envelope. "Here are copies of the President's itinerary from the moment he leaves the White House until he arrives back at the White House after his little excursion. The details change almost every minute but the main times are pretty well set by the railroad schedule. Even the President can't change that."

Luke nodded but remained silent.

"Do you have any further questions?" the congressman asked as he leaned back and stared at the figure across from him.

"One." Luke leaned forward in his chair, his eyes boring into the man who had done most of the talking. "How many people know about this plan?"

"There are four of us." It was the young congressman who answered.

Luke nodded slowly, as if considering this last bit of information. "Four. Five counting me."

"Then we can assume you'll accept this job?" The question came from the older man.

Luke nodded. "I'll do it.

Little more was said. There was some grumbling about Luke's demand for double payment but even that went without trouble. Luke took the thick packages of currency and packed them in his satchel.

The two men left first, individually and minutes apart, then Luke let himself out, locked the door and slid the key under the door. In a few minutes he was behind the Chesapeake Hotel, slipped his key into the old lock and twisted it carefully. The door lock opened with a muted snap and Luke let himself into the hallway, locked the rear door behind him and unlocked the door to this room. He would get a few hours sleep, get a hansom to take him to the train depot and get an early train out to Abilene, Texas.

He slept the first day on the train, exhausted by the late hours and the stress of meeting with the two men. The young man he figured was a politician of some sort by the way he talked. The older man was probably some rich business owner. But they had the money and had given him all the information he would need to do the job. He hadn't bothered to count the money; he knew that they were more afraid of him than he was of them.

* * *

Abilene, Texas

The train pulled into Abilene shortly past three o'clock in the afternoon. Only six people got off the train; and Luke tugged his satchel and gun case with him as he stepped onto the platform. The hotel where he was staying was only a few blocks from the depot and he walked there in about ten minutes.

He walked up the wooden stairs to the second floor, paused at his door, then knocked lightly at Ida's door. He heard the rustle of her getting to the door and it opened slightly.

"Oh, Luke!" she said softly as she opened the door and urged him into her room. "Oh, Luke! I'm so glad you're back!" She let him set the satchel and gun case down and then threw her arms around him pulling his lips to hers. "I've missed you!"

"I've missed you too, Ida," he said. It was true. He had missed her. He had missed her smile and her company and her eyes and their conversations. He had missed her in bed beside him. "I've missed you," he repeated. "Lets you and me go have dinner together."

She smiled, "I've been waiting."

CHAPTER 42

<u>Friday, February 20, 1903 Penacook, New Hampshire</u>
Clarence DePallin sat in the easy chair next to the window overlooking the Merrimack River. An open bottle of Tennessee Whiskey sat on the small table at his left and he held a tumbler still half full in his hand. He had sat there most of the morning, sipping at the whiskey and refilling his glass. Half the bottle was gone now but he was having trouble feeling the happy, relaxed glow he expected. Instead he felt heavy, burdened by the events of the last year. It took little imagination for him to envision the deaths for which he had been responsible. Now the real clincher, the death of President Theodore Roosevelt would soon be added to that list.

It was not that he particularly cared or not for the life of the President. After all the man did stand in the way of vast fortunes to be made in Nicaragua and had it been any other person he would still do the same thing. At least the blood would not be on his hands—well, perhaps figuratively it would be—as it was on Parker's and on Dunsworth's. Well, Dunsworth was already in the grips of everlasting *whatever* was waiting for him; probably not a comfortable seat in heaven. Now Culebra would take on the responsibility of pulling the trigger to abruptly end a man's life.

He had wondered about that moment. Would the assassin kill the President when he was looking toward him? Would the slug hit Roosevelt in the chest like a sledgehammer before the sound even reached his ears? Would he even know what happened? Would it be that moment of intense pain, then almost immediately . . . nothingness? Would Culebra shoot him when he was turned away, the slug perhaps severing the President's spine and crashing through his heart? Would Culebra watch the death and savor the last seconds of the President's life, storing the scene away for future memories. Would the whole attempt begin to unravel somewhere along

500

the line? Would the security detail be watching, scouting the mountain terrain for a sign of the killer, perhaps find him and gun him down? Would the killer reveal everything he knew? Is there any way that the trail would lead back to him? What would *he* do if mounted soldiers stormed this mansion to arrest him for treason or worse?

He sipped at the tumbler, emptied it and automatically reached for the bottle to refill. He hadn't slept well for three or four weeks now, ever since having to go after Parker and Ambrose for their share of the fee money. Both had revealed last minute concerns, doubts. If given the opportunity, both would have backed out instantly.

The killer, the assassin Culebra, had been an experience he would not want to repeat. The man exuded cold, deadly and evil fear. It was as if someone had held a copperhead snake close to his face with its mouth open, fangs bared, ready to strike and inject its deadly venom. He couldn't back away, distance himself far enough, fast enough. The night he and Ambrose had met with El Culebra in Richmond, he could not sleep afterwards; instead he spent the rest of the night tossing in the bed, his mind occupied by images he wanted to forget.

There were still three months of waiting ahead.

Besides that, his efforts to torpedo the Hay-Herran Treaty in the Senate appeared to be failing. The Senate was pleased with the terms, considering the United States was willing to pay $40 million for the New Panama Canal Company.

*   *   *

Del Rio, Texas

The Friday evening crowd was beginning to stream into the Longhorn where Sanford Parker was alone leaning onto the bar, his eyes roving the growing crowd for trouble makers. Two young Mexican men in their twenties popped through the swinging doors, caught one look of Parker and backed out immediately. Parker smiled. *That's right, boys. This place isn't for your kind.*

Two older men—Parker knew both of them—were standing down the bar several feet away. Their conversation had been intense and had grown louder as the afternoon had begun to turn to evening. They were arguing about the ocean to ocean canal and whether it should be built at all.

"Hell, they might ought to spend that money here in the United States!" one argued, "do something good with it!"

"Yeah? Like what?"

"Hell, I don't know! That's what them folks up in Washington get paid for!"

"Well, I'll say this: old Teddy's got a bull by the tail right now. Half is saying they should build a canal through Nicaragua. Half is saying they should build it through Panama!"

"And another half is saying they shouldn't build it at all!"

Both men roared with laughter.

Half and Half. Parker didn't need the reminder. He was in hock up to his arm pits and if the canal wasn't built through Nicaragua, he'd stand to lose most everything. Jennette knew nothing about his investment. She would be angry . . . no, not just angry . . . she'd come after him with her gun. She didn't like it here in the first place and would like it even less if they had to sell out and move to some sort of hovel. They'd be the laughing stock of the town. *Damn DePallin and his fancy money-making scheme! I should have never got involved with the Yankee sons-a-bitch.*

*   *   *

Chicago, Illinois

Ulysses Thaddeus McGarnet sat behind the huge desk that filled nearly a third of the corner office on the fourteenth floor. His window overlooked the busy Michigan Avenue stretch of large buildings; from the fourteenth floor he looked over most of them and had a view of Lake Michigan as well. Today, a thin layer of ice stretched out on the surface as far as he could see. The bitter cold of winter had hit the city in the middle of January and maintained its frozen grip on everything. Streets were layered with frozen snow and ice, making it difficult to go anywhere. The few pedestrians on the sidewalks huffed great plumes of steam as they hurried along, collars turned up against the frigid wind that coursed between buildings toward the lake.

McGarnet wasn't interested in the view outside his window. He was studying reports from the various steel mills and processing plants he owned at the lower end of Lake Michigan. Their furnaces lit the horizon at night and could be seen thirty miles away from Chicago.

Whether one looked at his position within the company as the top of the pyramid or the bottom of the funnel, everything having to do with the steel business under his command passed through him. Ships brought raw iron ore from Lake Superior. Huge smelters converted it to iron ingots. Furnaces converted the raw iron into steel which was then rolled into sheets and I-beams for future use. Workers, hiring and firing, wages and salaries, compensations and commendations all passed across his desk. Deaths and injuries, falling and rising prices and profits, status of their competition, all at one time or another were converted to numbers on paper awaiting his signature. He sat at his desk from seven in the morning until seven at night. His marriage had long since dissolved into a dull, live-in relationship with Eleanor, his wife of thirty years.

The steel business *was* his life. It had been his life for forty two years. It had made him one of the wealthiest men in the United States. It was a wealth that would be in his family for generations to come.

So, why had he, for God's sake, allowed that idiot congressman to talk him into making a risky investment in Nicaragua? It wasn't even the money; he could have funded the venture himself if he had wanted to. It was the risk that had increased geometrically and now he was involved in a plot to assassinate the President of the United States! He had provided twenty-five percent of the funds that would be used to pay the assassin. That alone could put him on the scaffold with a rope around his neck. With the extra pounds he was carrying, a fall to the end of the rope would probably rip his head right off. The last thought caused him to automatically reach for his tight shirt collar and run his finger around to loosen it. *Damn it!*

*   *   *

New York City

The railroad executive was having very similar thoughts while attending a meeting with other heads of departments of the railroad. Meetings seemed to be the bane of his life; especially in the last few years their occurrences brought with them hour upon hour of endless discussion in small cigar-smoke filled offices. Plans for future routes, right-of-way problems, changes in technology, government regulations . . . the list of topics was endless and John J. Ambrose used the time to let his mind sort out other, more timely issues.

Of immediate importance to the large man was the recent meeting he had attended with Congressman DePallin to meet with the man called El Culebra. The trip to and from Richmond had been covered under the guise of business. The meeting left him feeling sick and worried. He hadn't liked the man they had selected to assassinate President Roosevelt. He didn't like his manners or lack of manners. He didn't like being threatened. He didn't like the casual way in which *he* told *them* what he was going to do and not do. He didn't like the way the man had stuffed nearly a million dollars into the satchel as if was nothing. The man never said thank you or please or refer to either of them as sir. He didn't like the lack of respect. He was a paid assassin for God's sake! Highly paid! What would happen if he didn't do what he was paid to do? What if he just walked away with the money? What if this was all a swindle to take their money, perhaps turn them in to the government as having hired someone to kill the President?

Ambrose had started at the bottom rung of the railroads, swinging a hammer and laying track. He worked his way up through engineering, then supervision, finally management and then upper level management with division responsibility over the whole eastern half of the country. It had brought with it excellent salaries, benefits and a comfortable life. He could even retire if he wanted to in a few years, perhaps take his wife Lucile to Europe for an extended trip.

But the one issue kept scratching at the back of his mind: what if? What if they caught the assassin and he revealed everything he knew? What if the whole plot blew up in their faces? The questions swirled endlessly through his mind. Lucile had often inquired if he was not feeling right; the last time she asked he had snapped back at her so strongly she had retreated into the bedroom for the remainder of the day.

The more he thought about it, the less he liked Congressman DePallin and for that matter the Texan, Sanford Parker or Ulysses Thaddeus McGarnet. Damn them all!

Chapter 43

Luke used the time during the day while Ida was teaching school to think about and plan for his upcoming assignment.

Today he had the topographical map spread out on his bed. Fortunately, the United States Army had taught him some basic map reading and orientation using a magnetic compass. He had just recently purchased a field compass with a snap-down cover and now he set about placing the compass on the map, getting everything properly aligned. The Kaweah River he found pretty much centered on the left edge of the map and running northeast by north into the depths of the Sierra Nevada Mountains. He was somewhat surprised at the high elevations; he had never been at altitudes over three or four thousand feet above sea level. The topographical map revealed sheer cliffs and deep canyons, numerous rivers and creeks, some areas appeared to be bald, treeless rock. There were a few areas that were marked Not Surveyed in places where the altitudes reached above thirteen thousand feet.

With his finger he followed the canyon in which the Kaweah River ran, up the canyon several miles until his finger was just below the point on the map that had been marked with an X. The mountains rose nearly vertically on each side of the canyon at this point. He wondered how the President's party was going to get up that steep incline. He would have to look and find a faster, more sure way to reach his target. He came back to the mouth of the Kaweah River and ran his finger north a few miles, then studied the route east from that point. *Very rugged country.* The map did not reveal what sort of undergrowth he might encounter, or whether the hills and mountains were thickly or sparsely covered with trees. No trails were shown, no settlements or ranch houses. He looked for a long time, studying alternative routes that he could take going in as well as coming out. Should the exit route be the same as the entry route? How would the Presidential party be coming in?

After a long time he decided that the exit route would be a longer route, northwest in direction that would bring him out several miles north of his entry point. If anyone managed to see him enter then there was less chance of there being a greeting party waiting for him on his way out.

Horses would have to be rented or stolen. There were bound to be ranches or farms nearby that would supply that need. He didn't want to create too much of a ruckus on his way in. There would be plenty of time for that on his way back to the train.

He spent a half hour checking and sorting the currency. He was still unsure of how he would handle the relatively bulky container of money—half a million dollars. He couldn't just leave it somewhere to pick up on the way out. Unless . . . Ida.

* * *

He heard her familiar footsteps ascending the stairs and he greeted her at her door. She smiled, unlocked the door, stepped in and pulled him in after her making sure the door was shut before she hugged him.

"What's that all about?" he asked.

"I've been thinking today, a lot."

"So? What is it that you think about all day?"

She leaned back in his arms and looked at him. "I think about you all day and I think that I'm falling in love with you, Luke."

He stared at her for several long moments. "I . . . I'm not sure what to say, Ida."

She smiled at him. "Well, you could say that you're falling in love with me, also."

Luke smiled and shook his head slowly. "Ida, I never knew what love was. It's still kind of a mystery to me. I didn't know what it was like to be . . . loved. I never thought that a woman could or would love me." He hesitated, "I never thought that I could love someone. And yet, I think maybe that I've found someone who does love me and that I can love. And it feels . . . good."

"Do you love me, Luke?" she asked quietly.

He pressed his forehead to hers. "Yes, I do love you." The words came out as a whisper, as if he was afraid to say them. Then he pulled back, looked deeply into her eyes and the words came out boldly, "My God yes, Ida. I do love you."

* * *

Washington, D.C.

On March 3, 1903, the United States Senate approved the Hay-Herran Treaty and sent it to President Theodore Roosevelt for his ratification and signature. The treaty, if approved by the Columbian government, would give the United States, in perpetuity, a six mile wide strip across the Isthmus of Panama. The cost to the United States would be a one-time payment of $10 million and annual payments of $250,000. Panama at this time was a province of Columbia.

* * *

Los Angeles, California

The office of William Talbot, District Attorney, was always busy. The near constant flow of attorneys, legal assistants and law enforcement kept the door opening and closing and the secretarial staff busy scheduling meetings. On this particular morning, Bill Talbot, as he was most widely known, had just finished his third meeting and it was approaching eleven o'clock in the morning. He motioned to his secretary to hold any new meetings until the afternoon. He had planned to use an hour for a personal concern.

He pulled the letter he had received from his brother, J. B. Talbot in Del Rio, Texas, several months ago. He had read through the letter the first time, got a chuckle out of his brother's ranting about Sanford Parker. The rancher had been a relentless strain on J. B. for years and he delighted in sharing accounts of Parker's various eccentricities with the District Attorney. But after rereading the letter, Bill Talbot realized that his brother had been serious this time. Parker had said some very threatening things about President Theodore Roosevelt and had in fact, implied *there were men up north putting up money to fund a plot against Roosevelt, perhaps a death plot. Parker himself could be one of the financiers.*

Bill Talbot had sat on the letter for months, undecided as to what, if anything, to do about it. At that point it was clearly hearsay and drunken hearsay at that. But with the recent release to the newspapers of the President's planned trip to California, Talbot took a second look at the letter. In fact, he had sent his brother a letter asking for a little more information.

J. B.'s response, received just this morning, had provoked Bill Talbot into action. J. B. had written, *Parker was aware of Roosevelt's plans to visit California, even before these plans were released to the press. He also had inside information not given to the press; that the President would be spending several days in the mountains near some clod-buster town. He alluded to his own sources of this information. Parker himself had recently returned from an unaccompanied trip to California. The trip was apparently <u>not</u> associated with his cattle business.*

Talbot, as an attorney, could not just sit on this information. Though he had no power at the state level, nor had an actual crime been committed, he needed to take some minimal action.

He pulled a sheet of paper with his office's letterhead in front of him and began to write.

*   *   *

Washington, D.C.
President Theodore Roosevelt signed and ratified the Hay-Herran Treaty. It would now go to Columbia for approval by the Columbian Senate.

*   *   *

San Felipe—Panama Province of Columbia
Manuel Amador Guerrero's visit to the *Telegrafie la Oficina* in San Felipe rewarded him with a message from his unknown contact in Washington, D. C. It was once again in code that required the use of the Bible to decode the brief communication. It took him twenty minutes to decipher the message. The meeting with the ship that would transport him to his destination off the California coast would take place on April 16th. A small boat would pick him up at 3 a.m. at the spit of land, Las Bovedas that reached into the Pacific and take him to the ship. He should bring cool weather clothing and all the materials that had been previously sent. He

508

would be away from home approximately one month. This would be the last communication from his United States contact.

Amador leaned back in his chair. It was almost unbelievable! It was actually going to happen, after all this time and all those trips and meetings. This time, he would meet with the man who could cause things to actually happen! He would meet with President Theodore Roosevelt. But, was this all be an effort in vain? The treaty had already been sent to Columbia for ratification.

He carefully tore the telegram and the decoded copy into small pieces. He put the fragments in the ash tray on his desk and burned them, stirring gently until all that remained was ash.

*   *   *

San Francisco
Thomas O'Reiley had worked late that evening catching up on a number of projects that had recently received less of his usual attention. He worked steadily through the stack of papers, occasionally glancing out the office window as the afternoon faded into early evening, then darkness.

The past month had rushed by as the corporation had brought the new head of the architectural firm up to speed on existing projects and proposed projects. They were already missing Frank Barnwell who had consistently run a smooth operation but realized that Barnwell's replacement choice, the experienced architect Emerson Cartwright, was rapidly learning the management side of the business.

Thomas had stayed in touch with Sheriff McGee and Beck Weston in Santa Cruz and was disappointed that the trial date for Beck had been slipped once again by the District Attorney. It appeared now that the earliest Beck would be in the court room would be mid-May. According to McGee, the District Attorney was considering dropping the charges against Beck because of lack of direct evidence but was not ready to make that decision. The prosecution's case was slowly crumbling but public outcry demanding the resolution of Nelle Dunsworth's murder was very strong.

The investigation into Alexander Dunsworth's murder also came up with minimal leads. All they had in reality was an autopsy report that showed that Dunsworth had died as the result of a massive head wound cause by an almost point-blank large caliber pistol shot. No bullet or casing was found at the crime scene and rain had washed away any shoe or boot prints that could have provided a little insight into the murder. The stranger, Francis J. Watson, had disappeared from the face of the earth, leaving behind conflicting eye-witness statements regarding his appearance. For some, the man had been very tall, perhaps six foot two or three inches and quite heavy, especially around the middle. He had a dark brown beard, neatly trimmed. Oh and he wore glasses. Others saw him as normal height, perhaps five ten and rather on the thin side, cleanly shaven with a narrow, tightly clipped mustache. And no glasses . . .

Chinatown's outbreak of bubonic plague had finally caught the eye of the federal government and demands were pressed on California's recently elected Governor, George Pardee, to clean up the oftentimes squalid conditions in Chinatown in order to get the plague under control. Since this had been Pardee's intention all along, he was already at work on the issue by the time the federal government got involved.

* * *

<u>Monday, April 6, 1903, Washington, D.C.</u>
Reveille sounded at 5:30 sharp; the special guard detail scrambled out of bunk beds and into uniforms for muster in front of the barracks that housed them. Corporal John London was among the group that stumbled out into the early dawn and lined up facing Sergeant Gus Stoker. The detail couldn't help but look up at Sergeant Stoker; the man was six foot six inches tall with a build that nearly filled an ordinary doorway. The only decorative hair the Sergeant wore was a huge brown walrus mustache that covered the space between his nose and the bottom of his upper lip. He had a voice to match and seldom had to raise it above a normal shout to be heard several blocks away. His men both feared him and worshipped him. In dress uniform, he displayed a chest full of medals earned while participating in nearly every one of America's wars since the Civil War.

Today he informed the men they would begin a quarantine period that would restrict them to the post until they left for their far west duty with the President. He didn't have to tell them that this was to prevent any information being released, intentionally or not, to the public that might jeopardize the life of the President. The regular training schedule, meanwhile, was to remain in effect. Today they would have a twenty-five mile hike with full packs, rifles and ammunition belts. They would have rifle practice twice during the hike, each practice preceded by a one mile run.

John London grunted silently, as did most of the rest of the detail, at the restriction. But it was to be expected from Sergeant Stoker.

Just two days ago he had another visit from the Congressman from New Hampshire. They had walked to the far end of the exercise field out of earshot from everyone. DePallin had lavished praise on the young man, saying *history will prove that you have done the right thing,* and that *many of the world's heroes had gone into history not by name but by deed.* What he was asked to do, the congressman said, would someday be seen as a courageous act of heroism.

London listened without comment, nodding and saying *yes, sir* and *no, sir* at appropriate times and at the same time thinking *you're totally full of shit, sir.'*

The congressman had left after patting London's shoulder as if implying *good dog!*

*   *   *

San Felipe—Panama Province of Columbia

Manuel Amador Guerrero sat in the small room of his house that he shared with his wife Maria. It was dark outside and they had only a small oil lamp on a corner table to illuminate the room. Maria sat silently near him, as she knew he was deep in thought. Two nights ago, two policemen had come to the house. It had been almost midnight when they knocked at the door. Amador had gone to the door in his robe and the men had squeezed past him into the house. After casually looking around, they had faced Amador.

"Where's the telegram?" they had asked.

"Telegram? What telegram?"

"The one you received in March. March nineteenth, to be exact."

They knew about the message. "Oh, that telegram." He had laughed. "It was nothing, a small letter from my friend in the United States."

"What did your friend have to say to you?"

"Only that he would be coming to see Maria and me, sometime in the future, perhaps six or eight months."

"Well, perhaps you kept the telegram. We would like to see it."

"I did not keep it."

"What did you do with it?"

"I threw it away. In the trash."

The one doing most of the questioning frowned. "But we didn't find it in the trash."

"You searched through my trash?"

"So, what did you do with it?" The question continued.

"I have told you."

"You have told us nothing. It was not in the trash. What did you do with it?"

Maria stepped forward. "Manuel, is that the piece of yellow paper I used to light the kitchen stove? I remember one night I couldn't get it started. I had to use some paper to help start it. That may have been the paper the policeman is talking about."

"You may be right, Maria. Where did you find it?"

"In the trash. You had just crumpled it up and thrown it away."

The two policemen had stayed another half hour, questioning and looking through the house, pulling books off the shelves and food from the cupboards. When they finally left, Maria collapsed weakly in the arms of her husband.

"Manuel, when will this end? When will we no longer have to fear the police?"

"Soon, Maria. Soon." He had not yet informed her of his trip that was rapidly approaching. He would leave in five more nights.

Tonight they sat in the small room, half expecting the policemen to visit them again. He had made sure the small hiding place in his office was carefully concealed. Only two nights remained now. Maria had been very quiet and had asked no questions. *She knows,* he thought. *She knows I am leaving on another long, dangerous journey. She can feel it. She knows by my heartbeat, by my breathing. She knows by what I say and by what I don't say. She sees it in my eyes, smells it on my skin. And I know she knows because she asks no questions. Is this what happens when two people live together most of their lives?*

I do what I do for my country. For Panama. That it may be free from the heavy yoke of oppression that Columbia places on us. That it may end years of bloodshed. I do it for Maria.

* * *

<u>San Francisco</u>
The Western Union Telegram arrived at his office by a messenger at a little after eight in the morning. Thomas slit the envelope open and stared at the message inside.

> O'REILEY URGENT AND PRIVATE STOP URGENT
> WE MEET STOP COME AS SOON AS POSSIBLE
> STOP TRAIN TICKET IN YOUR NAME READY
> FOR YOU STOP URGENT REPEAT URGENT STOP
> GOVERNOR GEORGE PARDEE STOP

The Governor!

Thomas couldn't imagine why the Governor would insist that they meet—and as *soon as possible*! Train tickets were waiting for him! He read the telegram again, thinking he had missed something. Urgent and private! The word *urgent* used four times! It was pretty much right to the point—the Governor wanted to talk with him—right now.

Chapter 44

It was late afternoon when Thomas O'Reiley arrived by carriage at the steps of the Governor's Mansion at 1525 H Street. Today it was occupied by newly elected Governor George Pardee and his wife Helen. Built in 1877, the ornate Victorian home had just recently been purchased and refurbished by the State of California for its governors.

He was met at the door by Missus Pardee and was led immediately to the large study where he found the Governor seated behind a huge desk. When he came in, Pardee got up and came around the desk extending his hand to Thomas.

"Ah, Thomas! Thank you for coming so quickly!"

"Mister Governor . . ."

Pardee interrupted, "Let's dispense with that formality right away, Thomas! Call me George, at least as long as we're here in his room! Come on, have a seat here. We've got a lot to talk about!"

Thomas sat in the indicated chair and Pardee sat near him, not behind the desk.

"You're probably wondering why I asked you here in such a hurry. You will understand in a few minutes, at least that's my hope." He swiveled the chair so that he could reach some papers atop his desk. "I received a letter a few days ago. It's from the District Attorney in Los Angeles. I've never met the man but I have no reason to doubt his integrity. William Talbot. You know him or of him?"

"Never heard the name before."

"Same as me. Let me, if you would, read this letter to you, skipping all the up-front salutary mish mash. Let's see . . ." He paused, adjusted his glasses and then read. "It has come to my attention that there is possibly a plot in the making to harm or assassinate our United States President, Theodore Roosevelt. As you know, he plans to travel by train to visit our state and will be in California May tenth through May fifteenth, perhaps plus or minus a few days. I have been told by a reliable source that there is a group of men who are well funded who will perhaps take advantage of the President's trip to make an attempt on his life. The itinerary, dates and locations were passed to me prior to the press releasing that information. Also, this source mentioned the President spending several days in the mountains east of some *clod-busting town*. If genuinely true, this is new, un-released information. I wish that I could be more specific but that is all I know at this time. He goes on, etc . . ."

Thomas waited for Pardee to open it up.

"Well, what do you think, Thomas?"

Thomas shrugged. "Could be about anything, George. Someone blowing off steam. Somebody drinking too much and talking too much. Someone making it all up, wanting to stir up a little action."

Pardee nodded. "I agree, Thomas. That was exactly my reaction when I first read the letter. Then something happened. Yesterday I received a communication from Washington, D.C. that informed me that the President has planned a highly secret meeting with some foreign dignitary. It is to be held at an undisclosed location in the Sierra Nevada Mountains. The memorandum specifically states that California is to assume absolutely no authority in this situation; the President has his own security detail and they will be responsible for their own transportation and so forth."

Thomas whistled softly. "Well, that puts an entirely different slant on it, Mister . . . er . . . George. President Roosevelt is coming to California, plans a secret lay-over somewhere in the Sierras to meet with a foreign dignitary. It's so secret that he doesn't want anybody nosing around, providing *help*. Sounds like someone has access to inside information." He paused, "But why are you telling me all of this?"

Pardee smiled grimly. "You will see, soon enough." He reached for another paper. "This arrived this morning." He handed the paper to Thomas. "Go ahead; read it."

Thomas glanced at the paper and then at then Pardee. Something felt peculiarly unbalanced and his hands shook slightly when he held the paper. It was hand written in neat cursive black ink. There were no ink splatters and it had obviously been written with a sophisticated nib. The capital letters were quite ornate, lines level, words and lines neatly spaced.

It was undated and the paper was plain, though high quality, with no letterhead. It read:

The Honorable George Pardee, Governor of California
<u>Personal and Confidential</u>
Dear Governor Pardee,

I am sending you this message in strict confidentiality. I must remain anonymous, for my life will be in jeopardy if my identity is revealed. Therefore I pray and trust that you will study this message with maximum concern and consider it to be sincere and factual.

I am privileged to certain information regarding travel plans for our President Theodore Roosevelt. As you probably know, he plans a visit to your state in May, 1903. After a brief stop in Los Angeles, he will travel to San Francisco for an appearance there. I am most certain you are not aware that the President and his security detail will secretly get off the train in Visalia and travel by horseback to an undisclosed location in the High Sierras. During his brief stay in there, he will meet secretly with an envoy from a foreign country. The identity of that person and the reason for the meeting are of little or no immediate concern. What you must know, however, is there is a <u>plot to assassinate</u> our President during his visit to the mountains.

Preparations for this assassination have been ongoing for several months and involve an unknown number of very powerful men in our government and in private life. The assassination will be carried out by a paid assassin that goes by El Culebra.

That all I can disclose. Any more would cause my identity to be revealed and would cost me my life as well as the lives of others who are entirely innocent.

Please, Honorable Governor Pardee, take this warning to heart.

"My God!" Thomas whispered after he had read the letter.

"Yes!" Pardee said quietly. "Now I'm sure you understand my deep concern."

"George, I must tell you a few things that I know that may have some impact on this entire matter."

"I'd be most interested in what you know, Thomas. That's why I asked you to come here."

"First," Thomas began, "Regarding the President and his security detail getting off the train in Visalia. I've been there many times during the past several years. There is a family near Visalia that provides horses, tack, supplies, food, everything one needs to spend a few days in the High Sierras. I . . ." He hesitated.

"Go ahead Thomas. Whatever you say remains confidential."

"I know that they had visitors from the United States Government not long ago and they are very secretive about the meeting. I think that is the most likely place for the President and his security detail to get their supplies for such an excursion."

"So, you believe this note could be genuine?"

"I believe I would very seriously consider it, Governor. It appears to me that the person who sent it to you is fairly well educated, has a good command of the English language and is apparently well enough placed to give him accurate knowledge of the President's plans." He studied the letter again. "He talks about a group of *very powerful men*, similar to the comment made by the District Attorney and that the planning has been going on for *several months*." He looked at Governor Pardee, "Do we know where the letter was posted?"

"Washington, D.C." Pardee looked at Thomas. "Tell me what you know about this man El Culebra."

Thomas nodded. "I've heard the name Culebra before. What I know is that he's supposedly a paid killer and has used his skill many times both here in the United States as well as in foreign countries."

Pardee looked hard at Thomas. "Do you know a man by the name of Bret Solomon?"

Thomas frowned, nodded. "I believe I've read or heard about him. Is he the man whose wife was slain in a double murder in the foothills east of Sacramento?"

Pardee nodded slowly. "Bret has been a friend of mine for many years. He's very ill and I believe he's dying. He visited me a week or so ago; I think to maybe settle up old matters, you know what I mean?"

Thomas nodded.

"He told me a few things in confidence, made me promise that I . . . that I wouldn't take legal action against him." Pardee studied Thomas for a moment. "What I'm going to tell you must be in the strictest of confidence, Thomas."

"I understand."

"Some years ago Bret wanted to buy the property that was right next to his. He had offered the owner, Richard Manhauser, a lot of money for the property but Manhauser refused to sell. Finally, Bret got in touch with a man who would *take care* of Manhauser. He made this connection through a man named Alexander Dunsworth."

Thomas raised his eyebrows in surprise but didn't interrupt.

"Through Dunsworth, Bret contracted El Culebra to kill Manhauser. But at the same time El Culebra brutally murdered Bret's wife, Priscilla. Apparently Manhauser and Priscilla were more than just friends. Bret nearly went crazy. Eventually he decided that the assassin, this El Culebra, had to be dealt with. He made a deal with an ex-con named Clarence Chandler to kill Culebra."

Thomas nodded his head. "Chandler agreed to kill Culebra if Solomon would pay off his gambling debt to the Chinese."

Pardee looked surprised. "You know about that?"

"I heard about it six months ago, maybe a little more."

"How did you find out?"

"A private detective. It's a very long story."

"I'd like to hear it someday."

Thomas just nodded.

Pardee continued with his monolog. "Then you probably know the rest of the story. Chandler started hunting down the murderer but got himself knifed and dumped into the bay."

"And," Thomas interrupted, "we know the name of the man who killed Manhauser and Priscilla Solomon is Culebra."

Pardee leaned back and nodded. "That's the whole story, Thomas. And now supposedly, Culebra's on his way to California to assassinate the President."

"And Bret Solomon?"

"Bret Solomon will probably die in less than six months." Pardee stared at Thomas then went on. "Dunsworth, the man that had put Bret Solomon onto the assassin got himself killed as well. The man or men who killed Chandler and Dunsworth was never identified."

"It's a long chain of killings, Pardee. When you start with Chandler, you find his partner, Vernon Dyson is dead. The guard at the prison, Doggett I think was his name, is dead and now Chandler is dead. When you start with Dunsworth, there are three lawyers in Los Angeles he may have murdered, his wife Nelle he probably murdered and recently a man named Oliver Perkins he is said to have shot to death; and now Dunsworth is dead. This Culebra we don't know much about but we know he killed Manhauser and Priscilla Solomon. There are many stories that he's killed several political figures and possibly a few in Central and South America. He apparently has a nasty habit of ritually killing young women to satisfy some sort of fanatical rage."

"Well, Thomas, sounds like you know far more about this guy than I do."

Thomas told him about his meetings with the Nicaraguan detective, Santiago and how the detective had gotten his name from the corpse of Chandler. He also shared what he knew about the property scheme that Dunsworth was running and how Santiago had switched documents to sell the investment group and Dunsworth useless and valueless property.

Pardee chucked at this. "I guess I shouldn't, but I like that kind of retribution!"

Thomas waited. Finally he asked, "So, Governor Pardee, why am I here?"

Pardee nodded. "Fair enough question. Let's put together what we know, or at least think we know. President Roosevelt is planning a trip through California in May. He's bringing his own security detail and California has been instructed to keep our noses out of whatever's going on. Roosevelt's going to swing through Los Angeles, then travel by train up through the San Joaquin Valley to San Francisco, spend a few days there, then head back to Washington D.C. Two independent sources, neither identified, have suggested Roosevelt is planning an unpublished stop-over near Visalia, or some other *clod-busting* town and he and his security people are going to secretly travel into the Sierra Nevada Mountains for a secret meeting with a foreign emissary or diplomat or something. These same two sources tell us that someone is planning to assassinate the President, most likely during his brief foray into the mountains. Whoever is doing this is well financed and has been planning this for some time. I think that pretty well sums up what we know."

"And we think the assassin is *El* Culebra."

519

"That's it."

"So, where do I fit in?"

Pardee shook his head. "California has been ordered to stay away. Why? I think perhaps someone high up in the U.S. government is involved with this plot. In any case, my hands are *legally* tied. There's little I can legally do to prevent what could be the ultimate disaster for America, the assassination of another of its Presidents. On the other hand, the whole thing could be a massive misunderstanding or hoax. How would we look it we called out the cavalry and went charging off to save the President while he's peacefully camping in the mountains? On the other hand, how would we look if we did nothing and the President was killed while we were sitting on our hands, even though we had some indications that an assassination was being planned?"

"That's a difficult call for you, Governor."

"Well, Thomas, I've already made a decision. That's why I called you. At least one informant tells us that the President and his security people will get off the train in Visalia. I remember that's the area you where you killed that mountain lion several years back. I also know, through talking with my good friend, your father-in-law Handon McPherson, that you've returned there several times since. You are quite familiar with the area that the President presumably will be using for his meeting."

Thomas started to interrupt but Pardee stopped him. "Just wait, Thomas, I'm not through. There's nothing I can legally do to help prevent this tragedy but there *is* something I *can* do. I can send in someone who is familiar with the territory, who has an outstanding reputation as a tracker and hunter, who is already apprised of the situation and whom I fully trust. I want you, Thomas, to serve as my *Executive Deputy*, with my full personal authorization to hunt down and kill the man called Culebra as he attempts to assassinate the President of the United States."

Again Thomas tried to interrupt but Pardee stopped him with a raised hand.

"You will have no legal status. If you are apprehended during the execution of these duties, I will disavow any knowledge of you. Whatever the outcome of your efforts, the truth will never see the light of day, remaining instead deeply buried in the secret archives of the State of California. You will have no legal authority. No one must ever know what you accomplish or fail to accomplish. That includes me. I am sworn to uphold all the laws of this state. I would hate to have to turn you in for committing murder but that is what I'm asking you to do."

Thomas sat quietly, his mind in turmoil. The Governor of California was asking him to act as an assassin, to kill another human being in cold blood if necessary, to save the life of the President. He would not be allowed to seek the counsel and wisdom of Amanda or his father-in-law. It must be his decision. There was the distinct possibility, although Pardee hadn't mentioned it, that he could lose his life as well. Was he willing to take that risk? Could he just walk away and let the Governor find someone else? Perhaps he had already tried and others had refused to accept the danger. What about Amanda and the children? They would never know one way or the other. He suddenly felt strangely inadequate, unprepared, steeped in Indian lore that he abruptly seemed to have forgotten. What would Gray Hawk do? What would Gray Hawk advise him?

The feeling, the touch on his shoulder was so intense he turned in his chair to see who had laid a hand on him. There was no one in the room except him and Pardee.

Thomas swung back around. "When do you want me there, Governor?"

* * *

San Francisco

It was late afternoon by the time Thomas had taken the train back to Oakland and ridden on the ferry across to San Francisco. A hired hansom delivered him to his home on Nob Hill just as the sun was beginning to approach the far horizon.

He was greeted at the door by an exuberant Amanda who gathered him in her arms as if he had been away for months.

"Well, my important hero, what did the governor want with you? Did he offer you an important job?"

Thomas thought for an instant that she had somehow learned of the Governor's request then realized she was simply asking flippantly. "No such luck, my dear. Just a discussion between two friends."

"You're not going to tell me, are you?" Amanda asked accusingly.

"No, I can't tell you, Amanda. I've been sworn to secrecy."

"Are you serious?"

"Amanda, my dear and beautiful wife. Please trust me. I can't talk about it and that's the way it must remain. Please don't allow this to cause any distrust between us. I cannot talk about it, even with you."

Amanda leaned back in his arms, stared into his eyes. "Very well, my secretive husband. We shall never again mention it. Our lips are sealed, forever." She smiled, "now, come on in and have a bite to eat before we retire. Tell me, if you can, about your *old friend*, the Honorable Governor of California. Did you have an opportunity to see the new Governor's Mansion we've read so much about? I understand from my *private* sources that it is quite beautiful, perhaps even luxurious as befitting a state governor. And the grounds? Tell me about the lawns and gardens. Everyone will be attempting to duplicate them."

Thomas smiled and shook his head. "The house was nice and the yard was nice also."

"Thomas O'Reiley, you make me furious sometimes!"

Thomas decided it was time to head off further discussion. "How are you're your plans coming for the party? Have you made up the guest list yet?"

CHAPTER 45

<u>Wednesday, April 15, 1903, San Felipe, Panama Province of Columbia</u>
Manuel Amador Guerrero sat in the dark beside his wife Maria. He had a leather satchel on the floor beside his chair. Inside the satchel were his clothes and the envelope containing the papers he had received from his contact in the United States. If he was apprehended by the Columbian police with these in his possession, he could very easily end up standing before a firing squad.

He and Maria had spoken very little the past several hours. Both realized the danger that lay ahead of them both. The Panamanian government, a corrupt puppet regime operated and controlled by Columbia would not hesitate to convict him as a revolutionary and Maria as well, since they lived in the same house. There would perhaps be a little trial where evidence would be produced and the conviction would come quickly, as would the bullets of the firing squad. He pulled his pocket watch for the hundredth time and glanced at the time. Barely eleven o'clock. He had another three hours to wait. He had decided he would leave the house at two o'clock, walk to the end of the spit of land and wait there for the small boat to pick him up.

Restlessly, he stood and hauled the satchel into the bedroom and stuffed it under the bed. The bed cover fell over the exposed edge of the satchel. He had barely finished this when there was a loud knock at the door.

"*Madre de Dios,*" he whispered.

He heard Maria get up from her chair and go to the door. The door squeaked slightly as she opened it and he could hear Maria conversing with the men outside. He walked into the room and to the door where he stood beside Maria. "What is going on?" he asked.

Maria turned to him. "The *policia* are wondering why we are up so late and are fully clothed. Most people, they say, are in bed by now."

Manuel Amador Guerrero squeezed by Maria and stood in the doorway. "Who are you?" he demanded.

"*Especial de la policia*," the larger of the two responded. "You are Doctor Manuel Amador Guerrero?"

"*Si*. That is me. I am Doctor Guerrero."

"We have evidence that you are a revolutionary."

"That is absurd. I am a doctor."

"Even doctors can be revolutionaries, *señor*." He stepped forward. "We would like to come in. Please do not create a problem by refusing us entrance."

Amador swept his arm in a motion of courtesy. "Please, by all means, come into our most humble home."

The two policemen stepped in. The house was completely dark. "Why are you in the dark, *señor*?"

"We prefer the dark at this time of night. Lights on in a house this late at night invite the curiosity of the *policia*."

The large policeman grunted. He spent several minutes walking from room to room while the second policeman remained with Maria and Amador. They could hear books being swept from the bookshelves in Amador's office and rattles as the policeman attempted to move the furniture.

He came back into the room. "Where do you keep it?"

Amador frowned. "Keep what?"

"The telegram you received on March nineteenth."

"You have already searched our home for that telegram. My wife used it to light the stove. It is gone."

"Yes, that's what we were told. But we don't believe it. We have decided to sit and wait until you tell us where it is." He motioned to the other policeman. "Find a lantern and light it. We will wait. Perhaps time will help the doctor remember."

The two policemen sat in the only two chairs in the house, forcing Maria and Amador to stand. A lantern was lighted and sat on the corner table. Amador stood leaning with his back to the cool wall for support. Maria gave up quickly and sat on the floor next to him. No one spoke. The two policemen gazed impassively at the two civilians.

Amador estimated that an hour passed. The room remained quiet except for the soft snoring of Maria who slept with her chin on her chest, a position learned from being the patient wife of a doctor. The larger policeman nodded off a few times, the jerk of his head waking him with a start. The other policeman stared ahead unseeing; his eyes locked onto some small imperfection on the wall beside Amador.

Amador spent the time going over the list of names and places he had been provided. He was identified as *Juan Fernando Gomez,* a farmer from a small town named Verhalan, some thirty miles south of Pecos, Texas, on the Toyah River. His farm consisted of a little over three hundred acres on which he grew melons. The information provided included names of people in Verhalan who knew him, the name of his bank and the name of his wife, Abella. It was all a fabrication.

If he had been asked right now, he could have woven a convincing story of his life as a farmer on Texas. He went over and over the names, picturing the imagined person to whom each belonged.

Another hour had passed. "Sir, my wife is very uncomfortable. Please allow her to go to bed."

The large policeman shook his head. "No, she is to remain here."

Amador tugged at his pocket watch, made a show of displaying the time to the policeman. "Look! It is after two o'clock."

"We have all night, doctor."

Another long silence pervaded the room. The second policeman nearly fell off is chair when his head dropped suddenly. Maria's loud snoring soon acted on both policemen. The smaller of the two simply gave up and let his head fall back, closed his eyes and was soon fast asleep, his snores alternating with Maria's.

Finally the policeman kicked the feet of the snoring man beside him. "Bernardo! Wake up! We must leave."

The two policemen arose awkwardly and shuffled to the door. "Have a pleasant night's sleep doctor," the large one said. "We are sorry to have disrupted your night."

When they were gone, Amador pulled his watch out. The meeting at Las Bovedas was in less than thirty minutes!

He quickly retrieved his satchel, gathered his wife in his arms and kissed her. "Pray for me, Maria," he whispered.

He slipped out the narrow door that opened onto the narrow alley behind the house. The two policemen would be watching but where? He would have to throw caution to the wind. He didn't have time to do anything fancy. The walk to Las Bovedas, even for a young man, would take twenty minutes if not more. He could not be late! He started down the alley, his feet making crunching sounds on the gravel. He turned right at the end of the alley onto a larger street then cut across and through a vacant property. He walked quickly, not looking back. If the police saw him they may arrest him; or wait until he met with the small boat, then arrest others as well. He was sweating as he crossed the next street then turned onto the road that led to Las Bovedas. Trees lined both sides of the road and he could hear the waves of the Pacific Ocean brushing against the shore not far away. A noise to his left caused him to stop. It was a rustle from among the trees, a man's voice then a woman's. He started again. Many years past, he and Maria had spent warm nights among the trees as young lovers.

He was out of breath, his legs were growing shaky and weak from the pounding pace he was keeping up. *Not too much further.* He shifted the satchel to his other hand. Two hundred, maybe three hundred yards to go.

He saw a figure step out from the security of the trees. He was too far away to discern how the man was dressed. He could only continue toward the man. He glanced over his shoulder. There was no one behind him.

There was a quiet whistle from ahead, the call of a nocturnal bird but Amador sensed that it came from the man. He stumbled on, forcing one step after the other. Finally he saw the man raise his arm and motion to him. Three minutes later he stood panting beside the man who quickly took his satchel and led Amador to the small boat pulled up onto the beach. Amador helped shove the boat into the water and finally slid in, taking a seat as the other man grabbed the oars and began rowing. Amador was fully exhausted.

*   *   *

CHAPTER 46

<u>Friday, May 1, 1903, Abilene, Texas</u>

Luke turned quietly to the form of Ida, still asleep at his side with nothing on. *She is beautiful*, he thought, *something I would have never thought before.* He watched the slow rise and fall of her chest, the almost-smile that seemed to reside constantly on her face. He would have to awaken her soon, because she would arise and bathe before she dressed and walked to the small schoolhouse where she taught. He had put off the conversation he must have with her and he knew he was running out of time.

"Good morning, Sweetheart," he whispered next to her ear. "Time to wake up."

She groaned quietly, turned her head to face him before she opened her eyes. "Well, good morning to you, too." She reached across and stroked his face with her right hand. "It's a little early, isn't it? Or maybe you had something in mind?"

Luke chuckled softly. "I always have something in mind when I'm with you."

"Well, I like that," she murmured as she moved her face closer to his and tried to kiss him.

"Not yet, Ida. I have to tell you something."

"What? You're going to leave me for another woman?"

"Don't be funny. This is serious."

"All right, then. Let me put on my serious face." She frowned, formed her face into a scowl then said, "all right, I'm ready."

Luke smiled, "Ida, you are impossible."

"Well, do you want to be serious or what? We're running out of time."

"I have to be serious for a few minutes, then . . ."

"We'll see."

He hesitated, then, "Ida, I have to be out of town on business. I have to leave today."

"How long will you be away?"

"Two weeks."

She sat up in bed, the sheets falling away and revealing her nakedness. "Two weeks? Where are you going?"

"Los Angeles," he said. At least, that much was true.

"Why did you wait until today to tell me?" She sounded hurt, her voice about ready to break.

"I just didn't want to tell you but I had to."

She looked at him for several moments. "Is it your work?"

He nodded. "It's work. When I'm finished I'd like you to come out to Los Angeles to be with me."

"But . . . school."

"Your students will be on vacation in a week. You'll have all summer."

She smiled and it quickly spread into a grin. "I'd love to do that, Luke. I've never been west of Abilene."

"I'll take care of everything. There'll be a train ticket waiting for you here in Abilene. I'll meet you at the depot in Los Angeles."

She threw her arms around him. "Oh, Luke! That sounds so wonderful. I can hardly wait."

"There's one more thing, Ida. When you come out on the train, I want you to bring that box along with you. You know, the one with the padlock on it. Just buy a suitcase that it'll fit in and bring it with you."

"What's in it?"

"I'll show you in Los Angeles."

She nodded, "I'm so excited, Luke."

"And one more thing, Ida. If anything happens . . ." He shushed her interruption with a finger on her lips. "If anything happens and you don't get a telegram from me in three weeks . . . I want you to have what's in the box."

"You're scaring me now, Luke. What do you mean *if anything happens?* What . . . what could happen?"

Luke grunted. "Lots of things, Ida. I could get run over by a Los Angeles street car. I could fall off the train in the middle of the desert. I could fall into a California earthquake crack. I could get swept away by a huge wave and eaten by a whale. I could . . ."

She was laughing. "All right. But you must be careful and not let any of those things happen, Luke. What would I do without you?"

"You're going to be just fine, Sweetheart. Just fine."

She nodded and smiled. "Now, we still have a few minutes . . ."

*   *   *

Off the west coast of Baja California

The ship *Bonita* carrying Doctor Manuel Amador Guerrero rocked in the heavy seas. Only eighteen years old, *Bonita* was already far out of date in this age of steam powered ships. Originally she was a warship then sold off as the Brazilian navy, her original owners, updated their fleet. Modified several times, she was now engaged under many names in clandestine operations. Her two sharply raked masts and long bowsprit suggested more speed that she was actually capable of.

Amador had stayed in his cabin, fighting sea sickness as the ship sailed northwest along the coasts of the Central American countries, then the long coast of Mexico and finally that of Baja California. The seas had settled somewhat and he ventured out several times a day to stare at the miles of blue water that surrounded them. They were, he was informed, about forty miles west of land. On one of his forays topside he had seen a pod of whales off the starboard side, their huge backs breaking the surface when they vented. Another time they had sailed through a school of flying fish and he was amazed to see them dart out of the water propelled by their great speed as they sailed through the air for a hundred feet or more. Dolphins regularly raced them at the bow, darting and hurrying alongside in a playful contest of speed.

Amador visited the deck one more time before the sun set, watched the great golden disk as it approached the horizon seeming to squash out of shape as its lower edge reached down to touch the sea. The bulge grew even greater, the disk seemed to flatten just before it dipped out of sight behind the curvature of the earth. Light rays shot from the spot where the sun had been; then darkness approached rapidly. The stars seemed to pop out of the deep blue sky and suddenly it was dark.

The weather had been warm so far and he enjoyed the fresh air. The captain had assured him that the ship would be in position no later than

Wednesday. They would run in quickly under the cover of night, get the doctor ashore and then leave, returning two weeks later to pick him up and return him to his home in San Filipe.

* * *

Sunday, May 3, 1903, Los Angeles, California

The train from the east pulled into the depot with much squealing of steel against steel and billows of steam. Luke gathered the few things he had brought along with him; a small leather suitcase and the gun case holding the breakdown rifle. Anything else he needed he would purchase here in Los Angeles and simply discard after the job was finished. He had figured he had a few hours to take care of those needs before boarding the Southern Pacific train headed up the San Joaquin Valley.

A hansom delivered him to a large general store not more than six blocks from the station. He purchased two blankets, wooden matches, leather riding gloves and a Western style hat. Food supplies he would pick up in Visalia. By mid-afternoon he was aboard the train headed north.

* * *

San Francisco

Thomas was thinking over the conversations during last Friday's party as he was getting ready for the trip. The suggestions that President Roosevelt could end up with a bullet in his back sounded quite ominous, Thomas realized that for many, the President stood squarely in the way of speculative financial gain. The decision regarding the path of the canal was still to be made and strong forces were battling for the upper hand.

Thomas packed as he usually did for a trip into the mountains, trying very hard to not do anything that would upset Amanda any more than his occasional forays to the mountains did. The weather would still be cool, perhaps even some snow remaining. Days could be warm. He had to be prepared for either.

When Amanda was not present, he placed his knife deep in his luggage. He also took along his binoculars; at the last minute as he was getting ready to board the hansom for the ride to the train depot, he retrieved his Winchester rifle and a box of ammunition.

"Thomas, why are you taking that? You haven't taken a rifle with you for years."

"Thought I might do a little target shooting while I'm there. Haven't shot it in a long time."

Amanda shook her head. "Why is it I get a bad feeling when you take a rifle out of storage?"

"Mandy, please don't fret. I told you that I will be back in a few weeks at the most."

She looked at him skeptically. "This just isn't like you, Thomas. Something's going on and I worry for you." She paused, then asked, "Does any of this have to do with your meeting with Governor Pardee?"

"Can't answer that, Amanda. Maybe it does and maybe it doesn't." He shrugged his shoulders.

"Sometimes, Thomas, you infuriate me!"

"I'm sorry, Amanda. I don't mean to."

He had left shortly after that conversation. The train trip seemed especially long as they traveled down through the huge valley, still mostly green before the summer sun toasted everything to a golden color. It had been difficult to not tell Amanda what was going on, especially because her intuition seemed so keen that it was almost impossible to keep secrets from her.

He was met at the Visalia station by Angela; they hugged silently and not as closely as prior meetings. Angela was mostly silent on the trip back to the ranch; Thomas could sense the awkwardness between them. Finally, before they reached the ranch, he told her that he was aware of her and Frank's relationship and that he felt very good about it.

She turned to him, her eyes moist. "I never meant to hurt you, Tom. Ever. My feelings for Frank are just so much more different than what I have for you, even today. I think I understand how you were feeling and I understand the awful position I was asking of you. I hope you can forgive me, I pray that it has not harmed in any way your relationship with your wife. I still love you, Tom," she smiled sheepishly, "just in a much different way. I hope you and I can remain close friends for the rest of our lives."

"I'm planning on it, Angela."

"So am I."

He found the Gordon family to all be rather tense when he arrived but no amount of questioning could get them to tell him what was happening.

Hector inquired as to where Thomas was planning to go. When he told Hector that he would probably stay in the vicinity of the deer camp, the rancher blanched and let him know that another party of men would be staying there. Thomas assured him that he would not interfere in any way with others; they would not even be aware of his presence. Hector seemed only slightly alleviated by these comments, and only then did Thomas realize that the Gordons would supply the horses and tack for the President and his security detail. He kept these thoughts to himself, not wanting to further burden the family.

He and Angela spent a few minutes by the corral that evening but there was not the intimacy that had been there before and their conversation seemed stilted. They talked about the future of the ranch and Ramon's rapidly evolving plans to convert into citrus farming. She alluded to her and Frank's pending marriage and the probability that she would move to live with him in Sacramento. Every now and then a comment would pierce him bringing to the present memories, visions, thoughts that still seemed too close to the surface. Their parting was awkward. She came into his arms and put her arms around him, her face next to his. "I shall always love you, dear Thomas," she whispered. Then she was gone.

*   *   *

At sea, fifteen miles west of Morro Bay, California

It was near midnight when the ship's captain ordered the sails to be set again. It had wallowed for hours in the smooth swells, the light breeze occasionally causing the reefed sails to slap against the yard arms. The captain had now a Peruvian flag displayed. Its exact nationality and ownership remained intentionally vague, as its name changed quite regularly; for this clandestine operation its name was *Bonito* and if ordered, it could convincingly prove to be a Peruvian vessel on a business voyage to Vancouver, British Columbia. The fog had gradually lifted much to the relief of the captain. It was the first night of the new moon and the pilot was already aboard, ready to make the dash under the cover of near total darkness toward the coast and into the difficult harbor of Morro Bay.

Doctor Manuel Amador Guerrero leaned silently against the starboard railing, a thin unlit cheroot stuck between his lips. He wore heavy denim pants and a thick, sturdy shirt under his sheepskin jacket, its collar turned up against the cold, damp air. A thick, nearly white mustache covered his upper lip; otherwise there were very few remarkable physical characteristics surrounding him. A western-style hat with a narrow brim covered his head.

His mission had taken years in the planning and the man he was to meet could put the plan into motion that would politically, militarily and economically change this hemisphere and affect worldwide balance of power forever. Much blood had already been spilt and more was likely to saturate the soil of his country. Time was of the essence.

For the next several days, he would be known as Juan Fernando Gomez, a rancher from a small border town in southwest Texas.

He listened as orders were given and carried out in a surreal hush; men wore no shoes and orders were spoken rather than hollered. The sails dropped into place quickly, tightened and braced to take advantage of the small breeze that blew across the ship from the sea. He felt the ship heel to port slightly as the sails caught the current of air; he could hear the faint gurgle of the sea as the ship cut through quietly toward land.

The pilot used a few well-known lights on the coast to guide him in, though none of them was there for navigation. The stars were bright now that they were clear of the dense fog that had surrounded them for several hours. He could hear the gentle commands that were converted into directions to the helmsman, steering the ship on a narrow path through numerous shoals that could rip the bottom cleanly off the boat if it were allowed to come upon them. A huge black shadow appeared off the starboard beam; it would be Morro Rock, a monster boulder nearly six-hundred feet tall that nature had plunked in the center of the bay. It earned its name from its shape—*morro* being Spanish for a crown shaped hill. The rock slid by, a silent fortress, and then they were in the bay.

The captain touched Amador's arm. "It is time, Señor Amador. You must hurry; we cannot remain in the harbor."

Amador nodded silently as he grabbed his suitcase and followed the four deck hands to where others were already lowering a small boat over the side. He dropped his suitcase into the waiting hands of a seaman in the boat, shook the hand of the ship's captain and quickly climbed over the side and into the small boat. Silently the four sailors set their oars in place and began pulling hard toward the shore. The shoreline was dark and for the most part invisible. The huge Morro Rock was behind them on the starboard side. Amador could hear the sailor's labor breathing as they pulled hard at the oars. One looked over his shoulder and muttered, *"Existe la luz*". Amador saw the light also; apparently it was a small lantern swinging back and forth. Then it was gone. Moments later the boat ground into the gravelly sand and the men jumped out to pull it up further. A voice called softly from the darkness, *"Señor Juan Fernando Gomez?"*

"Si, yo soy Juan Fernando Gómez."

* * *

Washington D.C.

The train had pulled out of Washington D.C. with no fanfare. The President's Railcar was connected into the line of passenger cars along with the sleeping car that housed the special security detail. Between the two cars was the dining car for the staff and security detail. Corporal John London watched through the windows as the countryside swished by broken intermittently with small towns that the train pushed through without even slowing down. The train, they had been told by Sergeant Gus Stoker, would head west for several hours then turn south west for the long run across the lower states to Los Angeles, California. They were told to get a good night's sleep as they would return to a normal schedule of calisthenics under his personal direction in the morning.

Two cars back, the President of the United States of America rode comfortably in the specially made car, complete with overstuffed chairs and footstools and a full sized desk. His aide, James, sat at his elbow, taking notes and as usual, caring for the general comfort of the chief executive.

Roosevelt himself was reading over again the speeches he had prepared to deliver in Los Angeles and San Francisco, striking through whole areas and penciling in changes as he was apt to do. James would later labor with the typewriter to print them so that the President could read them easily. After they had been traveling for several hours, Roosevelt dismissed all but James for the night.

"James," he started when the car was clear, "if you would, bring me up to date on the gentleman from Panama."

"That would be Doctor Manuel Amador Guerrero, Mister President. According to dispatches we have received, he was picked up by the Bonita and will be delivered to Morro Bay, California on schedule assuming the weather holds. There is some indication from our agents in Panama that the Panama government was watching him very closely but he seems to be quite adept at maneuvering around them. We have two men watching his house around the clock to ensure that nothing happens to his wife in the way of reprisals while he is away."

"Very well done, James. Very well indeed." He tapped the desk top for several seconds. "Now, James, I've heard a few rumors from some of my, um . . . acquaintances . . . that there's the possibility of an attempt on my life while we're in the mountains. Have you heard anything about this?"

James looked stricken. "Sir, I've absolutely no knowledge of such an undertaking. We've been extremely vigilant regarding the secrecy of your movements. I should only hope that your friends are wrong, perhaps hearing and passing on an ugly rumor started by some malcontent. In any case, I'll alert the Security Detail."

"Well, that might be a prudent step. Let's hope it's only an *ugly rumor*, James. I certainly wouldn't like to be shot if we can avoid it."

"Indeed not, Mister President. I'm sure we all feel the same way."

*   *   *

The High Sierras

Thomas reached the top of the switchback trail up the steep canyon wall of the Kaweah as the afternoon sun was reaching for the mountains on the other side of the huge San Joaquin Valley. He had taken his time, letting the horse set the pace and using the reigns lightly. He studied the trail for any signs of other visitors to the area but the soil was unmarked, still plumped up by the winter's ice and cold. His horse left the only prints.

The season had been rough on the high country as well as the valley below. Many trees had been blown down by the high winds and some of the small streams still ran deep and swift flowing over their banks. But springtime had begun and wildflowers burst from the ground in colorful clusters and carpets of Lupine and Indian Paint Brush, Monk's Hood, Pussy Toes, Red Columbine and Dogwood.

When he reached the old deer camp, he waited for the old Indian but was met only by the silence of the surrounding forest. He glanced at the position of the sun; he had about three more hours of daylight. He clucked his horse into motion.

*   *   *

535

He found the shaman's campsite and was pleased to see smoke curling from the hole in the top of the shelter. The Indian must have heard him, for Thomas saw him emerge, bent over, through the small opening. The Indian waved across the distance and waited for Thomas to get nearer.

"Tah-moss! My friend. You are here. That is good!"

"Grey Hawk. It is good to see you. You have made it through another winter!"

"Long winter, Tah-moss! Much snow and too cold for this old man."

Thomas could easily see the tremor in the old man's arms and hands. He looked much older than just six months ago. The muscles in his face were slack and his eyes had lost their shine. His voice quivered slightly. "Old man maybe needs some fresh beef," Thomas said. "I have brought some with me for you."

"Ah! You make a soup with meat?"

"Whatever you want, my friend."

The Indian nodded. "Soup with fresh meat would make this old man very happy."

"That's what we will do, then."

Later that evening after they had eaten, the two men talked. Thomas mentioned feeling Gray Hawk's hand on his shoulder.

"Yes," Gray Hawk said quietly. "I felt you searching for counsel. I was there for you, Tah-moss."

Thomas told the shaman what was happening and the old Indian nodded. "Then it is as I saw in the omens last year. The white man's chief. Someone will come here to kill him."

Thomas nodded. "I must prevent that, Gray Hawk."

The Indian looked at Thomas for a long time. "I will help you."

* * *

Thomas awoke to the gentle snoring of Gray Hawk who had slept the night through wrapped in one of his bear skins. Thomas had used one of the skins as well and slept with his back against one side of the shelter. As he was drifting off to sleep, he thought about the responsibility that Governor George Pardee had thrust upon him. He hardly knew where to begin. Where would an assassin most likely attack? Where could he best gain an advantage over the President's security detail? What would be the most logical time of day to make his attempt? How would he plan an escape? Did he have any inside help and who might that be? When would he attack the President?

When Gray Hawk woke up, the two had breakfast and Thomas shared his questions with the Indian.

"What do we know about this killer, this man they call *El Culebra?*"

"Not very much, Gray Hawk. He has murdered many men and women. He uses a very powerful rifle. He can kill from far away. He also uses his knife."

"Where has he done these killings?"

"Mostly in large cities. He uses houses, buildings to hide his presence. He shoots quickly, disappears quickly."

The shaman nodded. "How does he disappear as you say?"

Thomas thought. From what little he had learned from newspaper articles he'd read, he used confusion and speed to cover his escape. "Confusion. He uses confusion and speed."

"Yes," Gray Hawk said quietly, "many people hear and see; but they all hear and see differently."

"That's right Gray Hawk. One person says the *shot came from such and such direction*, others say, *no, it came from that way*. One person sees the assassin behind a bush; another says no, behind that rock, another direction." Thomas nodded as he considered his words. "So, he will want to create confusion, perhaps use the echo of a rifle shot to confuse."

"You think very wisely, Tah-moss. How would this killer make himself invisible?"

"As you taught me, Gray Hawk, by blending in with the surroundings. By looking like the trees and the bushes around him."

Gray Hawk nodded. "Think of hunting animals, Tah-moss. You must remain downwind so the animal does not smell you. How must you position yourself so that the animal, or the man you hunt, cannot see you?"

Thomas frowned. He'd not thought of the placement of the assassin, carefully planned and utilized for the best effect. "Sunlight! He would place the sunlight at his back so that it would be in the eyes of those looking toward him!"

Gray Hawk nodded. "Yes! Late afternoon sunlight. Burning directly into their eyes, blinding them for the moment. And soon following, darkness falls. He makes a perfect escape."

"He would plan his escape route ahead of time, or he would waste time himself by getting lost or confused in the darkness."

"So, Tah-moss we are building an image of this man *El Culebra*. Do you think he is able to think in these same terms?"

"Yes. The man *El Culebra* has never been caught and no one even knows what he looks like. I will be looking for an evil ghost, Gray Hawk."

"He is a very dangerous man, Tah-moss, to have survived without being caught. My people have had to fight men like him. Many of my people have died terrible deaths at the hands of his kind. You must be very careful, Tah-moss but not so careful that it prevents you from being cunning and deadly like a snake. You must use every skill you have, everything I have taught you, without thinking about it. And when you get the chance, Tah-moss, you must kill this man without hesitation, without mercy, using any weapon you have. If you must beat his brains out with a rock then that is what you must do. If you must hold him under water and drown him then that is what you must do. If you must blind him with your thumbs and choke him with your fingers then that is what you must do. Do not pause, even for a heartbeat, to have feelings of mercy. He has taken many lives as you have told me and has shown no mercy. His hands are painted with the life blood of those men and women he has slain without warning, without pity. He is your enemy, Tah-moss. If you do not kill him, he will be quick to kill you; he will do that with great pleasure and will sing victory songs and dance over your body."

Thomas sat quietly. That was the longest discourse he had ever heard from the Indian. He realized it was what the shaman or the chief would have said to Indian warriors about ready to go into combat. *Show no mercy. Kill the enemy. Use any means possible. Otherwise, he will kill you.*

Thomas nodded. For the first time, he felt a mantle of confidence around him. For years now, Gray Hawk had taught him the Indian tactics of tracking, hunting and even some basic fighting skills. Now he was being called to use these techniques as well as every skill he had learned throughout his life.

He realized how far the two of them had come in their ability to communicate. The *language* they used had evolved over the years they had spent together. Using a few English words that Gray Hawk knew and the few Indian words he had taught Thomas, combined with hand signs that had evolved to illustrate some of the various actions such as hunting, sleeping, walking, seeing, eating, their vocabulary had gradually broadened. The two men sometimes added depth and substance to their conversation by simple stick drawings in the sand. The most difficult concepts were feelings or emotions such as want, hate, anger but over time these developed their own words, mutually accepted. As years went by, they could hold long conversations with little difficulty or awareness that they were moving easily from Indian words to English words to hand signs and to their own unique words. Meaningful sharing of ideas, concepts and actions of their lives had become possible.

CHAPTER 47

<u>Visalia, California</u>

Luke stepped off the train onto the platform. The town looked small and dried up, even though it was early spring. The weather was quite warm but he left his leather coat on, the revolver tucked into the belt of his pants. He carried a large suitcase as well as the small case for the rifle. As usual, there was a livery near the train depot and he made his way there gathering only a few curious looks from the townsfolk. A half hour later he rode out on a dusty bay, his bedroll and supplies tied behind the saddle. He carried the rifle still in its carrying case tied atop the supplies. He stopped at a small market and selected some easy to prepare food items to take with him, canned stew, canned salt beef, smoked pork, enough to last a week. It would make for slim pickings but he decided it was that or take along a second horse.

After studying the topographical map, he had decided there appeared to be enough natural water that he would not load himself with a canteen either. The man at the livery stable didn't ask questions as to where he was going. With all the state government men that had been in town recently because of the floods, he apparently assumed Luke was one of them.

Luke set the horse to a comfortable pace and headed toward the still-green foothills several miles west of the town. When he was still a few miles away, he stopped and pulled the map and the compass from his pocket and spread the map on his lap. He adjusted the map, lined it up with the compass and picked a few peaks as landmarks, selected the shallow canyon that appeared to lead upward into the high country. A few hours later he passed an old cabin almost hidden in the forest that appeared to have been recently repaired and occupied but there was nobody around. He let the horse forage for a few minutes, found the tiny stream behind the house and drank from it, as did his horse.

For just a moment, he thought he heard a voice. It was distant; it sounded like a young female voice. He gathered in the reins and led his horse into a dense thicket of trees as the voice got nearer. It was coming up the same canyon from below the old cabin. The young voice was singing and Luke could now make out the words. The horse and its rider came into view from behind by the cabin. When they emerged into the sunlight Luke drew an abrupt breath. The rider was a young girl, probably in her mid-teens. As she sang her voice was uninhibited and crystal-like in quality. He watched from within the thicket as she dismounted from the horse and stretched, unaware of his intimate closeness less than thirty feet away. She shrugged off her light jacket and rolled her shoulders to ease away tightness before she casually dropped the jacket to the ground. Luke's terrible and powerful obsessions quickly surfaced as the girl's adolescent but shapely breasts pressed against the thin cloth of her shirt; she ran her hands slowly through her long, dark hair and carefully lowered herself to sit beside the small creek.

*   *   *

Between Morro Bay and Paso Robles, California

Doctor Manuel Amador Guerrero, or *Juan Fernando Gomez* as he tried to think of himself, grimaced as the coach once again hit another rut in the road bouncing him clear off the seat. The coach had met him in the town of Morro Bay and they had gotten underway very shortly afterwards. The coach he soon found out had been arranged for by the government and he was its only passenger and would be for the entire trip halfway across the state to the town of Visalia. The driver told him they would pass through the settlement of Paso Robles before sunrise, then they would drop out of the coastal mountains into the valley. The trip this far had been over rough roads. The driver cussed and shouted at the horses as he pushed the coach as fast as it would go.

An hour later the road had smoothed and with fresh horses, they pushed steadily eastward. As the sun had come up, the doctor studied the dry countryside rushing past. The thin layer of grasses was beginning to turn brown and other than an occasional ranch or farm house, the terrain was bare and desolate. They rode quickly through one more range of low, rounded hills completely devoid of trees before the huge San Joaquin Valley opened before them.

Amador's mind went over the task ahead of him. Though he had verbal support from several high ranking government officials in the United States, it hardly defined approval. And approval, no, actually a promise of commitment, is what he so desperately needed. It would be absolutely essential if he was to achieve his dream and the dream of many of his fellow countrymen. He had never met the man he was to talk with; he had only read and heard about him. Men with his kind of power were frightening to Amador; he had seen that power abused far too many times during his lifetime.

The coach rocked as it sped across the flat land; Amador let his head rest against the wooden side of the coach and fell asleep, finally exhausted, his western style hat in his lap.

*   *   *

Aboard the Presidential Railcar

It was late evening as the train approached Yuma, Arizona. It would stop there for taking on coal and water for the run northwest into Los Angeles where they would arrive mid-morning. At each stop, the President's aide, James, checked at the Western Union office for telegrams addressed to the President and to dispatch any that Roosevelt had dictated in the hours preceding. The latest encoded message received revealed that the ship *Bonita* had made it safely and on time to Morro Bay. *Juan Fernandez Gomez* had been brought ashore and had boarded the stage for travel across the state. The President had merely nodded at that update.

Theodore Roosevelt sat in one of the deep chairs watching the scenery as dusk slowly settled over the countryside.

"It's a huge country we live in, James."

"Yes, sir. Truly magnificent and it seems to go on forever." The aide was getting tired of the constant rocking and clack-clack of the train's wheels. Other that a few short refueling stops, they had been on the move for over seventy-two hours. Although the Presidential car provided a few of the basic comforts of home, he also missed the opportunity to remove himself from the company of the President from time to time. Constantly being under the watchful eye of the President was a little unnerving.

"How does our schedule look, James?"

"I believe we're going to be right on schedule, Mister President."

"Good, James. Good." He paused, "I pray this meeting in the mountains is worth the effort, James. We've gone to a great deal of trouble to keep it tightly under cover. Should word leak out . . . there could be all hell to pay with Congress."

"I understand, sir. So far, we've had no indication of any leaks."

"Other than an assassin that somehow found out . . ."

"Yet to be confirmed, Mister President."

President Roosevelt nodded his head. "You are quite right, James. No use worrying about those things we cannot control, eh?"

The aide nodded. "Absolutely correct, sir."

*   *   *

Two cars ahead, Corporal John London and the others of the security detail had eaten dinner in the car right behind theirs. Talk had been a little subdued as the men were starting to feel somewhat cramped in their small quarters. The food had not been bad at all and Sergeant Stoker's insistence upon daily calisthenics relieved some of the tedium of hours of constant rocking movement. London sat near a window watching dusk fall over the desert. The past day had been pretty much the same scenery all day long, scrubby sandy dirt with an occasional dirt-street town that the train whisked through without even slowing down.

He thought about the assignment they had been given and was proud to have been selected to help protect the President but that pride was seriously blunted by the special orders given him by Congressman DePallin. He had thought hard and long about the congressman's comment that *history will show that you've done the right thing* and that *many have gone down in history not by name but by deed.*

What if the deed itself was criminal?

*   *   *

In the High Sierras
It was late afternoon when Luke spotted the huge tree even from a distance after coming up through the narrow, fern-filled canyon to the top of the mountain. He rode slowly past the huge redwood tree; he had never in his life thought something could grow that big; it was beyond his imagination.

Big wouldn't even begin to describe it. It dwarfed everything around it. He thought of Ida and wished that she could see the tree.

The narrow path leading past the tree wasn't visible to the assassin; the ground was firm and there had been only a few horses over the years; the path that had been pressed slightly into the earth was covered with forest debris and leaves from the trees. Rain and wind had obscured everything. He pulled the map and studied it closely. After making a few sightings with his compass, he felt he was in the right place.

He put the map away and looked around him, realizing he was very much out of his natural environment. He was familiar and comfortable with manmade structures, buildings with doors and windows, streets and alleys, sidewalks and hitching posts. He was used to the constant background of noise, the clanging of the blacksmith, of horses, of barking dogs; the smell of wood or coal smoke was a natural element of his usual surroundings. This was totally different. There were no streets, roads, alleys, houses. He felt disoriented; everything around him was different and was functioning under a unique and unfamiliar set of rules. Even his lungs felt the strangeness of the high altitude and he was consciously aware of taking deeper breaths, almost gasping for air. The thin air seemed curiously hushed; particles of dust too small to see hung suspended reflecting in the narrow shafts of sunlight that beamed through the tall trees. The silence was new to him, near total silence except for the occasional call of a bird. He clucked his horse into movement again. *I've got to be very careful*, he told himself.

He pulled the map out and checked it and his compass one more time. He was fairly certain he was close to the place on the map that the President had marked with an X. It would be ahead, maybe a half or three-quarters of a mile. *It would sure be easy to get lost up here*, he thought. He clucked his horse into motion and followed the center of the broad valley he was in. In a while the valley narrowed, as the map had indicated it would and he found the small creek that flowed down its eastern side. Within an hour he came into the small, secluded glen that matched the location the President had marked.

The small clearing was deserted and it appeared that there had not been anyone there for a long time. Some of the long poles that had formed a rough corral had fallen down; debris covered most of the ground. However, he found the circle of stones that delineated the fire pit and he was certain this would be where the President would die. There was certainly room for four or five small army tents.

On the southwest corner of the glen an immense granite wall appeared to thrust out of the mountain itself. Huge, the column of rock towered over him for many hundreds of feet. The granite rose in a thick, vertical column out of the slope of the mountain side; the back of the granite pilaster was firmly embedded in the mountain; the shear face dropped several hundred feet into the valley. The craggy rock surface of mottled gray granite hovered like a sentinel hundreds of feet above the valley. Eons of alternating freezing, ice and heat from the sun had caused segments to split away as massive stone shards, creating deep scar-like fractures that had pulled away from the face of the cliff. From the valley floor these marks were all but invisible, blending into the face of the granite precipice with the bands and streaks of quartz.

He spent the next hour surveying the campsite and the surrounding area deciding quickly from where he would fire the fatal bullet into the President of the United States of America.

Weather should not be a factor as long as it held as it was right now. Rain could present a problem but only if the Presidential party decided to break camp and leave. As long as the President was within sight, Luke was confident he could carry out his assignment. Of course, rain could work equally well in his favor, especially if the rain came after the assassination; it would make following him all but impossible.

Luke tried to envision the situation through the eyes and minds of the President's security detail. They would have been trained to constantly expect trouble. They would be continually looking for an indication of potential danger, on the lookout for anything that was out of the ordinary, anything that looked, sounded or felt unusual. However, human nature usually dictated that once an area had been declared safe or clear, the level of concentration on that area dropped. He had seen soldiers get killed when they stupidly adopted this attitude but nevertheless human beings tended to let their attention turn to more important things once they felt that their surroundings were secure.

He would have to plan and arrange his escape strategy and know it well. It couldn't be overly complex but could not be so simple as to expose his ultimate plans. Whatever the route, it would have to converge smoothly with his planned exit through the deep canyons leading to the foothills, the huge valley and the railroad beyond. Right now his priority would be to establish a base camp from which he could operate.

* * *

Los Angeles, California

The President of the United States of America, Theodore Roosevelt, received a tumultuous welcome as the train pulled into the railroad station. He rode in a 1903 Packard Model F closely followed by the California Governor, various state and city officials, a squad of cavalry consisting of Troop D First Brigade of the California National Guard and Signal Corp, and the First Brigade, California National Guard. The caravan followed a complex route through the city to the Westminster Hotel where he would meet with various dignitaries, including Governor George Pardee, dine and spend the night. His plans were to leave early Saturday morning, the ninth of May.

The President's security detail trailed very close behind, never more than twenty or thirty paces away from the President. Corporal London felt good to be outside in the sun and free of the restraints of the railroad car in which they had spent the last several days. They carried their Model '95 Winchester-Lee rifles with bayonets attached per the sergeant's orders. London let his eyes continuously scan the surrounding crowds and nearby buildings for anything that appeared out of place or abnormal; Sergeant Stoker had drilled this into them as they had practiced in Washington, D.C. London wondered, *if I was the assassin, where would I strike from? Perhaps from atop one of the tall buildings lining the streets, or from within the crowd of people lining the streets, or maybe from within the thick grove of trees in the small park we had just passed.* His eyes swept back and forth; an assassin could strike from many places.

* * *

Sierra Nevada Mountains

Thomas rode his horse into the higher mountains surrounding the old deer camp. Shortly past Standing Tall, he picked up the prints of another horse. He dismounted and studied the prints carefully. Very recent—perhaps less than an hour old. The shoe itself was not uncommon—perhaps slightly worn. No nails missing and the hoof itself had been well maintained.

Nothing about the prints to indicate the horse was uncomfortable . . . except, perhaps showing a slight hesitation. That could indicate an inexperienced rider . . . Thomas led his horse slowly, studying the prints. The rider had stopped quite often, probably to study his surroundings. Unfamiliar with the trail, the rider had urged his horse to follow the narrow stream.

Thomas slowly pulled his rifle from the scabbard and checked to make sure a round was in the chamber. The track followed the little creek, avoiding muddy areas but obviously the rider was unaware of the prints he was leaving. At one point the rider had dismounted and squatted beside the stream, probably for a drink. The horse had stepped up close and had probably drunk from the icy water, as well. Thomas studied the footprint. Thomas looked at the boot print—a riding boot from the cut of the heel. An almost new boot with clean, sharp sole and heel edges. He estimated the wearer weighed about a hundred and seventy-five pounds. He had used a twig to knock the mud from his boots before getting once again on his horse. Was he fastidious about his new boots or just an inexperienced horseman? From the position of the discarded muddy twig, Thomas guessed the rider was right handed. Thomas studied the man's prints carefully. There was nothing to indicate the man had anything unusual about his stride other than perhaps getting used to a new pair of boots.

Thomas led his horse across the creek and tied him within a tight thicket of trees. He followed the creek on the other side, away from the horseman ahead of him. When he arrived at the deer camp it was abandoned; the rider ahead of him was not in sight. Thomas stayed in the trees for several minutes, studying the area. He could see the tracks left by the horse and man as they had studied the area. They had visited the old corral and the fire ring of stones. Finally Thomas emerged and entered the camp site. His quarry had studied the granite cliffs that lined the southwest and western edges of the clearing.

Without any information it seemed to him that the camp would be the logical place for the President to stay for a few days. Water was plentiful and grazing for the horses was more than adequate; the area was essentially level and large enough to accommodate several fair sized tents. *Of course,* he realized, *the President may elect to go elsewhere.* From these higher mountains and ridges surrounding the general area, the assassin could look down on the trail leading in to the camp site and the campsite itself with its surroundings.

To the south and west of the campsite was the huge rock cliff that he had attempted to climb during his first trip here alone. Towering over the campsite, he could see from here that only a small part of the granite outcropping was visible; the largest portion remained buried out of sight in the mountainside. The top was fairly flat, though eons of weather had it rounded over the exposed edges.

South of the campsite the small creek snaked along the confines of the narrow valley; mountains on either side sloped into the valley. The valley would be a good place for an ambush. The mountain sides were densely covered with brush and trees; the western side eventually merged with the massive granite buttress. East of the camp, the mountain rose up sharply, its forested surface broken by several rock outcroppings that appeared to stagger unevenly up the mountain, presenting stone parapets or rough bastions that looked into the valley. Trees grew from some of the outcroppings. They were rough and weather worn with crevices and cracks caused by years of freezing and thawing. As the mountain face itself was quite steep most would be nearly impossible to reach without using ropes, but it would be good to look them over carefully. A sniper who carefully placed himself could see the entire valley from several of the outcroppings.

North of the campsite the ravine that held the small creek narrowed and deepened into a canyon bordered within densely forested mountains. Following the creek northward led in the general direction of Gray Hawk's year-round shelter. There was no reason to suspect that the President would choose to follow that ravine. The shaman had selected a heavily wooded location several miles north of the deer camp and his shelter was isolated among a labyrinth of small canyons and ravines, many with small creeks. A high granite bluff on one side provided only occasional glimpses of the old Indian's camp and shelter; most of his camp was hidden, even the smoke from his fire, by the heavy cover of trees.

The afternoon was getting late and Thomas decided to head back to the Indian's shelter to spend the night. He had scouted most of the area around the deer camp and had seen no further sign of another human being. The single set of tracks that he had followed eventually disappeared when the rider had cut across a vast sheet of granite. Recent rains had removed any layer of dust that would have enabled Thomas to track the horse across the granite.

When he got to Gray Hawk's shelter, the old Indian was not there but he arrived about an hour later with a freshly killed rabbit. That evening they roasted it over a small fire after stuffing it with various herbs and roots. It was dark when they ate sitting under the stars with just the last thin sliver of moon that peeked through the trees from time to time. Tomorrow would be the new moon.

Gray Hawk told him Indian stories about the beginning of time, where the moon, sun and the stars had come from, the creation of the earth, how the various animals came to be and the purpose of each species, how his people came to live on this land, the eventual arrival of the white man. The narratives were half myth, half history, stirred together with a little colorful imagination on the part of the story teller. They both laughed and talked about the legends and where and how they had originated. "These are very old stories," Gray Hawk assured Thomas, "passed down, father to son, through many generations."

Thomas then told the shaman what he could of American history; its discovery by Europeans, early settlements, the war to break away from George, the powerful King of England, a second war with the British in 1812, the terrible and costly War between the States, the war with Spain, the gradual westward movement and settlement of the people now called *Americans*, the building of great cities and the spread of the railroads.

Gray Hawk told Thomas he had never seen the Pacific Ocean, had never stepped foot in a white man's town or village, could not even imagine street cars or tall buildings or ships made of steel that carried hundreds of men and had huge guns that could shoot a heavy projectile several miles. He knew what trains were but had never been close to one. His knowledge of the white man was unfortunately based upon the six gold seekers who had slaughtered his family and friends. "The white man," Gray Hawk concluded, "is very hostile. They kill each other and they kill my people. My people never understood why the white man kills them."

Thomas shook his head sadly. "Neither do I, Gray Hawk. I hope those killing times are over and that we may live in peace."

The Indian nodded. "I would like that, too, Tah-moss."

*   *   *

Luke spent his first night in the mountains sleeping in a small copse of pine trees on the side of a ridge about a mile from the glen where he suspected the President would establish his camp. He spread his bedroll out on the ground and ate a cold meal of canned stew. He put off building a small fire as he was concerned that someone might see it. He had satisfied his thirst with water from one of the many small rivulets that crisscrossed the area.

He thought about Ida and his vague but emerging plans for the two of them. He would meet her in Los Angeles and they would board a steamer headed for South America somewhere. They would be wealthy and able to travel and live almost anywhere. He could imagine her joy shopping for clothes.

But he couldn't help contemplating his new-found relationship with Ida. It had abruptly bloomed into being, yet he had no doubt that she did care for him. He still struggled with what love really was and wondered if the feelings he had for Ida were in fact feelings of love. He hoped so. It would be very good to have her by his side.

He thought about the young girl on the horse but forced the thoughts away as he pondered the plan he had begun to form in his mind, studying it from all angles, looking for weaknesses, contemplating improvements. Before he drifted off to sleep he reminded himself that he must check his rifle sighting to account for the high altitude and the angle of fire. He wanted to do that before anyone else arrived in the mountains.

*   *   *

Visalia, California

The stage coach finally reached Visalia. It had suffered a wheel failure the previous day that had delayed the coach for several hours somewhere in the middle of nowhere. A new wheel finally arrived and it took no time at all for it to be installed. Juan Fernando Gómez was thoroughly worn out; his old body not used to the rigors of traveling by sailing ship and stagecoach. Joints ached, muscles cramped and his stomach growled with hunger. Sand gritted between his teeth. He needed to shave, he thought, and have a bath to remove some of the dust and grime he had accumulated during the long ride. His clothes felt sweaty and dirty and sand seemed to have seeped into every pocket and opening. He remembered to tell himself that the horseback ride into the mountains could be very much worse than this.

An attractive young woman approached him. *"Señor Gómez? Juan Fernando Gómez?"* she asked.

"Si. I am Señor Gómez."

The young lady stuck out her hand and said, "Welcome, Señor Gómez. I am Angela Gordon; I will give you a ride to our ranch."

Gómez took her hand in his for a very quick handshake, then picked up his suitcase; but Angela took the suitcase easily from him. "Our carriage is right over there, Señor Gómez. I hope you had a pleasant trip."

"It was very long I'm afraid and quite tiring. We had a breakdown yesterday that delayed our arrival. I hope that has not presented a problem for you."

She smiled as she put his suitcase in the back of the carriage. "Not at all, Señor Gómez. Please, get in and we will be on our way." She urged the horse into motion and expertly maneuvered the carriage onto the main street of the town. Gómez studied everything carefully for he had never been in one of the United States' small towns like this before. There were few masonry or stone buildings, instead everything appeared to be constructed of wood and of one or two floors, rather than the huge tall buildings in New York City. The walkways in front of the buildings were even made of wood. Glass windows fronted most of the structures and signs announcing the business within hung over the sidewalk. *Davidson's Hardware, Peakman and Chide—Attorneys at Law, Lucy's Women's Apparel and Visalia Mercantile* were just a few. In some ways it reminded him of the small towns in Panama but of course everything there was built of stucco and painted white with red tile roofs.

"Is this your first trip to California, Señor Gómez?"

"Si . . . . I've never been here before."

"I guess it's like Texas in many ways."

Her remark caught him off guard. "Oh . . . yes in many respects, especially the land itself." He had to remember to play the role the American Government had assigned him.

As they drove out of town, the great Sierra Nevada Mountains stretched before them from horizon to horizon. Hazy blue in color, the tallest peaks were still snow covered.

It took them about forty minutes to travel the narrow road to the Gordon ranch where he was enthusiastically greeted by Hector and Margarita Gordon, and shown to the extra bedroom where he would sleep until the rest of the party showed up. The Gordon family had been informed by the U.S. Government of the arrival of Señor Juan Fernandez Gómez from Texas and knew better than to ask questions of the new visitor. Instead they invited him into the main room to rest and nap in the large leather chairs after he had cleaned up, an invitation to which he immediately agreed and was soon fast asleep in the comfort of the Gordon home.

CHAPTER 48

<u>Thursday, May 7, 1903, High Sierras</u>

Thomas was up early in the morning. This time he would make his cautious route around the deer camp on foot, as it gave him a better opportunity to study the ground for tracks and perhaps further clues about the assassin. He took a different route, about a hundred yards above the previous day's route. By mid morning he was approaching the huge granite column on the southwest corner of the camp and was about three hundred yards above where the monolith merged into the mountain.

The horseshoe prints were plainly visible to his expert eye. He listened but the only sound was the buzz of insects and distant bird calls. The air was still and warm. He could smell the medley of odors that made up the natural smell of the forest: wildflowers, pine and redwood trees and the rich earthy smell of layers of loam underfoot. From somewhere upwind came the smell of deer urine. He let the air flow over and through him, memorizing the pattern of odors as if they were a painting of many colors. He could easily separate out individual odors and sounds.

He picked the trail up again at the flat expanse of granite where he had lost it the night before. After an hour of searching, he found the track again, leading upward into the tortuous assembly of valleys and ridges and single peaks surrounding the deer camp. He found where the rider had got off and let the horse stand free for some time. The horse had nibbled at the various wild shrubs and grasses, urinated and left a pile of droppings. Thomas checked and found the droppings to be rich in oats and hay; probably the sign of a rented horse. There was no trail to follow other than the meandering of the man on horseback somewhere ahead of him. Finally at one point, the trail led over the edge of a steep ridge into the dark blue-green forest far below. Thomas retrieved his binoculars and studied the dense woodland. There was no sign of the horse or the man and Thomas began to be concerned that he had followed a wrong trail—perhaps that of a hunter merely wandering through.

He retraced his steps until he was overlooking once again the deer camp site. Thomas took a few moments to study the surrounding cliffs and steep mountains. Several places presented themselves as possible sites where a sniper could very effectively hide. Assuming the sniper was not an experienced rider he would most likely select a site that he could easily get to and escape from. That would probably eliminate the several rocky outcroppings on the steep mountain east of the campsite. The sniper would likely not select a site from where he would have to make his escape by climbing further up the mountain. With his inexperience, that would take time and even possibly lead to a disastrous fall with his horse. No, the sniper would most likely stay high above the camp, firing down at his target before making his escape. That left several possible locations where the sniper could set up for his shot. The assassin, if not an experienced mountain man, was certainly experienced and successful in his occupation. Perhaps he would select not the best overall site, because that would be too obvious to the President's security people. Perhaps he would select a site that provided maximum cover for himself rather than the best shooting location. Perhaps he would rather risk a longer shot, or two or three shots rather than a shorter, guaranteed shot. Perhaps he would select a site that would offer him the best possible exit rather than the optimum shooting location. Perhaps even, the assassin would establish an obvious site to throw off anyone following him then switch at the last moment to a secondary site. He may even elect to assassinate the President before he arrived at the camp, as there were plentiful opportunities to do that as well.

The shooter, the assassin, the man Culebra, had the advantage at the moment.

The sharp crack and rumbling echo reached him and it sounded somewhat like distant thunder, echoing back and forth among the mountains. But it had a sharp edge to it that was not at all like thunder. It was not natural; Thomas knew it was a rifle shot.

*   *   *

Luke studied the results of his rifle shot carefully. He had figured correctly the new ballistic path for his shot. The thin mountain air would not slow the bullet as much and his compensation for the angle combined to affect the path of his shot. After making these minor adjustments to the telescopic sight, the bullet had hit exactly where he had planned. There would be no need for a second shot. He ejected the spent casing and slipped it into his shirt pocket, expertly broke the rifle into its component pieces and packed them carefully into the carrying case. Standing up, he took one last glance at the scene below. It very closely resembled the setup looking into the deer camp.

His horse was about a hundred feet away, hidden amongst the trees. Fifteen minutes later he was far from the site and riding along the edge of a granite ridge that ran for hundreds of yards along one side of the mountain. His stomach growled and he grunted in acknowledgement of the fact that he had not planned his food very well. He had already gone through three of his tins of stew and one tin of beef. That left not much to carry him through the rest of the week. He was in no mood to have to scrimp on food. He rode along the ridge, then cut to the right to the other side of the mountain and dropped down into the deep valley, followed a small creek to where he had established his camp and got off the horse, removed the saddle and blanket and tied the horse to a sapling.

*   *   *

Thomas jogged at an easy pace in the direction that he thought the sound of the rifle shot had come from. The further he went, the more concerned he became. Of course he could be wrong and this time he hoped he was because he was heading directly toward Gray Hawk's camp.

He knew the mountains well after being here year after year and he took short cuts, purposefully heading now toward the shaman's shelter. He was soon near the trail over which he had carried Gray Hawk when the old man had been cornered by Bear that Walks in Pain. As he got closer to the Indian's camp, he could smell the smoke from his fire and it reassured him and he imagined the old man sitting close to it to ward off the early afternoon chill in the air.

He saw the wisp of smoke that curled through the trees surrounding Gray Hawk's shelter and then was in the opening itself. He saw Gray Hawk sitting cross-legged with his head on his chest next to the fire pit and Thomas smiled. The old man could sleep anywhere nowadays. He walked over to the Indian and then stopped dead in his tracks.

The hole on the old man's back was just below shoulder level and centered on the spine. Thomas shut his eyes against the pain and anger that swept through him. He knelt next to the shaman and carefully felt his neck for a pulse. There was none.

Carefully he eased the old man onto his back. The wound where the bullet had exited was awful to see; a ragged hole in the center of his chest revealed where the bullet had exited. At least, Thomas realized, Gray Hawk had died instantly, his spinal column shot away and his vital organs shredded. He reached with his hand and gently shut the eyes of his friend, shaking his own head to clear away the tears of grief and anger. He stroked the Indian's hair gently. *Why? Why would anyone kill this old man in such a way?* Very carefully he lifted the Indian, held him in his arms, took him into his shelter, laid him out among his bear skins and covered him.

"My friend," he said quietly, "I know who did this. I am sorry I was not here to protect you but I shall come back soon to see that you receive a fitting entrance to your new hunting ground. Until then, I ask you to rest patiently and wait for me. I have something I must do in honor of who you are and who you have been."

Thomas removed his own clothing and walked naked to the small stream and bathed ceremoniously, carefully rinsing away the dust of the present time. He raised his arms and the words seemed to flow from somewhere deep inside him: "Aw-hi-hi-wa-hi-na-na-hi . . ." the lexis of the chant flowed as easily as the curious melody. The words had no immediate meaning to him but were of great importance at the same time. It symbolized Thomas's anguish for the cruel, brutal death of his friend Gray Hawk.

He returned to the shelter and tied on the breech cloth, slipped on the deer skin vest and the carefully handcrafted moccasins that the shaman had made. He pulled his hair back and knotted a small piece of vine around it. Then he reached for the small containers that held the colored powders they had used so long ago. He chose the black powder first and made jagged streaks on his face, his forehead, his chin, then on his arms, chest, hands and legs. He applied red, just a few dots and slashes here and there; a little white then the brown applied almost as shadow. Lastly, he fastened his knife to his breechclout and secured the lower end of the scabbard to his upper thigh with a leather thong.

"I'll come back, Gray Hawk."

He already knew where the shooter was hiding when he killed the old man. It took him twenty minutes to climb to the top of the ledge looking over the shaman's campsite. It didn't take long to find the place where the shooter had lain on the ground; the impressions of his knees and elbows were easy to find. Thomas lay down in the same place and looked at the scene below. The old Indian would have been in plain sight, his back to the killer three hundred feet above; the shot would have been from a distance of about a hundred and fifty yards. Not a difficult shot by any means and if the shooter was using a telescopic sight it would have been, to an experienced shooter with a high powered rifle, quite easy.

He studied the ground around him for other signs that might reveal something about the shooter. From the knee and elbow prints on the ground, Thomas figured that he was approximately the same size as the sniper. A disturbance on the dirt close to the shooter caught his attention. Something had been dragged across the dirt—a box, perhaps? Or a case for the rifle? Too small for a standard rifle though. Perhaps a rifle that could be broken into component pieces? The stock, the barrel and a telescopic sight? It could easily fit in a case for ease in carrying among crowds and on trains. It could be about the size of a standard business valise. Then there'd even be room for ammunition.

No sign of tobacco use. No sign of restlessness. The killer probably had not been there very long; just long enough to make the adjustments on the rifle to compensate for the wind, the angle, the distance to the target. He would carefully adjust the optics, center the crossed hairs on the center of the old man's back, squeeze the trigger to make the shot, retrieve the spent casing and then carefully dismantle and store his rifle. Thomas stood up and widened his search for clues to the man's character and ability. There were foot prints to and from the shooter's position. They were boot prints, the same relatively new boots with the narrow toes and higher, slanted heels of riding boots. There was even some indication that the wearer was having trouble with getting used to the boots; a slight hesitation in the footprint indicated he was favoring his right foot some.

The trail of boot prints led to the thicket of trees where the shooter had left his horse. The horseshoe prints were identical to those he had found the day before at the deer camp. The man had taken a few moments to relieve himself before he got onto the horse. There was nothing else to shed some light on the man who would try to kill the President.

Thomas followed the horse tracks as they led further up the side of the mountain then followed the ridge before they crossed over the top and down the other side.

The sunlight was almost gone and it would be dark in less than thirty minutes. Thomas decided to return to Gray Hawk's shelter and share the space with the shaman's corpse. The old man was entitled to the dignity of a watch on this, his last night on earth.

Thomas reached the Indian's shelter and entered. It was cool now without the benefit of the small fire but Thomas chose to not light a fire. Instead he elected to share the discomfort with his friend. He took up his place outside the small entrance to the shelter and put his back to the shelter wall. It was the night of the new moon and Thomas watched as the pale disk rose above the horizon, lit only by the sunlight reflected back toward it from the earth. Somehow the moon's ghost-like appearance seemed fitting for the death of the man called Gray Hawk. Thomas drifted off to sleep with images of the old shaman when he was younger, when they first had met and could scarcely communicate with one another. He dreamed that night of being in his small sail boat; he was sorely injured and the sea gull Frisco brought him a fish to eat and then spoke to him with the voice of Gray Hawk: *Be as cunning as a snake, Tah-moss.*

* * *

Visalia, California

The northbound train stopped a mile short of the train depot in Visalia. The conductor informed the train's passengers that the delay was caused by debris on the tracks and they would be on their way shortly.

The Presidential party took the opportunity to disembark from their two special cars at the back of the train into waiting carriages and their gear was transferred to two wagons. By the time the train lurched forward again toward Visalia, the President and his security detail were well on their way toward the Gordon ranch several miles to the east. They would spend only a few minutes at the ranch, just long enough to transfer their gear to pack horses. Theodore Roosevelt would use those few minutes to meet and become acquainted with the Panamanian, Manuel Amador Guerrero.

The mid-morning sun was already warm and Corporal London was sweating by the time they arrived at the ranch. They were greeted by

Hector, Margarita and Angela, offered tall glasses of cool water to drink and to wash down Margarita's homemade cookies. London glanced with curiosity at the young woman. He had never seen such a beautiful young lady in all his life. Her skin had a healthy bronze color with a natural sheen to it and her hair, black as rain-wet coal, came to the middle of her back in a single long braid. Her eyes were dark; he suspected they were probably brown in color and her long eye lashes flashed when she smiled, which she did when she looked toward him.

It took the party about an hour to get everything packed for the trip into the high country, including the four pack horses bearing food prepared by Margarita. The soldier's horses were equipped with scabbards for their rifles and were positioned two ahead and four behind the President who rode alongside *Juan Fernandez Gómez* and the President's personal assistant, there to be the official recorder of everything the President said or did.

The party started out, Hector Gordon taking the lead of the train of fourteen horses. He had agreed to lead the party to the top of the switch-back trail. From there, they could easily follow the canyon with the small creek to the old deer campsite. The route would take them past Standing Tall and enable them to reach the camp site before dark.

*   *   *

Thomas arose with the first rays of sun, washed and re-applied the marks with red, black and white powders. He chose to remain hungry this morning, for the old shaman had taught him that hunger also sharpened his senses. The Presidential party could well be on its way and Thomas could only guess what the assassin had planned for the day. Probably because the Presidential group would not arrive until late afternoon, almost dusk, he would not attempt a shot today.

He had decided to carry the old man to a mountain side overlooking the valleys below and bury him there. Not sure of the manner in which Indians handled their dead, Thomas decided to bury him wrapped in one of his bear skins along with his personal treasures; his small collection of enameled pans, his carefully constructed bow and the quiver of arrows, his precious knife and other small items including feathers and pieces of shell that the old man had collected over the years. Thomas knew the shaman would want him to keep the pipe.

It took Thomas the most of the afternoon to climb the mountainside carrying the body of his friend. When he finally rested, it was to look across the mountain peaks to the highest ridges, miles away and to the east. Most of the peaks were still layered with the winter snow and glistened brightly in the afternoon sun. Gray Hawk, he decided, would like it here. He could see the sunrise every morning and watch the seasons change in the valleys below.

He found a crevice between two huge boulders and into it he carefully lowered the bear-skin wrapped shaman, then gathered rocks and pebbles to pile on top to construct a cairn. It took him an hour to seal the crevice with enough rocks to keep animals from digging through to the body.

When he was finished, he stood silently over the cairn for several minutes, feeling the pain growing within him; finally he raised his arms as he had seen Gray Hawk do, raised his face to the sky and began to chant words that seemed to well up from deep within his very soul; *Hi-ya-wa-hi-so-wa-ha-wa.* The chant continued for several minutes on its own accord; bold, unscripted, heartfelt and sorrowful; Thomas saw visions of the old man when he was young and when he was a ferocious warrior chased by the United States Army. The chant seemed to Thomas to release the old man from earth's grasp on him and he could see him and Bear that Walks in Pain walking side by side. It seemed also to take away the hurt of the loss of his Indian friend. Tonight, he promised the shaman, he would reside in his shelter, smoke the pipe and tomorrow he would hunt down and kill the man who had done this.

It was late afternoon when Thomas reached the shaman's camp. He bathed once again in the stream and then fixed food for himself. Lastly, when it was dark, he sat in the shelter with the pipe and filled it with some of the herbs as the old man had shown him.

"I wish you were here with me, Gray Hawk," he said quietly as he lit the pipe with a stick he used to carry the flame from the small central fire to the pipe and puffed it into life, "I would like your thoughtful council, for tomorrow will be a difficult day." Soon the shelter became small and warm and the odors that the shaman had left behind filled him. A myriad of colors drifted by in unique, crystalline forms like colorful snowflakes and the sound they made was soft and reassuring. His own thoughts took form and had color and fragrance and sound . . .

He spent the late morning following the horse tracks but after losing them in the bed of a stream, he was not able to pick them up again. The rider and horse could have gone either upstream or downstream and there were numerous places where large, flat rocks could have provided easy cover for the trail. As the late afternoon sun set, he headed once again for Gray Hawk's camp.

*   *   *

The Presidential party had found its way to the deer camp and the soldiers set about erecting the tents and establishing a perimeter watch, an around-the-clock ring of protection around the President and his guest; always out of direct sight of the President, the soldiers kept a watchful eye on the surrounding forest. Of course, they had seen the granite cliff on the western edge of the vale and had studied it carefully with binoculars. With his troops at his side, Sergeant Stoker studied the solid column of granite then swept to the other side and the series of rock parapets that overlooked the valley.

"That's a lot of ground to try to reconnoiter, men." Stoker said as he held the field glasses to his eyes. "We don't have enough troops to do that. Just keep a close eye on everything. If you see, hear or sense anything strange, you call me immediately."

The soldiers nodded. Two of them would eat an early evening meal then get a few hours sleep before taking over the guard detail at midnight. They had done this many times and everyone was aware that Sergeant Stoker would be up and checking on his men at any hour of the day or night. There would be no slacking off among the detail guarding the President of the United States of America.

*   *   *

Luke had watched the party enter the enclosed campsite and saw the soldiers erect the tents for the President and his Panamanian guest as the long, deep shadows swept over the glen far below him. It was late afternoon and dusk was settling over the scene below. Smaller tents held soldiers and a medium sized tent that turned out to be the cook's tent were expertly erected. Oil lanterns were being lighted; the smell of beef roasting lingered tantalizingly in the still air. Luke silently cursed his mistake of not bringing enough food with him. His stomach had growled insistently all this day and would have to be satisfied with a chunk of dried beef and a hard biscuit or two when he returned to his crude campsite.

He had spent the afternoon constructing a camouflage of cut tree limbs and foliage behind which he could lay and gaze down at the President's camp. He had watched as two or three of the soldiers scanned the mountains carefully with binoculars. None had indicated anything unusual and none had pointed to where Luke would set up his sniper position. The shot would be tomorrow afternoon, shortly after four o'clock.

He crawled away from his hiding place and then walked to where his horse was tied, lifted himself into the saddle and headed for his own campsite, several miles distant in the quickly falling darkness.

Tomorrow would be a very busy day.

CHAPTER 49

<u>Friday, May 8, 1903, High Sierra Mountains</u>
Thomas was awake before the sun crept over the high peaks to the east of him. He had sprawled on one of Gray Hawk's bear skins; the small fire had burned out and he remembered only bits and pieces of the night. That was all right. He knew that he had spent it in good company with the spirit of the old Indian. He felt alive this morning; everything seemed particularly solid and well anchored. Even the air seemed exceptionally crystal-like and he could hear the individual cries of birds awaking to the new day.

He went to the small creek and once again bathed in its icy water, a ritual-like action that he had watched the shaman perform many times. The shaman had many reasons for this ritual and some he had never shared with Thomas but Thomas knew without explanation that it was preparing him for the day ahead. It had been part of his hunting ritual, it had been part of his teaching, had been part of the ceremony with the pipe and with the sweat ritual.

Thomas ate very lightly of the dried beef that Angela had packed for him. Once again he found the containers of colored dyes and began to stroke them on his face and arms and chest. His fingertips drew straight lines and jagged lines, circles and arcs of red and blue and white and black. He had no pattern in mind—he let his hands and fingers act as if they were in control of the design. He slipped on the breechclout and leather vest, the moccasins and tied his hair into a short braid, secured it with a piece of tough vine. Lastly he tied his knife in place and picked up his Winchester rifle. He checked to make sure there was a round in the chamber and set the safety. He tried not to think about what he was going to do this day—he was going to hunt down and kill another human being.

He tried to force his thinking on all that Gray Hawk had taught him over the years, to *be as cunning as a snake*.

He picked up the trail where he had stopped the afternoon before. The mountain side was steep and covered thickly with detritus from the trees which made it difficult to pick the trail of the horse and rider. A storm had recently knocked down many trees which lay battered where they fell, shorn of branches and left with sharp splintery spikes where the branches had once grown.

The trail became even more difficult to follow and Thomas knelt down to study it. It was heading northwest and generally away from the President's campsite. He looked ahead, trying to place where the shooter could have spent the night. Another ridge jutted perpendicular to the one he was on. Both ridges dropped sharply into a deep canyon, blue-green with thick trees a thousand feet below. Thomas decided that the shooter had probably set up camp on the other ridge, perhaps even on the far side of the ridge. He rose and continued to follow the trail which was slightly uphill from him. This side of the mountain was steep and covered with a thick carpet of undisturbed pine needles and required all of his attention to maintain his footing.

He didn't see the smooth rock surface below the layer of debris from the trees and it was too late when his foot started slipping. He reached out and grabbed for support but there was none. The entire pine needle surface covering the expanse of rock slid downhill and he was sliding with it. For a few startling seconds he was able to maintain his balance but the sheer slide became even steeper and he was suddenly plummeting down the side of the mountain crashing through thickets of bracken and saplings, falling, sliding, tumbling. Hurtling out of control, he got a quick image of the barb covered log ahead but there was no way to slow down or stop his forward fall. He slammed into the log with a brutal jolt that knocked his breath away. Merciful darkness closed in almost instantly.

He opened his eyes and was immediately aware of the intense pain. He remembered little of how he had gotten here; his stomach seemed to be pinioned against the rough bark of the fallen tree that was at least two feet in diameter; his arms and shoulders were laying on the top of the log and his hips and legs were under the log. A wave of excruciating pain swept over him and once again he passed out. When he regained consciousness he became aware that the angle of the sun had shifted. It was mid afternoon.

When he attempted to move savage pain lanced through his right side taking his breath away and forcing him to stop. He pressed his hands against the log and realized that his right hand no longer carried the rifle. He'd lost it somewhere in his fall or flung it away when he hit the log, he didn't remember. The dark green forest below him swam before his eyes and he tried to take a deep breath and remain awake. The pain was ghastly and he almost called out.

He shut his eyes and rested for several minutes before he tried once again to move. The pain in his side rose quickly to torture and he had to stop. He turned his head slowly to see what was causing the pain.

"Oh, God!" he groaned and let his head fall against the rough log. A spike of wood, the remaining splinter where a limb had broken off, had pierced his side just below his ribs. Nearly an inch in diameter at its base, the sharp spear of wood had gone all the way through his side and now protruded nearly a foot beyond. The rude entry and exit points were about five inches apart. The flesh was torn and bloody as was the razor-like splinter of wood. Thomas let out a low moan, partly of pain and partly of near hopelessness.

He shut his eyes and for the first time in years thought about the narcotic-like black seeds he had discovered on the island, their ability to almost immediately induce unconsciousness and relief from pain. He had none and had lost the last few he had when his little sailboat crashed against the North California coast.

His choices were immediately clear to him; stay where he was and die, or attempt to get free of the terrible spike of wood—and maybe die anyway. Without much thought, he knew that he would at least attempt to get free. He still had to find and kill the assassin before it was too late.

He forced his mind to center on the task at hand. He could either lift himself off the spear or cut the spear away from the tree and then pull it out. The first method seemed the most dangerous way as he could imagine having the spear half-way out then losing consciousness and falling again on it.

He studied the splinter and where it was still attached to the tree. Luckily, most of the limb had broken clear of the tree; only this single splinter remained and it had cracked where it attached to the tree when the tree fell. Perhaps he could continue that break with his knife and eventually pry the broken splinter away from the tree. He carefully reached for his knife with his left hand. Too drop it would be fatal. The movement shot jolts of pain through him and he had to rest between small movements for fear of losing consciousness, dropping the knife and watch it skid out of sight down the side of the hill. He would have to work with his left hand since any movement with his right arm brought slicing pain with it.

He finally got the knife even with his face then started across before he realized that he couldn't bring his left arm into the position he needed. He would have to get the knife in his right hand and do the work with his right arm and hand. He gritted his teeth and let a groan come out as he maneuvered his right arm into position. Sweat beaded on his face and he had to rest momentarily.

He took up the attack once again. Moving his right hand, he got the point of his knife onto the cracked and splintered wood and twisted the knife. Nothing happened. He drove the knife in further and twisted, groaning with the pain the movement caused. This time he could see the crack widen slightly and he drove the knife in again trying to not pay attention to the pain that accompanied the movement. He twisted the knife again and the fracture seemed to widen. He thrust and poked, then used the razor-sharp blade as a saw. His movements were close to frantic with waves of agonizing pain driving him. He swore at the spike of wood, at his knife and at himself for taking too long. The words seemingly lent energy and power to his movements. He was just about to let the knife rest while he regained strength when he felt the sliver of wood begin to give. With renewed energy he sliced at it, sawed at it, pried and levered it and suddenly he felt it separate from the tree.

He drew in deep breaths of air and stabbed the knife into the heavy bark to hold it. He knew that what he had to do now would be even worse.

*   *   *

Luke had spent the morning at his campsite. He would let the day pass into early afternoon before he made his way again to the shooting site. He didn't want to spend the day unprotected from the hot sun while he waited for late afternoon to come. He dozed some, nibbled on the last of his dried meat and walked to the little spring nearby and swallowed a few handfuls of water.

He assembled his rifle carefully, inserted one of the heavy .50 caliber rounds. He shouldered the weapon and put his eye to the telescopic lens, then shook his head in admiration. It was the perfect killing weapon. Today it would claim the life of the most powerful man in the world. In two or three days he would be in Los Angeles and with his woman Ida. He hadn't thought about her much the past several days—his mind had been occupied with other things—not more important things, just other things. She would never learn how he had come into this much money. They would travel to foreign countries, live in style. No family, though. He had already decided that he didn't want to be a father and have to raise a son like himself. He quickly shut that thought away.

The sky was pure cobalt blue, the kind of blue he had seen the few times he'd been aboard ship at sea. It looked like it went on forever, which some had told him that it did. He found it hard to believe that there was no end to the sky above. Infinity was beyond his power to even begin to appreciate. Nothing goes—or lasts—forever. Not even life. His mother had once tried to tell him about God and Heaven—*eternal life* were the words she had used—but again, he found it just too difficult to understand, so he gave up trying. He hadn't thought about his mother for a long time. It was too long ago to even remember what she looked like, exactly, probably pretty, though. Maybe dead by now, like the man who had fathered him. *Heaven* and *Hell*. He shook his head; can't have one without the other but if there really was a place called Hell, he would sure like to think that the man who had come home occasionally to beat his mother and him would be living there. He'd heard enough stories about Hell to be sure that it wasn't a good place to be, though that's probably where he'd end up also. *Now, wouldn't that be something,* he thought, *my daddy and me side by side in Hell.'*

*   *   *

The President of the United States of America sat at the small folding table across from the man from Panama, Doctor Manuel Amador Guerrero. They had been in conversation since mid morning with Doctor Amador doing much of the talking. He hadn't gotten very far into his argument when he realized what an excellent listener President Roosevelt was. So now he was careful in the words he chose, the phrases he used, for this man would hear and understand every nuance, every suggestion. The argument he was presenting would make marks on cultures and countries that would last for centuries.

The common people of the Panamanian Isthmus, presently a territory of Columbia, South America, were tired of civil war and wanted desperately to be free of Columbian rule. The two countries had virtually nothing in common and were largely separated by impassable mountains and jungle. A major revolutionary effort was being planned by the Panamanians to take place later in the year. They could win this revolution and would be happy to negotiate with the United States of America regarding building an inter-ocean canal across the isthmus. They *could* win. But Columbia had immense martial power in the form of the army and navy at their disposal. Brought to bear against the revolutionaries in Panama, such power would easily defeat the attempt to overthrow the puppet government set up in Panama.

What they really needed, said the Doctor, was help from the United States of America.

Roosevelt listened carefully. He had already been briefed by his staff about what the Doctor from Panama was going to ask for. He wanted to hear it right from the mouth of one of the chief architects of the revolution and so far he found this gentle old man, a well known and beloved physician, to be honest and well spoken. But the area in which he was beginning to tread was laden with traps, international and national, political and economical. Millions of dollars were at stake. Country borders were at stake. Public opinion was at stake. His own political future was at stake. The list seemed endless and he needed not only an awareness of each and every trap but plans and a means to avoid each one.

The two continued to talk. Hot coffee was brought in. Sandwiches were brought in. Some of Margarita's cookies were brought in.

*   *   *

Thomas leaned back against the log, exhausted by his efforts to get free from the tree. The spike of wood still protruded at both ends from the flesh just below his right rib cage. Thomas knew that it would have to be removed and the entry and exit wounds sewn shut. He sat in painful desolation, his mind not willing to think about what had to be done. He forced his mind to contemplate the steps he would have to take, just as he had on the island all those years ago. Be prepared to staunch the flow of blood as soon as the spear of wood was pulled out. Have something ready to close the two wounds and hold them closed. Have something ready to prevent infection from getting the upper hand. These were all problems simple enough to solve but his body revolted at the thought of moving.

Think, he ordered himself, *you can't just sit here!* He glanced around him for materials he could use. Vines. Broad leaves on ground-hugging plants. He recognized a few with medicinal powers. He started with the vines. Small and tender green, he stripped off the leaves, then split the vine lengthwise and split each half again and then again until he held several long strands, threadlike and strong.

From the nearby tree, he selected long splinters of clear wood that he would whittle into needle-like sharpness with his knife. Six of these should be enough. He picked the leaves of three different plants; one known by the shaman for its ability to help stop the flow of blood from a wound, one for fighting swelling that could burst taught skin and one that would drive infection away, at least temporarily.

Thomas prepared everything he would need and set his supplies carefully on a branch so they would not be disturbed. The awful pain in his side had started to become numb and that was good but the pain would reawaken when he pulled the huge sliver of wood out. He sat with his feet against the log, his supplies to his left, his knife still stuck in the bark of the tree. He selected a short stick and put it between his teeth, bit down hard on it and placed both hands on the end of the wood sliver. He shut his eyes and then pulled with everything he had in him. The pain turned red and white hot, shooting through every particle of flesh and bone in his body; he groaned loudly as the shaft of wood began to slide out. He screamed into the wood between his teeth as the last bit of wood finally cleared the wound; then the blood flowed copiously and he nearly passed out. But he couldn't and he knew he had to continue with the gruesome task.

He selected one of the splinters he had sharpened and pinched the front wound shut before he shoved the needle-like splinter through both sides of the wound. Quickly, he selected a second splinter and did the same thing, then a third. He reached for a single strand of the thread from the vine and looped it around each end of the three barbs, drawing the wound closed with X shaped loops, then tied off the loose ends. It was crude but it worked. Hastily, before he lost his nerve, the repeated the process with the second wound; it was more difficult because he couldn't see it as well. In five minutes he was through. His hands were shaking and his entire body quivered with the pain that shot through it. Much of the bleeding had stopped but he applied a layer of the leaves against the wounds, then a layer of those that would fend off infection. Using the vine

569

threads again, he tied the leaves over the wounds carefully then circled the thread around his rib cage three times and tied it tightly in place. Lastly, he drew the deerskin vest tightly over the wound and secured it in place the same way he had done the wounds.

He forced himself to rest for several minutes to get his breathing back to normal. His side felt like someone had branded him with a red hot poker. While he sat, he remembered he had lost his rifle somewhere during the fall. It could be anywhere above or below the log that had stopped him. He shook his head. Not now. Looking for it would have to wait; it could have slid all the way to the bottom of the canyon.

As long as he didn't move, the pain wasn't too bad. As soon as he started to get up it hit him in powerful waves that almost knocked him down. He struggled, retrieved his knife and made certain it was secure. Step by painful step he started up the side of the mountain. He glanced at the position of the sun as it approached the western horizon. *I'm running out of time. Culebra's going to kill the President and there's little I can do about it.*

* * *

Corporal John London stood at attention outside the President's tent. He could hear the low rumble of conversation inside but the words were too faint to make out. He had been selected by the sergeant to stand guard duty at the door of the tent to make sure no one interrupted the two men. He held his rifle at port position diagonally across his chest. As he stood thus, he thought about the words the Congressman had said to him: *History will prove that you have done the right thing,* and that *many of the world's heroes had gone into history not by name but by deed.* Not knowing what was transpiring inside the tent caused the young man to consider the validity of those words. He sensed that something historic was taking place, something beyond any one man's ability to change or control. He wondered just how the congressman fit into this scheme; what part of the puzzle was he? If this was so important for the congressman, why hadn't the entire security detail been brought in on it as well? Shouldn't the Sergeant be brought in on the plans? What would be the price he would pay if he didn't follow the congressman's directions? DePallin had made some ominous threats but could . . . or would . . . he actually do what he said?

*   *   *

Luke glanced at the position of the sun, reluctantly raised himself on his elbow and then stood.

"Time to go to work, Luke," he said to himself. "Easy money!" He chuckled and took out the three pieces that comprised his weapon, carefully assembled them checking each piece completely for any minor speck of dirt. Everything was in order. He confirmed that the elevation and distance settings on the telescopic sight were exactly where he had left them after shooting the old Indian. It appeared that wind would not be a factor; the air was motionless, stirred only occasionally by tiny eddies rising unseen from the sun-warmed rocks. He carefully disassembled the rifle once again, slipped each part into the carrying case and then tied the case behind the saddle.

Five minutes later he was nearing the location from where he would shoot and kill the President of the United States. The thought gave him a small thrill. Soon he would be famous but absolutely unknown to the world except for the two men with whom he had met in Richmond and the one who had tracked him to Abilene. That had been a serious mistake on his part.

He glanced at the sun once again and pulled his pocket watch. Three o'clock in the afternoon. He had an hour and a half, give or take. He pulled back into the shade of the forest and tied his horse, found a place where he could sit comfortably and watch the granite rock. It was bathed in sunlight right now and would be for at least another hour.

*   *   *

Thomas labored as pain seized his muscles; spasms shot through him like razor sharp arrows. Every step caused an agony-filled racking of his body—pain overlapped pain. He stumbled on, intent on finding the trail of the assassin. The route Thomas had chosen hugged the side of the mountain behind the monster granite column overlooking the Presidential campsite. As he struggled, his mind shifted through the possibilities; perhaps the shooter had opted for a different site, perhaps the sniper was already in place, his sites already on the President, perhaps all of this was a giant hoax, perhaps the shooter had set this up in such a way that the shooting would take place later, perhaps in San Francisco, perhaps . . .

571

The various options raced through his mind and he tried to think of only this one, singular option; the sniper was waiting to take his shot from the top of the granite cliff that overlooked the campsite. He tried to keep that single thought, that image, clear in his mind.

He slipped once and his feet went out from under him and he slid about ten feet down the steep mountainside before he was able to grasp the base of a sapling to stop his plunge. The slip had opened the fresh wounds and they bled freely, the blood running from under his vest and down his right side.

He rested for just a few moments, getting his breath back, letting the agony ebb back into unconscious pain that he could bury and ignore, at least for a while. He resumed his trek, gradually climbing toward the ridge that ran along the top of the mountain. If he had calculated correctly, he would come out several hundred feet north of the granite structure.

*   *   *

President Roosevelt leaned back in the folding camp chair, nodding his head. He had listened to Doctor Amador very closely and was impressed with his overall knowledge of the political reality in Panama and Columbia but also of the enormous problems the French Canal Company had run into during their ill-fated attempts to dig a canal across the Isthmus to link the Pacific to the Atlantic Oceans. The two attempts by the French Canal Company had nearly bankrupted France. Roosevelt knew that if the United States were to fail in the same undertaking, financial disaster could bury the United States in debt, political heads would roll and the United States would never again put a shovel in the ground to build a canal. The cost of failure was much more than financial catastrophe; it would relegate the United States of America to the legion of second-rate nations that were incapable of taking on history-altering ventures. Such failure would perhaps even imply to the world that the United States of America was unable to defend itself.

President Roosevelt listened as Doctor Amador closed in on the final points of his argument. Roosevelt knew what he must do. But first, both men needed a break from the intense discussions they had endured. "Doctor Amador, you have presented a very well thought-out line of reasoning. I want to respond to you in the same manner; however, this canvas seat is starting to feel quite hard and I suggest that we both take a break to *stretch our legs* as the saying goes. We've been in here several hours now. Let us re-group, shall we say, in an hour?"

"Mister President, I agree. A few moments to stretch will do us both good." Amador glanced solemnly at his pocket watch. "One hour, then?"

The two men stepped out of the tent, past the guard with his rifle at port arms and into the open air of the camp. It was already late afternoon; the sun had begun its slow arc across the sky and would soon be hiding behind the huge column of granite that rose a few hundred yards away.

*   *   *

Luke had just taken his position behind the thin camouflage of tree limbs he had constructed when he saw the movement below him. It was too early still; he needed the sun to be shining into the eyes of the soldiers when he took his shot. He carefully folded his leather coat into a long roll, laid down on the rock with the roll under his right elbow, raised the rifle to his shoulder and pressed his eye to the telescope. The figure of the President popped into view, startlingly close. He could see the President's mustache and the eyeglasses that hung by a ribbon poked into his breast pocket. The man looked solid, as if carved from a chunk of oak wood, and even over the distance his power and headship were reflected in his facial expressions, his walk and the manner in which he addressed those near him.

Luke fiddled some with the focus of the telescopic sight bringing everything about the target into bright and clear sharpness. He could see the button holes on the man's coat and could even determine that the President's suspenders were bright blue.

He glanced over his right shoulder; the sun would be in position in a half an hour. The air was still and warm and somewhere a bird made a noisy and raspy cry, almost like an infant's cry—'wah'. He would be glad to be out of these mountains, and by this time tomorrow he would be. He was getting hungry and tired of sleeping on the ground.

He studied the men below. He could locate four men in uniform—soldiers—but he was sure there were probably others. The horses were free to roam in the roughly constructed corral. He counted them, fourteen in all. He counted nine saddles astride one of the long poles that enclosed the corral.

Besides the President, Luke saw another civilian, an older man with white hair who chewed a cheroot but never lit it. This man and the President had apparently spent the entire day in the tent. There were two other men, one obviously the cook by his attire, the second was more formally dressed and seemed to hover around the President.

* * *

Thomas had to stop to get his breath. The pain that coursed through him sapped what little energy he had. He listened and heard a Stellar Jay give his warning cry to the animals in the area—*look out, there's a beast on the move . . .* '

Thomas wondered how much the assassin knew about the nature by which he was surrounded. If he knew, he would have taken the Jay's call seriously. He planted his left foot on the slope above him and levered himself forward. The wound in his side pounded and screamed with pain and before he had taken ten steps he had to rest again. He was sweating profusely and he tucked his right elbow against the wound. He took ten more steps and found himself at the top of the ridge; two hundred feet ahead of him and to the left was the top of the tall granite column. He could see the northern face and some of the top surface. He could only hope that he had correctly figured out the shooter's strategy.

He stopped once again to breathe deeply. He had planned on having his rifle with him at this point but now he had no weapon except his knife. He sniffed the air and smelled the musty odor of a horse. He glanced at the sun and was startled to find it nearing the horizon. He was almost too late! Still struggling for breath he started forward again, his eyes sweeping left and right. He saw the boot prints before he caught sight of the horse tethered in the trees beyond the granite. Culebra was here. Somewhere.

* * *

Luke peered through the telescopic sight, lined up the crossed hairs on the chest of the President just as his aide stepped into the line of fire to speak to Roosevelt.

"Damn!" he muttered, keeping the rifle in position. The man waved his arms in animation and the President nodded in understanding. "Come on," Luke whispered impatiently, "get out of the way!"

He watched as the President pulled his pocket watch, stared at it for a moment, then looked almost directly at Luke. Luke remained still; the only movement was his finger softly stroking the trigger guard. One of the soldiers joined the pair and Luke swore as the President turned sideways toward the new person. For a brief moment, the aide started as if he was going to move away, but then stepped back again cutting off Luke's vision of the President.

"Damn it!" he muttered again and watched as the other man, the white haired one, joined the small cluster, motioning toward the tent. He saw the President nod. "Shit! I'm going to lose 'em . . ." he whispered.

One of the soldiers walked into the scene and the aide and the older man walked away. President Roosevelt turned once again, this time to face the additional soldier. It placed him squarely in Luke's sites. Luke carefully lifted the rifle just a hair, placing the crossed hairs on the hollow of the President's neck, stopped brushing the trigger guard and moved his finger onto the trigger. His breathing was shallow, controlled as he began to feel the resistance of the trigger.

"Señor Culebra!" the voice behind him calmly addressed him. "If you move a single muscle, you'll be a dead man!"

Luke blinked in absolute disbelief. *One of the soldiers?* His finger relaxed just for a moment then he began to assert pressure once again on the trigger. "Hell! You know I can't stop now!" he said quietly to whoever it was behind him. But his aim had been disturbed and as he tried in vain to adjust the rifle, the President turned and was walking toward the tent.

"If you move, I will kill you! Give it up! Put the rifle down!"

Luke watched as the President opened the flap of the tent so that his visitor could enter first, then both flaps fell into position. The opportunity was gone, at least for the moment.

Luke let the rifle slowly drop to the rock and slid it a few inches to his right, then with his forearms resting on the rock, raised his hands, fingers spread, in a gesture of surrender.

"Don't move!" Thomas ordered. He stood directly behind the assassin, several feet away and out of the man's sight. He had to get his hands on that rifle, somehow. "With your right hand, push the rifle back, slowly!"

Luke moved his right hand toward the rifle, felt the barrel, grasped it then slowly pushed it toward the voice behind him. "You're making a mistake mister," he said quietly. "The name's Luke Sanders. I'm not El Culebra, or whatever you called me. You've got the wrong man."

"I don't think so. You killed my Indian friend."

"Huh? That old Indian was your *friend*? Hell, you should'a told me. I wouldn'a shot him if I'd known."

"Shut your mouth! Push that rifle closer to me."

Luke eased the rifle further down his side. His mind was already working on escaping this situation. He had to assume the man behind him had a gun. Well, it wasn't the first time he had to talk his way out of a fix, at least until the odds were a little more even. Surprise was his specialty. "There's my rifle. I can't get it any closer than that."

Thomas looked carefully. The assassin had not yet seen him but the chances were good if he bent to retrieve the rifle, the man would try a surprise move on him.

"Put both your hands on the rock where I can see 'em!"

Culebra nodded slowly and placed his hands with arms outstretched over his head. The butt of the rifle lay within Thomas's easy grasp. His shadow overlapped the assassin's prone body. Thomas began to bend down slowly, stretching his right arm toward the rifle. Watching the man for any sign of movement, using only his peripheral vision to see the rifle, his fingers found the stock and he gently lifted the weapon and then stood up again. After a quick glance, he realized the rifle was similar to his father-in-law's rifle. He held it next to his right hip, his finger on the trigger. The weight of the rifle pulled painfully on his right arm and the muscles on his right side quivered.

The words of Gray Hawk rang in his ears: *And when you get the chance, Tah-moss, you must kill this man without hesitation, without mercy, using any weapon you have.*

I could, Thomas thought, *put a bullet in him right now and fulfill my contract with Governor Pardee and my promise to Gray Hawk.*

He hesitated for a split second and then it was too late.

Culebra sprang up from his prone position in a violent flurry of arms and legs, swinging, kicking and slashing in all directions. His left foot made contact with the rifle barrel and the weapon flew from Thomas's grip and clattered onto the granite, slithered toward the edge before it stopped. Culebra quickly gained his balance and charged at Thomas, his arms still wind-milling. One fist caught Thomas on his left shoulder and pushed him toward the edge. Thomas stumbled, struggling furiously to regain his balance and stay on his feet. When he managed to get his feet planted solidly again he was on the angled edge with nothing but space behind him.

The shooter was fifteen feet away, a knife now gripped in his right hand. "I don't know who you are but you're a dead man," Culebra muttered. His eyes swept up and down, looking at the apparition standing before him. Face of multi-colors, dressed like an Indian warrior, blood streaming from under the deerskin vest. But he was a white man, not an Indian. He watched as Thomas quickly pulled his own knife with his left hand.

Thomas knew that he would have to fight the killer with his left hand; his right arm and hand were almost useless because of the painful wound on his right side. He kept his right elbow pressed against the wound to help stop the flow of blood. He had no experience in this kind of fighting, but using the basic techniques Gray Hawk had taught him, he bent his knees, left leg slightly in advance, taking a fighting stance. He held the knife, blade forward and left arm extended, took several deep breaths, rolled his shoulders and pointed the knife at the assassin's chest. He locked his eyes on Culebra's, seeing the rest of his body and movements with his peripheral vision. *Watch your opponent's eyes, they will tell you everything* Gray Hawk had taught.

Culebra moved to his right several feet, away from the curved edge of the granite and the deadly drop-off, the knife in his hand making circular motions. His face carried a frown, his eyes fastened on Thomas's trying to read his opponents intentions. Luke had been in many bar brawls, even bar brawls that had ended with only him walking away. This was different. The man facing him wasn't drunk or arrogantly sure of himself. There was no crowd of supporting men and adoring women. His opponent was cautious, maybe even naïve. He was wounded, but Culebra could see the steely determination in the man's eyes.

Culebra stepped quickly one step to his right and Thomas followed quickly, stepped forward in a sudden feint, watched as Culebra responded by stepping left, away from the line of attack. Now the assassin slid forward three steps, bringing the two men to within about five feet of one another. Thomas extended his left foot far forward and slashed sideways, right to left and Culebra leaned back away from the blade. Thomas stepped forward again, slashed again and this time Culebra leaned inside the arc and their arms crashed together, both blades pointed up. Culebra swung his left arm in a wide arc that crashed into the wound on Thomas's side and Thomas felt the hot poker of pain stab through his body. He grunted and smashed at Culebra's face with his forehead, once, twice before the killer backed away with blood pouring from his nose and mouth.

The two circled cautiously, their knives inches apart, waiting for the other to make a move. Thomas moved first; a quick feint to his right followed by a lunge and the knife in his hand cut across the right forearm of his opponent. It was a shallow slice that drew blood but didn't hinder Culebra's movement in any way. Culebra grinned a bloody, toothy smirk and made three quick feints then rushed with his knife low, aimed at Thomas's belly. Thomas stepped aside, transferred his knife to his right hand but Culebra's blade cut painfully into his right side. Thomas's blade, held lower, slashed deep into the assassin's hip as he lunged by.

Both men grunted in pain and surprise. Culebra paused only long enough to glance at this new wound then charged again, his knife pointed at Thomas's chest. Thomas spun on his left foot and thrust his right leg into Culebra's path. The killer tripped and stumbled headlong onto the granite but was almost immediately on his feet. Once again the two men circled. Both were bleeding but their eyes were intense, unflinching. Thomas feinted to the right then Culebra did the same. Their movements now were measured, deadly. Each step, each feint, every thrust was designed to learn something about the opponent or to inflict deadly injury. Thomas took advantage of the fact that Culebra had worn his riding boots and was unable to move quite as freely as he was. The moccasins felt every ridge, every tiny ripple and each grain of loose granite on the surface. He was quickly aware that on the northern side there was more loose granite that made the surface there more treacherous, especially to the hard soles of Culebra's boots. He eased carefully in that direction.

Culebra charged at Thomas and at the last instant kicked with his left foot at Thomas's right leg. Thomas grunted as pain shot through his body and his vision dimmed momentarily. Culebra's next kick landed on Thomas's right side and he stumbled backwards, fighting to remain conscious. But the pain overtook him and he sank to his knees. Once again the killer swung his left boot at Thomas's rib cage and Thomas doubled over, waves of pain pounding at him like the ocean's surf in a storm. And again the assassin kicked but this time Thomas fended off the boot by slashing at the leg with his knife. Culebra saw the knife too late and howled as the blade ripped across his left knee; he dropped his knife as the pain shot through him and Thomas rolled and kicked the knife away. Thomas tried to spin away but Culebra dove at him and bit

Thomas's hand that held the knife. Surprise and shock stunned Thomas for a moment and the knife slipped through his bloody fingers onto the surface of the granite.

Culebra pounced on Thomas and threw his right arm across Thomas's neck, leaning on it. Thomas couldn't breathe and his assailant's eyes were locked onto Thomas's; a bloody grin split his face as Thomas struggled under the choking hold. He couldn't make a sound; all air was cut off and he felt himself growing weak. He raised his hands and placed them on each side of Culebra's head, then moved his thumbs until they were squarely over the killers eyes. He pressed with the ends of his thumbs, feeling the softness of Culebra's eyeballs begin to yield under the pressure. Culebra attempted to squeeze his eyes shut but that move was too late. He groaned as the pain increased, finally jerked free of Thomas's grip and staggered to his feet, searched quickly to find his knife and scooped it up. But Thomas was on his feet also, knife in hand.

Culebra lunged again, his blade high in his right hand. The two men locked in place, arms intertwined and knives searching for an advantage. Culebra pulled his head back and butted Thomas on the forehead, a move that caught Thomas by surprise and he staggered backward. Culebra was all over him again as he fought for balance. Finally Thomas let himself fall backward onto the hard granite, curled slightly and Culebra crashed onto him. But Thomas used Culebra's own momentum to lift the killer right over his head and shoulders and Culebra hit the granite on his back with a loud grunt.

Thomas was on his feet almost instantly but so was Culebra, the knife still in his right hand, waving in tight circles. Thomas slid his blade from right hand to left hand and back again, several times, watching as Culebra's eyes followed the rapid movement. Finally the assassin threw his left hand forward and the handful of granite sand hit Thomas full in the face. He shook his head to free his eyes from the grit and Culebra laughed, stepped toward Thomas, his knife making broad sweeps. Thomas was still blinking hard and he feinted once and Culebra was drawn into his feint, knife held high but stepped back before Thomas could take advantage of his mistake. Thomas started the knife movement again and when the knife was in his right hand he lunged forward, his left arm held high to fend off his opponent's downward swing and at the same time he guided his own blade toward Culebra's belly. The two men collided but Culebra's face was contorted in pain and surprise. The blade had struck him, glanced off his lowest rib and buried itself in the flesh of his right side. It wasn't a fatal wound but it was painful and for a few seconds it took his breath away.

Thomas held onto his knife, twisting it and pushing it in as deeply as he could as his left hand grabbed the wrist of Culebra's right hand that held the knife. Thomas began to twist the wrist as hard as he was able.

Culebra grunted in pain and his hate-filled eyes locked onto Thomas's. "It ain't going to end like this," he grunted. He spat a bloody wad that hit Thomas in his left eye and brought his left knee up suddenly into Thomas's groin. Thomas was forced to let go as he staggered back, doubled over in pain and almost blind in his left eye. He saw Culebra lurch as he tried to regain his own balance and Thomas, head down, charged at him.

Culebra took the charge right in his midsection and the momentum knocked him flat onto his back. His legs scrabbled for a foothold and he suddenly rolled over onto his stomach as he slid toward the rounded, sloped edge of the pillar of granite. He held onto his knife as he skidded in the loose granite particles, his legs were already well onto the curvature of the edge. He got his right knee up and that slowed him some, then his left knee; and he was crouching on all fours, the toes of his boots scraping, searching for a notch, a seam or anything to hold onto. The fingers of his left hand were curled like talons, fingernails searching as well for imperfections on the surface. But he was losing, slipping toward the deadly drop-off.

Thomas watched in morbid fascination at the killer's futile struggle during his last moments of life on earth. "Don't move," he finally said. He turned and ran to recover one of the tree limbs Culebra had used to camouflage his shooter's position. He ran back with it in hand to where Culebra was straining to find a place to hold onto.

"Grab hold!" he shouted as he thrust one end of the limb out toward Culebra.

The assassin looked at him in surprise, "You can go to hell!"

"Let go of your knife and grab hold!"

Culebra's right knee slipped and he lost the bit of traction he had there. The left boot began to slide now and Culebra automatically struggled to regain a foothold.

"Take it! Grab the branch!" Thomas shouted but Culebra again sneered, his eyes focused on Thomas. The expression slid into a gruesome, bloody snarl of arrogance. His right knuckles were pressed hard against the rock, his fingers still curled around the handle of his knife but his hand was slipping on the rough granite.

"Hurry! Grab hold!" Thomas urged again as he held the branch close to Culebra's right hand. "Let go of the damn knife and take it!"

Culebra shook his head. He was still grinning, even as both hands were slipping, losing their scant grip on the rough surface. At the last moment, the bloody smirk was replaced with sudden awareness of what was happening, then with a look of horror as his body gathered momentum in its accelerating slide toward the edge.

Thomas could only watch now as the assassin slipped backward. There was an impulsive but ineffective scrabble of arms the last few feet and then Culebra's legs slid over the edge followed quickly by his hips and lower torso. The expression on his bloody face transformed into an obscene mask of terror, his eyes wide, bloody mouth open. Suddenly the only sound was the soft scuffing of his body as it slid on the granite. He slipped over the edge and was gone. Thomas knew the assassin would fall straight down for several hundred feet before crashing into one of the deep rock crevices that were around the base.

Thomas sat, exhausted. Pain rose from almost every part of his body. There had been no unusual sound or hollering from the President's camp and in all probability, they were entirely unaware of what had happened atop the granite column so close by.

And when you get the chance, Tah-moss, you must kill this man without hesitation, without mercy, using any weapon you have.

Thomas thought, *You've taught me well, Gray Hawk but I'm not a warrior like you.*

*　　*　　*

President Theodore Roosevelt stood, pushed the camp chair back and extended his hand. "Doctor Amador, I believe we've reached an agreement."

The doctor stood and grasped the President's hand. "It is so, Mister President. You have been most generous and it is something that my country will always remember."

"You do realize," Roosevelt continued, "that this discussion and our decision must be kept, shall we say, away from public eyes until the time comes."

"Of course, Mister President."

"Excellent! Well now, shall we avail ourselves to some of this beautiful California scenery?"

"A great idea, Mister President!"

* * *

Corporal London took the opportunity to scan the mountainsides with the field glasses. The sun had dropped over the rim of ridges and it would be dark before long. He was surprised that nothing had happened. According to the congressman, some unmistakable events were to take place today involving the President and the man from Panama. He had been instructed to say, under oath if necessary, that he had observed the Panamanian signal someone atop one of the mountain peaks by raising his hand and waving a white handkerchief. This was to have taken place before the unmistakable event that the congressman seemed convinced would occur but was obviously reluctant to describe.

The Panamanian had spent nearly the entire day sequestered with the President in the tent, coming out only for short breaks and at lunch time. At no time had he observed the Panamanian having any interest at all in the mountains around him. In fact, the Panamanian had been within ten feet of him all day. And now the President and his guest appeared to be the best of friends, laughing and talking as if they had known one another their entire lives.

Corporal London had done his duty the best he could and since the day had certainly been uneventful, he felt the congressman would certainly understand.

Tonight the Sergeant had planned a bonfire for the entire group of men to enjoy and had in fact agreed to lead the group in singing some selected camp songs that the President was known to be partial to. The security detail had practiced the songs on the train before they reached Los Angeles.

* * *

Thomas finally stood up, although his legs were wobbly. He needed to get back to Gray Hawk's shelter and take care of his wounds. He gathered up the rifle and made his way through the gathering darkness to the assassin's horse, still tied to a sapling. He found the carrying case for the rifle and determined how to disassemble the piece for storage. After that he tied the gun case behind the saddle and after several attempts, got himself into the saddle. The pain was nearly unbearable and the fresh wounds only added to his misery. He clucked the horse into movement and headed him toward the shaman's campsite.

He scarcely remembered guiding the horse through the labyrinth of canyons but was glad when he arrived. He slid carefully off the horse and led him to where he had the other horse tethered. He released the cinches and slid the saddle off as well as the few items the assassin had tied behind the saddle. Soon the two horses were tethered together, able to forage and get water from the creek.

Thomas made his way into the shelter, got a small fire started before he laid down on one of the bearskins and fell sound asleep. He awoke several times during the night and once helped himself to some of the medicinal root powder that Gray Hawk had told him would mediate pain.

He slept until after the sun came up the next morning. His right side was stiff with dried blood and pain. Carefully, he removed the vest. The wounds from the huge spike of wood appeared to be very raw and red. The new wound from Culebra's knife was a clean cut several inches long and that sliced through the outer layers of muscle and skin.

He helped himself to several bites of Gray Hawk's dried venison as he sat and watched the sunrise. In his pain and weariness he let the tears come for the first time as he thought about his Indian friend. Everything would be different now. He wondered if he would ever again return to this place.

He didn't hear the soft rush of footsteps behind him until the last moment and was barely able to escape the awkward swipe of the knife as Culebra lunged at him. Thomas rolled to the left and scrambled to his feet. The assassin stood there, his sneer ruined by the blood that ran from his lips and stained his teeth. Culebra stood staring at Thomas, shaking his head.

"You should'a checked, *Indian-man*. I got lucky," he said, "only fell a few feet and landed on a ledge. Now just look at you!" Culebra shook his head sadly. "You're in bad shape and I'm going to put you out of your damn misery!"

Thomas had left his knife in Gray Hawk's shelter. He had a sudden vision of the old Indian, trapped in the deep snow with the bear on its hind legs and Gray Hawk growling like a bear at the huge animal. The spontaneous roar erupted from deep in Thomas's chest—a visceral, discordant bellow that startled him with its ferociousness. He charged at Culebra, his left hand thrust out to seize the killer's arm that held the knife. He twisted Culebra's arm as the assassin was forced to back-peddle to stay on his feet. Thomas, still roaring, sensed the killer was losing the battle to remain on his feet. He grabbed at Culebra's right arm with his right hand as well, locked on and continued to twist, forcing the knife to turn toward Culebra. A look of panic passed over the assassin's face. His left foot slipped off one of the rocks surrounding the fire ring and he lost his balance. Thomas leaned hard to stay with him as Culebra fell backward onto the still-warm ashes.

The killer grunted when he landed on his back. His eyes widened in shock as the point of his own knife, gripped with his right hand, penetrated the soft spot below his sternum. Thomas looked straight into Culebra's startled eyes as he curled his left hand around the assassin's hand on the hilt of the knife and pushed against the killer's attempts to tug the knife away from his body. The man's strength was surprising and Thomas brought his right hand in as well, pressed it against the curved hilt of the knife, leaning hard onto the hilt. Culebra opened his mouth and clawed ineffectively with his left hand at the knife. Giving that up he reached for Thomas's face with his fingers bent into claws but the embers of life were quickly fading. Thomas kept up the pressure and the knife blade slid gradually through skin and muscle until it was buried to the hilt in Culebra's chest. His mouth opened and the assassin groaned softly and arched his back, his hate-filled eyes locked on Thomas's as life finally slipped beyond his grasp with a long, rattling sigh. Culebra slumped gradually to the ground; his body trembled as a single, involuntary shudder coursed through it before he died. Thomas had to look away from the open eyes and the blooded face of the killer. A surge of bile rose in his throat.

Thomas sat for several minutes with his head cradled in his hands, his breath coming in gasps. He had taken all that remained of life away the man. Had he done it because the man had attacked him, or he done it to punish the killer for all those whom he had killed? The many men he had shot? The women he had raped and mutilated? Had he done it out of anger? The man lying before him was well on his way to whatever happened after death. Did he know he was dead, or had he entered a vast place of darkness with no boundaries, no awareness, the ultimate, complete end of life? He finally got up and stumbled down to the creek, lowered his entire body into the icy water to let the current wash away the dried blood and cleanse the wounds. He scrubbed his face with handfuls of water and rinsed the bitter taste from his mouth. The water was frigid, but Thomas sat until he felt the cold had penetrated to his bones. Finally he stood, then sat shivering on a rock until the morning air and sunlight had dried him thoroughly. He washed the blood off the vest, moccasins and breach cloth and let them carefully dry in the sun before he placed them in a pile. He looked through Gray Hawk's supply of medicinal powders and selected three which he carefully applied to the wounds. He had nothing to bind the wound with, so he slipped on his shirt and pants, laced his boots on. It felt strange to him to be dressed like this. The clothing covered most of his body, shutting off the gentle breezes and the warmth of the sunlight.

He walked slowly to the cairn where he had buried his Indian friend and sat next to it.

"Gray Hawk, my friend. I'm sorry for what has happened. I know that you are now in a happy place, walking with your friend *Ha Sook Inya*—Bear that Walks with Pain. You will have many stories to tell each other. Perhaps you will find your family there, as well. I hope so. I found the man who did this to you, Gray Hawk, and he no longer walks this earth to harm others. I have learned much from you, Father Gray Hawk. You are an excellent teacher. I am a different man now. I am a hunter, a man with many Indian skills. I have tried to be the warrior you taught. I understand many Indian ways and see this world through new eyes. I understand my surroundings, the animals, birds and insects that are all part of this world. You have shared with me your knowledge of plants, roots, barks and their various powers over pain."

Thomas sat quietly for several minutes before he added, "I have one last task, my friend, and I ask you to understand why I do it. I want no white man to ever visit your shelter and take your things or celebrate and dance where the warrior Gray Hawk who evaded the soldiers for so many years once lived. I need to return all you have left on this earth to the earth. It will turn to smoke to be dispersed to the four corners and can never be assembled again. I have selected some few things I would want as memories of you; the pipe we have smoked and the moccasins, vest and breech-clout you made for me. I have left you with your bow and arrows, your knife and a few of your furs." He paused and listened to the breeze rustling through the trees. "My friend, I don't know if I will ever be back this way again. But I promise you that I will always hold your name in my heart. Now, I must say good-by."

Thomas stood for just a few moments, then turned and got back on the horse, steering the horse back toward Gray Hawk's shelter. There he gathered everything and carefully piled it in the old shelter. He dragged Culebra's corpse away and left it sprawled on a slab of granite for the animals to devour. He disassembled the ring of rocks that had once been the shaman's fire pit. He looked hard and found every fragment of the old man's living and placed them all inside the shelter and cut saplings and piled them on top of the heap, added firewood before he finally made a small fire and took it to the shelter to light the pyre.

He stood back while everything was burning watching the flames leap high until they had consumed everything. Thomas stirred the ashes to ensure there was no small piece of the Indian's life that could be discovered. It was late afternoon by the time the fire had died and the last coals had winked out. He stirred again, scattering the cooling ashes across the dirt. Finally, it was done. He would spend this night here and head for the Gordon ranch in the morning.

*   *   *

The Presidential party had packed up quickly and by late afternoon they were following the Kaweah River back toward the Gordon ranch. President Roosevelt studied the terrain with natural interest, pointing for whoever would listen, the various rock formations, the different species of trees and the plethora of wild flowers. Doctor Manuel Amador Guerrero rode near the President but his head bobbed in exhaustion as he listened to the President's monologue. He still had thousands of miles to cover to take the President's message to the revolutionaries in Panama. It was a message that would change everything. Amador would have to cross the great San Joaquin Valley once again, meet the ship Bonita at Morro Bay and return to the Columbian Province of Panama.

The Presidential party would spend the night at the ranch and board the train the next day as it drove through Visalia. That evening they would arrive in San Francisco where he would deliver a speech to the city's elite and before heading for Washington, D.C.

As they approached the ranch, Roosevelt drew his aide, James, aside briefly. "Well, James," he started, "it looks like the plot against my life was perhaps someone's imagination running loose. What do you think?"

"I think we were very fortunate, Mister President. It could have proven to be most disastrous if someone had actually attempted to assassinate you."

Roosevelt nodded. "You're right, James. We were very fortunate, indeed. Of course, we still have three thousand miles to go to get back to Washington."

The aide nodded. "We do at that, Mister President."

CHAPTER 50

<u>Sunday, May 10, 1903, Gordon Ranch</u>

It was late that afternoon when Thomas O'Reiley finally reached the Gordon Ranch. He was not able to remember much of the trip out of the mountains and somewhere he had slipped off the horse and lain on the ground for most of a day and night. He was burning up with fever and the wounds on his side were purple with infection. Bloody pus oozed from the deep wounds and his crude method of closing them had begun to spring open. He remembered reaching the river and falling in the swift current to let the cold water take away the heat of his fever and wash the wounds clean once again. He hadn't eaten, at least that he could remember.

Hector was the first one to see him coming down the tree lined lane, riding a horse and leading a second horse. He was barely holding on and his body was curled forward, his head swaying in rhythm with the horse's slow walk. Hector called for help and Margarita and Angela were there quickly to help get Thomas off the horse and into the house. Angela went to find the doctor in Visalia; Hector and his wife got Thomas in bed and cleaned up some. The doctor arrived an hour later and with Margarita's help, removed the crude closures that Thomas had put in and replaced them with careful cat-gut stitches—forty eight in all—to close the gaping wounds. He swabbed the entire area with carbolic acid in hopes of preventing further infection.

Thomas slept for nearly twenty-four hours and when he awoke he was ravenously hungry and ready to sit up in bed. The doctor visited once again, replaced the dressings and told him that things appeared to be healing well.

That afternoon Thomas surprised everyone by getting up and dressed and meeting them in the great room. They were full of questions but his answers were very vague and unsatisfying. He had fallen, he told them, onto a huge splinter protruding from a broken tree. He told them how he had closed the wound but claimed no memory of the second long clean wound below it, the one from Culebra's knife.

That evening as he and Angela sat in chairs in front of the fireplace she told him about the Presidential visit and asked if he had seen the President or his party.

"No," he said softly, "not a sign of them."

Angela told him about the brief encounter between Julia Stanton and the stranger on horseback, up behind Old Man Shingleton's cabin. Julia had told her parents that the stranger stopped her and asked where she was from. He seemed pleasant enough and mentioned to Julia that perhaps he'd see her again in a few days. The description Julia had provided made Thomas realize the stranger had been Culebra. He closed his eyes and shook his head, thinking how fortunate the young lady had been to not meet up again with the stranger.

Thomas felt well enough to travel two days later. He and Angela spent time together at the corral as they had in times now long past. She curled into his left side and he put his arm around her shoulder. Not much was said by either of them. She was now wearing the engagement ring, a Barnwell family heirloom that Frank had given her. She told him they would be married in six months. Thomas smiled and nodded, "That's wonderful, Angela. I'm happy for both of you."

There was a gentle good-night hug and Angela walked back to the house without looking back. Thomas spent a few more minutes in thought then walked to the bunkhouse.

Sunday, May 17, 1903, Panama Viejo, Panama

A personal friend of Doctor Amador, Victoriano Lorenzo, a guerrilla leader of the revolutionary Liberals in Panama, had been flushed from his mountain hide-out, forced through a farcical trial and was quickly executed by the Conservatives after he refused to accept the terms of agreement that ended the bloody civil war. The so-called Treaty of Wisconsin that ended the war was signed aboard United States battleship USS Wisconsin. Doctor Manuel Amador Guerrero learned of his friend's death while in Morro Bay, awaiting his return to Panama.

The same day Thomas boarded the northbound train for Sacramento. He had sent a telegram to Governor Pardee and requested a short meeting with him. Pardee responded that he was anxious to talk with Thomas and would meet with him at the Governor's Mansion.

Thomas arrived at the Governor's Mansion in Sacramento in the early afternoon. Shown into Governor Pardee's office, Pardee greeted him warmly at the door and offered him a seat. Both men sat silently for several moments. Thomas was aware that he could not involve the Governor in any way for the things that had occurred in the high country. Silently he took the gun case from his satchel and put it on the desk in front of the Governor. Pardee raised his eyebrows uncertainly then opened the case. He studied the contents of the case for several long moments then looked at Thomas.

"Looks like you were successful, Thomas."

"Yes, sir, I would say so." He pointed at the rifle, "Thought you might like to add that to your trophy collection."

Pardee nodded. "I don't know how the nation can ever thank you, Thomas. I spoke with President Roosevelt while he was in San Francisco. He described his visit to the mountains as restful and *simply grand*."

Thomas nodded, a slight smile touching his lips. "That's good." It was awkward, verbally skating all around the subject but he knew that Pardee could not discuss it without putting himself in legal jeopardy. "I believe I'm headed home now, Governor." He extended his hand. "Very nice to see you again."

"Good to see you as well, Thomas."

*   *   *

Thomas arrived at his home in San Francisco late that night. Amanda happened to still be up, sitting in the sun room reading when she heard his key in the front door lock.

"Oh, Thomas!" she cried as she threw her arms around her husband. He winced and she immediately let him go. "What have you done to yourself, Thomas?"

"It's nothing, Amanda. Just a little sore still."

She looked at him for a long time; her eyes were soft and her expression was filled with love. "Is it over now?"

"It's over, Mandy. It's over."

EPILOGUE

<u>1903 and Later</u>

On August 12, 1903, the Columbian congress failed to approve the Hay-Herran Treaty, mainly because Dr. Herran had negotiated this treaty with minimal oversight by the Columbia government. Unwilling to renegotiate the terms of the treaty, the United States then moved to support the separatist movement in Panama.

*   *   *

Congressman Clarence DePallin sat once again looking out the window of his mansion, gazing at the Merrimac River as it flowed by. The trees had begun to turn to their fall colors and grounds keepers raked them into huge piles to be burned. An empty bottle of Tennessee Whiskey sat on the table beside him. Corporal John London had been called to testify before a congressional hearing regarding Congressman DePallin's efforts to influence Congressional attitudes toward Panama. After the committee had heard the soldier's testimony the committee recommended a full hearing into the Congressman's actions. DePallin stared at the Navy Colt revolver on the table top. His political future was over. Much of his personal financial holdings had been mortgaged to enable him to purchase the useless land in Nicaragua.

The pistol shot startled the grounds keepers working just outside the window. They peered in to see the body of Congressman Clarence DePallin leaning back in the chair, a bloody hole in his right temple. It was Friday, September 4, 1903.

*   *   *

Rumors of a planned Panamanian uprising reached the Conservative government in Bogota, Columbia. On November 3, 1903, the Columbian government sent troops to Colon to be transported to Panama Viejo via the railroad. They are delayed in Colon by Panama Railroad authorities who were sympathetic to the Panamanian revolutionary cause. Meanwhile, the United States battleship USS Nashville helped delay disembarkation of additional troops off of Columbian ships in Colon. After a near bloodless uprising, the Liberal revolutionaries declared the Republic of Panama. Three days later, on November the sixth, the United States government informally recognized the new Republic of Panama. Ten days after the uprising, on Friday, November 13, 1903, the United States of America formally recognized the Republic of Panama, completing the strategy for the revolution that Doctor Manuel Amador Guerrero and President Theodore Roosevelt had discussed and agreed to high in the Sierra Nevada Mountains in May.

* * *

Five days later, on Wednesday, November 18, 1903, the United States Secretary of State John Hay and Philippe-Jean Bunau-Varilla, representing the Republic of Panama, signed the Hay-Bunau-Varilla Treaty. The Senates of both the United States and the Republic of Panama approved the treaty that established the Panama Canal Zone and authorized the United States to build a canal through Panama. This treaty, approved and ratified by both the United States and the Republic of Panama, effectively drove a stake through the heart of any Nicaraguan inter-ocean canal prospects.

* * *

On Saturday, February 20, 1904, Dr. Manuel Amador Guerrero was inaugurated before the Panamanian National Constitutional Convention as the first constitutionally elected President of the Republic of Panama.

* * *

On the same day, in Del Rio Texas, Sanford Parker was shot to death by his wife Jennette Parker after she discovered he was having an affair with the attractive sixteen year-old daughter of one of his Mexican ranch hands. Tried for murder, Jennette Parker was found not guilty after the jury comprised of local men had deliberated only ten minutes. One of the members of the jury was J. B. Talbot, the local banker.

*   *   *

Work began Wednesday, May 4, 1904, on the inter-ocean canal through the Isthmus of Panama under the direction of the United States Army Corps of Engineers.

*   *   *

Angela Gordon and Frank Barnwell exchanged marriage vows on Saturday, August 13, 1904, in a simple out-door ceremony attended by close friends and relatives. Among those attending were Thomas and Amanda O'Reiley. Over the years, Angela's family, Hector, Margarita and Ramon converted the ranch into a profitable citrus farm, raising oranges, grapefruit and lemons. After the death of Hector Gordon in 1919, the farm was managed by Ramon Gordon and his wife Sally. Margarita Gordon passed away in 1922. Descendants of the Gordon family still own and manage the farm.

*   *   *

Frank and Angela Barnwell moved to Sacramento where Frank remained involved in the conservation and distribution of water throughout the state. They had two children, both boys. Frank died in an automobile accident at the age of 62.

*   *   *

On Monday, August 15, 1914, the American Steamship SS Ancon made the first official trip from the Atlantic Ocean to the Pacific Ocean through the completed fifty-mile long Panama Canal.

*   *   *

Julia Stanton, once saved from a mountain lion by Thomas O'Reiley, grew up on the ranch owned by her parents and later studied voice and classical music in Los Angeles. She had a successful career as a soprano opera singer, traveling throughout the United States and Europe.

*   *   *

Miguel Esperanza-Vincente continued to live in the reconstructed family hacienda in Punta Gorda, Nicaragua and became very successful in the import-export business. His long-time friend, Gomez Santiago, remained in the private investigator business for six more years then moved to California, earned his Law Degree and set up his agency in Los Angeles.

*   *   *

Santa Cruz County Sheriff Joe McGee persuaded the District Attorney to drop the murder charges against Beck Weston. McGee remained Sheriff of Santa Cruz County for eight more years.

*   *   *

Beckley Weston went to Texas to be with his ill brother. He was never heard from.

*   *   *

Corporal John London was promoted to Sergeant and sent to Europe with the American Expeditionary Force during the Great War. London was killed by enemy gunfire at the Battle of Meuse-Argonne on October 17, 1918.

*   *   *

John J. Ambrose and Ulysses Thaddeus McGarnet were both wealthy enough to absorb the loss of their investment in Nicaragua property. When they heard of the death of their partner Clarence DePallin they decided perhaps it was time for each of them to retire. McGarnet lived in Connecticut until he died in 1933; Ambrose remained in Chicago and passed away a year later, in 1934.

*   *   *

Sophia Jenkins and Phillip Goode were married in San Francisco in 1906, just before the earthquake devastated the city. They worked as volunteers during the catastrophe, serving food and water to the thousands who had been made homeless by the quake. They later moved to Seattle, Washington and opened a small pub which they named *Shakers Pub*.

*   *   *

Bret Solomon passed away with cancer shortly after his visit from Santiago. He was never charged with complicity in the murders of his wife, Priscilla Solomon and neighbor Richard Manhauser. His property fell into receivership and was sold off for back taxes.

*   *   *

California Governor George Pardee took on the task of eradicating the bubonic plague from the city of San Francisco. By the end of 1904, he had been successful. Over two hundred lives had been lost to the plague. In 1905, Pardee established the state agricultural school that would eventually be known as the *University of California at Davis*. He was serving as Governor in 1906 when the monster earthquake devastated San Francisco. George Pardee temporarily moved his office to Oakland, across the bay from the stricken city, and spent the next twenty-four days coordinating relief efforts. During the 1906 elections, Pardee was quashed by his long lasting feud with the Southern Pacific Railroad and lost the election for Governorship. Pardee passed away in 1921 without ever revealing the assassination attempt on Roosevelt's life. The location of the rifle used by Culebra is unknown but the highly modified Mauser rifle is most likely in the hands of a collector.

*   *   *

President Theodore Roosevelt got to build his canal across the Panama Isthmus. His role in the Panamanian revolution would in 1921 cost the United States $10 million in compensation to Columbia for his personal involvement in the revolution. Twenty-seven years after its completion, in 1941, the Panama Canal would serve an important role in yet another world war, this time under the presidency of Franklin Delano Roosevelt, Theodore Roosevelt's fifth cousin. On December 31, 1999, responsibility and control of the Panama Canal was formally handed over to the Republic of Panama by Jimmy Carter, the 39th President of the United States of America.

* * *

The individual within the White House that provided information to the conspirators was never identified. Roosevelt's aide, James, resigned his position three weeks after the President returned to Washington D.C. from his trip to California, citing poor health. James retired in his home state of Georgia where he soon dropped out of public sight.

* * *

A few miscellaneous human bone fragments were discovered in the high country above the Kaweah River in 1973. Three quarters of a century old, the remains were never fully identified other than they were of a male about thirty five years of age. The bone fragments indicated that the man had been probably killed and eaten by a bear. The only artifact recovered was a rusted knife. Some speculation had suggested the remains were those of the Indian of lore, Gray Hawk, but that theory was eventually debunked. The remains of the shaman Gray Hawk have never been located.

* * *

Ida Hubbard waited for five months for Luke to contact her. At first the disappearance of her lover brought her great angst and heartbreak but as time passed she began to accept that he was probably dead. The wooden box he had left her had remained unopened until she finally decided to return to Kansas City, Kansas.

When she unlocked the container she discovered over a million dollars in paper money and gold. She did what most people in her position would do; she took the money and asked no questions about its origin. In Kansas, she invested wisely, spent carefully and became one of the wealthiest women in Kansas City. Ida Hubbard never got married and passed away at the age of 92.

* * * *
* * *
* *
*